Born in Morley, Yorkshire, David lost his father when he was only four years of age; and during school holidays, his mother had no option but to take him with her to the mill in which she worked as a spinner of woollen yarn. And here he experienced the sounds, sights, and smells of an industry that was etched into his memory.
It wasn't until he moved to Brighton that he decided to commit these recollections to print; and even though he is now an adopted Brightonian, this novel displays his enduring affection for England's largest county, widely celebrated as God's own country.

Author's Note

For the uninitiated, I have kept the idiosyncrasies of the Yorkshire dialect to a minimum.

The Mill Girl

David J Morris

In Loving Memory of
Sarah Morris
1914 – 1972
Peter Birks
1949 – 2011

Part One
The Girl
1936

1

Whilst the rest of the family slept peacefully, Emma Harvey lay awake listening to the constant clatter of caravan wheels and the snagging of ill-shod horses' hooves on the cobblestones below the bedroom window, and she was overcome with dread.

Even now, in the calm and comforting light of day, she could do little but repeatedly pace from the back door to the front one. Back and forth she crossed the stone-flagged kitchen floor, her hands clasped tightly together, fingers twitching, her mind battling against the emotions that had plagued her throughout the previous sleepless night.

It was an oppressively hot August day and both doors were wide open. Yet it wasn't just the unprecedented heat which had suddenly arrived in Collingley that, ever so often, caused her to raise her pinny and waft it in front of her plump, freckled face: it was also the prospect of hordes of gypsies descending upon the small West Riding town at the start of Feast Week.

Tonight, all the woollen mills were to close their gates, and then the workers would eagerly congregate on Stockwell's Field to enjoy the annual fair. But the event wouldn't hold any enjoyment for Emma. Last year her only son had been taken from her in the most horrifying of circumstances, and now she was reliving it all. Oh yes! her neighbours had often said that time would heal her grief, but it hadn't happened yet; and still her memories couldn't discount the fact that he was gone. But however hard it may be, she had to get on with life and look after her husband and the remainder of her brood.

She halted in her cyclical movements around the kitchen and went to the oval mirror above the sink. Taking three large U-shaped pins from her pinafore pocket, she held them between her lips before hanging her head to one side and twisting her red hair into a spiral, employing the pins to secure the result close to her scalp. Then after inspecting her reflection, she turned abruptly and went to the cellar head where she got out the bread she had baked earlier in the week, and a quarter pound of butter that Nelly had kindly brought her. She's a good neighbour is Nelly, thought

Emma. Kindness itself. But the only thing that made Emma shudder when she thought of her, was the off-and-on job she did: she laid folk out. How could she do it? And sometimes, even when she visited Emma, she'd get the call and rush off. Then, to cap it all, she'd be back within the hour and describe the state of the deceased. Oh! it fair made yer quake. And even though Nelly no doubt knew what this family had gone through over the last year, she did it every time. Still, she was a good lass for all that.

Emma placed the butter beneath an earthenware cooler before seating herself at the table, drumming her fingers on its pitted wooden surface, miles away in contemplation: Just look at the state of this place – a heap! Oh, aye, it's clean and tidy, but yer can't forever use yer flour up trying to stick the wallpaper back on when it keeps peeling off due to the damp. And the bugs…oh, the bugs! They'd creep in from next door through the cracks in the adjoining wall. Now that was a lark: trying to burn the buggers to death with a candle and having to stand the bed legs in tins of paraffin so they couldn't crawl up. Still, they'd been kept at bay.

Now her thoughts turned to her husband. George was lucky to still be in a job the way things had been going with this…slump, as they call it. They'd said the worst was over and that unemployment was going down now, but she couldn't see it. She'd heard that there were two thousand folk out of work in this small town alone – but it was worse in Lancashire where the cotton industry had more people unemployed than those who worked with wool. Even so, it was still a worry; and God only knew what they'd do if her husband was laid off. And then there was Sarah. Oh, Sarah! What a bloody handful she is! What sort of job could she get with all these folk on the dole? Oh, it didn't bear thinking about. But inevitably her thoughts returned to the loss of her son. Not just because he was taken from her – it was the way he was taken. Even now she could still sense his spirit flitting around the house, getting up to mischief, laughing with Sarah and Emily, but never at all wayward or disobedient. Aay, John lad, I do miss yer.

Of a sudden, she sensed a presence behind her. Jumping up from the chair, which crashed unceremoniously onto the stone floor, she clutched at her breast and spun around. "Nay, Nelly; yer nearly scared me half out o' me wits…I thought you were a gypsy."

Nelly Dicks thrust her sun-reddened face forward, saying, "Do I bloody well look like one?" Then, tendering a small smile, she said, "Anyroad, I just thought I'd bring yer this bunch o' flowers because of...well, today being...yer know...."

Emma's top lip trembled. But she pushed back her shoulders and said, "Bless yer, lass. They're much appreciated. Now, sit yerself down and I'll mash us some tea."

Nelly righted the chair, and seating her dumpy frame at the table, watched her neighbour as she took down a pottery vase from the shelf above the sink and lovingly arrange the flowers within. Then, as Emma scooped up a jug of water from a bucket at her feet, she observed her gently tipping it into the vase. Eeh, poor lass, thought Nelly. What this woman had gone through. Not only had she lost her only male child, but she'd also suffered greatly in her life.

Nelly had only lived next door for six months, but the women in the street who had lived here for much longer, had unreservedly volunteered the information as to Emma's past – particularly about Emma's first husband. Apparently, Henry Conlan was a beast of an Irish Catholic who treated Emma with a vicious contempt that was far from what any decent person would consider as being Christian.

He had come over from Ireland to work in the Liverpool Docks, and one day he received a message saying that his sister was poorly, and it was thought that she wouldn't last the week – she lived in Morley and worked in the same mill as Emma. Then, as life takes strange twists and turns, he was introduced to Emma at his sister's funeral; and, much to everybody's amazement, he packed in his dock work and got a job as a fettler at the mill – and married Emma three months later. But one thing that Emma refused to do was to take up the Catholic faith. And he never forgave her for that. Then in the summer of 1900, Emma gave birth to her first child – a girl who was christened Mary, and who became the apple of her father's eye. But three years later, a second daughter Katherine came along, and throughout their childhood, it was Mary this and Mary that and Katherine never got a look in.

Things changed dramatically though when Mary started work at a rag merchant's and, for some reason, Henry started drinking heavily. He always had been a drinker – but not to the extent that he did then – and he turned into a complete monster: coming in blind drunk and beating Emma so badly she tried to avoid the neighbours as much as she could – at least until the bruises faded. But they knew what was going on all right, even if they didn't catch sight of her. But Mary wouldn't believe it was anything to do with her father.

Then one evening, the back door burst open and Emma's neighbour, Leonard Barraclough, staggered up to the fireside and breathlessly said to her, 'He's 'ad it, lass: thee 'usband…yer're a widow now, Emma.…Eeh, I'm sorry, lass, but I thought yer'd best know.…He were workin' blind drunk, and tum'led head first into a vat o' vitriol. It's the talk o' t'Jubilee.'

It came as both a surprise to Emma's neighbours, and a shock to Mary, when less than a year later, Emma became engaged to George Harvey. But now, after sixteen years of marriage, their devotion to each other is unwavering.

"What d'yer think, Nelly?" said Emma as she placed the vase of flowers in the centre of the table.

"Grand, lass."

"Aye. Grand! Now, let me see to that broth on the fire and then I'll get the kettle on." With this, Emma Harvey marched across the kitchen to the black-leaded range where, after pulling a cloth from a length of string that was draped across the mantelpiece, she hoisted a pan of mutton broth onto the hob. "And why we have to have a fire goin' in this weather is beyond me…they've got gas over yonder" – she gestured in the direction of the street – "and we're stuck in these bloody hovels."

She's right there, thought Nelly. The cottages they lived in – well, existed in – may have been fine for the mill workers when they were built in the early nineteenth century, but together with the passing of time and the acidic and smoke-charged atmosphere, they were now the worse for wear. Originally constructed of blocks of locally quarried stone, they now seemed weighed down with a chronic depression. Cracks were appearing in both the outside and inside walls, and the doorsteps seemed to have twisted, and had sloped towards the cobbled street known as Victoria Row.

And apart from that, conditions were cramped. There was only a stone-floored kitchen-cum-living-room on ground level and a bedroom above – which often had to accommodate the sleeping arrangements of families of six or more. Granted, Nelly only had herself and daughter Jessie to cope with, but Emma was in a different position: there were five of them! And to top it all, none of Victoria Row's residents had either electricity or gas.

Nelly turned her attention back to Emma now. "Yer never know, lass, the landlord might get round to putting gas in for us one of these days."

Emma turned, her red hair appearing more fiery than ever in the glow from the grate. "Who? Stockwell? Nay, he's on his last legs so our George says. And besides, the place'll likely collapse around our ears before he pops his clogs." Emma lifted the lid off the pan, and taking a knife from the dresser, stabbed at the pieces of meat. "Oh aye, it'll do." She placed the pan into the side oven and grabbing the kettle from off the hearth, screwed it into the coals.

"Where're your two little 'uns, then?" enquired the neighbour.

Still holding the knife, Emma wiped it on her pinny and went to Nelly's side, saying, "Gone to our Mary's." She sat down and tossed the knife on the table. "It gets me how our Em dotes on that new babby o' Mary's – Sarah can't be bothered of course. And yer know what, Nelly" – she leaned forward – "George loathes the sight of her...our Mary, I mean."

"I'm not surprised," said Nelly; "not from what I've heard."

Emma's large green eyes widened, and drawing closer to Nelly now, said, "Well, I don't know how much y'ave heard, lass, but Mary and our Kath are from me first husband – he were Catholic – and whereas Mary follows the faith to the letter, our Kath won't have a thing to do with it. In fact, she can't abide anything that Mary stands for. But she loves George as if he were her own father, and George loves her an' all; but he can't abide Mary. Oh, he'll tolerate her, but like Kath, he doesn't go in for this papist nonsense....Now, lass," Emma slapped her hands on the table and pushed her ample frame out of her seat, adding, "you go an' keep an eye out for any of them damned gypsies while I mash the tea. Then I'll have to get cracking before the mill hooter sounds and he gets home to find me in me muck."

Nelly promptly pulled out a small stool from beneath the table and carried it to the front window where she mounted, peered above the lace curtain that covered the lower pane, and scanned the street – admitting to herself that although she had learned a lot about her neighbour's marital situation from the women on Victoria Row, they had never mentioned anything about her son. No, it wasn't through tittle-tattle how Nelly knew: it was gleaned from the free press close on a year ago.

The report in the Collingley Advertiser on the 23rd of August 1935, appeared to revel in the gruesome details of the Harvey boy's death. It told how when the fair held its opening night on some rough ground leased from Asa Stockwell, young John

Harvey was larking about on one of the rides and fell into a gap between the drive shaft and some broken decking. They said his body was mangled beyond recognition when they finally got him out. But Emma dismissed the claims of her son's misbehaviour because John was such a sensible lad. And it was her belief that some gypsy or other had pushed him to his death. But nothing was ever proved. Nelly shuddered now. Poor Emma. She must have thought when her only son died, that the sun would never rise again. But – as is the way of the world – it always did....

"Yer might as well come to the table now, Nelly...I found some seed cake in the cupboard. Just enough for the two on us. C'mon, love, lest tea gets cold....Did yer clock any of 'em? They usually come out of the ginnel next to Arnie's shop."

"Er...no, Emma. Perhaps they'll keep away this year?"

"Oh, aye! Like dogs keep away from a black pudding. Well I'm ready for 'em...I'll sit facing the front door just in case....D'yer know, they may have said what happened last year were an accident, but I know better."

"Well," said Nelly, "since I didn't live around here then, I can't really comment."

Emma banged a fist on the table, saying, "*I* bloody well can! He were killed by those rogues. And as God is my judge, I'll find out the truth one of these days and swing for the buggers."

Seated now, Emma poured the tea and handed her neighbour a slice of cake, which Nelly placed next to her mug, saying as she did so, "Me mother always kept the doors bolted when gypsies were about."

"Well not me," said Emma, mumbling the words over a mouthful of cake; and after washing it down, said, "It's bad enough having a fire in the grate without having the flamin' doors shut."

"Ah, well, yer see" – Nelly sipped at her tea – "me mother were worried that if she came face to face wi' one of 'em, and she didn't buy owt off her, then she'd be cursed."

"Cursed be buggered....I'll tell yer this for nowt," said Emma. "Last year I'd just gone down to the tap in the back lane to bring up a bucket, and when I got back this black-haired piece were standin' on me hearth rug with a basket of pegs. 'What the hell d'yer think yer at?' I asked. 'Buy some clothes-pegs, love,' she says, 'and maybe a bunch of lucky heather?' Eeh, I can tell you, Nelly, if it hadn't have meant me traipsing back down to the tap again, I'd have drowned the dozy-lookin' mare....Pegs, lucky heather, curses…tosh!"

Nelly watched in silence now as Emma finished the last of her cake, thinking, She's not convinced. She's not sure that the loss of her son wasn't due to her refusing the gypsy woman. And as she gazed at this kind-hearted neighbour of hers, she realised that there was a vulnerability hidden behind that stony façade, and wondered if she dare bring up the subject of her allowing the girls to visit the fair this very evening after the terrible events of a year ago. But, as if Nelly had spoken her thoughts out loud, Emma gently placed down her cup and cradled it between her trembling fingers before saying in hushed tones, "They'll pester the life out of me if I keep them from going to the feast, Nelly."

And Nelly nodded.

"It's not as if I worry about them…well…coming to any harm – our Kath'll see to that – but just thinking about what happened last year to, yer know…." And Emma's eyes glazed over.

"Aye, lass, aye….And our Jessie'll be there an' all."

Emma smiled through her tears. And then, after wiping her face on her pinny and tucking a strand of loose hair back into the bun atop her head, she said with a slight chuckle, "What wi' our Kath and your Jess, those gypsy lads won't know what's hit 'em….Aye, I suppose I'll let 'em go since Stockwell seems to have put things in order. And having said that, we don't know if it'll be the last Collingley Feast they'll see. Aye, they'll be safe enough."

Organising the thoughts in her head now, Nelly said, "I saw her from next door this mornin'" – she nodded towards the fireplace – "goin' into that Arnie's shop."

"Aye," said Emma, "she'll have found summat her dad picked up on his round and pawned it…she'll be wanting some brass to go to t'feast wi'."

"Well, it seemed to me as if she needs a new frock…the one she were wearing looked as if it'd seen better days."

"Oh, she's a right baggage, Nelly…and a trollop! Do you know" – Emma leaned across the table – "she'll have anything in trousers – or usually out of 'em. I'm surprised she hasn't ended up in the family way by now."

"How old is she, Emma, then?"

"Just turned sixteen."

"I'd have said she were older than that."

"She bloody well acts like it, lass….At one point she set her cap at young Wilf – Arnie's lad – but Arnie soon nipped that in the

15

bud. The lad's only fourteen after all.…She's damned brazen!"

"Eeh…! But what does her father think of it all?"

"Who Len? Nay, he's as daft as a brush. He'll be as drunk as a lord tonight – always is on feast night.…And have yer seen that horse of his? Emancipated it is! As thin as a rail!" Emma tapped the table. "D'yer know, lass; if the weather's bad, they take the bloody thing indoors and let it sleep in front of the fire. If yer put yer ear next to t'chimney-breast yer can hear it snorin'."

"Eeh, can yer credit it…!" Nelly turned now and looked at the large clock above the dresser. "Well" – she drained her mug – "I'd best be off, lass, and leave yer to it…times gettin' on."

Emma glanced at the clock herself now. "Aye, time flies when yer're busy." She rose now, and after scraping her high-backed chair over the stone flags, she began to side the table, saying, "Come up later, Nelly, when the kids are out. We can have a go at that list rug if yer like. A few more rows and it'll be done." And Nelly said, "George won't mind, will he?"

"Heavens no! He'll be engrossed in his Advertiser – and it's best yer're not next door on yer own."

"Right then, lass, I'll be up later.…Ta-rah then, Emma. And ta for the tea."

"Yer're welcome, lass. Ta-rah, Nelly."

Immediately Emma busied herself. She inspected the pan of broth in the side oven of the range and boiled a pan of water on the fire. Then she washed the pots, dried them, and put them away; wiped down the table and straightened the chairs; went to the dresser drawer to get the book out for Alex Stockwell to sign when he came for the rent; and after looking around her small kitchen to see if it was in order, went to the back door, leaned on the jamb, and gazed out across the fields.

Although the weather was stifling, the day offered up the hint of a breeze. The fields that stretched into the distance were still fresh-green from the rain of some days ago, and through the heat haze one could just see the church tower on the top of Thorp Hill. But looking beyond the rural nature of this part of town, the landscape rapidly gave way to the vast sprawl of industry as an incalculable number of chimneys thrust skyward, belching black smoke and acrid fumes from the bowels of Yorkshire's woollen mills.

George Harvey worked at Stockwell's – which he'd found hard to stomach after last year's events. But he had to feed his family, so had little choice in the matter. And besides, they rented this place from Asa Stockwell otherwise they'd be out on the streets.

Katherine brought in another wage, though – she worked in a clothing factory in Leeds. Yet the work was no less gruelling.... Oh! how Emma wished that her youngest two could one day find less arduous employment. But what else was there in this part of the country apart from the mills and skivvying for nobs?

She worried about Sarah the most since she'd shortly be finishing school. Sarah had a bright head on her shoulders and would find her way in the world with a steely determination that Emily just didn't have. Always a sickly child, Emily appeared like a lost soul, and God alone knew what would become of her...?

And as Emma stood propped against the door, she looked across the open fields and closed her eyes. There, with the warm rays of the sun washing over her face, and the happy sounds of small children playing in the back lane echoing in her ears, she convinced herself that, for once, the world was at peace.

But beneath her closed eyelids, where the softened silhouettes of the town remained imprinted, she was blissfully unaware of the dark clouds that were gathering along the horizon.

2

Resurrection nestled close to Barn Brook – a turbulent stream running from high in the hills above the village of Thorp, through Collingley itself, and on to the outskirts of Leeds where it joined the River Aire. Employing several sluices, Barn Brook had been dammed to provide the water necessary for the many processes used in the manufacture of woollen cloth; and the mill overlooked Stockwell's field, where now the fair was being assembled for the first night of the annual holiday. But at three o'clock on this August afternoon, William Crowther had other things on his mind.

William was the only son of J B Crowther who was revered as a model employer: he was generous to his staff and cared for their welfare and safety. William was the handsomest of lads: tall and well-built with a mop of hair that was as black as coal, and his dark eyes sparkled with a youthful confidence. Now, at the age of seventeen, he was taking a larger part in the running of his father's empire and would often be seen visiting the various departments of the mill, chatting to the workers and listening to any grievances they may have. The women adored him and, it had to be said, so did some of the men; and the younger girls would sit giggling together at break time as they speculated as to his masculine assets, wishing that he would court one of them – but they were in no doubt that his future had already been mapped out for him.

Being a mill worker was a hazardous profession: the mills were dangerous places. And although Crowther's was known for its good safety record, nevertheless accidents still happened. So, it had come as a blow to William as he rushed into his father's office and informed him that a young girl's hair had been caught in the cogs of one of the mules and was unconscious. Immediately J B went down to the shed and instructed the foreman and a lad to grab a pair of shears and cut off her locks. And after she had been released, the foreman and his doffing lad carried her to a pallet and transported it into the mill yard.

"Oi! Just hold on a minute, lad! I don't know where yer think yer're runnin' to, but me legs are goin' to buckle afore long."

"But we ought to get her home, Mr Fowler, before she goes an' dies on us. She's been out cold since it 'appened."

"Good Lord, lad, she won't die...I've seen worse injuries on lesser than her and they've been back at work within days. Mind you, if I don't take a breather, it'll be *me* who's laid out; and besides, we'll have to put her down to open the gates. She'll come to no harm."

With this, the old man and the boy lowered the hessian-covered pallet onto the cobblestones in front of the mill gate. The foreman then arched his back and drew in several deep breaths before shuffling over to the yard wall where he leaned against the soot-blackened stones and lit a Woodbine. And after drawing zealously on the cigarette, he gasped, "I wish I knew what the hell her mother feeds her on 'cos she weighs a bloody ton."

The boy looked up; his bright, blue eyes clouded over with concern, and said dully, "We ought to have recruited another pair of hands." He stood now, saying, "Shall I go back and fetch somebody?"

"Nay, lad!" – Geoff Fowler flapped his hand – "We'll be here all day if we wait for one of those gormless buggers." He thumbed up the yard. "Come to think on it, it would 'ave been easier to dump 'er in a skip and wheel 'er home." He chuckled now; but the boy remained pensive, saying, "But the skips were all full. We'd doffed two mules and were nearly ready for another when" – he pointed at their charge – "she started screaming like a stuck pig. It were a good job I were at hand to slip the drive belt or she might've been a goner."

Geoff approached the boy now, and wrapping an arm about his thin shoulders, said kindly, "Aye, I know, lad; I know....Eeh, I wish I had a tanner for every time I've told 'em to get their hair bobbed before they started at t'mill. But do they listen? Do they hell as like! And then look what happens. I'm worn out with it all, Wilf....D'yer know, lad; it's time I retired."

Making no comment at this, Wilf simply said, "D'yer think she'll pull through, Mr Fowler?"

"Course she will, lad; she's as strong as a carthorse is this one – and nearly as heavy. And" – he spun the young lad around and looked into his worried eyes – "yer did the right thing in stopping the mule. I'm proud of yer, Wilf. Really proud." The foreman placed a hand on the boy's head, saying, "I were only kiddin' about wheeling her home in a skip....Well I ask yer, can yer just see the two of us trying to lift this lump into a bobbin basket?" And the boy smiled. "Now, you dog out in case young Crowther comes down the yard while I finish me smoke, and then we'll get her 'ome." Geoff went back into the shadows beneath the high wall, thinking the while, I wish the lad wouldn't go to the feast tonight. Look what happened last year when some lad fell into the machinery just like her – he mentally nodded towards the pallet. Mind you, she'll survive; but that poor soul....Oh, it worried him sick that any harm should come to Wilf since he had the makings of a damned good piecener and could easily become head spinner one of these days. Granted, it would take a lot of hard work, but the lad were no shirker. Not only did he doff bobbins all day, but then had to go home and see to his dad's needs ever since his sister started work at the children's hospital. Hospital! Well that was a bloody laugh: more came out dead than went in living! No, Wilf looked after his dad – and the shop – without ever a word of complaint. And just look at him now: caring for a stupid girl who should have known a lot better.

"What's up with *her*?"

The sudden voice pierced Geoff's concentration, causing the glowing cigarette stub to shoot from his mouth as if he'd been slapped on the back. Focusing his eyes now, he beheld two round faces peering at him through the gates. Then the taller of the duo turned her attention on the lad, saying, "Is she dead, Wilf?" But before Wilf could respond, Geoff Fowler scurried to the pallet and confronted the boy. "Do you know these two?" he growled.

Wilf bit on his bottom lip. Then, moving his tongue around his mouth, he nodded, saying, "Aye, Mr Fowler. They're George Harvey's lasses. He works at Stockwell's. He's an overlooker."

"Well, overlooker or not" – Geoff turned to the girls – "it doesn't give you two the right to come waltzing up here as if you own the place. Now" – his arm moved in a circle – "be off wi' yer, you little tykes."

But the little tykes didn't flinch. Then, levelling her gaze at the old man, Sarah Harvey said, "We only came to see what had happened. We were on or way to our Mary's – she lives in one of those posh houses on the top road."

Geoff moved his head from side to side. "Well, la-di-bloody-da," he mocked.

"Nay," said Sarah; "don't be like that. I just thought I could help. My sister" – she gazed at the thin little creature by her side – "wouldn't be any good because she's not strong like me, but I could help a lot." She returned her gaze to the pallet now. "Are you sure she's not dead?"

"Does she look it?" This was Geoff again.

"Aye, I'd say so," said Sarah imperiously.

"And I suppose you're an expert when it comes to life and death?" said Geoff, his tone expressing incredulity.

Sarah took a step nearer the gate and tossing back her long auburn hair, said, "No....But I do know how somebody dying makes you feel: it's awful. Only last year...."

"Mr Fowler! Mr Fowler!" Wilf was tugging furiously at his foreman's sleeve.

"What is it for God's sake?"

And in a whisper, Wilf said, "Mr Crowther's comin'."

"Oh, Lord help us!" Geoff's usually ruddy complexion turned pallid and his long, droopy moustache visibly twitched.

William Crowther strode down the yard and leaned over the pallet; then as he looked at the assembled group, he said softly, "Is everything all right, Geoff...? You really should get the girl home and out of this hot sun. And from what I can observe, she seems to be coming round now...but probably still in shock. Now, get going, and tell her mother to get some hot, sweet tea into her. Oh, and by the way, make sure you stay with her until Doctor Griffiths arrives – I've just telephoned him – and be sure to tell her mother that the mill will settle his bill. Now, hurry along, Geoff, lest he gets to the house before you do. Father has always said one can set a clock by Sam Griffiths' punctuality."

The foreman whipped off his cap, and holding it close to his chest, said, "Aye, aye, Maister William...I'll do that. Aye, I will." Turning to Wilf now, he said, "Don't dawdle, lad," and ordered him to draw back the gates. And as he and the boy hoisted the makeshift stretcher out of the yard, Geoff curled his lip and hissed at Sarah, "Get yerselves gone!"

But Sarah was oblivious to his words: her attention was fixed on the young man who was now re-closing the gates. And as he did so, his sooty eyebrows arched, and smiling, he said, "Hello, you two."

"Hello, sir," said Sarah.

William Crowther placed both hands on the wooden rails of the gate and bowed his head slightly, saying, "And whom do I have the pleasure of meeting, young miss?"

Momentarily, Sarah was lost for words, taken as she was by the young man's friendly demeanour and his sparkling brown eyes.... It was now that she offered him her hand. "I'm Sarah Harvey, and this" – she looked to her side – "is my sister, Emily." And Emily flushed.

William drew back the gate, and coming out onto the cobbled street, wiped a hand on his brown corduroy trousers. Then, taking Sarah's outstretched hand in his, said gently, "Delighted, Sarah."

Oh! such a gentleman. And how handsome he was! His sun-tanned face was partly shrouded by his black hair, which in the bright sunlight bore hints of red. His lips were full, and his chin – showing the hint of youthful stubble – was firm but slightly rounded. And beneath his open-necked, linen shirt, his chest was already well-developed, sporting the fine strands of hair of a boy nearing maturity.

"Are you here to meet someone, Sarah?"

"Oh no, sir...we were just passing, and I saw the girl laid out and wondered if there might be something I could do to help."

"Well, I must say you have a noble spirit. Many people older than yourself would most likely have walked straight passed." Again he lowered his head. "But, would it appear immodest of me to ask such a caring young lady as to her age?"

"Thirteen, sir – fourteen next year – and then I'll be leaving school."

"And have you had thoughts of what you might do then?"

Sarah's mood darkened now as she said flatly, "I suppose I'll go to work in the mill...all the lasses do."

"Oh, no, not all of them. And from what I've gathered, I think you'll do better than that – although I shouldn't be saying so since look what *I'm* doing." And pointing back up the yard, he swept his arm towards the expanse of buildings that made up J B Crowther & Son – a domain that one day would be his. Turning back to the girls now, his long fingers cradled his jaw as he said, "Something's puzzling me though. I seem to know the name Harvey from somewhere?"

"My dad's an overlooker at Stockwell's," Sarah announced proudly.

William clicked two fingers. "Maybe that's where I know him from? Is his name John...or Joe, perhaps?"

Sarah lowered her head now, saying, "No...John was me brother. He was...killed...at the fair a year ago."

"Oh, forgive me. I do remember reading about it now. But I

didn't mean to upset you, Sarah."

"You haven't, sir." And she raised her head and smiled at him. He'd called her Sarah!

"I am so sorry for your loss. Please send my condolences and best wishes to your family – though it seems rather tardy considering the lapse of time."

"I will, sir; and thank you."

What an extraordinary girl this is, thought he. She's got a brain on her for certain....Thirteen, eh? He would have said fifteen – possibly sixteen! And gazing at her now as she wetted a handkerchief and wiped a mark from her sister's forehead, he concluded that she bore none of the coarseness associated with her class, exhibiting a certain pride in her own and her sister's appearance and social behaviour. And goodness she was pretty – nay, beautiful! Yes, she really was beautiful with those rare, green eyes and long, auburn hair which was now draped before him as she bent down to buckle Emily's shoe.

"She gets herself into a right state at times, sir." Sarah was erect now, smiling at him. And he returned the smile, saying, "And less of the 'sir' – it's William. Remember that the next time we meet.... But, for the moment, I really must get back to work or Father will think I'm slacking. Now" – he wagged a finger – "look after yourself...and you too Emily." Then, he passed through the partly open gates, closed them behind him, and walked slowly back up the yard, waving as he went.

May I ask a lady her age! The next time we meet! Look after yourself! And he'd called her Sarah...William and Sarah....Oh! how she wished.

Going to Mary's was a trial. The combination of her and her posh house was anathema to Sarah. This abhorrence of Mary had been instilled into her by Katherine....No, it hadn't! Sarah had made up her own mind about Mary without being influenced by others. By! she really thought herself a cut above the rest. But if the truth be known, for all her airs and graces, she was as common as muck! Granted, she lived in one of the new houses on the top road, but how had she got there? She'd married into money that's how!

Sarah tightened her grip on her sister's hand as they reached Mary's gate....Oh! coming here must be a punishment for something Sarah had done. She'd rather be locked in a dark cellar for a week than spend two hours in her half-sister's company. But

Emily wanted to see the baby, who some days earlier had just cut her first tooth, so what could she do but bring her?

The tooth-cutting had even warranted Mary getting a taxi – of all things – to Victoria Row to announce the event. Mam was overjoyed to hear the news. But the flustered way in which Mary had burst through the door, caused Dad and Kath to look at each other as if war had broken out. Then, when they discovered what all the fuss was about, Kath had walked out and gone to a neighbour's, while Dad had calmly refilled his pipe and stuck his head in the Advertiser. Later, after giving Mary a threepenny bit for the child and seeing her off, Mam had returned to her husband's side, saying pointedly, 'Yer could have said summat, George. After all it *is* your first grandchild!' And Dad had looked up at her, and beneath a halo of smoke had said, 'She's nowt to do wi' me.' And Sarah could understand exactly what he meant.

"Oh, c'mon, our Sal; let's get in." Looking at her younger sister now, Sarah forced a smile and unlatched the gate.

Mary's garden was just like her house: all flowers. Sarah hadn't seen a range of flowers like these before. All the ones she knew were in the fields at the back of her own house…and oh! how she loved walking through those fields – in all kinds of weather. There the flowers were beautiful: blues, yellows, and when the poppies came out she was in her element: they were red! She loved red – perhaps because it was the colour of her mother's hair? She didn't really know. But even though Mary had some red roses in her garden, it just wasn't the same! And apart from that, she had them indoors: in the fireplace when she hadn't a fire going; on the wallpaper; and even as patterns on the dresses she wore. Oh, how Sarah hated roses!

Hilda – the woman who came in to 'do' for Mary – answered the door. "Eeh, lasses; it's fair grand seein' yer both. Come in. Come in, do. She's out in t'back garden wi' t'bairn. You go through, Emily, and I'll see to yer sister.…But yer know where to go, Sarah, eh?" And Sarah smiled at this odd, but amiable body who 'did' for Mary, and followed her into the room.

Oh, it's worse than ever. She's gone and got a flowered carpet. It's like a house full of nothing but…flowers. Flowers, flowers, flowers! If her dad saw this he'd have a dicky-fit. Still, Dad would never again set foot in the place – once before was enough for him!

"Sit yerself down, lass, and I'll let t'missis know yer're 'ere…

Eeh what am I saying? She'll know that already since your Em's out t'back. Now, come an' plant yerself." Hilda let out a cackle now, adding, "Plant yerself…eeh, that's a good 'un: plant yerself! What else could yer do in 'ere? Eeh! that is a good 'un." And with this, Hilda scuttled through to the kitchen, saying as she went, "An' I'd best mash the tea, I suppose. D'yer know, lass, it's all go."

Now, seated beside the fireplace on a padded, brocade-covered stool, Sarah gazed up at the five-globed light fitting hanging from a brass centre-piece surrounded by a large, plaster ceiling rose, thinking, At least she's got electric. We don't even have gas!

Hilda had lain the table for afternoon tea. On a fine, lace cloth that draped majestically over the mahogany table, she had arranged Mary's best china cups and saucers, and plates edged in a gold trim, decorated – naturally – with tea-roses. Small silver forks with mother-of-pearl handles were placed neatly to the side of each, and a three-tiered, silver stand, sported a variety of dainty sandwiches and slices of cake. From experience, Sarah could guarantee that the sandwiches would contain cucumber, salmon paste, and some would be filled with Hilda's home-made potted meat. And the cake, whatever it was, would be sliced so thinly that you could – as her father had previously said – read the bloody Collingley Advertiser through it. Sarah giggled to herself on recollecting Dad's comment, and wished she were back home right now, waiting for him coming in from work instead of sitting in this overstuffed greenhouse.

Hilda reappeared from the kitchen carrying a teapot, which she deposited carefully on the table and covered with a knitted cosy. "Y'ought to come out to t'garden, lass. It's fair grand out there… your Emily's 'avin' a whale of a time wi' t'young 'un."

"Oh, I'm all right here, Hilda. I can't take much of this hot sun," Sarah lied.

"Well, I'll just take your Em a plate o' summat. Mary says she'll be in shortly and 'ave a word wi' yer."

A word with me, Sarah thought. What about? Oh! please, Em, don't want to stay too long.…Please!

Directly after Hilda had gone, Mary came in.

She was a pole of a woman – quite tall for a female – with a shock of raven hair that wreathed an overly made-up face. Much to Sarah's surprise, she was dressed in a plain, cream-coloured, summer frock with short sleeves; and on her feet, she was wearing a pair of open-toed sandals with a slight heel. And as she stood with her back to Sarah and poured two cups of tea, she said, "Come and sit at the table, Sarah. I don't want you getting crumbs all over the new carpet....Do you like it? It was very expensive – but of course we can afford it."

"Aye...er...yes! It's very pretty."

"Right, let's have something to eat and afterwards we can have a chat. There are a few things I'd like to discuss with you before you go home."

Oh, hell! I wish I were there now...!

After the two had taken tea, and Sarah was picking crumbs off the tablecloth and sprinkling them onto her plate, Mary spoke: "Now, I've been thinking of what you may do when you leave school – it won't be long now, you know....Well, last evening when Jack and I were dining with the Stockwells, I brought up the subject. And Edith said – provided there was a vacancy – she would certainly be willing to give you an interview shortly before you finish your education. Naturally, I can't promise you what the job would be – or even guarantee you success – but the offer is there. Now, what do you think?"

Sarah didn't know what to think – or if her brain was even working. But, clasping her hands together on her lap now, said succinctly, "I was thinking of going in the mill."

Mary immediately showed her disapproval by pursing her lips. "That's not for you, Sarah...Emily maybe, but not you."

Sarah could feel the blood pulsating through her veins. How dare she! How dare she think that Em was only good for the mill! What a cheek! Mary herself had worked in a rag merchant's of all places, so she had no room to talk....Oh, calm down Sarah, calm down.

Mary was talking again. "Now. It has come to my attention that you are spending some time in the company of that Barraclough girl."

"Her name's Alice," said Sarah.

"Is it? Well that's by the by." Mary leaned heavily on the table now and thrust her painted face forward, saying, "She's trouble, Sarah." Then, stretching her arms over the lace tablecloth, Mary's face took on the appearance of someone sucking a lemon. "I know for a fact that she mixes with all and sundry, and what she gets up to with them I dread to think! She lives in a pigsty – probably infested with...oh, the Lord only knows what – and I will not have a sister of mine associating with such trash. And another thing...."

Thankfully, Hilda raced in grasping the child – with Emily in tow. "I'll 'ave to change 'er...she's only gone and shi...messed herself." And she rushed out, holding the infant at arm's length.

At first Mary appeared insensible to the condition of her baby daughter – and even to Sarah's fit of the giggles – but then she turned, saying to Emily, "I'll go and see if Hilda needs a hand." And she stood looming over the youngster, adding, "I think you had better tell your sister what we will be doing, Emily; and perhaps then she'll decide to be on her way."

And when the lanky woman had gone upstairs, Sarah confronted her sister: "What was all that about? Have you two been planning something out the back?"

Emily drew nearer to the table, and fiddling with the edge of the cloth, said, "She said I could stay an' play wi' t'babby."

"But I've got to take you home, Em."

"Ah, but our Mary says she's going to a special Mass tonight – it being the feast week, like – and she'll bring me 'ome then."

"Oh God! Emily. Why didn't you say that I was taking you back? Mam won't like it...and Dad'll go spare. You just don't think at times!"

Emily was almost in tears. But Sarah pulled her close, and putting her arms around her, said, "Oh, it's all right, love; I'll face 'em. You stay if you want. After all, that little one needs you from what I can see....Now, you go back in the fresh air and I'll be off. ...Go on." She stood back and stroked her sister's face. "I'll see to it, love. Go on...go and play in the sun." And Emily went.

What was she to do? How on earth could she explain things to Mam and Dad? Perhaps she should go out and grab her sister and insist that she come home with her?

Sarah went and sat back on the stool beside the fireside and looked at the arrangement of flowers sitting in the hearth, and prayed for guidance. Katherine would know exactly what to do; but what would that be? Think! Think, Sarah Harvey!

Somehow, she knew she would have to pluck up courage before confronting her parents with the news....And then it came to her: she'd call in and see Alice Barraclough – despite Mary's protestations – and ask her what she should say to Mam....Aye, that would be the best idea. After all, Alice was three years her elder and oh! such a damned good liar. And as far as Mary was concerned, she could bloody well go and run up a shutter.

3

"Where the hell have you been? Have you seen the time?" Emma glared at her daughter. "And just look at the state of yer: filthy! Surely you didn't get like that at our Mary's?"

Sarah glanced down at her hands. "No; I called in on Alice on the way back and helped her sort through some of the stuff her dad had picked up on his round this mornin'."

"What?" Emma grabbed her daughter by the shoulders now. "I could shake yer till yer teeth rattle!" Then pushing Sarah aside, she bounded to the sink and picked up a bucket. "I've told you a thousand times not to set foot in that flea-ridden shack. She's a bad lot is that Alice Barraclough. Now, get yerself down to the tap and fetch up a bucketful. And it'll be cold water for you, me lass. There's just enough in the kettle for yer dad to 'ave a wash and I'm not boiling another one – not in this weather." She thrust the bucket into Sarah's arms. "Go on then! Don't just stand there looking gormless. Hey! and by the way, where's our Em? Not next door an' all I hope, or there'll be ructions I can tell you."

"Still at Mary's, Mam," said Sarah under her breath.

But her mother heard her. "What? Well how's she goin' to get back here? She can't walk home on her own. Somebody'll have to go and fetch her now, and....Oh, no!" She let out a lethargic groan. "Please don't tell me *Mary's* bringing her back?"

Sarah nodded; and after telling her mother the truth, she ran out into the back lane with the bucket, leaving Emma to hold her head in her hands....

Humping the bucketful of water back up the lane, Sarah spotted Len's horse standing in the Barracloughs' yard. Len must have finished for today now, she thought. And after glancing at her own back door which was wide open, she deposited the bucket and ducked down low, thinking, At least the water should warm up a bit. Then, crawling over the cracked and weed-ridden earth beneath the broken back walls of Victoria Row, she reached the Barracloughs' gate. Standing now, she dusted herself down and brushed the grit from her knees.

Ben had his head stuck in the midden, chewing on something

rank no doubt. She knew that Leonard, after his journeys of the day, picking up any bits of scrap that he could lay his hands upon to sell on to the gypsies over the next week, would be drunk and fast asleep by now; and that Alice would be tarting herself up for a night at the fair – to go looking for a lad!

Unlatching the gate now, she went into the rubbish-strewn yard, and slowly approached the emaciated creature and held out her hand. Ben looked up from the midden and ambled towards her. She stroked his hair, saying calmly, "Poor lad. I wish you were mine....D'yer know, I'd wash you and feed you and let you wander over yonder fields" – she indicated the landscape behind her – "and I'd love you, Ben, just like a brother." Her heart sank now. Aay! John, she thought, I wish you were here and taking me to the feast like you did last year. And as Ben nuzzled into her, she grasped him close and wetted his matted mane with her tears.

"Sarah! Sarah! Where're you at now? Yer dad's home....D'yer hear?"

"Oh, hell! I'd best be off....Mam's calling....Love you Jo...er, Ben." And after wiping her face on her frock, she retrieved the bucket and raced back home – forgetting to re-latch the Barracloughs' gate....

Emma had decided to let her husband have a wash, change out of his work clothes, and finish his meal before dropping the bombshell about Mary coming.

Katherine had arrived home. She had declined the mutton broth – as had Emma – saying it was far too hot to eat; but both George and Sarah had demolished all that had been put in front of them.

Katherine was brushing Sarah's hair now, and without turning to look at her step-father, said, "How about coming to the feast with us, Dad?"

Emma gazed at her husband.

Then George said, "I don't think so, lass; I'll be happy enough here tonight. But you and the lasses go and enjoy yerselves."

"Nelly's coming up later." This was Emma.

And George, mopping up the last of his gravy with a chunk of bread, said, "That'll be nice...I like Nelly."

Emma looked at this tall, broad-shouldered man of hers, thinking, I'll have to tell him before long.

"Where's our Em...? She bad again...? In bed, is she...?" George pushed his large frame out of his seat and went and put his bowl in the sink.

"No...she's...."

But Sarah interrupted her mother, blurting out: "At Mary's... she's bringing our Em back when she goes to Ma....Ow!" Katherine had dragged the brush through her sister's hair so hard that it had dug into the scalp. And immediately, the two elder women of the household turned to catch the expression on George's face, whilst Sarah tried to disentangle the brush from her locks.

A throbbing silence echoed around the kitchen. Then George, having swilled his plate and placed it on the set-pot, turned slowly; and after depositing himself in his chair beside the range, he took up his pipe. Striking a match on the grate, he lit the tobacco and drew in the sweet-smelling smoke until the bulb glowed red. All eyes were fixed on him, until he said softly, "Whenever you're ready, lasses, so am I....D'yer think I'll pass at the feast dressed as I am?"

And as Sarah and Katherine's faces lit up the whole room, Emma just gaped at her husband.

"Emma! George! Can I come in?"

"Door's open, Nelly."

"Aye, of course it is, lass...I just thought that...."

"Oh, do come in, Nelly, and get sat down for goodness sake."

Nelly looked about her neighbour's kitchen as if searching for spies. "You on yer own, lass?"

"Aye, I am....Kettle's just on t'boil. I weren't going to do another tonight, but there were enough embers left to see us by."

"Eeh! it's been a swelterer today. Our Jessie were drippin' when she got 'ome....George upstairs then?"

Emma sauntered over to the table with the teapot, and when she had seated herself, she breathed heavily, saying, "Pour it out, lass."

What's up here? thought Mrs Dicks, spooning two helpings of sugar into Emma's mug; she looks in a right state.

"Aay, I'm sorry, lass. It's been a bugger of a day." And Emma went on to tell her neighbour the saga of the girls' visit to Mary's; Sarah going into the Barraclough house; and that when her husband had found out that Mary was bringing Emily home on her way to Mass, he'd ushered his dearly loved girls out of the house and taken them to the fair.

"But I didn't think he'd set foot on the feast ground after last...."

"Neither did I, Nelly," Emma cut in. "But the thought of Mary being here for even five minutes was too much for him. He just finished his pipe and was off with the two of 'em before I could shut me gob. Anyroad, Mary arrived – and went – and then I clocked young Wilf coming across the street, and I asked him to take our Em down to the feast ground and drop her off with her dad."

"Eeh, I say…! Well, it's to be hoped that's all the trouble out of the way for t'present."

"Oh, please, Nelly, don't tempt providence – I honestly can't take any more today."

But Emma's words had barely left her lips when an almighty wailing emanated from the back lane, and before either could raise herself and go to the open door, Leonard Barraclough fell headlong over the threshold and landed with a thud on the stone floor.

Emma was up first and rushed towards her neighbour. Crouching over him now, she said gently, "Len, lad…eeh, Len, are yer hurt? What on earth's up, man?"

"Is he drunk, Emma?" Nelly asked.

"Course he's bloody drunk! I told you he would be. Mind you, I've never seen him in as bad a state as this before. Come and help me get him into an easy chair."

And when the two women had dragged him into George's armchair beside the hearth and forced him to drink a mouthful of strong tea, Emma knelt on the rug and shook him violently by the knees. "Len! What is wrong? LEN…! Here, Nelly, pass me a wet flannel out of the sink." And after she'd wiped Len's face and he appeared to be more lucid, Emma said, "Right then. Tell me."

Len leaned forward; and with a glazed expression on his damp face, said, "It's me 'orse…he's gone. Me livelihood, Emma; and he's gone. Gone!"

"Gone where? I thought he were locked up in the yard."

"He were! I put 'im there when I got 'ome. And he's too bloody dozy to open the gate 'imself….What time is it, lass? Please tell me what time it is. What's the time, Emma? What's the damned time?"

"I'll slap him before long, Nelly….IT'S NEARLY SEVEN!"

Len drew himself up now, saying, "It's those soddin' gypsies what's pinched him, Emma. Pinched me bloody livelihood….I'll have to go and look for him." He stood upright now – and stayed upright – saying, "I've left the rent with our Alice….Alex'll be 'ere afore long, won't he? 'cos t'lass wants to be off to t'feast….

31

Eeh, thanks, Emma, I feel better now. Best be off though, or they might think o' sellin' the old bugger....I *will* find him, Emma; I'll find our old Ben." And Len tottered out.

"Now. Where on God's earth is he goin' lookin' for an 'orse the state he's in?" said Nelly.

"I've no idea, lass." Emma pushed herself up from a kneeling position, and holding onto Nelly's shoulder, added, "What were you saying about all the trouble being out of the way for today?"

And as they looked at each other, they couldn't help but to burst out laughing....

They had finished the last few rows of the rag rug. And after they had swept up the bits of woollen threads that were scattered about the kitchen and made a further pot of tea, Emma said, "He's been next door a long time."

"Who?"

"Alex Stockwell – I caught a glimpse of him crossing the street when I was putting the trestles away. He's been in there well over half an hour, lass. We'll have spent the rent before he gets to us."

"Well, I'm glad I brought mine with me and locked up, what with 'em pinchin' 'orses and the like....D'yer know: it's not safe to be alive these days."

Emma still had Alex on her mind. "He doesn't stay this long when Len's around. Odd that...?"

A few minutes later, a knock came to open the door. "Oh, Mr Alex," said Emma. "Come in...come in. My, it's stuffy tonight, don't you think? Sit down for a minute while I get the book."

Alex Stockwell took a seat at the table, saying, "It certainly is a stifling evening, Mrs Harvey...especially to have a fire going."

"Oh, it's being left low now – what with the time getting on," said Emma handing him the rent book.

And as the young man pocketed the coins and receipted the book, he was apologetic: "I am later than usual I'm afraid, but Father's taken a turn for the worse and then...er...Miss Barraclough kept me talking. Did you hear that her father's horse has gone missing?"

"We did indeed. And I'm sorry to hear about your father."

"Well, it's only a matter of time now, ladies....But he has asked me specifically to let you know that, come what may, you will be connected to your own supply of gas before next summer."

Emma clasped her hands together, saying, "Oh, Mr Alex, that'll be wonderful – won't it Nelly?"

Without commenting, Nelly slid her own rent across the table towards this heir to old Stockwell's fortune, pondering as to the veracity of this tall, black-haired, and overly handsome young man. And as he passed the book back and smiled into her eyes, she knew he was hiding something.

When he had bid them both good evening, Nelly said bluntly, "That lad's not all that he seems."

It was shortly after eight and the sun was on its way to setting.

Nelly had returned home to prepare a bit of supper for when Jessie got in, and Emma was sitting alone in the twilight. She couldn't get her mind off the happenings of a year ago, and prayed that this year her family would soon be back home, safely by her side....

Emily was the first to run in, and as she went and clung to her mother, burst into tears.

"What in heaven's name is wrong?" Emma gently lifting her daughter's head and smoothed back her straw-coloured hair and passed a thumb beneath her eyes. "Now, come on, love...what is it?"

"Well...well...yer know Wilf took me to the feast because Dad had gone...." And Emily cried.

"Shush, love...go on...go on."

The youngster took in a staggered breath, saying, "Some lads picked a fight with him...and Wilf got bashed...oh, Mam."

"There, there, no more tears....But what about...?"

Then in came her husband, pushing Sarah before him. "Go on, take her up, lass." And taking Emily's hand, Sarah led her sister to the chamber steps and saw her up to bed.

Emma was on her feet now. "George, it's not just Wilf, is it?" She could see the pained expression on his face. "Is it Jessie? Oh, not our Kath. Surely not our Ka...."

George Harvey wrapped his strong arms around his wife. "No lass, everybody's fine....Well...."

Emma thrust him away. "What do you mean by 'well'?"

"Calm down, Emma, we're all all right."

"But where's Katherine? Where is she? I'll tell you, George, I've had my bloody fill of it today. Just tell me!"

He went to the dresser now and lit the lamp. Then striding over to the sink, he bent down and pulled out two bottles of ale that were cooling in the water bucket. He prised off the caps and poured the contents into two mugs. "Now," he said, "sit yerself on that chair, shut up, and have a drink. Then I'll tell you what's happened."

Emma was wringing her hands. "Oh, for God's sake I can't take much more of this after...."

"Emma. Sit! And drink!"

And Emma did as she was bid.

George swigged at his beer and wiped his mouth on his shirt-sleeve. "Right!" he began. "Katherine's next door with Alice." His hand was raised now. "Don't say a word. Just hold on a minute." Once more he quenched his thirst. "She's staying with her until her dad gets in...God knows where he is!"

"Somebody's pinched his horse," said Emma.

George resisted a smile, knowing what he had to impart next: "We were sitting outside the beer tent – me and our Em, I mean – Katherine had taken Sal on the Shamrock...you know that big swing thing."

"I know what it is, George...just get to the point."

George refilled his mug now, saying, "Well, then we saw Alice pass us, giggling and dancing with some of the gypsy lads, and she waved to us and then went off in the direction of the mill. But in the meantime, Wilf turned up with a real shiner – he'd been in some sort of scrap...I've just seen his dad running off carrying a length o' wood. He'll sort 'em out."

"Oh, for God's sake, George! Just spit it out."

George look into his beer before saying, "Well, when Kath got back with our Sal, she said *she'd* seen Alice an' all – going off with these lads." He took a further gulp of his drink. "Then, Kath said she was going to follow them – thinking Alice may be in some danger. And she was right."

"What do you mean she was right?"

George opened another button on his blue, cotton shirt and finished his beer. "It seems likely that one – or more – of those lads, just might have...well...yer know...."

"No, I bloody well don't know...! Oh God...yer don't mean she could've been...got at?"

George nodded.

Emma's mouth hung open. But she quickly closed it when her cheeks began to balloon involuntarily. Then, hurriedly pushing back her chair, she ran to the sink. And there she vomited.

4

"Eeh, Emma, will it ever stop raining? And it's cold with it for May."

Emma rammed the poker between the ribs of the grate and rattled it amongst the coals. "Well I'll say this, Nelly, I never thought back in August I'd be happy to see flames darting up me chimney....Sit yerself down, lass. Here, let me drape yer coat over George's chair to dry off."

"Seen anything of her next door, lately?" Nelly passed Emma her coat.

"Who, Alice? No, not really. Mind you, I can imagine that Len's given her strict orders not to set foot outside the place – being in the condition she is." Emma shook her neighbour's coat as a terrier would shake a rat and draped it over the back of the chair. "Pour the tea, Nelly, that's a good lass."

And when they were both seated, finishing off the last of Emma's home-made Simnel cake, Nelly said, "How long is it now, then?" She nodded at the wall.

"Nearly there, Nelly. Couple o' weeks now I'd say."

"Bound to be....I wonder what colour hair gypsy babbies have?"

"Black, I suppose. They all have."

"Maybe it'll pop out with a ring in its ear."

Emma laughed heartily. "Eeh, yer're a daft bugger, Nelly.... Mind you – and it's most odd – whenever I mention Alice's situation, our Kath clams up just like that!" She made a gesture with her hand. "She's kept it all too close for my liking...she knows something, that's for sure."

"Our Jess is the same."

"Ah, but – and I don't mean owt wrong in this, lass – our Kath and your Jess are as thick as thieves."

"Yer're right there, Emma."

"Kath's next door now...doing what, God only knows! Oh, I do wish my lot wouldn't set foot in that place." And Emma shuddered.

Nelly leaned forward; and sketching invisible lines on the table top, said, "D'yer think she's let on who the father is?"

"She might not know, Nelly....But I bet a pound to a piece of shit, if she does, she's blurted it out to Jessie and our Kath."

"So, d'yer think they do know summat after all?"

"Oh! like toast is bread....But, I'll tell yer this for nowt: whatever has gone on behind that wall" – she stabbed a finger toward the chimney-breast – "I'm determined to find out."

And the two women nodded at each other.

Next door, Katherine was sitting among the rubbish in Alice's kitchen. How on earth can they live in this lot? Fair enough being poor, but not to exist in such squalor. Her own family was poor enough, but at least her mam kept a clean and tidy house. Fancy! bringing a child into this bug-infested hovel. It didn't bear thinking about.

Alice Elizabeth Barraclough was an only child. But this would not have been the case if her siblings had survived the flu epidemic that had stricken her own and other families' households during the early 1900s. And then her mother, Florence, weakened by the raging virus and the conditions in which they were living, died giving birth to the only child of the Barraclough clan that would be fortunate enough to survive.

Alice was a hardy girl – and an intelligent one. She did well at school and could have gone on to great things if circumstances hadn't prevented her; and she was devoted to her father. Her role in life now was to take the place of her mother and take care of Len and the business – albeit if her standing in that so-called business was as a rag-and-bone man's assistant.

Alice came back from the outside privy, and struggling to find her way through the boxes of old clothes and cast-iron pans, she said, "I'm glad Dad found Ben...we'd have never been able to buy a new horse otherwise."

Katherine looked intently at this pretty sixteen-year-old who had been brought up solely by her father since she was born, and had to admit he'd done a good job: she was well-spoken and looked after herself. And even though her clothes were other folks' cast-offs, at least they were laundered and pressed....But then she'd gone and got herself into trouble!

"We're right out of tea, Kath, or I'd make you some."

"Oh, that's all right, love; I didn't come in for that...I just wanted to have a little chat." Katherine sat forward now, and resting her arms on her knees, put her hands together, saying,

"About the baby....Are you going to keep it?"

"Yes I am....And Dad's in agreement – whatever the consequences."

"It might be taken off you, you know."

"I'll never let them do that!"

"You might not have any choice, love. And what about the father? Has he said anything?"

Alice slumped forward. "He doesn't seem to care."

"Well, he bloody well ought to! He's played a part in all this for God's sake!"

The girl was close to tears. "Don't be angry, Kath. I can't bear it if you're angry. Apart from me dad, and you and your Sarah, I haven't a friend in the world."

Katherine grasped the girl's hands and shook them gently. "I'm not angry, love. I could never be angry with you....It's just that I care. And there are more people concerned about you than you might think. But it really riles me that he seems to have ignored things as if nothing ever happened between the two of you."

"Oh, well, Kath, I can't do anything about that; I've just got to take one day at a time and see how things turn out." Alice's reddened eyes widened now. "But y'aven't told anybody who the father is, have you?"

Katherine took exception to the remark. "Certainly not! What kind of friend do you think I am?"

"Oh, I'm sorry. It's just that...well...."

"Eeh, love, come here." And Katherine embraced the mother to be, saying, "We'll get through this, love. You and me; we'll get through it when the time does come."

And the time came a little sooner than anyone expected.

"Mam! Mam! Where's our Kath?"

"She's in the cellar fetching up a bucket of coal....And where the hell have you been? You're wet through!"

"We think the baby's coming."

"We? What baby?"

"Alice's of course. Whose do you think?"

"You haven't been next door? How many times have I....Come here this instant." Emma grabbed a towel from the set-pot, and dragging Sarah towards her, vigorously proceeded to dry her hair. "You get yourself into such a state at times."

"But it's comin'. She's bangin' her head."

"I'll bang *your* bloody 'ead afore long if you don't keep still."

Katherine appeared at the cellar head, only to see Sarah emerge from beneath the towel looking like a besom brush. "What's going on?"

Sarah attempted to flatten her hair. "Oh, Kath! It's Alice...the baby's comin'."

Katherine dropped the bucket. "I'll go."

"I'm comin' an' all," said Sarah, and she ran to her sister.

"Oi!" said Emma. "Get back here!"

"Oh, shut up, Mother!" and Sarah followed her sister out of the front door, while the stupefied matriarch was left holding the wet towel. Then she said aloud, "Shut up! Shut up? Well that's the bloody limit."

Katherine and Sarah raced next door to find Alice writhing about on the bed that her father had brought downstairs for her. "Oh, Kath. Fetch the...the doctor. I...think I'm....Oh, God, I can't stand this...."

Katherine took charge now. "Sarah, pull down those towels from off the range, and get a pan of water going the fire. Oh, and see if you can find a ball o' tough string and some scissors. Then tie the string onto the scissors and put both in the water when it boils – but watch out you don't scald yourself." And as Sarah did so, Katherine went to comfort the young girl who was about to bring a new life into the world. "I'm here, love. Squeeze my hand...you're doing fine."

"Oh, no I'm not...oooh...! Oh, Kath, I think I've...dear God...."

"Try and relax, love. Just breathe....A little faster...that's it.... Sal, come and help me with the towels and we'll try to get her in a better position." And as Katherine and Sarah pulled and tugged at the screaming girl, Alice repeatedly banged her skull against the bedhead. "It's going to take more than just us two to see to things, Sal. Run and get Jessie, love."

As Sarah fled the house, Alice grabbed Katherine's hand. "I'm... I think I'm...d...dying, Kath."

"You're bloody well not. Not if I've got anything to do with it. Just hang on...it's going to be all right, I promise." Alice's screams reverberated around the shabby, junk-filled kitchen....

Moments later, Jessie burst in followed by Sarah. "Good God! I could hear her when I was coming up the street. Is she...?"

"Get over here, Jess, and give me a hand. I think we're going to be in for a long haul."

At five minutes to three, on the morning of Sunday the 16th of May 1937, Alice Barraclough gave birth to a son.

"If he'd have been a girl, Kath, I'd have called her Florence after my mother."

"You're not disappointed at not having a girl, are you?"

"Good Lord no! I mean just look at him."

And Katherine smiled broadly at the lad, thinking, Aye you can see he takes after his father. Then she turned to Jessie and Sarah, saying, "Thanks for your help, you two; I couldn't have done it on my own....Now, you best be off while I tidy things up."

Jessie pulled down her sleeves. "I'll stay if yer want, love."

"No, you're on a Sunday shift in a few hours; I'll manage now."

Jessie leaned over Alice and, stroking the little boy's hair, she smiled, saying, "He's a real beauty, Alice. A real beauty."

When she and Sarah had left and closed the door against the unremitting rainstorm, Katherine sat on the edge of the bed and held Alice's hand. "Well, you did it, love....How do you feel?"

"Tired, Kath."

"I'm not surprised."

And as Alice cradled her son's head, she glowed with a love that Katherine had scarcely encountered before. Then the new mother asked, "How did you know what to do, though?"

"Don't forget, love; I saw three come into the world next door," said Katherine.

Alice nodded. "Now," she said, "I want you to do something for me before Dad gets up."

"Anything you want, love"

Alice raised herself higher on her pillows, saying, "There's a small, wooden box...just behind that pile of books on the window sill. Will you get it for me?"

And when Katherine found the object and placed it on the counterpane, Alice asked her to open it.

"Well, I never!" Katherine's eyes were wide with wonder. "It is stunning!" And as she held the sapphire and diamond cuff-link close to the lamp, she gasped. Then, turning it over in her palm she saw, engraved on its silver base, the letter 'A'. "But whose is it?" she asked.

"His now." And the young mother gazed at her son.

"But where did you get it?"

"From his father."

Katherine almost dropped the brilliant object onto the floor. "He *gave* it to you?"

"Oh, no...he lost it. Most likely he doesn't know where, but it's his all right....Well, Alan's now."

So, she's calling him Alan?

"But" – Alice continued – "I want you to keep it safe for him until he's grown....I trust you, Kath, you see. And, if anything should happen to me, then I know you'll look after it and pass it on when the time comes."

"But nothing's going to happen to you. Where did you get that idea from?"

Alice smiled the strangest of smiles. "I have a feeling, Kath; a very strong feeling that something dreadful's going to occur – not just to me, but to all of us."

It's what she's been through, thought Katherine; but looking deep into those extraordinarily penetrating eyes, something told her that she could indeed see the future. Now Katherine said firmly, "Don't think such things, love....But still, it'll be safe with me; I promise you that. In fact, it will never leave my side." And she replaced the link in its box, the while thinking, I wonder if the other one's around here somewhere?

"Oh, it's you! You're still up, Mam."

"Aye, it's me. And aye, I'm still up. Well?"

"Well what?"

"Don't pretend with me, Katherine. What did she tell you?"

"Like what, Mam?"

"Who the bloody father is! That's like what!"

Katherine seated herself at the table. "Look, I know as much as you do. Alice has no idea who he could be."

Emma shoved her hands into her hair. "She has no idea? Well, I've always said what a slut she is, but that proves it." She placed her hands back on the table. "I'll tell yer this, madam: if you're kiddin' me and you know more than what you're saying, I'll discover the truth and woe betide you when I do...! So, what colour hair has it got?"

"Mam, he's not an 'it'. He's a beautiful little boy; and the small amount of hair he has at the moment, is...well, dark...ish."

"I knew it! I bloody well knew it! A rotten gypsy!"

"Oh, I can't listen to you any more, Mam; I'm going to bed."

Emma waved her daughter away. "Aye, you do that. Bloody well go, 'cos I won't be."

5

It started with the semblance of a sigh.

Sarah had taken the ashes out of the grate and placed in their stead, paper, wood, and small pieces of coal, ready for the fire to be lit. She didn't know why she was the first up today...she was just restless. Looking at the clock now, she thought, Going on for four. It'll be light soon. Thank God it's stopped raining.

The rain had persisted for well over a week; and it reminded her of the torrential downpour that had drenched the town on the day that Alice Barraclough gave birth to her son. She recalled coming home afterwards and how her mother had scolded her for having been next door to witness such a spectacle, and how vigorously she had been towelled dry for a second time. Yet the experience of seeing a new child being born was something that both astounded and invigorated Sarah, and she would never forget that look of overwhelming love which the girl had shown toward her little boy after the struggle she had gone through....Still, she'd have to press on. Dad would be up soon and wanting his tea.

Taking the ashes into the back lane, she threw them in the midden; and through the weird, low, mist that had settled over the land, she could just about spot Len Barraclough's horse standing quietly in next door's yard as if he were still dozing. Poor old lad. He's been out in this wicked weather since it started. They ought to have taken him indoors like they used to.

It was now that she heard the first, unearthly murmur – much different from the strange lament she had noticed before. It was as if thunder was snoring in the fields below Thorp Hill. And then it stopped. But it started again, as if the distant land was groaning. As though it was in pain....

She had set the table for breakfast and the fire was roaring up the chimney when Katherine came into the kitchen. "Mam and Dad not up? I never noticed when I got out of bed."

"No. I'd better call them in a few minutes or Dad'll be on the last push up. He hates being late."

Katherine slumped into her father's chair in front of the fire, and staring into the flames, she said wearily, "I heard some peculiar noises in the night – but maybe I was dreaming?"

"You weren't, Kath. I heard them when I took out the ashes. They scared me." Sarah lifted the kettle into the grate. "It'll soon boil, Kath. Will you keep an eye on it till I wake them?"

"Of course I will, love." Katherine flipped her long brown hair over her shoulders, leaned close to the fire, and pushed her hands towards the heat. It was now she thought about Alice who last year had suffered the agonies of giving birth. What would become of her? And what of the boy? She couldn't help but think that fate *did* have something dreadful in store for them. And within the next hour she would be proved right.

The family – apart from Emily – was seated around the table. George Harvey had finished his soft-boiled egg and fried bread, and his wife was refilling his mug of tea. "That were grand, Sal," he said, wiping his mouth on the back of his hand. "Set me up for the day, it has." And Sarah blushed, saying, "Oh, Dad...it were nothing special."

"I wonder if I should take our Em to see the doctor?" said Emma changing the subject. "She's not going to school, George. That's for sure."

"Oh, just let her stay in bed, lass. It's nobbut a cold. Probably brought on with all the rain we've had lately. And besides, we can't afford doctors – 'specially now they're talking of us likely going on short time at the mill."

Emma remained quiet. Then Katherine said, "Alice were tellin' me that Len had been out on his rounds, and one of the lanes going up to Thorp had sunk so much he had trouble getting his cart through. He had to cut across a field; but that was as bad: full of holes."

"Well, he should have known better than to go out in that weather," said Emma as she got up and collected the breakfast plates. "He gets dafter by the week." She went and tossed the crockery in the sink.

"He hasn't been himself since the bairn came along."

"Well, all I can say to that, George, is that he should have brought her up better. Fancy letting her get into the family way at her age."

"Nay, lass, it were hardly his fault. And besides, he can't keep an eye on her every minute of the day."

"Well he ought to – knowing what she's like."

"That's not fair, Mam." This was Katherine. "And I don't know what you mean by 'knowing what she's like'. I know more about her situation than *you* do."

Emma paused in her dish washing, and turning, said, "Oh, you do, do you? Well you might let me in on it….What I do know is that she's a wanton piece." She pointed a soapy finger at the adjoining wall. "Fancy getting herself involved with one of those gypsy lot and now we're having to live next door to the…the thing. I'm surprised at you lot, I really am after all we've been through. I never thought that my own family would have truck with the likes of gypsies – or their offspring."

"They are all right, Mam," said Katherine. "I really don't know why you dislike them so much."

"Dislike! I detest them. They're filthy and crude and…." Her words were cut short as a momentous crash came from next door, followed by a high-pitched scream. "What on earth…?"

And then it began in earnest.

Sarah was the first to become aware of the abnormal disturbance when she noticed the ground beneath her feet start to tremble. "Dad! Can you feel…?" But her question was interrupted by an extended creaking of the beams above their heads. And as they all looked upward, a shower of plaster descended from the ceiling, covering the table in a layer of brown dust.

George was on his feet. "Go and get Emily, Kath; and throw a coat on her." And as Katherine sprang from her chair and raced upstairs, Sarah flew to her father and clung to him, quickly followed by Emma, who cried out, "What's happening, Geo…?"

Suddenly, waves of soot and lumps of stone surged down the chimney into the fireplace, scattering burning coals around the kitchen and setting fire to the hearthrug in their wake. George pushed his wife and daughter away. "Get outside! The front door! And as far away from the house as you can."

"What about our Em and Kath? We can't just…."

"Get out! NOW!"

Emma grabbed Sarah by the shoulders and both fled from the house as George ran to the sink, and clutching the bowl of dirty washing-up water, tried to douse the flames that had now engulfed the rug. And then he thought, What the hell are you doing, man? That was a bit pointless! Just get outside yourself! But suddenly, roof slates began to fly into the room, accompanied by clouds of black dust that billowed from the chimney. He was now half-blinded, and after touching the side of his face, he could feel the warm stickiness of blood dripping down to his chin. Yet although sightless and bleeding, his hearing was somehow enhanced, and the thunderous rumblings coming from next door sounded as if a storm was raging in his neighbours' house. And he soon realised that the same storm was about to engulf his own home if he didn't move. Then he heard Katherine's voice cry out above the crashing of crockery and the breaking of glass: "Dad! Dad!" And he shouted in the direction of her voice: "Get out of the…back door!" He was breathless, choking.

Unrestrained now, the stone flags beneath his feet began to crack and he could feel them loosening. If he didn't try to get out now he'd be following them into the cellar. Yet he was too late, as the floor, seemingly rising at first, buckled under him, and he sensed himself falling.

But somehow, he managed to grab hold of the fire grate with one hand and cursed as its remaining heat seared his fingers. He had to bear the pain somehow since his legs were dangling in air, thrashing about over the chasm that had been created in the middle of the kitchen. Now, feeling around him with his free hand, he detected the edge of a flagstone that, although sloping precariously, still appeared to be fixed to its brick supports that made up part of the cellar. He took his chance now. Holding on to the slab, he searched about with his foot until it rested on one of the bricks in the void below him, and without hesitating he released his hand from the grate and threw himself sideways until his hands came together, clutching at the edge of the flag. Then mustering all his strength, together with the aid of the brick support beneath him, hurled himself upward until he landed bang flat on the remains of the stone floor. He panted heavily, ignoring the pain in his burned hand; then began to slither like a snake in the direction of the back door. Above the noise of creaking beams – and the smashing of plates as they flew off the dresser – he could hear his named being called from every conceivable direction. He had to get up – and out – somehow.

Still sliding blindly over a section of the floor that incredibly had remained intact, his hand came across a large, moulded object directly in front of him: it was a leg of the table, still resting there in its usual position. Will it move if I try? he thought. But this was no time to think. He wrapped one arm around it, then the other, and slowly began to draw himself towards it. But the table *did*

44

move, and he was being dragged with it back into the depths of the cellar. But suddenly it stopped dead against one of the broken flagstones. This was his chance. He tugged violently against the table leg – which thankfully remained fixed – and pulled himself erect until he could feel its roughened surface. And then he navigated himself in the direction of the door, hoping that another gaping void was not in his path. But something *was* in his path and he tripped, landing flat on his face.

Blessedly it was the edge of the threshold and he could feel fresh air wafting against the back of his neck. "Keep going man," he said aloud; "you're nearly out; don't give up now." But the words had scarcely left his lips when a deafening and ruthless roar burst forth behind him as broken joists and floorboards came crashing down from the bedroom – one joist barely missing the sole of one of his work boots. God help me if one of the beds comes next! Then the pain in his hand intensified as if it were trapped in a vice.

"Dad! Take my other hand....Quick! The whole place'll come down afore long." It was Katherine who, possessed of a superhuman strength, began to drag him over the threshold and into the yard as if she were pulling a sack of coal up the cellar steps. She pulled and pulled until she reached the field where, releasing her grip, she gasped and dropped him onto the grass. Breathlessly she said, "Are you...are you all right? You're bleeding."

George's back was pumping up and down as he too tried to recover his breath. And then he managed to say, "I'm fine, love." He coughed the words. "At least I will be when I get rid of this dust out of me eyes and stick my hand in a bucket of cold water.... Is Em with you?"

"Yes, she's standing in the middle of the field. C'mon let's get you up and further away...But what about Mam and Sarah?"

"They got out the front," said her stepfather.

Helping him to his feet now, Katherine began to wipe his eyes with a moistened handkerchief. "There. Any better?"

He nodded; and when he felt young Emily wrapping her arms around his waist, he fully opened his stinging eyes and stroked her fine, mousy hair. Turning around now, he placed a hand above his eyes and looked directly before him at what remained of the row of terraced houses.

The end one, the Barracloughs', was totally razed. It was a mound of rubble. Here and there were broken beams, planks of decaying wood, and an odd chimney pot perched precariously on top of the whole mess. He rubbed his eyes and focused on his own home which, at least from the outside, appeared to be still standing. But it couldn't be anything other than a ruin. He could speculate with confidence now as the roof caved in and it collapsed like a house of cards.

The three of them fled further into the field, away from the bricks and shards of glass which appeared to have grown wings and were hurtling towards them. Then there came an eerie silence as if the world had ended.

Through sore and watery eyes, George Harvey now turned to his daughters. Emily was weeping uncontrollably, while Katherine appeared to be staring into oblivion – and that was not far from the truth. "Come on. Let's try and find a way round the front." And taking Emily's hand, he said, "Don't cry, love....Let's go and find Mam and our Sal."

They skirted the end of the Barracloughs' yard which was buried in blocks of stone several feet high – the only thing remaining being the battered old gate lying abandoned. Climbing over the fence that separated Victoria Row from Low Field, they staggered over the oddments of what remained of people's homes until they reached comparative safety.

The street was packed with neighbours and bystanders: men in open-necked shirts with sleeves rolled up over their elbows, and women with arms tucked into their aprons. But where was the rest of his family?

Then he spotted Arnie Sutcliffe and young Wilf. "Have you seen Emma and Sarah, lad?" Wilf shook his head. "Go an 'ave a look for 'em," said Arnie. "I'll keep the lasses wi' me." And George barged his way through the crowds.

"What a bloody mess, eh, lass?"

Katherine nodded at Arnie. Then turning about, she saw for the first time the extent of the devastation. The Barracloughs' place didn't exist. And their own home was barely recognisable – apart from the iron range and its surrounds, wherein, even now, smoke could still be seen emerging from the grate. A small part of the front wall that joined their house onto the Dicks' still remained, but Nelly and Jessie's place seemed to be leaning onto the next-door neighbours' one further down the Row. And it suddenly dawned on Katherine that if they would have had gas, things could have been terrifyingly worse.

"Emily! Kath!"

"Sarah! Over here!" Katherine pushed two burly men aside and caught hold of her sister's arm, pulling her into a protective embrace. "Where's Mam?"

Sarah raised her head, saying, "Dad's with her. They're on their way back with Jessie and her mam....What are we going to do, Kath? Where will we all go?"

"Shush, love...we'll all get through this somehow."

"But what if they split us up?"

Katherine grasped the girl's hands, and bending close to her, said, "They'll never do that. Never!" And she wiped away Sarah's tears. Then raising her head, she saw the others approaching.

"So, we're all here then?" George ushered his wife and two neighbours forward, whence Emma pulled her children to her bosom and sobbed.

"Eeh, it's a real bugger all this, George," said Arnie Sutcliffe. "How could it have 'appened?"

"God only knows, Arnie; but at least we're alive....Yet, I don't suppose we can say that of the Barracloughs."

Now, unexpectedly, the crowd thinned around them, opening a narrow corridor to allow Alex Stockwell through. "George, are you all safe? I was just passing the end of the Row on my way to see Mr Crowther when I saw what was happening."

"We're a bit battered and bruised, but safe enough, sir. But I don't think I can say that about those poor folk." And he pointed at the pile of rubble that once was home to his neighbours.

Alex looked in silence at the scene before him. It was a full minute before he turned his face – drained of every drop of blood – back at George Harvey. "We must try everything we can to see if...if anyone's still...still alive."

"Aye, we must do that, sir. And as soon as possible I'd say."

Alex nodded nervously. "I'll send for some men from the mill." And he looked around the dumbfounded group.

Wilf Sutcliffe stepped forward. "I'll go, Mr Stockwell. I'm a fast runner."

"Right. But be as quick as you can."

"I'll be that all right. I'll cut across the field." And Wilf sped off.

"Now, George," said Alex. "We'll still need as many hands as we can muster. Are you all right to help? And maybe enlist others?"

"Aye, I can manage....I'll just get my hand seen to and then I'll be free to do what I can."

"Of course. And thank you."

George Harvey asked Arnie if he'd take his family and the Dicks into his shop whilst he gathered some of the men together.

"Of course I will, lad....I'll mash us all some tea – think I'll have enough cups – and they can all have a wash an' all."

"Can I stay with you, Dad? I want to see if I can find Ben."

And when George looked at Sarah, his heart missed a beat. How proud he was of this fine girl of his. But he said, "No, love. You go with yer mam and the others. It'll be too dangerous."

"Well, I'm staying, Dad, and nobody's going to stop me." This was Katherine.

"Don't be daft, lass; it's men's work."

Katherine moved forward and faced him. "Believe me, I'm capable of doing anything a man can do. And besides, you'll need all the help you can get to sort that lot out." And her arm was thrust in the direction of the downfall of their lives. "Now, get some salve on your hand and cover it well and we'll crack on." And George nodded without saying a word.

She, sixteen men from the neighbourhood and another twenty from the mill, worked throughout the day. They shifted heavy stone slabs that had once made up the walls; beams that had supported the upper floors; broken furniture and smashed crockery, and manually deposited them in Low Field. Then, at five in the evening, a voice rang out: "Here's another one of 'em!" And before much longer, Alice Barraclough's body was lain next to her father's in the field and covered with a sheet until transport arrived to take them away.

Even then, no one gave up, and as the light began to fade, a young child's cry was heard. And as six of them, including George, carefully removed the final beam and several splintered planks, there, speared through his small hand with a long, rusted nail, was the boy. George, dripping sweat and tears of complete and overwhelming emotion, threw back his head, and looking into the vastness of heaven, cried, "Yes!"

Seven pairs of eyes were trained on George and Katherine.

Cradling his bandaged hand, George carried on with his news: "Anyhow, the parish hearse took...Len and Alice away."

"Poor souls," said Nelly. "It's a good job it isn't like the old days when the resurrection men used to pilfer the corpses and...."

"Oh, shut up for God's sake, Nelly!" said Emma. "And anyroad, how bloody old *are* you? Did yer still have cock-fighting in the back yard and a lock on the tea caddy? Jesus!" She turned back to her husband now. "So, what about the lad, George?"

George inhaled deeply before saying, "Well, some man in an ambulance came and told us not to remove the nail from the child's hand – it would be best left in and taken out at the hospital in case of infection. So I helped to carry him away. Then, shortly after, Katherine had a word with him and off he went."

"What did yer say, love?" Emma addressed her daughter.

"Oh, I can't really remember, Mam. I was in such a...a confused state...I just don't know."

Sarah went to her father now. "Did you find Ben, Dad?" And George wrapped an arm around his daughter, saying, "No, love. He probably bolted over the fields somewhere. He'll be safe enough, so don't fret."

A long silence ensued before Emma, as pragmatic as ever, said, "Well, what the hell are we to do now? No house, no clothes but the ones we stand up in, and no bloody means of getting *either*."

Katherine stood now; and with hands tucked in her coat pockets, walked the length of the long room above Arnie's shop, the while turning between her fingers, the small box containing the precious cuff-link. And as she paced back and forth the others watched her every movement, waiting for the words that were forming in her mind. Then she said abruptly: "Mary's. We'll go to Mary's."

Now the deathly hush that greeted her words crept around the room like a stalking beast.

Emma swung round and looked at her husband's face. It was a face she had never seen before in all their years of marriage. And when he spoke she flinched.

"WHAT?" George was on his feet now, his arm outstretched. "That's the most ridiculous thing that's ever come out of your mouth. I've always thought of you as a level-headed woman, Katherine, but that remark really takes the biscuit."

Katherine ran forward. "But...."

"NO! And by God I mean that."

And the beastly silence returned....That was until a small voice said, "Dad. They can stay here. We've got plenty o' room."

Arnie Sutcliffe looked at his son's beaming face. "Well, bugger me...why didn't *I* think of that...? What about it, George lad? There are mattresses in the shop and me and Wilf can bunk up – our Lily can have Wilf's bed....Oh, and there's a big stove to cook on.... Well?"

Emma watched her husband walk to a corner of the unfamiliar room and bow his head. She was well aware how much today's frightful occurrence had affected him, and just hoped that his physical strength could help him overcome the profound loss of the home that he had worked hard to maintain and bring his family up in. And still they all waited for what seemed an eternity for his reply to Arnie's suggestion.

Eventually, George slowly raised his head and said quietly, "Thanks, Arnie."

6

The two families had been living over Arnie Sutcliffe's shop for less than a week, but to most of them it had seemed like a lifetime.

It wasn't that Arnie had proved difficult – far from it: he had been the perfect gentleman and left them to their privacy. But for Emma and Nelly, living in strange surroundings had caused some friction between them – particularly when it came to cooking. They were constantly under each other's feet. And then, to rub salt in the wound, the men undertaking the demolition of Victoria Row, had retrieved most of Nelly and Jessie's possessions leaving Emma and her family with the simple basics since most of their things weren't worth saving.

Katherine had managed to come across some rejects from the tailoring warehouse – which at least had provided a change of clothing. And, unbeknown to George, Mary had visited and brought some of her husband's cast-offs. Even so, existing as they were, was testing everybody's patience.

Then, on the Friday evening, Jessie came rushing in from work with news that would lighten their hearts: "Oh, just let me sit down and catch me breath…I've run all the….Just a minute…and then I'll tell yer." She dropped her ample chassis into an armchair and rested her head on the back.

"What is it, lass? Come on, tell us." This was Nelly; but the other three females present echoed her curiosity.

"Well," Jessie began, "I was 'aving me snap – those sandwiches were lovely, Mam – and who walks into the weaving shed but J B himself, and he comes straight up to me and plonks 'imself next to me on a box. Oh, I can tell yer, I were struck dumb….Anyroad, after tellin' me to carry on wi' me dinner, he planted a hand on me knee just like this." And Jessie demonstrated – much to the disbelief of the others who were standing around her open-mouthed. "Then he says to me: 'Now, Jessie Dicks, I've heard of your plight after the shocking events of some days ago, and I have some news for you.' He took his hand off me knee then, and looked straight into me eyes, saying, 'Early next week, two of the mill houses on Long Lane are being vacated and I immediately thought of you – and your neighbours of course. So, if you want to move in – they're furnished, with running water and gas; no electricity at the moment I'm afraid, but no doubt we'll get round to that at some point – then they're yours.'

"Oh, I can tell yer, I couldn't speak. I just nodded me head like a rag doll. Then he said, 'Good. Good. I'll send William around with the keys – probably Sunday if that suits – and he can make arrangements for you to move in....Right then, Jessie,' says he, 'I'll go and let you get on.' And he patted me knee again and walked off."

Emma and Nelly were already bouncing up and down in their excitement, hugging each other like two friends who hadn't seen each other for years. And when they ran out of steam, Emma gasped, "Eeh, I can't wait to tell George and our Kath."

And Sarah smiled broadly at Emily, thinking, William Crowther's coming here. He did say we'd meet again, but I didn't think it would happen so soon.

The name Long Lane was strangely enigmatic. It only ran from The Hollow – a local colloquialism for the dip in the land where four stone-built arches supported one of the two rail lines which served the town – to the Wesleyan Chapel at Town End; a distance of no more than thirty yards. But puzzling over why it was so named was of no concern to George Harvey who, on this bright, July morning, was pushing Arnie Sutcliffe's cart up the slope that thankfully levelled out at their new front door.

"Eeh, I say!" exclaimed Emma, standing back to get a good view of the three houses. "They certainly look solid enough. And it seems as if they've got garrets! I wonder what they're like inside?"

"Well, woman, if you get the key out we can see," huffed George.

Emma dug deep into the pocket of her green woollen cardigan and pulled out the set of keys – which had not left her sight since William Crowther had brought them on the previous Sunday afternoon. Running up to the newly painted door now, she tried one, then another, shaking nervously as she did so.

"Oh, come on, lass. I haven't got all day. I've got to go back and fetch Nelly's stuff, yet. And then get to work!"

"I'm tryin' me best....And anyroad, they've given you a bit o' time off to do it. Don't fuss me....There! We're in."

Emma entered their new home with caution, as if breaking in.

"Eeh! George. Come and see this!"

"I will if yer'll shift yer carcass." And after parking the cart, he followed his wife inside.

"Oh, just look, love; it's fair grand....Eeh, I say!"

The house was similar to their old home: one main room which served as a living and kitchen area, with a sink and tap in the far corner, and a set-pot between it and the range for doing the laundry. It was generously fitted out with cupboards and a fair-sized table with six chairs; two easy chairs and a brown leather settee pushed back to the wall; it was neatly decorated with a cornflower-patterned wallpaper, and from the ceiling hung a gas fitting with two mantles.

"Oh, George! What d'yer think...? Let's have a look upstairs, eh?"

"It's an improvement I'll say that. But look, lass, I want to get going. I'll bring the things in off the cart and go back for Nelly's stuff. You have a bit of an explore." And when her husband had left, Emma did just that.

On the floor above the kitchen were two bedrooms. The larger one looked out on to the lane, which in turn was succeeded by green fields; and on a hill in the distance there appeared to be a large mansion house. The room contained a metal-framed double bed with wooden head and footboards, and two wardrobes; and though the walls were only whitewashed, it had a feeling of freshness and cleanliness about it.

The smaller bedroom was much the same, but with two single beds almost touching each other. They'll manage in here all right, thought Emma. Or maybe they could move one of the beds into her and George's room for the two young 'uns....Aye, that'd be better, and Kath can have her own. She mounted the steps into the attic now, which ran the whole length of the property. It was sparse with bare floorboards – but at least there was a cast-iron fireplace. The girls could come up here perhaps? She'd have to see....

Back downstairs, she began to sort through their few paltry possessions. Arnie had been kind enough to let them have a kettle, a collection of pots and pans, and items of cutlery which she stored away in cupboards and drawers – all but the kettle which was heating on one of the gas rings next to the sink. "Now," said Emma aloud, "thank the Lord I remembered to bring some tea and sugar. I just hope the milk hasn't gone off." It hadn't. And when the tea was mashed, she seated herself in one of the armchairs and beamed with delight. By 'eck, Jessie, it were a blessing you worked at Crowther's or we wouldn't be here now. And she looked at the ceiling, saying, "Thank you."

She finished her tea and washed her mug with the remainder of the hot water, and cleared their clothes away, before thinking, Oh, hell! Where's the closet? Then, picking up the keys, she opened the back door and scoured the long yard, eventually spotting a brick-built structure with two doors. That'll be it I suppose. Well it best had be or I'll pis....

"Emma! You there?"

"Aye, Nelly, just comin'." God, she does pick her moments.

"Well, aren't we the lucky ones. Eeh! look at your place....Ours isn't as big as this; but it'll suit for me and our Jess."

"George got your stuff up, then?" Emma enquired.

"Aye....Well, not all of it. But Arnie says he'll store it and we can bring it up bit by bit. We've got what we need for t'present. I'll tell him to get rid of the bed since we've got one 'ere."

"Oh, don't do that, Nelly; we could use it for our Kath, and then the two young 'uns won't have to share. Apart from mine and George's, there are only two singles upstairs...I'll pay yer for it."

"Yer bloody well won't," said Nelly. "We're neighbours for God's sake...! Oh, by the way, George says he's taking the cart back and goin' straight to t'mill....Eeh, aren't we blessed Emma... gettin' these places. 'Ave yer seen the view out front? Yer can see right over to Crowther's place."

"Is that the big house on the hill over yonder?"

"Aye. And I'd like to see inside...bet it's like a palace."

"Well, I don't think we'll ever get an invite, do you?"

"Yer never know. Besides, I think old J B has a glint in his eye for our Jessie....And what about William and your Sarah?"

Emma's forehead crinkled. "What about 'em?"

"Oh, don't pretend wi' me, Emma Harvey. You saw as well as I did how they were looking at each other when he brought us the keys. C'mon, you must 'ave done."

Emma gently shook her head. But smiling now, she wagged a finger, saying, "You're a right bugger, Nelly Dicks. Now, get that kettle on while I go to the closet...."

On her return, Nelly was pouring the tea. "I knew I had something to tell yer, Emma."

"What's that then?" Emma sat at the table.

Following suit, Nelly sat and pursed her lips, saying, "Just before leaving Arnie's, some chap or other that I think must work at Providence, had told him that Asa Stockwell had passed on during the night. The chap had been working the late shift apparently, and said that the news spread like wildfire."

"Well, he had been ill for some time," said Emma, "so I don't think it would have come as a great shock to anyone. And anyhow, what he put us through lately, I've little sympathy."

"I wonder how she's taking it?" Nelly sipped at her tea.

"Oh, Edith's such a hard-faced cow I doubt whether she's shed a solitary tear. And knowing what she's like, I'm loath to let our Sarah go and work for her."

Nelly almost dropped her cup. And when she'd placed it safely back on the saucer, said, "Oh surely, Emma; Sarah's not going to work for the Stockwells of all people?"

"Well, it's not settled, Nelly; but our Mary's put a word in for her. So, we'll just have to wait and see what happens when she leaves school in two weeks...God help us!"

Nelly took a drink of her tea. Then said, "I suppose young Alex'll be in charge now."

"Well, he is the oldest; so, I should imagine he will. Mind you, he'll likely do a better job of running the place than that brother of his – the scoundrel."

"Oh, I think Alex is a bit of a rogue an' all....Do you know, Emma, for nearly a year now summat's been preying on me mind."

Emma looked at her neighbour enquiringly. "What's that then, lass?"

"Well." Nelly leaned forward. "Do you remember that night of the feast when Alex came for the rent?"

"Eeh, what a night that was" – Emma gazed up at the ceiling – "poor old Len losing his horse and Alice being molested."

"Ah, but was she?" Nelly searched Emma's face for a similar hint of doubt. Emma's response was: "What d'yer mean by that? Alice were got at by a gypsy lad and that's all there's to it. Anyroad, what are yer trying to say wi' all this?"

Nelly stretched her lips into a wry smile. "Well, Alex Stockwell spent a lot o' time in the Barracloughs' place. And, Len was out looking for his 'orse, so it gave Alex plenty of opportunity to...to, yer know...." Nelly wagged her head from side to side.

Emma looked blank. Then it hit her: "You don't mean to say that you think Alex and Alice got up to some sort of...hanky-panky?"

Nelly nodded. And now the seed had been sown.

7

There was a woman and two young men in the room.

She was impatiently waiting for a response as they continued to look down at the floor. "Well! Do you not agree with me that you hastened your father's death? Speak! Speak! I order you!"

Joseph didn't raise his head, but his shoulders *were* raised periodically in an uncontrollable bout of sniggering.

"Oh, so you think it's funny, do you?" Edith Stockwell strode around the table, her black satin dress shimmering in the candlelight, and slapped her youngest son hard about the ear. He winced, but his attitude maintained the same stubbornness he had shown from early childhood. "Your father knew all too well it was your stupidity that led to the death of that boy at the fair two years ago, but he kept it close. Nevertheless, it caused him heartache from then until the day he died." She turned her attention to her eldest son now. "And what have *you* got to say for yourself?" She shoved her face close to Alexander's. "Well?" But there was silence.

She traversed the carpeted dining-room and halted at the large, marble fireplace where, stretching out her arms, she leaned heavily against it. But she didn't remain there for long before spinning on her heels. "Something has got to be done about that little…that little bastard."

Alex threw back his head and glared at his mother.

"That's struck a chord, I see. Well, my lad, that is exactly what it is. You're nothing but a damned fool, Alexander. Fancy! getting involved with a guttersnipe like her. Thank God she's dead; and I pray that son of hers follows her to hell as soon as possible."

"Stop it!" Alex was on his feet now, his physical swarthiness translated into the darkness of his words. "You knew nothing about her. She was beautiful. Gentle. Not like you: a wizened woman – old before her time." His hand was raised now, the palm directed at his mother. "Oh no! you've had your say. It's my turn now." He strode to the far side of the table where he picked up a dirty knife from off his mother's plate. "I've thought over the last year of using one of these on myself, but now, as long as my son remains on this earth, I'll be there for him." He threw the knife back on the plate, where it bounced, flew off, and landed at his mother's feet. But she never moved. Then Alex, more calmly now, said, "She was no guttersnipe as you put it, and anything you may have thought of her being responsible for, I was responsible too." He walked to the bay window and peered out across the grey town over which the sun was slowly sinking. "Father should have been ashamed of himself for allowing decent, working people, to live in those harrowing conditions." Turning now, he smiled wryly. "As you see, Mother, his first grandchild, or 'bastard' as you wish to call him, has no mother to nurture and love him now – as she most certainly would have – and why? Because, by allowing those houses to get into the state they were, my father – your husband – murdered her. Maybe that will strike a chord with *you* now?"

"Damn you! You know perfectly well that those houses collapsed because the old mine workings beneath them collapsed. After all that rain we had, they flooded! And besides, it was your great-grandfather who built the houses in the first place."

"Oh, and do you really think my father knew nothing about that? He should have rehoused those poor families years ago. You close your eyes to everything going on around you, Mother – that is only if it doesn't affect you and your standing in this town. You're perverse, you really are." And now Alex Stockwell stormed out of the room, slamming the door behind him.

The prematurely grey-haired, forty-three-year-old woman, her face as red as the velvet drapes at the windows, staggered to a chair where she sat and planted her palms on the polished, oval table and groaned. Then, looking directly at her younger son, said quietly, "And you can get out as well; and send Maggie in to clear this lot." She indicated the crockery on the table.

Oh, this was a complete nightmare: losing her dear husband only days ago, and now her son had turned against her. What had she done in her life to deserve this? But Edith Stockwell was a resolute being, determined and at times formidable, and had to find a way out of this dilemma regarding the child....

When Maggie came in to clear the dinner plates, she said to her: "First thing in the morning, I want you to go and fetch Doctor Griffiths to see me."

"Oh dear! Are you ill, madam?"

"Don't be ridiculous, girl! And make sure you're early tomorrow. Now earn your wages and get this lot out of the way."

The following morning, Doctor Griffiths entered the drawing-room where Edith Stockwell was reclining on the settee reading a copy of the Collingley Advertiser. Without looking up, she said, "Do sit, Samuel. I've ordered coffee for us." And when the aged practitioner took a seat opposite, he leaned forward slightly and peered over at the headlines, which after nearly two weeks were still highlighting aspects of the disaster in Victoria Row. Yes, it certainly was a tragedy for those pathetic people; and if Asa had got his fat backside out of bed, he could have prevented it.

"Would you care for breakfast, Sam?"

"Er...no, Edith....I ate earlier."

"Well, I've told Maggie to bring up some buttered pikelets if you feel like one."

What is wrong with this woman? Samuel Griffiths asked himself. Just lost her husband, ignoring the headlines in the newspaper, and talking about crumpets of all things. Still, he'd best keep on her good side if he wanted his practice to continue since she provided the majority of the funds that kept him going.

Yet, he felt past his time. He was weary. Not only did he have a general practice but spent the rest of his time as the resident doctor at the local children's hospital. That's where they brought that poor little mite after the catastrophe. Sam had taken to the child: he was a bonny bairn – so much like Alexander was at his age – but he remained very poorly. And Sam knew quite well that if blood poisoning set in or the child developed lockjaw, he would certainly not survive.

"Right then." Edith Stockwell deposited the newspaper on the coffee table and raised herself. She walked slowly towards the fireplace and turned about to face the doctor. Then, clasping her hands together, she looked directly at him and said, "How is the... child? And I'm sure you know the one I mean."

Doctor Griffiths did not face his benefactor as he said, "Quite ill, I'm afraid....Not well at all."

"Good. I'm pleased to hear that at least."

His eyes were on her now. This hard-hearted woman was beginning to irk him. And even if she did withdraw her funding, he'd be well shot of her. "I've always thought you a generous woman, Edith," he said, "but to wish harm on the boy is reprehensible."

Unclasping her hands now, she slapped one hard on the mantelpiece. "Don't underestimate the influence I have in this town, Sam. I could destroy you and your business with a click of my fingers." She looked down at him. "Not only would you have no income but also your reputation would be in tatters....You have a sister, don't you? Somewhere down south, I believe?"

Where was this leading? His previous determination to be rid of this woman had foundered. And when he spoke, his voice trembled. "Yes...but how did you...?"

"I know everything, Samuel Griffiths." Her eyes were wide with a conceited fervour now, as she went on: "I'd hate for her to find out for certain – how shall I put it – misdemeanours of yours over the last few years. One being only last August as I recall?" And she smiled. "Oh, yes! I see that rings a bell."

She moved across the floor now with a gliding motion, and upon reaching the piano she lifted the lid and struck a key. Then, seating herself there, said, "You must remember the young girl who was injured at Crowther's mill....Surely? Well, my dear doctor, if it hadn't been for my intervention – hush money if you like to call it – then you would have been hauled before the court on a charge of...well...molestation?"

Sam was on his feet now. "I did nothing of the sort; I had to examine her. That's what doctors do!"

"Oh yes, only when you'd dismissed her mother from the room – who I might add, went straight round to the mill and expressed her suspicions of what you might have got up to while alone with the girl to J B himself. After all, although she was fifteen, she was – from what I've heard – somewhat simple." She stood and went to the window where she adjusted the drapes. Then, without turning, said, "I didn't believe it of course...but thought it best to nip it in the bud. So" – she swung around – "I decided it should go no further." Sauntering back to the couch now, she clasped the back, saying, "After J B informed me of what – or what not – had happened, I thought that, in the interests of all concerned, it was my duty to keep the woman's mouth shut. Five pounds should have come in very handy for her and her daughter I should say – wouldn't you?" She came and sat down now, and looked at her doctor with questioning eyes. When he made no comment, she spoke further: "I would hate it if the rumour should still get around – especially if it reached your dear sister."

The man opposite was numb. She had worked it all out. Even if he denied this falsehood she would make sure it was made public. But why would she want to? What was her motive in threatening to spread such vicious and unfounded lies? Well, Samuel Griffiths was about to find out.

The door creaked open and Maggie entered with a tray, which she duly placed on the low table and was about to leave when Edith said, "Oh, I want you to do something for me."

"Madam?"

"Go to Mr Stockwell's wardrobe and clear it out. He won't be wanting what's in there any more." And she let out a manic laugh.

"Yes, ma'am…but what will I do with them?"

Edith's tone changed now. "Don't be so damned stupid, girl. Burn them! Give them away! Sell them if you like…anything! Now get out."

Sam watched the girl scurry away, thinking, How does she keep staff, treating them in such a fashion? And now she's removing every trace of her dead husband. It beggared belief.

After handing a cup of coffee to the doctor, she inclined her head towards the plate of buttered crumpets. Sam shook his head.

"No, I don't think I will either," she said. "I haven't the stomach for them after all." She sipped at her drink. Then placing it back on the tray, said, "It must die." Edith stared at him. "Yes, I'm talking about that child which was regrettably rescued from Victoria Row. And do not question my reasons, Sam, just do it! You have it in your power to see it off; and you can carry it out without anyone being the wiser. You will see to it that everything would appear as if it had died of its injuries. And I hope you grasp what the consequences would be if you don't, eh…? Now, I suggest you finish your coffee and get to it.…Oh, and by the way" – her finger wagged – "I'll want to see proof; be assured of that. Total and irrevocable proof!"

Driving back through the town, Samuel was unaware of what was going on around him; his mind was elsewhere. He couldn't understand why she wished to be rid of the boy since he wasn't in any way connected to her or her family. Maybe she hated gypsies; or perhaps she wished to rid herself of any link with her husband, the houses he had so obviously neglected, and all their inhabitants? After all, she had just got rid of Asa's clothes. She had not a pang of conscience whatsoever about what she was suggesting. Yet he had no other option open to him but to carry out her demands.

He pulled the car to a sudden halt and leaned on the steering wheel with his head bent low. After some minutes, he raised himself and looked directly ahead. There in the distance was the clock tower of the hospital – *his* hospital. Good God, man! you're a doctor: you were put on this earth to save lives not destroy them! And it was in that very moment that Samuel Griffiths determined to find a way out of his dilemma. He had to come up with a plan to save both his own skin and that of the poor child.

8

"I look stupid!"

"No you don't. Katherine got this for you cheap. Be grateful."

"It's too tight."

"Oh, for God's sake, come here." Emma dragged her daughter forward and released the top button on Sarah's tweed coat. "There, that's better." She stood back and made an inspection. "You'll do. Now, I'll just get me hat and we'll be off."

"I don't want to go, Mam."

Emma rammed the floppy-brimmed, brown felt hat so far down on her head that her eyes were not visible, saying, "You're going!" She pushed the hat back and glowered at her daughter. "You don't realise, madam, how lucky you are to get the chance of a job the way things are; so now that you've left school, you'll work like everybody else who's fortunate enough to be employed, so there. Now march!" And as Emma escorted her daughter out of the house and through the town, no further words passed between them – that was until they reached the bottom of the cobbled rise which led up to Edith Stockwell's house. Then she said comfortingly, "Oh, come on, lass. If I think the job's not right for yer, then I'll say so. And we'll look for somethin' else." Emma took her girl's hand and they proceeded up the slope.

It was a forbidding place. Built of locally quarried stone that at one time would have shone with a golden grandeur, it was now blackened with age and the smoke-laden air that hung over this small town like a filthy blanket. And beyond the rusted iron gate, the broken path that led up to the front door was interspersed with dandelions and tufts of couch-grass.

Mounting the steps now, Emma glanced at the tall stone pillars of the portico and wondered if they also bore the weight of someone's untold sadness in this cold and sullen place. Oh, give up woman, she thought. Let's be inside and see what happens. And she rang the bell.

Presently, the large oak door was opened by a small woman wearing a black dress covered with a white apron. "Can I help you?" she enquired.

"Yes," said Emma. "We're both here to see Mrs Stockwell. She is expec...."

"Oh, aye. Come in an' I'll tell 'er yer're 'ere." She drew back the door and Emma ushered Sarah into the hall. "We're a bit short-staffed wi' Maggie gettin' the push," said the little biddy. And in a whisper now, said, "The silly girl only went and pawned Mr Alex's clothes when t'missis meant for her to get rid of her husband's stuff." She shook her head and giggled. Then after closing the door, said, "If yer'll just wait here, I'll go an' tell 'er yer've arrived."

"She seems pleasant enough, doesn't she?" said Emma after the woman had disappeared through a door to the left.

"I suppose so," Sarah sighed.

"Oh, for God's sake shape yerself, girl. And stop looking so bloody miserable."

Shortly the woman stuck her head around the door and beckoned them forward. "She's not quite ready for yer," she whispered. "She wants me to show you to the drawing-room. This way."

Once inside the room, both mother and daughter surveyed the place. They had been shown to a chintz-covered settee with lace pieces draped over the back and arms. Beneath their feet, a pale-green, embossed carpet stopped short of the skirtings by two feet – the space being taken up by highly-polished wood on which, dotted here and there, stood small, marble-topped tables with an assortment of potted plants perched upon each of them. And in the bay window, stood a grand piano with a stool covered in, from what Sarah could judge at a distance, red velvet, which reflected the fabric of the floor-length curtains.

"Well, I must say the place looks nicer inside than it did out." Emma spoke in hushed tones. "They must be worth a bob or two – especially now he's gone. It's a pity he didn't spend some of his brass on those so-called houses of his."

"They've got wallpaper," Sarah observed.

"So have we!"

"Ah! but yer can see through ours....What's that rope for, Mam?" She pointed. "There! Next to the fireplace."

"I think it's one of those ringing things to get someb'dy to come when yer pull it."

"Oh...! I see...! Shall I go and give it a yank?"

Emma looked askance at her daughter. "I'll bloody well yank you in a flamin' minute if you don't stop pesterin' – she'll be here afore long, so keep it shut!"

Sarah looked around the room before saying, "I wonder what she'd want me to do if she took me on? Perhaps it'll be a seamstress like our Kath. What d'yer think, Mam?"

Emma shuffled in her seat. "I don't know…! I suppose we'll find out afore long. And anyroad, Kath's not just a seamstress – she's a supervisor." She narrowed her eyes now in order to see the time on the cabinet clock in the middle of the mantelpiece. "I wish she'd get a move on; I've a load o' washin' to get in…it won't do itself. Mind you, I bet *she* doesn't do her own." And she nodded in the direction of the door.

"I wonder why she wanted you to come with me?"

"Well, I wasn't going to let you come up here on yer own, was I? Besides, our Mary said she'd like to meet me and have a chat."

"What about?"

Emma turned to face her daughter. "How the hell do I know? You do ask some daft things at times."

"I thought Mary would have said something since she seems to be thick with this lot."

"Well she didn't. And keep yer voice down in case she.…"

The door swung open and Edith Stockwell stood there. "Oh please, don't get up, Mrs Harvey." Emma had sprung to her feet when hearing the door click. Sarah remained seated, her hands clutching the edge of the sofa. "This is Dorothy – my youngest. I thought she could show Sarah the garden until you and I get acquainted." And from behind the woman's black, calf-length skirt, a blonde, wavy-haired creature appeared. "Go and shake hands with our guests like a good girl. Go on." Edith pushed the girl towards the settee where she shook the visitors' hands.

She looks scared to death, thought Emma; but a pretty little thing. About Sarah's age she guessed, but very timid looking – unlike her own daughter.

"Right," said Edith, "take Sarah's hand and show her the way. When I've spoken with Mrs Harvey, I'll send Gladys to get you."

And the child followed her mother's instructions with a brave smile on her face. But as they reached the door, Sarah turned back and looked at her own mother with an expression resembling that of someone being led to the scaffold.…

The sun had come out, and the house didn't look as threatening as it had done when Sarah first arrived. Even the garden, which sloped gently down to a privet hedge, appeared more welcoming.

There was a small shed at the bottom of the slope, nestled neatly in a corner, and through the doorway Sarah could see the figure of a man bent over a bench; and he appeared to be busy at something or other. "Let's go and see Philip," the girl said suddenly, and taking Sarah's hand, led her across the lawn and into the shed.

"Philip, this is our new maid."

Sarah stared at the girl. Maid? Me a maid? Well, we'll see about that!

"He's backward, you know....But he's mother's younger brother, so we put up with him."

Backward? They're all bloody backward if you ask me. And Sarah had already decided not to work here...but, just to please her mam, she'd go along with this insanity.

"Philip spends most of his time out here," said the girl. "He likes weaving mats out of blades of grass – we never use them of course – and he's interested in things to do with wirelesses and such. He's always playing about with wires and batteries and stuff. And he does carpentry. Now, let's go and look over the edge."

Sarah was in a bit of a daze as the girl grasped her hand and pulled her out of the shed towards the bottom of the garden. Here, behind the hedge, a narrow path riddled with stony outcrops and canopied by overgrown trees, led down to a smooth, sunlit ledge.

But when Sarah emerged from the shade and adjusted her vision, she threw herself backward against a raised, mossy area, and recoiled in horror. Not five feet in front of her, the rocky ledge gave way to a drop of such proportions that she thought she might faint.

"Come and look, Sarah! A train's coming...we can watch it go into the tunnel. Hurry!"

And as Sarah clung to a tuft of grass, the girl danced about on the very edge of the ledge like someone demented. I'll never be able to get back up that slope, thought Sarah, as her heart raced and her mouth became dry. I'll be stuck here till somebody comes and carries me out. Oh, Mam, come and find me. Please get me out of here.

"You missed it, Sarah." The girl was back in front of her now. "You should have come and seen....Oh, what's the matter? Don't you like heights?"

Sarah shook her head.

"Come on then. I'll take you back....Mother will be wanting to see you now. Here, take my hand."

And with one hand clutching at Dorothy and the other grasping at clumps of grass, she managed to reach the arbour where, dragging the girl along with her now, raced back to the garden.

Gladys was standing on the doorstep. And when the two girls reached her, she said to Sarah, "She's ready for yer, lass....Eeh, yer're covered in green stuff. Quick, let's get yer hands washed an' I'll take yer back in...."

Sarah was clean and calmer now as she entered the drawing-room.

"I hope Dorothy looked after you, Sarah?"

Sarah nodded at her prospective employer. But Emma could see that there was something wrong.

"Right then. Sit down and I'll go through what your duties will be," said Edith. "I've outlined them to your mother and she seems to think them suitable. In fact, we talked about other things as well, but that shouldn't concern you....Now" – Edith Stockwell leaned forward in her chair and rested her forearms on her knees – "you won't be expected to live in, but you must be here by five in the morning to lay the fires.

"Then" – she indicated the floor with a sweep of her hands – "you can clean the carpets in here at first, and then in the rest of the house when my sons have left for work. But don't worry" – she gave a slight laugh – "I won't expect you to be on your hands and knees: we have recently acquired a Goblin to help you out."

Leaning back now, Edith placed her hands together as if she were in prayer and went on: "During the day you can serve refreshments to my guests – many of my acquaintances are here most days – and you can help Gladys in the kitchen...baking and suchlike."

She doesn't want much, thought Sarah sarcastically. Oh, but she did...! Edith continued: "Then in the evenings, I'll expect you to help me with my toilet before you finish for the day. The wage is a very generous ten shillings for the week....So, how does that sound?"

Both women looked for a response. And when Sarah said, "Er, yes, it sounds...all right," the two women smiled.

"Good." Edith Stockwell stood now. "I won't expect you to give me your final decision at the moment. Go home and discuss it further with your mother and let me know in a few days....Right then, I'll just ring for Gladys to show you out and leave it at that for the time being. But be assured, Sarah, the job is yours if you decide to take it...."

Going down the lane now, Emma said, "Well, I must say you've fallen on your feet there, lass. Ten bob a week an' all. What do you think?"

Sarah stood facing her mother and, her face flushed with ire, said, "No, Mam; she can stick her job. I'm not working for a set of loons like *them*!" And she stabbed a finger back at the house. "Not only have they got a nutty man in a shed who weaves grass and fiddles with wires and stuff, but...also a...a blonde-haired...wotsit of a thing who nearly got me killed."

Emma stared open-mouthed at her daughter's vociferous outburst and then said, "Got you killed? But...."

"No, Mam. And if that woman thinks I'm working alongside some" – she waved a hand around her head – "some elf or whatever – that for all I know they keep locked in an attic – she can think again. And then she expects me, after a day's work, to help her wipe her own arse. Well, no thank you!"

Elf? Arse? What is she rambling on about? Emma knew her daughter looked uneasy when she came back from the garden, but something serious must have addled her brain. "But what else will you do, Sal?" she said with despair.

Sarah was walking away now. But as her mother called to her, Sarah looked back and shouted, "I'll go in the bloody mill. That's what!"

9

Katherine was bent over, unable to breathe for laughing.

"Oh, stop it for God's sake, Kath. I'll never be able to live this down. I'll be an outcast...a damned pyorrhoea!"

"Mother, the word is pariah; pyorrhoea's a disease of the mouth." Katherine was aching with unfettered amusement.

"Is it? Well, same thing...I won't be able to open me bloody gob if this gets out – and it will you know....Eeh, I really thought that our Sal was the intelligent one in the family."

"Oh, thanks a lot, Mam." But Katherine was still giggling.

"Fancy, thinking that one of those carpet cleaning things was a... a creature or summat. And then when she said about wiping Edith Stockwell's backside; well, I ask yer." And Emma joined in the boisterous laughter.

"Oh, Mam, that's the best laugh I've had all year. Aay, dear me." Katherine wiped the tears from her eyes and took in a breath. "Now, you were going to tell me what Edith was quizzing you about."

Emma sniffed. "Oh, aye. Well, it were odd really, but she wanted to know a heck of a lot about Alice Barraclough for some reason." Katherine's face straightened as her mother went on: "All manner of things, like: did she have any other relatives besides her dad; did I know where they lived if she had; did I know who her baby's father was, and other things that I can't quite remember at the moment. I had to say I didn't know much – apart from that I thought her dad had a sister somewhere, but she'd probably be dead an' all by now. I think Len said she were in her seventies... and that were years ago."

"Well, Alice told me that her father was the only one left of her family," Katherine responded. "That is apart from the baby of course, and now the poor mite's on his own in that excuse for a hospital."

Emma looked down at the table. "Aye....Oh, I know I've said things about Alice, but I wouldn't wish the young 'un any harm.... Do you know though, I've been pondering over something that Nelly said to me the first day we moved here, and that was that she had an inkling that Alex Stockwell may be the father of Alice's baby...but I think it's total rubbish meself. If I had thought it were true, I'd never have taken Sarah there for a job."

"Of course it's rubbish, Mam." Katherine quickly changed the subject now. "Talking about jobs, I suppose Sarah'll be there by now. D'yer think she'll be set on?"

"Jessie thinks so," said Emma, nodding. "She says they're short-handed at Crowther's for some reason – you wouldn't have thought so these days. Thank the Lord this family's been luckier than most. So, lass, here's hoping that we'll have another mill worker in the family afore the days out."

Maurice Butterworth entered Jeremiah Crowther's office.

"Ah, come in Maurice, lad, and let me introduce you to Sarah. She's after a piecener's job – well recommended by Jessie Dicks I might add."

"Well, that's a recommendation indeed, J B."

"Right then, go and show her around and see what she thinks."

J B Crowther glanced at Sarah now, and smiling, said, "Maurice here, will look after yer, lass, so don't fret."

Sarah smiled back at him. "I won't, Mr Crowther...and thank you."

"Yer're welcome, lass." And Maurice led Sarah into the depths of the mill....

The first place they went to was the engine room. Sarah was impressed by the size and brilliance of the massive machines: they shone better than any diamond could ever shine. Two men, stripped to their waists with wide leather braces supporting grey corduroy trousers, were shovelling huge amounts of coal into furnaces – the heat of which hit you full in the face. They never faltered in their work when she and Maurice entered the boiler room – and still didn't when her guide said, "Aren't they fair grand, lass? One" – he pointed at the first steam-powered machine – "is called Fanny, and t'other one is Laura." Sarah giggled. "What's up, lass?" asked Maurice.

"Oh, it's just that me aunt Mary has a little girl called Laura – but nob'dy in the family has a Fanny." It was Maurice who chuckled now. "Eeh, yer're a right card, Sarah; a right card.... Mind you, don't ask me why they have girls' names, but it's always been the case in the mills....Perhaps it's because they're beautiful...and reliable." And Sarah could see exactly what

Maurice meant.

The great wheels that ran the belts to power the mill's mules and looms and other machinery, were painted a brilliant red, whilst other moving parts gleamed in gold. The long, steel pistons were so highly polished that they reflected the other parts of the vast machine, causing one to believe that everything else in the boiler room was in duplicate. Oh yes, Mr Butterworth was right: they were indeed beautiful! "We'd best move on, lass. I'll show you every process from start to finish, and by then you'll be as knowledgeable as I am." And as he laughed heartily, Sarah beamed with delight.

As names were often given to the great engines, so they were to the mills themselves: Fortune; Perseverance; Providence; and then there was Crowther's, which was renamed Resurrection after a huge fire in 1883 destroyed the rag warehouse.

It was found to have been caused by the metal toe-cap on a workman's clogs creating a spark on the stone floor, which, unnoticed at first, ignited the grease-soaked cloth, and rapidly turned the place into an inferno. Several other buildings were caught up in the conflagration, but much of the mill was spared. Afterwards, the warehouse was rebuilt; and added, was a new weaving shed with a saw-toothed roof. Then the workers often went about barefooted. But today, as Sarah was shown around Resurrection, they were all sensibly shod in stout boots.

Maurice Butterworth escorted Sarah through the whole mill and explained everything about the process of making woollen cloth. Initially, he enlightened her as to the role played by both Resurrection and Providence – which was owned by the Stockwells. At Crowther's mill, everything from beginning to end was carried out on the premises, whereas the Stockwells only dealt in weaving, dyeing and finishing, and imported wool from outside sources – of which a substantial percentage came from Resurrection.

The two families had agreed that the Stockwells could purchase rags from any source and have them processed by the Crowthers at a discounted price, with the condition that Providence used Resurrection as its main supplier of spun yarn.

"Right, Sarah," said Maurice. "This is where it all starts." They were in the rag warehouse. "All the stuff in here which comes from the rag merchant – or from the Stockwells – has to be sorted into different batches: colour, quality, new or old, and so on; then it goes to the willey 'oile." Maurice paused now and smiled at the quizzical look on Sarah's face. "I know it's a funny name, lass; but all it means is the place where the rags are opened up before being scoured or blended....D'yer know, Sarah; at one time, fullermen used to go round the local pubs and collect buckets o' pee to use for the scouring, 'cos it were like ammonia, and one of 'em were called, 'Piss Harry'." He chortled now. "Things are different these days, though – thank the Lord."

In the willey 'oile, a great teeth-bearing machine ripped up the various pieces of cloth, minimising small defects, and lubricating the resulting material which then went for carding. The carding machine was covered in staples, which disentangled the fibres and separated them into ribbons known as 'slubbings'. Thus divided, the slubbings were then see-sawed onto huge condenser spools, which were over two feet long and some ten inches in diameter – and could be quite weighty. These were placed in cradles at the back of the mule, and the threads pulled under cylindrical weights known as drafting rollers, before being attached to the hollow, take-up bobbins, which slipped over spindles at the front of the mule.

"Now," said Maurice, "comes the part which'll be more of interest to you, Sarah, and that's the actual spinning process."

Whereby she had been fascinated by what she had seen already, Sarah became overawed by what met her as she entered one of the many spinning rooms: the place was vast; and down one side, directly facing one another in pairs, four huge mules were in motion, and the noise of them was deafening. Multiple metal rails were bolted to the wooden floor on which the mules ran back and forth. And right where Maurice and Sarah were standing, curved armatures, similar to sickles, were attached to long steel rods that stretched the woollen yarn upward, which was then spun onto the bobbins slotted onto wheels at the base. Here, the wheels were joined to one another by twine or 'wheely band'. The machine itself held a hundred or more wooden bobbins; and after the armatures slammed back down, the mule returned to the rear of the machine where the process was then repeated. Maurice picked up one of the bobbins from a basket, saying, "This is what you'll end up wi'. It's a weft bobbin that pops into the shuttle on the loom. C'mon, let's go and see, eh?"

To the left of the mules at the far side of the shed, stood a dozen or so looms, rattling away as picking sticks belted their shuttles

across between the warp threads with the aid of a leather strap –
the threads alternately being switched up and down by the clacking
heddles.

At this point, Wilf Sutcliffe came running up. "We need some oil
for one of the pieceners, Mr Butterworth; and her mule's gone
dicky on 'er an' all."

"Right, lad, I'll be with yer in a jiffy." He turned to Sarah now.
"C'mon, lass; come wi' me." He led her to one of the looms, and
here they encountered Jessie Dicks. "Ah, Jessie lass, yer know
Sarah don't yer? Well shut yer loom down and get off home – it's
almost time anyway – but on yer way will yer take the lass to see J
B for a minute and call in the stores and tell 'em to get some oil
down 'ere sharpish. Here" – he dipped into his top pocket –
"there's a chit for it. Now, shut down and then yer can toddle off."
Looking back at Sarah again, he said, "This is it then, Sarah: this
will be your little domain. What do you think?" Maurice yelled
above the din. "Will we see yer Monday, then?"

"Yer will, Mr Butterworth...aye, yer will."

On their way out, Jessie took Sarah's hand, saying, "Well, we're
going to be neighbours at work as well as at home."

Sarah smiled. "I never thought they'd set me on, Jess. I thought
they'd have to think about it and then let me know later."

"That's because they recognise a good 'un when they see one,
Sal. Now, let's get that oil sorted out first, then I'll wait for yer till
J B's had a word."

"What will Mr Crowther want to see me about, Jess?"

"Well, what d'yer think, love? To tell yer about yer wages of
course."

Eeh wages! thought Sarah; my very own wages. I can't wait to
get home and tell them all.

10

"Hello, love. I'm Lily; Lily Sutcliffe."

"Maggie Gledhill. Pleased to meet you."

"Likewise. Now, sit yerself down for a minute and I'll tell yer what'll be expected of yer. Have y'ever worked in an 'ospital afore?"

"Er…no.…I was in service before."

"Well, that'll probably come in handy. Would yer like some tea? We're allowed four a day, but you're new so this'll be on the house so to speak."

"That would be nice. Thank you."

"Right. I'll just pop to the kitchen.…There's a pamphlet on the desk, so have a quick read. It tells yer all about the place."

When Lily had left, Maggie glanced around the sparse, little office, with its cream-coloured walls and green tiles, thinking, I'll never last in this job either. The place had a sickly smell about it: like a mixture of chemicals and children's pee. She hoped she wouldn't have to do any smelly jobs. Cleaning and serving meals was her lot – she knew all about those things from doing for the Stockwells. Oh, that nasty woman! How was she to know that Edith meant for her to get rid of Asa's clothes and not Mr Alex's? Besides, she'd always been taught that when the head of the household died, the elder son was then known as the Mister.

She picked up the pamphlet upon which a picture of Doctor Samuel Griffiths was prominently displayed. He looks a kind man, she thought; and even though she'd only met him on a few occasions, he'd always smiled at her. But if he had a hand in killing that child to satisfy the vile and criminal designs of Edith Stockwell, she'd expose him along with the grey-haired old witch. Oh yes, she knew what she'd heard outside the drawing-room door, and if she could help save that little mite's life, she'd do it. And however much she may dislike this job, she'd just have to take it.

"There y'are, love." Lily came back in carrying a tray, which she deposited on the desk. "Had a good read?"

"The doctor looks like a good man."

Lily poured out the tea. "He's a treasure, lass; a real treasure.… In fact, since I've been here, he's shown nothing but kindness t'ward me. He'll be in shortly to take you around and show you what's what. But he's left it up to me to explain just what's expected of yer.…'Ere, 'ave a biscuit." And she handed Maggie the plate. "Go on; take two if yer like." But Maggie declined. "Right then. Now, yer'll take the meals to the wards – some of the kids have special stuff, but yer'll soon get used to who has what – and if they need help then just give 'em an 'and." Maggie nodded. "A woman comes in to see to the babbies, but only at certain times – she used to be a midwife, but not any longer. Nonetheless, she loves to help out. Then there's the cleaning – it's done around two in the afternoon just after they've had their dinners. Oh, and there's the washing-up to do of course, but I'll help yer with that so you won't be up to your neck in suds." Lily chuckled now.

And smiling, Maggie said, "I hope you don't mind me asking, but what is *your* job, Lily?"

Laughing again, Lily said, "Jack of all trades, that's me.…Well, I sort through the letters first thing and see if there's owt urgent for Doctor Griffiths to look at – he writes all of his own replies – and I do some filing and stuff, and then go and help the nurses. The head one is Miss Carlisle. God! she's a terror; but we keep on her good side – if she has one – since she came on Mrs Stockwell's recommendation. There is another nurse who does days and one who comes in for the night-shift. Still, even then, Doctor Sam is likely to be called out if there's an emergency – poor man.… Anyroad, as I said, I help them out at times – nothing medical like; just general things. Oh, and I change the bedding – you can help me wi' that, and.…"

The door opened now, and the doctor came in. "Ah, Miss Gledhill, we meet again." And he shook Maggie's hand. She noted though that he didn't smile at her. "I hope Lily has told you a bit about our little place?"

"Oh, yes…sir. She has told me what I'll be doing."

"Good. But one thing you mustn't do is call me 'sir': Doctor or Mr Griffiths will suffice – whichever you like. We don't stand on ceremony here, do we, Lily?"

"Oh, heavens no. Just one big happy family."

And Maggie thought, Not for long I should imagine.

"Right, Maggie; let's do the rounds." Doctor Griffiths did smile now, and linking Maggie's arm, led her from the office.…

There were only three wards in the Collingley Children's Hospital: one on the first floor and one on the ground, with an annexe attached for the younger and most serious cases who had either been orphaned or abandoned. It was here that Maggie encountered Betty Saville – who came in to give the babies their feed – and Nurse Carlisle. Betty was a jolly, red-faced woman; whereas the nurse was the total opposite: pale, skinny, and miserably long-faced.

"Regretfully," said Doctor Griffiths as he escorted Maggie around the ward, "we have nine under a year old at the moment; but as you can see, we just don't have the room for any more. Still – and this might sound harsh, Maggie – there are a few who, alas, won't see the month out. Peter and Simon, here, were found on the streets, and Luke and Rosy, both gypsies, are fighting croup and… this poor soul.…" He pointed at the small child in front of them; and, his voice wavering now, said gently, "He was found in the destruction of Victoria Row.…He doesn't seem to be showing any signs of improvement yet…but we live in hope. Betty says she'll come up with a name for him since we only have his surname, and she dotes on him as you can probably see."

So, this is the boy! thought Maggie; and she could see how the elderly lady cherished the child. He was a bonny lad, no doubt: a dark-haired little chap with a quiet contentment shining from his large, and unusually piercing, blue eyes. And that rotten Edith Stockwell, for some unknown reason, wanted rid of him.…Well, whatever it took, Maggie would make sure that it would never happen.

She had worked solidly for ten days; and on this bright, September Thursday, Maggie Gledhill had a day off and determined to treat herself to a shopping trip in Leeds.

She had resisted the temptation of entering her namesake's shop, Maggie Doyle's, on Albion Street, after checking the contents of her purse: she only had the option of gazing in jealous admiration of the fine Crown Derby and Worcester ornaments and plates in the window. Nonetheless, when she visited the vast Kirkgate Market where Marks and Spencer had first set up their Penny Bazaar in 1884, she could not resist purchasing two oven-bottom cakes for herself and her mam.

After looking around C & A Modes and deciding to buy a woollen scarf for the winter, Maggie set off for Commercial Street towards the junction with Lands Lane, where right on the corner sat Betty's Tea Rooms – the best place in town for éclairs and cream horns in this art deco age.

As she was approaching the entrance to the shop, a voice from behind brought her to a sudden halt: "Maggie! Maggie! I thought it was you."

Maggie turned around. "Well, blow me, it's Katherine! I haven't seen you since I worked at Rosenberg's.…You still there?"

"For me sins, love. But it's my half day off so I thought I'd have a look around town.…Are you fixed up with work?"

"Oh, thereby hangs a right tale.…Here! How about joining me in Betty's and I'll tell you all about it?"

"You're on, Maggie…but it's my treat.…"

Before long, they were seated at a window table in the high-ceilinged establishment and the smartly attired waitress was taking their order. "Two cream horns and a couple of éclairs," said Katherine, "and a pot of tea for two, please." She put the menu aside and smiled at Maggie. "So, tell me all your news."

Maggie leaned forward. "Well, it's been quite an eventful six months, Kath.…After I left tailoring, I was at a loss as what to do next, but fortunately – or *unfortunately* as it turned out – I managed to get a job as a sort of maid-cum-dogsbody for the Stockwells." Katherine's mouth turned down at the corners now. "Aye, I thought you'd react like that," said Maggie. "Anyhow, I got on all right – at first that was – and Asa was a kindly man even though he was desperately ill at the time, but Edith could be a pain in the backside I can tell you."

"Oh, I can believe it, love. Our Sarah went after a job there but refused point-blank to work for the woman. She went in the mill instead."

"Wise move," said Maggie.

Now, the waitress brought their order, and after Katherine had filled their cups, Maggie continued: "Well, the time came when dear Asa passed away and Edith turned from just an irritating woman into a total cow. She had a massive argument with her sons one night and asked me to fetch Doctor Griffiths the following morning – and she had a bit of a set-to with him an' all.

"Then, while he was there, she only went and told me to throw out Mr Alex's clothes – or so I mistakenly thought. You see, I assumed that when she said, 'Go to Mr Stockwell's wardrobe and clear it out,' she was referring to Alexander and not his father. I suppose I acted a bit daft at the time, but I didn't want to rile her more than she was already. And besides, Alex *was* the master of the house....So, I took the clothes to Arnie Sutcliffe's and pawned them."

Katherine almost choked on her éclair. And after wiping her mouth on a napkin, she roared with laughter – causing Maggie to laugh along with her. Then, when they had both composed themselves sufficiently, Maggie said candidly, "So she gave me the sack."

"Eeh, Maggie! So, what happened then?"

"Well, I heard about this job going at the children's hospital, and although I hadn't any medical experience, I thought I'd give it a go. Anyhow, I got the job – which is like a general help – and this is my first day off in ten days. But I had a sort of purpose in wanting to go there in the first place."

"And what was that, love?"

"Well...." Maggie hesitated. "Oh, I suppose I can tell you; I know it won't go any further."

"Not from me it won't," said Katherine. So Maggie went on to relate the conversation she'd overheard between Edith Stockwell and Samuel Griffiths – of which she begged Katherine not to divulge – whereby Edith had tried to persuade the doctor to dispose of some poor bairn who was rescued from the disaster in Victoria Row.

Katherine slapped a hand hard on the table causing the crockery to rattle. The other diners turned to look at her, whence she smiled and whispered an apology; then leaned over to Maggie, saying, "He hasn't done it, has he?"

"Good heavens no! In fact, I don't think he ever will, whatever hold Edith Stockwell has over him; nevertheless, I'm keeping an eye on things. You know, Kath, it puzzles me why she wants to do such a...such an evil, evil thing."

"It doesn't *me*, Maggie; not in the least....Now it's my turn to confide in you. The boy's mother was one of our neighbours, Alice Barraclough, and was in fact fathered by...Alex Stockwell."

Maggie looked at her in disbelief. "But I thought the father was a gypsy?"

"Aye, we all did at first until Alice told me personally that the child was Alex's. But now you do know, it's got to remain just between us two."

Maggie nodded her head vigorously. Then she said, "Come to

think about it, it makes sense now what with Alex storming out of dinner one night. Well, I never! Mind you, it puzzles me why Lily Sutcliffe never said a word about it?"

"She probably doesn't appreciate that Alex is the father. And I can't imagine anybody does besides you, me, and the Stockwells. I know for a fact that none of my family don't." Katherine refilled their cups before chewing on an eclair and washing it down with tea. "Now, Maggie," she said, tapping the table. "Would you know if Arnie Sutcliffe's still got the clothes you pawned?"

"Well, I haven't redeemed the ticket yet. To be honest, I never will."

"Good! Then give it to me and I'll do it. After all, Dad could do with something new, and Alex is about his height and build so they should fit. I'll go and see Arnie tonight and get them off him."

Edith Stockwell smiled as she walked away from the hospital. At last the boy was dead and she was overjoyed. The dark shadow that had been hanging over her like a storm cloud had disappeared and now the sun was out. She buttoned her astrakhan coat and walked to the car.

"That's that over with." And she slammed the door behind her. "Now, let's be off....I've that girl to see at four. I only hope she's got better sense than the last one – and the one before her, come to that – and takes what she's offered. Fancy, turning down my generous offer just to go and work in a mill. It just shows the stupidity of people who are raised in the gutters."

Philip never uttered a word. He simply started the engine and drove his sister home.

11

Edith pulled the tasselled rope that caused a bell to ring in the kitchen, and shortly her new employee entered the drawing-room.

"Come in, Ethel. How are you settling in?"

"Fine, ma'am."

"Good. Now, I want you to run an errand for me."

"Ma'am?"

Edith waved an envelope. "This is a note that I need delivering to the children's hospital. I want you to go there and present it personally to Doctor Griffiths – just say who's sent you and they'll allow you to see him. Ask him if he would read it while you are there, and then come back and let me know his response. Can you manage that?"

"Course, ma'am."

"Right. Then get your coat on and be on your way...."

When Ethel returned, she was, much to Edith's surprise, accompanied by Samuel Griffiths. "Oh, Sam, I didn't expect you to accept my invite so soon. Nonetheless, I'm delighted to see you." She bade him to be seated, and turning to Ethel now, said, "Prepare some tea for us, love, will you?" And as Ethel withdrew, Sam thought, She called one of her staff, 'love'! What's come over the woman?

Edith seated herself on the settee beside him and entwined the fingers of her hands. "Congratulations, Samuel. I did think that you would refuse to carry out my wishes, but on my visit to the hospital a few days ago – you were out at the time – and although Nurse Carlisle was off work with a tummy upset, your secretary, Lily, informed me that the child was dead and buried." She inclined her head towards him. "Obviously, I could not dig up the grave, but I was shown around the wards and, sure enough, an elderly woman called Betty confirmed that the child was gone. The poor woman was distraught, and I was then left in no doubt that my wishes had been fulfilled....So, my dear doctor, it is my intention to reward you for your good work." She stood now and walked to the fireplace. "I have decided" – she faced him now – "to increase my donation to the hospital by...."

A knock came to the door and Ethel entered with a tray, which she placed on the low table in front of the settee. "Shall I pour, ma'am?"

Edith came forward, saying, "No, dear. I'll be mother." And she gave a slight laugh.

She's flipped, thought Sam. Totally flipped.

After tea was served, Edith continued her conversation: "As I was saying, I intend to make an extra contribution of one hundred pounds per annum."

"That's most generous, Edith. It will certainly help."

"I thought you'd be pleased. Now" – she got up and went over to her desk in the bay window – "here is the full amount in advance." She returned and handed Sam a cheque. "It's made out to yourself as per usual, so just put it in your business account and when it is cleared, well, use it for the good of the children in your care."

And Doctor Griffiths pocketed the cheque, thinking, You aren't as clever as you thought you were, woman.

The whole town was buzzing with the latest gossip.

It was Nelly who first brought it to Emma's attention: "As God is my judge, Emma....I were coming from our Minnie's along Park Street and there he was – driving like a mad thing out o' t'ospital grounds. He had to stop for a bus to pass, so it gave me a chance to get a closer look, and the car were packed wi' stuff: boxes an' cases an' chattels and the like."

"Maybe he were going on holiday?"

"What! wi' all that lot...? Nay, Emma, you tell me who takes pictures – and lamps – with 'em just to go to Blackpool? And a cat!"

"A cat?"

"Aye! A cat! I didn't see it, but I heard it."

Emma pondered for a moment before changing the subject. "By the way, Nelly; did your Jessie tell you the news about us getting electricity put in?"

"Aye," said Nelly with outright indifference, "but what about this doctor business?"

"I don't know...! Mind you, I know two people who might be able to shed some light on it and that's Lily Sutcliffe and Maggie Gledhill. I'll pop down to Arnie's and see if he's heard owt, and get our Kath to go and see Maggie...."

The news that Emma got from Arnie was that Doctor Griffiths

hadn't said a word about going anywhere to a soul. He'd cleared all his possessions from the hospital and when Lily went round to his house to see what was going on, it was empty – stripped bare. A neighbour had come out and asked Lily what she wanted and when Lily told her, the woman said that a moving van had arrived at two in the morning – of all times – and cleared the lot.

Then when Katherine met Maggie, she garnered further information....

"Well, this is becoming our usual meeting place, Maggie," said Katherine as they made their way to a table in Betty's Corner House and ordered tea.

Maggie smiled weakly, saying, "We'll have to make it a regular thing, Kath." And then her face darkened. "Although, I've no idea if I'll have a job afore long with the situation as it is."

"What situation's that?" Katherine was not letting on that she knew anything about Doctor Griffiths' departure.

"The doctor's disappeared. Nobody knows where he's gone or why. But that's not the worst of it, Kath." She looked down at the floor; and when she held her head back up there were tears in her eyes.

"Oh, love; here take my hanky. Whatever's wrong?"

Maggie blew her nose. "Well...I thought I was keeping an eye on things, but it...well, it all went wrong." She shook her head with discernable anguish. "The morning I went back after my day off – before I found out about Doctor Griffiths – a heavy-set man was shovelling earth into a hole in the garden where the orphaned youngsters who have died, are buried." She sniffed now. "Anyhow, when I approached the nurse who was standing by the grave with the chaplain – she was a new one because, as I found out later, Carlisle had been taken ill. Then she took me aside and told me that two little 'uns had passed away – one at noon the day before and another during the night when she was on replacement shift. But when I asked her which ones, she said she couldn't tell me. That was daft really, because all I had to do was to go to the ward and check – unless she thought I'd be too dim to figure out who they were. Well, when I got there, I almost ran into Edith Stockwell who was just coming out. I don't think she saw me – or even if she recognised me – because she just waltzed away down the corridor. So, when I had the chance to look around and ask Lily what had happened, I was shocked to find out that the boy had... died." And the tears came on her again.

Katherine stared at her in total disbelief. And after a while she said, "Oh, Maggie; I'm so, so sorry....So it looks like Edith got what she wanted after all? Damn and blast the woman! I only wish I could get my hands on her: I'd wring her scrawny, bloody neck. Well, I'm sorry to say it, love; but what with Griffiths bolting, it certainly looks like he had something to do with it after all."

"Well, what do you think, Dad?"

George Harvey ran his hands over the suit jacket. "It's a fine piece of cloth, lass. And you made it at work you say?"

"Aye, I did," said Katherine. "Will it be all right for you?"

"More than all right. And the shirts are fair grand an' all."

"I'll have to get you a pair of cuff-links, though – for special occasions."

George hugged his stepdaughter, saying, "You're a grand lass, love. Thanks so much....Mind you, I can't imagine me havin' any special occasions."

"Yer never know, Dad. Yer never know...." But thank the Lord he didn't know what she'd had to do to get this lot.

She'd sworn Arnie to secrecy over the clothing coming from his shop and who had owned them. And she'd had to sneak them into the house without anyone noticing. But when she'd inspected the bundle, it dawned on her that Arnie couldn't have gone through it, for lo and behold she came across what she had hoped against hope she may find: the second link. There it was – still in one of Alex Stockwell's shirt cuffs – an exact match to the one Alice had entrusted her to give to Alan when he grew up. And it was engraved with the letter 'D'. She had the pair. Still, even having both was pointless now. All they were good for was as a sad and worthless keepsake since the poor boy would never be able to use them – not now that he was rotting in the damp, Collingley earth.

12

J B Crowther had called Sarah to his office.

"Please sit down, Sarah....Oh, my dear; don't look so worried. Would you like some tea?"

"Er...yes please, sir."

J B poured out the tea for them, passed Sarah her cup, and sat down. "Aay, it's a bit of a worry what's going on in the world lately, Sarah." He stroked his long, grey beard. "What with parliament being recalled, and then, only yesterday, Russia signing a pact with Germany. But I haven't called you in to talk about politics...although events over the past months do have some bearing on it. Our turnover has increased dramatically since the need for cloth has gone up, and, as you've probably noticed, we are having to take on extra staff – from whatever source, but mainly females – to cope with the demand.

"Now, you've been here for just over two years, and I've had glowing reports from your foreman about your work. I have noticed that your timekeeping is, without exception, faultless; and you have not been off sick for one single day." He took a gulp of his tea. "So, it is my intention to increase your wages to one pound and four shillings per week." Sarah smiled.

"And," J B Crowther added, "because of the knowledge you have so quickly grasped of your piecening duties, I would like you to consider training any other newcomers that take up employment. If you decide to accept my proposals, I am prepared to add another half crown to your wages. Well, what do you think?"

"Oh, sir; I'd be glad to do it. And thank you for considering me."

"Good. I must say, Sarah, that your the only who I trust to do the job. So, let's finish our tea, eh?"– he looked at his pocket watch – "and then you can get off home. I'll let Maurice know of your decision and he can set thinks in motion...."

Back in the shed, Sarah ran over to Jessie who was waiting for her and told her the news. "Eeh, that's grand, lass. I bet yer mam and dad'll be chuffed to bits. C'mon, let's grab our coats and be off...and let's not forget our gas masks."

The following Monday, Sarah met her first recruit. "Hello, love. And what's your name?"

"Amy Broadbent, lass." And she shook Sarah's hand. By, thought Sarah; for a woman, she's got a right grip on her. "Eeh, I bet yer truly feel a bit awkward havin' to show me the ropes at my age. But old Mr Crowther were willin' to give me a chance, so I'm glad on it. And what wi' all the men either on standby or joinin' up, I suppose it's up to us women to do our bit an' all."

"You're spot on there, Amy. Well, so long as you don't mind me being your tutor, so to speak, I'm sure you'll do fine. And after all, J B has a canny judgement when he sets somebody on, so if you're good enough for him, you're good enough for me....What kind of work were you doing before, then?"

"I've been in service since I were thirteen. Mind you, I only stayed at me first job for two year. But, I found another one and were with 'em for nearly fourteen until they moved away last January. Then I thought I'd never get another position – knocking on thirty, like – and I were right. I had to find summat though 'cos I've got me old mother to take care on."

"Well, Amy," said Sarah, "you've got another job now. So, how about we get started and see how it goes?"

"Fair enough, lass. You show me the ropes an' I'll have a go at it."

"Right. You stand there in front of the mule and I'll go and get it going." Sarah went to the side of the spinning machine and pulled a lever, then returned to Amy's side. "Watch now," she said.

Shortly, steam began to hiss from a large pipe attached to the wall and the huge machine started up. It hummed at first, then began the process of spinning yarn: it advanced towards them and stopped just short of their feet. "Just look what happens now," said Sarah, and the mule went through its cycle: drawing out the threads and adding twist; gradually filling up the wooden bobbins on their spindles; moving back and forth, back and forth on its iron rails.

"I'm not sure if I'll get the hang of all this, lass...not at my age."

"Nay, Amy, you're still a young woman. And listen, love; if I can do it so can you....Now, when the bobbins are full and the mule is in the forward position, we can doff the bobbins – that just means taking them off and putting them in skips ready to be taken to the looms. Right" – Sarah gazed at the movement of her mule – "everything seems to be going all right for the moment, so I'll show you around for a bit." Sarah shouted above the din: "Wilf! While yer're doffin', can yer keep an eye on my mule till I show Amy around?" And Wilf yelled back: "Right, Sal!"

Sarah grinned at the newcomer now, saying, "I'll show you the most important thing in the mill, Amy." She pointed over to a distant corner. "The kettle! We have a break about ten, and then dinner's between half twelve and one. Then we have another break at three-thirty. Now, come over to one of the looms and I'll introduce you to Jessie."

Sarah led Amy between Wilf's mule and her own and took her over to where Jessie was loading a new bobbin into her shuttle. "Jessie. This is the new lass, Amy."

"Oh, hello, love. How are yer gettin' on?"

"Well it's all very new at the minute."

"Don't worry, lass; you'll soon get the hang o' things…and we all help one another in here, so don't be afraid to ask if yer get stuck." She glanced over Sarah's shoulder, saying, "Don't look now, Sal, but Mr William's just come in…he's got a girl with him. Maybe she's new an' all."

Sarah turned around anyway, and indeed William Crowther had arrived in the shed. But she doubted if the girl was a potential employee, for it just happened to be Dorothy Stockwell.

"Hey," said Jessie, "don't yer think yer'd better get back to work, Sal?"

"I *am* working, Jessie."

"Well whatever; it's too late now: he's coming over."

The nineteen-year-old man approached Jessie's loom, and when he arrived with Dorothy attached to his arm, he said, "Hello, Sarah." And Sarah calmly responded: "Mr William."

"I think you know Dorothy, don't you, Sarah? She's Edith Stockwell's daugh…."

"Aye, I know her," Sarah interrupted him; "and this is Amy. She's a new 'un."

"Hello, Amy. I hope you'll get to like it here."

Amy appeared to have been struck dumb, her eyes fixed on the girl at William's side. But then said, "Oh, I'm sure I will, Mr Crowther. Sarah's a good teacher."

William smiled at the group, saying, "What I really came over for, was just to let you know that Dorothy" – he turned to the girl on his arm – "and I are engaged." Dorothy smiled; but Sarah's face was immobile. Then he said, "Well, ladies, I'll leave you to get on with your work. Come along, Dorothy." And the couple turned and walked away.

"Eeh," said Jessie, "that's a turn up for the books."

"Quite!" said Sarah. "Come on you two; it's tea-time."

"Don't take it to heart, love. You know what they say about more fish being in the sea."

"I don't want another fish, Mam; I wanted him."

Emma placed a hand on her daughter's shoulder. "Aay, love, it could never have come about. They're a different breed to us, and people like them wouldn't consider marrying out of their class."

Sarah stood up from the table now. "Class? Bloody class! I don't see what class has to do with it…not if people…." And she broke down in tears.

Emma drew her daughter close and held her. "Oh, love. You'll see it could never have been. In time, you'll appreciate he wasn't for *you*." She stroked Sarah's bobbed hair. "One day a man will come along, and you'll know he's truly the right one. Now, come on, lass; time's gettin' on and you've got to be gettin' ready for work."

Sarah pulled away from her mother. "I'm not going. I'm never going back to that place."

Emma's tone changed now as she said, "You are! You've got responsibilities. You can't leave that Amy to manage on her own just after one day."

Sarah picked up her plate and went and washed it in the sink. And she stood there until she heard her father's voice as he entered the kitchen. Straight away, he walked over to the dresser and turned on the wireless. "Let's see what the news is today," he said. "Bad again I suppose."

"I really don't know why you accepted that thing, George," said Emma.

"I told you: Alex Stockwell brought it in and said I could have it. Apparently, his Uncle Philip cobbled it together – he's good wi' things to do wi' wirelesses – and just look at his grand woodwork. I surely wasn't going to turn it down."

"Well, I want nowt in this house to do with the Stockwells."

"Oh, give over, Emma. The kids love it; and I can listen to the news. Things are getting bad. We might be at war afore long." George stroked the polished wood and stood back to admire the workmanship. "He's very clever, don't yer think? Edith's brother."

"Clever!" Emma glanced over at the sink. Then turning back to her husband, continued: "Good God, George; even our Sal knows he's tuppence short of a bob. He's likely got all the things in it the wrong way round and it'll blow up....And anyroad, we've other things to concern us other than war and wirelesses."

"Like what?"

"Our Em, that's what! You might have noticed she's been seeing a lot of Wilf Sutcliffe lately and I don't like it." Now Sarah raced passed her parents and bounded up the bedroom stairs.

George threw his wife a puzzled look. "Summat wrong wi' our Sarah, lass?"

"No! Don't change the subject. Em's barely fourteen and oughtn't to be carrying on wi' lads...especially one who's eighteen."

"She could do worse than Wilf if the truth be known."

"I don't want her to be doing worse – or better – wi' anyone at her age."

"I'll have a word with her, lass. Now let me listen to the wireless before I get off to work."

Emma threw the tea-towel on the set-pot and shook her head.

Presently, Sarah came back down to the kitchen. "I suppose I'd best be goin' lest I'm late and get the sack."

"All right, love. Keep yer chin up," said Emma. "I'm doing stew and dumplings for yer tea. Yer like that don't yer?"

"Aye, Mam...ta-rah then...ta-rah, Dad."

"Ta-rah, lass."

During the weeks that followed, Sarah concentrated on her work – but not without experiencing some sickly heartache whenever William showed his face in the mill.

The family were enjoying a sunny Sunday after the previous night's storm. Nelly and Jessie were helping Emma with the vegetables for dinner, to which they both had been invited; and Sarah, Emily and Katherine had gone for a walk over to Thorp, promising they'd be back by twelve. It was almost eleven now, so George switched on the wireless.

"He's in his element wi' that thing, Emma," said Nelly with a smile on her face.

"It's not been off since he got it, Nelly. And all you hear on it is war, war, war...it'll never start."

"Don't be too sure. That bloody swine Hitler has invaded

Poland, so we could be next," commented Jessie. "He won't back down yer know."

"Shush! Shush you lot," said George; "the Prime Minister's on."

The women put down their knives and went over to the dresser.

'I am speaking to you from the Cabinet Room at number 10 Downing Street. This morning, the British Ambassador in Berlin handed the German government a final note, stating that unless the British government heard from them by 11o'clock that they were prepared at once to withdraw their troops from Poland, a state of war would exist between us. I have to tell you now that no such undertaking has been received, and that consequently this country is at war with Germany....'

Emma looked at her friends' faces. Nelly was staring blankly at the wireless as Jessie rested her hands on her mother's shoulders, and her husband had his hands clasped together with his head hung low. They listened to the rest of the broadcast, then stood quietly throughout the national anthem.

It was Emma who broke the silence. "I'm glad I finished those blackout curtains – we should have had 'em up on Friday – and got in extra candles....Now, I'd better go and sort out those gas masks and check the cellar...then I'll get on and mix the Yorkshire pudding."

13

On Monday the 8th of January 1940, housewives were obliged to use their ration books for the first time.

"Bloody hell!" said Emma, "what am I supposed to do with four ounces of soddin' bacon? It's no good, George, we'll have to pinch a pig."

But rationing got far worse, as did the war. The conflict that many had thought would shortly be over, intensified. In June, almost two hundred thousand troops were rescued from Dunkirk, France surrendered, and then during the following May, London suffered a massive onslaught in the Blitz. But its citizens, with the continuing presence of King George and Queen Elizabeth, rallied with their customary stoicism and unflagging British spirit. Yet a bitter blow was dealt to many a household when, in December of 1941, unmarried women over twenty were directed into essential war work. And those aged nineteen to thirty were liable for call-up to the Forces.

High Ridge House had been requisitioned for the billeting of troops; and William Crowther – now in the army – and his wife Dorothy, had moved to the Stockwell's house, whilst his father went to live with his brother at Tingley. And though Resurrection continued spinning and weaving cloth, Providence had been taken over for the production of armaments.

Then in 1942, Britain began preparations to welcome the Americans into their midst; and the Collingley drill-hall was in readiness for their imminent arrival – and so were all the single women. "God help us when they come flitting around town," said Emma. "None of us'll be safe."

"Well, I don't think they'll come after you, Mam."

"Don't be so bloody cheeky, Katherine Conlan. I might be nudging sixty, but I'm not bad for me age."

"Well, I don't think there'll be any of 'em even *half* that age, so don't count on it, Mam."

But Katherine was wrong, for when the troops had been in town for less than a week and a welcome dance was held for them, Katherine met a thirty-six-year-old GI. And when she arrived back home, she said, "Can I bring him to tea on Sunday, Mam?"

"Don't be ridiculous, Katherine. I can barely get *us* by with what we get in rations – least of all trying to feed a big American."

"How do you know he's big?"

"They all are! Built like brick sh.…"

"Aye, yer've made yer point, Mam."

After a moment of silence between the two women, Emma draped the tea-towel over the set-pot and, turning to her daughter, enquired, "What's he…er…like, then?"

"Oh, Mam, he's charming. Tall, handsome, and a real gentleman – and he's a sergeant an' all."

"Well, that's a recommendation I must say. He must have some go about him to reach that position."

"So, can I then? Bring him on Sunday?"

Emma looked at her daughter. "Aye, I suppose so. I'll see if I can eke out what we have in.…Oh! but how can I give him a cake made from custard powder or those bloody awful powdered eggs?"

"He'll likely bring something with him, anyway," said Katherine. "They seem to be well-stocked with stuff."

"No! I'm not havin' that." Emma was piqued at Katherine's assumption. "No guest – an American one at that – is coming into my house and bringing his own food. I won't have it. And anyway, Mary'll be here, and I don't want her thinking I can't cope."

"Oh, does she really have to come? She'll put the mockers on the whole thing."

"Aye, she does.…D'yer know, I thought this hostility towards your sister would have been settled by now. You're a thirty-nine-year-old woman an' act like a spoilt kid."

Katherine walked to the back door and looked out on the yard. "I just can't abide the way she bangs on about the Church and what it stands for, Mam. I'll say one thing about Jonas and…well, it doesn't matter."

"What doesn't?"

"Nothing, Mam; nothing."

Sunday arrived. The sun was beaming down on the small town and one wouldn't have thought there was a war going on.

Emma had done her very best with what she had in the way of food, but Nelly and Jess were coming and had provided something as well. She had told her husband to dress in the clothes that Katherine had made for him at Rosenberg's, before she had to leave after being directed into a munitions factory at Thorp Arch.

Sarah, herself having opted to go into munitions instead of biting her finger nails waiting for her call-up papers to drop on the mat, had cut and dressed Katherine's hair in the style of the day, and she and sixteen-year-old Emily – who was now a weaver at Crowther's mill – were sitting on the front doorstep talking about Wilf Sutcliffe.

"You like him don't you, Em?"

"I do, Sal; I like him a lot....In fact, he's asked me to marry him."

"No!"

Emily smiled and nodded her head.

"Oh, Em!" Sarah pulled her sister to her and hugged her tightly. "Have you told Mam yet?"

"Shush! No, only you. After all, I don't know if he'll change his mind."

"He won't...I know Wilf and he won't; and you'll not find a better one. Mind you, it's about time our Kath got herself a fella and settled down before she's left on the shelf."

"Maybe today'll be the day, Sal?"

"Aye, yer never know. C'mon let's go in...time's gettin' on." And the two girls went indoors.

"I hope you two haven't muckied those frocks," said Emma. "I used up me best curtains to make 'em – all hand sown, yer know."

"Now, how could we mucky 'em, Mam?" said Sarah. "You've only scrubbed the steps three times today after all." And she laughed.

"Less of your cheek, madam....Now, pop next door and see if Nelly and Jess are ready 'cos he'll be here afore long. Oh, me heart's goin' twenty to t'dozen."

But before Sarah had the chance to go next door, Nelly and Jessie Dicks appeared on the doorstep. "Can we come in, lass?"

"Aye, course yer can, Nelly."

Once inside, Nelly glanced at the table. "Well I must say yer've done a lovely spread – considering."

"I just hope he'll have enough, Nelly."

Katherine drew Jessie to one side, whispering, "I haven't told them yet, Jess. D'yer think it'll come as a bit of a shock?"

"I don't see why. After all, what if he is...."

The conversation was promptly muted as all heads turned when a knock came to the door. Emma clasped her breasts, her heart racing, and then let out a gasp of relief as Mary stepped into the room. "Oh, Mary; I thought you were a man...I mean *the* man... you did give me a turn."

At this juncture, George appeared at the bottom of the bedroom stairs, looking immaculate in Alex Stockwell's pawned suit he'd had for four years. "Glad you could come, Mary," he lied.

"Well, how could I not George? It's a rare occasion indeed when our Katherine draws a man's attention." She smiled at her younger sister who gritted her teeth as she and Jessie passed both Mary and her father, calling back to Emma: "Just going for a little walk, Mam."

"Well be quick about it," said Emma. "It's going on for four already...."

Standing in the field at the other side of the lane, Katherine said, "I'll kill her before the day's out, Jess."

"Oh, don't take any notice, love; you know she relishes seeing you nettled, so just keep calm. After all, you don't want to be having a barney on today of all days."

"I wish I'd never suggested him coming to tea."

"Well you did, and he is, so make the best of it."

"Aye, you're right, Jess. But I won't sit back and say nothing if she makes any nasty comments."

"I can't see her doing that, love. Whatever else she is, she's a respectable, God-fearing woman."

Katherine gave Jessie an intense look. "Well if you mean that Mary's sanctimonious, then I agree; but I don't think the word respectable could, by any stretch of the imagination, be applied to her."

"Well try and not let it get to you, love...because" – she took Katherine's arm – "if I'm not mistaken, I think your visitor's just coming through The Hollow." She pointed down the lane.

Katherine spun around. "Oh hell! Quick, Jess, I can't let him see me stood in the middle of a bloody field." The two raced indoors, where Katherine said breathlessly, "He's coming up the lane."

Emma ran to the mirror, patted her hair, whipped off her pinny, and slung it in the set-pot. George was seated in his armchair puffing on his pipe, while Mary sat quietly on a stool near the back door. Sarah and Emily were standing together at the table, and as Jessie went and stood by her mother, Katherine paced the floor... until a knock came to the door. Nobody moved.

Now Emma said, "Well, go on, Kath. Don't keep him standing

there, for God's sake!'"

Katherine straightened her back and walked slowly to the door. After a few moments of subdued chatter, Katherine admitted the GI.

It was a crash from the back wall that drew everyone's attention away from the tall American, as Mary lay prostrate on the stone floor. Emma scuttled to her, saying to Nelly: "Have yer got any smelling-salts at home, lass? She's fainted."

"Aye. I'll run and get 'em."

Sarah and Emily ignored Mary's condition and looked back at the confused soldier. "He's very handsome," whispered Emily. "He's that all right," Sarah responded.

George was out of his seat now and walked over to their visitor. "Pleased to meet yer, lad."

"And you, sir....I hope you'll accept this gift from the US for you and your family. There's butter, a can of corned beef and some sliced meats, cookies and chocolates, tobacco, and a carton of Lucky Strikes....Is the lady okay? Not ill I hope."

"That's very kind of yer, lad; I'll put them on the dresser....Who, her?" – he nodded at Mary – "No, she's just passed out. She'll be right afore long."

As George took the parcel to the sideboard, Nelly returned and began to administer the salts to Mary's nostrils, whence the patient suddenly shuddered back to consciousness and was helped to her feet.

Now Katherine said to her stepfather: "Let me introduce you properly, Dad. This is Sergeant Jonas Williams. Jonas, my father, George." And the two men shook hands warmly. Then she introduced him to the rest of her family and friends. It was when she came to her sister that she hesitated, for Mary's eyes were wide with disbelief. And when the man asked her if she was feeling better, Mary merely nodded her head; and when he held out his hand, she just touched the tips of his fingers and leaned back against the wall.

As Katherine and Jonas mingled, Emma went to Mary, whispering, "What on earth is up with you today?"

"Me? Me? In heaven's name, Mother, haven't you got eyes in your head? Surely you can see what he is!"

"Aye. I can. He's a fine, well-mannered individual – which is more than I can say for you. What the hell is wrong?"

"Just look at him! He's black, Mother. Black!"

Mary didn't stay to tea.

But before she departed, she asked Katherine to go outside because she wanted to speak to her. And so as not to cause a scene in front of Jonas and her family, Katherine complied. "I thought you were ill? So what do you want now?" she barked at her elder sister.

"What I want," said Mary, "is for you to come to your senses. How could you bring disgrace on us all like this?"

"I have no idea what you're rambling on about. What disgrace?"

Through gritted teeth, Mary said, "You know full well what I mean! Not only do you soil any reputation you may have had by having truck with a common soldier, but by having it with a black one. I suppose now you'll be telling me it was the fault of the blackout that you couldn't see who was feeling you up in some back alley or other. You're nothing but a...."

Mary's diatribe was suddenly halted when Katherine's hand landed on her sister's face. "You bloody loathsome cow!" she roared. "It's you who's a disgrace. Now get out of my bloody sight before I'm tempted to lay you out."

Mary could find no words to express her shock at her sister's actions. She hurriedly adjusted her coat, clasped her handbag to her breast, and plodded off down the street. Katherine watched her for a moment, then arched her spine and went back indoors....

After an enjoyable meal, Emma and Nelly were moving the tea things, and Jonas was happily talking to George, Sarah and Emily – and nobody, apart from Jessie, noticed the fury in Katherine's eyes.

"Oh, don't tell me you had a row with her?"

Katherine leaned close. "All that nonsense about fainting, Jess. She ought to be ashamed of herself basing a judgement on somebody because of the colour of their skin. It's what's inside that counts." She stabbed at her chest. "Well that's it with our Mary. I hope I don't see hide nor hair of her ever again."

George glanced over at his stepdaughter, then looked back at Jonas who was seated now, and drew on his pipe. "So, where're yer from in America, lad?" he said.

"Chicago, sir. I was born there, and have lived there ever since."

"So how long have you been in the army?"

"Since I was nineteen: seventeen years in total."

The smoke hovered around George's head and he watched it sail up to the ceiling. Then he looked through the haze directly at

Jonas. "Do you...now how can I put this without it sounding hurtful, 'cos I don't mean it to be, lad...do you have mostly black lads under yer?"

"It's not hurtful, sir. Yes, the majority are. But one thing I will say is that the people in England treat us as equals and not like outcasts as they do in the States."

"I wouldn't say everyone around here would feel like that, lad... no, not everyone."

Emily leaned forward now, saying, "Are yer going to marry our Kath?"

As George sniggered, Sarah nudged her sister. "Yer can't ask him that!"

"But I want to know 'cos it's about time. I'm only sixteen and I'm gettin' wed soon."

George dropped his pipe; and after retrieving it off his lap, stared at his youngest child. "What was that? Getting wed? Who to?"

Sarah excused herself and went to Katherine and Jessie. And after exchanging quiet words, the three turned towards the fireplace and Katherine beckoned Jonas over to join them.

George was talking animatedly to Emily. Then his voice was raised. "Emma! Get over here." A stunned Emma threw down her tea-towel and went over to her husband who asked, "Did you know about this?"

"Know about what? And keep your voice down; they'll hear you all the way down the street."

George pointed. "She's gettin' wed to Wilf Sutcliffe."

"Oh don't talk wet, man. I've never heard anything as daft in me life."

"Well ask her. Go on, ask her."

Emma directed her gaze towards her youngest. "Owt to say?"

"Well...well, he's asked me."

"Then he can damn well unask, that's all I can say."

George nudged his wife. "Not when we have company, lass."

"Well that's bloody good coming from you." She turned towards Emily now. "I'll talk to you later my girl." And Emma walked away.

Jonas leaned towards Katherine; and in a whisper, said, "Is there a problem? Am I intruding?"

"Good heavens, no. It's just that Em's been proposed to and Mam and Dad probably think she's too young to be thinking about marriage just yet."

"And she's sixteen?"

Katherine nodded

Jonas looked over at the thin Emily – and then at her father, before saying to Katherine: "Look, I think I'll take my leave."

"Oh no! Don't go yet."

"I think it may be for the best. I'll just thank your parents for their hospitality and be on my way....Can I see you again, Katherine?"

Katherine smiled into his eyes now, and said, "I'd like that, love. I'd like that very much."

Jonas went to George and thanked him. And then to Emma where he shook her hand. "Thanks, ma'am. I've enjoyed being in your home and...oh! look: you've burned yourself. You should have it attended to."

Emma glanced at her knuckles. "Well, I'll be damned! I don't know when that happened, but I don't remember doing it." And when she felt her hand, some of her fingers were numb.

Katherine had decided to walk Jonas back to The Hollow. Nelly and Jessie had helped Emma tidy the kitchen and then they'd gone home. Meanwhile, Sarah and Emily had taken two stools outside and were sitting in the field across the lane discussing their parents' reaction to the news about Wilf Sutcliffe; whilst indoors, George and Emma were talking about Mary.

"That daughter of yours is a damned bigot if you ask me."

"I'm not asking you, George. Still, I must agree with you....You would think with her being so religious, she'd have a bit of...well, humanity about her."

"Mary's never been human, lass. And as for her religion, I haven't heard the Pope condemning what's going on in Europe."

"D'yer think it's because Mary hasn't seen a black man before – apart from Al Jolson – or maybe she doesn't think he's suitable for Kath?"

George sucked at his pipe. "God knows! Anyroad, Al Jolson were white."

"Were he?" Emma cradled her chin. "Well he certainly looked black to me." It was now that George noticed the burn on Emma's hand. "What've yer done there, lass?" He indicated with the stem of his pipe.

"D'yer know, love, I'm not sure....I were tellin' Jonas that I didn't know I'd even done it. He said I ought to have it looked at."

Emma turned her hand over. "Funny that."

"He's right though. Y'ought to go to see the doctor."

"Nay, George, I've burnt meself before and haven't needed a doctor. And anyroad, we can't afford it."

"Look, love; I've got a bit o' brass put aside, so why don't you go and get it checked out – just to be on the safe side?"

Emma looked at this man of hers. And when she answered him, her voice wavered. "Aye, love....Aye, I think I might."

14

Emma Harvey considered that the headaches she'd been having for some time had been brought about by three things: the continuing war and the effect it was having on her family; Katherine's involvement with a black American soldier and Mary's reaction to their relationship, and the bombshell that Emily had dropped about marrying Wilf Sutcliffe.

But it had concerned her more, when she started feeling nauseous and kept losing her balance. Yet – and bearing in mind her phobia of doctors and hospitals – she had decided to have herself checked out. The doctor had referred her for tests, and today the results were disclosed to her. Now she had to face her family and give them the news.

They were all seated at the table waiting for her to speak, and when she did they had no idea how to react. "Oh, I might as well come straight out with it: they think I might have a growth on me brain." She paused and drew in a deep breath. "And they've told me…well, they've told me that they will have to operate as soon as possible."

"So can they remove it?" Katherine asked.

"They don't know at the moment, love. I was told it all depends on what they find.…One thing that did upset me though, and that was when they said I'll have to have me hair shaved off – and it'll probably stay off if they have to use radium."

Sarah went to her mother, and throwing her arms around her, said, "Oh, Mam."

Emma patted her daughter's arm. "Oh, yer never know. It might grow again, love. And besides, I can wear a turban like women do these days."

She's putting on a brave face about it, thought George; but she always does about everything. Then he said, "Can they do owt for the headaches?"

Emma smiled weakly. "Well, they have a lot of new stuff these days and they've put me on the strongest tablets available at the moment. But yer see, the pain comes and goes, and if they find something, they say the pills won't help me much.…Well, I can't sit here thinking about things. I'll get us some dinner going."

Sarah pushed her mother back onto the chair. "No you won't. I'll do it."

"You will not! You're on the night shift at Thorp Arch and you might miss the train if you start cooking. I can't understand why you went into war work when there's work aplenty in the mill.... And besides, I need to keep meself busy. Will you want owt, Kath, or are yer meeting Jonas?"

Katherine hesitated before saying, "Well, he's asked me to go to a dance they've laid on, but I'll cancel it if you like."

Emma stood now. "Don't be daft, lass; you get yerself off. Besides, he's being moved down south or somewhere soon, so grab every chance while yer can. Now, let's see what I can rustle up for us."

Less than three weeks later, Emma was admitted to hospital and within two days was operated on. The procedure went well, but it could not yet be considered as being a success until she had recovered enough for further tests to be carried out.

Nevertheless, after seven more weeks in Leeds Infirmary, and three weeks of convalescence, she was able to return home. "I feel fine you lot; don't fuss."

"You know they've told you to take it easy, Mam," said Sarah, "and I'm going to be here to make sure you do."

"But what about being on munitions?"

"Well, with Dad being busy at Providence and Kath working all the hours that God sends, I'm the only one old enough to look after you. So they've laid me off on compassionate leave."

"Oh, I see....Well, I must say I'm glad on it. I used to worry myself sick that the two of you might lose your fingers or get blown to bits at that place. Now at least I've only got Kath to fret about."

"Don't fret about owt, Mam. Just get yourself better. I'll pour us some tea."

Emma smiled at her girl. Then she asked, "What's been happening since I've been away? They had the wireless on all the time in the home, but I couldn't concentrate on it."

And when Sarah was seated, she reported every piece of news she could bring to mind – apart from a conversation that had taken place between herself and her father:

"What on earth were you thinking about, Dad?" she had said.

"I can't see what the problem is, Sal. She just happens to work at the same place and we get on, that's all."

"Get on with what? Mam's lying in a hospital bed not knowing if she's going to get better and you're messing about with another woman!"

"I'm not messing about; it's nothing like that. What with your mam being laid up, and her not being here for over two months, I needed a bit o' company."

Sarah slammed his dinner plate on the table. "Here! Get yer potato pasty....Company indeed. We're all after a bit o' company as you put it, but we don't all go about it like you've done."

George picked up his knife and fork. "I wish I'd never told yer now."

"Well y'ave....I only hope it doesn't get around. And believe me, Dad, if it does and me mam finds out, then it won't be pasty yer'll be having for yer dinner, it'll be arsenic. Now, I want you to promise me faithfully that you won't have anything else to do with her. Well?"

Her father had looked at her sheepishly, saying, "Aye...aye, lass; I promise."

Three months after Emma had returned home, the tumour on her brain had recurred, and any further operation was out of the question. It was just a matter of time now.

Emily cried uncontrollably when her mother took to her bed, but Sarah demanded that she be brave and not let their mother see her in this state. "She needs us all to be strong now, Em."

"But she's going to die, Sal...she's going to die."

Sarah shook her sister. "Don't let Mam hear you saying that, Em. And besides none of us know it for sure."

"The doctors must know."

"Well, Mam hasn't said owt about it, so we'll just have to hope things'll be all right. Now, you get yourself ready and go and meet Wilf as planned – we've got to get on with things, love, as best we all can."

Then things took a surprising turn when Jonas came back to Collingley on leave and proposed to Katherine. "I'm pleased for yer, lass," said Emma, as Katherine plumped up her mother's pillows and proceeded to brush her thinning hair. "He's a good man, love; you're lucky to have one like him. You'll have to find a house I suppose?"

"Well" – Katherine sat on the bed and took hold of her mother's hand – "now don't get upset, but I think I'll be going back with him to America, Mam."

Emma looked blank for a moment; then said, "Aye, a new start away from all this, eh? Probably be for the best....But it won't be just yet will it?"

"Heavens no! Who knows how long this war will go on? And he may be...."

Emma drew herself upward. "You were going to say killed, weren't you? Yes, that's a possibility. But none of us know if any of us'll survive if it boils down to it. No, love, look on the bright side – I do, even with all my problems."

"Aay, Mam." Katherine snuggled into her mother's shoulder. "Do you know how much I love you?"

Emma held her daughter close. "Eeh, I do, love....Now listen: me hair's not like it was, but I'm not bald and I'm feeling all right. Okay, I'm in bed at the moment, but I think I feel good enough to get up...so I will!"

Katherine drew away. "Don't, Mam; don't!"

"Look, love; I can't just sit here waiting for...the end. There's a war on and I could do me bit to get us all through it. So, I am going to get up and, tomorrow, go and ask Mr Crowther if he'll set me on part-time."

Katherine leapt from the bed. "Don't be so stupid!"

"Oi! Do you really think I'm not capable of doin' owt? Believe me, in the morning I'm out and gettin' meself some work."

The following day, Emma went to talk to J B Crowther and near demanded that he set her on. And he unreservedly agreed to her ultimatum, granting her a weaving position for two and a half days a week.

"You haven't lost your touch, Emma," said Jessie as they sat on their boxes and ate their dinner.

"Like riding a bike, love. In fact, I think I'm better at it now than when I was younger."

"And it's pay-day...Mr William and Dorothy'll be round later with our wages."

"Dorothy Stockwell – well, she as was?"

"Aye! She's the cashier. Been here now for about five weeks."

"Well, well! The last time I saw her was when she was nobbut a scared little girl hiding behind her mother's skirts – and that must be six or seven years ago."

"She's a fine young woman now, Emma. And they're so well suited to each other – her and William. He's on leave at t'moment; but how the hell *she* wangled it to get out of doing war work is beyond me."

And Emma remarked, "Oh, no doubt Edith had summat to do wi' that...."

At four o'clock, William and Dorothy Crowther entered the shed and began to distribute the week's wages. When they reached Emma and Jessie's looms, Jessie said, "Hello, Mr William, Mrs Crowther; this is Emma Harvey, Sarah's mam. She's started part-time."

"Well this is a pleasure I must say," said William; and Dorothy smiled, saying, "I thought I recognised the name when I was doing the wages. And I remember you now when you brought Sarah to our house and I showed her around the garden. How are you?"

"Oh, as well as can be expected," said Emma.

"We do miss Sarah, Mrs Harvey," said William now. "It's a pity she went into war work at such a young age. She was such an asset to the mill."

"Well, to be honest with you, sir, she's finished on munitions now. I shouldn't really be saying this, but she was given leave to stay at home and look after me. I've been poorly you see; but I was going crackers being at home all the time and I twisted your father's arm to set me on a few days a week. But if they find out, they'll likely make her go back."

"Well, I for one won't let on. It's such a pity that young girls should have to work in such dangerous conditions – however many arms and shells are still needed. It's much safer working here I'm sure."

"I won't argue with that, sir."

But the whole conversation that had taken place, presaged imminent tragedy when Emma had to send a lad to find a tuner to look at her loom, which didn't seem to be functioning properly. Due to the war, most men were away fighting for their country, and tuners were in short supply – the result being that routine maintenance in the mills had to be deferred. Yet, before a tuner was available to attend to her loom, Emma carried on weaving. This proved to be a reckless mistake. With alarming force, the picker suddenly dislodged from its fixing and shot across the loom, smacking Emma directly on her right temple.

Jessie flew across to her. "Emma! Emma!" But Emma was sprawled on the raised platform in front of her loom. "Maurice!" she cried to the foreman. "Get an ambulance quick! Emma's hurt."

After a further spell in hospital, Emma came home and had to return to her bed.

"I begged her not to go back to work."

"I know, Dad; but you know what she's like: stubborn as a mule," said Sarah. "Now, what d'yer want to take to work for yer dinner? We've got some mucky fat from the butchers if yer like."

"Aye, a bit o' drippin' wouldn't go amiss."

As Sarah made her father some beef dripping sandwiches, George sat and stared at his hands. The hospital had said that the accident at work had exacerbated the damage to Emma's brain and the time she had left to her would be brief. What would he do without her? He just couldn't bear the thought of losing her. Throughout their twenty-three years of marriage, she had not only been a wife and a devoted mother, but his constant companion. He was convinced his life would also be over when she lost her own.

"There y'are, Dad." Sarah handed him his snap.

"Ta, love." And as he watched his daughter mashing her mother's tea, his heart almost burst.

"I'll just take this up to Mam and see if she wants owt to eat." And as Sarah took the tea up to the bedroom, George dropped his head onto the table and cried....

Sarah placed the mug on the bedside table. "There, Mam. Dad'll be up to see yer before he goes to work. Do you fancy a bit o' breakfast?"

Her mother let out a small noise. Seeing that Emma was still asleep, Sarah went over to the bed and stroked her hair. "You know what you were saying last night, Mam: about Dad taking up with another woman and you wouldn't really mind if he did? Well, what with me and our Kath keeping an eye on him, he'll never get the chance. But of course, he wouldn't do anything like that because he loves you much too much, Mam...Mam?" Sarah took hold of her mother's hands. They were extraordinarily cold, so she rubbed them between her own, saying, "I'll bring up a hot water bottle." But after gazing at her mother for the longest of moments, she drew close and gently placed her fingers on her lips. And then it dawned on her that every spark of life had gone from the woman lying on the bed.

She raced downstairs and stared blankly at her father.

"What, lass? What is it?"

Sarah ran into his arms. "Oh, Dad." And when he felt her sobs drumming against his chest, he knew that his cherished Emma had left them.

15

Martha Roberts was born in South Wales in 1885. She met and married a soldier at the start of the First World War, and had moved to the outskirts of Wakefield where he shared a house with his sister; and here she bore him a son. The two women did not get on – which came as some surprise to those who knew Rachel Halliday because she was one of the nicest and most respected people in the district. Then in 1916 when her brother, serving with the 13th Battalion of the Yorks and Lancs Regiment, was killed at the battle of The Somme, Rachel immediately dismissed Martha and her child from the house that was now her own.

Martha Halliday though, was a resourceful individual, and it took her little time to find a job in a local mill as a bookkeeper and pack her son off to her family in Wales to be brought up by them. She never remarried, and at the age of fifty-eight remained an elderly widow who, when the need for women to carry out essential war work – despite their ages – were employed in diverse jobs including the production of armaments, she moved to the converted Providence mill where she met George Harvey.

"He seems smitten with her, Nelly. He talks about her constantly. I never believed that even before my mother died he'd ever get involved with another woman as long as Mam was still on this earth."

"That's men for yer, Sal. Unpredictable!"

Sarah poured out the tea. "He says he's going to bring her to meet me today, but I hope he doesn't. I can't bear the thought of having her in the same house where Mam lived. And on top of that, he seems to have ignored the fact that he's a grandfather now. I only hope he's going to act like one and stop behaving like a big kid. Do you know, he hasn't been to see Emily since she had Kevin, and I doubt whether he ever will now that he's got other things to occupy him."

"It'll be a flash in the pan, love. I can't see him being serious about a woman of her sort."

"What sort?" Sarah was astonished by her neighbour's remark. "Do you know something that I don't?"

Nelly leaned forward and tapped the table. "She packed her kid off back to Wales when he was nobbut a babby – to be looked after by her relatives after her husband died in the First War – and then her sister-in-law chucked her out of the house. Rachel Halliday was a saint of a woman, so this one must be a devil and a…."

They both turned abruptly when the door opened and George Harvey walked in. "Oh, hello, Nelly!"

Nelly nodded, saying, "George."

Sarah's father averted his gaze as he stood back from the open door and said, "Come in, Martha."

Nelly and Sarah remained seated as the woman entered. She was a small body – not more than five foot four – and as George ushered her into the centre of the room, Sarah noticed that Martha Halliday walked with a slight limp; and standing now, said, "Er… I'll pull up a chair for you."

"Thank you, dear. Most kind," said the woman.

When she was seated, George leaned over her saying, "Are you all right there?" The woman nodded, whence George said, "Let me introduce you. This is my daughter, Sarah; and this lady here is our very good neighbour, Nelly." Martha then acknowledged each in turn.

"Would you like some tea?" said Sarah with a total lack of concern.

"Yes, my dear; but only a weak one with a small amount of sugar."

Nelly spoke now. "It'll have to be, lass; what wi' stuff being rationed."

"Oh, I appreciate that. This war is affecting us all and none of us know when it will ever end."

Sarah called from the sink area where she was filling the kettle. "Would you like another, Nelly?"

"No, ta, love; I best get off and leave you to it." Nelly stood now. "Pleased to meet you, missis. And I hope your leg gets better soon."

"I doubt it," said Martha. "It's ulcerated you see."

"Oh, how awful.…Well, Sal, George, I'll go and let you all get acquainted. Ta-rah for now.…"

After Nelly had gone, George sat next to Martha and patted her hand. "Sarah's been a big help since Emma died."

"Yes, she seems an able young woman. You must be a very proud man, George." And Martha gazed at him and smiled.

"There you are," said Sarah as she passed the visitor a cup. "And some seed cake I managed to get hold of."

"Not for me, dear," said Martha flapping her hand. "I can't stomach the stuff. Caraway doesn't agree with me you see."

"But that's all we've got, so...."

"Never mind, lass," said her father; "just tea'll be fine." They all drank in silence; during which, Sarah was surreptitiously making an analysis of the woman. She had a small, sort of flat face, with a small nose and grey eyes that appeared not to have any emotion behind them. Her hair was also grey, tightly waved against her skull, and her hands were mottled with age. And even though Sarah's mother had been seriously ill in the later months of her life, her hands – and appearance in general – were still youthful.

But holding the knowledge that she had gained earlier from Nelly about this woman, she wondered what kind of person she really was behind the exterior. Not nice at all! She'd sent her son miles away to be looked after by relatives after all. No caring mother, however desperate, would do that! Even Alice Barraclough in the position she had found herself, had sheltered her son against the prospect of him being taken from her. Sarah wondered now what this woman's son was like, and whether or not she had been in touch with him over the years – or even if she'd in fact visited him? But she certainly had no intention of asking!

Suddenly George said, "We were thinking of going to t'Jubilee tonight, lass. D'yer want to come?"

When Sarah roused herself from her thoughts, she was about to refuse, but suddenly changed her mind: "Aye, I think I will, Dad. It's ages since I had a night out. Will it be okay if I ask Jessie along?"

"Course, lass. The more the merrier, eh Martha?"

Martha gave a weak smile. "I suppose so, love."

She's calling him 'love', thought Sarah. How bloody dare she!

As they walked towards Town End, Sarah and Jessie kept their distance from the couple in front. "I can't believe it, Jess. He seems to have gone dippy over her."

"They do seem close, lass, I must admit. D'yer think he's got... sort of...designs?"

"I bloody well hope not. In fact, if this carries on, then I move out – and I don't care where I go either. I'll sleep on the streets if it comes to it..."

When they entered the Jubilee, all eyes turned on the four of them. Then, through the smoky haze, a figure approached. "Hello, Sarah!" It was Maurice Butterworth.

"Oh, hello, Mr Butterworth. How are you?"

"Fine, lass....Eeh, I'm glad yer're comin' back to t'mill. Have they let you off munitions, then?"

"Yes, they have. They let me off to look after Mam, and after she died they never forced me to return; so, instead of lolling about at home, I went and saw Mr Crowther and he was eager to have me back."

"Aye, things are on the up now. And after the recent successes of our forces, it looks like we'll be going like hell makin' cloth for demob suits afore long."

"Well, let's hope so. This war's gone on long enough....Oh, look at me stood here rambling and I haven't introduced you." Sarah turned to her side. "You know Jessie of course; and this is my father and...a friend of his."

Maurice shook George's hand, saying, "Pleased to meet yer, Mr Harvey. I were sorry to hear from Jessie about yer loss."

"Thanks, lad....Can I get you a drink while I'm gettin' ours?"

"Aye...aye, go on then. Tetley's for me."

As George went to the bar, Maurice said, "Now, you ladies come wi' me; there's room over yonder." And the three women followed him to a table beside a frosted glass window....

They were on their second round of drinks when Maurice excused himself to go to the gents, and while he was absent, George said, "Sarah, I have something to tell yer."

Sarah put down her pale ale and looked at her father.

"I know it's not long since yer mother passed on, but...well, I'm thinking of settlin' down again." He paused and stared at his daughter whose face was like flint. "I'm thinking o' weddin' Martha, here."

Sarah did not respond at first; but then she stood, and without saying a word, picked up her handbag, threw back her chair, and pushed her way passed a bewildered Jessie.

"Nay, lass," said George. "What's to do?"

"You are, Dad. You are! And when you get back home I won't be there; then maybe you'll consider carefully why I've walked out."

And without further words to anyone, Sarah stormed from the public house.

16

"I don't think I can bear living with them any longer, Em – especially now that Kath's back at Rosenberg's and has moved in with Maggie Gledhill. Dad's a changed man since he took up with that...that thing! Oh, God, I wish I'd have stayed here when you took me in in the first place."

"Well, if the fiasco of him deciding not to get married and live over the brush was owt to go by, *I'd* have been out of that house like a shot an' all. Talk about bloody mutton dressed as lamb! In fact, I've seen better-looking sheep than her."

Sarah laughed at her sister's remark, but said, "The reason he gave was that he didn't want her to get her hands on anything after he died."

"Like what?"

"I don't know, Em." said Sarah. "After all, he must have paid a lot out for Mam's operation....Anyhow, how's the little one and Wilf?"

"Teething – Kevin I mean, not Wilf. Ha! Oh, he does bawl at times, Sal, whatever I rub on his gums. And bloody 'ell, when I put him in that gas chamber thing he screams the cellar down...Wilf's still on fire watch every night. Eeh, I wish it would all end."

"It will, love. Things are bound to get better before long....Now, would you mind if I just go for a little walk? It might clear my head a bit."

"Course not! You do what you want if it makes you feel better. Don't be *too* long though, 'cos the cake – for what it's worth – will be out o' t'oven in twenty minutes."

"I won't, Em...."

Across St Mary's Road, there was an area known locally as The Docks – she and Emily used to come here when they were younger and bring a few sandwiches and some pop. It was an odd name because it had nothing to do with sea and ships: it was just an area of sloping land covered with sycamores, where, at the latter part of the year, the winged seeds came sailing down from above like miniature spinning tops.

They'd sit and have their makeshift picnic and watch the trains in the distance come trundling along the line from Wakefield on their way to Leeds. They were happy days – unlike now when the whole world had just gone insane. And as Sarah walked beneath the tall trees and felt the glossy-leaved rhododendrons, she wished desperately that her father had not latched on to that woman, and she could be with him on her own. What was she to do? She didn't really know. One thing that she did know for certain, and that was she could have a home with Em – but would she be settled?

She sat down and stared into the distance and wondered now if William Crowther was safe serving in France. And there again, she also wished that he hadn't married, and he may have asked herself to be his wife; but now that would just not happen. God, was she an evil person? Why had she lost so many people in her life whom she loved? She still thought about her brother – even after nine years – and then of course, there was the loss of her mother. Aay, Mam, whatever will become of me? You were always there to guide me – even though it was often forceful. And what if she lost her father? Oh, God forbid! Would she end up a sour, old spinster…? Then, in this moment of fitful contemplation, she came to a determined conclusion: she would marry any man who asked her, just so that she wouldn't be left alone. She lay back on the moist undergrowth and, looking up at the vast, open sky, pondered as to her fate – and to the rest of humanity if this war didn't end soon.

But during this summer of 1944, Germany unleashed the V1 rockets on Britain, and it would surely make the prospect of an early victory over Hitler's dictatorship, much more unlikely.

George was on lates at the factory.

Sarah had made something that she'd been able to cobble together from what she could find in the cupboards – and the woman had actually eaten it. Then, Martha said, "Would you mind awfully, Sarah, if you could change the dressing on my leg? and then I'll go to bed."

Sarah boiled another kettle after washing the pots, and then proceeded to clean Martha's leg. The pus was fetid. "You're hurting me!" squealed the woman. "Give me the water and I'll do it myself. I wish your father was here because he'd be more gentle."

"Oh, do shut up moaning! You're lucky you've got somebody here to do it at all."

"Stop it! Stop it now! Just bandage me up and help me up to bed." So Sarah did.

When Martha had retired, Sarah sat close to the fire and stared into the flames. "The swine woman." However much she disliked her father for entertaining her, she wished that he and herself were on their own and out of this nightmare. Why, oh why, did he have to take up with her…? She rose to make some tea for her father coming in…and then she heard it. It was a buzz bomb: one of those she'd heard about that the Germans had built. It was overhead. But why no air raid siren? Yes, they'd been over London before, but not here! She turned off the kettle and ran upstairs.

Martha was sitting bolt upright in bed. "We're done for!"

"No we're not. Look, let me get you up and we'll go into the cellar."

"I can't move. It's the leg. It's the leg!"

Sarah began to drag the complaining woman out of bed when the sound of the bomb ceased. It was going to drop on them. She pulled back the blanket and slid in beside Martha who cried, "Oh, love, what's happening?"

"Shush," said Sarah. "Hold on to me. We'll be all right." And then they waited until the explosion came.

Sarah was now convinced that the V1 rocket was certainly *not* off course. And as she pressed herself close to Martha, she reckoned it must have been intended for the mill. And she was right.

The bomb descended into the middle of Stockwell's Field just missing both Providence and Resurrection. But it had not missed the shift workers who were on their way home, killing most of the thirty men and women – one of whom was George Harvey.

Sarah and her siblings were now without both mother and father – and what on earth was the future for them all?

She had been faithful to her father's wishes and never opened the letter he had entrusted to her before his death. Before the family set off to the church, Sarah sat on his bed, and in this quiet and personal moment, began to read his words: 'Sal, my very special girl. I have kept a little something for you, which you will find at the back of my wardrobe. Keep it safe – it might be valuable one of these days.'

She broke off now and went to find that which her father had left her. And when she unwrapped the article, she stared at the framed painting with one thought in her mind: It looks as if a child's done it....Still, she didn't care. If her dad wanted her to have it then she'd make sure nobody else got their hands on it. She returned to the letter now: 'Also, I want you to know one thing now that I am no longer with you. I am in need to tell you this because I would never rest peacefully in my grave if I didn't.

'You must have wondered how I was able to pay for Mam's operation since we hardly had a spare copper. I want to tell you now – and please, never tell a soul about this – I didn't....It was Mary.

'Don't be as harsh on her like Kath has been. She really doesn't deserve it. You will make something of yourself, Sal, won't you? Please don't be sad; I'm off to see Mam now...Dad.'

The ink on her father's letter soon became blurred as tears cascaded from Sarah's eyes. "Oh, Dad," she sobbed. "You daft bugger."

The church was packed. So loved was George Harvey that not just his family, but friends and colleagues from far and wide, were present to pay their last respects to a man held dear. For the moment, war was forgotten; it was George's time now, and what was still going on in Europe and the rest of the world would just have to wait until he was laid to rest.

The singing of Abide With Me ended a tearful ceremony, and in the churchyard of St Mary in the Wood, three pained sisters held each other close as earth was scattered onto the coffin. Mary, together with her husband and daughter, remained at a distance. Martha was at Sarah's side, her arm linked with Nelly's; and Jessie stood next to Katherine, whilst Wilf tried to comfort a grizzling Kevin.

Then the families made their way back to Long Lane where Nelly had laid on the best she'd been able to manage. Martha refused anything to eat and drink and retired to bed; and within half an hour, Wilf had excused himself to take his son home; and Mary, Jack and eight-year-old Laura soon followed.

"Well, will you be staying on now, Sal?" asked Emily. "You know there's always a home for you with me."

"I know, love; and thanks...but I suppose I'll have to stay put," said Sarah. "Now that Kath's not here, there's only me left to look after Martha...and she's getting worse. Mind you, she gave me her son's address and I've written to him asking if he could come and see her, but I haven't heard anything yet."

"He might not *want* to see her," said Emily. "Well, not after farming him out to her sister thirty years ago."

"I suppose it depends how much she's kept in touch with him... I'll go mental if he doesn't reply."

Katherine came up behind them. "You two okay?"

"Aye, Kath," said Sarah. "Considering."

"Ah, well, I hope this isn't an inappropriate time to give you both something." She handed her two younger sisters an envelope each.

"What's this?" said Sarah.

"Open it and see."

Sarah pulled out the flap of the envelope, took out the printed card, and read. "God in heaven, Kath!" But she was smiling. "A wedding invitation! You and Jonas...and at Christmas."

"Well, the twenty-third; he'll be back on leave then, so we decided to take the plunge."

Sarah flung her arms about her. "I'm so happy for you...aren't you, Em?"

Emily smiled. "All I can say is it's about bloody time." And the three girls laughed together.

"What's this all about?" said Nelly as she sidled up to them. "It's supposed to be a solemn occasion you know."

"Sorry," said Sarah, "but Kath has some good news."

"Come on," said Katherine taking Nelly's arm. "Let's go over to Jessie...I've got something to give you both." And as she led Nelly away, Sarah watched her sister hand the two women their invitations and thought, Not only has she left this house but no doubt she'll be leaving the country next. And then, apart from our Em, I'll be completely abandoned.

17

Nelly Dicks was a sweet woman. She attended to Martha regularly while Sarah was at work, refusing any compensation for baby-sitting the invalid.

And one evening as Sarah and Jessie were on their way home from the mill, Sarah said, "I don't know what I'd do without your mam, Jess. She's been a brick over the past few months."

"She doesn't take any nonsense, though. And believe me, she can give better than she gets."

Sarah chuckled. "Now, come in and have a bit of something to eat. I managed to get some sausages from the butcher. It'll be a bit of a treat for us all."

"Aye, lass, I will...I'm starving."

Sarah opened the door.

However, not only were Nelly and Martha seated around the table, but also a dark-haired man who stood when Sarah and Jessie came in. They both looked on in silence, waiting for somebody to say something. It was Nelly who spoke: "Sarah, this is Martha's son."

The man came forward and offered Sarah his hand. "John. John Halliday. Thank you for your kind letter, Sarah. When I read of your situation, I thought it my duty to make the long journey. And, if it is of no inconvenience to you, I would very much like to stay for a few weeks and maybe lend a helping hand?"

Sarah was lost for words. He was not as she'd expected – although she didn't know what to expect with him being his mother's son. He was certainly well spoken...and ruggedly handsome in a way. "Er...well," she said, "I think that would be all right....But where will you stay?"

John turned and looked at his mother. Then addressing Sarah, said, "Well...here I thought – if you have the room."

"Oh, I couldn't let you do that! No, it's out of the question."

"Oh, I'm sorry....Perhaps I can find a hotel for a while."

"Around here?" said Sarah. "We don't go in for hotels in this neck of the woods." She turned away now and went to the door, where she removed her coat and hung it on a hook. "Hang your coat up, Jess, and I'll get on with tea." But she hesitated when she reached the sink. Lend a helping hand, eh? she thought. Then turning around, said abruptly, "All right, John; perhaps you can stay – but not for long, mind. I suppose we could take the spare bed up into the attic and maybe get a fire going to air the place."

John smiled showing a set of fine, white teeth. "That would be ideal for the time I'm here?"

"By the way, this is Nelly's daughter, Jessie. We work together in the mill."

"Pleased to meet you, Jessie," said John.

Jessie shook his hand. "Likewise."

Sarah approached Jessie now, saying, "Set the table for me will you love? and I'll get those sausages on."

"Aye, lass, I will."

When they had eaten, Sarah began to clear the table, but Jessie held her back, saying, "Me and Mam'll wash up lass; you see to your company."

Sarah sat back down, and turning to Martha's son now, said, "Well, John; and what kind of work do you do?"

"I'm an accountant. They wouldn't take me into the army when I applied – I didn't pass the medical – but Mother was pleased about that, weren't you, Mother?" Martha nodded. Then after a moment of silence, John said suddenly, "Would you be up to taking a walk, Sarah? It's a lovely evening and perhaps you could show me a little of the area."

"There's not much to see, really – apart from a few fields to wander in just across the road. It's nearly all mills around here."

John turned to his mother. "You wouldn't mind if Sarah and I take a little stroll, would you?"

"But….Oh, no, go on if you like…but don't be long. You can help me to bed soon."

"We won't be. Come Sarah, let's walk for a while."

As they were departing, Sarah turned to Jessie and Nelly, saying, "I won't be long. Will you be all right for half an hour?"

"Aye, lass," said Nelly. "You get off and Jess and me'll stay on till yer get back."

Once in the lane, John said, "Mother must have been a bit of a burden to you, Sarah – particularly since your father died."

"Just a bit."

They took the path across the field that led over to High Ridge. It was a fine evening with a descending sun, and starlings were sweeping across the western sky. "This is quite a haven for you, I expect," said John.

Sarah glanced sideways at her companion and noticed a distant look in the man's brown eyes. "I suppose it is," she said, "considering how built-up the rest of the town is."

John halted at the stile, and facing Sarah now, said, "You know, even though Mother and I have not spent much time with each other over the years, I do care for her and her welfare. And, with that in mind, I'm going to take the opportunity while I'm here over the next fortnight, of looking for a job."

"For two weeks?"

"No, permanently. I want to be nearer her now that I've seen how frail and dependent she is."

"You mean you'd move from Wales to come and live here?"

John nodded. "And if it works out – and of course that is all down to yourself – then I was wondering if you might consider letting me take up residence in your attic room? I'd pay the rent of the house of course, and recompense your neighbour for seeing to Mother's needs while we're both working – or even get a helper in if it was really necessary."

"Oh...I don't really know....I'd need to get permission from the landlord and I can't be sure he'd agree."

"But you will consider it?"

Sarah bit on her bottom lip. And after a moment's hesitation, said, "Let me sleep on it, John....And talking about sleep, we'd best get back and get your mother seen to...oh! and get the spare bed up to the attic."

John Halliday had been lucky in his search for employment in the area and had been offered a position with an engineering firm in Leeds; and the kindly J B Crowther had been generous in agreeing that Sarah could certainly accommodate John in her home for as long as the situation warranted it – although some eyebrows had been raised at Sarah having a single man come and live under the same roof. But nonetheless, Nelly had said she'd be agreeable to carry on seeing to Martha's needs.

But during the time that John was absent arranging his affairs back in Wales before his move, Martha had turned in on herself – believing that it was the last she would see of her son. "Well! that's bloody charming!" said Nelly when Sarah passed on the news.

"She gives him away when he was knee-high to a grasshopper, and now wonders if she'll ever see him again. Well, I'll tell you this, Sal: she's making my life hell. I don't know if I'll be able to take her moaning any longer."

"I'm sorry, Nelly; but I do know what you mean. She drives me up the wall at night!"

"Don't be sorry, lass; after all, it's not your fault." Nelly took hold of Sarah by the arms now. "Look, love; I'll carry on till he gets back, but after that I don't think I'll be able to...."

When John returned in late September, he told Sarah that he'd get a nurse in to look after Martha during the day and then they'd share responsibilities for her welfare at other times. But he was taken aback by Sarah's reaction: "Oh, no, John. Responsibilities? I don't have any responsibilities towards that woman. She's *your* mother not mine; you see to her. And you may as well know now, I'm going to live with my sister within the next few days, so Martha's your problem now."

"But...."

"I've sorted it with Mr Crowther that you can stay on as a proxy tenant for the foreseeable future, and now I'm going to start and pack my belongings."

"What's he like, Sal?"

"Gorgeous. And such a charmer. We went dancing at Mark Altman's in Leeds last night...I hope I didn't wake you when I got in."

"Course you didn't....So, are you seeing him again?" Emily asked.

"I am. He says he can't live without me."

"Oh aye...they all do, these Americans. I only hope you don't decide to wed him and go running off across the other side of the world like our Kath'll probably do."

Sarah laughed. "There's no chance of that....It's all just a bit of fun."

A knock came to the door. "Now, who's that on a bloody Saturday morning?" said Emily as she went to answer. "Oh...er, yes, she is....D'yer want to come in?"

Sarah turned about in her seat to see John standing there. "Hello, Sarah," he said humbly.

"Go and sit down, lad, and I'll make us some tea." This was Emily. And as she went into the scullery, John took a seat opposite

Sarah and rubbed his hands in front of the fire. "It's cold out," he said. "It wouldn't surprise me if it snowed – even at this time of year."

"How's your job going?" said Sarah, ignoring his remark concerning the weather.

John leaned away from the fire now. "Oh, fine. They're a good crowd to work for…and Mother's not too bad at the moment: she seems a lot brighter in herself." He raised his head to look straight at Sarah now, and said, "She misses you."

Sarah's jaw dropped. "Me? She misses *me*? She hated my guts when I lived with her to be honest!"

John shook his head. "No, that's not true. In fact, she said only yesterday that she wished you'd come back – or at least pay us a visit. What do you think? Perhaps you could come to tea tomorrow?"

"No, sorry; I'm going out. And if you really want to know, I'm seeing someone. His name's Marty. He's an American soldier."

"Oh, I see…well it was only a suggestion."

Emily came in with the tea. "There y'are; this'll warm you up.… Now, Sal; if you'll pour, I'll go up and see to Kevin and leave you two alone for a while." With this, Emily went up the bedroom steps and closed the door behind her.

Sarah poured out the tea and handed a cup to John. "How's the woman doing you got in to see to Martha? Still there is she?"

"You're being sarcastic now, Sarah; it doesn't become you."

Sarah slammed her cup on its saucer. "How dare you! The sarcasm is coming from yourself: she misses me; she'd like me to go back. Why for God's sake? So she can have me running around after her? Being her servant? Her slave? Well I'll tell you this" – a finger was pointed at him – "I've had to move out of my home because of her, and however long it takes, I won't set foot in the place as long as she's there. Now, I think enough's been said on the matter, so I suggest you finish your tea and get back to your precious mother."

Some days later, Sarah received a letter.

'Dear Sarah

'I am so sorry if I upset you when I came to see you at your sister's, but I promise you my intentions were honourable. My mother really is a changed person and she appreciates all that you did for her after your father died, and she really would like you to come and visit us whenever is convenient.

'How is your friendship with the American going? I hope you are happy. He's got himself a real treasure in you.

'Anyhow, maybe you would care to write back or send a message through Jessie that you may possibly consider calling upon us.

'Sincerely,

'John.'

"He's got a bloody nerve!" said Emily. "How could he expect you to go and sit in the same room as that awful woman?"

Sarah folded the note and slipped it back in the envelope. "I don't know what to do, Em....Maybe I will go and see if she has changed as he says."

Emily sighed. "You said you'd never go back if she was still there." When Sarah did not respond, Emily said, "Well, it's up to you, that's all I can say."

The following Sunday, Sarah went to Long Lane and back into her old home. Martha really was a changed woman after all: she was mobile, and welcomed Sarah with open arms. "Oh, my dear, I'm so glad you came. We have missed you. Come and seat yourself. Do. Do." And John smiled.

Then a woman appeared at the cellar head. "Hello," she said. "Eeh, well I never, it's Sarah! It must be goin' on...what? five years since I saw you last."

"Amy?"

"Aye, lass; it's me. I moved in next door – not Nelly's; this side." She thumbed towards the wall. "And I'm looking after yer stepmother now."

"She's not my stepmother, Amy."

"Oh, right...well, it's still grand to see you, lass."

"So, what did you do after you left the mill, Amy?"

"Eeh, yer'll never believe this, but I've been helping to make planes – bombers, like. But since things are on the up now – as far as the war's going – they laid me off.

"I could have gone back in t'mill, but I could never get the hang on it – nowt to do wi' your trainin' o' course, I just couldn't fathom it. Anyroad, lass, Mr Crowther were kind enough to let me rent one of these 'ouses after my little stint, and 'ere I am tending to t'sick."

Martha came forward now. "Sarah, why don't you come and sit down? Tea is nearly ready and then we can have a little chat."

The prospect of talking to Martha seemed tedious to say the least; but after they had eaten, Martha promptly fell asleep, and while Amy was doing the dishes, John took hold of Sarah's arm, saying, "Can we do what we did when I first met you, Sarah, and go for a walk?"

"It's bitter out yonder," Amy called out. "Best wrap up!"

And Sarah found herself acceding to John's wishes.

Now, he helped her on with her coat and wrapped a scarf about her neck, and when they were out in the lane, he said, "Come on, let's walk to the stile like we did before."

The sky on this occasion was threatening, and darkness was almost upon the land; yet strangely enough, Sarah's heart had lightened.

"It seems ages since we first did this," she said plaintively.

"Almost two months," said John. "But a lot seems to have happened during that time."

"Yes," said Sarah, "it has."

"Are you still courting your American?"

Sarah smiled, saying, "Oh, I wouldn't have called it 'courting' as such. It was just a friendship of sorts."

"You said *was* just a friendship?"

"Yes," said Sarah. "I'm not seeing him now. In fact, he's gone back on duty somewhere."

"Oh," said John....

They were at the stile now, and Sarah leaned against it and stared over at High Ridge. But her thoughts were neither on Marty – nor even William – but on the man who stood beside her. She shivered involuntarily.

"You're cold," said John taking her hand. And when he gently turned her towards him, he took the other one and held them both in his.

"No. I'm not cold. Not now," she said; and as she looked into his warmly intense eyes, all her senses appeared to abandon her.

John suddenly averted his gaze now and glanced skyward as the first few flakes of snow began to descend from the heavens. And as one landed on Sarah's cheek, he loosed his hands from hers and tenderly brushed it away. "Sarah?" he said.

"Yes, John?"

"Would you...would you consider becoming my wife?" He held up his hand as Sarah was about to speak. "Yes, I'm aware I haven't known you for long, and you have to love someone to accept his proposal, but...."

Sarah slowly turned away from this man who had asked her to marry him, and in surveying the darkening, barren land that stretched before her, she couldn't believe what came into her mind. She could see herself sitting in the sunlit Docks across the road from Emily's house, and hear herself saying that, for good or ill, she'd marry any man that asked her.

Now she looked at him once more, saying, "You must have thought during the time we have known each other, that I have tended to reject you out of hand and, at times, been quite rude toward you. But, if I'm really honest with myself, the truth is, John, I think I fell in love with you from the very first day when we dragged that stupid bed up into the attic. So – as to your proposal – yes, I will marry you."

And in the ensuing twilight, as the snow fell around them and the earth became suddenly still, the two of them embraced.

On Saturday the 23rd of December 1944, a double wedding took place in the church of St Mary in the Wood.

Sarah Halliday and Katherine Williams were both embarking on a new life and, within six months, so would their very own part of the world, when peace was declared in Europe.

18

"Now look here, Martha. It's no good trying that with me! I'm going to work and that's an end to it."

"But think of my son's child you're carrying."

Sarah leaned over her mother-in-law and placed her hands on the arms of the rocking-chair. And pushing her face forward now, said, "I am doing, woman! That's the reason why I'm going to work: to give him – or her – a good start in life. One wage isn't enough to keep three of us let alone four."

"And what about me? I'm ill! This…this thing that I'm suffering from could…well, it could kill me….Oh, but of course, that doesn't seem to matter to you."

Sarah stood erect now. "No, as a matter of fact, it doesn't. I couldn't give a monkey's. Kill you indeed – what? Ulcerated legs…? Do you know, you've been a blight on my life ever since you took up with my father. And the only good thing that came out of that ill-fated encounter, was that after his death I was lucky enough to meet John."

"Yes, but you just wait until I tell him how you treat me and see if…if he doesn't witness another side to you."

"Listen, madam" – a finger was pointed at the seated woman – "if you ever try to meddle in our lives you'll regret it – I'll make sure of that. And it won't be the damned ulcers that kill you, it'll be me!" Sarah tramped to the door now, and taking her coat from a hook, turned back, saying, "I'm going or I'll be late. Amy will be in as usual to see to you, so be thankful for that. If it was down to me, you could sit there and starve." And she went out with a slam of the door.

Jessie was waiting for her outside.

"Did you hear any of that?"

"Most of it," said Jessie. "That's why I didn't knock."

They swiftly set off down the lane. "She's a sly old bitch, Jess. And an ungrateful one at that."

"You shouldn't let her upset yer like she does. And anyroad, she has a point: yer know for a fact you shouldn't be working in your condition."

"Oh give over, Jess. You know perfectly well that I'm more than three weeks off my time – although if John hadn't thought it was longer, he would have stopped me going to work. But at least nobody at the mill knows I'm expecting, not with this bloody tent on." She grabbed at the overall under her coat.

"But that's the point: you are! Folk notice things, yer know."

Sarah grabbed Jessie's arm, pulling her to a halt. "Now look, if you dare say a word to anybody, I'll...well...I'll never forgive you."

Jessie pulled herself away now, saying, "Aye, maybe not; but I'd never forgive meself if yer lost him....Aye, him! There's a lad in there." She nodded. "Oh I know you think I'm just a daft sod, but so many times in my life I've known when a woman's carryin' a lad – and this is one of 'em. So, get yerself back 'ome and I'll cover for yer."

Sarah shook her head. "That's not my way, Jess. And besides, I'll need all the money I can lay me hands on in the coming months."

"Well, it's up to you; but, mark my words, you'll do no good to either on yer" – she nodded towards Sarah's belly – "leaning over those mules and the like. Anyroad, if yer're so determined, it's time we got a move on before we're both out of a job and short o' brass."

When every thread coming from the condenser spools to the bobbins, break, it is known in the mill as a 'fell' – and shortly after she had set the mule in motion for the morning session, Sarah got one. Every single one on the line of a hundred bobbins snapped and she had to wait until the mule reached the half-way-point on its travel back to the condensers and then stop it. This was all she needed: having basically to start again from scratch. But her troubles didn't end there, for she spotted William Crowther striding into the shed accompanied by his wife who, unlike Sarah, was evidently near her time. The couple already had a four-year-old son, Mark, who was born when his father was abroad, and Jessie had been right in her prediction that Dorothy would be having a boy. Sarah wondered if Jessie could forecast the outcome this time?

"Oh dear, Sarah," said William, "you have a fell. Never mind, these things happen. I'll go over and get one of the other pieceners to come and give you a hand."

"Oh, it's no problem. I can manage....How's your leg?"

"On the mend – although I still have a slight limp after taking that bullet. Mind you, I was lucky compared to others in the regiment....And how are you, Sarah?"

"Very well, Mr William."

"And how's married life, eh? No doubt you'll be starting a family like us before long." He smiled at his wife.

Sarah laughed. "I expect so."

"Well," said William, "I'll leave you to get on while I take Dorothy to meet the new cashier and show her the ropes. I only hope it doesn't put too much of a strain on her." He took his wife's arm. "Bye for now."

"Bye, Mr William; Mrs Crowther."

"Bye, Sarah," said Dorothy. "I hope you get your machine sorted."

And the two women exchanged smiles....

At dinner time, Jessie said, "She's 'avin' a lass this time."

"How the hell do you know?" said Sarah. "If I didn't know better, I'd swear you travelled to work on a broomstick."

Jessie chortled. "I just seem to know these things. Mind you, when Mr William was talking to me I sensed there was going to be a death around him afore long."

"Oh don't, Jessie. You're giving me the creeps."

"Just wait and see. I'm never wrong...."

It was shortly after two o'clock when the news spread through the mill that J B Crowther had passed away. Jessie scurried across to Sarah's mule. "Didn't I tell yer?"

"What a shame," said Sarah. "He was such a lovely man."

"And when one departs, another arrives." said Jessie.

"Oh, don't start that again, Jess. And don't say 'I'm never wrong' or I'll throttle yer."

Maurice Butterworth approached them now. "Have you heard the news, ladies?"

"We have, Maurice....I was just saying to Jessie what a nice man he was. Well, I suppose it's all down to Mr William now."

"Aye," said Maurice. "Him and his Uncle Jim'll be partners now."

"I've never come across Jim," said Jessie. "What's he like, Maurice?"

"Much like his brother really, but quieter. He's mostly on the sidelines as far as the family business goes and is plannin' to move to New Zealand; but for now, I think he might have to take a bigger part in the running of the place – at least till young William finds his feet."

"It's a big responsibility, though," suggested Sarah. "After all, William's still only....Oh...oh, my God...!"

"What is it, lass? Are you...?"

"Oh, Jessie...Jess, I think...." Sarah bit on her bottom lip and bent herself double over the mule, the bobbins sticking into her.

"I bloody well knew it!" said Jessie. "I told her to get herself home but she's as stubborn as a mule – and I didn't mean that as a wisecrack, Maurice."

"But what's wrong wi' her?"

"She's having a baby, lad. That's what!"

"Bloody hell! I'll go and phone for an ambulance and get her to hospital."

But when Jessie saw the mess on the floor she said, "Nay, lad, I think it's much too late for that. Quick! Go and drag over an empty skip and pull down the front and...and throw some sacking over the bottom. She'll be going to no hospital I can tell yer."

John Halliday got off the train at Collingley Top and walked the short distance home where he was surprised to see Jessie waiting there.

"Oh, hello, Jessie. I didn't expect to see you here. Is Sarah home? And what about Mother?"

"Hey! One thing at a time, lad....Yer mother's next door with Amy and Sarah's in bed."

"Why? Is she ill?"

"Well, not exactly....Come on up and see her."

John was worried. What had happened? He couldn't bring himself to speak as Jessie led the way upstairs and into their bedroom. And what greeted him was a sight that almost stopped his heart.

"Go on then, lad," said Jessie. "Meet the new arrival." And she smiled broadly. "I'll leave yer to it and go put the kettle on."

John walked slowly to the bed where Sarah was cradling their son. "But...I thought...I didn't....How on earth....?"

Sarah placed a finger to her lips. "Shush. He's asleep." Then she patted the edge of the bed. "Come and take a closer look."

John eased himself onto the bed beside his wife and leaned close to his boy. "He's got my nose," he said with pride.

"Aye, he has that. But my mother's hair – more golden though, don't yer think?"

"I don't know what to think just now, love. Apart from how... how beautiful he is....But how...when did you...?"

"I had him at work." Sarah nodded now. "Aye, at work! And you'll never guess where – in a bobbin basket of all places, with half the bloody mill watching....Then they brought us home in a delivery lorry, which seemed appropriate in the circumstances." She smiled now.

"But surely you should be in hospital so they could check you out. And more to the point, you should not have been working, you know!"

"Oh, don't fuss, love. My mother had me and four others at home without any bother and Jess knew exactly what to do: she has helped deliver babies before. And besides, our little 'un here didn't hang about when it came to it. Now, would you mind dropping a line to Kath? Her address is in the dresser downstairs. She'll be chuffed to bits."

"If you want....Yes, I'll do it straight away and post it tomorrow." John was once more drawn to his son. "We've got ourselves a fine boy, Sarah....What are we going to call him?"

"I haven't had a chance to think about that yet."

"No of course not. You look tired, love, so I'll leave you and go and do that letter to Katherine." He smiled and stroked his wife's cheek.

Sarah nodded. And after her husband had left the bedroom, she gazed at her fair-haired son, saying, "I think yer dad's a bit annoyed with me, love. Still, never mind....Now, what are we going to call you? Well, whatever it is, I have a feeling you're going to be a champion. Aye, my little beauty, a real champion."

19

Sarah turned from the sink and gazed at her son who was seated at the table, drawing.

What a lad I've got! she thought, and smiled at his concentration. He could already read, write, and tell the time, and he wasn't yet in the infant's school. Sarah spoke now: "You'll have to be finishing off soon, Paul. I'll have to set the table for when yer dad gets home."

"I'll just finish this, Mam. I'll only be a minute." He turned now and looked at the clock on the wall. "It's only six o'clock, and he said he'd work late tonight."

He's right, thought Sarah. But after this morning's distressing episode, it wasn't surprising that she'd forgotten that her husband was preparing for the month end, and would be extra busy until he'd got all the figures out for the bosses at the foundry. But did she really care? "Well, if that's the case," she said, "I'll make your grandmother something and take it up to her."

"She won't have owt, Mam; not until me dad gets home. She said so."

"Oh, did she? Well she can bloody well wait then. I'll just make us summat."

"I'll wait for Dad an' all, Mam."

Good God! She was the only one who wasn't waiting for him coming home – not if he was still in the mood he was before leaving for work. Sarah couldn't understand why he always took his mother's side – particularly when he knew how much she could embroider a situation and turn it into something that always made her appear as the victim. She was such a scheming so-and-so.

After her marriage, Sarah had moved back to Long Lane and took on the role of a caring wife. The household had enjoyed a joyous Christmas when Emily and her family, and Katherine and Jonas had joined them – Jonas providing most of the food for a sumptuous Christmas dinner. They were equally cheered by the continuing news that the war was hopefully drawing to a close. But Sarah's happiness was short-lived when her mother-in-law demanded that she give up her job at the mill and stay at home to look after her.

"I refuse to, Martha. The mill is my life and I won't give it up for anyone. Amy will see to you during the day as she has been doing, but I will continue working."

John had not been happy with the situation, but he accepted his wife's decision, knowing that one day they would be starting a family and the money would come in handy when the time arrived. Nevertheless, Martha reverted to her old self and barely shared a civil word with her daughter-in-law; and even on VE Day when the whole town turned out for a celebration, Martha had remained indoors sporting a long face.

Early in 1946, Katherine had said her tearful goodbyes and she, Jonas and their young son, had sailed for America to start a new life. Then in the spring when Paul was born, Martha suddenly began to smile again. She doted on her grandson, and took to giving him his bottle. She would talk gently to him, and sing to him – but in Welsh, which annoyed Sarah greatly since she could not understand a word of what she thought of as nonsensical.

Martha did not consider Sarah as being the mother of her grandson: it was as if only her son had a part in his conception, and her resentment of her daughter-in-law grew into an unmitigated hatred. This had a profound effect on John: he blamed Sarah for any animosity that existed between the two women, and accused her of ignoring her young son just that she could carry on working. Sarah took exception to his remarks, and initially, without her husband's knowledge, started taking Paul to the mill with her and laying him in a bobbin basket while she carried on with her work.

Martha believed he was being looked after by Nelly; but when John somehow discovered what was happening, he raced round to Resurrection and informed William Crowther that his agreement in letting this happen was against the law, and that if he did not refuse Sarah permission to bring Paul to work with her, he would inform the authorities. And William had to meet his terms.

Sarah was remembering all this as she continued to watch her son drawing contentedly at the table. But her mind could not get away from her mother-in-law.

This morning she had gone and told her son that Sarah had deliberately tied the bandages on her leg too tight – just to hurt her.

"You shouldn't have done that to an elderly lady, Sarah," John had said.

"I did nothing of the sort," said Sarah. "She makes things up just

to make life difficult for me. She's a bitter and twisted woman…
and a liar."

John turned on his wife. He grabbed her by the arms and shook
her. "Take that back!"

"John, you're hurting me!"

"Now you know what it's like. If you ever hurt my mother again,
you'll have me to answer to."

"Oh, playing the big man, eh? Well, it's about time you did.
You're just like her lapdog most of the time."

He released her arms and raised his hand. "Well, well. So that's
how you treat a woman is it?" said Sarah. "Threaten to strike her if
she tells the truth and it doesn't suit you?" Her eyes were wide and
dark with anger.

"Oh, I'm going to work.…"

"You do that," said Sarah. "And don't bother coming back."

It was well after eight o'clock and John had still not arrived home.
The last train from Leeds was due in at eight-thirty. Sarah stared at
the clock and waited. Paul had nipped next door to see Jessie and
her mam, so she sat on her own – waiting.…Then, on the half-
hour, she heard the train's whistle and got up to put the kettle on.
She had just lit the gas when the most ear-splitting noise emanated
from the street: it was as if the war, which had ended five years
ago, had resumed and a bomb had dropped on them. She raced out
into the lane where the other neighbours were gathering. Paul
came running to her. "Look Mam! There's something happened in
The Hollow."

Sarah grabbed her son's hand and walked next door where Nelly
and Jess were craning their necks to try and see what was going
on. "Did you hear that awful noise, Sarah?" said Jessie. "Well, I'm
not standing here wondering what's 'appenin'. I'm off down to see
for meself."

"Oh, do be careful, love," said Nelly. "It could be dangerous.
You don't know what's happened."

"That's why I'm off, Mam: I'm nosy."

"I'll come with you, Jess," said Sarah. "Nelly, do us a favour and
go next door to see if Martha's all right and look after Paul till I
come back."

"Of course, lass." She took Paul's hand, saying, "Come on, lad;
let's go and see to yer Gran."

When Sarah and Jessie reached The Hollow, Sarah's worst fears were confirmed: the last passenger train from Leeds had collided with a goods train carrying coal and gas from the colliery, and both had crashed into the parapet surrounding the top of the arches that supported the line. One engine was perched on the very edge of the devastated bridge, its wheels contorted, still billowing smoke and spilling burning coal onto the street, catching some onlookers unawares who then had to race backwards as the stuff cascaded about them.

The first carriage of the Leeds train still had its lights on and one could catch a glimpse of the passengers staggering about inside, whilst the second and third carriages had jack-knifed and were in darkness, swaying perilously close to the perimeter of the bridge's walls, groaning with each slight movement. And on the far side, where the goods train stood, fires were breaking out.

"Dear God in heaven!" said Jessie. "I think I'm going to be sick." Sarah put an arm around her waist, but Jessie could feel her friend shaking violently.

After what seemed an age of waiting, distant sirens and fire-engine bells emanated from the area beyond The Hollow, and then police vehicles approached from behind them coming from the direction of Town End. The crowd, of which Sarah and Jess were only a small measure, parted as the police moved forward. "Get back! Move well away! Come on folks; move well back, well back now."

Jessie took Sarah's hand and they shuffled up against the wall of the White Horse from which men had emerged holding pints of ale, whilst ambulances were being escorted through to what was thought of as a safe, but suitable, distance to be on hand to attend to the injured. But then a shrill grinding of metal like a giant's finger-nails on a blackboard came from above, and amid the screams and gasps of the assembled multitude, the two jack-knifed carriages plunged over the parapet, crashing headlong into the street below, dragging a further carriage with them.

Most of those assembled scattered in various directions, but Sarah and Jessie remained clinging to each other as though they were glued to the pub wall. A burly policeman ran towards them. "Come on, ladies; this is no place to be hanging about. There could be an explosion any minute." He took hold of Jessie's arm. "Get yer big mitts off me, lad!" Jessie barked. "This woman's husband could 'ave been on that train, so give her some respect."

"I am doing, lady. But I insist that you move on out of harm's way. Now, if you refuse to leave the area, I'll get some of my men to come and carry you."

"Yer bloody well won't," said Jessie. "And if yer dare lay a hand on...."

"Leave it, Jessie," said Sarah. "He's just doing his duty.... C'mon, let's go back home and wait there." And as they walked back up the lane, Sarah turned back and stared at the tangled mess in which it was possible her husband lay injured – or even worse.

Paul and Martha were both sound asleep in bed. Sarah, Jessie and Nelly had been up all night drinking copious amounts of tea, wondering what was happening back in The Hollow.

Every now and then, Sarah went and stood in the lane and reported back that they had brought arc lights and cranes to help clear the wreckage, the while praying that after this morning's argument, John may have decided not to come home after all, and had stayed in Leeds and gone for a drink with his mates at work. Yes, that would be what he'd done without a doubt.

Then shortly after midday, two policemen came to the house and asked Sarah if she would accompany them to the drill-hall where a temporary mortuary had been set up for the bodies of the victims of the crash. They had found papers with her husband's name and address on, and believed he could be one of those killed.

And an hour later, Sarah returned home with news that shocked both her family and her neighbours.

20

The day of John Halliday's funeral had arrived.

Paradoxically, the day itself could not have been nicer: the early sun had extended its long, golden arms across the vast sky, and here and there it supported buds of fair-weather cloud in its open palms – but there was a fire in the grate and Sarah was sitting so close to it she had to continually rub the heat away from her legs.

"It was me, Jessie. I wished him dead: I told him not to come home on that very morning and he didn't....Oh, they may have said it was a tragic accident, but it was me, Jess. Me!"

"Oh, love." Jessie leaned over the back of the chair and held Sarah close as she sobbed uncontrollably. "It wasn't you. Come, love, don't cry. We have to get through the day one way or another. Here, take my hanky."

Sarah wiped her face. "How am I going to live with myself?"

"You'll have to, lass. You've Paul to take care of now."

"I don't want to take care of him – not now. Martha can do it. Every time I look at him he reminds me of his father."

Jessie took hold of Sarah's shoulders and shook her. And moving to face the distraught woman now, said, "Oi! We'll 'ave none o' that talk. D'yer hear me?"

Sarah pushed back her chair now, and after a deep sigh, said, "You're right, Jess. What am I thinking about? Yes, Paul has to be my priority now; but I feel so alone."

"Look love, you're far from alone. I'm here and I always will be." But Sarah seemed unaware of Jessie's words as she said, "Look at the flames darting up the chimney, Jess; and those little dancing men between the ribs....Do you see them? And there's a tree there – just there" – she pointed into the fire – "a large oak with swaying branches. Oh, oh; Paul's climbing up to the top to escape from the heat. That's it: he's at the very top now."

"Love, time's getting on...don't yer think y'ought to go upstairs and get yerself ready? They'll be here afore long."

"He's always been a good climber has Paul," Sarah said, as she nodded her head. And then she fell silent and her eyes dimmed. "But not good enough. He's going to need my help." Then she swung her head at Jessie, saying, "He'll get all the help I can give him."

"Of course he will, love."

"Do you know" – Sarah's fingers began to drum on the chair arm and she appeared not to breathe as she spoke – "whatever I do in the life I have left to me, I'll do it for him." Now she sat bolt upright and grabbed Jessie's arm. "Jess, listen to me! Never let me forget those words; and if I do – when I'm recovered – remind me of them."

Jessie nodded desperately.

"My life at the moment is like a worthless rag: full of holes – perished! But I'll make sure Paul doesn't perish. Whatever it takes me to do for him to reach the top of that burning oak" – she stabbed a finger at the hearth – "I'll do it. No one will destroy him as I am destroyed. For every ounce of life he lives I'll provide a pound, and mark the cards of anyone who tries to stop him. I will help him climb that scorched oak with all the strength I can muster and with any trick I can use....Now, I'm going upstairs to get the three of us ready."

And when Sarah had gone, Jessie wept.

Cars had assembled outside the house on Long Lane, and the hearse was amassed with flowers. Sarah walked to the first vehicle and, when she was seated, an attendant helped her mother-in-law in beside her; Paul and Jessie Dicks sat behind. Those following included Jessie's mother, Sarah's sisters Emily and Mary with their families, and subsequently other close neighbours and friends.

The cortège slowly progressed, passing the Catholic church and The Jubilee, along Victoria Row where Jessie pointed out to Paul the open ground where once she and his mother used to dwell before their homes collapsed, and then they turned into Bridge Street. Presently, on the right-hand side, Crowther's mill came into view and the cars paused. The workers were on their break and having their snap in the sunshine. Some of the men were lighting up cigarettes and leaning against the mill wall, but when they caught sight of the funeral procession, they walked to the gates and took off their caps, holding them close to their chests.

"Why have we stopped, Jess?" asked Paul. "And why are those men taking their hats off?" Jessie held the boy's hand, saying, "As a mark of respect, love. They want to spare a minute to express their condolences."

"For me dad?"

"Aye. And for you and yer mother an' all." And then the cars set off again, moving slowly across the bridge that spanned Barn Brook, and to the junction with Thorp Lane where the cars stopped once more to allow for passing traffic.

Paul sat back in his seat, his legs barely curling over the edge, and watched his mother gaze woefully out of the side window. She was dressed in a black woollen coat with padded shoulders and a cloche hat with a feather attached to the side; and the small veil that partially covered her eyes, fluttered gently in the breeze from the half-open window. And then she turned and looked ahead as the hearse moved forward. Paul glanced up at Jessie who said quietly, "Nearly there now, love."

Compared to Collingley's parish church, Woodkirk was small. But the area in which it stood – on the brow of a gently rising hillside near the boundary with the village of Thorp, surrounded by a multitude of ancient trees and bramble hedges, was the most beautiful in the area, and well-chosen to lay a man to a peaceful rest.

The congregation stood as the coffin was carried in, and Sarah, taking her son's hand, walked to their seats and were followed by the other mourners. The service was a punishingly solemn affair – as most funerals are – but to Sarah it was exceptionally distressing. Throughout the ceremony, the words she had said on that wretched day were ceaselessly on her mind, and she knew they would haunt her for an eternity....

As the service drew to a close, John's mother had been granted one concession to Sarah's personal arrangements, and Myfanwy was sung as her son's final music. And as it was played to the congregation, Martha's face appeared like stone, her usual expression unchanged. But Sarah, her emotions unbounded, held her head in her cupped hands and shed an abundance of tears. Paul felt his mother shaking, and after turning to look at her, dropped himself onto her lap and cried along with her....

Outside, the clouds had gathered, and a cold wind had set in. And it was here, before her husband's body was carried to the graveside, that Sarah caught sight of William and Dorothy Crowther. It was Dorothy who spoke: "William and I wish to extend our sympathy to you and your family." And she kissed the widow's cheek.

William held out his hand now, saying, "I am so sorry for your loss, Sarah. And perhaps, when you are feeling up to it, you might consider returning to work? We do miss you, you know."

Holding tightly on to William's hand, Sarah smiled gently. "You are both very kind," she said. "Thank you. And yes, I probably will come back to work…well, maybe one day."

Part Two

The Boy

1956

1

Paul excelled at school. This year he had been presented with a copy of We Didn't Mean To Go To Sea by Arthur Ransome with the dedication: 'To Paul, top of Form 3A. Midsummer 1956. With best wishes. Doris Beevers'. Next year he would sit his 11 Plus exams and his teacher had no doubt that he was destined for a grammar school education.

Yet, the six years since John Halliday's death had been no less harrowing than 1950 itself. For one thing, Paul had contracted scarlet fever and had been admitted to an isolation hospital on the far outskirts of Leeds, during which time he missed Christmas at home – and for another, Nelly Dicks had passed away. Then, less than three months later, Martha had also died.

Shortly afterwards, it was decided that instead of running two separate households, Jessie should move in with Sarah and Paul. The arrangement suited Paul most of all. He had discovered a new playmate in the guise of the elderly Jess, and used every available opportunity to take advantage of the situation.

On certain days, when a prevailing south-westerly wind had dispersed the overnight rain clouds and the sun bathed the town in an unsullied light, one could easily be persuaded that the place was some rural idyll instead of an industrial heartland. This was even more evident to the residents of Long Lane whose front windows overlooked a panorama of green fields and smooth-topped hills that acted as a town boundary, before the earth finally descended into the meandering river valleys of the West Riding. And today was one of those special days.

"Oh, do come on, Jess, I want to be off. It's a beautiful day out there and you're messing about looking for shoes."

"Now, look here young man; I can't be trampin' about in them there fields with me best ones on....Mind you, I've only got two pairs and me others are for special, so these'll have to do. I only hope we don't come across anybody we know....Now, I warn yer"– a finger wagged – "no adventurin'. I'm not climbing any trees at my age."

"Can I take me kite?"

"No you can't! The last time you did, you had me – *me*! at my age – running along with a thing on a string!"

"Well this time I could pull it. You could launch it."

"I'll bloody well launch you in a minute....Right, that's it; I'm ready. Go on, out wi' yer while I lock t'door." Paul smiled affectionately at Jessie Dicks, pleased as punch that she'd come to live with him and his mam after her mother and his grandma had died.

Now he bolted out of the house, raced across the lane, and threw himself into the field, pulling clouds of rosebay over him as one would a blanket on a cold night. But the sun was out now, and he smiled broadly, thinking, I wonder what we'll see today? Maybe hares – or even horses? But what did it matter: he was in his element and his heart ached with a kind of sickness that was brought about by an extreme and overpowering love of life. On his feet now, he brushed away the fluffy white seeds of willow herb from his brown corduroy shorts and shook his head.

"You're covered in the stuff," said Jessie as she neared him. And after shuffling her fingers through his bright blond locks, she straightened the collar of his white cotton shirt, thinking, This is going to be filthy before the day's out. "Now don't get too far ahead of me – do y'hear?" She was holding his thin, freckled arms now, and as she gazed in awe at those sparkling, blue-green eyes, her heartbeat suddenly faltered. Undoubtedly the boy was not of this earth: he was surely some being from a far-off place where only beauty existed and time stood still....."Listen, young man, wait for me at the stile." And as he bounded away, she called after him: "Do you hear...?" Jessie shook her head in desperation as Paul raced off into the distance.

At fifty-four, Jessie Dicks was in relatively good health, and though she had given up working in the mill – mainly to look after Paul while his mother carried on her own job – she still did part-time cleaning for the well-to-do folk in the town. And there were enough of those around to keep her going into her old age. But it worried her to think of Paul having to be cared for by his aunt Emily when she had to go out to work – even though the individual jobs only lasted for a couple of hours.

Paul and his cousin Kevin – who was two years his senior – fought like hated enemies. Kevin was spoilt something rotten and looked down upon Paul as though he was a poor and beleaguered stranger instead of a close relative. And he had a vicious streak to him: calling Paul things like 'mummy's only baby' and 'pretty little pansy-boy'. But Paul – even though he was on the skinny side – could stand up to his cousin: he'd always come out on top when they fought – either with the use of his fists, or his words. He took after Sarah's mother for his mettle, and was so much like Emma Harvey in many, many ways.

Paul was waiting at the stile. "Look at these things in the wood, Jess. There are little red spiders and ants and things. Look!" And he pointed out the crawling creatures to his companion.

"Aye, I see 'em....But lad, I'm lathered. Let's be going back," said Jessie, pulling out a handkerchief from her short-sleeved frock. "I could do wi' splashing meself wi' some water or summat."

"I know!" said Paul brightly. "Let's go down to the beck at the back of High Ridge and you can have a paddle."

"Me! Paddle? I'd never get me shoes back on. And besides it's too far...and it's a fair pull back up these fields."

"Oh, come on, Jess; I'll help you back." And he took her hand.

Eeh! how can I refuse the lad? she asked herself.

"Why didn't you get married, Jess?" said Paul. And as she walked gingerly down the stony path midst the fields, Jessie said, "I never found anybody I liked, I suppose."

"Somebody would have loved you, Jess – if they'd known you as long as I have. Of course, I can't marry you, now can I? In fact, I know I'll never get married, because I don't like the smell of girls. They smell different to lads – not whiffy like – just different."

This lad is so deep, thought Jessie. Where does he get these thoughts and senses from? She'd never come across another boy of his age who knew so much, and felt so profoundly, about the things that surrounded him in this vast and disturbing world....

They eventually reached the stream that ran along to Tyler's Barn. Here it cascaded over the stones and boulders at the back of the Crowther property. "Come and paddle with me Jess...come on!"

"I've told you already, if I take me shoes off I'll never get 'em back on."

The boy was already in the middle of the beck, standing on a rock, throwing water over himself as his hair gradually darkened. "Oh, Jessie, at least come and feel the water."

And reluctantly, Jessie did.

"See! I told you...it's fair grand," said the boy, imitating her speech as he proceeded to toss droplets of water towards her. And then he was at the far side, standing proudly on a grassy pinnacle like a young prince lording over his domain. "Come over, Jess… look!" He had turned to his right now. "A rabbit, Jess…there's a rabbit. Look!"

When Jessie looked, she saw that indeed the lad was right: it was a rabbit. Not a wild hare or such, but a rabbit that children would keep as a pet. Where was it from? She gazed upward at the imposing house known as High Ridge, and looking back now at Paul's glowing face of wonder, she knew she must cross the beck in an attempt to hold both her charge, and some other wayward creature, close to her breast for safety. Slowly she stepped onto an outcrop of York stone and it seemed to be well secured so she balanced there, judging the distance to a further piece in the middle of the beck. But it was slightly beneath the surface and glossed over by the trickling water. Oh come on woman, shape yerself; and she stepped out.

"Somebody's coming, Jess!"

Paul's outcry alarmed her. She looked up and faltered in her step as she saw two figures racing down a path that led from the big house, and in this moment ended upon her knees in the beck, twisting her ankle in the process. Her cry brought Paul racing to her. "Jess, are you hurt?" he said, jumping into the water. "Let me help."

"I've…I think I've…."

"Here let me try and lift you onto the bank."

"You'll never be able to lift me, lad….Let me try to….Oh, dear me…."

"Put an arm on my shoulder, Jess, and I'll…." But Paul's words were stifled as a voice said, "You hold her hands and I'll go behind and take her shoulders."

Jessie looked up. The young man who was hovering above her, smiled down, saying, "You won't be offended will you?"

"Er…no…but I'm…well, a bit of a weight."

"No problem. Have you broken anything, though?"

"I don't think so…just twisted my ankle."

"Right. When we get you upright you'll have to keep your weight on the good foot and then we'll get you up to the house…. Jane!" he called to the young girl standing on the opposite bank. "Hurry! Get the rabbit back in its cage and go and get Max…he's cleaning the car. Go on then!"

As the girl ran off, the young man said, "I'm Mark by the way. Best to be introduced before manhandling a lady." He looked at Paul now. "As I say, take her hands and I'll lift...okay?"

Paul nodded.

As they reached dry ground, Mark Crowther directed his words to Paul: "Right, take hold of my arm and we'll support her about the waist whilst she leans on our shoulders." And as they moved slowly toward the house, Paul held on to Mark's arm for all his might, thinking, He's a strong lad is this one...and he smells nice...much nicer than girls.

Jessie was sitting in the Crowther's kitchen. The chauffeur had come to the boys' aid and was now making a pot of tea as Dorothy Crowther bandaged the visitor's foot. "There. I don't think it's too bad. Have a cup of tea and when you're feeling better, Max will drive you both home, won't you Max?"

"Certainly, ma'am. I'll just finish the car...shouldn't take me more than a half-hour."

"Good." Dorothy raised herself now. "There it should be better in a few days. Is your dress drier now?"

"Oh, aye missis...madam...it's very warm in here."

"There's your tea, love." And as Dorothy handed Jessie the cup and saucer, she said kindly, "And it's Dorothy to you, Jessie....Is Paul your son, then?"

"Oh, good Lord...heavens no...I just look after him while his mam's at work. In fact, she works at your husband's mill. Sarah Halliday's her name."

"Oh, Sarah. Well, I never! I last saw her at her husband's funeral. And Paul's her son you say?"

Jessie nodded.

"Well, he's certainly grown out of all recognition over the years. ...Now, you drink your tea while I go and see what the children are up to." And as she walked to a door opposite, she turned, saying, "Mark and Jane seem really taken with Paul. I must say he's a good-looking boy and he'll be quite a catch for somebody one of these days."

As she was leaving, Jessie thought, Well certainly not from a household as posh as this! But for once, Jessie's intuition had failed her. This foreign occurrence had set in motion a train of events which was to impact on the lives of both her, her loved ones, and on those who dwelt in this fine house.

2

Going to Emily's was a nightmare for Paul. For one thing, Kevin had appeared to harbour a new grudge against his younger cousin ever since Paul had passed his 11 Plus exams; and for another, his auntie Emily always fussed over him and told him to stay indoors – even in the nicest of weather.

Jessie was just following Sarah's wishes though; and that was, while his mother was in hospital, Paul should spend a little time with his relatives. So, on the brightest of early August days, they set off. "Let's cut a corner, lad, and go through the allotments."

"Oh no, Jess! He'll be there helping his dad dig stuff up or wringing hens' necks, and if he catches sight of us he'll come back with us to Aunt Em's and bash me or summat."

Jessie stopped walking. And facing Paul now, said, "Hey!" She shook him gently. "If there's any bloody bashin' to be done, it'll be me doin' it! Now! I'm not walking all the way back from where we've just come from and be traipsin' down Zoar Street just to please you. So, we're going through the allotments and that's an end to it!"

To Paul's blessed relief, Kevin and his father were neither in the allotments nor at home. "They've gone to the station to pick up some boxes of new chicks," said Emily. "And Wilf's goin' to bring me back a bit o' shoppin'…I'm not feeling so good today, Jess. And 'ow's our Paul then? Well, yer're lookin' right. Jess's takin' care on yer I can see that. Aye I can see that."

"How's Sal, then?" said Jessie.

"Well, I managed to get there to see her last eve and she's fairin'. In fact, Jess, she looks a lot better than I feel. Now! Let's get t'kettle on. I've got some angel cake. Yer like that don't yer, our Paul?"

"Yes, Aunt Em." Oh, she still treats me like a child – but they all do come to that!

While Emily busied herself in the scullery, Paul whispered, "Can I go out, Jess? Just for a while?"

"Yer Aunt Em won't like it, yer know. But aye, I suppose so. But don't go far; and don't mess yourself up – that's yer best shirt…I'll tell her yer need some fresh air. Go on then before I change me mind." And she smiled as he crept quietly out of the open door.

At the end of the landing, Paul looked up and down the street – deciding which direction may be best for a brief adventure. He turned right, and ran down St Mary's Road until he arrived at the entrance to the old, dilapidated mansion house. It had been bought by the council when its owner died and converted into flats for displaced families, but it had not been maintained to any reasonable standard. He entered, walking slowly along the dirt track until he spotted a sloping, grassy path that meandered between lines of horse chestnuts and elders, clumps of groundsel and toadflax. And as he strolled along the path, he gazed up at the great trees and then down to the tall, waving grasses and wild flowers, whence he fell among them and stared up at the patches of blue sky.

How he wished Mark was here to share the moment with him. It had been almost a year since he and Jess had made the journey over to High Ridge, and in the short time they had been there, he knew deep within his soul that what he felt for Mark was much more than just a brief friendship. Sometime – and somehow – he must find an excuse to go and be with him for much longer, and to try and figure out what these feelings really meant. If he didn't, he truly believed he would go out of his mind.

It was now he caught sight of a length of knotted rope dangling from the upper branches of a tree directly in front of him, and despite Jessie's warning not to get messed up, he raised himself and went over to inspect it. And without reluctance he began to climb....

"Oi! What the bloody 'ell d'yer think yer're doin'?" Paul swung around when the voice startled him, and there below him stood a shabby youth. "Get off! That's my bloody rope an' nobody else's."

Paul hastily jumped to the ground.

Facing him, with hands on hips, stood a boy who appeared to have been up a chimney. His face was almost as black as his hair, and his long, grey trousers were held up by string.

"I...I was just having a look," said Paul.

Rolling up the sleeves of his ragged shirt, the boy said, "Well, don't – unless I say yer can. And anyroad, who are yer and what d'yer want?"

Paul extended his hand, saying, "I'm Paul. I was just having a look around. Sorry if I did anything wrong."

The boy made no attempt to shake Paul's hand but simply said, "I'm 'Arry; 'Arry Carr. I live in one of the flats up yonder." He pointed up the grassy slope, adding, "So, Paul, eh? Yer're a posh 'un all right – I can see that."

"Not really....Me mam works in the mill – but she's in hospital at the moment having an operation – and I'm visiting me auntie; she just lives up St Mary's Road."

The boy stared directly at Paul now before saying, "D'yer want to see me den? It's just down 'ere at the bottom." He thrust out his arm.

"Er...yes."

"C'mon then. But don't trip over t'tree roots."

At the lower end of the path, beneath a high stone wall, a shaded glade contained a roughly constructed hide-out with an old hearthrug spread out on the grass. "Sit on that while I have a pee." The youth ran to a tree where he undid his buttoned flies and relieved himself on the bark. On his return, he looked down at the seated Paul. "D'yer ever faddle?" he said.

"I don't know...what is it?"

"This," said Harry, and taking hold of his penis, he stroked it repeatedly. "Me dad showed me 'ow to do this when me mam were out. It's not a bad size for a lad o' fifteen, is it?"

Paul was at a loss as what to say, but ventured: "Er, no, I suppose not."

"C'mon then, let's 'ave a look at yours."

"Oh...I...I don't think I...."

The boy was at Paul's side now. "Oh c'mon, there's no 'arm in it; all the lads do it. Lie down and I'll show you what to do. Go on!"

Paul was mesmerised by the whole situation and, to his astonishment, found himself submitting to this youth's demands.

Harry knelt now, unbuttoned Paul's worsted trousers and, together with his white cotton underpants, pulled them down to his knees. "I've seen me mam do this to me dad, an' all." And his tongue journeyed over Paul's genitals.

"Oh, no don't...no Harry, I'll...I'll have to...to go. Me auntie will be wondering where...." But words failed him when the youth took Paul's penis in his mouth and made repeated sucking motions, before promptly masturbating on the moist rug.

Harry rolled over on his back. "That's better," he said. "Been wantin' that all day." And he ran his tongue over his lips.

Paul hurriedly adjusted his trousers and sat bolt upright. Then, after flicking nervously through his fine, blond hair, said slowly, "Er...so...so, which school do you go to?"

"School? Ha! Never been. Nobody's ever sent me or even come for me...what about thee?"

"Well...I think I'll be going to Morley Grammar in September."

"Oh, clever bugger are yer? Well, all I can say is it's a bloody good job yer're not goin' to one o' those fancy boardin' schools or yer would 'ave been buggered. They say they're doin' it to one another like rabbits. Me dad's done it to me a few times." Then suddenly he pushed his face to Paul, saying, "I'm starving. I 'aven't eaten owt for two days. Got any chocolate or summat?"

"Er, no. But...." Paul found himself strangely warming to this boy who had shown him things he would never have even guessed could happen between two people. And he began to feel sympathy for him as he said, "Well, I'm sure me auntie would make you a sandwich if you like?"

Harry didn't respond at first, but after springing to his feet, said, "Aye, okay then; I could do wi' summat in me belly after laikin' wi' meself" – he patted his crotch – "C'mon then." And he pulled Paul upright....

Kevin and his father had returned from the station and were cutting up wood in the front garden. His cousin totally ignored Paul but, dropping his saw, he scowled at the scruffy individual who was accompanying him.

"Hello, lad," said Wilf. "And who's this then, eh?"

"My friend Harry," said Paul and, glancing at his cousin, smiled. "Come on, Harry, let's go in and see Jess and me Aunt Em." And the two boys entered the house.

Jessie sprang out of her chair when she saw her dishevelled charge. "Just look at the state of yer. Come here!" Paul went and stood in front of her. "Yer're covered in grass and dust and stuff. I told yer not to mess yerself up. Here, before yer aunt Em comes up from the cellar." Jessie ruffled Paul's hair now and brushed the dust from his clothes. "There, that's better. Now...." In her fussing over Paul's appearance she hadn't noticed the stranger in their midst. But she did now. "What the hell is this?"

"It's Harry," said Paul. "He's come for a sandwich. He hasn't eaten for two days."

"Well it'll be three as far as I'm concerned."

Emily emerged from the kitchen now carrying a sack of potatoes, which she dumped carelessly on the stone flags. "God in heaven who's this?"

Paul went to Harry's side. "This is Harry, Aunt Emily; I met him in the flats down the road. He showed me his" – Harry nudged him – "...his den."

"He looks as if he's been down the pit, the mucky tyke. So what's he doing 'ere?"

"Well, he hasn't eaten for days and I thought you could make him a sandwich or" – Paul looked at the sack on the floor – "maybe some chips?"

Emily thundered towards the pair. "Chips! I'll chip him all right. Now get rid of him before yer uncle comes in and turfs him out."

"Me mam'd feed him; but she's in hospital, isn't she?" said Paul.

Jessie noticed the sudden change on Emily's face: her nephew's words had humbled her at the mention of her sister, so Jessie decided to intervene. "Look, Em, why don't yer rustle summat up for the lad while I...well...tidy him up a bit?"

"Er...aye, all right. But it'll have to be some haslet...I'm not peeling these!" She kicked the sack of potatoes and went to the table where she proceeded to butter some bread.

"Come on then, lad; let's get yer in the scullery," said Jessie.

"Oi! Get yer 'ands off me, missis."

She pushed him forward, saying, "If yer want to eat then yer're 'avin' a wash – and I'm doing it so it's done properly. Now get in there!" Harry was thrust in the small kitchen where Jessie closed the door behind them.

"Thanks, Aunt Em. He's not a bad lad really."

"I'm doing this for yer mam since, apparently, *she'd* do it. But it's the last time" – she waved the butter knife – "I don't want you bringing any more waifs and strays 'ere for sandwiches or owt else. D'yer hear me?"

Paul nodded.

"What yer makin', Mam?" Kevin had burst in from the garden. And bypassing Paul, went and sat at the table.

"It's a few sandwiches for Paul's...Paul's friend."

"What? For that rag he dragged back with 'im?"

"Harry's not a rag!" This was Paul. "He's twice the man you'll ever be."

Kevin sprang off his stool. "Man? Man? He's a bloody shirt button if yer ask me – and a tatty one at that. Man! That's a laugh! And I suppose he latched on to you because you're just a little

148

girl." The word was drawn out and said with a sneer; but Kevin's malevolence was halted as Paul flew at him and, grabbing his cousin by the hair, pulled him to the floor where he commenced to punch him with an unrestrained rage.

"Oi! Oi! Wilf, get in 'ere fast!" shouted Emily.

Directly her husband came bounding in. "You two not at it again?" And he went to pull the pair apart, whence Jessie rushed out of the scullery with Harry in tow. "What in heaven's name is goin' on?"

"Fratchin' again they were," said Emily breathlessly; "and it's all his fault." She pointed a finger at Harry Carr.

"It was nothing to do with Harry, Jess...it were him," said Paul, and a finger was directed at his cousin.

"Oh, shut yer gob, yer nelly." said Kevin, whence Paul moved forward and was about to attack his cousin again. But Harry barged his way passed him and punched Kevin full in the face, sending the dazed boy reeling into the sideboard.

"Right, that's it! Out!" Wilf grabbed Harry by the scruff of his neck and led him to the door and down the short path to the landing.

"And don't come back!" screeched Emily.

At this, Paul ran to the open door and called out: "Uncle Wilf, wait! Just wait a minute." Then he hurried back to the table where he picked up the haslet sandwiches for his new-found friend, and raced back outside. "Harry! Harry! It's me! Look, I've got yer something to eat."

3

Paul couldn't come to terms with what had transpired between himself and Harry. He had an ache inside – but not really a pain! It was a…a sort of queasy and confusing feeling. And each day – and night, come to that – the event was paramount in his thoughts. But in those moments of fear and, oddly, ones of sheer delight, he couldn't help but wish it had happened with Mark.

"He's not coming down wi' summat an' all, is he?"

"He's come down with it, Amy. It's probably after the both of us got drenched last week coming back from Emily's. Still, apart from him catching a cold, I think he's missing company – his mam, I mean. A lot of it is in his mind I'm sure, but just to be on the safe side I'll stop off at the druggist and pick him up some cooling powders."

"Are yer goin' to call in and see Emily after what happened?"

Jessie shook her head. "No. I've other things to do that'll take up all me time. Now, lass, if you'll just keep an eye on him till I get back, I'd appreciate it."

"I'll see to him…now you get off and do what yer need to."

Jessie had arrived at the gate that led into the flats – although there wasn't a gate as such, but just two large, stone columns, embedded with rusted hinges where a gate used to be. It was a miserable place: overgrown with grasses and weeds and thickly-leaved trees that, in parts, kept the grounds shaded from the light of the sun. In the distance, she could hear the sounds of children playing – which reminded her of the reason she had come to this dismal and unearthly place. The vast, old house must have been a grand residence at one time, but now it contained what she could only describe as 'the dregs of society'. And she was here to find one of them.

As she approached, a number of the children fled in different directions like terrified creatures – all except one who remained rooted to the spot on the broken stone steps that led up to the front door. Jessie stared down at the girl who she ascertained could not be more than six or seven yet appeared like a shrivelled old woman. Her long, matted hair wreathed a face that looked as if it hadn't seen soap and water for months. Just like Harry, was Jessie's thought; then she spoke: "Do you live here, love?"

The girl nodded.

"Well, I'm looking for Harry…Harry Carr. Do you know him?"

The girl nodded again. Then, wiping her nose on her cardigan sleeve – where Jessie could perceive that there were already several crusted snotty snail trails – she fled through the battered and paint-crazed door leaving Jessie to wonder if she was out her mind coming here just to pacify Paul. Looking about her now, she wondered how anybody could live in this…this utter desolation and filth – yes filth! Granted, she, Sarah and Paul lived in a small mill house with not all the conveniences of the more well-to-do, but at least it was kept respectably clean and the windows shone in the sunlight. Here was like a dark and different world to the one they inhabited.

Presently the girl returned, followed by a little woman with a large nose and black hair swept harshly away from her face. "Well, what yer sellin' then? 'cos whatever it is we don't want owt!" she exclaimed.

Jessie took a step back. Then, moving forward again, said, "I assure you, madam, I'm no gypsy."

"No, I can see that. So what's yer business, then?"

Jessie put on an affected voice. "I'm looking for Harry Carr. Do you know of him?"

"Aye, I bloody do. He's given me nowt but trouble since I born 'im – just like his father. That good for nowt, dozy-lookin' bugger ran off wi' some young slattern when I were labourin' wi' me second. I lost her – and it were all down to that nasty sod. 'Arry yer say? What d'yer want from 'im?"

Jessie coughed. "Well, I'm looking after a young lad whose mother's in Leeds Infirmary, and…well…he's in need of some company to cheer him till she comes home, and I were wondering if your son might like to come and see him?"

"Oh, I clock it all now. He said he'd been up t'road last week wi' a lad, and some woman or other 'ad give 'im a wesh. Well, whoever she were, she did more than I can. He won't let me near 'im wi' a flannel and carbolic."

Jessie lowered her head slightly, saying, "That were me. I gave him a wash and combed his hair and…."

The woman let out an unconstrained cackle. "Eeh, well I'll be buggered. I'll tell thee this: if yer can 'andle our 'Arry yer can 'andle owt....Aye, he can come and cheer the lad since 'is mother's badly. When d'yer want 'im?"

"Well, today if it's convenient."

The woman shook her head. "Can't do that, missis. He's out rabbitin' an' won't be back for hours. Just tell us yer address and I'll send 'im along termorrer."

"Oh, right; I'll just jot it down and then...."

"Nay, missis, that's no bloody good. None us in these parts can read. Just tell me an' I'll tell 'im...I can't read but I can remember."

After Jessie had given her their address, she thanked the woman and, bidding her goodbye, turned swiftly and hurried away from that dark and depressing place, thinking, I hope I haven't made a rod for my own back with what I've just done.

Jessie hadn't slept a wink. Yet, the early morning sun and Paul asking for some porridge had cheered her. She had told him that Harry might – and she emphasised 'might' – come to see him today. But it wasn't just that: Paul knew that his mother would be coming home soon and that he had to try and be well enough to greet her. Wilf had called unexpectedly last evening saying that Emily had been to see her sister, and that the doctors had said she was well enough to come home within the week.

Before taking Paul his breakfast, Jessie opened the door to the lane and brought in the milk. It was a beautiful morning, and apart from plumes of smoke emerging from the mill chimneys, there was not a cloud in the sky. Leaving the door wide open, she prepared the porridge and took it up to Paul's bedroom and sat with him until he'd eaten. She had to admit he was looking brighter, and although he couldn't manage the whole bowl, at least he'd eaten most of it.

On her return to the kitchen, she almost dropped the tray when she encountered a figure standing at the bottom of the bedroom stairs. "Eeh! yer nearly scared me out of me wits....What d'yer think you're doing coming into folks' houses without a by your leave?"

"I did shout, missis...honest."

My God! It was him: Harry Carr! She could scarcely believe her eyes. He was as clean as a new pin. His face shone like a mirror and his hair was neatly trimmed and combed. And, though his clothes didn't look as if they were meant for him, they were presentable enough. "Oh, well, yer'd best come in. Let me put these things in the sink and I'll make you some tea – or would you like a glass of pop?"

"Aye, pop'll do," said Harry, following her into the room.

Jessie went to the sink and after plunging the spoon and bowl in cold water, poured out a glass of dandelion and burdock for the unexpected caller. "There, lad…will that suit?"

"Eeh, missis, I haven't 'ad this for years."

My goodness, he's stopped dropping his aitches – well, at least most of 'em. And then Jessie thought, I might have underestimated this common young man. After all, he was cleaned up and almost well-dressed – and didn't speak at all bad.…Maybe his mother had hidden something from her.

Harry downed the drink in one go. "Thanks, missis," he said, and wiped his mouth on the back of his hand.

"D'yer want another?"

"No ta! Is Paul in?"

"Aye. He's in bed. D'yer want to go up and see him? I'm sure he'll be glad to see yer."

"Aye, I'll do that. D'yer mind?"

"Not at all. First one at the top of the stairs." Harry deposited the empty glass on the table. And when he had gone upstairs, Jessie poured herself a cup of tea and sat down. Well, I'll be blowed. Fancy him turning out like he has in such a short time. What was all that business about when Paul brought him to Emily's house last week? He talked with such a broad Yorkshire accent even *she* could hardly understand what he was saying. Oh, a right Jekyll and Hyde – that's what he is…! And in the course of time, many people would experience these two sides of Harry Carr – and to their cost.…

It wasn't long before Harry descended the bedroom steps followed by a dressed Paul.

"Eeh, lad, d'yer think y'ought to be up yet?"

"I'm feeling a lot better, Jess. And I can't help Harry with his reading and writing while I'm lay in bed."

Where did all this come from? thought Jessie. Teaching the lad now?

"Sit at the table, Harry," said Paul, "and I'll get some paper and pencils. Is that old Rupert Bear annual down here anywhere, Jess? I can't find it upstairs."

"Er…aye, it's around somewhere." Jessie went to the dresser and opened a side cupboard. "No…er, no…oh aye! here it is. Bit frayed round the edges though." And she took the book to the table. "Now, I've got to get on with some washin' so I'll leave you twos to it." She had already lit the fire under the set-pot and the water was bubbling away nicely, so she went to the cellar head and brought out a basket of bedding; and, lifting the set-pot lid, emptied the sheets and pillow cases into the tub. "I'll leave that to stew and go and make the beds. Will you two be all right?"

"Yes, Jess," said Paul as he opened the annual and spread it out in front of Harry. "Right. Let's start here."

Jessie began to ascend the bedroom steps, but looked back at the two boys leaning over the book. Eeh, just wait till I tell his mother about this, she thought. And smiling to herself, she raced upstairs.

Two weeks later, Sarah arrived home and had recovered nicely. "Well, no more kids for me, Jess – not now I've had it all taken away. Mind you, it's unlikely I'll ever get married again so what does it matter?"

"Nonsense! There's somebody out there for yer, mark my words."

Sarah laughed. "Still making predictions I see, Jess? But, I must say from what you've told me, that it's unbelievable what Paul's achieved with young Harry. My lad's got the makings of a teacher by the look of it."

"Oh, he'll likely lay his hands to anything, lass. He's a marvel when it comes to figure work."

After a moment, Sarah said, "Has he been over to High Ridge since I've been away?"

"Not that I know of," said Jessie. "At least not when I've been out walking with him."

"He was off like a shot this morning after breakfast," commented Sarah. "I wonder what the rascal's up to this time?"

"Well, whatever it is, Sal; no doubt it'll be wholly for the good."

Paul and Harry were crossing Barn Brook. "They usually play out in the back garden – or come down here."

"D'yer think they'll let me into the house, Paul? I put me best clothes on this mornin'."

"I can't see why not," said Paul. "Mrs Crowther did say I was welcome anytime and I could also bring my friends for a visit, and really you're the only one I've got – apart from Mark and Jane.... No, you'll be all right."

They had negotiated the stream and were going up the slope to the Crowthers' garden when a young girl appeared. "Oh, hello Paul! It's nice to see you after so long...come on up." Jane beckoned them forward.

"This is Harry, Jane. I've been busy...." Paul was about to say he'd been teaching Harry how to read and do sums, but thought better of it.

The eleven-year-old waited until they were on her level, before saying, "Hello, Harry. Now come on you two and meet my father. You didn't see him when you first came Paul, did you? Regrettably, Mother and Mark are out now – Max has taken them into Leeds to buy Mark some new clothes. Come on...Father doesn't bite." And Jane showed them into the small back garden where William was seated reading a newspaper. "Father, we have visitors."

William looked over the top of his paper, and removing his glasses, said, "Oh!" He stood now as Jane said, "This is Paul, Father. I told you about meeting him when the lady fell into the brook."

"Ah! So, you're the famous Paul who my two have never stopped talking about from that day to this. And your friend?"

"This is Harry, Mr Crowther. I hope you don't mind me bringing him with me?"

"Not at all!" William shook Harry's hand. "Sit down both of you and I'll get Jane to go and ask Annie to bring out a jug of lemonade."

Both Paul and Harry draped themselves on the lawn in front of William Crowther. "Mark's not here at the moment, I'm afraid. He'll be sorry he missed you." He sat again. "So, how are things with you, Paul? Getting on well at school?"

"Yes, sir. I'll be going to Morley Grammar School next month."

"Oh, so you got into grammar school too, eh? That certainly is an achievement....Mark will be entering the sixth form at Batley next year, and his mother and I want him to go on to university afterwards. But he won't be pushed into anything he doesn't want – and I for one am certainly not going to push him. He says he would like to come into the mill and learn the business, but I personally believe he could do well in the arts – designing or painting or even music....Still, I'm sure he'll find his niche

155

somewhere."

William turned his attention to Harry now. "And what of you, young man? Are you still in education?"

"Er...no...sir....I...I've finished now."

"And what are you planning to do, Harry?"

"Don't really know."

"Have you been looking at career prospects?"

"Er...."

Paul jumped in now. "Harry wouldn't mind being a builder."

"Really!" said William. "Well everyone needs a good tradesman these days." Then Jane appeared accompanied by Annie who was carrying a tray. "Ah, boys, refreshments have arrived."

Annie placed the tray on the garden table and poured out four glasses. "There we go," said William as he handed one to each of the boys and, bringing her own, Jane came and sat on the grass next to Harry.

"Our housekeeper, Bessy, makes a fine lemonade," said William. And after each had sampled their drinks, William spoke again: "Harry's been telling me he wants to be a builder, Jane."

Jane pushed her long blonde hair over her shoulders and smiled at the fifteen-year-old by her side.

"Do you know," said William – he addressed Harry directly – "I may be able to help you." He sipped at his drink. "I've just had some work done at the mill by a building firm who have done a sterling job, and the owner is a real gentleman and most accommodating. I could, if you like, ask him if he might take you on as an apprentice. What do you think?"

Harry stared at the man. Then Paul said, "That would be smashing, Mr Crowther...wouldn't it Harry?"

"Er...yes. Yes, it would! I'd like that, mister."

"Good! I'll find out for you and let you know as soon as I possibly can...oh, but how do I get in touch?"

Paul was the one to answer: "I could come over now and again to see if you have any news. And then I'll let Harry know."

"Well, if you don't mind, Paul."

"I don't mind, sir. I like coming here."

"That's settled then," said William. "First thing Monday morning, I'll get on to it."

Bessy appeared at the kitchen door now. "The missis is back, Mr William...laden down wi' stuff an' all."

"Oh dear," said William looking at the two boys. "I suppose I'd better go in and lend a hand. You three stay and enjoy the sunshine...and have some more lemonade." And as he walked across the lawn and entered the house through the kitchen door, Mark passed him and came into the garden. "Hello, Paul!" he called out as he approached.

"Hello, Mark," said Paul. "We were just talking to your father. He's going to try and get Harry a building job...oh, this is Harry: he's a friend of mine."

"Oh, I see....Hello, Harry."

"Hello."

"Did you buy anything nice in Leeds?" This was Jane.

"Yes, quite a few things," said Mark. "Mother's got something for you as well."

Jane sprang to her feet. "Oh, I must go and see. Come on Harry; come with me and I'll show you around the place as well. There's a much bigger garden at the front."

Harry hesitated, looking awkwardly bemused.

"Go on," said Mark. "It'll be all right. Nobody will mind."

So Harry followed Jane into the house, and Mark took his place on the grass next to Paul. "I'm glad you could come, Paul. It seems ages since you were here last. I would have come over to see you, but I didn't know if I'd be intruding."

"Course you wouldn't. Jessie would have loved to have seen you – and I could have introduced you to Mam. I've told her all about you, you know."

Mark smiled slightly. Then he said, "Is Harry a...a close friend?"

"Well...no not really – I met him once when I went to my auntie's. And when I was getting over a cold, he came to see me. He hadn't been to school though, and – now don't let on I've told you this – he could hardly read or write or do any arithmetic. So I taught him!"

"So, do you think you'll become a teacher?"

Paul shrugged. "I don't know what I'll do when I leave school. What about you?"

Mark heaved a sigh. "Mother and Father want me to go on to college or university. I might take a course in design or something similar, but it may mean I have to go to Huddersfield or Manchester or somewhere like that."

Paul's heart sank. He knew he hadn't seen Mark for such a long time, but at least he knew he was only at a distance of a couple of fields. What if he went miles away – or even to a different county?

"Anyway," said Mark, "nothing's settled yet." He stood now. "Come on. Let's go down to the stream where we first met and cool down a bit." And Paul gladly went with him down to Barn Brook....

Once there, they stood throwing stones into the bright waters; and pieces of twigs that floated to where the stream disappeared beneath a copse of trees. "If we scratch them with a stone like this" – Mark demonstrated – "then we can follow them and see how far they get."

When they had marked the pieces of wood and watched them sail away, they walked along the bank, checking as they went, until they reached the shade of a thicket. Here they peered into the shadows dancing on the water, but saw nothing but their own undulating reflections.

They sat now, pulling at blades of grass and pieces of turf. Then, suddenly, Mark put his arm around Paul's shoulder. "I've missed you, Paul," he said, his voice almost tearful.

Paul wrapped an arm around his friend's waist, saying, "And I've missed *you*...a lot."

"Oh, Paul! I can't believe I found you like I did. Will you...will you always be my friend?"

"Of course I will. But really, it was Jessie who found *you* by falling into the stream."

Mark chuckled, but said, "No. It must have been fate. Something extraordinary happened to bring you to me."

Then the two of them lay back beneath the overhanging branches, and mid the dappled shade they moved close. And there, for the first real time, they explored their burgeoning love for each other.

4

It had been snowing heavily all day.

Sarah was sitting close to the fire darning some of Paul's socks, and he was at the table writing Christmas cards.

"Shall I send one to Mr and Mrs Crowther? And Mark and Jane?"

Sarah didn't look up from her work, but said, "If you like...but nice words, mind! And I'll want to look at them before they're posted."

Paul laughed. "Eeh, Mam, sometimes you must think I'm some sort of idiot."

Now she glanced over at this extraordinary son of hers and was about to say, Oh no, lad, you're no idiot: you're your father's son all right. But she just smiled as he focused his attention on the task before him as he occasionally straightened his back, then dipped his head again to carry on writing.

"All done," said Paul. "Oh, no, I've forgotten Harry!"

"Do you know his address then?"

"No...but I'll just take it to him."

"Right," said his mother.

"There, I've written them all now...apart from Jessie's of course, but that's one you're *not* going to look at because...."

The sound of a car's wheels crunching on hardened snow in the lane, brought Paul's words to an abrupt halt. His mother quickly deposited the tumbler – covered with a half-darned sock – beside her chair, as Paul raced to the window and peered behind the curtain. "It's Mr Crowther."

"Oh, Lord. Get yourself back here, lad, and help me tidy these bits up. Surely he can't be coming here?"

"He is! He's coming to the door, Mam."

"Here, quick, shift those cards while I put the wool in the dresser." Then came a knock at the door. "And I look such a sight," said Sarah. "What d'yer think he wants?"

"Go and find out, Mam. Or shall I?"

Sarah glared at her son. "Oh, just get out of the way and let's see, shall we?"

When Sarah drew back the blanket along its pole and opened the door, William Crowther was standing there. "Ah, Sarah," he said. "I hope I'm not disturbing you, but the children practically forced me to come and see you...and on such a night as this." And she looked upon this man who employed her, thinking, He hasn't changed really. Granted she'd been in his presence when he came round the mill, but that was work. Now she remembered the very first day she'd met him when she was thirteen. Then she'd had only one thought – and that was of him being hers.

"Oh...er...yes....Oh...sorry; do come in." She directed him into the room. And in closing the door she caught sight of two faces peering at her through the car's windows. "Oh, you have the children with you?"

"They insisted in tagging along I'm afraid."

"Well, they can't stay outside in this weather. Paul, go and tell them to come inside." And as her son scuttled passed her, Sarah ushered William to the fireside chair she had vacated earlier, saying, "I'll put the kettle on. Will the children have some?"

"Don't go to any trouble...it's only a quick visit just to ask you if...."

Suddenly, Paul and William's daughter bounded in and stood beside the table leaving Mark to close the door behind him and draw the blanket across.

Then William spoke further: "As I was saying, Sarah, it's just a brief call." And at this point he reached into his overcoat pocket and withdrew a small, white envelope, saying, "We would like it very much if you would accept this invitation to spend Christmas Eve with us at High Ridge – that is if you don't have anything else planned?"

"Well...er...no....We usually go to me sister's on Boxing Day... but that's all really."

Paul's face beamed with delight. And as he and the children exchanged looks of animated glee, William stood, and handing Sarah the envelope, said, "It includes an invite for Jessie as well if you could let her know?"

"Oh, yes, of course...although I don't know if she'll be able to make it – I think she's going somewhere, but I will tell her."

"Good....Well" – he beckoned to his son and daughter – "we'll be off and hope to see you all on Christmas Eve....Oh, and by the way, I'll send the car for you at around seven, so you don't have to worry about getting there – especially if the weather is as bad as it is at the moment. So, for now, I'll bid you goodnight, Sarah.... Right, children, say your farewells and we'll be off."

When all goodbyes were exchanged, and Paul returned from waving the visitors off, Sarah looked in dismay at her son, saying, "What on earth am I going to wear?"

Sarah longed for the car to be early. Under no circumstances could she walk into a house full of people she didn't know – or even wanted to know. She only hoped it was just the Crowthers – at least then she'd only have to become more acquainted with his wife. Oh! but what if Dorothy's mother was there and her two brothers? That would be a complete nightmare. How she wished Jess was going, but she was spending Christmas with her cousin in Morley. The clock seemed to be rushing her. It was going on for seven and she'd not yet dressed.

"What are you wearing, Mam?"

"God knows!"

"That black one's nice...the one you got for Dad's funeral."

"Good Lord, lad, it's seven years old. And besides, I don't know if it'll still fit. Oh, aye, I must find a suitable coat if I can find one."

"Nay, Mam, we won't need coats. It'll be warm enough in the car – and at the house."

However awkward Sarah felt about his suggestion, she would go along with her son's plan. He was always right in these matters. "Right then. Have you washed behind your ears?"

Paul groaned. "Yes, I have, Mother – and behind everywhere else. Now, get upstairs; the car'll be here soon."

But it was almost twenty minutes late, further fuelling Sarah's anxiety. Nonetheless, the inside of the car was exceptionally comfortable – and as warm as toast. Both she and Paul – he with a wide grin on his face – felt like royalty. Sarah thought she ought to say something; so, after a short unnecessary cough, said, "It's still very cold just now don't you think...? But at least it's not snowing. ...Still, I think it does threaten."

The smartly liveried chauffeur said, "It looks like it, madam.... I'm sorry I am a little late, Mrs Halliday, but I had an important errand to run for Mr Crowther. He sends his apologies."

"Oh, yes...he must have other things to see to." She felt awkward now. She wanted to be back home before she even got anywhere. And then unexpectedly, Paul reached over to his mother and squeezed her hand. This small and affectionate gesture reassured her; and she was content in the thought that whatever happened on this special night, her son would be by her side.

She knew that Paul, and also Jess, had been inside High Ridge – although Jess had only been in the kitchen. Paul, from what she had gathered, had been with the children somewhere or other, and he hadn't furnished her with much more information other than playing with a train set – an item which she'd scrimped and saved for to buy him, even though it brought back horrible memories of her husband's death....

High Ridge House stood in an acre of land. Between it and Long Lane, stretched the undulating fields through which Barn Brook meandered. It was a refreshing and welcoming place amid the otherwise pulsating, grime-ridden atmosphere of this small, West Riding town. In contrast to the bland and unimposing appearance from the rear, the main approach from Ridge Road showed the house in its full splendour.

Built in a Georgian style out of solid Yorkshire stone, it was surrounded by a relatively squat stone wall that gave it a welcoming and unassuming appearance, belied only by the imposing wrought iron gate through which they now passed. On one side, a large, rectangular lawn now covered with a blanket of snow, led up to a paved area in front of the four-columned entrance; whilst on the other, forming a barrier against the prevailing westerly wind, there stood a row of majestic cypresses.

As Sarah and Paul would eventually find out, the ground floor consisted both of a large dining-room and drawing-room, each leading off from an imposing hallway; a library and kitchen at the rear – separated by a small vestibule, which opened out into the back garden where stood a well-stocked greenhouse. On the upper floor, directly above the drawing-room, was the main bedroom; whilst opposite at the other side of the atrium, were two smaller bedrooms for the children. Then at the back of the house, there were two further rooms classed as bedrooms one and two, and a small spare room next to the servants' quarters with its own adjoining bathroom. A further bathroom and dressing-room was situated between the main bedroom and bedroom number two. But it was one special feature that always prompted favourable comments from visitors: an open area that joined the two landings leading off the huge mahogany staircase and ran along the front of the house: it was known as 'The Parade'.

Sarah gasped as they went through the gates, marvelling at the sight before her. High Ridge House was nothing less than a majestic palace in some wintry, foreign land. Ahead, lights blazed from every window, and in a particular one, at the far downstairs right, stood an enormous Christmas tree bedecked with a rainbow of twinkling lights. She heard Paul almost yelp with delight. Yet her eyes did not turn to him in admonishment, but they remained trained on the spectacle emerging before her, as the car turned into the front drive and came to a slow and stately halt.

The driver exited and opened the doors for the visitors.

"Paul! Mrs Halliday! Up here!" Both looked up to the balcony above the great front door, to see the Crowther children. "I'll come down, Max. Annie's busy in the kitchen with Cook." And Mark disappeared – dragging his sister behind him – shortly to appear at the door. "We're so glad you could make it. Jane's so excited she's had to go and change her drawers." He laughed loudly. "Come on in." He turned to the chauffeur now, saying, "Father says could you go and pick up Grandmother and Uncles Alex and Joseph now, Max; but be sure to join us later, won't you?" Max tipped his cap. "Thank you, sir. I'll be off straight away."

Sarah took her son's hand and together they proceeded up the steps, her heart beating so hard she believed it may burst. Then they were in the large hall, only to be confronted by an enormous crystal chandelier hanging from the high ceiling; and straight ahead, there was a wide, red-carpeted staircase that divided left and right at a landing. And there on the landing wall hung a portrait of J B Crowther smiling down at them. "You recognise him don't you, Mrs Halliday?" Mark said. And Sarah nodded. "Oh, yes, I certainly do. It was your grandfather who first set me on at the mill. Such a lovely, kind man."

Paul looked at Mark now, thinking, Just like his grandson.

"Right! Let me take you to meet Mother, Mrs Halliday…she's in the drawing-room. Father's finishing off some paperwork in the library but he shouldn't be too long. You're the first to arrive so it won't be too nerve-racking." Sarah guessed he knew how she'd been feeling over the last two weeks; but she mentally straightened her back, and holding tight to Paul's hand, followed Mark Crowther through a door immediately to the right of them – trembling as she went.

The room was sumptuous: a high ceiling was decorated with plaster cornices and swirling mouldings, while the furnishings included green, velvet-covered chairs and settees and highly-polished tables and bureaus. The walls were bravely painted in a deep shade of red, upon which hung numerous portraits and landscapes in large, gilded frames. And within the ornately carved, white marble fireplace, logs sparked and crackled in the grate.

In all this elegance, Sarah was unaware of an approaching figure; but when she heard her name being mentioned, she regained her senses, and her trepidations about coming here were suddenly, and strangely, dispelled when she acknowledged William's wife. And though she had met her on several other occasions, she only now noticed how petite and pleasing she was. "Sarah, dear, you are most welcome."

But as Sarah shook the woman's hand, she sensed a cold, clamminess about it; and her face – even though tinted by a slight amount of make-up – looked pale and drawn as though she was concealing some sort of ill-health. "I was just admiring your lovely room, Mrs Crowther."

"Thank you. But, as an honoured guest, I insist you call me Dorothy." And she smiled.

Then the door opened and in walked William. Sarah was taken aback by his presence. He was dressed in black trousers and a white blazer with gilt buttons, and he looked more handsome than ever. Then he spoke to her: "Sarah, I'm delighted that you and Paul could make it." His voice had taken on a boyish tone: just like she'd heard when she first encountered him. And as she stared into his brown eyes, she was lost for words – until Paul said aloud, "Will Jane be here soon? Mark says she's gone to change her knickers."

Sarah now wished the floor would open up and swallow her. But seeing William throw back his head and let out a roar of laughter, she giggled inwardly at her son's guileless remark – nonetheless wishing she could wallop him. "She'll be here, young man…be patient." And inclining his head toward Sarah, said under his breath, "A romance in the making don't you think?" Sarah merely looked at him. Then, a smiling Dorothy, said, "I'll go and bring her down. She is a trouble at times, Sarah. Now, William, give our guests some drinks before the rest descend upon us and quaff the lot." And as she proceeded to the door she laid a gentle hand on Sarah's shoulder, but uttered no further comment.

Sarah requested an advocaat and a lemonade for her son, and seated herself on the settee facing the fire. William presently returned, and after handing Sarah her drink, sat down beside her. "They get on so well together – your Paul and my two. It's almost as if they were made to be together, don't you think so, Sarah?"

Sarah glanced over at Mark and her son who were admiring the tree. "Well, I have to admit that they do seem to have taken to each...or should I say...one another."

"Do you know, I'm convinced it was meant to be," said William. Then, after a long pause, he said, "I can't help but think that fate plays a great deal in our lives." He leaned forward now and looked enquiringly at her. Thankfully she had no time to venture a response as noisy chatter emanated from the hallway. "Oh, please excuse me; that'll be Alex and Joe by the sound of it." He stood and beckoned to his son. "Come, Mark, and greet your uncles." And as the pair disappeared, Paul came and sat next to his mother and held her hand.

Shortly, a small, young woman opened the door. She was clad in a black uniform covered with a white pinafore and sported a white, maid's cap. She smiled kindly, then stood back against the wall, holding the door handle in her small hand. William and Mark returned with Alexander and Joseph Stockwell who were then introduced.

After greetings were exchanged, William led his brothers-in-law to the drinks cabinet and poured out their choices. And as the three men began to chatter away, Sarah began to carefully study the two young men who now ran Providence mill.

She had not met Alexander since he used to collect the rents from Victoria Row. He was eighteen then; now...what? Probably forty? Mind you, he looked much younger and was a stunningly handsome man. And although she herself hadn't noticed them when he stood over her and shook her hand, that he had the most beautiful of eyes. Katherine had mentioned this, and now, as she watched him raise his glass to his mouth, Sarah wholeheartedly agreed with her. As for his brother, Joseph; well, she considered him a chilling individual. He was not ugly by any means, but she had decided there was a disagreeable nature hidden beneath his outwardly pleasant disposition.

Sarah cast her eyes to the door now, as Jane ran in accompanied by her mother and another woman. The elderly woman who entered was unmistakeably Edith Stockwell. Sarah recognised the sour face of the one who tried to employ her when she was a fourteen-year-old. But Edith appeared not to notice the two figures seated on the settee as she turned to the maid and straightened the girl's headgear. Then, she walked across the room to the Christmas tree where she deposited several gaily-wrapped boxes at its base. Turning now, she stared at the sofa, and in a strident voice, said, "Don't you have the manners to stand when a lady enters a room, boy?" Paul was about to rise when his mother tightened the grip on his hand and forced him down into the seat. "I see," said Edith. "Well, I have the measure of you....Mark! come and kiss your grandmother."

Jane immediately skipped over to the seated pair and sat beside Paul, whilst Mark went to his grandmother and kissed her on both cheeks, as Paul watched his every move. How handsome he looked: dressed in a red checked shirt and grey worsted trousers, and highly polished, black lace-up shoes. Oh, how Paul wished something would happen so he could stay here all night with his friend!

Mark noticed Paul staring at him now, and after excusing himself from his grandmother's presence, went and knelt on the floor in front of his sister. "Grandmama can be a bit overbearing at times," he said under his breath. "In fact, at all times. I only wish it had been just you and Paul coming tonight, Mrs Halliday; we could have had a much better time."

"I'm sure we still will," said Sarah. "Oh, I nearly forgot!" She picked up her handbag from off the carpet and took out two small packages and handed one each to Jane and Mark. "Just a little something for you both. Why don't you go and put them under the tree with the others?"

"Oh, thank you, Mrs Halliday. Come on, Jane; let's find a prominent position for them." The two ran off, but not before Jane had thrown her arms around Sarah's neck and kissed her on the cheek.

This show of affection had not escaped Edith's attention, and she came across the room, her long, powder-blue, silk gown undulating about her. "May I join you, Mrs Halliday?"

"Yes, of course....Paul, why don't you go and join the children?" And Paul did not hesitate.

Edith settled herself next to Sarah and said, "Did you meet my sons?"

"Yes, briefly...they seem nice young men."

"Hardly young any more. But yes, they are. Although Joseph can be rather wayward at times – a bit like your own son."

"My son is far from wayward, Mrs Stockwell."

"Maybe not; but his manners when a lady enters a room leave something to be desired."

"Paul is very well-mannered. And if a lady *had* entered the room, he would most certainly have stood."

Edith gave a slight grunt, before saying, "I see he gets on well with Mark. Quite the pair, aren't they?"

"He gets on with Jane and Mark very well, and your daughter has told me how much they both enjoy his company."

Edith Stockwell shifted in her seat. "But they are from such different backgrounds it has to be said, and friendships on that basis should not be encouraged. Don't you agree?"

"Not in the least. Any friendship needs fostering if it is genuine, and theirs certainly is. There seems to me to be too much insincerity in people these days." Sarah took a sip of her drink. "Having lost his father when he was four, Paul was brought up to value every moment of affection that is handed out to him before it is gone forever. I had to bury my husband after five short years of marriage, so I know what I'm talking about; whereas you were married for nigh on twenty-five."

Edith eased herself to the edge of the settee and looked directly at Sarah. "How do you know that? My family's business is not broadcast to all and sundry."

"Oh, please; don't pretend to be so naïve. I have got eyes and ears like the rest of the population in this town. And besides that, my father worked for Asa's father from the age of twelve and knew everything that went on – both in the mill and out of it."

Edith stood now. "I think we have talked enough. I will have to go and have a word with my daughter. Excuse me." And she drifted away. Then, seeing he had the opportunity to rejoin Sarah, William came and sat beside her. "Has she upset you? She can be an irritating woman at times."

"Not at all. We were just chatting about the old days."

At this point, Max entered, and approaching William, said, "Excuse me, sir, but I think there's a problem with the car. I've had a quick look over her, but I don't think she'll be going anywhere again tonight especially with the weather worsening."

"Oh dear." William considered the situation before saying, "Right, Max" – he stood now – "you can't be wasting your time on Christmas Eve; leave it until the morning. Now, get yourself changed and come and join us. Oh, and on your way out, will you ask Bessy and Annie to come and see me."

Seeing a look of distress on his mother's face, Paul returned to her side, whence William said, "Well, I'm afraid you're stuck here for the night."

"But…we need to.…"

Paul nudged his mother, saying, "We can't go out in this weather, Mam."

"He's quite right, Sarah. You're not going anywhere." His wife and son came over to join them now. "Is there anything wrong, sweetheart?" Dorothy said.

"Max is having problems with the car.…So it looks as if we are having guests for the night. Bessy and Annie should be here in a moment, so I'll make the arrangements. Now, I think you'd better go and break the news to your mother." Sarah's heart sank. Dear God! I've got to spend a whole night – and who knows how long tomorrow – in the presence of that woman. "Let me get you another drink, Sarah," said William.

"Oh, yes please," said Sarah, and after he had departed, she looked at Paul who said, "Don't worry, Mam; we'll be fine."

"He's right," said Mark. "After all, we couldn't let you walk back home, now could we?" William returned with Sarah's drink, and sat down beside her, whereby she turned her attention away from Mark and thanked her host. "Ah!" he said, "here are Bessy and Annie." He stood as they approached. "Right, Bessy; it looks as if we may have five more people for Christmas dinner tomorrow – or at least for breakfast depending what happens about the car. Will you be able to cope?"

The cook pushed out her chest. "Of course, sir," she said. "We've plenty in, and Annie can lend a hand. Five more won't make any difference to us two, will it, lass?"

Annie shook her head. "Right," said William. "Now, let's get the sleeping arrangements sorted out. Jane can keep her own room and Alex and Joseph can go in number one." Annie nodded. "Sarah here, can have number two next to the bathroom, and I'm afraid Mrs Stockwell will have to settle for the spare. And as for you two" – he looked at the boys – "you'll have to bed down together."

Paul swallowed hard, whilst Mark's heart fleetingly missed a beat.

"So," said William, "I think that's all. Will you both see to things?"

"We will," said Bessy; and turning to Annie now, said, "Come on, lass, let's get cracking."

Now Dorothy said, "Don't look so worried, Sarah. You've nothing pressing to get home for have you?"

"Well...no...not really."

"Good. Then it's settled."

Jane rushed forward and knelt at Sarah's feet, saying, "I'm glad you can't get home. We'll have so much fun tomorrow."

William smiled broadly. "Now, since it is Christmas, I think you two young men could have just a small sherry to keep out the cold. You wouldn't object if Paul indulges, would you, Sarah?"

Sarah had resigned herself to the fact that she and her son had been kidnapped, so responded: "No. But only the one, mind...."

Presently, with Dorothy accompanying on the grand piano, they sang a selection of carols; then, everyone enjoyed a variety of canapés and hot roasted chestnuts. But now, Edith Stockwell was addressing her daughter. "It's scandalous! Fancy; she gets one of the better rooms in the house and I'm shoved in the spare one next to the servants."

"Mother! It's only the one night. Surely you can manage?"

"It looks as if I'll have to...but I'll tell you this: I'm asking Alexander to phone Philip and tell him to bring our own car over in the morning whatever the weather. To be brutally honest, I don't relish the prospect of spending more time than I have to in the woman's presence and that disrespectful son of hers. I really don't know why you have to associate with such...such...."

"Oh, you can be malicious at times, Mother. I don't see why you have a problem with nice and decent people."

"What? Decent! Decent? Oh, you've a lot to learn, Dorothy. A hell of a lot!"

"Do you know, Mother, your behaviour often makes me think that you really aren't my parent and that I'm somebody's... somebody's flyblow. Are you sure my father didn't have a mistress?"

"How dare you!" Edith slammed her drink on the mantelpiece and swiftly left the room.

Mark was at his mother's side, now. "What's up with Grandma?"

Dorothy smiled. What's 'up', she thought. That's what comes of mixing with a 'disrespectful' boy; but said, "Nothing, sweetheart."

"Anyway, we're going up now, Mother. It's getting late."

Dorothy bent over and kissed her son. "Very well, darling. See you in the morning. Sleep tight."

"Have you any pyjamas, Mark?"

"I have. But they'd be too big for you. Look, it's awfully warm in here, so let's just get undressed and get into bed."

"Oh, I couldn't!"

"Well, *I'm* going to....Oh, come on, Paul, and let's get some sleep; it's going to be a busy and exciting day tomorrow."

Paul turned his back, shyly peeled off his clothes, and dived into bed, soon followed by a naked Mark who slid in beside him.

After a short while, Mark said, "I know you can't be asleep yet, Paul." But his young friend didn't answer; so Mark pulled the eiderdown under Paul's chin and snuggled down. Then, waiting momentarily, he whispered, "Paul, do you remember when we chased twigs down the brook?"

He felt Paul draw in a long breath. "Of course I do."

"Then let's pretend we're there now in all this snow."

Paul shivered.

"You're not cold, are you?"

"Not now."

Mark turned and unashamedly rested his hand on Paul's belly. And in this warm and precious moment, he drew his friend close.

5

"Never!"

"It's true, Jess. We stayed the night – *and* for Christmas dinner. Thank the Lord the Stockwells weren't there; I'd had enough of Edith the night before. Do you know, she even got her brother to drive over the following morning – how he made it in those conditions I'll never know – and she refused to have any breakfast that the cook, Bessy, had kindly prepared. Mind you, I did find out from Dorothy, that our Mary had been invited to Edith's for Christmas dinner."

"Well, I'll be buggered. Jack an' Laura an' all?"

"The lot of 'em....Anyway, as I was saying, on Christmas morning, a knock came to the door and the maid – Annie was her name – came in, saying, 'There y'are, madam. Cook's sent up a little breakfast for yer.' So, she places a tray on the bed, opens the curtains, and comes and plumps up me pillows."

"Eeh! Treated like royalty, eh? Go on then."

"Well, there was bacon and sausages and tomatoes, toast, and two poached eggs...oh, and a pot of coffee – I only had the one cup – and then she says, 'I've put out clean towels for you.' The bathroom was directly next door to my room, which I might add, was absolutely beautiful. And then she says, 'The rest 'aven't stirred yet, but the fires are nicely up the chimleys' – she tickled me how she pronounced chimneys – 'but I am surprised 'cos the kids are usually up before *me*. Mind you, Mark's grown out of the Santa Claus phase: he's quite the big man now. Well, I'll leave yer to it, madam. Just come down when yer're ready.' And she flitted out."

With this, Jessie poured them another cup of tea and demanded to know more. And Sarah obliged.

"After I was washed and dressed, I left the nightie that Dorothy had lent me on the bed, picked up the tray, and eventually found my way to the kitchen where Annie was stuffing a bird. 'Oh, hello, madam. You're still the first up....Cook's just taken Max a cuppa – he's trying to get the car going.' And then she told me I should have left the tray in my room for her to collect, but I was truly ignorant of what you *did have* to do in the circumstances. Anyhow, she suggested I go and sit in the drawing-room and she'd bring me a cup of tea shortly.

"My! it was a cosy room, Jess, and the tree was already ablaze with lights at such an early hour of the day. I walked to one of the tall windows and looked across the snow-covered garden, wishing that Paul would make an appearance, hoping he'd managed to sleep all right in a strange bed. Thankfully it had stopped snowing, and my wish was that the driver had managed to fix the car, so we could get back home that day and not have to spend another night with the Crowthers. Not that I wasn't grateful for their kindness – far from it – but I just wanted to get back here to my own surroundings."

"I know what yer mean, lass. I enjoyed me cousin's company of course, but it's nice to be back in our own place. Anyroad, where *is* Paul?"

"He's gone back again. Max picked him up earlier. Mind you, I gave instructions that he be back here for his tea because I'm not wasting that stand-pie....Oh, by the way, the cook up at the house – such a jolly little woman – packed us up a huge box of sliced turkey and a great big jar of pickled onions. I was reluctant to accept it at first – feeling like a charity case – but Dorothy wouldn't take no for an answer. Anyhow, me and Paul had some yesterday with the bread you'd baked; there's still loads left since the poor woman had prepared enough for the Stockwells – who hadn't stayed of course.

"And talking about Paul; d'yer know, Jess, he's not been himself since we got back on Christmas night: moping about, biting his nails – and at one point bursting into tears for no reason. All he wanted to do was to sit and stare into the fire. And you know how he loves to play in the snow – well not a bit of it. But then when he heard the car draw up this morning and Mark came to the door, he was different all together: as happy as Larry – that's why I let him go over for the day. I was just glad to see him back to his old self. I only hope, Jess, that he stays that way."

"Oh, he will do, lass; after all, they go through phases do lads. Talking about lads, I saw Harry Carr while I was at me cousin's and he seems to be doing well since Mr Crowther got him that job with the building firm."

"That was such a kind thing that William did for Harry....One thing that does puzzle me though, and that is how quickly Harry took in everything that Paul taught him. Surely he must have known something before to learn so fast?"

"Aye, I've thought about that meself....D'yer know, I honestly believe – and I've said it before – that there's much more to Harry Carr than meets the eye."

Edith Stockwell was seated in the drawing-room of High Ridge House talking to her daughter.

"You don't look well, Dorothy."

"Oh, I'm all right, Mother. I think I overdid it the last two or three days."

"Well, if William hadn't invited Sarah Halliday and that...that odd child of hers, then things may have been better."

"Mother! Don't start that again. Sarah's a lovely woman; and Paul's not odd as you put it. In fact, he's at grammar school, so he's a clever young man. Mark may never even take up an offer of a place at university, so does that make him even odder?"

"You're twisting my words, Dorothy....Anyhow, with my influence, I could persuade him to go without any problems."

"How? Through bribery?"

"No!" Edith pulled in her chin. "I don't know how you could even suggest such a thing."

Dorothy stared at the fire without saying a word. Then she sat forward in her chair, saying, "Anyhow, Mark's gone over to collect Paul and he'll be bringing him back here, so I don't want any nasty comments or disapproving looks directed at any guests that are invited into this house."

Edith sprang out of her seat. "You overstep the mark, Dorothy. I cannot sit back and see my grandchildren manipulated by what are – to all intents and purposes – common strangers."

It was Dorothy who was on her feet now. "Nonsense! They are neither common nor strangers. If it wasn't for the 'common herd' as you deem to categorise them, neither you nor my husband would have any kind of business worth its salt.

"And as for Paul, he is both a virtuous and respectable boy who Jane and Mark have grown very fond of – and he of them – and I won't have their happiness jeopardised by your insane prejudices. Now, before Mark and his friend arrive, I suggest you make a hasty exit. After all, I wouldn't want you to catch anything from a common grammar school boy that may prove fatal. Now, I think you're capable of showing yourself out."

That same day, Dorothy Crowther cancelled the invitation to spend New Year's Eve with her mother, and William had gladly bowed to her decision after hearing of Edith's irrational opinions. And when the children found out that as an alternative, she had sent Sarah and Paul a card requesting, if it was convenient, they – together with Harry Carr and Jessie Dicks – should attend a small get-together on the same night, they were over the moon.

"Well, I never thought I'd be here again a week later," said Sarah as she sat on the settee next to William's wife enjoying a glass of cream sherry.

"You're more than welcome," said Dorothy. "Both William and I could not wish for better friends to celebrate the New Year with us."

"That's kind of you," said Sarah. "I just hope we don't get stuck here like last time...oh! that sounds awful. I didn't mean that we weren't grateful for your hospitality, it's just that...."

Dorothy lay a hand on Sarah's knee. "I know. Still, we were all happy for you to stay – especially the children. Just look at them: in their element, and Jessie looks as if she's enjoying herself."

"I think she might be boring the life out of William, though."

"Oh, no," said Dorothy. "I haven't seen him laugh so much in ages. And Jane's taken with Harry by the look of it."

Sarah looked over at the four youngsters huddled together near the fireplace, and couldn't help but think that Paul was even more taken with Mark if the truth be known. And then, when she noticed them move into a private corner, it was obvious to her that there was more to their relationship than just being friends....

"Paul," whispered Mark. "Why don't we disappear for half an hour?"

"We can't," said Paul. "They'll notice."

"I could make some excuse. Nobody would mind."

"No, Mark, it wouldn't be right." He glanced over at his mother and he knew she was watching. "I think we ought to try and not make things look too obvious. It's supposed to be a secret between us two, and if we don't...well...calm it down, then others might find out and we'd be in real trouble."

"Have you gone off me all of a sudden?"

"Don't be daft!"

"You have; I can tell. I bet you've a hankering for that Harry Carr you taught how to read and write. Did he thank you in some way for your trouble, eh? Did he stick his hand down your trousers and play with it? or do something even more than that, like fu...."

His jealous ravings were brought to an abrupt halt when he caught sight of Sarah leaning over his mother. And then when Sarah turned and beckoned him, he ran to her. "Mark! Something's wrong. Get your father. Get him quickly!"

But William had noticed and had already rushed over. "Sarah, what's wrong?"

"She's fainted or something. I think we should get a doctor – she's very pale."

"Mark, go and phone," said William.

Sarah felt Dorothy's forehead, and knew that something was seriously amiss.

Then Jane came bounding over. "Father. What's the matter?"

"I don't know, sweetheart. Mark's gone to phone for the doctor." William leaned over his wife now, and holding her by the arms, said quietly, "Dorothy, love...Dorothy?"

6

Spring had truly sprung for Paul's thirteenth birthday.

Sarah had managed to buy him a bicycle for the three-mile journey to school after Mark had taught him how to ride. The two were inseparable and spent all their spare time in each other's company.

After refusing to stay on at school and study for university – much to the annoyance of his grandmother – Mark was learning the family business, and Sarah often saw him pottering around the mill – always with a broad smile on his face like someone deeply in love. Many outside observers had commented that he and Paul appeared to be more than just friends; and although the sentiments had not accessed Sarah's ears, they *had* reached Jessie's.

"I've got something to tell you, Sal."

Sarah placed the washing-tongs by the sink and put the lid back on the set-pot. "And what might that be, Jess? Nothing serious I hope."

"Well," Jessie patted the table and continued, "it could be.…Yer see, me cousin's in a bad way, and I wondered if yer'd mind if I went and stayed with her for a while. I don't think she'll be with us for much longer."

Sarah came and seated herself at the table and reached for her companion's hand. "Nay, Jessie, why should I mind? Of course, you *must* go."

"Well…I was thinking – what with you working – that there'd be nobody here to see to Paul's tea till you get home from the mill."

"Now listen here, Jessie Dicks: he's thirteen for God's sake and I'm damned sure he can get his own – and if he can't he'll just have to wait."

"I know, but he's still young and I wouldn't want him to…well, come to any harm."

Sarah leaned back in her chair now. "You worry too much, lady. And besides, what harm could he possibly come to? The nights are lighter now. It's not as if it's the depths of winter and crackpots are wandering the neighbourhood. Now get your body up them stairs and pack a case. There's a bus to Morley in an hour."

Jessie smiled weakly. "Aye, I'll do that, lass. I just wish we had a phone so I could let you know how things were goin'."

"Now look! Harry's coming over tomorrow to carry on his arithmetic with Paul, so I'll ask him to call and see you every day since he's working over that way, and he can get a message to me. He'll be only too glad to keep me informed. After all, he owes me – or Paul, rather – for teaching him his sums. But nevertheless, he'll be as pleased as punch to keep popping over since it's quite a while now that he did, what with that lad o' mine spending most of his time at the Crowther's these days."

He did that all right, thought Jessie; and folk have noticed. But she said, "Right then, I'll go and get meself ready." And as Sarah watched her amble off to the bedroom, she couldn't help but feel that she'd soon be back.

Jessie returned eight days later, after Harry had brought Sarah the news that her cousin Beatrice had died two days earlier. But on her return, Jessie also brought further tragic news.

"They say these things come in threes...well, that's two gone already."

Sarah wondered what further news of death was being dropped on her doorstep....Well, she was about to find out.

"I was just coming up Bridge Street from the bus stop, when this woman stopped me. 'I hope yer don't mind me asking, love,' she says, 'but are you that lady who came up to High Ridge two or three years ago when you fell in the brook and the missis saw to yer? I didn't see yer when yer came at New Year when Mrs Crowther was taken ill – I had the night off – but I think I remember yer from before.' Well, I told her I was, and she told me she was Bessy, the cook from High Ridge – such a lovely woman apart from the moustache – and if I could let you know."

"Let me know what?"

"Dorothy Crowther died earlier this mornin'."

Sarah's mouth fell open and, after dropping her sewing into her lap, said, "But...but she's only about the same age as me."

"Aye, thirty-six. That's what the cook woman told me. Apparently, she'd caught some infection or other and pneumonia set it....Mind you, she must have had a weak constitution for it to take hold of her so young."

"I don't believe it, Jess; I thought she'd got over that bad bout of flu she'd had....I wonder how William's taking it?"

"Not too bad apparently. But she told me that the children are really distraught."

"Oh God! And Paul's just taken a walk over there."

"Well, he weren't to know, love."

"I suppose not…I'll have to go and get a sympathy card for them."

"Sit yerself down. I'll go down to the newsagent's and pick a nice one out for yer."

"You will not! You've enough to think about with your cousin's funeral coming up without flicking through black-edged cards. Put the kettle on while I get back."

"Okay, I will, love. I think we both need a strong one."

"There's a half-bottle of brandy in the cupboard, so slop some in an' all."

William Crowther was seated next to Paul in the drawing-room. "I would like you both to be there, Paul – and at the reception afterwards. Dorothy loved both your and your mother's company when you came for Christmas, and often talked of you. And Jessie must come too." He turned and looked Paul square in the face. "I think Mark couldn't cope at the funeral without you being there."

Paul smiled tearfully. "Is Mark all right?"

"As well as can be expected, son. He and Jane are spending a few days with my Uncle Jim. I thought it might help them…but they'll be sorry to have missed you."

"And what about you, Mr Crowther?"

"Well…lonely I suppose…."

Paul looked at the downcast expression on William's face, and in a moment of uninhibited compassion for the father of his dearest friend, he threw his arms about him.

With tears dribbling down his face, William managed to say, "I can see why Mark loves you, Paul. You're a very special young man, and your mother must be very proud of you."

Paul was at a loss as what to say next. But as he pulled away from the distraught man, he said, "I'd better go home now, Mr Crowther. Mam'll be waiting."

"Yes, of course. But tell her what I said, won't you? And do try to come on Friday."

"We will, Mr Crowther. We will…."

Once outside, Paul stood quietly in the garden. Then, in a sudden moment of total despondency, he ran over the fields and into the town, where in no time at all he found himself standing at the gate to the flats where he first met Harry.

The spring flowers were out – waving gently in the warm breeze – and leaves were already beginning to clothe the branches of the trees. The place itself though, was as silent as the grave: no sounds of children emanated from the surroundings, nor any yapping of dogs or chirruping of birds; and not one wisp of smoke sailed from the broken chimney pots – it was as if the earth had not yet been woken from a long, long sleep....

"Well, well!"

Surprised by the voice close behind him, Paul turned around to see Harry standing there. "So the teacher comes to his pupil now, does he?"

Paul coughed up a laugh, and smiling now, said, "You scared me, Harry."

"Sorry...so what yer doin' here?"

"I...I just wanted to come and see you....I went to see Mark, but when I got there, William told me Mrs Crowther had died and the children had gone to stay with his uncle. So, when I came out, I ran all the way here."

Harry took his arm. "I'm sorry to hear about Mrs Crowther. Look, come wi' me and we can have a talk if you like."

Paul nodded; and the two of them walked slowly along the stone-pitted path and down to the shaded area beneath the high, stone wall. "God!" said Harry. "It's ages since I came down here. D'yer remember, Paul?"

"Well, I can hardly forget...not after what happened."

Harry laughed, but he could not hide his blushes. "I don't know what came over me."

"It's what nearly came over me that springs to mind," Paul chuckled.

"Now you've really embarrassed me," said Harry.

"Don't be daft. As you said at the time: 'all lads do it' and I've found out how true that is. Come on; let's sit for a while."

When they were seated, with their backs pressed against a tree's roughened bark, Harry brushed the building dust from his overalls, saying, "They only had a couple of hours work for me this morning, so they sent me home. Still, I'm glad Mr Crowther got me the job, and the foreman told me there's lots more work coming along and...."

"Harry," Paul jumped in. "Can I tell you a secret...? But you

179

can't tell a soul."

"Course. What is it? I can see it's botherin' yer whatever it is."

"Well...." – Paul hesitated – "Well; it's me and Mark. We're... we're sort of together."

"How d'yer mean?"

"Well, like the two of us were sort of together that first day I met you: here on that sticky, mucky hearthrug."

"Oh" – the word was drawn out – "I see....Does anybody else know?"

"God! I hope not. I think Mam has her suspicions, but that's all."

"Mothers do know these things. Take my own for instance. She keeps asking who I'm seeing at the moment, as if she's been a fly on every bloody wall."

Paul grabbed at a piece of long grass and began to nibble on it; and looking into Harry's bright, blue eyes, said now: "And are you? Seeing someone?"

Harry averted his gaze. "I am....And now I'm going to tell you *my* secret." He looked back at Paul now. "I met somebody two or three weeks ago in the White Horse. And, one thing led to another and we ended up in bed together – not here! We rented a room for an hour and...er well, I suppose I'd better come clean and tell you: I slept with your cousin."

"Kevin!?"

"Oh, Paul, for God's sake, no...! Your Laura."

"You are joking!"

Harry shook his head.

"Aunt Mary's Laura? Well I'll be buggered – no I don't mean that!"

Harry bent over in laughter. Then when he looked up, his face became serious. "Now! Don't you say a word. D'yer hear me?"

"Our Laura, eh?" Paul smiled, then said, "Don't worry, Harry, nobody will find out from me, I promise you that."

"So," said Harry, "we've *both* confessed something today."

Paul nodded. "And I feel better for it....Look! Why don't you come back with me since you're not working – we could brush up on some maths and you can have a bit of dinner with us?"

Harry considered the invitation for a moment. "Aye, why not?" He pulled Paul to his feet. "C'mon yer little bugger."

"Oi! Less of the 'little'." And as Harry swung his arm about Paul's shoulders, they walked back up the slope, laughing together.

Sarah took a bunch of flowers to the funeral; not for Dorothy Crowther – she'd already sent those – but for her late husband. And when the service was over, and Dorothy had been laid to rest in the family plot, she prepared herself to visit John Halliday's grave. Paul asked to be excused – and his mother concurred, knowing how upset he would be. But the conversation between them was overheard by William Crowther.

He came to her, and gently taking her arm, said, "Would you like *me* to come with you, Sarah? Or would you prefer to be on your own?"

"Oh, I can't take you away from your family on such a day as this."

"It's no problem. They're thanking the vicar; we can join them shortly."

She smiled at him. "Well, if you're sure."

"I'm sure." And they walked together to the stone that was engraved with John Halliday's name. Sarah knelt beside the grave and placed the bouquet on the shale that was scattered between the black marble boundaries that contained her husband's remains.

"Do you still miss him, Sarah?" William was kneeling with her now.

"I'll never stop missing him, William. He meant a lot to me; much more than anyone – even Paul – will ever know. Yes, there were disagreements – arguments at times – but I suffer daily thinking of something I said to him on the morning he died." She turned to look at him now; and in saying, "I don't think anyone will ever take his place," his eyes darkened, before he said softly, "Whenever you're ready, Sarah, we'll make our way back. But please, take all the time you need."

Sarah gazed down at the grave. And when she raised her head, she said, "I'm ready, William. I'm ready now." William stood, and taking Sarah's hand, helped her to her feet....

Arriving back at High Ridge, everyone assembled in the drawing-room. Jessie was expressing her condolences to William as Paul stood patiently at her side; whereby – at a distance – Edith Stockwell mopped her brow and addressed her sons: "How could he walk off with that woman after just burying your sister?"

"His wife! Mother," said Alexander.

Edith gritted her teeth. "My daughter...!"

Over on one of the settees, Jane was sitting with Sarah, her head pressed close to the only woman in the room who could comfort her. "Don't fret, love; it'll turn out fine in the long run...I can promise you that." And Sarah wrapped her arm around the thirteen-year-old girl.

Mark arrived in front of them now. "Thanks for being here, Mrs Halliday. Is she okay?" He nodded towards his sister.

"She will be, son. She will be."

Mark looked at her in astonishment; and after a moment, said, "You called me 'son'."

"Did I? I'm sorry. I wasn't quite thinking straight."

"But it's nice...I already feel like Paul's elder brother, so it doesn't actually seem wrong."

And as Sarah looked at this dark-haired, handsome young man, she felt as if she had to ask him something that she desperately craved an answer to – a question that she had wanted to ask for some long time. Now, much to Mark's astonishment, she suggested that Jane should go and be with her father, and then asked Mark to take his sister's vacated place beside her. And, when she looked at him, the boy knew something profound was about to come from this astute woman's lips. Oh, and how right he was when Sarah said, "Do you love Paul?"

Now, with little hesitation, he said solemnly, "You know, don't you?"

Sarah nodded.

"Does it show so much?"

Sarah nodded.

Mark appeared to show some alarm, before he said, "So am I to suppose that everyone else knows as well?"

"Why should they? Paul is my own son and nobody else's. I practically know him inside out, so it's of no surprise to me."

"And you disapprove of course." Mark's head was drooped onto his chest.

Sarah's hand was on the boy's shoulder now. "You underestimate me, Mark – as do so many of the others in this room – but I'm beyond their petty prejudices and hatred...yes hatred, Mark. I truly am above all that – and more.

"All I ask is that you treasure what you have and let no one dissuade you from holding on to what you believe in. People will hurt you; they'll likely call you foul names and say that how you feel is against the laws of nature; they'll try to destroy your and Paul's relationship with all the means they have at their disposal, but fight them! And if you ever need a friend to fight them with you, then I am here."

She looked directly at this youth who was weeping at the loss of his mother and pulled him to her as those around them looked on. "Now, come on, love," she said as she manoeuvred his long black hair from off his face, "dry those tears, and go to your family."

7

Laura Wilson was nearly twenty-four, and her mother had been trying for five years to find her a husband. But both she and Laura's father, had been unable to come up with a favourable suitor, because Laura tended to be attracted to the lower classes such as tradesmen, builders, and builders' labourers – one such being Harry Carr who was six years Laura's junior. But all this would change when the three were invited to dine with Edith Stockwell.

Edith had also been attempting matchmaking for her sons. Alexander, she was sure, would never marry – he was the archetypal confirmed bachelor – and as for Joseph…well, he'd certainly sown his wild oats over the years but still, at the age of thirty-eight remained without a wife.

And so, on a balmy spring evening in 1959, she had invited the Wilsons to dine. It was not just the meal that Edith Stockwell had designed, but her intention was to push Joseph in Laura's direction.

Despite her true sister having hastily run off with an American, and her half-sisters – who were nothing to write home about – Edith had a certain respect for Mary who was not as common as the others. And although the house she lived in was not as regal as her own, it was fitting for a woman who was married to a man like Jack Wilson. The only drawback to this potential union between Mary's daughter and her youngest son, was the tricky situation of Laura's religion. Nevertheless, that could be overcome – and if need be, Joseph would have to trade his faith for hers.

"Mary, dear. Please come and sit down next to me." Edith Stockwell patted the vacant space next to her on the settee.

"Edith, may I say how very sorry I am for your recent loss. It was a total tragedy – and her so young." Mary Wilson seated herself and took the woman's hand.

"It was so unexpected, Mary. And goodness knows how the children are coping with the loss of their mother." She smoothed down the skirt of her black satin dress, and without looking up, said, "Your half-sister and her son were at the funeral you know."

"I did hear of it," said Mary.

Edith sighed deeply. "I cannot understand what William was thinking about; after all, she wasn't close to my daughter. In fact, it is my belief that Dorothy – and forgive me for saying so – didn't care for the woman's broad-minded and plebeian attitudes. And that nephew of yours seems to have cast a weird and aberrant spell over Mark that has completed affected his judgement. I sincerely believe it was he who coerced Mark into not working toward a place at university."

Mary shook her head. "I don't really know what to say...."

Edith sat upright now. "Anyway, where are Jack and Laura?"

"Jack's just turning the car around, and Laura took the opportunity of visiting the powder-room before she made an appearance. And what of Alex and Joseph?"

"They should be back from the mill shortly. But – and I've made this a stipulation before they sit down to dinner – they must both bathe and get changed before coming into the presence of guests."

Mary offered up a clipped smile. However much she respected Edith Stockwell – and enjoyed the hospitality she extended to her and her family – she couldn't but feel some resentment when she maligned Sarah and young Paul. Despite Sarah's liberal way of thinking when it came to life and its idiosyncrasies, as her sister, she respected her views whatever they may be. Sarah had worked hard all her life and brought up a fatherless son who demonstrated a sensitive and caring character, and, be it through Sarah's own personal coaching or the boy's innate intelligence, there was no doubt she had done a fine job.

The drawing-room door opened, and the young maid shepherded in Laura Wilson. Edith immediately got to her feet and went to greet her. "Laura, my dear; how charming you look. Come and take a seat." She showed Laura to a chair beside the fireplace.

"Thank you, Mrs Stockwell."

"Oh please, dear; call me Edith."

Laura addressed her mother now. "Dad's just hanging up his coat, Mum. Although I can't understand why on earth he wanted to wear a topcoat in this weather."

"My husband was just the same," said Edith as she resumed her seat next to Mary. "Always chilled to the bone however clement the conditions. Now, as soon as Jack arrives, and Alex and Joseph get in and make themselves presentable, we'll take drinks and then go in and dine."

Dinner was over, and while the ladies went back to the drawing-room, the men had remained in the dining-room with brandy and cigars.

"Alex," said Jack Wilson. "I hate to bring it up on an occasion like this, but I must broach the subject of your outstanding rag account." He puffed on his cigar. "I recognise that your cash flow may be causing you a little difficulty at present, but I'm afraid I cannot extend you credit for much longer without at least a part payment."

"But I don't understand, Jack. We should have been able to finalise the account at the end of last month...Joseph! What have you to say about this?"

Joseph went and replenished his drink. Then he returned, saying, "I believe the cashier drew a cheque for the full amount on the twenty-fifth."

"Well I didn't sign it! You're supposed to keep an eye on the accounting procedures as you well know, but in this case, you apparently haven't." Alex turned to Jack now. "I will personally look into it first thing Monday morning, Jack, and get it sorted. And I apologise for any inconvenience it may have caused."

"That's fair enough, Alex. And I'm sorry I had to bring the matter to your attention....Well, shall we go and see what the women are up to?" And the three of them went to the drawing-room....

"Ah," said Edith when they entered, "I was just saying how nice the garden's looking. Philip has done it beautifully....Joseph, it's such a lovely evening, so why don't you take Laura for a look around? I hear she's a bit of a horticulturist."

"Oh, I wouldn't say that," said Laura, "but I do like a nice display of flowers." She gazed at Joseph and smiled.

"All right then," said Joseph. "Would you care for a little stroll, Laura, and leave this lot to get on with whatever?"

"That would be nice." And Joseph escorted the young woman into the garden....

"It's certainly a lovely evening, Joseph; don't you think? And your uncle *has* done a good job: the garden really is beautiful.... Why wasn't he at dinner?"

"Uncle Phil doesn't like get-togethers. He says it's a meal spoiled by idle chatter. He usually stays in his room."

"What a pity. I would really like to meet him for once."

"Oh, there's nothing to recommend him, Laura. He's not good

company at all."

The two strolled around the garden – Laura commenting on the various blooms – until they reached the shed. "Uncle spends a lot of time in here," said Joseph, "doing one thing or another. I often wonder if he's got a slate or two loose, the things he gets up to."

Laura stopped walking. "Don't be unkind, Joseph."

"I'm just saying what I think that's all.... Would you like to go and have a look over the valley? It's just around this bend, but it's a little dangerous so you'd better take my arm." Linking him now, Laura looked up at the tall, well-made man and, for all his faults, thought him a handsome and charming individual. And although he was fourteen years her senior, she considered that he would make a most acceptable suitor.

"Well, what do you think of this view, Laura? It's quite something, eh?"

She turned away from the landscape and looked directly into his eyes. "Wonderful.... But that sounds silly overlooking a railway line. Nevertheless, the valley itself is quite romantic and in such a lovely setting." And as he gazed into her sultry eyes he noticed her pupils dilating.

Now, without hesitation, he took her hand, saying, "You're lovely too, Laura." He now ran his fingers down the side of her face and pushed her long, dark-brown hair over her shoulders. Then, leaning forward, he kissed her gently on the lips, soon to become aware that her response was immediate and powerful when her tongue slid into his mouth. She cradled his head, pulling him hard to her as they fell backward onto the mossy ground beneath two overhanging trees. Releasing the grip on his face, she moved her hands beneath his shirt and stroked the soft, thick hair that covered his strong torso; and as her hand went further and caressed his firm belly, he let out a deep moan.

She knew without doubt that he was longing for her as she fumbled with the buttons on his linen trousers; and as she drew them down, she could see that beneath his white, silk underpants, his body was hungry to take her. And in exposing him, she recognised the tell-tale bead of moisture a man generated when he was aroused. So, with the experience she had gained from knowing Harry Carr, she put her mouth down and tasted him, moving back and forth towards his musky hairs until the liquid intensified on her tongue. But he stopped her now and let his underpants fall to the ground, his body yearning for her.

Now Laura leaned back on the carpet of moss and pulled up her dress and underskirt. Then, raising her buttocks, she slid down her drawers and, spreading her legs wide, showed herself to him.

He could see the glistening readiness that sparkled there, and immediately he was upon her, entering her with such force that it caused her to gasp loudly. His pulsating senses were heightened by the feeling of the soft moss and long, delicate grasses caressing his inner thighs as he thrust at her, but he knew if he didn't hold back, he would soon not be able to stop, and destroy his reputation of giving women pleasure; so his movements slowed, until he could sense she was almost at her peak, and allowed himself no restraint, knowing he was taking her to a height of passion that would engulf her. And in a wild and shuddering moment, their bodies became as one; and when Laura began to screech like a feral cat, Joseph emptied himself into her.

8

"You idiot!"

Edith Stockwell paced up and down across the drawing-room floor. And when she reached the piano, she slammed down the lid.

"But I never thought she'd become pregnant!"

Edith rushed towards her son. "You never thought? You never thought! My God, idiot's not the word for you. What the hell did you think that...doing what you did to her might result in? Well, that's it! You'll marry her – and soon before it becomes too obvious."

"Oh no, I won't, Mother. I have no intention of marrying the woman. And it's fine you telling me *that*, considering your darling Alex fathered a bastard. You never forced *him* to marry the girl."

"She was a slut! I could never have condoned a union between a son of mine and such a low piece. And that applies to that obnoxious Halliday woman who William is now about to marry."

Ignoring these remarks, Joseph said, "Do you really think that Laura Wilson was blameless in all this? Well let me tell you: she was dripping for it."

"Shut your filth!" Edith came close to his face now. "You will marry, or the money you would have inherited on your fortieth birthday, will be forfeited."

Joseph walked away from her, saying, "It won't! It will become mine by law."

Edith gave a guttural laugh. "Oh, my dear, you're very much mistaken."

"What?" He was back next to her now and, taking her by the arms, shook her. "What did you say?"

She removed herself from his grasp and walked to the settee where she leaned against its back and fixed her eyes on her son. "There was a stipulation in your father's will, that if just this kind of thing should happen, you would be disowned if you didn't do the honourable thing and marry."

"But why has this not been mentioned before – and why didn't I know about it at the time?"

"Because you never turned up for the reading of the will. You

189

were too busy out whoring!"

Joseph turned red in the face and the veins in his neck went rigid. But words wouldn't fall from his lips as he stared in anger at his mother.

"You *will* marry her, Joseph…and in a Catholic church!" Seeing the look of dismay on her son's face, Edith said, "Don't worry. You won't have to convert. Mary has agreed to that."

"What? You mean you've discussed the situation with Laura's mother?"

"Naturally. After all, I had to find out if she and her husband had no objection to their daughter marrying somebody so much older than she is. And before you interrupt, any objections they may have had were soon dispelled when they found out about her condition."

Joseph took off his tie and threw it on the floor, before walking to the bay window where he looked out across the miserable town. And calmly he said, "And where are we supposed to live and bring up the child?"

"Here of course.…It would be unthinkable for the child to be born and live anywhere else."

He faced into the room now. And as he leaned on the piano, he said, "You have it all figured out, don't you? Every single aspect. Well, all I can say, Mother, is this: you've already lost a husband, a daughter, and now a son…because believe me, I will never – as long as I live – forgive you for all this. And then you and your precious Alexander can spend eternity in glorious and untroubled harmony, because you most certainly deserve each other."

9

"I was thinking, darling; now that you and Paul will be moving in here tomorrow, and Bessy is retiring from service at the end of the month, that Jessie may wish to step into her shoes. What do you think?"

"Oh, William, that would be perfect. I've been worrying about her since you first proposed to me. She's never said anything of course, but I've known by her expression that she's been wondering what she might do being on her own in that place. Naturally, I'll have to see if she wants to take on the responsibility, but my guess is she'll jump at the opportunity; and Paul will be over the moon. He dotes on Jess."

"Good. And there'll just be enough time for Bessy to help her settle in and show her how things are run. Also, I'll get on to my solicitors and an estate agent to get the ball rolling in order to re-let the place. Now, get ready, and Max can take you home and you can give her the news."

Sarah leaned over to her husband-to-be and kissed him. "I do love you, William."

"Well, I hope so, or I'll have to let the church know that the wedding's off."

She chucked him under the chin, saying, "Oh get on with you, Bill Crowther. Now, let Max know I'll be ready in two shakes of a lamb's tail."

As she walked to the drawing-room door, William called after her: "You better had be, Mrs Halliday; we have a date in the morning." And she turned and smiled at him.

Sarah was wearing a pale-blue silk dress that came just below the knee, a pair of white court shoes, and a white pill-box hat.

"You look a picture, lass."

"Will I do then, Jess?"

"Do...? I'll tell yer what: I'd marry yer meself if yer weren't spoken for."

"Oh give over, Jess....I only hope Wilf's not late, though. Eeh, I wish Dad was here to give me away....Aay, love, how did this all happen? Only five months ago, William was burying his wife and I was putting flowers on John's grave."

"I knew then what his intentions were."

"How?"

"Oh, I noticed how he was looking at you when you were comforting his kids – and not because he was just wanting a new mother for them – it was obvious he'd fallen head over heels for yer, lass."

"Jess! His wife had just died!"

Jessie wagged a finger. "It wasn't just then. He'd set his cap at you long before that."

Sarah walked to the window and looked across the fields to High Ridge. "Do you think I'm doing the right thing?"

"Nay, bloody hell! Don't be 'avin' doubts now for God's sake!"

Without turning, Sarah said, "Oh, there are no doubts, Jess....It just seems to have happened so quickly."

"Aye, it has, so let's get on with it."

Sarah drew back from the window; and turning, she said calmly, "Wilf's here."

"About bloody time an' all. Now" – Jessie went over and placed her hands on Sarah's shoulders – "stop frettin' so much. Everything'll be fine."

Wilf came in. "Well, well, I've got to say, Sal, I'd marry yer meself if I...."

"Weren't spoken for...I know; Jessie's just said that. Are our Em and Kevin all right?"

"Aye. They set off for the church half an hour ago. By the way, who's the best man?"

"Alex Stockwell," said Sarah. "Now don't look so alarmed! Just thank the Lord it's not Joseph or he'd have sold the rings by now. ...Are Jane and Annie here?"

"Waiting in the second car, lass," said Wilf Sutcliffe. "Come on then, take me arm and let's get to it. By! yer do look a bobby...."

"Dazzler?" said Sarah, and she linked Wilf's arm.

The parish church of St Paul's was an awesome sight. Its proportions were almost like those of a cathedral. It stood at the far side of Collingley Park close to the town centre and – but for the town hall and mill chimneys – it dominated the area.

One would have thought royalty was arriving in town, because on this warm, late September Saturday, the streets were packed with onlookers and those out for their weekend shopping. And as Sarah's car came to the end of the park avenue, she not only caught sight of the assembled hordes, but heard the church bells peeling audaciously.

"Oh, hell, Wilf!"

"Calm yerself, love." He patted her hand.

"But there are so many people here. What are they all doing?"

"Come to see you…yer're famous now…best get used to it."

They got out of the car now to 'oohs' and 'aahs' from the crowd, and one voice could be heard saying, "Well done, lass. Yer nabbed 'im." Sarah attempted a smile as she grasped at Wilf's arm. "Help me, lad. Help me in."

The organ was already playing in the background; but as they entered through the large oak doors, they were met by a blast of sound as the mammoth organ; the orchestra of the Collingley Music Society; Collingley Brass Band, and the bells of St Paul's rang out the final thunderous minutes of Théodore Dubois' Fantaisie Triomphale. Sarah's heart was pounding, and she suddenly stopped in her tracks when she saw that every single pew, without exception, was occupied in this overwhelmingly monumental building. And as she looked around, she thought, He's bloody well gone and closed the mill for the day. The whole workforce is here! But she had forgotten that waiting patiently to follow her down the aisle, were Jessie and Sarah's two bridesmaids, Jane and Annie.

Jessie poked her in the back, whispering, "Get a move on, lass. He won't wait forever yer know." And when she heard Jane and Annie giggling at Jessie's remark, she took in a breath, and went on the long walk, which would culminate in her becoming Mrs William Crowther.

William had hired the ballroom of Collingley Town Hall for the reception. It was bedecked in every imaginable bloom – apart from roses which he knew Sarah had a dislike of – and a canopy of red and white ribbons hung from the ceiling, whose moulded cornices depicted scenes from the town's past and more recent history. And the mayor was present. "Welcome, lass. And may I say what a grand lass y'are….Eeh, that husband of yours is a lucky devil…. D'yer know, if I weren't spoken for I'd…."

"Marry me yourself?"

The mayor howled with laughter. "Aye! Aye, I would an' all.

Well, enjoy yerself, lass. Enjoy!" And he walked away still laughing.

"He's not right in t'head," said Jessie. "D'yer know, he used to have the tripe stall on the market. Can yer bloody well credit it? Eeh, I don't know."

Several waiters started to bring round champagne, and when one paused in Sarah's presence, she took a glass for herself and one for Jane who whispered, "Am I allowed?"

"Just this once, sweetheart. But don't let your father see."

Jane took a sip and shuddered. Then after her second tasting, she said, "Now that you're married to my father, do I call you Mother?"

Sarah looked at the pretty thirteen-year-old and replied, "If you want to, love. Or just call me Sarah if you prefer."

Jane pondered for a moment. Then she said, "If you don't mind, can I call you Mam like Paul does?"

Sarah touched the girl's cheek. "I'd be honoured....By the way, who caught the bouquet?"

"Annie here!" said Jessie. "She nearly floored me to cop it."

Annie giggled. "Oh, don't lie, Jess. I did nowt o' t'sort."

Jessie took Annie's arm. "Come on, lass; let's go get summat to eat. I'm starvin'."

After they had left, Jane said, "Mam?"

"Yes, love?"

"Do you think Paul likes me?"

"Likes you? He loves you; I know that."

"Really?"

"Yes, really....Why do you ask?"

Jane shuffled her feet. "Well, I was wondering if...well...well maybe when we're both old enough, do you think he'll marry me like Father married *you*?"

Sarah was stumped as to what to say at first; but then said, "I don't know, sweetheart. None of us know what will happen in the future. It's like what Prime Minister Asquith once said – look! that's a picture of him over there – and that was: 'wait and see', so that's all we can do."

Over at one of the side tables, Jessie picked up a plate of smoked salmon sandwiches. "All that?" said Annie. "I told you I was hungry," Jessie answered.

"But you're supposed to have one – two at most – not a whole plateful."

"Look," said Jessie, "there's always stuff left over at any sort of do, so why waste good food?" She began to eat – just as Edith Stockwell arrived. "Ah, it's Jessica."

"Jessie! That's what I was christened and that's what it is. Go grab a waiter, Annie, and get us another drink, that's a good lass."

"So," said Edith, "she managed to wangle her way into my family at the earliest convenience."

"Who's she? T'cat's mother?"

"Don't play that game with me. You know exactly who I'm talking about. My daughter has been dead barely six months and not only has your so-called friend seduced my son-in-law but my grandchildren as well."

"Look, woman! If any seducin' were done it weren't on Sarah's part. And as for your grandchildren, where did they go when they lost their mother, eh? To William's uncle's, that's where! And more to the point, they'll have a better life havin' Sarah around them now than havin' you! God knows why you were ever invited to the wedding in the first place."

Edith Stockwell gave a sickly smile. "How could I not be invited when my son was the groom's best man...? I do have to say though, that Bessy has arranged a fine reception, don't you think?"

"It was me who arranged it if you want to know."

"Ah, so that's the reason why you're eating for two...not in the family way are you?" Edith laughed.

"What? Like Laura Wilson were before she married your son...? Oh, don't look so appalled. Only me and Sarah know – and Laura's mam and dad, of course. But believe me, Mrs Edith God-Almighty Stockwell, if you don't shift your carcass out of my face, I'll get up on that there stage and announce it to the whole bloody town. Now, why don't you just go and bother the mayor – he's used to dealing with tripe."

As Edith slunk away, Annie crept up behind Jessie and tapped her on the shoulder. "What was all that about?" She handed her a glass of champagne.

"Nothing, love. Nothing at all....Mind you, I'd forgotten cow was on the menu."

Paul and Mark were seated at a table by themselves. Paul was watching his friend as he gazed about the room with a broad smile on his face. He looked more handsome today than Paul had ever seen him, and the black suit and wing-collar shirt he was wearing was exceedingly becoming.

Paul had reached an age when certain feelings were starting to overwhelm him at times. Things seemed different now since they met three, long years ago; and though Mark was older than him by four years, he still acted as a boy and not as the man he would soon become.

They had been close to each other – very close on occasions – but nothing had gone beyond their boyish experiments with what grown-ups called 'sex'. The time had come for Paul to press his intentions towards this stunningly attractive boy, but he didn't know how. He wished Mark would behave like the other seventeen-year-old boys he knew from grammar school: they had no qualms about having encounters with either girls *or* boys – although the rumours were never confirmed. Perhaps it was just youthful exaggeration?

"You look miles away," said Mark.

"Oh…er…I was just thinking."

"What about?"

Paul lied by saying, "About when I should give Mam and your father their wedding present."

"Really? Oh, tell me what it is! Have you brought it with you?"

"I brought it last night, and it's being kept safe by one of the staff in the main office. But I can't tell you because it's a secret."

Mark pinched him gently on his hand. "You're a tease, Paul Halliday. A total tease."

"You'll see it eventually.…Actually, it's for all of us now that we'll be moving into High Ridge."

Mark leaned back in his chair. "Gosh! I'd totally forgotten about that." He came forward now saying, "Do you realise we'll have to share a room until the other ones are redecorated."

"Unless I sleep with Jane or Jessie.…Of course I realise, you nit. Don't mind, do you?"

Mark's eyes reflected the sparkling lights hanging from the ceiling. "Mind? I can't wait."

As was the tradition, William and Sarah led off the dancing when the orchestra struck up, and presently the other guests joined in. "Well, Mrs Crowther, has it been a good day all told?"

Sarah looked deeply into her husband's eyes. "The best, love. I couldn't have wanted more."

"But there is more: the honeymoon."

"But you said you were too busy at the mill and that you.…"

"I told a fib.…Want to know where we'll be going?"

"Of course I do!"

"Chicago! Since your sister couldn't come here, I'm taking you there."

Sarah pushed him at an arm's length. "Katherine! We're going to see Katherine?"

"Got it in one, Mrs Crowther." And he picked her up in his arms and whirled her around.

"Just look at those two," said Mark. "Like two kids."

Paul smiled. "They love each other." He turned now and winked. "Just like two kids."

Mark unexpectedly took hold of Paul's hand. "Come on. Let's go and get this mysterious present of yours...."

On their return, everyone was seated at their tables. "Come on," said Mark. "They'll never guess what you got them." And as they walked together across the polished floor, all eyes watched them as they approached the newly-married couple.

"Mam," said Paul, "and William – my new dad – we've got a little something for you." He handed the gaily-wrapped box to his mother.

"Oh, Paul," she said sternly, "it's full of holes."

"Just open it, Mam."

Sarah undid the ribbon and lifted the lid. "My God!" She slowly reached inside and lifted out a black Labrador puppy. "Aw, the sweet, little thing. What's her name?"

William laughed. "I can see from here, sweetheart, it's definitely not a girl!"

"I hope it's all right, Mam," said Paul, "but I remember you telling me how upset you were when the Barracloughs' horse was lost. So – and please don't be angry – I've given him the same name: Ben."

Handing the puppy to William – which immediately proceeded to wash the man's face with its floppy tongue – Sarah pulled Paul and Mark to her, saying, "Angry? I'm absolutely delighted. But I hope you both understand you'll be responsible for his welfare while we're away? Make sure you really look after him until we get back."

William stood now, and stroking the puppy's head, said, "And Mark, you make sure you look after Paul."

Mark smiled broadly at his father. "Oh, I will, Father. Believe me, I most certainly will."

10

Sarah's honeymoon had been an experience she would never forget. She had been delighted beyond her wildest dreams to see Katherine and Jonas; but oddly enough, their son, Josh, had left on a visit to Europe with his school on the very morning they arrived, so she hadn't been able to meet him.

When they returned home, Sarah was surprised how much Paul had matured in the six weeks that she and William had been away. He had a certain look of adulthood about him, and he and Mark appeared closer than she had ever seen them. And how Ben had grown! He was a beautiful boy, and so obedient. He doted on Paul and hardly left his side – apart from when he was demolishing his food. And then there was Jess, dearest Jess, who had kept the house in fine order and paid any bills that had come in, and retained every invoice and receipt for inspection – as if that was really necessary!

It shortly came about – mainly to relieve William of some of his many duties at the mill – that Sarah decided to take up the role of mill manager after Maurice Butterworth retired. She loved being back in an environment that she had grown up in, and relished her new position. Yes, the past few months had been a happy and fulfilling time for all the inhabitants of High Ridge House…but all that was about to change in the January of 1960.

Paul was in the garage talking to Max.

"Do you like your job, Max?"

Max looked up from under the car's bonnet and smiled at the young man. "Of course I do, Mr Paul. I wouldn't do it if I didn't. Why do you ask?"

"Oh, I don't know. I'm just bored."

"Bored? At your age?"

"Yes! Bored! Do you know, everyone seems to have disappeared apart from you and Annie – and without even saying a word to me about going."

Max threw the spanner aside and reached for a cloth on which he wiped his hands. "So Annie and me aren't good enough company for you, then?"

"Oh, Max, I didn't mean it like that."

"No, I know you didn't....Well everybody's probably out getting things for this evening, and that's something to look forward to, isn't it?"

"You're right, Max. Yes, I'm looking forward to Mark's birthday party of course, but...well, I am really, really *bored.*"

The tall chauffeur ran his hand over the car's bonnet. "Look, it seems as if the old girl is fine now, but I want to give her a long run to see how she's ticking over. So, how about you tagging along, and we'll see if me and her can cheer you up? We can have a trip out to Harrogate if you like."

Paul brightened now. "Oh, yes please, Max. I've never been to Harrogate before....Can we take Ben?"

"Only if you get a blanket; I don't want dirty paws all over the seats....Right then! I'll just go upstairs and get changed and we'll set off before the weather turns – it looks as if we're going to have some snow. Won't be long."

"I don't know where he's got to, Jess. Just look at the time; and they'll all be here before long."

"Hasn't he phoned or anything?"

"Not a word. And William's furious that Max has gone missing – he was supposed to go and pick Edith up half an hour ago – and the dog's nowhere to be found as well."

The telephone rang. Sarah ran to the desk and picked it up. "Where? And what on earth are you doing *there*...? Oh, I see.... And it's all right now?"

Jessie waited.

"So, you're just on your way back....How long will you be...? Right. See you soon." Sarah put the phone down.

"Well?" asked Jessie.

"They're in bloody Harrogate! He was bored, and Max suggested they have a run out. They'd just got there and the car broke down, so they had to be towed to a garage...anyhow, it's fixed now and they're on their way back."

"William will go berserk," said Jessie. "He could dismiss Max over this."

"I'll have a word with him. After all, it was Paul's fault, and I know how he can wangle things with people. Bored indeed! I'll bore him when he gets back."

"Now don't start, Sarah. You know William can have a temper at times, and we don't want to spoil it for Mark – not on his eighteenth."

Sarah sighed. "You're right as always, Jess. I'll just have to bite my tongue."

"Mind you," said Jessie, "we've still got to consider what'll happen now the dog's gone missing an' all."

"Oh, I forgot to say: he's with them. The poor thing'll be starving by the time they get back." The doorbell rang. "God! that'll be the Stockwells. I bet her brother's brought them. I'll rush upstairs before Annie gets the door and see if William's ready – *and*, tell him the news. I just pray to the Lord he doesn't throw a fit."

Edith Stockwell came into the drawing-room and kissed her grandson. "Happy birthday, sweetheart. I hope you have a wonderful time."

"I'm sure I will, Grandmother." But his look was sullen.

"What's the matter? Looking so sad and it's your special day as well."

"Nothing really. It's just that Paul seems to have disappeared... and Max and Ben aren't here either."

Edith smiled as she placed a hand on his shoulder. "Well, surely that's no loss, love."

Mark stared at his grandmother with fire in his eyes; but he ignored her remark, saying, "I'm going to get myself a beer."

"You can get me a sherry as well, darling; after all, the service in this house is apparently non-existent....I'll just pop to the library and see if your Uncle Alex has finished chatting to William."

As she went out, Mark poured himself a drink, and had finished half of it when Sarah came in. "Hello, love. I've been looking all over for you." Mark carried on drinking. "Paul's on his way back from Harrogate. He should be here before long."

"Harrogate?"

"Yes. He persuaded Max to take him for a ride out and the car broke down...Ben's with them."

"Oh, that's wonderful! Why did he have to go on today of all days, Sarah? He's done it just to spoil my birthday."

Sarah approached the disconcerted boy, and laying a hand on his arm, said, "Paul wouldn't do that, love. He wouldn't upset you – particularly on your birthday; surely you know that by now?"

"No, I suppose not…it's just that I miss him so much when he's not around."

"And do you think I don't know that? Now, your father will be coming in soon and…."

But it was Edith who re-entered the drawing-room. "Ah! Sarah. I notice you've seen how upset Mark is because of your son's antics. I've always said he was a wayward child."

Yet before Sarah could defend her son, Mark spoke: "Oh shut up, Grandmother! You really get on my nerves at times." And after downing his beer, went on: "Uncle Alex has always said you're a stirrer. Anything that allows you the opportunity to have a go at other people who don't happen to be in your circle of friends, totally suits you down to the ground."

Sarah had to admire the out-of-character spirit in her stepson, and mentally waved a fist in the air; but Edith was silent, her face reddened with pique – and she remained so when William and Alex entered the room. "Very quiet in here, isn't it?" said William. "This is supposed to be a celebration not a wake. Mark, put some records on for goodness sake and pour me a drink."

"I'll get you one, love," said Sarah. "Whisky?"

"Yes please, darling; I need one after today. And by the way, it's snowing to high heaven, and it looks as if it's set in for the night. I only hope they get back before it gets any worse."

Jessie was sitting next to William. "It seems to break down a lot – the car I mean. You ought to get a new one. At least then you could probably rely on it."

William flipped his head and stared at Jessie.

"What?" She shrank as he looked at her.

"Jessie, what a brilliant idea! Do you know: you're much more clever than people give you credit for."

Jessie smiled – but blushed. "Well, at least I'm good for most stuff. Now, you weren't too harsh on Max when he got back, were you?"

"I said what was needed to be said and left it at that."

"Paul can be very persuasive when he wants to."

"It wasn't Paul, Jessie. Max said it was *he* who suggested that Paul go for a ride with him….Anyhow, they're all back safe so that's all that matters. Isn't it, Ben, lad?" He patted the dog that was sitting at his feet. Then he looked up. "I see Edith's collared Sarah. I wonder what she's spouting on about this time?"

"Probably a load of shite as usual. Oh, deary me! I'm sorry, Mr William; that just slipped out." Jessie slapped a hand over her mouth while William let out a raucous laugh that turned heads. "Oh, I love your candour, Jessie. You really say it as it is – and no doubt you're perfectly right. I must remember that for future reference."

"What are you giggling at, Daddy?" Jane came and sat down beside her father. "Oh, just something that Jessie said."

"Tell me."

"Listen, why don't you go put something nice on the radiogram instead of this rock and roll stuff."

"But it's Elvis Presley. I like him. Mark says he prefers Cliff Richard, but *I* don't."

"Nevertheless, let's have a change for a while, sweetheart. Something more gentle – like some Mantovani so that Jessie and I can have a dance."

At the prospect of seeing her father dance with Jessie Dicks, Jane did not hesitate in racing across the room and flipping through the record rack.

"I hope you were joking, Mr William," said Jessie.

"Not at all. Let's show this lot how it's really done."

"But you ought to be dancing with your wife, Mr William, not me!"

"Now look, Sarah has my full attention most of the time; it's your turn now. And please stop calling me 'Mr William'; just William will do." And when the music began, William stood, and taking hold of Jessie's hand, said, "Would you care for this next dance, ma'am?" And Jessie accepted.

Well, I never!" This was Edith Stockwell. "This is totally improper: the master of the house dancing with a servant."

"Jessie's not a servant," said Sarah. "She's part of the family."

"Family? Well, if my Dorothy were still alive, she wouldn't have allowed it."

"Nonsense!" Sarah sipped at her drink. "Dorothy was a fun-loving woman – something that you have never seemed to grasp."

Edith faced Sarah. "You have no right to…."

"Excuse me, Mother." Alex had approached and interrupted the conversation. "Would you mind if I had a private word with Sarah for a moment?"

"Take all the time you want," said Edith, and pushing her shoulders back, walked away.

202

"Being her usual self, was she?"

"Nothing I couldn't handle, Alex. Now, what can I do for you?"

"Let me get us a drink first." And when he returned, he handed Sarah her glass of sherry and said, "William is thinking of investing in Providence. It won't be for a few years yet, but I was wondering what you thought?"

"Me? Why me?"

"Well you are married to him – and in a way married to the business – and he did say he'd discuss it with you."

"The business is totally his responsibility, Alex – and so is what he does with his own money."

"I think you'll find that that's not *his* attitude, Sarah; and he did say that any decision would have to involve the two of you."

Sarah was bowled over. It had never occurred to her that her husband wanted more from this marriage other than for her to be a wife, mother – and stepmother – and run the household with Jessie by her side. Granted she was now the mill manager, but she considered it more of a hobby than an obligation. "Well, as you say," she said, "that won't happen for a few years, so we'll wait until then."

Meanwhile, Paul and Mark were having their own discussion as they gazed out on the falling snow that had already substantially covered the garden. "It's beautiful," said Paul.

"Do you think so?" said Mark, his speech obviously slurred. "I see it like it is: cold and uninviting....A bit like you at times."

"I don't understand, Mark."

Mark confronted him now. "Why did you go off with Max?"

"I....Well, everybody was out and I didn't know what to do: I was bored. And then when Max said he was going to take the car out and that I could go along, then...."

"Oh, so Max invited you to go out for a bit of a jaunt, did he? And, naturally, you accepted his proposition."

"Well, yes....I did make sure Ben wasn't left on his own."

Mark threw back his head. "Then that makes it all okay, does it? What about *me* being left on *my* own? wondering where the two of you had got to and, more to the point, what you were getting up to."

"I don't quite understand what you're trying to suggest, Mark, but I don't like it."

"Oh, you understand all right, so don't play the young innocent with me. You might be four years younger than me – five now –

but by Christ, you're much, much older."

Paul turned away; but Mark grabbed him and pulled him to him. "And where do you think you're going to this time, eh?"

"Leave me alone. I'm going to talk to Mam."

"That's it. Go and run to mummy because you can't handle the truth."

"Let go of me, Mark, or I'll...."

"You'll what? What? Go on, tell me what you'll do....Well?"

William had seen what was happening between the two boys and he went over. "Hey, you two, what's all this about?"

"Ask him!" Mark stabbed a finger into Paul's shoulder, whence his father took hold of his son's wrist. "You've had more than enough to drink, my boy, and if you don't calm down I'll have no option than to take you upstairs and *make* you calm down."

"Oh, really? Well go on and do it and let them all see how you treat your real son over...over this thing."

By this time, the assembled company had noticed the raised voices coming from near the window, and halting their conversations, turned their eyes on the three of them. "Get upstairs this instant!" William pulled Mark into the centre of the room as Paul went and stood by his mother. Suddenly, Mark extricated himself from his father's grasp, smashed his glass on the floor and, raising himself to his full height, yelled, "Fuck off, Father!"

William, stunned as much as were the others present, glared wide-eyed at his son. But Mark had not yet finished: "You damned idiot! Fancy taking up with that cunt" – he pointed straight at Sarah – "and her bloody whore of a son....You should be grateful that she can't have any more kids, or they all might turn out..."

But his outburst was promptly arrested when William, with a force that knocked Mark sideways, slapped his son hard about the face. "Get out! Get out! Get out of this house at once and...and never set foot in it again!"

Mark, his dark, tousled hair covering his eyes, raised his hand to his face where the imprint of his father's fingers still burned upon his cheek. Then, sweeping back his long black locks, he walked slowly from the room.

William stood staring at the open door that led into the hallway; then he turned and surveyed those who yet remained. "I'm sorry, ladies and gentleman," he said, "but I regret this little party is over."

Sarah, Jessie and Paul were seated in the kitchen with the dog.

It was shortly after midnight, and Max – having been ordered to keep the driveway free of snow since he returned from his ill-fated trip – had driven the Stockwells home; and William, Annie and Jane – she in floods of tears – had retired to bed.

"I've never heard the like of such language that Mark came out with."

"Oh, Jessie, please!" said Sarah. "You worked in the mill for God's sake: we've both heard worse than that."

"Well, be that as it may, it was a dreadful thing to do and – apart from the vile word he called you – fancy saying Paul was a…well, you know what."

Sarah cradled her mug of cocoa between her hands. "It was worse what William did, though: dismissing his only son from the house into freezing conditions…I wonder where on earth he's gone?"

Paul stood now. "I'm going to try and find him."

"Where?" said his mother. "And in this weather?"

"I'll put an overcoat on, so don't worry; but I've got to go." Paul walked out into the hall and closed the door behind him.

"Paul!" his mother called after him, as the dog went to the door and began whining. "Oh, shut up, Ben!" she said. And the dog sat, then lay down.

"You know what Paul's like, Sal. He'll do what he wants to – as you well know."

Sarah slammed her fist on the kitchen table. "Kids! Who'd have 'em?"

"You did…well, one of 'em at least."

"But I ask you, Jess; where's he going to look?"

Directly, Jessie went and took her coat down from the back of the kitchen door, pulled on her boots and wrapped a scarf around her neck. "What are you doing?" said Sarah. "Going after him," said Jessie. "I might have an idea where he's gone to." She reached into a drawer and took out a set of keys.

"Those are for the house in Long Lane. What do you want them for? The place has been closed for two weeks having new electrics put in."

"Trust me. You stay here in case anybody calls. I'll take Ben with me; he'll be able to pick up Paul's scent."

"In snow?"

"Aye, in snow. Now, I'm off; I'll take a torch to find my way across the fields."

"I'm coming with you."

"No, you're not! Get yourself a brandy; I won't be long." With this, she opened the back door and called the dog....

At least it's stopped snowing, thought Jessie as she took the path at the side of the greenhouse and descended the slope to Barn Brook. I only hope I don't bloody well fall in. "Find, Ben lad! Go find Paul." And the dog bounded off before her.

The snow hadn't frozen solid, but it was four to six inches deep. She managed to negotiate the brook and proceeded up the slope at the far side, every now and again holding her chest before calling the dog back to her side. Together they reached the field, which succeeded the brow of the hill; and after a further half-hour trek, Jessie sighted the lights of Long Lane. She shone the torch in front of her and once more told the dog to 'find'.

Presently they were in the lane, and as Jessie fumbled in her pocket for the keys, she noticed that Ben had bounded through the open door of their old place. She breathlessly staggered forward, and once inside, flashed the torch around the darkened kitchen. "Ben! Paul!" And when she heard the dog barking above, she mounted the bedroom steps to the landing, looking in both bedrooms. There was nothing but cables and workmen's tools. Then she heard paws padding about in the attic, so she climbed the steep, narrow steps and entered the top room.

Shining the light about her, she finally saw them: Ben sitting licking Paul's face, while he nuzzled into him. "Oh, love," she said as she walked over to them. "You'll freeze up here." She knelt beside the crouching boy, saying, "Come on, love. Let's get back home and in the warm."

"I thought he'd be here, Jess...we both had spare sets of keys made. We've been coming here occasionally just to escape and...."

"I know, love; I know." Jessie took off her scarf and tied it about Paul's neck. "Now get yourself up and let's be off before the electricians arrive in the morning and find the three of us frozen to the floorboards."

Paul attempted a smile before saying, "Do you think he'll come back, Jess?"

"I don't know, love; we'll see....Now, come on; your mam'll be worried sick."

They then left the house, and after locking the door and crossing the lane, Paul turned back and looked at his old home. "Things were happier when just you, me, and Mam lived here." And as Jessie put her arm around his waist, she said, "They will be again, love. You'll see."

Paul lowered his head and shook it from side to side. "Oh, I doubt it, Jess. I doubt it very much."

11

The library door was flung open and Jessie bustled in. "Well, that's the bloody latest."

Sarah looked up from the letter she was writing. "What?"

"All his clothes have gone....Yer see, since Paul doesn't sleep in that room these days, I went in this morning to take the bedding off for a wash, and Mark's cleared his stuff out – the lot! Not even an odd sock is left."

"He must have come one night when we were all in bed, Jess."

"Aye, like a thief."

"Oh well, maybe he's gone for good....Still, I've got to go to Edith's this morning. Maybe she'll shed some light on things. Thank God Mary persuaded her to see me."

"I don't know what you think you're going to achieve, love; you know what that woman's like."

"I've got to do something, Jess," said Sarah. She stood now and began to pace the room. "I can't just sit around here while two people who I love dearly are suffering. And you never know, Mark might be staying there."

"Well, all I can say is that I wish you luck....What time are you going?"

"I'll get there for eleven."

"Right, I'll make you some breakfast."

"Oh, Jessie, I couldn't eat a thing the way things are."

Sarah arrived at the Stockwell house five minutes early. "I'll try not to be too long, Max."

"No worries, madam."

"Wish me luck!"

Max nodded, and Sarah got out of the car and walked up to the front door where she rang the bell. Eventually she was admitted by an elderly woman who asked her to take a seat in the hallway and she'd announce her.

It hasn't changed since I was here twenty-three years ago, Sarah thought. Mind you – she ran a gloved finger over the hall table – it could do with a damned good clean. She smiled now, thinking, I wonder if that elf still lives in the attic?

The elderly woman returned. "Come through, madam; she's ready for you." And I'm ready for her, thought Sarah.

Edith Stockwell was standing by the fireplace. "Do sit down, Mrs...Mrs Crowther." And she indicated the settee. "So what can I do for you?"

Sarah sat. And taking off her gloves, placed them on her knee. "I've come to see if you know where Mark is?"

"What...? Oh surely, you can't be so worried. After all, my grandson means nothing to you."

"He's my stepson, and I care as much for him as I do for my own boy."

"Ah" – Edith went to a chair beside the fireplace and sat down – "your son. Well he was the cause of all this. If he hadn't had gone off with that chauffeur of yours, Mark wouldn't have been so upset that he caused a scene. I can't blame him for that."

"Mrs Stockwell, I haven't come here to discuss my son's actions – or even Mark's – I'm here to see if you know where he is?"

Edith smiled. "Oh, my dear, I know where he *might* be...but that's all." She stood again and walked to the window and without turning to face Sarah, said, "He came here that night, you know; but he left after three days. He said he was going to visit an old school friend of his, but wouldn't say where. And" – she fingered the velvet curtains now – "he specifically told me that he would not be returning."

"His father's worried about him," said Sarah quietly.

"Then he shouldn't have struck him like he did." A silence ensued between the two women before Edith spoke again: "Your driver's getting bored out there." She spun on her heels now. "I think you'd best be off before he sets off for Harrogate without you."

Sarah sprang to her feet. "My! you certainly are an offensive woman. Thank God I never came to work for you." She slipped on her gloves and walked to the door where, turning back, she said, "But be assured, I'll find Mark somehow, and if I discover that you do know his whereabouts, I will not be responsible for my actions." Sarah walked out and left that dismal place....

On her arrival back home, she was surprised to see William there. "Hello, love," he said. "Why have you been to the Stockwells?"

"Oh. So Jessie told you?"

"No. In fact, Edith phoned me at the mill and said you'd been."

"Ah, well, so now you know. I only did it to try and help the situation. I've seen how you've been for the last week and hoped that maybe I could help build bridges so to speak."

"Look, love." He took her hands in his now. "I appreciate your concern – and I've also notice how down in the dumps Paul is about things – but what Mark said was indefensible. No son of mine – or daughter if it comes to it – can come out with sentiments like that without having to bear the consequences."

"Sweetheart, I do see your point...but to dismiss him from the house was, well, rather extreme to say the least."

William released Sarah's hands and went and poured himself a whisky. "Want one?"

"No thanks, love...I'll just pop into the kitchen and make myself a cup of tea. Do you know if Jessie's still in?"

"She was when I got back...But I'm not sure at the moment...."

Jessie *was* in the kitchen. "Have you seen him, lass?" she said.

"Yes, Jess. He's worried; I can see that, however much he tries to hide it."

"Well, pains in the chest aren't to be taken lightly. I know...."

Sarah interrupted. "Now just hold on a minute. What pains in the chest?"

Jessie put down the filled kettle on the gas ring and turned about. "Oh dear. He hasn't told you, has he?"

"Told me what?" Sarah took a seat at the table. And when Jessie joined her, she said, "Well, first of all, he's gone and bought a new car, and...."

"Hang on! A new car?"

"Aye. A posh 'un an' all. Then, he came back from the mill because he was feeling unwell: these pains in his chest and down his arm." She demonstrated. "I told him to phone the doctor, but he said it was nothing to worry about."

"God! not something else now, surely." Sarah stood now. "Well, whether he likes it or not, *I'm* calling the doctor."

"Don't you think you should tell him first?"

"Phone first. Tell afterwards." But before she had chance to pick up the telephone, it rang. "Hello, Sarah Crowther....Oh, hello, Mary....What? When...? Oh, love, I'm so sorry....Yes, of course I will. I'm on my way right now....Bye...bye, love." She put the phone down and looked at Jessie, saying, "Laura's lost the baby."

Sarah was sitting at Mary's table while her sister prepared some tea in the kitchen.

This was the first time she'd been in this room since she was thirteen and it had changed dramatically. No more floral wallpaper or carpets: now the walls were decorated with a creamy shade of paint, and a carpet the colour of butterscotch, complemented the modern furniture and fittings. And Mary no longer had a woman to come in and 'do' for her. But Sarah wondered how long that would last? Not long, she fancied.

"Would you like a scone, Sarah?" said Mary as she brought in the teapot.

"No thanks, love; just tea will be fine."

Mary sat down opposite and sighed deeply. "It was a little boy as well." And she looked down at the table-cloth.

"I am so sorry, love....How is Laura coping?"

"Oh, not too bad." Mary poured out the tea. "She seems to have accepted it better than I could have hoped."

"And what about Joseph?" asked Sarah as she poured milk into her cup.

Mary looked up at her sister now, saying, "Who knows? Nobody's seen him for a week....Edith is furious. She says she's had her fill of him."

Sarah raised the cup to her lips; and after sipping at her tea, said, "What will Laura be doing when she gets out of hospital? Will she go back to the Stockwells?"

"Oh no! She's made that clear....No, she'll be coming home; and I'll be glad of it." Mary drank some tea before saying, "The things that are happening with their business at the moment would not be beneficial to Laura's well-being."

"What do you mean?"

"Well apparently, things are in a right mess. Jack's stopped supplying them – mainly because he had to keep chasing them for money. And now some firm in Bradford has bought into the mill at a knock-down price."

"But surely that means it's not the business that's failing, but more likely that they're short of cash."

"I don't know; but according to Jack, these people are known for turning family businesses around and bringing them back into profit."

"Oh, it all sounds a bit odd to me," said Sarah, placing her cup down. "Still, it would be interesting to find out how big a stake they hold in the place?"

"Well, we certainly won't find out; I'm sure of that....Anyhow, how are things with you all, Sarah?"

"Oh, as well as can be expected....You probably heard that Mark left." Mary nodded. "And only this morning I heard – from Jessie I might add – that William's been suffering from chest pains, which he has never mentioned to me. I phoned the doctor before coming to see you."

"He probably didn't say anything so as not to worry you, love."

"Well I am worried....But that reminds me: I'd better be getting back. I left without telling him where I was coming." Sarah stood now, and picking up her gloves, said, "Send my love to Laura. And wish her a speedy recovery from me."

Mary herself got up now, and coming to her sister, kissed her on the cheek. "I will...and thank you for coming, Sarah. It's very much appreciated."

Sarah was uncharacteristically quiet as Max drove her home. So, somebody's bought into Providence, she thought. And after the conversation she'd had with Alex, she wondered if she should let William know before he invested money himself? That's another bloody thing to fret about.

12

Jessie was pummelling bread dough. "I think he's doing too much."

"But you know what he's like, Jess."

"Aye, I do! But you're his mother, so can't yer tell him? His schooling will be bound to suffer."

Sarah placed a hand on her forehead. "Look! William's not well and the doctor's told him to take some time off; Mark's not here; and two of the accounts staff are off – one with a broken ankle and the other one expecting. So what am I to do?" She went to the sink and poured herself a glass of water.

Jessie wiped her hands and laid one on Sarah's shoulder. "I'm sorry, love…it's just that I can't abide you and Paul takin' on so much. You'll both be poorly an' all before long."

Sarah touched Jessie's hand. "I know, Jess; I know." She turned to her now. "The only reason Paul offered to step in, is that it takes his mind off not knowing where Mark is. He's been like a lost soul for over a year since he left." She went and sat back at the table, and her head drooped. "How I wish he'd never got so involved."

"That's my fault."

Sarah looked up. "How do you mean?"

Jessie joined her at the table. "If I hadn't fallen in that bloody stream, then we'd have never come into this house in the first place."

Sarah extended an arm and patted Jessie's hand. "You daft, dozy, bugger.…Look! If John was still alive, I wouldn't be married to William. If Bessy hadn't retired from here, you could still be stuck on your own in Long Lane; and, if William hadn't thrown his son out, Paul and Mark would still be together. We can't keep saying 'what if' all the time; we've got to get on the best we can with what life's doled out to us.…Now" – she took a sip of water – "I'm going to the mill to see how things are."

Jessie watched her dear friend leave and worried for her.…

When she arrived at the mill, Sarah walked into the burling room where the women workers were busy removing any vegetable matter from the woollen fabrics, and rectifying any faults that were present with the aid of burling irons.

"Morning, ladies."

"Mornin', Mrs Crowther," they responded in unison. Then a lone voice said, "How's Mr Crowther doing?"

"Having a damned good rest at the moment," said Sarah.

"Well he needs it, lass. He's been doin' too much lately...never stops. You just make sure he doesn't come back before he's properly better – strap him down if needs be." The other women laughed. And Sarah, smiling, said, "I'll do that, Maud."

She went and inspected some of the work being carried out, and when she reached the youngest member of the crew, she leaned over and ran a hand over the cloth, saying, "Fine work, Daisy. Very fine indeed." The girl looked up and smiled. "Thank you, Mrs Crowther. By the by, I caught sight of your Paul this mornin'. Eeh, he's a good-lookin' lad. But he seemed a bit down in the dumps."

"Oi!" said an older woman at her side. "You mind yer tongue. It's no business of yours makin' comments about Mrs Crowther's son. Get on wi' what yer paid for."

"Oh, it doesn't matter," said Sarah. "It's kind of you all to think about the welfare of the family....Now ladies, I'll get off and leave you to it. Thanks for doing such excellent work."

And a chorus rang out: "Thank you, Mrs Crowther."

"Oh, Mrs Crowther!" Maud called out before Sarah reached the door. "A man came lookin' for yer about an hour ago, so I sent him up to t'offices."

"Really?" said Sarah. "Well, I'm going there now, so I'll find out what he wanted...."

When Sarah reached the offices, the staff stood as she entered. "Please, do sit down ladies and gents." She walked over to Paul who had his head bent over one of an assortment of ledgers; and pulling up a chair, she sat at his side. "Everything all right, love?"

"Yes, Mam. I've nearly finished the books and then I'll go through the bank statement later. It shouldn't take me long to do a reconciliation."

"Good. Now, I was thinking: it's a beautiful day, so why don't we all take a drive out into the Dales or somewhere? We all need a break from work for a change. We could even take a picnic."

"Yes, I'd like that. But as long as we don't have to go through Harrogate."

Sarah watched her son totting up the columns of the cash book and thought, He'll never get over that day he went out with Max.

That's how all this sad business came about.

Paul threw down his pen. "Oh, I nearly forgot. A man came in looking for you earlier. He said he was from some company in Bradford – he didn't leave his name or anything, but said he'd try and catch you another time."

"Well, who could that be? I don't think we have dealings with any people from that neck of the woods." She thought deeply for a moment; and then a bell rang inside her head: Mary had told her something about a firm in Bradford who had put money into Providence mill...I wonder?

She was not used to all this.

Sarah Harvey – as she was once known – had found it hard to come to terms with all these changes in her life: things seemed to have happened so quickly. She had grown up in a happy home; found a job as soon as she had left school; married and raised an affectionate and intelligent boy, and remarried into money.

Then, only yesterday, William had informed her that he had been to their solicitor to change his will, and now – as if he wished her to simply accept it – she was riding around in a Rolls-Royce. No, she was not used to this at all, and wondered if she ever would be.

They entered Wharfedale by taking the road through Otley and Ilkley, and soon afterwards arrived in the hamlet of Bolton Abbey.

After safely parking the car, Max took the picnic basket out of the boot; and when Paul had put Ben's lead on, he, Max and William walked ahead to Bolton Priory; and then down to the side of the river Wharfe where they found a suitable spot on the grassy bank to seat themselves.

"I wonder why Jane didn't want to come?" said Sarah to Jessie. "She seems to be in a world of her own just now."

"Well, for one thing," said Jessie, "it would've been a bit of a squeeze – even in the new car – and for another, you've been spending too much time at that bloody mill and haven't even noticed a thing that's going on at home."

Sarah stopped walking; and taking Jessie's arm, said, "What do you mean?"

"What I mean, lass, is that she's lovesick."

"Who for?"

"I told you that you don't see what's staring you in the face at times. Harry of course."

"Harry Carr?"

"Now which other bloody Harry do we know?"

"Well, she hasn't said anything to me about it."

"Nor me. But it doesn't take a blind man runnin' for a bus to know what's in front of him."

Sarah began to walk again. Harry Carr of all people! Well I never saw that coming....

"You two took your time," said William. "Gassing away back there. Anyway, we're just off for a walk along the river. Can you manage to lay the food out?"

"Oh, I don't think so!" said Jessie. "We are only women after all."

William laughed.

"Don't be too long," said Sarah. "And take it easy....And Paul! Don't go near The Strid. The river's notorious just there: people have been drowned before now."

"I'll be careful, Mam; don't worry." And the three men and the dog walked off.

Sarah and Jessie proceeded to lay out the tartan blanket on the grass. "It was a grand idea of yours to suggest we come out for the day, lass. Even William seems to have perked up – and Paul seems brighter an' all."

Sarah looked at the four disappearing into the distance. "I only hope William remembered to take his pills and doesn't overdo things. I was worried sick when he said he'd been to see his solicitor about changing his will."

"Look, a bit o' fresh air will do us all the world of good – what with him staying indoors most of the time and you and Paul in that dismal mill."

"That reminds me, Jess; Paul said a man came looking for me this morning, but never said who he was or what he wanted. The only thing I know is that he came from some place in Bradford."

"Have you mentioned it to William?"

"No. I thought it best not to trouble him with it at the moment."

"Well," said Jessie; "let's get the stuff laid out, because no doubt they'll be ravenous when they get back...."

The dog was the first to return, and readily sniffed at the food. "Oi! get yer nose out," Jessie warned the Labrador. "Your stuff's still in the basket so sit down and wait." And the dog obeyed.

A few minutes later, William and Max arrived, and William sat down next to his wife. "How are you feeling, love?" she asked.

"A bit breathless, but all right."

"Let me make a plate up for you, and when you've eaten you can have a nap. Max, help yourself; there's plenty to go around.... Where's Paul got to anyway? I thought he was on his way back with you?"

"He got talking to somebody," said William, "but said he'd be along shortly." Well that's something, thought Sarah. At least he's coming out of his shell a bit more now....

It was over half an hour later when Paul appeared.

"You've been a long time," said his mother. "I've been worried sick that you may have been swept away."

"Well, I got talking to this lad, and he wanted to see if he could cross the river. I told him how dangerous it was, but he ignored me, and waded in and slipped on one of the rocks – but I managed to grab his arm and drag him back to the bank."

"And is he all right?"

"Oh, yes. We just fell back on the grass and started laughing about it."

Laughing as well? thought Sarah. At last he's beginning to laugh about things! "Well," she said, "get something to eat before Ben pinches your share." She looked at her husband now, and tapping his arm, said, "Would you like some tea, love? Or a bottle of beer perhaps? William?"

"Oh, don't disturb him for a while, lass," said Jessie. "Just let him sleep."

...But it was here, in the verdant surroundings of Bolton Priory, where the cascading River Wharfe thundered its way over The Strid, that it soon became clear to all those who loved him, that William Crowther had drawn his final breath.

13

Sarah was seated at the library table with her hands spread over the blotter and her head lolling onto her breasts. Presently, she looked up at Jessie and, forcing an imitation of a smile, said, "I suppose I'll have to get on with the arrangements, Jess."

"Aye, I suppose so. It's been a week now....D'yer need a hand with anything, love?"

"Oh" – the sigh was long drawn out – "everything." She pushed herself out of her seat and walked slowly to the window.

Poor lass, thought Jessie. It's bad enough having to bury one husband, but now two! Eeh, life's a bugger...a right bugger! She went to Sarah's side and rested a hand on her back.

"So...I'm supposing it's mine now, Jess: over yonder, that great big lump of a mill....What the hell am I going to do with it?"

"You've got two options, lass: sell it – or run it."

Ah...Jess is being as matter-of-fact as ever, thought Sarah. So, what's it to be?

"Look! I'll make us a pot o' tea and we'll crack on wi' things. Yes?"

Sarah nodded.

The last will and testament of William Crowther was yet to be read. But he had left instructions with his solicitor that on his demise, a letter deposited with him should be passed on to 'my beautiful and darling Sarah' without delay.

When Jessie returned with the tea, Sarah bade her friend to draw up a chair and seat herself opposite at the library table. She then slit open the envelope.

"Even though I have no idea of what's in this, Jess, I couldn't have read it without someone being present – and you're the best person I would wish to share its contents."

Jessie Dicks offered up a weak smile as Sarah unfolded the two foolscap sheets of paper and began to read:

'To my Darling Wife

'I write this with a heavy heart – knowing that when it is read, I will no longer be with you. Yet I know that you, my dearest love, will carry out my wishes with the resolve and determination you have shown since the day I first met you as a girl of thirteen. I knew then – even though the path I subsequently took led me in a different direction – that one day you would most assuredly be mine.' Jessie blew her nose on her apron and Sarah paused momentarily to take a sip of her tea.

'I intend to follow a tradition in these parts and that is to close the mill for the day, so that those of the workers who wish to do so, may attend my funeral at Woodkirk. Unfortunately, the church itself will not be able to accommodate everyone, so I would very much like it if, at some later date, a memorial service could be arranged and held in the parish church of St Paul which has the capacity to hold the whole workforce, rather than just those who could be present at Woodkirk. Also, I would wish for a large orchestra and choir to perform part of Mahler's Second Symphony. There is a good reason for my choice – apart from it being a favourite of mine – and that is in its given name: "Resurrection".

'As you know, I have long been a patron of the arts – mainly music – and having been a member of the Hallé Concerts Society for many years, I have been in touch with them concerning this particular wish of mine, and they have most generously agreed to do everything in their power to grant my request – provided a suitable date can be arranged. This, my love, I must leave down to you.'

Now, Sarah turned over the page and placed it on the desk. "I don't think I can go on with this, Jess. I thought I could get through it as usual – but it's really getting to me."

"Oh, lass." Jessie was on her feet now, saying, "Then leave it for now, love. After all you need to give yerself time to sort things out." She leaned forward and placed a hand on Sarah's.

"No...no, I can't leave it...I've got to press on. But could *you* read the rest, Jess?"

"Me?"

"I've just caught sight of your name cropping up....Please! Will you?"

Jessie could not refuse this long-term and faithful friend of hers. So, taking the sheet that Sarah handed her, she sat again, took out her glasses from her apron pocket and continued the reading of William's words:

'And I'd be grateful, sweetheart' – Jessie gulped – 'if you could place an advertisement in the Yorkshire Post indicating that all those who knew me would be welcome to attend St Paul's. Also, I have made a list of those I would like to be present at the house afterwards.

'As for the catering arrangements, I would – if she wouldn't mind – like to leave these down to our dear Jess.' Jessie looked up and removed her spectacles, her face displaying a look of trepidation. But when Sarah indicated a desire that she carry on reading, Jessie replaced her glasses and continued: 'Naturally, I would not expect her to do it all herself – tell her to find the best caterers she can and give them a list of what she thinks would be required, and to employ extra staff to welcome the guests and serve food and drinks. I know full well that she will do an excellent job.

'Finally, I would like to extend my eternal love to herself, my sweet daughter Jane, stepson Paul and, of course, to you – my Darling Sarah.

'God Bless, my Love,

'Your William.'

"Oh, love!" Jessie rushed to the grieving widow now. And holding her in the tightest of embraces allowed herself to weep along with her.

Later that very same day, Sarah contacted the Hallé Concerts Society and made arrangements to travel over to Manchester and speak to their manager at a mutually convenient time; then, together with William's uncle James who had travelled from his home in New Zealand immediately after receiving the news of his nephew's passing, attended a meeting with the heads of the various departments of the mill.

After they were all assembled in the large main office of the premises, Sarah seated herself at the head of the long, highly-polished table and addressed her workers: "The events of the past week have come as a great and unexpected blow to us all. And though I am – as you all must be – still in a state of shock, I cannot allow my hollow emotions to cast an air of hopelessness over this fine enterprise of ours.

"It would be William's wish that not only does the mill continue without hindrance to its output or to the welfare of its employees, but his desire would also be to see it flourish and expand. After all, it is not called Resurrection for nothing; and we must all give everything we have in our very cores to prove to this little town of ours that it will not just be another producer of woollens, but the best producer of woollens in the whole of the West Riding."

Chants of hear! hear! echoed around the room, after which Sarah continued: "Jim has kindly offered to stay on for a further month to help me through any difficulties that I may encounter, but – and I say this with my deepest respect and gratitude to him – I know the workings of this place like the back of my hand. I know the loyalty of its workforce – and those who aren't so loyal – and I can put my hand to anything from fettling a carding set to burling a piece of fabric.

"As you can appreciate, I have a lot of organising to see to at the moment – of one thing and another – so I'll leave it at that for now. But be assured, I will be here as the head of this mill now; and as its head, I will not waver in upholding both its reputation and the reputations of those who have given their unremitting loyalty to it as an institution, and to William himself. Thank you."

After the department heads had left, Jim took Sarah's hand, saying, "I admire your resolve, love. And as a partner, I have no doubt you'll succeed."

"Have you, Jim…? Well, I'm not so sure that I will."

"Now, are yer going to be able to cope, Amy?"

"Aye, course I am. You go get yerself ready."

"The caterers'll be here at seven, so be prepared! There's half a dozen stand pies in the pantry and all you have to do is cut 'em up – not like doorstops, mind – and supervise the setting of the tables. …D'yer hear me?"

"Oh get gone…I'll be all right."

And Jessie went and got ready.

Going upstairs, she met Paul coming down. His appearance took her by surprise. He was not dressed in black as at the funeral, but in a light-blue suit, pale-pink shirt and purple tie. Oh, but he certainly looked immaculate. His red-blond hair was still long – curling over his collar – and, considering it was a depressingly wet July day, he smiled broadly at her. "Well, Jess, here we go again."

"Aye, lad.…How yer fairin'?"

"I'm fine, Jess. Mother looks a picture." His face changed now as he said despondently, "Oh, Jess.…"

"Hey, no tears now." Jessie knew now how much he was suffering despite his attempt at an outward show of composure, so she pulled him close to her, saying gently, "Come on, let's straighten yer tie." But he continued crying. "Nay, lad, be strong for yer mam. She needs you now more than ever. After all, you're all she has now."

"But I miss him, Jess." She stroked his long, silky hair, saying, "Aye lad, he was a good dad to yer. I can understand you being...."

Paul drew himself back. "Not him! Mark! He should be here!"

Jessie placed her hands on his shoulders, and grimacing now, said, "What Mark said about you and your mam was unforgivable; and besides" – her manner softened – "nobody knows where he is."

Paul bit on his lower lip. "Somebody *must* do." He pointed at her. "And in this day and age there are ways and means of finding out such things."

"Now look! He's not here – and he won't be – so get over it! Now, out of me way and let me get changed."

Sarah looked around the sheer vastness of the church, remembering how terrified she was when first entering the building on her wedding day. Above the altar, suspended from one of the oak beams, hung a huge gold cross, inlaid with scarlet velvet and bearing the figure of Christ. The large stained glass windows were lit by spotlights from outside, and both they and the huge number of candles amassed on tall wrought iron holders, cast a myriad of assorted colours up into the vaulted ceiling and over those gathered, as if vying with the summer flowers laid out in front of the raised stage for everyone's attention. Here, the Hallé Orchestra, soloists, and the Leeds Festival Chorus, were now assembled. And every five seconds, the bells of Saint Paul's chimed mournfully.

Beside her sat her son and stepdaughter. Then came William's uncle James, and next to him sat Jessie who was flipping nervously through the order of service. Across the aisle, sat Edith Stockwell and her two sons, brother Philip and presumably other members of her late husband's family. The rest of the congregation consisted of Sarah's sister Emily with her husband Wilf and son Kevin; half-sister Mary, who looked as if she'd applied make-up with a trowel, and who had half-heartedly agreed to attend a non-Catholic service, together with Laura and Jack. Also, there were members of the town council and those of the Collingley Music Society; the entire workforce of the mill, and other mill owners and dignitaries. And not one seat was vacant.

"I feel uneasy, Mam," whispered Paul. "It's as if something

unpleasant is going to happen. I'm sure Mrs Stockwell can feel it as well: she keeps looking to the back of the church."

"It's just the occasion, love. I think we're all a bit..." Sarah's words were interrupted when suddenly torrential rain began to batter the roof, as if God had decided He was not pleased with the whole set-up. Several of the outside lights fused in sequence, causing many of the congregation to gasp in horror. And then the church door slammed shut. Paul looked at his mother. She grasped his hand, saying, "It's all right, love. It's nothing...just this evil weather."

But, unbeknown to those assembled, the door had been closed by Mark Crowther. He stood there, at the back of the church, gazing about him, trying to see who was present for his father's memorial service; but, naturally, it was like looking for the proverbial needle in a haystack. Moving to a darkened corner he concealed himself there – but still continued his visual search for the one he most wanted to see.

Then he was taken unawares when, unprecedented in a place of solemn prayer, a mounting round of applause greeted the orchestra's conductor, Sir John Barbirolli. And after acknowledging the audience's appreciation, he turned, raised his baton, and led the now standing congregation in Hubert Parry's Jerusalem with words by William Blake.

After a short sermon, readings of tributes and prayers, the time had arrived for the orchestra, soloists and chorus to commence the final section of Mahler's Second Symphony. The piece began with Wieder sehr breit, and for those who happened to read Gustav Mahler's words quoted in the order of service, the sentiments would live with them interminably: 'O believe you were not born in vain! Have not vainly lived and suffered!'

Mark Crowther knew nothing of these words. He was experiencing a mounting and frantic reaction brought about by the prolonged musical crescendo that had gradually welled up inside him.

He was physically drained. His emotions were in turmoil. He began to shake violently, his hands thrusting his head from side to side as the music built to its inevitable climax.

Suddenly, removing his hands from his face, he staggered to the tall, oak door, lifted the heavy, ringed latch, and fled into the night – his tears being lashed from his cheeks by the unremitting rain.

The will was to be read after the buffet meal. Those present would soon know what William Crowther intended to do with his wealth, possessions, and business.

"The caterers have done us proud, Jess."

Jessie smiled at Sarah. "Aye, and all the pies've gone an' all."

"What did you think of the service? Was it all right?"

"More than all right....My it were fair grand! William would have loved it."

Sarah hesitated before saying, "Have you seen Paul anywhere?"

"Aye, he's over yonder talking to Jane and Harry. Mind you, why William wanted Harry Carr to be here is beyond me."

"Well," said Sarah, "I suppose it's because he helped in doing that building work at the mill for him. But why he's been listed to attend the reading is a bit of a puzzle. Mind you, that goes for the Stockwells as well."

"I think we'll soon find out, lass; the solicitor's just arrived."

Sarah glanced at the doorway where Francis Parker now stood, casting his eyes around those gathered in the drawing-room of High Ridge House. He then caught sight of Sarah and approached her. "Mrs Crowther." He took her hand. "What a magnificent service! You certainly did your dear husband proud; and once again, may I express my, and my firm's, condolences for your loss."

Sarah nodded. "Things have been set up in the library in readiness," she said, "so whenever you want to get started we can go in."

"Well, the time's getting on, so if you can arrange for those involved to make their way there, then we'll proceed."

Chairs were arranged in two semicircular rows in front of the library table where Francis Parker was now seated, sipping at his pink gin. He pulled a black-edged file from his attaché case and placed it before him, adjusted his pince-nez and looked around momentarily before stating: "The document I have before me has been signed by two witnesses and legally stands." He took a further sip of his drink. "I would like to specify at the outset that the provisions avowed in the enclosed document were made by the said William Baines Crowther freely and in a perfect state of mind, as confirmed by those who attended to him during the treatment for his heart condition; and, as such, is lawfully binding." He now gave a slight cough.

"The usual and general wording of the will has been slightly changed for rescheduled precedence and clarity's sake, but that does not constitute a breach of its validity. Having so said, I will continue...."

'This is the last will and testament of William Baines Crowther of High Ridge House, Collingley, in the County of York, West Riding, made on this eighteenth day of July nineteen hundred and sixty-one, and I hereby revoke all former wills and testamentary dispositions made by me, and declare this to be my last will. I appoint Mr Francis Roland Parker, solicitor with Messrs Parker and Harrison of The Lodge, 16, Park Street, Collingley, to be the executor of my will.

'All bequests are subject to the payment of my just debts, funeral and testamentary expenses and all taxes and duties payable, and are to be free of tax liability.' The solicitor took a further drink before resuming: "I will now proceed to the provisions made by the testator."

'Provided they are still in service at High Ridge, I devise and bequeath the following: to my maid Annie, and chauffeur Max, I give one hundred and fifty, and five hundred pounds respectively.' A small squeak emanated from the back row. 'Should either – or both – not be in my household's employ when this is read, then these amounts will revert to the residue of my estate, and that proviso will also apply to any other similar bequests.

'I hereby bequeath one thousand pounds to Harry Frederick Carr, and a further three thousand pounds' – Francis Parker paused momentarily and took a further sip of his gin – 'to a dear and dedicated friend who has been with me since my marriage to my wife Sarah: Jessie Dicks.' Seated at her left-hand side, Jessie grasped Sarah's arm – and Sarah patted her friend's hand. Now Francis drained his glass and looked over the top of his glasses. Sarah turned and beckoned Annie forward. And when the girl had retreated with the solicitor's glass, he recommenced:

'The two paintings hanging in the hall, which my late wife Dorothy brought with her on our marriage, will be returned to Edith Miriam Stockwell, together with any other articles that pertain to the Stockwell family – which may be ascertained at a mutually convenient time to be arranged between Edith's elder son Alexander and my wife Sarah....' Edith Stockwell leapt to her feet and was about to speak when Alex forced her back into her seat. Now Annie reappeared and placed the glass of pink gin in front of Francis Parker, who then carried on: 'To my daughter Jane, I leave my late wife's jewellery, together with ten thousand pounds to be held in trust until her twenty-first birthday. Any interest accrued between now and when she reaches maturity, will be apportioned – as and when it is deemed to be necessary – by the trustees.' Francis Parker raised his eyes. "The trustees judiciously appointed by the aforementioned William Baines Crowther are myself, Mr Francis Roland Parker and Mrs Sarah Crowther."

Edith Stockwell was back on her feet, and this time she would not be silenced. "This is an outrage!" she bellowed. "I will not tolerate it! To have this woman running my own granddaughter's affairs cannot be allowed. As long as I still have the breath in my body to prevent it, I will!" Alex's intervention at his mother's outburst went unheeded as Edith went on: "And as for you, sir" – she pointed directly at the perplexed solicitor – "binding or not, I will do my utmost to see that this total travesty be rectified without delay. From what I can gather about this whole charade, is that I have deliberately been brought here under a falsehood, simply to be humiliated."

Francis Parker sat upright. "Madam, please be seated. This is not the time or place to be expressing your views in front of an audience, so kindly retake your seat and allow me to continue." And as Edith reluctantly sat, Sarah looked at Jessie and shook her head.

The solicitor began again: 'I now come to my son Mark who, as you all no doubt know, left the house at my insistence in the January of 1960. But, it is my intention to set up a further trust fund of ten thousand pounds until he attains the age of twenty-five, provided he returns to the house and makes his abject apologies to those he so blatantly wronged. Should this not be fulfilled to the satisfaction of those involved, the fund will once again revert to my estate on the day following his twenty-fifth birthday. Furthermore, a similar fund will be administered for my stepson, Paul Halliday, who....'

"Enough!" This came from Edith once more. "I will not stay in this house another minute longer and listen to this rant. Alexander, Joseph, we are going!" And as the three were escorted from the room by Max, Sarah turned to Paul now, saying, "Take no notice, love. I've always said she was off her rocker and that's just confirmed it."

The rest of the will was delivered in an air of calm. In it, William had confirmed that the ten per cent share in Providence mill bequeathed to his daughter by his late wife, and of which he was the trustee, would now be in the care of the previously named trustees until her coming of age. Also, the thirteen per cent share held in the business by his uncle James would remain, with the other eighty-seven per cent being inherited by Sarah, together with the residue, which included the house and its contents, the Rolls-Royce Silver Cloud, the three houses on Long Lane, all other investments, and residual monies held in insurance policies and current and savings accounts.

"Well, ladies and gentleman," said the solicitor, "I have kept you far too long and, though the hour is late, I do believe it to be appropriate to rejoin the other guests and partake of a drink or two...don't you?" He removed his spectacles, stood, and proceeded to the library door. But before exiting, he took Sarah aside and said quietly, "Maybe yourself and Jim would like to make an appointment to see me and discuss the options open to you regarding his share of the business? Now, Sarah, don't think of this as an ending." He took her hand now. "You have been through a lot and it may seem as if your world's collapsed about you. But I know – and I've seen – what you are capable of. You're a strong-willed woman, Sarah Crowther, and everyone knows that; and there's a fine future ahead for you, I'm sure. You have a loving family around you and many, many friends who will support you – including me – and if you ever need my advice, I'll always be there to help."

Sarah looked at this dear man and squeezed his hand. "Francis, I'm certain that I will need all the help I can get."

14

"I love him, Mam. I've never felt like this about any another man I've ever met."

Sarah looked directly at her stepdaughter and shook her head. "Sweetheart, some of the young men you've brought here have been charming and polite and of a good background, but – and I say this even though I love the young rogue – Harry Carr has none of those qualities."

"But you've said it yourself: you love him, so why shouldn't I?"

"Because you're mixing one kind of love with another."

"But surely there's only one kind?"

"Oh, believe me, darling, love has many faces....Anyhow, apart from him just being here on the odd occasion – and one in particular was very odd – how come all of a sudden you seem to be so attached to him?"

"Oh...well, I just came across him one day when I went out. And we've been seeing quite a bit of each other lately."

"Really...? Why on earth haven't you asked him over? After all, he knows all of us, so it wouldn't be like walking into a house full of strangers."

"I think he can be a bit shy."

Sarah slapped her hands on the desk and laughed. "What? Harry Carr, shy? You need your senses sorting out, love. If Harry is shy, then I'm Greta Garbo."

"Who?"

"Oh, it doesn't matter....Now look, if we are still going into Leeds to do some Christmas shopping, then go and get your coat on while I see if Max is ready."

Jane rose, saying, "I'll put my best one on. After all, we never know who we'll bump into, do we...?" And she went out with a smirk on her face.

Max dropped them at the corner of Boar Lane and Lower Briggate. "We'll get a taxi back, Max, since we don't really know how long we'll be."

"Very well, madam." The chauffeur got back in the car and drove off towards City Square....

Briggate went from Boar Lane to the Headrow, and Sarah and Jane made their way along it, looking at the shops and decorations in Queen's and Thornton's arcades that led off the main thoroughfare. Then they went into Lewis's department store on the Headrow where Sarah bought Jane a new pair of shoes and a beaded handbag, and Jane bought some cuff-links for Paul. Next, they crossed over the road to Lands Lane and eventually arrived at Schofield's Department Store. "I love this place," said Sarah. "I'm going to buy some Chanel – and probably other things as well, knowing me. Do you know love, I never believed when I was your age that I'd even be able to afford the tram fare to come to Leeds, let alone to buy anything."

"Well, you deserve it, Mam," said Jane; and after taking her stepmother's arm, they went in and explored....

Forty-five minutes later, they came out weighed down with bags. "I'm parched after that lot," said Sarah. "We should have stayed in the shop and had a coffee."

"Fiddlesticks. Wouldn't you fancy something say...a little stronger, eh? Go on, you would really, wouldn't you?"

Sarah stopped walking. "You're trying to lead me astray, young lady," she said. "But yes, I would. I wonder where we could go?"

"Let's try Whitelock's. I've heard that it's really old and quaint – and you get a lovely crowd of customers."

"But we've no idea where it is!"

"We can ask!" So they did. And they found it in a narrow alley just off Briggate.

"Well, what you heard about this place is certainly true," said Sarah. "Oh look! there's a seat there. Take the bags, love, and I'll get us some drinks. Orange juice?"

Jane nodded and went to their seats where she deposited their shopping by her feet. And then she scoured the place to see if Harry was in.

"There we are," said Sarah when she had been served. "Oh yes! I like this place. We must come here again when we're in Leeds."

Suddenly Jane jumped, almost toppling the glasses. "What on earth...?" said Sarah. And then it was that she spotted the young man standing before them. "Hello, Jane," he said. And Jane, looking down to her lap, said quietly, "Hello, Harry."

"Harry?" Sarah leaned over the table. "Harry Carr?"

He held out his hand. "Grand to see you, Sarah, after – what is it now? Eighteen months?" He shook Sarah's hand, saying, "Can I grab my drink and join you?"

"Well...er...yes. Yes, of course you can." And when Harry had retreated to the bar, Sarah turned to the sheepish Jane and said, "You planned this didn't you! You knew all along he'd be here."

"Don't be angry, Mam. You're not *really* angry, are you?"

"I'm bloody well...." And then a smile broke across her face. "No, I suppose not....He's changed though. Do you know, the last time I saw him was at the reading of your father's will....I wonder what he did with the money that William left him?"

"He has his own business now," said Jane.

"No!" Sarah turned to look the girl in the face.

"Well, it's a sort of partnership with another man."

"You seem to know more about him than I do, young lady. How long has this been going on?"

"Shush, Mam; he's coming back."

Harry placed his drink on the table and drew up a vacated chair. "Cheers, ladies."

After clinking glasses, Sarah said, "So, young man, what have you been getting up to since we saw you last?"

We saw you last, thought Harry. She knows quite well I've been seeing Jane. But nonetheless, he told her about investing his legacy in a small business, and that he and his mother had been given a council house shortly before the old flats were due to be pulled down. "She couldn't settle though," he said now. "And then about six months ago she became ill and died shortly afterwards."

"Oh, I'm sorry, lad," said Sarah. "So, are you living on your own?"

"Yep! Thankfully the council let me take on the rent after me mam died, but next year – what with the business doing well – I'm going to buy a little place. Still, being on your own *is* lonely." He glanced at Jane.

Sarah finished off her drink. "Let's have another, eh? After all, it's nearly Christmas, so why not? And thinking about that, why not come and spend it with us, Harry, instead of being on your own? Paul and Jess would love to see you again...and I'm sure this young lady would as well." She turned to look at her stepdaughter. "Wouldn't you, sweetheart?"

"Well...yes. Yes, I would. That's If Jessie could cope."

"Oh, she'll cope all right, love. So that's settled then. Now, let me go and get those drinks."

"I was utterly gob-struck!" said Sarah.

"And he's got a business you say...? Well at least he hasn't squandered the money....D'yer know, I never thought we'd see him again after he got it."

"Yes, a business, Jess – well a partnership essentially. And he says they've got a lot of work coming their way and he's planning to buy a house."

Paul leaned over the kitchen table. "Has he changed much, Mam?"

"Like you'd never believe. I wouldn't quite say he was excessively handsome, but he's turned out a good-looking lad. And he was smartly dressed – casually like, but very well turned-out."

"Did he mention me at all?"

"Oh, he did that. He said if it hadn't had been for you teaching him how to read and write and do arithmetic, he wouldn't be where he is today. Anyhow, taking the bull by the horns, I asked him to come to dinner tomorrow."

"What?" This was Jessie. "Oh, Sarah; that means I'll have to traipse out to the butcher and greengrocer again. I haven't enough in to feed an extra gob."

"Oh, don't get all worked up, Jess. Max can run you into town. Oh, and while I remember, Harry will be spending Christmas with us."

"Well, I can see you've got it all worked out, madam. So, I'd best get to it before the shops are shut. I think I'll pop over to Morley – they'll probably have a better selection....Oh, and by the way, Alex Stockwell phoned while you were out."

"What did he want?"

"He didn't say; but he'd like to come and see you as soon as possible. He's going to phone back."

"Well, if he can make it this evening, I'll see him and get it over with."

Paul got up from the kitchen table. "If that's the case, then I'll come with you and Max, Jess. Maybe we can stop off and have a drink in the Queen Hotel?"

"Why not? What's good for the goose...." Jessie gave a sideways glance at Sarah.

"Oh, go on you two." Sarah flapped her hand. "But only a soft drink for you, my lad!"

"Of course, Mam. Just a soft one." And he winked at Jessie.

Before they returned, Annie was showing Alex Stockwell into the library.

"Thanks for seeing me, Sarah. I sincerely hope it's not inconvenient."

"I wouldn't have asked you to come if it was. No, everybody's out – except Jane who's up in her room wrapping a gift for Paul. Please, have a seat."

"How is Jane these days? Is she coping?" said Alex as he sat.

"As well as we all are, Alex. She must miss both her parents and brother – especially at this time of year."

Alex averted his eyes as he said, "Mother told me you'd been to see her about Mark."

"Yes, I had an audience with her majesty."

Alex chuckled, whereby Sarah wondered if she dare broach the subject of Mark's whereabouts; but knowing Alex, he would have told her anyway without bothering what his mother thought about it, so she simply said, "Now, what can I do for you?"

Looking directly into Sarah's eyes, he said, "Well, on that night that, well...er...on the night of Mark's birthday, Joseph and I had a private chat with William about investing some money in our place. He told us he may consider it in a year or two, but, naturally, that can't happen now, so...."

"You're wondering if *I'm* prepared to do it?"

Alex nodded.

"The plain answer, Alex, is no. Granted the mill is at full capacity and the business is flourishing compared to some others in the area, but every penny is needed to keep us at the level we are – and for any future investment."

"So, you're thinking of expanding?"

"It all depends. We need to consider the possibility of introducing man-made fibres, and using only pure wool – which, as you might be aware, could involve new machinery for a start, and necessitate some restructuring. So, I'm afraid I must refuse your request....But why not try other sources? I hear that a company in Bradford has been buying shares in other family businesses which still leaves the owners with a controlling stake." She watched Alex's face redden. Then she said, "Naturally, Jane's ten per cent that Dorothy left her, can't be touched until she's twenty-one; and even then, it would be on her say so what she wanted to do with her shares. And, even though she will receive the money held in trust for her at the same time, she has confessed to me that she has plans for that. No, I think that place in Bradford would be just the answer?" She opened her desk drawer and took out a business card. "Here, that's their address – and who to contact."

"But…well, I just thought that maybe if you *would* consider it, it could pull our two businesses closer together – and our families."

"Oh, love, I think the prospect of bringing our families closer together disappeared years ago. No, I'm sorry, Alex, but you've had my final say on the matter."

And when Annie was showing Alex out, he thought, She knows! She knows already about our situation. But how?

It was Christmas Eve and High Ridge House was a place of light and glitter when Harry arrived.

"Well, I never thought I'd see the day: Harry scruffy Carr in a suit. D'yer remember when I washed you in Emily's sink."

"How can I forget it, Jessie? I've still got the bruises."

Jessie flapped her hand. "Rubbish! Anyhow come here and give us a hug.…Oh, by the way, you remember Annie, don't yer?"

"Yes, I do. Hello, Annie."

"Well, go on, lass; say summat instead of just gawpin'."

"Hello…Harry."

"She's one o' few words is our Annie," Jessie remarked. "Now, lad, Sarah's just popped to t'mill to have a drink with the staff – she'll be back afore long – and Jane's upstairs" – she nudged him – "having a bath. But Paul's in the library catching up on his school work if you want to go and see him. He deserves a bit of a break, and no doubt he'll be chuffed to see you. You know your way, don't you?"

Harry nodded, and went to the library where he found Paul with his head stuck in a book. "Working on Christmas Eve, you little bugger?" he said.

Paul looked up, and pushing himself out of his chair, said, "Harry! How are you?" He went and hugged him now. "My God you've altered – for the better I might add.…Fancy a bottle from my secret store?"

"Why not?" said Harry.

Paul went to unlock a cupboard; and, after prising off the caps on two bottles, passed Harry a beer. "Jane says you're doing well for yourself – and she's really taken a shine to you."

Harry swigged his drink. "She's a lovely girl, Paul. I'm very fond of her and, in fact, I've brought this with me for her." He placed the bottle on the desk and delved into his jacket pocket and produced a small box that he opened. "What do you think?"

"It's beautiful! She'll love it. Friendship ring is it?"

"No! It's an engagement ring. I'm going to ask Jane to marry me."

Paul's mouth fell open, but he couldn't speak.

"Well? Do you think it'll go down all right if I do?"

Regaining the use of his tongue now, Paul said, "She'll jump at the chance, Harry. I'm delighted! Fancy me having you as a brother-in-law – well almost." And he shook Harry's hand before saying, "Mind you, you know you'll have to get permission from my mother."

15

"I met him at Leeds University," said Harry; "when I was doing some work on their new block. He's just gained his Bachelor of Arts degree in – now let's get this right – Special Studies in Textile Management. And he told me he wouldn't mind getting some practical experience in a mill, so I said I'd have a word with you."

"Well, I can't see why not," said Sarah. "Do you still see him?"

"Aye. He goes to Whitelock's of an evening, and we often have a drink together…that's when Jane allows me out, of course."

Sarah smiled. "So how are you both settling in your new place? Keeping up with the mortgage, I hope?"

"No problems. And thanks again for helping with the deposit."

"Well, as long as you're happy. Now, about this friend of yours; I suggest you ask him if he'd like to come over for Sunday dinner and we can have a chat about him looking around the mill. You and Jane are still coming, aren't you?"

"Oh, you know how she looks forward to Jess's Yorkshire puds and onion gravy. Wild horses couldn't keep her away….Well, I'd best get going or that wife of mine'll be wondering where I've got to."

"Okay, love; but do let me know about the lad coming and I'll make sure Jess gets enough food in."

David Allen was decidedly mature for a degree student, but he was an amiable and darkly handsome young man. He had come up from Bristol to study at the university, and was keen to see the workings of a real woollen mill.

He and Sarah were seated in the library having drinks. "I thought it best we talk in here, love – out of the way of the others. So, you're all the way from Bristol? Do you have a family?"

"I live with my mother and father, Mrs Crowther; no brothers or sisters though, just me."

"My son's in a similar position…although in a way he inherited siblings through my second marriage….Do you intend to return home now that you've finished your course?"

"I will do initially since my mother's not very well. But I

235

wouldn't mind coming back here eventually and maybe put down new roots."

Sarah chuckled. "Well there's enough muck for rooting anything around here. But surely you wouldn't want to leave there to come to a dull and dingy place like this!"

"Why not? It's really strange, but I feel as if I belong here for some reason."

"Well, I know *I* do…and it's not such a bad old place for all its faults. Where are you staying in Leeds, by the way?"

"I have a flat in Headingley. It's small but it suits my needs, and there are some.…"

The telephone rang; and Sarah excused herself. "Sarah Crowther. Oh, hello, Bert.…Yes, quite…! No, it's not inconvenient…will about an hour do…? Okay, Bert, see you then…bye." She replaced the telephone receiver. "Sorry about that, love, but there's a slight problem at the mill – nothing serious. But, maybe we could kill two birds with one stone? How about you coming with me before dinner and we can have a look around. It's not busy Sundays – apart from when we have huge contracts to fulfil – so we could do that if you like?"

"That would suit me fine, Mrs Crowther. I'm really looking forward to it."

"Good! Oh, and by the way, please call me Sarah."

David smiled.

"Right," said Sarah, "Drink up and we'll be on our way.…"

The first place she took David to was where her life as a young piecener began. "I started in this very shed when I was fourteen: twenty-six years ago this very month. How the time flies, David." She turned and observed this young man, and in him she could see her own past. "Still, let's move on, eh?" she said.

Walking through the various departments, Sarah explained the various stages in the manufacture of cloth. "Although, I'm probably telling you things you know already," she said to her companion.

"I have learned a lot at university, Mrs Crowther – sorry…Sarah – but there's nothing like seeing somewhere first-hand. Learning is all very well but, in reality, to smell the atmosphere of a place and touch the machinery is truly invaluable."

Sarah came to a halt. "David, I recognise that you've finished university now and you may wish to return home soon, but what would you say if I said I'd be willing to take you on as a…a sort of apprentice? You could be involved in every stage of the manufacturing process from start to finish if you like, and I can leave it up to you when you'd want to start, depending on your family circumstances."

David's enthusiasm was immediate. "I would jump at the chance."

"Really? Well I must say I admire your confidence. Now, I have another suggestion. If you don't have to rush back to your digs tonight, why don't you stay over and get to know us a little better? After all, you may wish you hadn't accepted my proposal if you decide you don't like us."

"I doubt that very much. And yes, I'd like to stay over; I don't relish the prospect of going back to my little place tonight."

"Right! that's settled. Now, let's go and see what Bert wants me for and then we can get back and sample Jessie's cooking."

"Did you see Paul's eyes light up when he heard that David was staying the night."

"Jane, you read too much into things."

"Harry, it's two and a half years since Mark left, and Paul's still got feelings – and wants. He is a man after all."

"Look, love; I've known David on and off for a while now, and I can tell you he wouldn't be interested in Paul. *You* maybe, but certainly not Paul."

"You'd better keep an eye on things then, in case he makes a play for me." Jane giggled and playfully slapped her husband on the arm.

"Best be coming in you two," called Jessie from the kitchen doorway. "Dinner'll be out in fifteen minutes. Oh, and bring that rug in with you!"

"Come on, love; Sergeant Dicks is dishing out the orders again." Harry picked up the rug off the lawn and took it inside.

"You've both got time to freshen up before it comes out if you want," suggested Jessie. "Annie's already put out fresh towels in both bathrooms."

"Are you eating with us, Jess?" asked Harry.

"Not today, love. Me, Max and Annie'll have ours here in the kitchen." She turned to Annie now, saying, "Let's get the cutlery out, lass, and go and set the table."

After the meal, sated by Jessie's excellent cooking, they all retired to the drawing-room for coffee. Paul had readily planted himself on one of the settees next to David, with Jane and Harry on another. Sarah sat in a high-backed easy chair, next to the fireplace.

"So, David," said Paul. "Mam says you're considering coming up here to work at the mill. Do you think you will?"

"Oh, definitely...as soon as I know everything at home is ticking along all right – and my mother is in good health – then I'll be back."

"What about somewhere to live? There aren't many places around here available."

"Well, your mother says she might be able to pull a few strings. And if it comes to the crunch, she said I'd be welcome to stay here until something came about."

"Really? That would be a treat: to have another man in the house. I'm constantly in the presence of three women....There's Max of course, but he's usually out and about, and in the evenings spends most of his time in his quarters above the garage."

David sipped his coffee before saying, "I'm sure I'll be able to find a little place of my own."

Paul leaned back on the settee. "Would you like to go to a pub in town?"

"Pardon...?" said an uneasy David. "Well, not really. It would be rather rude of me to just disappear, don't you think?"

"Oh, Mam wouldn't mind."

"But you're not old enough to go into pubs."

"Believe me, I can get away with it. There's a pub called The Lantern that'll let anybody in."

"No, sorry. It's out of the question."

Paul got up now and proceeded out of the room through the double doors that led to the library. And his mother's eyes followed him.

In the meantime, Jessie entered from the hall and, much to David's relief, came and sat in the vacated seat. He thanked her for the meal – to which she flapped her hand – then he said, "How long have you known Sarah, Jessie?"

Jessie raised her head in thought. "Lord, love...it must be going on twenty-seven years now. Me and me mam moved in next door to her and her family in 1936. She were thirteen at the time – hot-headed at times, but nevertheless a grand lass."

David glanced over at his hostess. Indeed, she was grand. He'd only met her eight hours ago, but his attraction to this forty-year-

238

old woman was becoming stronger by the minute.

"Anyroad," Jessie continued, "after her first husband died – he was Paul's dad – and me mam died when Paul was ten, I moved in with 'em. Then, to cut a long story short, she married Mr Crowther who owned this house and the mill. Unfortunately, he died of a heart attack; and here we all are."

Sarah came over now and said, "Have you seen Paul, Jess? I saw him go into the library but he's not there now."

"Shall I go and see where he is, love?"

"Please, Jess."

Sarah now noticed the distant look on David's face and sat down beside him. "Are you all right, love?" she asked her guest. "You look troubled."

"No, not really."

"Don't feel embarrassed. If something's bothering you, then tell me."

David placed his coffee on a side table. "Mother is on my mind. I think it would be best if I return home tomorrow."

Sarah placed a hand on his arm. "Of course. I understand it must be a worry for you as mine is for Paul at the moment."

"He was trying to get me to go to some pub or other," said David casually, "but I didn't think it fair on you and the others."

"He can't go into pubs at his age....Oh, he can be a trial at times. Do you know, David, if his father was here now, he'd sort him out."

David looked sideways at this woman who had welcomed him into her home without question, thinking, She still thinks of Paul's father. And he wondered if, out of her two marriages, whether or not he was – and would remain – her only true love?

Jessie rushed in. "I've looked everywhere. I even knocked on t'closet door, but he weren't there. Then I went up to Max, but *he* hasn't seen him either."

"He's damned well gone out," said Sarah. She turned to David. "Did he say which pub?"

"Er...I think it was The Lantern that he mentioned."

"Oh, no! It's the most notorious in town. The dregs of society go in there." She beckoned to Harry. "Harry!"

When Harry came over she told him what she knew: "He must have walked there because Max hasn't seen him."

"Well, even *I* would be wary of going in that place on my own," said Harry. "Right, I'd best go and see if I can find him."

"I'll come with you if you like," said David. "We'll go in my car."

"Thanks, lad. Yes, I'd be grateful for that, I must admit."

David parked the car discreetly a short distance from the pub, and he and Harry went inside.

The decor was plush – but the customers certainly were not. And all eyes descended upon them as they approached the bar.

"Hello, sweetheart," said a painted woman, pressing herself close to David. "Up for some fun, lover? Cheap rates."

"No thanks."

"What about yer friend?" she said, turning to Harry.

"Me neither," said Harry.

"Bloody 'ell, yer're not another couple o' them there queers are yer?"

"No, but we're thinking of becoming ones." Harry pushed his way to the bar where he described Paul to the landlord and asked if he'd seen him.

"Aye," said the greasy host pointing at the bar. "That's his drink there. He went to the closet a while ago. Just out the back yard over yonder." And he pointed again.

Harry and David followed the landlord's direction and went outside. Apart from the dim light of a street lamp at the end of the alley, the place was in darkness.

Harry called out: "Paul! Paul! Are you out here?"

But there was silence.

Harry called Paul's name again. But still nothing....

Then, a faint groan was heard from further down the ginnel, and as their eyes became adjusted to the gloom, they spotted a body scrunched up against the wall.

"Oh, Jesus!" cried Harry. "Come on, David."

When they reached him, they found Paul covered in blood.

"Paul! Paul, can you hear me?" Harry yelled. And when the groan came again, he pulled Paul up to his chest and, taking a handkerchief out of his jacket pocket, carefully wiped his face. "You'll be okay, sunshine. We'll get you home now." He turned to David, saying, "Go and get the car started, lad. I'll manage him all right."

And as David ran ahead, Harry carried Paul out of the alley.

Back at High Ridge, Paul's wounds were cleaned and he was

tucked up in bed.

"We ought to have got the police, Harry," said Sarah.

"That wouldn't be a good idea under the circumstances – or a doctor come to that in case he suggested the same thing. He looks worse than he is though, and nothing seems to be broken as far as I can see. Just let him rest. He should be fine in a few days – apart from two massive shiners."

Sarah leaned on Harry's shoulder. "Thanks, love…and you David. I owe you two so much."

"Honestly, you owe us nothing, Sarah," said David. "Well… maybe a stiff drink?"

"I think we all need one, love. Come on, let's all go down." Sarah sighed now. "This son of mine certainly won't be going anywhere else tonight – or for the foreseeable future by the look of him."

"Will he be okay on his own?" said David.

Sarah offered up a smile. "Oh, he won't be on his own, love: I'll send the dog up to stay with him. After all, Ben is the only boy around who loves him now."

"And me," said Harry.

Sarah grasped Harry by the arms. "Of course, sweetheart. But you know precisely what I mean."

She inclined her head towards David now, and with a penetrating look, said, "And I'm sure you do as well, young man."

16

It was almost six months before David came back to Collingley, during which time his mother had sadly passed away.

He stayed at High Ridge for just a week, before Sarah was happy to tell him that the tenant who occupied her old house in Long Lane, had not renewed the lease and the place was now his. He was overjoyed at the news and now took up his position at the mill with an indebted vigour.

Paul had quickly recovered from the assault, and was enjoying his final year in the sixth form at Morley Grammar – and he'd been made a prefect. Sarah hoped that the beating he'd received had made him more aware of the dangers around him, and that he'd think twice in future before acting so recklessly. But knowing her son, she surmised that there was a distinct possibility of him taking further stupid risks.

It had snowed relentlessly during the night, and this morning the land around High Ridge was under a shroud. The heavily burdened sky held the prospect of more to come, but even on this inclement Friday, nothing would keep Jessie Dicks away from Collingley Market.

Every week, whatever the weather, she would meet up with Amy and do some shopping – and visit the Co-op café. But today she couldn't rely on public transport and would have to set off early and walk.

"Surely you're not going out in this lot?" said Sarah as she reached for the coffee-pot.

"I am, lass. Nothing less than Noah's flood would keep me away."

"But what if you get there and Amy doesn't turn up?"

"You're joking of course. Amy Broadbent not turn up for market day? She'd put on a pair of skis if she had to. No, she'll be there all right – if only to dish out the latest gossip. D'yer know, where that woman gets all her information from is beyond me: she's like a walking encyclopaedia of scandal."

Sarah smiled to herself before saying, "Well, you just be careful. Negotiating that track over to Long Lane is bad enough in fine weather let alone on a day like this."

Jessie buttered the toast. "So," she said, "what are you up to today, lass?"

"Well," said Sarah, "hopefully – if Max has managed to negotiate the roads over to Bradford to pick up the head of Anderson's – I'll be discussing some sort of business arrangement: he's eager to have a look at some of our new designs. Do you know, when he first wanted to see me, I honestly believed he was going to let me in in on the fact that they'd bought into Providence – but none of it of course. He still hasn't said anything about it, so whether or not they really are the company that was involved, he's keeping it under wraps."

"Well, be that as it may, I've got to say from seeing the samples, you've done a grand job, love; and if he doesn't like them he's off his rocker. Right! I'm going to get meself ready and get off before it starts snowing again. Good luck, love...hope it all goes well."

"Thanks, Jess. Now you take care over them fields – I'll be worried to death about you not getting there in one piece."

"You worry about the mill, lass: that's more important. See you later, then."

"Bye, Jess."

It took Jessie almost an hour to reach the Wesleyan Chapel at the far side of Town End, but thankfully the High Street was almost clear of snow – although the kerbs were piled high with the stuff. She looked up at the Town Hall clock, which was approaching ten and paused to draw in a breath. Not bad, she thought; just about spot on. And as she approached the Market Hall, she spotted Amy who was chatting away merrily to another woman; and as she neared them, Amy turned, saying, "Ah, yer made it, Jessie," and then looked back at the woman, saying, "Nice talking to yer, love. Ta-rah then. Ta-rah."

"Who was that, Amy?"

"No bloody idea....She just started talking as she was coming out the market. But good God! the stuff she's been telling me about would make yer 'air curl. Some women are right gossips, Jess. And they do talk a load of rubbish....So where'll we start first."

Jessie concealed her amusement as she said, "We'd best get to the butchers first before they sell out...."

When they had bought all the shopping they could carry, they planted their bags in the Co-op café and ordered tea and fatty cakes for two.

"Now, before I forget," said Amy; "I've something I want to talk to you about that might be serious." She tore at the fatty cake and rammed a piece in her mouth; and after washing it down with a gulp of tea, she went on: "It's about Harry."

"Harry who?"

"Your Harry of course. Your Jane's Harry!"

"Oh, aye. What about him?" asked Jessie.

Amy looked over the top of her glasses. "I were coming back from me sister's last night and it was starting to snow. Anyhow, I was just turning the corner into the Bottoms, and I spotted him in a taxi which were waiting at the traffic lights."

This woman's just like me mother used to be, thought Jessie: obsessed about looking into parked cars, but she said, "Aye, he said he were getting one into Leeds to see a client about some building work, so I can't see why you think that's serious as yer put it."

"I did when I saw who were with him."

"Who?"

"Laura Stockwell!"

Jessie put down her cup. "I think you need to go back to the optician, Amy, and get yourself a new pair o' specs."

"That's right, make fun o' me, Jessie Dicks, but I know what I saw and *who* I saw. It were her all right: as bold as brass. Cuddled up next to him, dressed to the nines, grinning like a Cheshire cat."

"You're mistaken, Amy. Why should Laura be taggin' along with Harry? They barely know each another."

Amy tapped a finger on the table. "She were after him at one time like a dog on heat."

"Good Lord, woman, that were years ago. They were both young. And in fact, I don't think they've met since."

"Well, they have now. By! that fatty cake were good...."

Jessie couldn't help but ponder over Amy's words as she was on her way home. She'd managed to get a Morley bus that stopped at the top of Bridge Street – it was only a short walk from there to High Ridge. But as she opened the kitchen door and kicked the snow off her boots on the bottom step, Annie raced to her, and taking some of the shopping, said, "I'm glad you're back, Jessie. There's murder and mayhem going on 'ere."

Jessie's heart sank. And after bringing in the remainder of the bags and depositing them on the kitchen table, she took off her coat and looked at Annie. "What is it?"

The girl wrung her hands. "Jane came while you were out. Harry's not been home all night and she's frantic wi' worry, and the missis is at the mill and I didn't know what to do....Anyhow, I made her some strong tea and she went to the drawing-room."

"Right," said Jessie, "I'll go and see her...."

When Jessie entered the room, Jane was seated by the fire; and when she turned around and saw Jessie standing there, she sprang to her feet and rushed at her in floods of tears.

"Shush, love; shush now. Tell your Jess what's wrong. Come on, sweetheart, it can't be all that bad." But in her heart of hearts she knew it was – and that Amy was right after all.

Sarah was delighted that Anderson's had ordered the whole of the new designs of woollen cloth and that they were going to market them under her own name – and, she would be reaping a share of the profits. It had also given her ideas of setting up her own tailoring business on the premises, but that would mean building a whole new department. And she knew exactly who could carry out the work: Harry Carr! But her elation at the prospect suddenly collapsed when she arrived home and was confronted by Jessie: "Harry's run off with your Laura."

"Oh, stop trying to rile me, Jess. Sometimes I wonder if you do it on purpose."

"Far from it. Amy saw them canoodling in a taxi."

"Oh, Jess! you know what Amy's like. I would take everything she says with a pinch of salt."

"Well this time it looks as if yer'll have to take it with a full sack. Harry never went home last night and Jane's here, crying her eyes out...she's upstairs now trying to get some sleep after being up all night waiting for him."

Sarah began to pace the room. Back and forth she went until she stopped in front of Jessie and said, "I'll phone Mary and see if she knows anything." And when she had done, she turned to Jessie, saying, "Laura packed her bags and left her mother a note saying she was going to start afresh somewhere else. She never said who with though."

"That's it then," said Jessie. "They've bloody gone off together."

"Well, he kept it damned quiet. He never showed any signs of what he was up to. By hell! Jess, what in heaven's name are we going to do now?"

"Tell Jane."

Sarah's hands flew up in the air. "But how?" She adjusted her dress now. "How can I tell her that her husband's run off with my niece?" She wagged a finger at Jessie now, saying, "She'll blame it on our entire family, you know."

"Why should she? After all, Laura isn't *really* your niece. She's more like...oh, sort of a half-niece if there is such a thing?"

Sarah put a hand to her forehead. "I can't see that will make any difference, Jess....Oh, fetch me a brandy will you, love, before I go up and see her...."

Ten minutes later, Sarah knocked on Jane's old bedroom door and slowly entered. Her stepdaughter was curled up into a bundle on the eiderdown. She looked up saying, "Oh, Sarah, what's happened to him?" She sat bolt upright. "Should we call the hospitals and see if he's been hurt somewhere?" And as the tears flooded down Jane's pale cheeks, Sarah went over and comforted her, saying, "That's not necessary, love."

Jane pushed her away. "What do you mean? Tell me what you mean!"

And after Sarah related everything that Jessie had told her, Jane's tears were replaced by a flush of passion. "Laura! Laura Stockwell? But she's twenty-nine...and a married woman. You're lying! Why would he want to run off with her of all people – and where've they gone?"

"I don't know, love; I really don't know."

Jane leapt from the bed. "I'll go and ask your sister – she'll know. And when I find that bitch of a daughter of hers, I'll kill her with my bare hands!"

Sarah went to Jane now and rested her hands on the young woman's shoulders. "I called Mary, and she doesn't know any more than *we* do."

"I don't believe you. You're all in on it." Her eyes appeared to pulsate with anger. "Harry would never have left me for her if you hadn't persuaded him. You never wanted Laura to marry my uncle in the first place, so this is your way of getting what you want: by pairing her off with my...my husband." And the tears began again.

"But love, that's just not true. I would never...."

"Get your hands off me! I only wish you hadn't married my father and he was here now." Wiping her eyes, she inhaled deeply, and throwing back her shoulders, said, "I'm going home. And then – if your lousy rotten sister can't tell me where they are – I'll go and stay with my grandmother." She ran from the room and slammed the door behind her.

Sarah flopped back on the bed; and holding her head in her hands, cried out loudly: "Oh William! William! Why in God's name did you have to leave me?"

17

A heat wave breezed into Collingley in mid-July. It had been five long months since Harry had disappeared, and no word had reached them as to his and Laura's whereabouts. Jane had gone to live with her grandmother, leaving the small house that Sarah had loaned them the deposit for – and of which Harry was the sole mortgager – now in the process of being repossessed by the bank. Sarah had considered keeping up the payments, but she needed every penny to strengthen the business. And why should she help Harry when he had jeopardised both his chance of a home and that of a stable marriage? One redeeming thing though, was that his business partner was able to carry on in Harry's absence, convinced that he'd soon be back. Another sad departure had been that of David, who had returned to Bristol at the end of April on an open-ended leave. His future plans were uncertain: it all depended on the health of his father.

One particular morning, as Jessie was clearing away the breakfast dishes, Sarah came into the kitchen. "Where's Annie, Jess?"

"Don't you remember, lass? You gave her a couple of weeks off to visit her parents in Scarborough."

"Oh, yes; it completely slipped my mind. Well, she's certainly got the weather for it."

Jessie appreciated that the incident with Harry, and Jane's leaving under a cloud, had affected Sarah more than she'd admit, and that she could do with a holiday as well, instead of spending so much time at the damned mill.

Sarah picked up a tea-towel and began to dry the dishes that Jessie had washed, the while staring blankly out of the window. Then suddenly she said, "I miss the old house, Jess – especially at this time of year. Do you remember how we'd sit at the open door on summer evenings and watch Paul racing in and out of the tall grasses on the other side of the lane? And how he kept disappearing, and all we could hear was him whistling from different directions to try and fool us?

"Then, when the light began to fade, we'd all go back indoors and watch the moths come in and hover around the gas mantles. It's those little, simple things that I miss most of all."

"Ah, but just look what we have here, lass. Surely it's better than what we had to put up with in that poky hole....I only wish that coming here could have happened earlier when Paul was younger." But now, after handing Sarah a wet plate, she too looked out across the fields to Long Lane, thinking, She's right though: the three of us were happy there....

After Sarah had left for the mill, Jessie retired to the back garden and began working on her crochet. The day was hot without a cloud in the sky, and it reminded her of her childhood when every day seemed to be just like this. Then, the sun was so strong it used to melt the tar between the setts in the street, and even buckle the railway lines. In the distance, she could hear the tinkling of the brook as it trickled over shiny stones; and close by, the sound of chirruping birds. There was a calm stillness over the land and she hoped for all their sakes that it would last....

It did until Paul came bounding out of the kitchen yelling at the top of his voice: "Jess! Jessie! David's here!"

Jessie threw down her work. "Oh, hell, I do wish you'd give me some warning before scaring the life out of me. Look! I've made a mess of me crocheting now."

"You'll sort it out, Jess. As I was saying, David's just pulling up in the drive. I'll go and bring him out." And Paul raced off, shortly to return with their surprise visitor who was attired in a blue, open-necked shirt and sharply-creased, white cotton trousers.

Jessie was on her feet as he approached her. "Eeh, just look at you!" Her arms were outstretched. "Come and give us a hug. Goodness you're as brown as a nut – and as handsome as ever!"

"Oh, don't, Jess; you'll have me blushing." And he embraced her affectionately.

"Paul, go and get him a chair from the kitchen, that's a good lad. ...So what brings you here? I wish I'd known yer were comin' – I could have made you something special."

"It was a spur of the moment thing: I just got a few things together, threw them in the car, and came. I haven't even been to the house yet."

"Well, it's in good fettle; I've seen to that."

"Thanks, Jess."

Jessie flapped her hand. "It were nothing, lad; just a bit o' dustin' now an' again....So how's yer dad fairing?"

"Oh, he seems to have gone downhill since Mum died. But, he insisted I come back and get on with things here."

"Aay, bless him...."

Paul returned with a chair and placed it on the lawn. "Right," said Jessie, "you two have a chat while I go and fetch us a jug o' summat."

When she'd gone, Paul sprawled on the grass in front of the visitor who was now seated. "Well," David said, "I don't know about me being handsome, just look at *you*! How old are you now, Paul?"

"Eighteen. I'm waiting for the results of my 'A' Levels; although I do spend a lot of time at the mill with Mam – she never stops!"

"Are you going to apply for university?"

"Oh, no. I was born in the mill, David, and that's where I'll probably die....And to be honest with you, I'm sick of schooling; I want to concentrate on the business."

"You're staying out of trouble, I hope?"

Paul flushed and let out a protracted: "Yes...."

David grinned. Then he said, "So, tell me, how's everything else?"

"Well, the house is a bit empty at the moment. Max is still here, but Annie's gone to Scarborough, and Jane never visits any longer since she and Harry...."

Paul was interrupted as Jessie returned with a tray perched on a small table. "There! Something refreshing. Now" – she turned to David – "have some orangeade and then bring in your bags and you can get settled in your room and freshen up."

"But I'll be going to my place."

"No you won't, my lad! You'll stay here for tonight." She flopped into her garden chair. "Well this is a rare treat: having company for a change." She leaned forward and poured out three glasses of home-made juice.

"Paul was saying how empty the place is now," David remarked.

"It is that, lad. Oh, some things have happened since you were here last, I can tell you – mainly about Jane and Harry." And Jessie related the story.

But David did not show an iota of surprise. Then he said, "I know all about it, Jess." Jessie was rocked by this knowledge. How could he know? David went on to explain: "About two hours ago, I was driving through Wakefield on my way here, and spotted Harry coming out of a newsagent's – I had to stop because he looked so old and down in the dumps. Anyhow, I got out, locked the car, and ran after him down the street. He didn't recognise me at first, but then it dawned on him who I was, and he threw his arms about me like a long-lost brother.

"He was almost in tears, so I persuaded him to come to a café and have a coffee. And there he told me what had happened between him and Jane – and Laura, who had gone back to her mother's this very morning."

Jessie was on the edge of her seat. "No!" she gasped. David nodded, saying, "Apparently, they were living in a small, rented house and it was too…well, spartan for Laura's taste. And, not just that, but the relationship had turned sour a couple of months after they got together. He was in a bit of a state, Jess, I can tell you.

"Anyhow, he wrote down the address of the place and a phone number and said he'd be glad to see me whenever I could get over. I did tell him I was coming here, but it didn't appear to upset him – in fact, he smiled for the first time since I'd caught sight of him. And he sends his love to everyone."

"Well, I never! And are you going to get in touch with him, love?"

"I don't know, Jess. What do you think?"

"Do it, lad. Go back and see him right now – well, when yer're up to it. And, if I can be so bold as to suggest, take Paul with you. Harry's always had a soft spot for Paul since they were kids." She turned to Paul. "What do you say, lad?"

Paul did not hesitate in saying: "Drink up, David, let's be off… I'll go and get changed."

As Paul raced off, David said, "Do you think it's a wise thing for us to be doing this, Jess?"

"Course it is! If there's any chance of getting Jane and Harry back together, then Paul's the one to do it. Now, take your bags upstairs, have a wash, phone him, and then get off."

The two lads had some difficulty in finding the place. But eventually they did, and Harry was at the door to greet them.

"Aay, Paul, I'm glad to see you. Come in. Come in both of you."

The house was small and dark. But, apart from newspapers scattered about on the settee, it was tidy and certainly appeared clean enough. They sat down, whence Harry said, "I'm having a bottle of beer. Will you join me?"

Paul nodded whilst David said, "Only one though: I'm driving."

As Harry handed them the beers, Paul said, "Well, Harry, you've really got yourself into a right pickle this time."

Harry smiled, saying, "You sound just like Jessie, Paul; but you're right: it's turned out a bit of a mess. How is she – and Sarah of course?"

"As well as can be expected."

"And...Jane?"

"Back with her grandmother. God help her!" Paul sat forward now. "Why did you do it, Harry? How could you leave Jane for Laura Stockwell of all people? I know she's my cousin and I am very fond of her, but dear God she's an old tart in comparison to Jane."

Harry shrugged his shoulders. "I don't know. It just seemed to be right at the time. But thinking back, I must have been mad to do it."

"You can bloody well say that again!"

David was astounded at the way Paul was talking. I don't know about him being eighteen, he thought; he's behaving older than his years would suggest. And then it suddenly occurred to him that this shrewd young man could possibly have a trick or two up his sleeve.

"Could I have another please, Harry?" And Paul handed him the empty bottle.

As Harry was fetching another beer, David said in a whisper, "Don't drink too much, Paul."

"Just another...that'll be enough for my purposes."

When Harry returned, Paul said bluntly, "Do you still love Jane?"

Harry hesitated – more out of embarrassment than indecision. Then he said, "More than ever. I only wish I could...well...do something to get her back....But that won't happen after what I've put her through."

"Bollocks!" The expletive astounded the other two males. But Paul carried on: "I know Jane all too well and she'll be reasonable enough about things. And besides, I can guess she's regretting how she behaved towards Mam when she found out about you and Laura. But I still intend to tear her off a strip when I see her."

"And are you...going to see her?" Harry asked.

"I am – whether the Stockwells like it or not. Believe me, she'll see me all right even if I have to break the bloody doors down to get in. Just leave it to me. Now, David, if you don't mind driving me over to the house and waiting for me, I'll go and see her right now." He downed the beer.

"But...."

"Look, will you take me or not?"

"Do I have a choice?"

"No. Come on; let's get going before the drink wears off." Paul stood and went to Harry and hugged him. "I'll do my best, Harry...if that's what you really want?"

"Yes. Paul. That's what I want."

"Right, my trusted chauffeur" – Paul bent down and grasped David's knees – "let's be off."

18

The nights had drawn in now. Brittle autumn leaves were whirling around High Ridge, and the low sky was leaden and swollen with rain clouds; it was a scene of perpetual gloom. But not so for the eighteen-year-old Paul Halliday, whose blithe disposition lightened the darkest of days and lifted the spirits of all those who encountered him. He had not only celebrated his exceptional exam results some months earlier, but was also jubilant at the outcome of his visit to the Stockwell house in July.

On that occasion, the door had been opened to him by an elderly lady who informed him that Alex and Joe were at the mill, and Edith had gone on a shopping trip to Leeds and would be attending a matinée at the Grand Theatre. But Miss Jane was in and she'd check if it was convenient for her to see him. He was then shown into the drawing-room – which was decidedly cold considering the beautiful weather – and seated himself on the settee.

Presently the door opened, and Jane walked in. She greeted him warmly. "Paul, it's good to see you. I've missed you terribly."

"And I you."

She moved awkwardly across the room and seated herself beside him, saying, "You took a chance coming here, didn't you?"

"A big one. But I've had a few drinks, which helped."

She smiled now. But her mood changed abruptly when Paul told her he'd just come from seeing Harry. She was on her feet and walking to the door as Paul said, "He's desperate, Jane; in a right state....Laura's left him."

She turned about. "I can't say I sympathise with either of them."

Paul went to her now, his face showing tinges of annoyance. "I can't blame you for that," he said, "but I can for upsetting my mother by holding her responsible for the situation."

She bowed her head now, saying, "I didn't know what I was saying or doing, Paul; and believe me, I've suffered untold guilt about what I said ever since."

"Then don't you think you should go and apologise?"

She looked at him, her eyes in pain. "She'd never see me.... Would she?"

Paul took her by the arms. "You know full well she would. Now, I'm going to make a suggestion and I won't take no for an answer. David's outside in the car and I want you to go and do whatever women do with themselves to go out, and then come back with us to see Mam."

"I couldn't! I just couldn't."

Paul shook her gently. "You can, Jane. You're not a child any more. Now, go and get ready and come back home."

The tears welled in her eyes and Paul pulled her close to him. "You are coming, aren't you? I won't forgive you if you don't."

She raised her head and, wiping away her tears, nodded....

That was four months ago now, and with his mother's help, both Jane and Harry had been reconciled and were back living at High Ridge. Paul closed the ledger he was working on and smiled with satisfaction. But his happiness was not to last for long.

Mary Wilson scowled at her wayward daughter who was sitting in front of the fire. "How could you have brought such shame on the family, Laura? First you marry a Stockwell because you had to, and then you run off with a common labourer who you dumped and is now back with his wife living it up at High Ridge. And look, here you are, back with us in total disgrace."

"Mother! Will you never stop going on about it? Anyhow, it was you who wanted me to marry a Stockwell in the first place just to promote your standing in the town."

"That is just not true! Well, I'll tell you this: there'll be no divorce – the church wouldn't allow it."

Laura got out of her seat and went to the bedroom stairs. "And where do you think you're going now?" said her mother.

"I'm going to get ready and visit Aunt Emily. After all, you're certainly not prepared to let yourself be seen in that neighbourhood just in case your reputation suffers – she does have cancer you know!"

"Well, I see that Sarah – her full sister – doesn't appear to have made much effort to go and see her from what I've heard."

"Aunt Sarah's got a business to run, but I don't doubt that she's been as often as she can. And at least she's not too proud to be seen in the area like you are." With this, Laura stormed off upstairs....

Meanwhile, back at High Ridge, Jessie and Annie were busy in the kitchen. "You know how to cream butter and sugar together don't you, Annie? Make sure it's pale and fluffy before any of the eggs are added. Now while you do that, I'll go and get the fruit from the pantry – it's had a good week's soak in dark rum, so it should be nice and plump."

Annie smiled and began to stir the contents of the bowl.

"Just smell this, Annie," said Jessie on her return, thrusting the bowl under Annie's nose. "By! it fair knocks yer 'ead off....You're doing a grand job with the creaming, lass. Keep at it!"

"Hello, you two." Paul entered the kitchen. "Do I smell booze?"

"Aye," said Jessie, "but you're not getting any."

"I haven't time, Jess. I'm going to give Harry a hand doing a bit of work on the house next door to David's now that the tenant's left – and good riddance. He was a right old bugger."

"Hey! Have some respect for your elders....Still, I've got to agree with yer."

Paul ran around the large, kitchen table and, putting his arms around Jessie's broad waist, squeezed her tightly. She responded by slapping his hand with a wooden spoon. "Look, you rascal, Harry's outside polishing his car, so when he's finished, get yerself gone."

Shortly, Harry entered through the back door "You ready, Paul?"

"Aye, he is," said Jessie. "Now get him out of here before I lather him good and proper."

"Promises, promises," said Paul as he and Harry went out to the car.

"Jessie," said Annie. "Weren't you going to tell Paul about Emily being taken into hospital?"

"Oh damn, blast, and set fire to it....Paul...! Oh, he's gone now; I'll mention it when they get back...."

As Harry proceeded along Ridge Road on their way to Long Lane, Paul said, "So, how are things with you and Jane?"

"Oh, not too bad, Paul. We've both had to adjust since...well, since it all happened; but I think she's forgiven me – and it's all down to you and Sarah. But...." He hesitated; and didn't speak further until Paul pressed him. And then slowly he said, "She's gone off...yer know...."

"What? Suet pudding?"

"Paul! This is no joke."

Through laughter now, Paul said, "Sex!" He patted his friend's knee. "Give it time, love. She'll come around. Anyway, how's the house hunting going?"

"Oh, it looks as if we'll have to rent somewhere for now. I still owe your mother for the deposit on the *last* one."

"Well, when this place we're going to is done up, I've no doubt mother will offer it to you and...." His words were promptly abandoned as they approached the junction of Top Road and Commercial Street, and there waiting at the bus stop he caught sight of Laura. "Oh, Jesus!"

"What? What is it, Paul?"

"It's Laura. There" – he pointed – "at the bus stop. Keep going Harry before she sees us."

But Paul's words were ignored as Harry pulled across the road and drew the car to a halt in front of Laura Stockwell. He rolled down the window. "Hello, Laura."

"Hello, Harry." Then Laura lowered her head to see into the car. "Hello, Paul. You all right? And Aunt Sarah?"

"Er...yes. Yes, we're fine....So, where're you toddling off to?"

"I'm going to see Aunt Em. She's not so well I understand?"

"No, she's not. I think Mam was going to see her today."

"Oh, well, I'll probably see her as well when I get there – if this bus hurries up." She shivered now.

"Get in. We'll give you a lift." This was Harry; and Paul thought, He's at it again. I wish he really would stop.

"If it's not out of your way?" said Laura.

"Course not." Harry opened the back door; and after Laura was settled, he reversed, turned into Commercial Street, and proceeded on their way to Emily's house....

When they arrived in St Mary's Road, Harry parked the car, and Paul and his cousin got out and walked along the landing to the front door. But after a few minutes when they couldn't get a reply, they returned to the car – only to spot Sarah, Wilf and Kevin coming round the corner. And as they approached, Kevin ran passed his cousins without saying a word. Wilf stopped though, saying, "Hello, Paul; Laura. I'd best go see to Kev." And he sped off.

Paul looked questioningly at his mother. "You can't have heard then, love," she said. "Your Aunt Em was rushed into hospital last night. We've just got back....I'm afraid she...died two hours ago."

Paul stared at his mother in shock, while Laura, choking on her tears, threw herself into her aunt's now open arms.

19

None of them had enjoyed Christmas. How could they after Emily had not been there to share it with them? Sarah took her younger sister's death the worst of all of them and had castigated herself for not visiting Em more often. Even the onset of spring had not lightened her heart, but she still had to attend to her immediate family and the running of the mill. Also, her heart had been saddened further to see David leave as well, having had to go home to see his father who was ailing. And he didn't know how long he'd be – or indeed whether he would return or not. He'd instructed Sarah that it might be best to re-let his home because of the uncertainty of his situation.

Now, on this Monday morning at the end of March, she strode across the polished library floor and threw open the french windows. There before her, lingered the bustling, black-faced West Riding town that she had been born and brought up in. The battalion of mills, whose chimneys pierced the vastness of a blue, spring sky, were belching out smoke that would soon settle into wispy trails when the boilers were fully fired up. And the sight of them prompted her to recall when she gave birth to her son on a piece of hessian, draped over a basket of bobbins recently doffed from the mule, nineteen years ago this very day.

It had become the custom during the four years since William's death, after taking a light breakfast with the family, for Sarah to retrieve the letters from the hall table and retire to the seclusion of the library to go through her correspondence. Now, seated behind her desk, she slipped on her reading glasses and sliced open the envelopes – praying that on today of all days there would be little to have to deal with in depth. Taking up her gold-nibbed Sheaffer pen from its silver and crystal stand, she perused the papers with the alacrity of a woman intent on seeing the back of them as quickly as possible so that she could give all her attention to the arrangements for Paul's birthday.

There was little of importance to cause her concern, so she lay them in a tray, with a note for Jane of any relevant detail that may need to be sorted out. It did irk her at times that she had been landed with this responsibility of running the business, for after all she had married William for love and had not given a thought as to what her role would be other than that of a devoted wife. Nonetheless, she had undertaken these duties with the assiduity of a woman determined to prove to those misguided critics who thought her incapable of coping with the undertaking, that they were wrong.

Sarah had been raised to believe that nothing was impossible if you set your mind to it, worked hard, and never gave in to others who doubted your abilities. And yes, it *was* the years of circumstantial drudgery before her marriage, that had instilled in her a self-reliance that could outpace both the mental and physical attributes of any injudicious party who considered her unworthy of William's expectations of her.

She now opened the shallow drawer of her desk, withdrew her diary, and began to scan the day's entries. It was when she reached the final one that she slapped the diary down on the blotter and said aloud, "Damn! I'd forgotten that." The entry that had slipped her mind was regarding a new tenant taking over David's residence this evening when preparations for Paul's party would be in full swing.

At this point, her son came in. "I'll be off now, Mam. I've a busy day ahead of me at the mill taking into account that *it is my birthday!* I think I should be back about six-thirty, though."

"Ah!" said Sarah. "I might just have another little job for you. There's a new tenant taking over David's place today. He should be there by seven; so will you pop over, love, and show him around."

Paul assumed a resentful pose. But smiling now, he said, "Course, Mam. What's his name?"

Sarah flicked through her papers. "Ah, here it is...Steven... Steven Clark. He's an architect – or something of the sort. Only twenty-three, so you should get on famously with him. Oh, apparently, he's looking for someone to see to his books. There might be a little job going for you there, eh?"

Paul smiled at his mother. "Oh, you do work me so, Mam."

And Sarah smiled back, saying, "Go on with you, you rascal. And ask Jess to come in on your way out."

"Love you, Mam."

"Aye....Now on your way before I give you the sack." And when he had left the library, Sarah thought, He has no idea how much I love *him*. And though he didn't resemble his father one bit – apart from his head for figures – she could see in him her own mother: in looks, and the way he had managed to handle life after losing a loved one.

"Yes, love?" Jessie came in.

"Does he suspect anything?" Sarah said in a whisper.

And when Jessie approached the desk and placed her hands upon it, she leaned forward saying, "Not a thing."

Sarah rested her back against the chair. "Do you think I'm doing right in having a party for him?"

"Course you are. After all, it is his last one as a…teenager. That's what they call 'em these days, isn't it?"

Sarah smiled broadly. "Aye, that's it, Jess. Now, there's something I want to run by you to see what you think."

"Fire away, lass."

"Well, since Emily died, Laura has gone into an abject depression. Em doted on her when she was little, and I hate to think of her living in that house moping away, being at her mother's beck and call all day long, so…well, I was thinking about giving her a job here – only part-time though. Well? What do you think?"

"I…I don't know *what* to think."

"You must have some opinion, Jess."

"Well, it seems to me you'll be rubbing Jane's face in it after what happened with Harry."

"Look, his business is flourishing; he's paid me back what I loaned him; they have their own place in Park Street now; and Laura would only be here when they're not. And besides, you know for a fact that nobody will hold me to ransom when I make up my mind."

Jessie knew that all right, but went on to say, "So, what would she do?"

Sarah smiled. She had won Jess over. "Well, we no longer employ a gardener and the grounds are in a bit of a state. Laura loves flowers and pottering." When Jessie appeared to show no objection, Sarah said, "That's settled then. Now back to more pressing matters. Is everything in order for tonight?"

Jessie arched her back. "Yes! It is." Then leaning over the desk once more, said, "Amy's made a grand job of the cake…it's beautiful. She's getting on with cleaning the bedrooms now everyone's left.…Mind you, Jane and Harry seem to spend more time here than in their own place. They've had it over a month."

Ignoring Jessie's retrospective dig at their previous conversation, Sarah went on: "I did consider getting the caterers to make the cake, but I didn't want to put Amy's nose out of joint."

A knock came to the door and Amy entered. "Oh, excuse me, but...."

"Come in, Amy. What can I do for you? Jessie says you made a grand job of the cake."

Amy flushed. "I did me best, love. It's hidden out o' t'way in t'pantry."

"Look, why doesn't Jess get you a cuppa before you carry on with the bedrooms?"

"Oh, no thanks, love; I just came in to give you this to pass on to young Paul." She thrust a hand into her apron pocket and pulled out a small, wrapped parcel. "It's nothing much, but I hope he likes it." And a nervous liquidity filled her eyes.

Sarah reached out and took the gift. "This is most generous of you, Amy. But why not give it to him yourself tonight?"

"Me? But I didn't really expect to be...."

Sarah took hold of the woman's hand. "You didn't think that you weren't invited, did you?"

"Well...I...I didn't think you'd...."

"Amy Broadbent, you'll be here – that's if you're not doing anything else, of course?"

"Oh...no...no, I'm not. Thank you, ma'am...Sarah. Eeh! I'll right look forward to that, I will....Aye, I'll really look forward to that."

"Right, you crack on with your work, Amy, and I'll expect you about seven."

Amy beamed with delight and raced from the room.

"Bless her, said Sarah. "She's a good soul."

"Aye, and dizzy with it."

Sarah cuffed Jessie on her arm. "I know you don't mean that, Jessie Dicks. Now, let's carry on from where we left off." And Jessie sat at the desk.

"Right, the caterers are due at six, aren't they?"

"They are, love....But won't Paul be here, and wonder what's going on?"

"Ah, Jess, it couldn't have worked out better. I'd forgotten there's a new tenant coming into our old place – fortunately round about seven o'clock – and I've asked Paul to show the young man

261

around and to see if it's acceptable to him. Mind you, it ought to be after the money I've put into it. So, that should delay Paul until at least seven-thirty I should say."

"Young fella is he? This new tenant?"

"Twenty-three I'm led to believe. And by all accounts he's quite a looker."

"Really? Single is he?"

Sarah leaned back in her chair, and waving her pen at Jessie, said, "Don't you be getting any ideas, young miss."

"Ha! I wish."

"Oh, I know you've always had an eye for the lads, Jessie Dicks. I often remember you in the mill chasing all and sundry."

"Aye, but it didn't bloody get me anywhere." She lowered her head now and feigned disappointment.

But Sarah could hear the chuckles. "Oh, be off with you, you minx. We've both got lots to do before tonight."

"Aye, we have, lass....Let me know if you want any errands running. I'll get Amy to do 'em."

Sarah shook her head and smiled.

Paul had become frustrated recently. He couldn't cope with dealing with this-and-that without having some sort of sexual encounter to quench his unshackled desires. Okay, he'd experienced sex with Mark, but Mark had been gone for five years now and he desperately wanted a male body to cuddle up to. Ever since he was a young boy he had yearned for a man in his life. Even being taken on trips to Blackpool when he was about seven or eight, he had wanted the young men selling ice-cream and hot dogs to make love to him. But, of course, it hadn't happened....

Max picked Paul up from the mill and drove him to the house on Long Lane.

"I don't know how long I'll be, Max....You can wait can't you?"

"Of course, sir. I've nothing else pressing."

"Good. I'll be as quick as I can...."

Harry Carr had made a wonderful job of the place. Their old sparse living-room was now a spacious lounge with modern furniture, carpets, and strategically placed wall-lights which gave a comforting glow to the place. And there was a new, tiled fireplace, which had replaced the blackleaded range that his mother used to clean so diligently until it shone like polished jet. This feature was the only new thing that Paul regretted having been installed, for the memory of sitting before a roaring fire on winter evenings stirred warm memories of his childhood. He shivered now, thinking, It's damned cold in here. I'd better turn on the heating before the new chap arrives or he'll walk straight back out again.

The cellar was a revelation: being converted into a large kitchen with all the necessary equipment befitting a new, young tenant. Paul went to the boiler and read the instructions on the side; and after fiddling with one knob after another, he admitted defeat. "I know I'm a wizard with figures," he said to himself, "but this thing's beyond me. I'll have to chase up Harry and get him to come over."

The doorbell rang. Immediately, Paul ran up the basement stairs and went to the front door. He drew back slightly when he caught sight of the man standing on the step.

"Good evening, I'm Steven Clark. I've come to view your property."

"Oh, er, yes...please...please come in." And as Paul allowed the young man into the room where he placed a suitcase and a holdall on the floor, he stared at him in wonderment. This future tenant was not just any ordinary man: he was a Greek god, and his long eyelashes framed eyes of the brightest blue. An abundance of blond hair fell to his shoulders in a cascade of curls; and his broad shoulders sported a black leather jacket; whilst his muscular legs were clad in pale-blue denim. And as he turned about to face Paul, the birthday boy decided that after all this time without Mark, he was most certainly in love.

"It's been a bright day, but cold don't you think?"

Paul coughed. "Oh, yes it has been...it is...er....Oh, that reminds me: I've been to have a look at the heating, but it doesn't seem to be working. I can get you a cup of tea though if you like before I show you up to the bedroom...I mean, around."

"No thanks; I'd rather have one of these." He reached into his bag and pulled out a bottle of Scotch. "Like to join me?"

"Well...er, yes; considering it's my birthday."

"Really? Well let's celebrate then."

Paul rushed to one of the wall cupboards and brought out two glasses and filled a small jug with water that he placed on the table. "Please, Mr Clark, do take a seat."

The young man sat, saying, "Please, call me Steven – it's got a 'v' in it instead of 'ph' for some reason. And you are?"

"Paul. It's my mother, Mrs Crowther, who owns the house."

Steven extended his hand. "Pleased to meet you, Paul. And how old are you today?"

Paul shook the man's proffered hand, saying, "Nineteen."

"Just four years younger than myself, so not much difference in our ages." Steven poured a generous amount of whisky and a little water into both glasses. "Happy birthday, Paul," he said. "Here's hoping we can become good friends for the time I'm here." They touched glasses – whence Paul thought: Jesus! so do I.

Sarah looked at her watch. "He's late getting back, Jess. It's getting on for eight and the caterers are becoming edgy."

"They're getting paid, so let 'em. Anyroad, the man's train to Leeds might have been late and then the traffic gets bad in the rush hour."

"Maybe you're right, Jess....Nevertheless, I wish he would get a move on...."

Twenty minutes later, Paul bustled into the drawing-room with Steven following on behind. His face was flushed and as he spoke his words were almost incoherent: "Mam, this is Steven. I've had to bring him back 'cos the heating's not working and...and he can't stay there tonight. I'd best find Harry and get him to go and look at it and...."

"There's no need for that. And have you been drinking?"

Paul giggled. "Oh, Mam, it is my birthday after all, and it doesn't look as if anything else is going to get me merry tonight."

Sarah stood and went to her son where she took him by the shoulders, saying, "Get upstairs and have a wash and get changed for goodness sake. And be quick about it!"

"But...."

"Just do as I say." And Sarah pushed her son into the hallway and directed him up the staircase.

On her return, she closed the door behind her and said to the man still standing there: "I'm sorry about that, Mr Clark – I bet they've been pouring drink down him while he was at the mill. Please sit down."

Steven took a seat. "Actually, it's I who should apologise, Mrs Crowther, since...well, it was me who gave him the drink."

"Oh, I see." Sarah smoothed down her blue silk dress and went to the settee.

"He only had a few glasses," said Sarah's new tenant, "and he seemed all right in the car coming here. I really am very sorry."

Sarah patted her hair. "Well, it's done now. Maybe some cold water on his face will sober him up. You see, Mr Clark, alcohol goes straight to his head and he probably hasn't eaten all day knowing him....Now, there's a problem with the heating over at Long Lane? Well, be assured it will be seen to tomorrow, so you'll have to spend the night here if it's all right with you? I'll get it arranged at once." She stood and went to the side of the fireplace where she pressed a button. "I really am so sorry for all this, but I'll have the heating sorted out for you as soon as possible – and your rent will be deferred until the end of next month. That won't put you out, will it?" She glanced at the young man waiting for his response, but she was taken unawares when, without speaking, he merely returned her gaze and smiled at her, his eyes widening and his young, pale face taking on a glow of intense gratitude. And when he shook his head as a reply to Sarah's enquiry, the curls of his fair hair flopped onto his forehead.

Jessie entered the room now. "He's back then? Eeh, he almost fell up the stairs."

"Well, there's a bit of a problem, Jess. I'm afraid the heating's not working over at Long Lane, so we'll be having a guest to stay the night. When you go back, ask Harry to go over in the morning and sort it out, will you? But, before you do go, let me introduce you. This is Mr Clark, our new tenant."

Steven stood as Jessie went to shake his hand. "Lovely to meet you, lad. By! you'll be a right catch for the lasses around these parts I can tell yer."

Sarah said quickly, "So, Jess; since Jane and Harry are staying overnight in Jane's old room, I think Mr Clark would be better in number one instead of the spare. What do you think?"

"Suits me, lass. After all, we can't let the poor lad stay over yonder in the cold – not on a bitter night like this...I'll get Annie to turn down the bed and put some clean towels in the bathroom. Oh, and by the way, don't you think we ought to get this shindig started?"

"Yes, we'd better," said Sarah Then she turned to the unexpected guest, saying, "Well, if you'd like to freshen up, Mr Clark, Jessie will show you to your room – the bathroom's directly next door – and then you must come down and join the party. After all, it *is* my son's birthday." She raised her eyebrows and then smiled, saying, "Don't forget your bags."

The party was in full swing, but Paul was forbidden to drink alcohol – which he seemed quite relieved about.

"You all right now, Paul?"

"Thanks, Steven; yes....But I'd better stick to orange juice – for a while at least." And a mischievous smile spread across his face.

"I shouldn't have let you have three glasses," said Steven.

"It wasn't your fault; it's me. I do get a bit greedy for things at times – and I just don't mean for drink."

Steven looked at the boy's shining eyes and thought, He's flirting with me. He is downright flirting with me! And I like it. But I certainly can't respond however much I'd like to. At least not here!

"Hey you two! Ready for a fill up?"

"Thanks; I'll have another beer." Steven handed Harry his glass.

Paul followed suit; and when Harry began to walk away, he said, "Now don't you be getting drunk, Mr Clark, or I'll have to put you to bed."

The boy is positively blatant, thought Steven, but nevertheless damned attractive. Oh stop it man! This will never do. And he thanked Harry when he returned with the drinks.

"Cheers, Steve. I'll have the heating fixed first thing in the morning."

"Thanks, Harry; I'll be grateful for anything you can do. But I must admit it was a blessing in disguise since it enabled me to come to the party." He looked at Paul and smiled.

Paul stared at this beautiful man looking at him, and his heart raced. Then he said, "Excuse me, but I just want to have a chat with Mam."

Steven nodded, and as he watched Paul walk away, he took a swig of his drink, thinking, This is totally wrong considering he's only nineteen, but I want that boy. I really, really want him...!

And later that night, when the party was over and the house was silent, two young men lay back after their love-making was complete, and drifted peacefully off to sleep, cradled in each other's arms, exhausted by their exertions and sated of an unreserved and consummate passion.

"Did you wake in the night, lass?"

Sarah took the tea from Jessie and placed it on the bedside table. "To be honest with you, love, I slept the sleep of the dead."

Jessie sat on the side of the bed. "I didn't. I was awake most of the night."

Sarah sat up now, saying, "Well, I'm surprised at that, what with the stuff you take....Anyway, why? Were you not feeling too good? You should have woken me."

Jessie stood again now. "I couldn't have, love; I just couldn't."

Sarah pulled her pillows higher. "Jessie Dicks, there's something wrong. Now you get your body back on this bed and tell me."

"You wouldn't want to know."

"Oh, for God's sake pass me my dressing-gown." Sarah flung back the eiderdown and adjusted her nightdress. "I can't do with you prevaricating at this early hour." She was on her feet now. "And I'd appreciate it if you'd go and run me a bath. We'll talk when I'm dressed...."

Fifty minutes later, Sarah was sitting at her desk with Jessie seated opposite. She pushed the tea and toast aside and said, "Now! What is it?"

Jessie appeared to be embarrassed, but Sarah was having none of it. "Look, I've known you for far too long, Jess, to know that whatever troubles you may have will come to my attention before long – whether it be from yourself or someone else – and I'd prefer to hear it from the horse's mouth rather than hearing it second-hand."

Jessie straightened her back. "Well, if you're so determined to know what's on my mind, then you'll get it from me and nobody else."

Sarah inclined her head and exposed her palms.

"It's Paul." Jessie looked for a change in Sarah's expression but there was none: she retained the indomitable bearing of a woman that could take anything that was thrown at her. So Jessie threw it: "I got up to make myself a mug of Ovaltine and as I was about to go downstairs, I saw that...that Steven coming from his room and going along the far landing....Anyhow, I nipped back and sidled along The Parade to the other side and saw him going into Paul's bedroom." Sarah nodded now, but did not change the unswerving look that she had maintained throughout the conversation. "Then – early this morning – I went to his room to take the young man a drink, but my knock wasn't answered. So, naturally, I opened the door – only to find the room empty and his bed unslept in."

Sarah shrugged her shoulders. "So?"

"Well...I...."

Sarah leaned over the desk and clasped her hands together. "Jessie, I could easily say to you it's none of your business but I won't, because I know that won't satisfy you. So" – she stood now and walked behind her chair and leaned upon its back, saying swiftly, "I know that Steven spent the night with Paul because Paul asked me if he could. Now, Jessie Dicks, don't give me that look of disbelief as if butter wouldn't melt, because I know you've seen it all in your life. You always knew that Paul was in love with Mark so don't pretend you didn't, and I have constantly respected your discretion in the matter. But Mark's not here and Paul's happiness is my foremost concern, and if that's what he wants now, then so be it." She returned to her seat, bit into the toast and sipped at her tea.

"Oh, lass, they only met each other yesterday so you can't tell me that, straight away, they…they…just fell in…."

"Love? And why not? I fell in love with William when I was thirteen after speaking to him for the first time for…what? twenty minutes or so. Of course, I didn't know at the time what love truly meant and of all the implications and pitfalls it could entail, but yes, I loved him and, though he's gone now, I still do. But that doesn't mean to say I'll never love another.

"Jessie, in Paul, others have found a special kind of light that doesn't just flicker momentarily but intensifies – until it either can no longer be sustained or develops into something special. I only hope for both those boys' sakes, that the latter is the case."

Jessie leaned over and took Sarah's hands in her own saying, "But this is different, lass. They're in a different situation entirely and, to be blunt, could get in a lot of trouble – with the law, I mean."

Sarah pulled her hands away now. "Sod the stupid law! It's a law constructed by bigots and hypocrites. They sit in their bloody ivory towers, pretending they are whiter than white, when all along they are as corrupt as they come. There must be some politician who knows the law must change – or are they all as gutless as one another?"

"That's as maybe; but if their situation gets out, then…."

"Who the hell's to know what Paul and Steven are getting up to if no one says anything. I know I won't – will *you*?"

Jessie half stood now, and slapping her palms on the desk, said, "You know damn well I wouldn't, Sarah." She resumed her seat. "You know I wouldn't wish any harm on Paul – or anyone he cares for, as a matter of fact – it just worries me that he could get hurt if he's not too careful."

"I know, love; it worries me an' all. But, he's nineteen now and I can't keep him wrapped in cotton wool all his life, so he'll have to get on with it the best he can....Now, I think enough's been said on the matter so let's get on with other things, eh?"

"Aye, I suppose we best had." Jessie raised herself and pushed the chair back under the desk. "I'm sorry if I spoke out of turn." Sarah came to her now, and holding her gently, said, "You're a special friend to us all, Jess, and it's me who should be apologising to *you* for being a little abrupt."

"No, love, I shouldn't have been so daft about things....Right! I'll be off and get that bacon on for when Harry gets back from sorting the lad's heating out."

And Jessie walked out quickly.

20

"I can't think why he wants to come and see me, Jess. After all, I've barely seen any of them since the fiasco at the reading of William's will – oh, and that time he came to ask me if I wanted to invest in their mill. Mind you, I know investment has come from somewhere since he's planning a new warehouse."

"Really...? Anyhow, what time's he due?" Jessie asked.

"Ten, he said."

"Well, it's nearly that already."

"Right, when he arrives, show him straight to the library...."

Alex Stockwell arrived on the dot of ten o'clock and, as instructed, Jessie took him to the library. "Would you like some tea, Mr Alex?"

"Don't go to any trouble, Jessie."

"No trouble at all. I'll be making some for Sarah."

"Yes, all right then. Thanks."

Sarah entered as Jess was leaving. "Well, it's quite a while since you were here last, Alex." She seated herself behind the desk and faced him. "So, what's the reason for your visit? Nothing serious I hope?"

"Oh, no, no...well, maybe only to me."

Looking at this man sitting facing her, Sarah saw in him something she had never really noticed before: his eyes. In the clear, warm light of the library, they were almost lavender in colour – a colour similar to....

"Are you all right, Sarah?" Alex said suddenly.

"Oh, yes; I'm sorry I was miles away....please, go on."

He sat forward and clasped his hands together. "The mill's in a bit of trouble: more money seems to be going out than coming in from what I can gather, and I'm a bit of a dunce when it comes to figure work. I tend to concentrate on the working of the place and the quality of the end product. But something's not right somewhere along the line."

"Surely, isn't the best person to ask about it is Joe since he runs the financial side of things?"

Alex lowered his eyes. "There lies the problem." He looked up now, saying, "I believe he's highly in debt to certain people, and all I can think of is that's where the money's going."

"Have you confronted him?"

"Well, I have mentioned it. But he denies any wrongdoing, of course."

"And what about your bookkeeper? Has he come up with anything?"

"To be honest with you, Sarah, he's an old soak – and it wouldn't surprise me if he were in on it as well."

Sarah looked at him in amazement. "Surely not! Are you certain about this?"

"No, I can't be sure; but the signs are there."

"But this is eating into your profits – not to mention the tax situation which you are still liable for. And that's a burden just now for everyone in the woollen industry."

"That's why…well…I'm here to seek your help."

"Not money again? I told you last time that…."

Alex shook his head. "No, no nothing like that. I…."

Jessie entered now and placed the tea tray on the desk. "Shall I pour, love?"

"No thanks, Jess; I'll see to it." And after Sarah had poured the tea and handed her visitor a cup, she said, "You were saying?"

Alex hesitated in his response; then said, "I was wondering if you might allow Paul to come and look over the books for me – that's if he wouldn't mind."

Sarah took a sip of her tea before saying, "That may prove awkward. For one thing, Paul might refuse; and for another I'm not sure I could go along with it." She leaned forward. "Our two firms, whether you consider it so or not, are in competition – as are the rest of the mills in this town. Now, how do you think I'd react if some outsider came inspecting the accounts of my business? No, Alex, I find the whole thing rather distasteful – both legally and morally. And besides, what would Joseph, – and more to the point your mother – have to say about it? After all, they both consider my son and I a blight on their lives."

"But they wouldn't know a thing about it. Joe would be off on his usual jaunt to the Red House in Leeds, and my mother never sets foot in the mill. The only two people who would be there at the time would be Paul and myself."

"What about the boiler overseer? Surely he'll be there to damp down for the night?"

"I'll give him the night off. I can see to things myself if needs be while Paul gets on with the books."

Sarah sat back now and repeatedly drummed her fingers on the desk. "I don't like it, Alex; I don't like it one bit."

It was Alex's turn to lean over the desk as he said, "I'm in earnest, Sarah, and I don't know where else to turn." He looked down at his calloused hands and without raising his head, said, "I know our families have had our differences, but I personally count on you as a friend – I always have." His head came up and he looked at the woman who he had wanted to become his wife after William had died, and with a tremor in his voice, said, "Please. Please, Sarah, I'm begging you to try and help me through this."

Sarah Crowther looked at the forlorn figure before her, and her heart suddenly ached with a genuine sadness. Should she go along with his wishes and take a chance on his plan not being discovered or refuse him outright? "Look," she said, "let me think about it. Give me a ring in a few days and I'll give you my decision. But I can't promise you that Paul will want to be a part of it."

"Thanks. Thank you so much. I'll be in touch." He stood now; and after draining his cup, said, "I'll be off...I really appreciate you seeing me." He held out his hand. And Sarah took it, saying, "Take care, Alex."

When he had left, Jessie came back in to collect the tray. "So, what did he want this time?"

Sarah told her. "But I'm not sure what to do, Jess. If anybody finds out it could cause problems all round."

"I can't see that anyone *could* find out. I know the Stockwells have devious reputations, but at least Alex is as honest as the day is long. He'll keep everything close to his chest; I'm certain about that....But of course it's up to you and Paul to decide what to do."

The discussion went on, and after ten minutes, a knock came to the door and Annie entered. "Excuse me, but Joseph Stockwell's at the door....Sorry to say this, ma'am, but he looks the worse for wear."

"Oh, in heaven's name not another one," said Sarah.

"Do you want to see him, lass?" said Jessie.

"I suppose I may as well...I only hope Edith doesn't turn up next or you can tell her I've got some sort of infectious disease."

"I'd best get the kettle on again, then."

"Don't bother, Jess. He'll be after a Scotch knowing him – but he's not getting one!"

272

"Right, Annie," said Jessie. "I'll come and see to him, love." And after she had retrieved the tea tray, she and Annie left the library before Jessie returned moments later accompanied by Joseph Stockwell.

God! he looks rough, thought Sarah. Thank the Lord Laura left him when she had the chance. She indicated that he should take a seat and looked at him without saying a word.

Joseph smiled. "How are things with you?"

"Better than with you by the look of it," said Sarah.

Joseph, still smiling, inspected his attire. "Yes, I need a new suit, don't I? But money's tight I'm afraid."

Here we go again, thought Sarah. Money!

"How's Paul these days? What is he now? Nineteen?"

Where was this leading? Sarah felt her stomach beginning to churn. "Look, Joe; I've a busy day ahead of me so whatever you've come to discuss just get on with it instead of talking about my son."

"Oh, but what I've come about *is* your son – and one of your tenants." He reached into an inside pocket of his rumpled jacket and pulled out a manila envelope which he slapped on the desk. "In here are some photographs that may be of interest to you." He pushed them towards her. "Go on; take a look. I'm sure you'll be quite fascinated by them."

Sarah stared at the square envelope in front of her. Now her hands began to tremble as she reached for it and lifted the flap.

The first picture she came across showed Paul and Steven Clark entering The Hart public house in Leeds – a place notorious as a meeting place for homosexuals. She placed it face down on the desk before looking at the second. This one was of the interior where it appeared that some sort of party was in progress; and Paul and Steven were in the thick of it, drinking and laughing. She looked up at Joe Stockwell who had an evil smirk on his face. "It gets more interesting," he said. "You really must see the rest."

Sarah returned to the stack of photos. One after another showed her son and his friend in a situation that could never be interpreted as anything other than sexual, as they embraced each other in the most intimate of fashions. She was repulsed – not at the sight of Steven and her son acting as they were, but with disgust at the impudence and sick-mindedness of the man in her presence. She replaced the pictures in the envelope and threw it at him. "Get out! Get out of my sight and my house." She was on her feet now. "You heard me! Out!"

"Oh, you can't get rid of me so easily – not at least until you've heard what I want. And that is, Mrs Crowther, five thousand pounds in order that these photographs don't reach the newspapers – *and* the police. Just five thousand, and they, and the negatives, are yours. Put them in an album if you like or send them out as Christmas cards." Joseph's head flipped backwards as he let out a malevolent laugh.

Sarah sat down and, picking up the phone, rang through to the kitchen. Her voice did not falter as she said, "Jess, send Max in to me at once."

"Going to show them to your chauffeur, eh? Well I'm sure *he'll* enjoy them from what I've heard." Joe thrust his face forward. "I'll give you ten days to come up with the cash. Five thousand or you know what I'll do with them."

Max entered the library.

"Max, get this…this thing out of my sight."

The chauffeur strode forward and grasped Joe's arm. With his other, Joseph Stockwell retrieved the envelope, saying, "Ten days I said. Remember that! Ten days!"

"Get him out, Max! And please come back when you *have* done. Max nodded and pushed Joseph through the doorway.

In his absence, Sarah picked up the phone and rang Harry Carr.

"Harry!" Her voice was forceful. "Whatever you're doing tomorrow, cancel it. I want to see you.…Right…bye, love."

She slammed down the telephone and drummed her fingers on the desk, her mind in turmoil. But she wouldn't allow herself to be beaten up over her attitude towards her son.

When Max returned, she had already made up her mind about how she would deal with Joseph Stockwell. Now she looked directly into her chauffeur's eyes and said with unrestrained venom in her voice: "Max! If you ever see that reprobate near High Ridge again, run the bastard over!"

21

Leeds was well known for its majestic Victorian Town Hall and arcades; its variety of shops both large and small; the parks such as Roundhay; historic houses like Temple Newsam, and, on its northern outskirts, Harewood. There were art galleries, museums and churches; theatres including the magnificent Grand, and the intimate City Varieties Music Hall – and its pubs. Some were old and filled with history; some new and popular with the young and outgoing generation; and others infamous for those who frequented their beery and smoke-filled atmospheres – and it was the latter that were now of an interest to Sarah Crowther.

"You're a man of the world, Harry Carr, and a bit of a scoundrel as well."

Harry nodded and smiled.

Sarah shook her head, saying, "But I haven't asked you to come and see me just to tell you what you already know – I want you to do me a favour."

"Anything, Sarah; you know that."

"Right! Let me ask you this: do you care for Paul?"

"Care…? Sarah, you know I love him like I would a younger brother."

"Well, it's more for him really – the favour. Yesterday, Joe Stockwell – of all people – paid me a visit, and it wasn't a very sociable call at all. To come straight to the point, he wants money from me to keep his mouth shut."

Harry's face took on a fierceness. "Shut about what, for God's sake?"

"To keep quiet about Paul and Steven." She looked over the top of her glasses. "You're no fool, Harry Carr, and I'm sure you've speculated about their relationship."

Harry gave a slight nod.

"Well," said Sarah with unreserved composure, "he produced a set of photographs of the two of them going into The Hart in Leeds – and you probably know what kind of place *that* is."

"Aye, I've been in it myself. In fact, if the truth be known, I've been in nearly every pub this side of the Pennines."

"And what about the Red House behind the markets? It's notorious for its prostitutes and illicit gambling I do believe?"

"Oh hell...! Yes, I admit it. I've been there an' all. But what on earth is all this about?"

Sarah removed her glasses and, standing now, she proceeded to pace the room. "Harry," she said without looking at him. "If those pictures that Joe Stockwell has in his possession land in police hands, I dread to think what might happen to the two of them. I'm not sure about Paul, but because of his age, Steven would no doubt be sent to prison."

Harry got up out of his seat and went to Sarah's side. "But a few photos of 'em just going into some pub or other doesn't prove anything more than they would if the pictures were of *me*."

Sarah turned to face him now and her voice lowered a tone as she said, "Oh, but there's more...."

A knock came to the library door and Jessie called out: "It's only me!"

"Come in, Jess."

"I just came to see if yer'd both like some tea?"

"No thanks, love; just bring us two glasses and a bottle of whisky."

"Oh...right....Aye, I'll do that." And Jessie scurried out.

Sarah returned to her desk and indicated that Harry should retake his seat. "As I was saying," she said, "there's more to it than that. Apparently, it was somebody's birthday and a bit of a party was going on; and, a photographer was present to take pictures of the event – and unbeknown to the revellers, he'd been hired by Joe Stockwell. Joe didn't say as much, but it was obvious to me he'd put the man up to it on some pretext or other. He must have been planning it for weeks, Harry; and believe me those pictures would certainly incriminate both Steven and Paul."

Harry was on his feet again. "I'll kill him. I will! I'll bloody well kill him."

Sarah raised her hand. "That won't help matters, lad. Those photos will still be around for others to use if they so wished, and I know of one person in particular who would wish harm on both Paul and myself."

"But surely you're not going to pay him off?"

"Oh, he won't get a penny out of me, Harry, I promise you that! That's why I need your help."

Jessie entered. "Everything okay then?"

"Yes, Jess. Harry and I are just having a bit of a chat. Thanks, love."

Jessie placed the tray on the desk and immediately departed, whence Harry poured out two glasses of Scotch and swallowed a mouthful. "So, what's to be done?" he asked.

Sarah sat back in her chair. "Two can play at his game, Harry. Now" – she leaned over towards him – "we're going to set *him* up. You know how pleased he was when you ran off with Laura – he was rid of her at last – so I'm certain he'd enjoy your company for a while, and may likely thank you for providing him with an escape from a loveless marriage. Well, I have discovered from a reliable source – namely his brother – that he likes to frequent the very same Red House, and I want you to meet him there."

"I can't see where you're going with this, Sarah."

"We – no, *you!* – are going to snap him at it just like that photographer did with Paul and Steven. Oh, I know I've had some crazy ideas at times, Harry, and this is by far the most outlandish I admit, but the stakes are high, and I'm afraid it will mean you being involved in this charade.

"Now, forgive me for saying this, but I know that you are probably acquainted with every kind of life that walks the streets of Leeds, so I want you to hire one for the night."

"Surely you don't mean a prostitute...? Look Sarah, any photographs of Joseph Stockwell wouldn't make any difference whatsoever to him – or to those who know him – because he already has a reputation for shagging women from any walk of life – and at any age. Everybody would probably say: 'that's good old Joe for yer!'"

"Exactly! But what about if we really turned the tables on him, and had him...shagging, as you've so delicately put it, not any kind of prostitute, but a male one? And no doubt The Hart is the place to find more than just one."

Harry laughed. "Sarah, are you mad? Joe'll never go for that however drunk he gets. He'll never entertain a man."

"What if the man is dressed as a woman? Dragged up, as I believe they call it....Well?"

"Well, I must say that some of the ones I've seen in there can't be distinguished from women, but it's still going to be hard to carry out. I mean he's bound to discover the truth before the nights out when he...gets down to it."

"Not if he's away with the mixer before he *does* get down to business. Look!" She opened the desk drawer and pulled out a small bottle containing a quantity of clear liquid. "This will knock out a horse – I purloined some from Jess; she's got loads of the stuff to help her sleep, so she won't miss this little bit. Slip some in his drink just before you make your way to the hotel – I'll arrange that – but you'll have to hang around for a while and go in without him noticing.

"I'll get two adjoining rooms, so you can be on call with the camera when you get a knock on the wall from you accomplice. You'll have to take her – him, rather – into your confidence of course, and offer the going rate whatever it is, but I'm sure you can do that?"

Harry took a further mouthful of his drink. "Look! If he's out for the count, how could he possibly be capable of doing anything with anybody?"

"You're missing the point, love. He doesn't have to actually *do anything*. There's a phrase being bandied about these days – mainly in the case of politicians, I might add – and that is: 'found in a compromising situation'. So, as long as they are both starkers and in one of these, so-called, situations, then that's all that's necessary. I've already arranged with a photo shop to get the pictures printed – the man'll do anything for a consideration with no questions asked."

The woman's addled, thought Harry. This business has totally turned her brain, but what was he to do about it? Go along with it he supposed. After all, Paul would certainly suffer if he didn't, and he couldn't bear that. "Right! How long have we got?"

"Stockwell gave me ten days, so it'll have to all be arranged this weekend and carried out sometime next week. Do you think you can organise it, love?"

"I'll try my best, but I can't be sure I'll run into Stockwell on the night we arrange."

"Harry, I had to phone Alex last evening about something, and he didn't hold back in telling me that his brother goes out every night of the week to play cards – and other things. That's probably why he's after money: to pay off his debts; and he couldn't let an opportunity go by thinking he could possibly recoup some of his losses from somebody he believes to be a novice at card games."

"Well, I'm certainly not that!"

"You are now! You'll have to resist temptation, Harry, and let him win. Just make sure he has enough cash for later."

Harry gave a sigh. "Okay...I'll go tonight and maybe I'll be able to fix it to join in with his card-playing mates on a definite day next week. One thing though: I'll have to let Jane know what's going on or she'll become suspicious at my comings and goings."

"She already knows, love; and she only wished it could have been herself doing the deed."

Harry almost choked on his drink. "*What?*"

"No! Not with Joe!" Sarah huffed. "She's his niece for God's sake! And I'm sure he'd recognise her – even if she was dressed as a male prostitute pretending to be a woman. What I mean is, taking the photos!"

"Bugger me! Eeh, she's a dark one at times." Harry finished his drink and put his glass back on the tray. "Well, I suppose I'd best get to it and see what I can sort out."

"Bless you, lad; I knew I could rely on you. Good luck."

And after bidding Sarah goodbye, he proceeded from the house with one thought in mind: Good luck! I'm bloody well going to need it.

22

Although she had agreed to Alex Stockwell's request that Paul go through his mill's books, Sarah was worried that Joe may get wind of it and do something to prevent it, before she'd had chance to retrieve the photographs he had in his possession. Nonetheless, Paul had said he had arranged with Alex to go over this very evening – which just happened to be the same night that Harry had fixed to meet Joe. Still, they could be sure he'd not be at the mill to interrupt the inspection of the accounts.

Sarah had invited Steven over for the evening, and they were joined by Jane and Jessie for drinks and a bit of supper – although how she was going to keep her mind on the proceedings with what might be happening elsewhere was beginning to bother her. Still, she'd have to get on with it and do the best she could in the circumstances.

She was wearing her favourite black, jersey dress, set off by the diamond brooch William had bought her for their first anniversary; her hair was carried away from her face and held with a floral clip, and the string of pearls which Katherine had sent her for her wedding, hung delicately around her neck. She was checking her appearance in the large ornate mirror above the fireplace when a knock came to the drawing-room door and Jessie entered.

"Steven's here, love. My! the lad looks a real cracker an' all."

"Send him in, Jess, and then go and see if Jane's nearly ready, will you?" She'd had to lie to Jessie and tell her that Harry couldn't join them because he was going to see a client in Headingley about a building job. All this intrigue was getting to her.

Presently, Steven entered carrying a bunch of freesias. Jessie was right: he looked a prince in his midnight-blue velvet jacket and white dress shirt. His hair had been further lightened by the sun, and as he approached she could understand Paul's attraction to this beautiful young man. Then her mind wandered, and her heart skipped a beat, considering that she may have been too liberal in her thinking regarding their relationship after what had happened recently; but she smiled and took the flowers from him, saying,

"My favourites."

"Well, I have to confess, it was Paul who gave me the hint."

Sarah placed the flowers on a side table before saying, "I'll get Jessie to put them in a vase....Right, let's have a drink before we go in to eat. What would you like?"

"Oh, whisky and dry please."

After pouring the drinks, Sarah seated herself on the three-seater settee and offered Steven a chair. "I must say it's a beautiful evening." She glanced at the window. "We'll have a fine sunset by the look of it."

Steven could see she was feeling awkward – but why, he didn't know. She had usually been so comfortable in his presence on other occasions but not so on this one for some reason. He took a sip of his drink before saying, "I delivered the plans of the new warehouse to Alex and the work began on it last week. I must say I was grateful for him putting it my way – all thanks to you."

Sarah smiled. "He's a good man is Alex – more than I can say for the rest of his family."

Then, an extended silence began to unnerve the young man; but fortunately, the door opened and Jessie walked in. "Everything's ready if you want to come through, love."

"Thanks, Jess. Come on, Steven, let's go and eat. Bring your drink with you." Sarah stood and walked to the door where Jessie allowed her to pass, and when Steven approached her, Jessie said, "Everything all right, love?"

Steven smiled. "Yes, everything's just fine."

The meal went well, and Sarah had brightened. She had chattered throughout, and relaxed sufficiently to make those around her laugh heartily at some of the recollections of her childhood.

Now the four of them were back in the drawing-room where Jane was at the window chatting merrily to Steven, and Jessie was at Sarah's side consuming her fourth port wine. "He's a lovely lad." Jessie nodded towards Steven.

"Indeed he is, Jess....I hope things go all right with him and Paul for both their...."

"Mam! Jessie! Come and see this weird sunset; it's not like anything I've seen before." Jane beckoned them to the window.

Before Sarah rose, she looked at her watch in bewilderment since the sun would surely have gone down a while ago; and as she and Jess joined the youngsters at the window, her heart sank.

Looking out across the fields in the direction of Providence, the glow in the evening sky was all too familiar to those who had lived their lives in the West Riding. "That's no sunset, love," Sarah announced. "It's the mill. Providence is on fire."

Momentarily they remained transfixed, before Sarah said, "Jessie, quick, run and tell Max to get the car started."

"Shall I phone the mill as well?"

"No time for that, Jess." She turned to Jane and Steven. "Now you two stay here while me and Jessie get over there and see what's happening."

Steven rushed forward. "You're not going without me." And Jane echoed his words....

When they arrived on Stockwell's Field, the back of the mill was belching thick black smoke, and through most of the windows, fires could be clearly seen raging. Three fire-engines were at the gates, and two burly firemen wielding axes were hacking away at the woodwork. A vast crowd had gathered – amongst which Jessie caught sight of Amy Broadbent. She fought her way through with Sarah, whilst Steven and Jane followed at their heels. "Jessie! Eeh, Jessie," said Amy. "I saw it through my bedroom window about half an hour ago. But what are you all doing here?"

"Paul's inside," said Jessie.

"Oh, Lord no! But why?"

"No time for explanations just now, Amy."

Sarah spoke now. "They ought to be round the back not trying to break through the gates. That's where the offices are."

"They'd never get around," said Steven. "They've started demolishing the old warehouse already and it's a mass of rubble back there....Surely they must have keys or something instead of trying to hack through those heavy gates. Haven't they been in touch with Alex?"

"Alex is in there with Paul," said Sarah. "He would have locked the place up."

"Well, it's no good. I can't stand here doing nothing. Here, take this." Steven threw his jacket at Sarah.

"But what are you going to do?" she asked.

"When I came to see Alex about setting up plans, he showed me where the new warehouse was going to be and took me down a narrow passageway between the offices and the main part of the mill. It's over there." He pointed over to a tall, green gate set in the mill wall. "I can get over that and find my way from there."

"It's far too dangerous, Steven. Look, why don't we try and get to the gates and let the firemen know about the other way in?"

"We'd never make it through this crowd. And the police would likely stop us getting any nearer if we could. No, I'm going, Sarah, and no one's going to stop me. Paul's somewhere in that lot and I can't stand around without trying to do something." And he fled the women's presence and skirted the crowd until he reached the green gate.

Balancing on the protruding stones of the surrounding wall, he easily scaled it and dropped down to the other side. Thankfully the smoke was billowing away from the passage, but even here he could feel the heat. He raced along the narrow alley, his hands touching the side walls to propel himself forward, until his left hand hit a void and he stumbled: this was the turning that led up to the lower office door. Upon reaching it, he could spot flames flickering between the cracks of its wooden planking, but he knew he had to try to push the door ajar and take a chance on what lay behind. The door was locked; and even if he tried to break in, no doubt the fire would be directly behind, and he himself could then be at risk.

His mind was working overtime now, wondering what he should do. Then it came to him: here the passage turned left again and led along to the old warehouse. If he could negotiate the mounds of rubble, which no doubt were there, he may be able to climb over them and reach the pilings which had been put in place for the new building, and get up to the floors above. He went in earnest, catching the sound of fire-bells behind him, his thought being that the engines had finally entered the mill yard and were speeding up to the front of the main building; nevertheless, they would first have to fight the flames, which would have leapt over from the offices to the closely-set sheds behind the core of the mill by now, before they could finally reach the back. He scurried down the passage.

Shortly, he was scrambling up tons of rubble – helped by the fact that the moon in the clear summer sky was faintly lighting his way. Soon he reached the newly forming shell of the warehouse. The fire appeared to be concentrated at the front of the office building from where he had just come, and this gave him hope that the rear may be free of danger. Calmly, but speedily, he crept along a partially concreted level – grabbing a discarded length of reinforced channelling as he did so. His breathing was laboured now, but his heart was set on the one goal which was spurring him on: he must get Paul out alive or his very own life would undoubtedly be ripped apart.

He was on a broad, window ledge now, and after shielding his face with one arm, swung the metal bar hard at the glass, which immediately shattered. He repeated the action until the space created was large enough for him to climb through without the prospect of him tearing his flesh to ribbons. Inside, some of the overhead lights were still on, and he could clearly see the offices through a row of glass partitions. Running along their length, he finally reached a door that led through to the office rooms, but it wouldn't open. Something was wedged behind it. Sweat was pouring down his chest, the shirt clinging to him. Throwing the metal rod to the floor, he tore at the buttons and ripped the shirt from off his back, then thrust his shoulder at the wood. Once more he used his strength to wrestle with the door until, bit by bit, it moved. Reaching through the gap now, his hand could sense a body jammed behind. Now he summoned up a strength he would never have guessed he could possibly have, until he could squeeze through. The place was filled with smoke, stinging his eyes, causing him to retch, but the flames appeared to be concentrated much further forward.

The figure beneath him suddenly stirred. Then in a cough it said, "Paul....Through there...."

Now he managed to help Alex out through the door and into the relative safety of the corridor, whence he went back to see if he could find the boy he adored. But then a low rumbling occurred above his head, and through sore and narrowed eyes he looked upward.

The ceiling began to groan, and heave, and buckle. And now he knew instinctively that he was about to lose his beloved Paul.

23

Harry returned to High Ridge at three-thirty in the morning to discover the place still with all the lights on. He entered by way of the kitchen where Jane and Jessie were seated at the table.

"Oh, Harry." Jane rushed to embrace him with tears streaming down her face. "I'm...I'm so glad you're back."

"Whatever's wrong?"

"Look," said Jessie, "sit yerself down and I'll pour us all a cuppa."

Harry led his wife back to the table and took a seat beside her. "What's happened? And where's everybody else?"

Jessie handed him the tea, saying, "Sarah's at Leeds Infirmary. Paul's had an accident, and apparently he's unconscious." She sat now and went on: "There was a fire at Stockwell's mill. We waited until they brought him out and then she went with him in the ambulance. Alex didn't seem too bad – apart from cuts and bruises and a choking cough – but, I'm afraid, it does look that...Steven may have died."

"Oh my God!" Harry covered his face with his hands.

"The firemen are still searching the place," said Jessie plaintively; "but, as of yet, we've heard nothing."

Harry stood. "I've got to go and be with her."

"Look, love, yer won't be able to do anything if you do go," said Jessie. "Max's with her – he followed the ambulance in the car. Maybe we should all try and get some sleep for a few hours?"

"I couldn't sleep a wink. And I so wanted to tell her the good news."

"What good news?"

"Oh...about the building contract I managed to secure tonight, that's all."

"Well, I'm sure she won't be in any mood to hear about that, lad. Not yet anyway."

Sarah arrived home shortly before nine. Her face was dark; her hair dishevelled; her eyes raw with emotion; and she slumped into an armchair while the others stared at her, waiting to hear any news – but she just sat there staring at the carpeted floor. Then of a sudden she raised her head, saying, "I'll phone Katherine."

Jessie looked at her in astonishment. Why Katherine? Granted, she had kept in touch with her over the years, but what was the urgency now?

"Would you make some tea, Jess, and bring it to me in the library."

"Aye, lass, but...."

Sarah turned to Jane and Harry. "Get to bed you two; you look all in. I'll see you later."

"Go on," said Jessie, "and try and get some rest." And she looked at Harry and inclined her head towards the door.

"NO! I'm going out. He was responsible for all this: that bastard Joe Stockwell. Oh, he planned it all right. And believe me, when I find that piece of shit – and I will – I'll kill him!" Harry raced to the door.

"Harry! No!" This was Jane. "How could he be responsible? He was with you!"

Jessie was thunderstruck. Was she going mad? Who was with who – and where? Apparently, everybody knew something apart from her. Yet still she yelled, "Harry, lad. Come back here!"

Sarah just sat there and never said a word.

When Jessie took the tea to the library, Sarah had opened the french window and was standing on the patio watching the sun rise higher in the sky. She put down the tray and went to her side. Resurrection was emerging from a low mist, but Providence remained beneath a pall. "Oh, I only wish I'd never let Alex persuade me to allow Paul to go to the mill, Jess." They both looked into the distance where faint trails of smoke hovered over Stockwell's Field. "Come on in, lass," said Jessie, "let's go and have our tea."

When they were seated, Sarah picked up the phone and dialled Katherine's number. She waited and waited, until she said, "Katherine? It's Sarah. Look, I'm sorry it's the middle of the night where you are, love; but I had to call you with some bad news."

Jessie sat patiently and watched her telling her sister what had happened: "...and the doctors say Paul may remain in a coma for some time and that maybe...maybe he won't come out of it." Jessie could feel her heart being crushed as she listened further to the conversation. "They say it all depends on the extent of any damage to the brain, but can't say anything at the moment until, hopefully, he wakes up....Still, whatever the outcome, they did say that some patients have rallied with the help of family and friends being with them and talking to them – even though no response is forthcoming. Anyhow, all we can do is try.

"But they wouldn't let me see him, Kath. My own son and I couldn't be with him....And another thing...well, it looks as if Steven may have been...killed. He went in to try and get Paul out. But do you know, I've still got his jacket that he left with me. I'll take it back with me to the infirmary when I'm allowed – who knows, it might help if Paul has something belonging to Steven there with him....Yes, love, I'll keep you informed; and I'm sorry I've disturbed you at such an hour....Oh, thanks, Kath...bye for now. Bye, love."

Joseph Stockwell staggered down the garden in a daze. What on earth had happened last night? He'd woken up to find himself in a hotel bedroom in the middle of Leeds with not a stitch on. Dressing as quickly as he could in his drugged state, he ordered a taxi at the reception desk – baffled to discover that the bill for the room had been paid in advance. But the news that was passed on to him by the taxi driver, was even more of a shock when he learned of the fire at the mill – and of its consequences.

On his arrival back home, he bounded into the house where he discarded his jacket and went to the kitchen. Here he drank a large glass of water before racing back to the hallway where he encountered his brother standing by the open front door. No words passed between them as Joseph barged passed Alex and ran to the bottom of the garden, almost falling into the shed where his uncle was bent over his bench. He rushed at him. "You damned, bloody fool! Didn't you check if anybody was in the place before you set fire to it? God man! the plan was to get the insurance not to murder anybody. Yes! Murder!" He grabbed at the confused man and forced him outside and dragged him down the path that led to the shaded area out of sight of the house; and here he said, "I'm going to teach you a lesson you'll never forget. And if you say a word to anyone, then there'll be nothing left for me but to kill you. Now get on the ground. GET ON THE GROUND! I don't intend any bruises being evident for others to question how you came by them." His breathing was laboured as he forced his uncle to his knees and kicked him hard in the back, whence Philip fell prostrate on the rocky ledge. Blow after blow landed on the man's lower body as he writhed on the dusty ground and squealed like a pig. "Shut up!" said Joseph as he turned Philip on his back and straddled him, his face pressed close as he uttered obscenities and spat at the weeping man. "Go on, you bloody idiot, cry like the fucking, stupid bastard you are. Cry, cry, cr...."

Joseph's words were cut short as Philip grabbed at his nephew's crotch and squeezed hard. Joseph rolled off, holding himself in agony. Quickly now, the roles were reversed; but Philip didn't stand on ceremony when it came to causing indistinguishable marks on Joseph's face, as he punched him repeatedly. The pain in Joseph's groin was now transferred to his jaw, but his hands were free to grab Philip around the neck. "I *will* kill you now....Die you bastard. Die!" But they were both rolling precariously close to the edge of the outcrop.

Now, hovering on the edge of the abyss, both men yelled for the other to stop, but neither would give in. Then a sudden and acute pain tore through Joseph's back, and as he pulled his uncle close to his face, he attempted to speak. But just before his throat filled with blood, he could only croak the few words: "Forgive me... Sarah," before the two men rolled off the ledge.

24

Tuesday the 13th of September 1966 – the day of the inquest into Steven Clark's death.

During the period following the tragedy, Harry had told Sarah about the success of their mission concerning Joe Stockwell, but the report seemed pointless now that he was dead and those incriminating photographs were somewhere other than in Sarah's hands.

And not only that, after police investigations and post-mortems had been carried out on Joseph Stockwell and his uncle, it was discovered that Joseph's death had not been caused by the fall, but by a deep wound to his back, which was caused by some sort of sharp instrument that had pierced his lung. The date of that inquest had yet to be announced.

Harry had now been given the contract to refit the new offices at Providence. He'd had to take on more staff – including Sarah's nephew, Kevin, who had a penchant for woodwork – and subcontract some of the work, but he was pleased with the progress. And though Harry came into regular contact with Alex Stockwell, he would never divulge anything about his involvement with his brother.

As far as Paul was concerned, everyone had been to see him, and had talked to him for hours as advised, but with no response from the injured boy. Nonetheless, he was stable, and any brain damage would have to be assessed when he regained consciousness.

Some good news had come Sarah's way, and that was that Katherine was coming on a visit at the end of October and planned to stay over Christmas with them. Sarah was looking forward to that – although she was praying that Paul would have recovered by then. Still she had to get through today first.

Jessie and Amy Broadbent had decided to attend the coroner's court where Sarah was to appear as a witness. "Do shape yerself, Amy, or we're going to be late – it starts at eleven and Sarah'll be there already."

"Oh, stop yer fussin', Jessie Dicks. The bus isn't until twenty to."

"Well, wi' you dawdlin' so bloody much, we'll never get to the bus stop in time."

"Nay, it's only at t'bottom o' t'road. Now, are we ready?"

"Oh for God's sake, woman, get yerself gone and I'll latch yer door."

Sarah was seated on one side of the courtroom with Harry at her side, while Alex Stockwell and his mother sat opposite.

"I can see her down the front, Jessie."

"Aye, so can I. Now, sit down, Amy, and shut yer face."

The proceedings began with the fire officer's report: "Upon reaching the premises, it was discovered that the main gate was locked. This is not unusual in investigations of this kind; but in most cases, prior knowledge of other access points into the buildings involved are on file and spare keys are available – this wasn't the situation as regards Providence mill.

"As far as the fire itself is concerned, it is my conclusion it started in the shaft that runs from the basement, where various artefacts and important documents are stored. I have ascertained from Mr Alexander Stockwell, that the main ledgers and books were also kept there under lock and key.

"On the evening in question, Mr Stockwell and Mr Paul Halliday had placed the documents they required for their work in the open-topped electric lift that ran from there to the top floor of the office building. Then, the two of them had gone up the stairs where they retrieved them.

"Some half an hour later, Mr Stockwell smelled smoke and noticed it emanating from the open shaft which was situated at the far end of the long group of offices that made up part of the building. In our investigations, it was concluded that an electrical fault had produced a spark and ignited a large number of papers that had been left in the lift cabinet, causing the ensuing flames to set light to the wood of which the lift was constructed. The design of this structure would have acted like a chimney, the draught – and the oily surfaces – causing the flames to spread rapidly and unhindered."

Amy placed a handkerchief over her mouth and, looking at Jessie, shook her head, before the coroner asked the fire officer whether or not he could determine if, after the fire was brought under control, that the lift – or what was left of it – was still in the basement. The answer was in the affirmative.

Alex Stockwell took the stand and the coroner began to question him: "Mr Stockwell, my first question to you is why – apart from the main gate – other approaches to the interior of your premises were not known to the fire authorities and keys were not made available?"

"I have no idea, sir. I must have assumed that my late father had taken care of such matters."

"Really? But surely it would have been prudent of you to check such an important issue when – and I make an assumption here – you took over the running of the business?"

"I suppose so, but at the time of my father's death other matters were also of concern to myself and my family."

"I see," said the coroner. "Now, it is my understanding that when the fire officer finally reached the door that led up to the offices, it also was locked. I really cannot see the point of you locking this door since the main gate itself had already been secured. Nobody could have entered the premises anyway."

"I can assure you, sir, that I did not lock the office door."

"Well somebody did! Tell me, does anyone other than yourself hold keys to the premises?"

"Er…well, yes. My brother had a set."

"So, it could have been possible that he also entered the premises on that particular night?"

Alex coughed. "No, sir. He had an important appointment in Leeds. He could not have been anywhere near the mill at the time."

The coroner remained silent for a moment; then said, "Alas, I am unable to question him, since other factors, which I may touch on later, makes this impossible. Now, may I ask you what yourself and Mr Halliday were doing working in the mill at that time of night?"

Alex hesitated in his reply at first, then said, "Well sir, being the main shareholder in the business and the head of our family, I believed it my duty to investigate certain discrepancies in the accounts."

"At ten o'clock at night?"

"Well…the mill – apart from the boiler overlooker – would be unstaffed so that we could get on with things without hindrance."

"But surely you must employ workers who are qualified and capable of the task? And more to the point, why ask someone who has no affiliation with your business to come in and sort out your accounts?"

Alex looked directly at the coroner and said, "I thought he was the best person for the job, sir."

"For goodness sake, Mr Stockwell, do you honestly believe that to bring in a relative outsider would aid you in this? You must be aware that this young man you drafted in to sort out any problems you may have had, is now lying in a coma just because of your actions. What have you to say to that?"

Alex didn't answer.

Then the coroner continued: "Tell me, Mr Stockwell, is it true that at one time the lift where the fire started was operated manually by a rope and pulleys?"

"It was, sir"

"And when it was electrified, I presume a reputable tradesman carried out the conversion?"

Alex bowed his head. "My uncle did the work."

"Pardon?"

Alex raised his head now, saying more clearly, "My uncle did the work."

"And is he a qualified electrician?" the coroner asked.

"No, sir. But he is – was, rather – experienced in such matters."

"Well, be that as it may, the court will not be able to question him since I am informed that he died in the most suspicious of circumstances the day following the fire – along with your brother."

Alex nodded.

"Now tell me, Mr Stockwell, are fire-alarms installed in the mill?"

"Yes, sir."

"And did they go off?"

"They did, sir."

"And were these alarms installed by your 'unqualified' uncle as well?"

"Oh no, sir. They were put in by a…er…a professional."

"Ah, I see. Put in by a professional, eh?"

Alex did not respond to the caustic remark.

"So why were you and Mr Halliday not able to get out when the alarms went off?"

"Well, the fire was too intense by then," said Alex. "And we could not have used the stairs because they were directly next to the lift."

"Were there no other means of getting out – like fire-escapes?"

Alex stared at his mother as if seeking her advice, before saying, "I'm afraid the fire-escapes for the offices were unfortunately removed to facilitate the demolition of the old warehouse."

"Unfortunate indeed," said the coroner, his voice deepening. Then he paused and wrote something in his notes; and, after going back over previous pages, continued: "Now, from your previous testimony, you said there was one other person in the mill at the time – in the boiler room. Is that individual in court?" He looked around the room. "Apparently not." The coroner faced Alex again. "What is the name of this person, Mr Stockwell?"

Jessie nudged Amy when Alex took out a handkerchief from his jacket pocket and mopped his brow, and they and the others present waited for his reply.

"Well...actually....Er...he wasn't in the boiler room at the time." A tide of murmurs washed over the court, and when the coroner had restored order, he turned a critical eye on Alex Stockwell who, after drawing in a long breath, said, "I was attending to the boiler room myself."

"Have you deliberately misled the court, Mr Stockwell? If that is the case, then maybe your other evidence could be taken as being inaccurate?"

Alex was silent.

"So," said the coroner, "let me return to the fire officer's report. He stated that you – and I quote – smelled smoke and noticed it emanating from the open shaft. So, at the time, the boiler room was unattended?"

Alex nodded.

"Well, Mr Stockwell, I must admit that I am not conversant with the workings of the mills in the area, but I am frankly quite astonished – apart from what appears to have been an adequate alarm system at your premises – at the lack of due care and attention given to other safety provisions.

"Now, also in the same report, it is asserted that several documents had been left in the lift which, when the electrical fault occurred, had ignited. Why were such papers left behind after you had taken what was required up to the offices? After all, we have learned that these were always kept under lock and key by the nature of their importance, so why were they not returned to a safe area instead of being left exposed in such a manner?"

"I can assure you, sir, that Mr Halliday and I took everything out of the lift."

"I must take your word for that since Mr Halliday cannot be present to corroborate your assertion. One thing mystifies me, though: did this lifting device have something built in to it whereby it went up and down under its own volition?"

Several of those present began to giggle. "No, sir," said Alex. "One has to press a button to operate it."

"And did you press the button to send it back to the basement?"

Alex bit on his lower lip. "I cannot remember, sir. But why should I? It would have been pointless, since when Mr Halliday and I had finished checking the accounts, the lift would have been in place for us to simply place the documents inside and *then* send it back to the basement."

"Exactly! But it *was* sent back at some time before the fire started. Do you not agree?"

Alex *had* to agree; whereby the coroner proceeded to make notes again; then said, "That is all, Mr Stockwell. You may stand down." And Alex returned to his mother's side.

The coroner now addressed those present in court: "I think we should adjourn for forty minutes and carry on later."

Amy looked at Jessie saying, "Co-op café, then?"

"Might as well," said Jessie. "Better than sitting around here I suppose."

"Shall we see if Sarah wants to join us?"

"No, I won't bother her – and besides, I think she'll want more than tea to see her through this lot."

They exited the court and walked across the road to the café where they ordered tea and buttered scones. "He didn't put up such a good show – that there Alex Stockwell," said Amy.

Jessie bit into her scone. "He looked terrified to death, poor man."

"What d'yer mean, 'poor man'? It was him that put your Paul where he is now. And fancy getting his uncle of his to do the electrics....Oh! and that reminds me o' summat."

"What's that, lass?"

"It's just come back to me. On the night of the fire, before I saw you on the field, I were gettin' meself ready for bed; and I were about to draw the bedroom curtains when I saw this figure hurrying along the lane. I thought it odd 'cos he were all muffled up in a long overcoat – and on such a stifling night as it were an' all."

"So what's this got to do wi' owt?" said Jessie.

"Well, it were Edith's brother. Muffled up or not, it were him all right: I recognised that funny gait he has. And he were racin' – well, trottin' – from the direction of the mill….It were then that I copped sight of the fire."

Jessie put down her cup. "I don't think I'm totally dim, Amy, but what the hell are you going on about?"

Amy Broadbent tapped the table. "Think about it, lass. It was him who electrified that lift thing and, from what Alex said, he knew how to do it, qualified or not. So, if he knew how to do it then surely he knew how to *undo* it; mess it up; cause it to fuse, or whatever they call it. And he *was* in the lane after the fire started."

"So, are you telling me that you think Alex's uncle caused the fire that put Paul in hospital and killed Steven?"

"I am! Remember what that inquestin' fella asked Alex about the lift goin' up and down on its own, and Alex saying he didn't push the button, well then somebody else did!"

"Well, all I can say to that is you go and stand up in court and tell 'em what you think."

Amy's mouth fell open. "You must be bloody mad, Jessie. What? Me tell 'em what I've just told *you*? Oh, no, no, no…! Besides, he's pushin' up daisies now so what does it matter?"

"Well, be it on your own conscience, Amy Broadbent. Now, sup up and let's get back."

The inquest resumed as the coroner said, "I would now like to call Mrs Sarah Crowther."

Sarah stood and slowly walked across the courtroom. And after she entered the stand, she adjusted the short jacket of her black two-piece outfit and touched the brooch on its collar.

"Mrs Crowther, I thank you for your presence in court today and I pass on my sympathies to you regarding the condition of your son."

Sarah inclined her head.

"On the night in question, you were at home at the time that the fire started with other members of your family and one of your tenants: the said Steven Clark."

"I was, sir."

"Could you tell me, in your own words, what you did when you became aware of a fire in the mill where your son was working with Mr Stockwell?"

Sarah went on to describe how she, her stepdaughter Jane,

Steven and her companion of many years, Jessie Dicks, had been driven to Stockwell's Field to a position far back from the main gate.

"I am led to believe, Mrs Crowther, that shortly after your arrival, Mr Clark took it upon himself to enter the building unaided in order to see if he could...help in some way?"

"Yes. I tried to dissuade him, but he was determined to do so."

"Was Mr Clark a friend of Mr Stockwell?"

"Not really, sir – more of an employee. He had drawn up plans for Alex – Mr Stockwell – for a new warehouse, which was under construction at the back of the mill."

"And can I assume he had some knowledge of the layout of the premises."

"Yes, sir. He knew that there was a narrow gate at the far side of the mill where he could gain access to the offices on the top floor."

At this point the coroner glanced over at Alex Stockwell. Then, turning back to Sarah, he said, "I think it would have been wise of Mr Clark to pass on this information to the members of the fire brigade who were still engaged in breaking through the main gate."

Sarah was quiet for a moment. Then she went on to say, "It would have been impossible for him to reach them from where we were standing: a large crowd had gathered. No, he couldn't have reached them."

The coroner poured himself a glass of water. "I won't keep you much longer, Mrs Crowther; but one final question: do you think that Mr Clark acted somewhat rashly in his attempt to enter burning premises?"

"No, sir. I would have done it myself if it meant I could have saved my son."

Whispers were now heard from the well of the court; and after the coroner had asked for quiet, he dismissed his witness and retired to come to a decision....

Twenty minutes later he returned; and after removing his horn-rimmed spectacles, he clasped his hands together and addressed those assembled. "This case has proved to be a convoluted and distressing one for all those concerned. I have personal criticisms of some of the actions of certain people, but my duty here is to make a judgement. And the obligation I now have is to declare, and record, a verdict of misadventure."

25

Max had driven over to Ringway airport to pick up Katherine and bring her back to High Ridge.

The journey took her up into the hills of Yorkshire, over the dark and brooding Pennines where, apart from the odd isolated farmhouse and a few scattered homesteads, the land was cold and empty. Clouds, heavy with rain, passed slowly over a low and weak autumn sun that, now and again, managed to peek through and bathe the West Riding valleys in a brief, but incandescent light. The roads twisted and turned as they climbed upward, with a sudden sheerness catching one unawares at a turn in the road as the earth fell away and sloped back from whence they had come. And then they were over the top and descending, passing the villages of Marsden and Slaithwaite and on into Huddersfield where the air was dense with the smoke of industry. And here, the dark clouds were punctured by row upon unending row of mill chimneys. Sadly, many were into a decline, but no doubt those tall bastions of the Woollen Industry would still stand proud for many years to come....

It was Jessie who greeted Katherine on the porch at High Ridge House. "Kath! Well, this is something I must say. Come in; come in, lass."

"Jessie, love! My, you don't look a day over ninety."

"Oi, madam; don't you start!"

"Oh, come here you ninny." And Katherine kissed her on both cheeks. Turning to Max now as he carried her luggage into the hall, she said, "Just leave the lot in here for now. I'll see to 'em later....Here!" She handed him a note. "A little something for your trouble." Turning back to Jessie now, she said, "I'll have to get used to this money all over again, I guess."

Jessie smiled, thinking, Apart from a bit of a twang in her voice, she hasn't lost her Yorkshire accent after all these years. Then she said, "Let me take your coat, love...ooh, it's a beauty an' all."

"Sable, Jess. Just throw it on the cases for now."

"I'll do nothing of the sort! It's going up to your room. Leave the cases for now if you must, but not this coat. C'mon, I'll show you up and then I'll take you in to see Sarah and mash us a pot of tea."

"Oh, tea! Music to my ears. Do you know, I haven't had a decent cup of tea for…what is it? twenty years. The Americans were wholly useless after Boston."

Katherine followed Jessie up the impressive, deeply carpeted staircase and had to marvel at the huge crystal chandelier, which gave the impression that it was floating in mid-air. Well, the lass has really fallen on her feet here, thought Katherine. Fancy, coming from being a humble mill worker to go on and have her own place – and particularly one as fine as this.

After showing Katherine her room, Jessie led her to the kitchen where she prepared a pot of tea, and then to the drawing-room, where Sarah rushed to embrace her half-sister with tears in her eyes. "Oh, I didn't hear you arrive. Oh Kath, Kath."

"Now, now, little one; no tears. Big Kath's back and everything'll be fine – you'll see. Come on, let's sit down and have some tea; I'm gagging."

Jessie deposited the tray, poured the drinks, and then left the two sisters alone.

When they were seated closely together, Katherine took Sarah's hand, saying, "Now, tell me everything that's happened."

And Sarah did. She told her how Paul was fairing; Jane and Harry's marriage; Laura's unfortunate relationships; the result of Steven's inquest, and the saga of Joe Stockwell.

On hearing the latter, Katherine howled with laughter. "Oh, I've got to see the photos you got of him. How did you come up with such a harebrained scheme? But it worked – you got the swine."

"But it doesn't end there, Kath. Joseph died the following day and those photographs of Paul must still be around somewhere."

"Yes, but surely somebody must have come across them by now. You haven't heard anything, have you?"

"No."

"Then I wouldn't worry about it.…So have they had an inquest into Joe and his uncle's death, yet?"

"Yes. It took place last week. But the police requested an adjournment whilst further investigations are carried out, and it was granted. From what I heard, Edith Stockwell's outburst at the decision saw her being forcibly ejected from the court, demanding that the authorities find out the truth once and for all without further delay."

"Well, what a tangled web…! Still, talking about the Stockwells, could you let me have their phone number?" Katherine drained her cup.

"Why?" Sarah asked.

"Never mind for now, sweetheart; you'll find out in due course. But for now, I'd like to keep it private."

"Of course. I'll show you into the library – the number's in an index book on my desk and you can phone from there...."

When Katherine returned, Jessie was sitting next to Sarah on the settee. "Right, that's done," said Katherine. "Do you think Max would run me over there on Thursday?"

"Where?" said Sarah.

"To Stockwell's house."

"Oh, Kath, are you sure about this considering what their family has just been through?"

"I'm more concerned about what *this* family has been through. Yes, Sal, I'm certain....So?"

Jessie glanced at Sarah with scepticism in her eyes. Then Sarah said, "Well, if you're determined, I'll make sure he keeps the day free."

"Good." Katherine threw herself into an armchair. "You'll be going to visit Paul soon, won't you?"

Sarah nodded, saying, "In about half an hour – I want to relieve Jane and Harry for a while. Do you want to come?"

"Not now, love. But I will do for sure in a day or so. Anyhow, I've got Jess to amuse me while you're out."

"Oh"– Sarah turned to Jessie – "have you mentioned to Kath about this weekend?"

"Not yet, lass. I've been too busy trying on Kath's coat." She laughed now.

"What's happening at the weekend?" asked Katherine.

"We've a bit of a welcoming party planned for you," said Sarah. "Everyone's coming."

Katherine leaned forward. "Everyone? Please tell me you haven't invited Mary, for God's sake."

"Yes, I have. It's about time you two buried the hatchet."

"I'll look forward to doing that – deep into her rotten skull!"

"Kath!"

"Don't 'Kath' *me*, Sarah Crowther. You know how I hate her guts....Still, you can't go back on it now, I suppose. I'll just have to get on with it."

"Yes, you will. She's a changed woman, Kath, after that business with Laura."

"For the worse no doubt."

Sarah stood now. "Right, I'm off to the hospital. Max'll be bringing the kids back so be on your best behaviour." And she went over and kissed her sister.

Two days later, Max drove Katherine over to the Stockwell house.

She was led into the drawing-room by a young serving girl who seemed to have lost the power of speech, and there she encountered Edith who was standing by the piano. She didn't look at Katherine as she said, "The only reason I let you come here is because Alex insisted upon it. The Lord only knows why?" She moved to the centre of the room. "Please, be seated," she said, and pointed to the settee. "Now, what's the reason for this visit? Not about that despicable niece of yours?"

When Katherine was sitting, the two elderly, grey-haired women faced each other, and when their eyes met, Katherine said, "No, that's not the reason: this is business."

Edith walked to the fireside and sat in an armchair. "Business? What kind of business would you have with me?"

"Oh, it's not just you – this involves several people, the first being your grandson."

"Mark? What on earth has this to do with *him*?"

"I want you to tell me where he is."

Edith Stockwell was on her feet again. "Never!" Her eyelids trembled rapidly. "Mark's whereabouts is nothing to do with you or any other, apart from myself. How dare you come in to my house and demand from me?"

"Oh, do sit down woman for God's sake and let me speak."

Edith sank back into her chair, whereby Katherine changed tack. "At the present time, your business is experiencing numerous difficulties: output is down; credit is restricted; and money is tight. This is not entirely irreversible and, with the proper people at the helm and new investment, you can reverse this trend.

"I know that your family – not including yourself – only owns a fifty-nine per cent stake in the business, which includes ten per cent held in trust for your granddaughter that is not available to her until next year when she reaches the age of twenty-one. And may I remind you, Mrs Stockwell, that at present my sister is a trustee of these shares; so, if Jane should decide to rid herself of them other than in Alex's direction, then his holding of forty-nine per cent is tenuous to say the least."

Edith Stockwell leapt to her feet. "How dare you! How dare you talk to me about my family's affairs in such a blatant fashion! And how are you privy to all this?"

"I am privy – as you put it, Mrs Stockwell – because I'm the kind of person who finds out. Now, please let me continue."

Edith retook her seat.

"Your late husband – although he left your younger son a small legacy – did not entrust him with a share in the mill. This was a very astute judgement on his part, considering the amount of debt your son ran up before his death."

Edith did not know how much more of this she could take. But she realised she had no option but to hear this woman out since she appeared to hold all the cards. Everything she had said was manifestly true.

"To pay off these debts," Katherine continued, "you sold your own shares – which amounted to forty-one per cent of the business – to a company in Bradford called Anderson's, for a ridiculously low price. Now, if you'll permit me to digress for a moment, I want to take you back to before the war. I was thirty-five at the time and worked in a tailoring factory in Leeds where I met a man who I grew very fond of – and who wished to marry me. I would have done anything for him. And I did. He wanted to start his own business, and I was glad to loan him part of the money for his venture from the savings I had managed to put by through hours of sheer hard work.

"Shortly after his business was established, he not only married another and fathered a child with her, but refused point-blank to repay the loan. I vowed I would never trust another man again.... But then I met an American soldier – and the rest is history. Now, Mrs Stockwell, I am a very wealthy woman in my own right, owning the Williams and Mitchell Corporation of America.

"This is particularly relevant to my next point, which is that, through my contacts here, I heard some years ago, that a particular business was up for sale. I snapped it up; and now I am the sole owner. And just to rub salt into the wounds of the brute who robbed me so many years ago, I retained the company name.

"He is in his seventies now and dying an abysmal and deserved death in Leeds Infirmary. And I was privileged to witness his suffering at first hand when I visited my nephew, Paul, yesterday. Now, that brings me back to the reason for my visit. When you sold your shares to an outsider you were unaware who you were really dealing with since I, Mrs Stockwell, am that outsider."

Once more Edith was on her feet, this time pacing the room with her fingers jerking. She halted, saying, "I have never heard such nonsense in my life." Her head went up in a laugh. "Ha! You a shareholder? You're out of your mind."

It was Katherine's turn to stand now. And as she approached the seething woman, she said calmly, "It's perfectly true."

"But I sold my shares to Anderson's in Bradford," said Edith. "Which, apparently, you already know."

"Ah, but you see, the name of that pathetic specimen lying in hospital awaiting death, is a one Albert Anderson. And hence, Mrs Stockwell, I am the proprietor of the very same Anderson's of Bradford. Check it out if you like. Also, I installed my own accounts manager in your mill, since the bookkeeper was in cahoots with your younger son and they were robbing the business blind; and I had to protect my investment."

Edith went and leaned heavily on the piano, her face ashen, her stature seemingly shrunken.

"I will now tell you of my proposals." Katherine retook her seat. "I am prepared to sell you twenty-one shares – no more, no less – of the ones I hold. The remaining twenty I intend to retain as sort of...collateral. After all, they may come in handy for any future – well, how shall I put this? Negotiations! But my offer comes with one condition."

Before Edith heard any more, she said, "Sell? But that is out of the question: we could not afford to buy them."

Katherine raised a hand. "Just let me finish. As I said before, I am a very wealthy woman and acquiring extra cash is of very little interest to me; so, I am prepared to let you have your shares for one American dollar – which at today's rate of exchange amounts to seven shillings and tuppence – and afterwards it will be up to you as to what you do with them. As for the condition, it is this: you now proceed over to your desk and write down Mark's address."

Edith Stockwell gripped the edge of the piano, and biting on her lower lip, remained silent for a full minute; after which, once more, she began to pace the room. Then, slothfully, she went over to the semicircular desk in the bay window, reached for a pen and notepaper, and began to write. Presently she handed Katherine a small blue envelope. "There. Take it."

"Thank you. I'll have the necessary documentation drawn up and it should be with you within a week or so – and then you can write a cheque for the amount you owe me. Now, I will take my leave of you for I have other things to attend to. Oh please! Don't bother to see me out – I'll find my own way."

David arrived early on the Saturday morning. He had driven up overnight from Bristol especially for the occasion, and Jessie and Annie were the only two up to greet him.

"Eeh, yer look worn out, lad."

"It's a hell of a drive, Jessie; but I'm glad I could make it."

"Look, I'll make you some breakfast and then you can go and have a nap. Your room is all made up for you – Annie did it."

Annie smiled and her face reddened.

"That sounds most welcome – but don't let me sleep too long." But he slept until two in the afternoon....

"Who is this David person, Jess?" Katherine and Jessie were washing and drying the dinner plates – or as Katherine insisted: lunch plates.

"Didn't Sarah mention him, Kath?" said Jessie. "Well, Harry were doin' this job at the university and they sort of got talking, and Sarah said he could come and have a look round the mill – he was doing some sort of course on textiles and such. And, to cut a long story short, he got to know us all and just became like part of the family. Mind you, I'm not surprised, 'cos he's a grand lad – you'll see for yourself when he eventually gets up."

"Right, love, that's that lot done with." Katherine dried her hands. "I'll put the kettle on and we can sit down for a while before we start and get ready for tonight....Oh! but I'm certainly not looking forward to meeting Mary and Jack. I'd have much preferred Em's husband and her son for company."

"Just you be on your best behaviour, madam – for Sarah's sake. She's got enough on her plate without you adding to her troubles. And anyroad, Wilf and Kevin have booked to see a show at the City Varieties."

Katherine held up her hands. "All right, Jess, I'll behave. I only hope I'm not sitting next to her – or facing her come to that – or it'll put me right of my food....I've got to ask, though: who's making this dinner?"

"Well, Amy Broadbent's coming in to help Annie – she's a good lass is Amy. A bit dippy but good. And...." She was stopped in mid

303

flow as a knock came to the kitchen door and David entered. "Ah! Come in, lad, and I'll introduce you to Sarah's sister – she's come all the way from America on a visit."

Katherine shook the young man's hand, whence he said politely: "Pleased to meet you. I hope you had a pleasant trip."

But Katherine could not answer. She just stared at the dark-haired creature standing before her and her heart began to pound in her ears. For the longest of moments, she could do nothing but be mesmerised by him. Then she mentally shook herself before saying, "Oh, it was pleasant enough as flying goes, but I was glad to have my feet back on terra firma as they say. I'm still trying to get used to the difference in time."

"Well, I can't comment considering I've slept half the day, and I've only come a few hundred miles."

"Look," said Jessie, "a few hundred miles is no cock-stride. And travelling all that way in the dark is not my idea of fun, so you deserve some sleep. Now, there's a bit of dinner in the oven if you'd feel like some?"

"No thanks, Jessie; I think I'll have a bit of a walk and save myself for this evening if you don't mind."

"No, of course not. But wrap up well 'cos even though it's sunny, it's bitter cold."

"I'll do that. It was nice to meet you, Mrs…?"

"Katherine, love – and the feelings mutual. I hope we get the chance to chat further, later."

"I'll look forward to that." And when he had left the kitchen, Katherine said, "You were right, Jess: he is a grand lad…."

David tucked his scarf into his tweed overcoat and went down to Barn Brook. The sun's reflection danced back and forth over the clear, tinkling water as he stepped across the stones to reach the other side.

Once there, he proceeded up the slope until he reached the brow of a small hill where he stood and gazed about him. He could see in the distance the line of houses on Long Lane where he once lived; and beyond, he sighted the varied and irregular outlines of the many buildings that made up Collingley town centre. And this was where he was heading.

He had decided to buy Sarah a small gift. He pondered as to what might be suitable, because he didn't want to press his intentions at this difficult time for the woman who was constantly on his mind. On his visits to High Ridge, he had grown to like

Sarah more and more, and now he knew deep down that he was in love with her. Even so, the situation was fraught with insurmountable problems: he being fourteen years Sarah's junior; Paul's condition; the fact that the death of her husband may still be raw in her mind, and furthermore, that she may not have the same feelings for him that he had for her. So, the gift wouldn't have to be too ostentatious or overly sentimental at this stage – just a thank you present for welcoming him into her home.

The cold was making his eyes water, so after reaching for a handkerchief, he wiped them dry and continued at a pace until he eventually reached the Hollow; and then took the first road into the centre of the town.

"You can sit there, Kath, between me and Sarah," said Jessie. "I'll shove Jack next to me, and Mary next to him; then Harry – he'll keep her in check – and Jane, and then David next to Sarah opposite you. How's that?" Katherine surveyed the seating and nodded her approval.

The oval, mahogany table sported two, large, silver candelabra holding ten green candles; slim, cut glass flutes each containing a single white rose; two silver condiment sets and cutlery; tall champagne glasses and brandy bubbles, and dark-green napkins tied with white silk ribbon.

"It's quite stunning," said Katherine. "I've never seen anything as beautifully set out for dinner in my life. But I thought Sarah wasn't fond of roses?"

Jessie shrugged. "She seems to have changed her mind for some reason. Anyhow, love; I'd best go check on Amy and see how things are coming on – we're supposed to be sitting down at eight." And she toddled off.

Katherine sat in her assigned place and nodded at the other positions, saying in her mind the names of the others surrounding her. So, David's directly opposite me? she thought; I won't be able to stop looking at those gorgeous eyes of his. Oh, but thank God, Mary would be out of her vision. She rose now and proceeded to the drawing-room where Sarah had poured them each a sherry.

"Here, love; try that for starters," Sarah giggled.

"Oh thanks, Sal; I can do with it. And that's a point: I've hardly seen anybody apart from Jess and Annie today – oh, and young David – what with you and the kids being at the hospital. Come on let's sit; we've got half an hour to spare."

Seated next to each other on one of the long settees, Sarah turned to her sister and said, "So, how was the encounter with Edith Stockwell?"

"Oh, fair enough."

Sarah remained silent for a moment before saying, "Look, no doubt you want to keep this – whatever it is – private, but I only hope it was nothing to do with Mary or Laura."

"Nothing like that, love – just a bit of business, that's all."

"Kath, what kind of business could you possibly have with Edith Stockwell?"

Katherine tapped her nose.

"All right! I know you're never going to tell me, so that's it as far as I'm concerned."

Katherine moved forward and faced her sister now, saying, "Never say never, Sal. It's just that it's difficult for me to explain things in case my plans go awry. I hope it's not the case, but it could be a let-down – not just for me but for other folk as well. Just trust me for the moment and whatever transpires, I'm hoping it may work out for the best."

Sarah smiled. "Okay, we'll forget it for the moment. Now, come on let's have another sherry before we go in for dinner."

When they eventually exited the drawing-room, Annie was taking Mary and Jack's coats. "Mary, Jack, glad you could make it." And Sarah went and kissed her half-sister and her husband.

"Hello, Sarah," said Mary. "Sorry we're a little late, but Mrs Stockwell kept me talking on the phone for ages."

Katherine glared at her sister, who turned to her now, saying, "Katherine."

"Mary....And how are you, Jack?"

"Not bad, lass. Looks like America's treated you well. I was sorry to hear about your husband, but you remarried I'm told?"

"I did, Jack. But whereas Jonas was a little younger than myself, Frank is two years older: he'll be sixty-six next year."

Mary sniffed. Then glancing to the staircase, she spotted Jane and Harry making the long descent, followed by a man she didn't know.

"Oh, Mary, Jack," said Sarah. "Come, let me introduce you to a friend of Harry's – and to us all come to that." And she led them over. "Mary this is David. David, my other sister Mary and her husband Jack."

Pleasantries were exchanged, after which Jessie entered from the kitchen. "Right you lot! Dinner's coming out, so into the dining-room lest Amy gets annoyed and decides to eat the lot herself." So Sarah ushered the group into the room and indicated where each was to sit.

Amy, with a great deal of help from Jessie it had to be said, had done a wonderful job. They began with a poached egg on a bed of spinach with Hollandaise Sauce and toast triangles; followed by shoulder of lamb in a rich gravy, sautéed potatoes, mashed carrots, and savoy cabbage with juniper; the pudding being lemon syllabub with almond biscuits. Champagne was served throughout.

"Well, Amy, Annie," said Sarah, as the last dishes were being cleared, "you did us proud."

"We just made it, lass," said Amy. "It were Jessie who planned it all."

"You all did brilliantly. Thanks, Jess."

Jessie nodded and smiled.

"Now," said Sarah, "let me pour us some drinks while we rest for a moment; then we can retire to the drawing-room – Amy's going to play the piano for us."

As Sarah went around the table, Katherine turned to Jessie saying, "Is it my imagination, Jess, or were Sarah and David just a little too pally with each other?"

"I never took much gorm of 'em, Kath. But she likes David a lot – like we all do."

"Oh, Jessie Dicks, are you blind? There was more than a liking there from what I could see."

Jessie turned her face to Katherine now, saying quietly, "What are you hinting at, Kath? 'cos I know a hint when I hear one."

"Oh, it's probably just my imagination."

But when they were all seated in the drawing-room and Amy had finished vamping out music-hall tunes on the piano, everyone was a little surprised when David asked for hush and walked over to Sarah's position on the settee. Looking about him, he began to speak: "I'm sure you'll all wish to raise your glasses and thank our charming hostess for giving us such a delightful evening. To Sarah!"

"To Sarah!" echoed the other guests.

Then turning to Sarah, David continued, "I would, as a personal thank you, hope you will accept this small token of my appreciation."

The room fell silent as Sarah nervously unwrapped the long, slim box and gently opened it. "Oh, my goodness! It is lovely." She held up the garnet and seed-pearl pendant by its fine, gold chain. "I don't know what to say." She stood and kissed David on the cheek. "Thank you so very, very much…and when I wear it – which will be often – I will always think of you."

Katherine nudged Jessie, who said, "God! let me go and fill up these glasses."

Mary now made her way to where Katherine was seated. "I was most sorry to hear of your husband's death, Katherine."

"Really! Well it would have been nice to receive some sort of sympathy from you at the time."

Mary sat down now. "I was unaware of his death until several weeks later."

"So! It wouldn't have been beyond you *then* to send me a card or a letter."

"I didn't have your address."

Katherine slammed the arm of the settee. "For God's sake, you've got a tongue in your head. Why didn't you ask Sarah?"

"I didn't think."

"You never bloody do!"

Katherine shifted in her seat as Mary went on: "I don't know what this unjustified animosity is that you've always held toward me."

"Well, let me tell you straight, shall I? Our damnable father for one thing, who you appeared to love so much and who treated Mam like a punch bag. Oh, don't look the innocent with me because you know it's true. And another thing, you took your faith to manic extremes: all this claptrap about hell fire and damnation – I suppose Paul's lying in a coma is due to him being…." Katherine bit her tongue.

"Due to him being what?" Mary asked; but Katherine was saved her embarrassment when Jessie returned. "I thought there wasn't going to be any arguments tonight, Kath."

"Sorry, Jess, but…oh, I'm going to bed…!"

As Katherine hurried from the room, David looked enquiringly at Sarah. "Oh, take no notice, love," she said. "And thanks again for your lovely gift."

David placed an arm around her waist. "Anything for you, Sarah," he said. "Absolutely anything."

26

The following day, Katherine expressed her apologies to her sister and they were graciously accepted – although Sarah did suggest that the apology should really be directed toward Mary. Nonetheless, they both agreed that the incident should now be forgotten.

Katherine then went to her room and wrote a letter to Mark. Her words were factual and to the point. She told him of Paul having suffered a hairline fracture to his skull and had been in a coma for ten weeks, and that Sarah had long forgiven Mark for the harsh words he had said about Paul and herself. And now, more than ever, she would like to see him back home where he belonged.

She paused. Sitting at the dressing-table with the pen dangling between her fingers and her eyes staring out of the window in the direction of Long Lane, she could just see, over the brow of the hill, the faint outline of the bedroom window where her mother and father used to sleep; and below the dark and ponderous sky, the chimney stack that was now devoid of smoke – the last time it had emptied its fiery lungs was when Steven lived there, for Sarah had not yet re-let the place. Now, like Paul, the hearth lay lifeless and devoid of someone to rekindle its flame.

Was she being foolish to think that by wresting the whereabouts of Mark from his grandmother that some miracle could now happen? After all, it was only theoretical that the doctors believed that by talking to someone in a coma could – maybe in time – bring them out of a state in which they may really wish to remain. What if Paul's still active mind knew of Steven's death and wished to dwell with the memory of him instead of once again facing a world without him?

Or on the other hand, was it Mark inside his head? And did he know it would be pointless to make any effort to waken from a realm of sweet recollections and sun-filled days? No one could possibly know

Katherine grasped at the pen; and focusing on the task at hand, went on with the letter.

"She has always had a thing about Mary, David. I believe it stems from something that happened in their childhood and of Mary's Catholic faith, neither of which Katherine will ever come to terms with. The daft thing is, is that Kath's second husband is a Catholic – which she only told me some years after her marriage – and made me swear never to divulge the fact to Mary. I have a strange lot in my family!" Sarah looked at the man before her and knew he hadn't heard a word she had been saying. "Are you all right, love?" she asked.

"Er...oh, yes; it's just I've a lot on my mind. You see...well, I really don't want to go back home just yet – even though my father may not be with us for much longer. He'll be eighty-two next year and is sadly bedridden with a permanent nurse in attendance. I did have a long chat with him before I came here – he's quite lucid – and it was he that suggested I should get away for a while. Having said all that, Sarah, I still want to stay here."

"I'm sorry, love; but you know you'll regret it if you're not with him when the end comes – particularly now that your mother's gone."

David leaned forward in his chair and stared at the floor. "Yes, I would regret it. So, I reckon I'd best return in a day or two. But" – he raised his head and faced her now – "may I ask a great favour of you...? Would you allow me to buy the empty Long Lane house? I know you haven't got a tenant for it, so if I *could* buy it, I'd be most happy to do so."

Sarah was motionless; her eyes were wide and her mind suddenly void of thought. But she galvanised herself, saying, "I... er...I must admit I haven't really considered that option before – and it does seem a bit pointless it lying empty. I know my concerns have been elsewhere over the last few months, but I suppose I should do something about it now." She sat back and looked up at the ceiling. Then she lowered her head and said, "At the moment you have your father to think about; but, if you still feel the same about moving up to this dreary old town when you get home, then yes, David, I'll sell you the house." She reached forward and offered a hand. "Shall we shake on it?"

David beamed with delight. "Thanks, Sarah. Thank you so very much."

Sarah got up. "Right. Now, if we're going to the hospital we'd better get going. I'll go and see if Max is ready for us." And as she walked out of the room, David's eyes followed her every step....

When they arrived at Leeds Infirmary, the doctor and a nurse were attending to Paul.

"Ah, Mrs Crowther, we won't be a moment."

"How is he, doctor?"

"Stable. But very little change really." The doctor looked at Sarah's companion who he had not seen before.

"Oh, this is a very good friend of ours," said Sarah. "Is it all right him coming?"

"Of course it is. Right, we'll leave you now so you can have some time with your son."

When the medical personnel had left them, David drew up two chairs and he and Sarah sat at the side of Paul's bed. "He looks as if he's just sleeping peacefully, Sarah."

"He does, doesn't he? In fact, he looks better today than he has done for a while." She took her son's hand. "Hello, love. How are you feeling? I've brought David with me – he's visiting for a few days – and he's going to buy our old house." Paul was unmoving, and even his eyelids remained passive.

"Do you think he can hear us, Sarah?"

"I believe he can; I *know* he can, love."

The room door squeaked open, and when Sarah turned, she saw her nephew standing there. "Kevin!" She pushed back her chair and went and hugged him.

David was at her side now. "I'll go and sit outside for a moment."

"Oh no, no; stay. Kevin this is David."

Kevin shook the man's hand. "Aunt Sarah has told me about you. Sorry me and Dad couldn't come and meet you at the party."

Sarah took her nephew's arm now. "Come on, love. Come and see Paul." She led him to the bed where he looked closely at his unconscious cousin, and unashamedly began to cry. Sarah grasped him about the shoulders, and pulling a handkerchief from her coat pocket, offered it up. "He's going to get better, love; it's all right."

Kevin wiped his face. "We used to fight like cat and dog when we were kids, yer know." His words were directed at David. "I never knew at the time how much he meant to me, and now just look at him."

"Look, love; David and I will go and have some tea and leave you alone for a while." And as the two proceeded down the long corridor to the tea-bar, Sarah said, "Well, David, I've said this many times before: wonders will never cease."

David left Collingley three days later. But before he went, he had knelt before Sarah and asked her if she would consider becoming his wife.

She declined to give him an answer, but the week since his departure had seemed like a month; and during this time, she hadn't mentioned David's proposal to a soul. In fact, she had convinced herself that the whole episode hadn't happened – but it had, and she couldn't keep it bottled up inside her any longer.

Katherine had decided to pay a visit to Wilf's to see him and Kevin, so it gave Sarah the opportunity to summon Jessie to the library where the two of them could have a moment to sit and chat without any interruptions.

"Jess! I've got something to tell you."

"Well, I just hope it won't take long because I'm in the middle o' making a shepherd's pie and he's starvin'."

"No jokes, Jess. This is serious."

Jessie plonked herself on a library chair and folded her arms. "Go on then! I'm listening."

Sarah leaned over the desk and clasped her hands together. "Over the last year things have changed my outlook on life. It's been a rough ride for all of us but, for myself, events have thrown me about like Ben would do with one of his toys. I've not known whether I've been coming or going. But when Katherine arrived, I felt as if things were settling down; then someone had to go and throw a spanner in the works."

"Who?" Jessie unfolded her arms and pulled her chair nearer the desk.

"David."

"Oh, give over. What could he have done to upset the applecart?"

"Well for one thing, he wants to buy our old place on Long Lane" – Jessie didn't appear thrown by this remark – "and the other may come as a shock, Jess."

"Well?"

"He's asked me to marry him."

Jessie slapped her hands hard on the desk and, throwing back her head, laughed. "And about bloody time!"

"You mean you...?"

"I have got eyes in this old head, love, and I've seen what's been going on between the two of you. Sometimes I wonder if you think I came sailing down Barn Brook in a wash-tub. Yes, I've seen all the signs – and so has Kath."

"Kath?"

"Aye, Kath – your sister, if it's come to your attention. She mentioned how you and David were close at the do we had, but I brushed it off. Then, when he gave you that pendant...well that put the tin lid on it."

"But it never dawned on me at the time."

"Well, love, you had a lot on your mind....Anyhow, have you said yes?"

"No! I mean...oh, Jess, I just don't know. For one thing, I'm forty-three and he's only twenty-nine – that's a big difference."

Jessie leaned over the desk. "But do you love him?"

"Oh, I...I....Yes I do! There! I've said it. Satisfied?"

"It's not me that's going to be satisfied, is it? After all, he's young and good-looking and likely a bit of a stud."

"Jessie Dicks!"

"Oh, don't play the prude with me, Sal. It's all part of being married, and sadly, I missed out on it. Now, don't keep the lad on tenterhooks forever: make up your mind and tell him – and as soon as possible."

Sarah looked down at her hands. "I wonder what Paul would say about it?"

"Well, nothing at the moment I should imagine; but, when he gets better, I'm sure he'll be thrilled for you, lass."

"I do hope so, I really...."

At this point, the library door opened and Katherine appeared. "Oh, sorry, I didn't know...."

"Come in, love," said Sarah; "Jess was just leaving – she has a shepherd waiting for his dinner."

Jessie giggled and trotted off.

When Jessie had gone, Katherine took to the vacated seat and said, "Well, have I got news for you! When I got to Wilf's, he and Kevin were at the allotment; but Wilf's sister, Lily, was there and what she told me will make your hair curl. Apparently...."

"Hold on, Kath. Can I tell you something first?" And after Sarah had told Katherine about herself and David, Katherine threw her arms around her sister and said it was the best news she'd had all day. And then came to a decision that Lily's staggering revelation would just have to wait.

27

Three women were trimming the Christmas tree.

"It was sad about David's father passing on," said Jessie. "When's the lad due to arrive, Sal?"

"New Year's Eve, apparently. But" – Sarah sighed now – "I'm thinking about cancelling the party."

"Why?" asked Katherine.

"Well what will people think of me having a celebration when my son's lying in a coma?"

Jessie and Katherine glanced at each other, before Katherine said, "But it's all been arranged now. Think of all the people you'll be letting down."

"And what about letting *myself* down, Kath? I was hoping beyond hope that Paul would have recovered in time." Sarah stood back now. "Well, we've done a good job on the tree. I only wish he were here to see it."

"We all do, love," said Jessie. "We all do."

Annie came in now. "Excuse me, ma'am, but there's a gentleman to see you. He wouldn't give his name, but he said it was important. I showed him into the library since yer were busy in here. He's got a black beard and the dog's going nuts at the door."

"Well, lasses, keep a good hold on yer valuables: a pirate's aboard," joked Jessie.

Sarah smiled. "All right, Annie. Take Ben to the kitchen and I'll come through." Then turning to Katherine and Jessie she said, "I wonder who on earth it could be?"

Sarah went to the library, where the man was standing with his back to her, gazing at the books on the shelves. "May I help you? I'm Mrs...." She staggered backwards and grasped at the door handle when the man turned to face her.

"Hello, Sarah. I hope you don't mind me dropping in without prior notice, but I just had to come."

She hung on to the door. "Mark...! It is you, isn't it? My Lord how you've changed. But even with that facial hair I had no doubt who it was – and after all this time."

"Yes, it's nearly seven years, Sarah. I'm an old man now."

"Oh, give over...you're not yet...twenty-five, is it?"

"The thirteenth of next month. That really is an unlucky number for me." He came forward now, and taking Sarah's hands, said, "I've just come to apologise to you for what I said all those years ago, and, if you'll allow me, I desperately want to go and see Paul."

Sarah gazed at this tall and still attractive young man, and she could see his father standing there. "I...I don't know what to...." She broke off and threw her arms around him. "Oh, love, I knew what you said was in the heat of the moment....And of course you can go and see Paul." She stood back from him and looked into his dark eyes; and holding him by the arms, said, "But how did you find out?"

Mark Crowther lied diplomatically now. "Well – and I know this may be hard to believe – grandmother wrote to me and gave me the news."

Sarah's arms fell away from him. "Edith! She let you know about Paul?" He nodded. "Well, I've heard everything now. Edith Stockwell of all people....And did she let you know about your father's funeral?"

Nodding again, he said, "I came...well, to the memorial service that is. I hid at the back of the church in the darkness as that awful storm raged outside. And then, like a coward, I just disappeared again."

Sarah took both his hands in hers now, saying, "But where have you been all this time? And what on earth have you been doing?"

Mark raised his eyes to the ceiling. "Well" – he looked at her once more – "I've been living in Manchester, and I did go to university after all. I studied textile design as part of a degree course in Textile Industries. And one day when I was in town, I saw you. You were going into the Hallé offices in St Peter's Square."

"Yes! I was there to settle the arrangements for the orchestra to play at your father's service."

"Oh, I wanted so desperately to speak to you, but was much too ashamed after what I'd said to you and Paul."

"Look, love. That's all in the past, and there it should stay. Now, you must come through and meet my sister. I've told her so much about you...and then we'll get you settled in." And as she linked his arm, she said, "You're back home now, Mark. Home to stay – because I'm determined not to let you disappear this time."

Mark Crowther left for Manchester the following morning to arrange for his belongings to be transported to High Ridge. Sarah had nigh on demanded him to do so, and he had not hesitated in agreeing to her wishes; and two days later he was installed in his true home. He did not unpack a single item, but immediately got into his car and drove to Leeds Infirmary where Sarah had informed the staff of his imminent arrival.

He was shown into Paul's room, and was alarmed to see all manner of tubes, wires and drips connected to him. Slowly he went to his side, and after sitting, gripped his lost lover's hand and pulled it to his face. He could smell his strangely sweet scent, and the unanticipated warmth of his fingers as he passed them over his mouth. "Paul, my Paul. Oh, how I've missed you; but I'm back now and I want you back with *me*...please!

"I'll do anything if you'll forgive me – anything. Just get better quickly and come back to me so I can love you all over again. Life's been unbearable without you to hold and be by my side as you used to be....Do you remember that first Christmas? I don't think anybody imagined what we were up to...do you? And then that time when we lay together by the brook where it runs under the trees? It was then I appreciated just how passionate and special you are. Oh, Paul, please get better...and I promise you, I'll never leave you again."

Mark remained there for two hours with no interruptions from the hospital staff, and he never stopped talking for one second; but there was not a glimmer of a response from the injured boy.

Eventually a nurse appeared at the door and, looking at the clock on the wall, nodded; and then went back out. "I have to go now, Paul; but this time, I won't be very far away." He leaned over now, and kissed Paul tenderly on the forehead, whispering, "Goodnight, love."

It was Christmas Eve, and all the family was present – only Paul was conspicuous by his absence. Then the telephone rang, and Jessie went to answer it. "Yes?...Oh, yes she's here. I'll just get her for you."

"Jess?"

"It's the hospital, love," Jessie said quietly, and as Sarah went to take the call, all eyes were upon her and the room fell silent. "Mrs Crowther. Oh, hello, doctor. Yes...yes...! No, I understand...and... and thank you for letting me know. You have all been so...." She dropped the phone and collapsed to her knees; and, placing her hands over her face, sobbed uncontrollably.

Katherine raced to her sister. "Sal, what's happened?"

Sarah gradually raised her head, and with tears streaming down her face, said, "It's Paul."

Mark rushed over now and knelt in front of his stepmother. "What is it, Sarah? What?"

Sitting there before him, Sarah took in a deep breath, trying to quell her tears; before she gasped, "He's come round. Paul has come round." And the shrieks of joy must have been heard in Collingley Town Hall.

"Oh, tell us, lass!" said Jessie. "Tell us what the doctor said." Mark helped Sarah to her feet.

"Well" – she wiped away her tears – "he said that Paul opened his eyes about an hour ago. He can't have any visitors for a while because they want to monitor his progress; but, if he goes on all right, there's a possibility he could be home within the week. Oh, for God's sake will somebody get me a drink!"

Mark rescued Sarah's glass of port from beside the telephone and handed it to her. "Thanks, love." She took a large swig and then was able to smile. "Apparently, he can't remember a thing about the fire, but can recall people going to see him and, peculiarly, what everyone was saying to him....Oh God in heaven! This is the best Christmas I've ever had. He's coming home. My lad's coming home!"

And on the 30th of December, her lad did.

28

Had she done the right thing? Had she disregarded the health of her son even though he wished to celebrate his freedom from oblivion? After all, he'd only been home one day and had been advised by his doctor to rest. But, as Katherine had said, the occasion had already been arranged, and she had agreed that she could hardly change her mind now and let so many people down. And then there was David. No doubt he'd want an answer from her tonight; but what would she say?

The town hall ballroom had been beautifully decorated, and the large Christmas tree was dressed totally in silver and white; and a fine net stretched across the width of the room filled with multicoloured balloons. And the place was packed. Families and friends – and as many of the mill employees of both Resurrection and Providence who had not made other arrangements, were chatting away merrily waiting for the festivities to get into full swing as members of the band began to tune up.

"Well, I'll say this," said Jessie; "they've turned out in force." But when Sarah made no comment, she glanced at her and noticed that she was looking at her son who was seated at the next table with Mark, Jane and Harry.

"He's certainly been through the mill, Jess – if you'll pardon the pun – but he insisted he wasn't going to miss tonight at any cost."

And as Jessie followed Sarah's gaze, she said, "He's very pale, love; but happy....Oh look...here's David!"

Sarah's heart and mind suddenly faltered. Nonetheless, she took in a breath and stood as he came over.

"Not too late, am I? What a swine of a drive up it was – but I'm so glad I could get here....I stopped off at the house and freshened up and got changed. Max hung on till I got ready; then he, Annie, Amy and myself got a taxi here." He looked around the ballroom now. "It's quite a spectacle, Sarah...you've done everybody proud."

"Thanks. But haven't you forgotten something?" said Sarah. As David looked questioningly at her, she patted the side of her face.

"It is New Year's Eve after all." He grinned, and kissed her fondly on the cheek.

"Don't I get one then?" asked Jessie, and David skirted the table and bent over her. "You jealous, Jessie? Oh, come here...!"

"That's better! Now, I'll leave you two alone and go and join Amy and the others."

At the Stockwell table, Edith said to her son, "You've never stopped staring over there since he walked in a few minutes ago."

"There's something about David that fascinates me," he answered her.

"Oh, Alexander, please don't tell me you've gone the same way as Mark after all these years? I've often wondered why you never married."

"Don't be ridiculous, Mother! Anyhow, if Joseph's feeble attempts at settling down were anything to go by, I'm glad I didn't."

Edith turned to where Mary, Jack and Laura were sitting; and nodding, said, "I wonder what she's up to these days apart from so-called gardening? After that episode with Harry Carr, one would have thought she'd have learned her lesson. But just look at her: eyes all over the shop."

"Well, she is free after all. And who knows, I might even ask her to go out with *me*."

Edith spun her neck around. *"What?* Oh, do tell me you're joking!"

Alex spluttered with laughter. "Oh, Mother; of course I am." Then his expression saddened, as he said, "No, I think the woman who's stolen my heart is already spoken for...."

Now, the bandleader tapped his microphone. "Ladies and gentleman, please take your partners for the first dance: a waltz."

Paul turned to Mark. "I do hope they don't play the Gay Gordons or I won't be able to control myself." Mark laughed, before Jane said, "Maybe now that the Labour government's in power and Leo Abse has proposed that Bill in Parliament, they may change the stupid law next year."

"Well, it's about time," said Harry, and he and his wife raised their glasses to the boys....

"I wonder where Jessie's got to now?" said Sarah.

"Didn't you see her?" David said. "She's dancing with Max. You know, considering she's never married, she's not backward in coming forward."

"She never had the time or the inclination to settle down, love. There was her mother to look after – and then Paul of course – and now she's devoted to looking after all of us."

David went silent for a moment. Then, without looking at Sarah, said, "Talking about settling down; have you...well...have you thought any more of what I asked you before I had to go back to Bristol?"

"Well, to be brutally honest, I seem to have been occupied with other thoughts over the past few months."

"Oh, yes of course...."

Sarah reached across and took his hand, and as he looked at her now, she said, "But that doesn't mean I haven't been considering it – and it's definitely not a refusal....In fact, I've thought more about it tonight than ever – and the night's not over yet."

The night went on, and the members of the band had played their hearts out. Deservedly, they were acknowledged with a roar of appreciation from the audience. Now, upon hearing another round of applause after that for the band had faded, Sarah looked towards the stage as the mayor approached the microphone. "Ladies and gentleman," she announced. "It has been my pleasure this evening to welcome one of our community's most successful and revered businesswomen.

"Her life has been burdened with much toil and sadness, but she has borne both with an unrelenting fortitude. Her consideration for her employees is always paramount – as is readily apparent with tonight's fantastic turn-out. So now, I would ask you to raise your glasses and toast your hostess: Sarah Crowther."

The tinkling of glasses followed by cries of 'To Sarah', brought an embarrassed blush to the recipient's face; but Sarah rose and acknowledged the outpouring of affection from those present.

The mayor now raised her hands. "Ladies and gentleman. It is fast approaching midnight, and before the town hall clock strikes twelve to herald in a new year, I want to introduce to you a surprise addition to our festivities. Maestro...." She indicated to the bandleader. And when the introductory music began, a young man walked onto the stage and approached the microphone where he spoke: "Ladies and gentlemen, I have had a request from a member of the audience, which he would like to be dedicated to a very special lady who has given us an evening to remember." He looked out into the audience. "Sarah. This is especially for you.

Originally sung in Italian as L'Edera, it became a worldwide hit for Cliff Richard under the name: Constantly. It is a song of love; so all those who find themselves in that fortunate state, I dedicate it to you."

Sarah smiled as she took David's hand and joined the others already on the dance floor where he held Sarah close; and as she looked into his eyes, she whispered, "A member of the audience indeed. It was you who asked for this, wasn't it? But how did you know it is one of my favourites?"

Leaning away from Sarah now, David said, "It wasn't me – honestly. But I only wish it had been." And after the song was over, they both returned to the table, where Sarah said, "I wonder who did suggest it? I feel more embarrassed than ever now."

"Why?" said David. "There must be a host of people here who would wish to express sentiments like that, so what's to be embarrassed about?"

Katherine appeared now. "Well, how did you enjoy my little addition to the proceedings?"

Sarah shook her head and smiled. "I knew you were up to something. My God! you've always been secretive.... Who was the singer though?"

"I'll go and bring him over."

"Oh, no don't, Kath...!"

Ignoring her sister, Katherine went toward the stage as David said, "You'll have to excuse me for a minute as well, love. Nature calls."

Alex Stockwell, noticing Sarah was now on her own, walked over to her table. "May I join you for a moment, Sarah?"

"Of course! Please do, Alex....How are you enjoying the evening?"

Alex drew up a chair. "Tremendously. But I just came over to give you something." He reached into his inside pocket and pulled out an envelope, which he placed on the table. "It's taken some time I'm afraid, but I've just got around to sorting through Joseph's belongings. Well, I came across a key to a desk in his bedroom, and inside I found these." He pushed the envelope towards her. "They belong to you." He stood now; and leaning close, kissed Sarah on the cheek. "Happy New Year, love. And I hope you liked the song I chose for you." He then smiled and walked away.

So it was him! thought Sarah as she watched Alex return to his table. Then, gathering herself, placed the envelope on her lap and opened it. And inside were the photographs and negatives of Paul and Steven at The Hart. She looked over at Alex who raised his glass, and then hurriedly put the envelope in her handbag.

"Now, love." Katherine had returned with the young singer. "Let me introduce you. This fine specimen of manhood standing here, came specifically to see you." She put her hand on the young man's shoulder. "This, Sarah, is your nephew, Josh."

"Josh? This is your Josh? Your son, Josh?"

Katherine nodded. And when she pushed her son forward, he went to his aunt, and in a soft, American accent said, "I wasn't going to miss you this time, Aunt Sarah." And Sarah stood and embraced him....

It was five minutes to midnight, and while David took Joshua around and introduced him to everyone, Sarah said to Katherine, "How did he get here?"

"He swam the Atlantic....How on earth do you think he got here? Max went over to the airport and picked him up this afternoon and snuck him into his quarters."

"So that's why Max wanted some time off!"

"You catch on quick, love; I'll give you that. Now, I'd better go and rescue David."

Sarah watched as Katherine strolled across the floor of the ballroom and took David's arm. But she didn't bring him back immediately: she walked him over to a corner of the room and entered into a deep conversation.

When David returned, Sarah didn't have the mind to ask him what he and her sister had been discussing, and as he said, "You must be over the moon to see your nephew," she put her curiosity on hold.

"Yes, I have to admit it was a wonderful surprise. I just can't believe all the things that have happened over the last few days."

"Well, I hope you'll believe this." He delved into his jacket pocket and pulled out a small box, which he handed to Sarah. "Go on; open it." And when she saw the diamond engagement ring, she said, "What on earth...?"

"Now, I'll ask you again, Mrs Crowther...will you marry me?"

She returned the ring and offered him her left hand. "Well, go on, Mr Allen. See if it fits." And as he placed the ring on her finger, she noticed for the very first time, a scar on his right hand....

The town hall clock struck midnight and Auld Lang Syne had

been sung, during which a thousand balloons cascaded down from the ceiling. The party-goers were still dancing, but Katherine and Sarah were alone at the table. "Oh, sweetheart, that's some beauty." Katherine admired the ring. "You said 'yes' then I guess?"

"I did, Kath. I made my mind up when Josh sang that song. But I've known for ages. I believe it's what I've always wanted."

"Oh, come here!" Katherine hugged her younger sister. "Now, you must give him something to seal the deal."

"But I don't have anything…well, not on me."

"*I have!* I knew they'd come in handy ever since I first met David. Hang on a minute…." She reached into her handbag and handed Sarah a padded box in which sat a pair of sapphire and diamond cuff-links. Sarah inspected them closely. "They have his initials on the back."

Katherine nodded. "Go on, love; go over and give them to him. He's chatting to Paul and Mark."

And when Sarah did, and saw the unbridled delight on David's face, she began to access her memories. She was now aware who this man really was, and it stung her with a spark so powerful it caused her mind to ignite. Now approaching her forty-fourth year on this earth, she could not help but to look back on the happiest periods of her life….

Her childhood:

'Sarah! Sarah! Where you at this time? Yer dad's home….D'yer hear? You haven't been next door? How many times have I….'

'Mam! Mam! Where's our Kath?'

'She's in the cellar fetching up a bucket of coal….And where the hell have you been? You're wet through!'

'We think the baby's coming.'

'We? What baby?'

'Alice's of course. Whose do you think…?'

Her work:

'If that woman thinks I'm working alongside an elf – who for all I know they keep locked in an attic or somewhere – she can think again. And then she expects me, after a day's work, to help her wipe her own arse. Well no thank you…!'

'What will Mr Crowther want to see me about, Jess?'

'Well, what d'yer think, love? To tell yer about yer wages, of course…."

Her marriage to William:

'I do love you, William.'

'I hope so or I'll have to let the church know that the wedding's off.'

'Oh, get on with you, Bill Crowther....'

'Will I do then, Jess?'

'Do...? I'll tell yer what: I'd marry yer meself if yer weren't spoken for....'

And her son:

'It's Mr Crowther...he's got Mark and....'

'Oh, get yourself back here, lad, and help me tidy these bits up. Surely he can't be coming here?'

'He is! He's coming to the door, Mam.'

Oh, the joy a woman had in giving birth to a son! And now, as Sarah looked into David's stunning eyes, she could envisage Alice Barraclough lying on a bed, surrounded by boxes of old clothes and cast-iron pans, cradling her *own* beautiful and extraordinary boy.

29

On the 28th June 1937, Victoria Row had been destroyed.

Katherine had toiled with a gang of men to see if she could help in the recovery of the bodies of her neighbours. And when Alice and her father were discovered, they were lain out in Low Field and covered with sheets until the municipal hearse arrived to take them away.

Subsequently, a parish burial was ordered since there were no other relatives, and no ready money available for anything other than a pauper's funeral – the grave itself only indicated by a small, roughly-hewn stone.

Now, on the 1st January 1967 as celebrations continued for the new year, Katherine, Sarah and Lily Sutcliffe were seated at a table on their own.

"My mind was as sore as my fingers," said Katherine as she recalled that inauspicious day. "I was numb. And then when I heard Dad scream to high heaven and the boy was pulled from the rubble, I knew not where I was or who I was! Then when some man appeared – who said he represented Doctor Griffiths – and told me that the child would be taken to the children's hospital and he wanted a name for the records. Well, stupidly, I just told him it was Alan. 'Baby Allen, then?' says he, and I nodded...."

Having gathered her thoughts now, she said, "On the day I went to confront Edith about the whereabouts of Mark, I went to the municipal cemetery and searched for a grave. The place was almost derelict – and so overgrown I thought I was on a pointless mission. But as I tugged at the weeds and grasses like someone demented, I discovered this small, eroded stone with the words just about visible: 'Allen, Father and daughter'. But I won't dwell on the moment....Anyhow, I'll get to the saga about Anderson's and Edith Stockwell. I bought Anderson's six years ago this very month, and I...."

"Didn't tell *me*!" said Sarah. "Do you know, when one of your cronies eventually got to see me – and wanted to accept my new designs and make them up – I never could have believed that you were behind it."

Katherine's head shrank into her shoulders. But she grinned, saying, "I wanted to keep it to myself. You see, I wanted to do something just for you without the complications of you knowing where it came from. I know it may sound silly, but it was my way of...giving you a little back for you just being you....And then I surreptitiously bought a stake in Providence.

"Anyhow, when I got here in October, I went and saw Edith and gave her back some of her shares – well, sold them to her for a dollar. It was only to find out the whereabouts of Mark so that he might possibly be able to help in bringing Paul back to us. Of course, it may all have ended in failure; but thank God it didn't. Nevertheless, I held back twenty per cent of the shares as a bargaining chip for"– she winked at Sarah – "certain photographs?" Then, if I'd voiced my suspicions about David, well...."

"Suspicions! About David?"

"Yes! You may have not wanted to have a thing to do with someone who had Stockwell blood in his veins – and I could see how much you were in love with each other."

Sarah took a large mouthful of her drink. "Okay then...now let's have the whole story about that."

Katherine's eyes began to sparkle now. "Well, it all started that night of the feast when Alice's father went out looking for his horse, leaving Alice to give Alex the rent....Well, I can tell you, she gave him more than just the rent that night." Sarah delved deep into her memory again. God, it was all my fault! I left the gate open! If I hadn't have done – allowing Ben to wander off – Len would have been at home! It was me who was totally responsible for all this.

Katherine continued now: "Anyhow, strangely enough, I wasn't totally convinced about Alex's involvement with Alice – taking into account the apparent assault on her at the fairground. But when I met David, it was obvious that his face was the image of his mother's, and also that he just had to be Alex's son. Everything about him is the epitome of his father: his voice, his hair, his mannerisms, and those eyes....Oh, I fell in love with those eyes of Alex Stockwell when I first met him. And what a lover he was!"

"You don't mean to say you *slept* with him?" said Sarah.

"Only the once!" said Katherine. Lily chuckled. And smiling, Katherine went on: "It was shortly after his father died and he came to Rosenberg's touting for business and...well we started talking, and he took me out for a drink, and one thing led to another as they do....He told me he preferred older women, so why he got involved with Alice Barraclough is beyond me. But he did tell me something that, apart from me, only his family knew: his middle name was Daniel; and when I discovered the second cuff-link still in the shirt I got from Arnie's shop, it all fitted into place. So you see, the initials 'D' and 'A' were not inappropriate for David."

"Surely his name being Allen is pure coincidence?" said Sarah. "I'm sure there must be thousands of people around with that name."

"But, Sal, you've seen the scar on his hand. That must shorten the odds. No, it's obvious from what I've said, everyone must have taken it as being the family surname at the time....Anyway, when I met Lily here, at Wilf and Kevin's place a few weeks ago, she completed the story.

"Apparently, shortly after the child had been taken to the hospital, an elderly woman who went in part-time to see to the youngsters' needs, had named the boy David after her own son. And also, that the boy hadn't been got rid of at the behest of Edith Stockwell, but that actually Sam Griffiths had substituted a dead gypsy baby – which was buried in his stead – and then disappeared taking the child with him. Lily was in on all this, of course."

Lily nodded, saying, "He knew quite well that one youngster was on his way out, but had to pick the right moment to make sure the dreaded Nurse Carlisle wouldn't be there. So, he poisoned her dinner – not much like – just to make sure she were off for at least a couple of days. And of course, when Edith Stockwell went to check up on things, Carlisle wasn't there – because if she had been, she would have told Edith the truth. Still, we had to tell the replacement nurse that came in for the night shift, that *two* babies had passed away – one being buried during the day, and that the one she'd then witnessed being laid to rest early the following morning, was David – but was really the one who *had* died. Then it was fortunate when Edith came in to have a look around, she saw how distressed Betty Saville was – we had to fool the poor soul an' all – and when Edith came to see me, and I told her that indeed David was gone, she was then totally convinced."

"But what about the day nurse? Sarah asked. "Surely she would have known that a little one hadn't died the day before?"

"She did!" said Lily. "Carlisle made her life a misery while she was there; and, knowing that she was in the pocket of Edith Stockwell, was more than happy to help us in the deception."

"And you've actually kept this a secret all these years?" said Sarah.

Lily nodded. "I have never uttered a word about it from that day to this. I even told me dad that I'd been round to the doctor's house and a neighbour had told me he'd flitted at two in the mornin'."

It was Katherine's turn again to speak: "Now, shortly before David's father died, he confessed on his death-bed that David was adopted and that he wasn't his real father – nor was his mother his mother. The people who David had believed for years to be his parents, were in reality brother and sister. And when he was barely over a year old, they moved from Salisbury to Bristol, changed their names to Allen, and took on new identities – David told me all this when I took him aside earlier."

"So who was this so-called father of his?" Sarah asked.

"Samuel Griffiths of course! Doctor Sam!"

"Never!"

Katherine nodded. "Sometime, it must have become apparent to Sam that the boy who Edith wanted rid of, was obviously Alex Stockwell's son since she was so adamant that he carried out the deed....At this point, Sam determined that David should return to his roots; and so he arranged for him to take a course in textiles at Leeds University. And no doubt during the time he's been here, David began to put two and two together – particularly tonight when he came face to face with his real father."

Now Katherine looked directly upon the face of her half-sister whose reaction to her disclosures was abnormally screened; but said, "Well, now that you *do* know all that, will you still want to marry David?"

Sarah, her sparkling green eyes now filled with unmitigated assuredness, didn't say a word. She turned away from the two women at her table and surveyed those she loved in the ballroom. There was Jess, the droll and devoted Jess; Harry and Jane, happy at last; her nephew Kevin who had grown into a pleasing and caring young man, sitting with her old friend Wilf; David, the one who now wished to make her his wife; and then her son – her dear, dear son – who had rediscovered the love of his life. And how akin were the circumstances in which those two men now found themselves: both brought back to her from the dead as though resurrected.

Looking back at Katherine now, she smiled broadly, saying, "Will I still want to marry him...? Oh, without a doubt, Kath....If only to see the look on Edith Stockwell's sour face when it dawns on her that I'm going to wed her grandson."

And now the three women clinked glasses and laughed.

Part Three
The Family
1967

1

Sarah was seated at the patio table drinking coffee. At her feet, a black Labrador lay snoozing in the sun; and to her right, on a cast-iron chair without a cushion, was a discarded copy of the Yorkshire Post headlining the closure of another woollen mill.

The late 1960s were proving to be difficult years for the Yorkshire Woollen Industry. Many family businesses in the West Riding had not survived – and what else was left for them to do? They knew little other than the manufacture of cloth. Apart from cheap foreign imports, taxes on profits were at a crippling level. But Sarah possessed an unyielding determination that astounded many who were still struggling to carry on, and would fight like the lioness she was to keep her own enterprise afloat. Sarah was determined not to allow her business to go under – as had been the case with so many of the mills in her home town of Collingley – and had resolved not only to save her empire, but also to expand it: eventually by acquiring Providence mill which was owned by the Stockwells. Yet to achieve her ultimate ambitions, she also needed to make further substantial purchases and form a new limited company.

She looked at her left hand now and began to turn the rings on her finger. One was a slim gold band that John Halliday had placed there in 1944 when they were married in a double wedding alongside her halfsister, Katherine. The second ring – a platinum and diamond cluster – was William's way of telling her how much he valued her love. And then there was the small, less showy, diamond engagement ring that David Allen had presented to her on New Year's Eve. He – in one way or another – would become the major shareholder in Providence on the demise of his father. But only the Almighty knew when that would be; and, if Alex did indeed stipulate in his will that David would so inherit, then no doubt it would be contested by the manipulative matriarch, Edith Stockwell. Sarah though, was determined that this would never happen – but she didn't want to take any chances as far as Edith was concerned, and resolved to buy out the Stockwells at the earliest opportunity. But that was for the future. For now, the present was her concern.

It was a beautiful spring morning: not one brazen cloud had dared to corrupt the cerulean aspect that greeted her when she stepped out of the library into the sweetly-scented garden. Yet still there was a nip in the air, persuading her to wear a thick, navy blue jacket over her favourite black woollen dress. Jessie had brought her a pot of coffee, saying she would join her shortly to discuss the arrangements for the arrival of Sarah's sister Katherine and her son Josh who were last here at New Year, and those for the upcoming celebrations of her son, Paul, who was about to reach his twenty-first birthday in a few weeks' time. Now, staring across the garden in the direction of the mill where smoke billowed from its tall chimney, and sporadic pulses of steam burst forth from vents in the stone walls, Sarah smiled a contented smile knowing that her son would be there, happily working on the accounts.

Paul was finally in a stable relationship with Mark, and they had moved from High Ridge into a house of their own. The two boys were polar opposites: Paul being the mathematician and Mark the artist; one blessed with hair the colour of the sun, the other with that of the blackness of night. At one time, it was touch-and-go if their deep bond could ever survive, when his father had dismissed Mark from the house after a tactless remark had poisoned William against his son and, heartbreakingly, neither had ever seen the other again.

Mark stayed away for nearly seven years, during which time Paul discovered another love in his life. Steven Clark was an architect who took over the tenancy of one of Sarah's houses on Long Lane – which just happened to be the one in which Paul was brought up in and where now he and Mark lived. Steven was a truly beautiful young man – both in his physique and his heart – and Paul was smitten from the first moment they met. And Sarah regretted that she hadn't had more time to get to known him better.

After the tragedy at Providence mill when Steven was killed, Sarah was left with a monumental problem. For one thing, she had the turmoil of knowing that Paul lay in a coma, and the other was having to leave it up to social services to find out if Steven had any family to see to his affairs and funeral arrangements. Eventually a relative was found – an aunt she believed – and Steven was buried somewhere in Leeds without her knowing anything further, and which was heart-breaking to her still. Paul recovered of course, and although he was perfectly cognisant of his family and friends, he could neither remember the fire – nor Steven. At least, he had never admitted to it. Oh! how she wished she could have done more for the man who loved her son – the son who now was loved by another.

But Sarah's happiness at Paul's ordered condition was transient, in the knowledge that even though it was rumoured that the obscene law regarding homosexuality would soon be repealed, Paul and Mark were technically still breaking it. Nevertheless, Sarah had supported Paul through his struggles even when Edith Stockwell's youngest son, Joseph, threatened her with blackmail. Then, when he and his uncle died, and Alex had returned those incriminating photographs, she believed her troubles to be over, only to hear that the police were now in the process of investigating the deaths. Now, the previous smile that had blossomed on her lips, inextricably wilted....

"Oi! Have you dropped off out here?" Jessie toddled onto the patio and took a seat. "Oh, these bloody chairs are a bugger on the arse. I don't know how you can sit on 'em."

Sarah gazed lovingly at the sixty-five-year-old and the smile returned. "Look. Before we press on with things, Jess; I've been thinking."

"Aye! You do more thinking than is good for you."

Ignoring the remark, Sarah went on: "Well, I was wondering if Paul and Mark should come back and live here. After all, there's plenty of room. What do you think?"

"Why? They seem happy enough where they are to me. And Amy and the other neighbour really get on well with them."

"But will it last? You know perfectly well that there are some malicious people out there who, given the chance, could possibly do something to harm them both. It has been tried before."

Jessie waved her hand. "Well, all I can say is that it's up to them. I for one would love to have them both back here, but" – she wagged a chubby finger in Sarah's direction – "it should be their own decision."

"I suppose you're right, love. We'll just have to see how things go. So, is everything just about ready for when Kath and Josh arrive?"

"Aye! But it surprises me that they've only been gone a couple of months. Why on earth do they want to come back so quick?"

Sarah shrugged, and her eyes widened. "I have no idea. She did say that she and Josh were coming for Paul's twenty-first; but, as you know, there's always something devious about my sister's plans....Now, I'll ask you again, is everything ready?"

"Oh, for God's sake. Yes...! Amy's nearly finished their rooms and I've worked out what we'll be havin' for dinner, so that part's sorted. All that's left now is for you to do the invites. Is that all right for Madam?" She smiled; but Sarah seemed lost in thoughts. Oh, how Jessie admired this strong woman who was so much like her mother? And though her hair was not as red as Emma's was – it was more auburn – she certainly had her temperament. Folk had often said there was something of the Viking in their ancestry, and Jessie could quite well believe the sentiment.

"Do you know, Jess, I can't say I remember much about Josh. To me, he just looked more like a...a suntanned, young Kath."

"Nay, don't tell your sister that, or she'll think you believe she used to look like a fella."

Sarah chuckled now. "Well, whoever Josh is like, he's certainly a looker. That means we're going to have to keep an eye on Annie – and Paul no doubt." Then her face altered. "Oh, I do hope that son of mine behaves himself, Jess. I don't want a brouhaha going on."

"A what-haha?"

"A ruckus."

Jessie leaned forward and stared at her friend. "I do wish you'd talk sense at times instead o' speaking in tongues." But observing Sarah's dull and pained expression, she thought, Oh, so do I. Jessie knew how hot tempered both the boys could get; and Paul, even though he doted on Mark, had a roving eye when it came to the lads. She now said, "Well, this is no good; I'll have to get on instead of prattling on 'ere." She pushed her portly frame up from the seat; and before taking her leave, said, "And you'd best get going an' all before another bloody mill shuts down."

As she walked away, Sarah thought, However much I love the old trout, she can really put the mockers on things at times. She leaned down now and patted the dog. "Come on, Ben, lad; things need to be done...."

Seated at the library desk now, Sarah picked up her pen and hovered over the invitation cards. Now! Who should she invite? Well, certainly not Laura – even though Paul was fond of her – since Jane and Harry would be back from holiday. And why on earth Harry had an affair with Laura, the Lord only knew! So, not inviting Laura meant not inviting her parents, which no doubt would please Katherine who – it had to be said – hated her sister

Mary with a detestation that bordered on the psychotic.

Well, I'm not getting far with this, thought Sarah as she leaned back in the chair. And as she remained there contemplating on the task before her, Jessie came in from the small vestibule that connected the library to the hallway. "Sorry to interrupt, love, but two bobbies are here to see you. They're at the front door. A young 'un and an older one. Shall I show 'em in?"

"Oh, not again." Sarah stood. "This thing about the Stockwells has been going on far too long. I cannot understand why the police are asking questions – particularly of us – when it was obvious that they fell over a hundred feet to their deaths."

Jessie Dicks folded her arms over her breasts. "Well it mustn't have seemed so obvious at the inquest since it were adjourned to a later date. Anyroad, we don't know they're here for that."

"What else could it be...? Sarah hesitated now, before saying, "You'd better take Ben to the kitchen or he's liable to rip their throats out."

"Well, I'll tell yer this: if he doesn't, I will! I hate the soddin' police. If they're not clippin' wayward kids' lugs, they're forever holding their flamin' balls; and now they've decided to have a go at *us*. It really pisses me off."

Sarah smiled, saying, "Go on. Show them in."

After taking the dog with her, Jessie returned a few minutes later and admitted the two policemen. The plain-clothed inspector took off his hat and went over to Sarah who was seated at her desk, while the other – young and uniformed – remained beside the library door. "Inspector Ackroyd, Mrs Crowther, and this" – he turned his head slightly – "is Constable Jarvis." She stood, and taking his hand, said, "Inspector. Please be seated. What can I do for you?"

The inspector placed his hat on the table and coughed as Sarah retook her seat. "This is somewhat of an embarrassing situation I find myself in, Mrs Crowther; but I have to ask you if you recall the death of Mr Steven Clark in the fire at Providence mill?"

Sarah leaned back and clasped her hands together. "Inspector, I could hardly forget it. And also, my son was in a coma at the time."

The inspector coughed again.

"Can I order some tea for you?" said Sarah. "Your throat sounds very dry."

"No thank you. I'm fine....Now, you no doubt have heard that we are still investigating the suspicious circumstances surrounding the deaths of both Joseph Stockwell and his uncle after that fire – particularly that of Mr Stockwell."

"I have heard rumours…but what has that to do with *me*?"

"Oh, not you directly. But it could involve your stepdaughter's husband."

"Harry?"

"Mr Harry Carr; yes. You see, in our investigations, it would appear that Mr Carr spent the night before Joseph Stockwell's death in an illegal card school. Several witnesses have confirmed that both he and Mr Stockwell participated, and that Mr Stockwell won quite a bit of money from Mr Carr – which may be construed as Mr Carr having a score to settle."

"Oh, but surely you're not suggesting that he had something to do with what happened to both Joseph and his uncle?"

"Mrs Crowther, I am not suggesting anything; but I do need to interview Mr Carr, and I would be obliged if you could furnish me with his address. He does not appear to be on the electoral roll."

"Oh, how remiss of him." Sarah looked directly at the inspector, her eyes critical and vibrant. "And I suppose if I refuse to supply his – and my stepdaughter's – address, then you may also *construe* that I could have an ulterior motive in concealing their whereabouts?" Sarah reached for a piece of notepaper and pen. "May I ask why you wish to interview Mr Carr?"

"You may ask, madam; but I am not at liberty to answer – as you may appreciate."

"And what if I was to say that I also am not at liberty to furnish you with his address? And please don't call me 'madam', it makes me sound as if I'm running a brothel."

The inspector was nonplussed, and he detected that his colleague was sniggering behind his back. Once more he coughed – this time it sounding almost as if something was lodged in his throat. But he answered forcefully: "I would say…Mrs Crowther…that you had something to hide."

Sarah looked down at the pad on her desk, and after picking up her pen, languorously began to write. "There you are: Mr and Mrs Carr's address."

The inspector thanked her.

"But," said Sarah; "you won't find them in." She smiled now. "They are taking a second honeymoon, and none of us know where they've gone." And after Sarah had summoned Jessie, the inspector picked up his hat, and without speaking further, he and his subordinate departed.

"What was all that about?" asked Jessie when she returned from showning the police out.

And as Sarah repeatedly tapped her pen on the desk, she said, "Trouble, Jess. Trouble."

2

"That's where I used to live when I first met your father. And soon, coming up on the right, is Aunt Sarah's mill. There! That's Resurrection."

Joshua looked out of the window of the Rolls-Royce Silver Cloud. "It's very big," he said.

"The biggest in the West Riding," said Katherine.

"What does it mean – riding?" asked Josh.

"Ah, it comes from the Norse meaning 'third'. And because Yorkshire is so big, they had to divide it up to administer the place, so it was split into three – hence: third. That's why there isn't a South Riding – only West, North and East....As far as the mill is concerned, I'm sure Sarah will show you around the place if you like."

"Yes," said Josh with genuine enthusiasm. "I'd like that...I'd like it very much. But why is it called Resurrection?"

Katherine was thrilled that her son was showing so much interest, so she explained: "Ah, well. It didn't have a name like the other mills in the area, so after a fire last century, it was decided to give it one, and they came up with Resurrection."

She gave a little sigh now. "It was such a pity we had to leave so soon at the beginning of the year," she said. "Still, now we can see the town in spring instead of in the freezing cold, eh?"

Josh didn't respond. But then, completely out of the blue, asked, "Do you think Aunt Sarah likes me, Mom?"

Katherine puzzled as to her son's sudden distraction; but said, "Oh, don't have any worries on that score, love. Sarah likes everybody – well, there are exceptions."

"You mean the Stockwells?"

"Mainly. But there are others that get her back up."

After a moment of quiet, Josh said, "From what you've told me about her, she seems quite liberal in her attitude."

"You could put it that way." She leaned forward and placed her hand on the chauffeur's shoulder. "What do you say, Max?"

Max turned his head slightly. "Mrs Crowther is certainly a free-thinking woman, madam; nevertheless, she doesn't suffer fools gladly."

Katherine chuckled. She liked Max. He'd been a chauffeur at High Ridge for going on fifteen years and was the sweetest of men. Apart from Sarah herself, Jessie Dicks, Annie the maid and Amy Broadbent who came in occasionally as cleaner and general help, he was the only other member of the household. Annie was a timid, little thing; and at the age of twenty-seven, still hadn't found herself a man. Oh! she'd forgotten about Laura – her niece – who had reverted to her maiden name of Wilson, and was employed as Sarah's gardener. Now that was a strange set-up if *ever* there was one.

"And what about Paul?" said Josh.

"What...?" said his mother. "Oh, well, I've got to say that Paul can be a bit of a scoundrel; but Mark keeps him under control. They're a smashing couple."

"But doesn't Aunt Sarah mind Paul being" – Josh nudged his mother and whispered, "gay?"

"Sweetheart, you don't have to whisper. Max is the soul of discretion – like Sherlock Holmes' Watson. So, to answer your question: of course not! Why should she? Naturally she worries about people having wicked notions about that sort of thing and that they might hurt both him and Mark; but, your aunt – as Max says – doesn't suffer fools gladly. And after all, we all have to die one day, love; so we've got to make the most of the lives nature gave us."

"What would my stepfather think about it?"

"Good Lord! For heaven's sake, love, you know he's a dyed-in-the-wool Catholic – and they're a weird lot. I know that from your Aunt Mary."

Josh laughed derisively. "But still you married him?"

"Yes! But that was business. I have only ever loved one man and that was your father....Oh, look, Josh! We're here! Back at High Ridge." This was a relief to Katherine since the conversation with her son had soured. "Wow! what's happened to it? It's sparkling."

"Mrs Crowther had the masonry sand-blasted, madam," said Max as he manoeuvred the car through the wrought iron gates and proceeded slowly down the drive.

"Gee, Mom," said Joshua, "it's fantastic! I didn't see much of it in the dark when I arrived last New Year. And then I slept most of the following day before we had to fly back to Chicago."

Katherine patted her son's hand. "Well this time, love, you'll be seeing quite a lot more, I promise you."

Max pulled up at the majestic stone porch and exited the car. He went around to Katherine's side and opened the door for the woman who was of a similar age to Jessie; and watching her closely as she emerged, he thought his employer's half-sister a statuesque woman; and though she was possessed of a mop of silvery hair, she had the manner of a much younger and vibrant personage.

Now, as Joshua emerged from the Rolls, he stood back to admire the grandeur of the building.

"Well? What do you think of the place in daylight?" said his mother. And Joshua said, "It's beautiful. But I have to admit I'm terrified."

"Why? There's nothing to be scared about. After all, you know everybody. Come on, let's get inside."

Max rang the bell and shortly Annie appeared. "Oh 'ello, madam. Lovely to see you again. Come in. Come in and I'll tell the missis you're here. Are yer seeing to the bags, Max?"

The chauffeur acknowledged Annie's enquiry and proceeded to unpack the boot, as Katherine and Joshua followed Annie into the hallway. "Oh, I say! It's been redecorated," said Katherine. "It's so much brighter."

"It was finished a few weeks ago," said Annie. "The missis chose the wallpaper and the paint."

"What do you think, Josh?" Katherine asked.

Joshua was lost for words as he looked around. The floor was tiled with a creamy-coloured marble, and above, casting what seemed like a thousand sparkling lights in every direction, was the newly restored great chandelier. The wide, central staircase was deeply carpeted in a vivid red, and on the walls, there appeared to him what looked like silken wallpaper with a delicately interwoven, pale-green leaf design. "It's something else, Mom."

"Oh, by the way, Annie; you remember my son Josh, don't you?"

Annie dipped slightly, saying, "Aye, madam. I do."

Max was depositing the last of the suitcases. "I'll leave them here for now, ma'am, and take them up to your rooms later."

"Thanks Max. Thanks for everything," said Katherine, and Max tipped his cap.

"Right," said Annie, "let me take you through. I think the missis is in the drawing-room."

As they walked across the hall, Katherine said, "Jessie not

around, Annie?"

"No, madam," Annie replied. "She's over at Paul and Mark's helping them choose some curtain fabric. The missis said it was time they had a spruce up an' all." She knocked on the drawing-room door and showed the guests in.

"Sweetheart!" Immediately, Katherine raced and embraced her sister. "Well, here we are back again. And Josh is staying much longer this time."

Joshua approached his aunt and kissed her on both cheeks.

"My! you're more handsome than ever," said Sarah. "Now, let's have some drinks, eh? Annie love, be a good lass and bring in a new bottle of port and maybe one of whisky as well...."

Later, while Katherine was engrossed in deep conversation with her sister, Joshua remained quiet; and, sipping occasionally at his whisky, he began to engage himself in a scrutiny of his aunt. He had to concede that at the age of forty-four she was a striking woman: her auburn hair showed no sign of greying and was dressed to perfection; her large, green eyes sparkled with each word she uttered, and her posture was that of an assured and dignified human being.

The room itself was as impressive as the hallway. Sumptuous chairs and couches were covered in dark-green velvet; highly polished tables sported vases of daffodils and tulips; various cabinets housed shimmering glassware and porcelain; and on the cardinal-red walls were ornately framed pictures of Yorkshire landscapes. But one particular work of art stood out from the rest, and that was a painting by L S Lowry.

His mother had mentioned how Sarah's father, unbeknown to the family – including Sarah herself at the time – had hidden it from view, and it only came to light when he bequeathed it to her on his death. It was the only thing George Harvey had that was of any value, and now must be worth a fortune. And as Josh stared intently at the painting, his eyes slowly closed, and he drifted off into a world of mill chimneys and people as thin as matchsticks....

"So," said Katherine, "tell me what the police wanted."

"Oh, Kath," Sarah sighed, "things don't get any better." She took a mouthful of port. "They are still investigating the death of Joe Stockwell – and his uncle. And, as you know, the night before it happened, I sent my stepdaughter's husband on a fool's errand to cajole Joe into a situation which he couldn't possibly wriggle out of."

"But it wasn't foolish: Harry got the photographs you could have used against Stockwell like those he had of Paul and Steven when he tried to blackmail *you*."

"Yes, but the police have found out that Harry was in an illegal game of poker with Joe on that same night. They may be thinking that Harry was seeking revenge after losing money to a shark like Joseph Stockwell."

Katherine leaned forward and rested a hand on her sister's knee. "Well, if that's the case, I'm sure they could come up with at least a dozen people who'd wish to harm him. Try not to worry, sweetheart. Anyhow" – she sat back now – "how's married life going for Jane and Harry?"

Sarah half-closed her eyes and jerked her head. "It's not, to be honest. They're away at the moment: I made sure they took a break to try and sort things out."

"What sort of things? Harry's not been messing about with Laura again, has he? I don't know why you employed that niece of ours knowing what a fast cat she is."

"Oh, it's nothing like that. Laura's a good worker and never comes into contact with Harry and Jane. No, it's not that, it's... well, it's...sort of awkward."

Katherine leaned forward again, and Sarah knew her sister would press her if she didn't deliver. So she said quickly, "Jane doesn't want any kind of intimacy." She glanced at Josh who had fallen asleep on the settee, before saying, "They're not...you know...." She moved her head from side to side.

"Oh, I see," said Katherine, reaching into her bag and pulling out a packet of cigarettes. And as she lit up, she asked, "So, how long has this been going on – or not? And more to the point, how do you know?"

Sarah sighed. "A long time apparently. Harry told me. And, from what he said, it seems to have stemmed from the time her uncle Joe died."

"Perhaps it's grief that's put her off?"

"Oh, I doubt it, Kath. She detested him as much as *I* did. And, don't forget, she was totally behind me when I told her what I planned to do to trap him."

Katherine dragged on the cigarette. "And what about Kevin? How are he and Wilf getting on?"

"Oh, they're both fine." Sarah sipped at her port. "Kevin's a partner in Harry's building business now. His dad is so proud of him."

"Our Emily would have been an' all. What is it now? Three years since she passed?"

Sarah nodded. "And how I miss our little Sis. I'm sure Josh would have loved her as much as we did." She gazed over at her nephew now. "He's tired. In fact, you both must be after your journey. Why don't you go and have a nap?"

Katherine stubbed out her cigarette. "I think that sounds like a very good idea, love"

"Right! I'll show you to your rooms and then get Max to bring up your luggage." Sarah placed her drink on the coffee table, and standing, walked across to her nephew, rescued the whisky from his sagging hand and gently stirred him. "Bed time, young man – for a while at least."

Joshua awoke slowly to the scent of white jasmine and his aunt's eyes sparkling knowingly in front of his face. And the look she gave him now, was as if she were able to read the contents of his very soul.

3

Harry lay in bed next to his wife, thinking not of her, but of Sarah and Paul.

Sarah – the reason only known to herself – had sent he and Jane away, likely to see if they could sort out their marriage which, if all was to be told, was on the rocks. She had never hinted at this, but he could see in that wonderful woman's eyes that all this was her intention. Oh! how he regretted having had harsh words with her after Joe Stockwell had died.

At the time, she had said to him: 'Dear God, Harry. Please tell me you had nothing to do with Joe's death.'

'How many more times do you want me to say it, Sarah?' he had replied. 'Yes, I went there; but I hid behind a wall at the side of the house. Nobody could have spotted me....Anyhow, as I waited, I saw Alex coming up the garden path and I watched him go inside. This surprised me, since I was under the impression that he would still be in hospital after being injured in the fire. Then – a few minutes later – Joe rushed out of the front door and went straight to the shed at the bottom of the garden. I was about to follow him when Alex reappeared and stood looking about the garden. I ducked down behind the wall and waited until I thought he had left. I waited...and waited...and finally fell asleep. And when I woke up, it had begun to rain; so, I turned up my coat collar and fled the accursed place. On Paul's life that's the truth, Sarah. I thought better of you than to even think I would do anything like that. You bloody disappoint me. You really do!'

And here he was, with Sarah's blessing, lying by his wife's side in the early morning at the best hotel in Scarborough, thinking not only about his love for Sarah but also for her son. Yes! he had to admit he was in love with the lad – not in a sexual way, but as in a way that maybe Alexander the Great and his Hephaestion were in love. Paul had taught him their story – along with many others when they were young.

He recalled with affection when he first met the special young boy who taught him how to read, write, do sums; and how he had dragged him into a world that changed his life. On the day they travelled to High Ridge, Paul had introduced him to William Crowther – and the kindly man had got him a job as an apprentice with a builder who had carried out some work at his mill. This was a fortuitous journey in more ways than one – he met William's daughter, Jane, who became his wife.

But on the day he met Paul, he had unashamedly used him as a warm body to masturbate next to. Now he only had the option of a private wank since his wife had rejected his advances.

She had not been the same since his short-lived affair with Laura Wilson, and things seemed to have got worse after her uncle died. Sex between them had been put on the back burner, and he could count on one hand the number of times that he and Jane had made love. And on those occasions, none had ever resulted in a shuddering climax.

He slipped from the bed and placed the eiderdown gently back over his wife. Then he put on his dressing-gown and went to the window. There he drew back the curtains and stared out over the grey North Sea. It looks as miserable as I feel, he thought. Going back and forth over the insignificant sand which darkened with its every ebb and flow. Repetitively going back and forth in a pointless and boring rhythm just like his infrequent sex life.

Then he heard a yawn from behind him; and in turning, Jane was smiling at him. "What's it like out, love?" she said, and yawned again.

"Dull," he said.

"It might brighten up."

"Aye...perhaps."

"Come and sit beside me, love, before I get up. Just for a while." And when he returned to the bed and sat facing her, she pushed back her husband's long, black hair. "You're still thinking about what Mam said, aren't you?" She stroked the stubble on his chin. "Oh, she didn't mean anything by it, love, but all this business about...." She paused and looked down at the floral coverlet. And when she returned her gaze at her husband, she breathed heavily before saying, "This business about Uncle Joe is affecting us all. It's only that she cares about the two of us. You must also know that Sarah won't blame you for what you said – she's not the kind of person who would."

Harry rested a hand on her thigh. "You're right of course. I shouldn't have spoken to her like I did. But since Joe's death, everything seems to have changed – even you. You've scarcely wanted me. It seems as if his dying has affected you so much that your love for me has died as well."

"No, it hasn't. I love you so much, Harry Carr. And if it all boils down to it, even I would have had every right to…." She stopped talking. And when she didn't start again, Harry stared at his wife's moist eyes and said, "Every right to what?"

Jane shook her head. "It's nothing important." Smiling now, she said, "Look. It's our last full day, so let's make the most of it." She glanced at the window. "The weather seems to be brightening. We could go and look for a present for Paul and then take a boat trip – they've got a bar on board. Eh?"

Harry remained morose; but presently he nodded, saying, "Yes. Let's do that."

The late March sun had burned away the clouds, the sea was calm, and the views from the ship were spectacular. The cliffs between the North and South bays glistened in the spring light, and the ruined castle still guarded the wonderful Yorkshire coast.

Whilst Harry ordered drinks, Jane surveyed the scene. How peaceful it all seemed from what she felt inside, and she knew the time had come to tell her husband the truth. Over the years, she had kept her secret close to her breast. Sometimes she would convince herself that what had happened to her was just a dream, but the nightmare was real enough and now she had to relieve herself of its pain.

"There you are, Mrs Carr," said Harry as he placed the glass in front of his wife. "One very large snowball."

"Thanks, love…I hope Paul likes the cologne we bought him."

"It cost enough," said Harry.

Jane turned to her husband. "You don't begrudge him it, do you?"

Harry chuckled, saying, "Of course not. I just mean it would be a shame paying the money if he *doesn't* like it. I'd have paid even more if I knew it pleased him, so let's hope he loves it rather than hates it. Mind you, Paul would say he loves it even if he doesn't."

Jane tasted her drink now. "Ah, that's nice," she announced. Then she stared out to sea as if she were searching for something on the horizon – which wasn't far from the truth. She had to pluck up the courage to confide in her husband; but as she looked at him with his eyes closed facing the sun and bearing a wistful smile on his face, she decided that this just wasn't the time.

4

They were on a trip to Leeds – specifically to buy birthday presents for Paul. But certain snippets of conversation that occurred during their outing would come as a total shock to Katherine.

"I haven't been on a bus in years," she said. "I think the best place to get off is at the bottom of Briggate if my memory serves me right. It's just after we go over the river, so keep a look out."

Josh had hardly spoken a word during the half-hour journey. "Are you all right, love?" his mother enquired.

"Oh, yes…just thinking."

"What about?"

Josh stared out of the window. "I can't really say…all sorts of things, I suppose."

"Tell me."

"We'd better get off, Mom. We're just going over the river."

After an hour exploring the shops, during which Katherine had bought Paul a most expensive wrist-watch and Josh had purchased a recording of the complete Wagner's Ring Cycle, which, hopefully, his cousin didn't already have. And now they were having a well-deserved break in a bar next door to the City Varieties Music Hall. "We'll have to catch a show here sometime. And also at The Grand." Katherine suddenly turned to her preoccupied son, saying, "You know I won't rest till you tell me what's on your mind, so get on with it."

Her son took a swig of his beer. "Well, I'm thinking of coming to live here, if you really want to know." His long, dark eyelashes fluttered.

"You are kidding!"

"No, I'm not! I hardly slept last night thinking about it. And I really want to do it."

"But you're going into our American business next year. You can't just throw that away."

Josh looked directly at his mother. "I still can go into your business, Mom. But at Anderson's….I could run that place for you."

Katherine was taken aback by her son's suggestion. Granted she could do with a member of the family keeping an eye on her design and tailoring company in Bradford, but why Josh? He lived a comfortable and rewarding life in the States and had never even hinted at anything other than wanting to stay and work there. What sudden occurrence had so fuelled this change of heart? "You are a weird one at times, Josh," she said now. "You certainly don't take after your father."

"Mom, all I want is to come and live and work here. Other guys of my age – and younger – go all over the world; and at least I was born here and have family who I know and trust."

"Well, you've certainly put me on the spot I must say."

Josh placed his hand on his mother's. "At least will you think about it?"

Katherine forced a weak smile. "Yes, I will....Now, let's be off. I want to go to Kirkgate Market before we get the bus back...."

Josh was captivated by the huge market, with its ornate iron pillars and the incalculable number of stalls bursting with meat, poultry, fish and vegetables; bread, cakes and chocolates; cheeses of every kind; linens, clothing and hardware and every other item one could possibly wish to buy. And when they came out burdened with bags of foodstuffs, he was on a high. "I want to go to The Hart. Aunt Sarah mentioned it last night and I want to see what it's like."

His mother grabbed at his arm. "The Hart? It's a dive – at least it used to be. And what was she doing telling *you* about it?"

"Oh, come on, Mom. Let's live dangerously for once." And Katherine surprised herself by agreeing; thinking, I am a little curious about the place myself, since it was there that Joseph Stockwell had those potentially damning photographs taken....

The pub was far from what she had expected. It was small, but cosy in a curious sort of way. There was amber-coloured flock wallpaper, and a dark-blue carpet with 'The Hart of Leeds' picked out here and there in gold; and the bar was horseshoe-shaped as it curved away from where they were standing, into another area at the rear. And she was surprised to see an elderly barmaid serving drinks to the few customers present. Shortly the woman approached them, saying, "What can I get yer, love?"

"Oh...I'll have a glass of sherry – a large one – and...."

"A pint of beer," said Josh.

The woman went about getting the drinks; and when she returned, said, "You're not from these parts are yer, young lad?"

"Er...no. I'm from Chicago."

"Not a gangster I hope!" The woman laughed.

"Not yet," said Josh, smiling.

"He's a bit of a wit the lad is," said the barmaid. "Grandson, is he?"

"Son!" said Katherine, scowling.

"Eeh, I'm sorry, lass...that'll be four and six."

Katherine handed the woman a ten-shilling note, and after getting her change, she and Josh went to a table and deposited their bags. "It's not too bad in here is it, Mom?"

"The cheeky mare," said Katherine. "Grandson indeed!"

Josh chuckled. "It's a mistake anyone could make."

"Oh, really?"

"Just sit down, and I'll go and bring the drinks over." And Josh returned to the bar with a smile on his face.

Katherine sat and delved in her handbag for her cigarettes; and when she had lit one and taken in the first puff of smoke, she looked about her thinking, So this the place where Sarah's trouble with Joe Stockwell began. Right here in this very room he must have hatched his plan to blackmail her using Paul as bait. Well, he deserved all he got by plummeting hundreds of feet from a stone ledge at the back of his house – God pays back.

"One large sherry, ma'am," said Josh as he returned; but his mother never said a word: she was staring open-mouthed at a framed photograph on the wall beside her. "Mom...?"

"It's him, Josh!" she gasped. "That's a picture of Steve – Paul's friend who was killed in the mill fire. I'm certain of it. Sarah showed me an exact copy – although she keeps it under lock and key in case Paul may come across it and it stirs any awful memories." And before Josh could make a comment, Katherine was on her feet and striding to the bar.

"Another sherry, love?" said the barmaid.

"No thanks. That photograph on the wall over there" – Katherine pointed – "Can you tell me who it is?"

"Aye, he is a good-looker, isn't he? It's my nephew Steven – well...was, before he were killed in a fire. He was more like a son to me after his parents died – and he told me everything. Anyhow, after finishing his studies in London, he came back to live up here. He rented a place over Morley way – or somewhere of the sort –

and had, to put it bluntly, found a lad of the same persuasion of those that come in here. And he loved that lad dearly – whoever he was."

Katherine looked at the woman in disbelief, before leaning over the bar, saying, "That lad is *my* very own nephew too."

"Never. Surely not?"

Katherine nodded.

"Hang on. I'll come an' join yer without folk hearin' us." With this, the diminutive, grey-haired woman came from behind the bar, shouting as she did so: "Oi! Tommy! Come and look after things for a bit, lad." And as she joined Katherine and Josh, she pulled out a padded stool from beneath the table and sat and faced them. "Well, I'm flabbergasted. Fancy your own nephew being the one't Steven tried to save. Eeh, lass, this has come as a bit of a shock meeting you like this."

"Oh, I'm so terribly sorry. I didn't mean to…."

"Nay, love, it's all right." She flapped a hand. "But, between you, me and the gatepost" – she stabbed a finger at the table now – "I've always had my doubts about what really happened at that mill. I went to the inquest, yer know, and there were lots of odd things that didn't seem to make sense to me. I still believe the fire were started deliberately – and I said at the time, that however long it took, I wouldn't rest till whoever did it was made to pay."

Katherine touched the woman's hand. "I think that may have happened already."

"Aye, I gathered that." The barmaid turned her head now, and called out: "Tommy! Bring us a whisky, lad." Turning back to Katherine, she said, "My heart went out to the lad's mother that day. In a way, she had lost a loved one an' all.…But now, you comin' 'ere is nowt less than a miracle. Yer see, I have summat for the lad if I could bring it for him. I won't go into details but it's most important."

Josh kicked his mother's foot and she acknowledged the reason for his action. So after the woman grabbed the drink from her stand-in who had approached, she drank feverishly as Katherine said, "He doesn't remember Steven after the fire, love; and, well, to be honest, he's with somebody else now. You must understand the implications if you contact him." She picked up her drink and drew on her cigarette.

"Aye, I do, lass. And I wouldn't want to upset him, but I'll 'ave to do summat. Perhaps I could see his mother?"

"Well…I suppose I could ask her since you say it's important," said Katherine. "Tell you what, give me your phone number and I'll mention it to her and then she can contact you. How about that?"

"Grand, lass." With this, the woman pushed herself off the stool and raced to the bar, shortly to return with a beer-mat on the reverse of which were two telephone numbers. "That's me home number" – she pointed – "and the other is the pub's. She should get me on one or t'other. Anyroad, I'd best get back or Tommy'll sup the place dry." She laughed now and scurried away.

"What do you make of all that, Mom?" Josh said quietly.

"I don't know what to make of it. She seems genuine enough, but it's odd that Sarah has never mentioned anything about Steven having a family – or that anyone who knew him was at the inquest."

"And what was the inquest's outcome?"

"Misadventure.…But from what your Aunt Sarah said, there were a lot of unanswered questions."

"Like what?"

"Oh, it was all a bit odd from what she told me. Apparently, the fire began in a lift shaft which was used to hoist books and documents up to the offices where Steven was killed trying to rescue Paul and Alex Stockwell.

"Alex's uncle, who really wasn't qualified to do the job but had a knack of dealing with such matters, had installed new electrics. Anyhow, these electrics must have caused a spark that set the shaft alight.…Another thing that's always puzzled me, is what Jessie told me about Amy Broadbent.

"She told me that Amy had expressed her belief that Philip – Edith Stockwell's brother – was acting strangely on the night it happened. She'd seen him scurrying up the lane in front of her house coming from the direction of the mill. She thought it odd that he was all muffled up on such a hot night and why he was even *in* the lane, since the Stockwell's house is at the top of a slope behind the mill itself."

"And did he give evidence at the inquest?"

"He couldn't, love. He was found the day after the fire lying on the railway line with every bone in his body smashed because of the height from which he fell – or, because he was pushed?"

Josh took a mouthful of his drink; and in this moment, decided that he *was* going to come and work here. Apart from being fascinated by this enigma surrounding the events that put his cousin into a coma, he wanted to be close to him regardless of the relationship he had with Mark. Yes! Now he had definitely made up his mind.

"And there was his picture," said Katherine, pushing her palms forward, "stuck up on the pub wall. Hasn't Paul seen it?"

"He never goes in the place these days – and he doesn't mention Steven," said Sarah. "I don't know whether that's because he doesn't remember much about him after his accident, or if he doesn't want to think about him now that Mark's back....So what's all this with Josh?"

Katherine shook her head. "I don't know what's come over him since we arrived. He's determined he wants to come and live here and work at Anderson's."

"And what are your thoughts about it?"

"Oh, I don't know....There's a place for him back home – and I don't think I could bear to lose him."

"Well, love, you probably will have to one day. They all fly the nest at some point."

Katherine approached the library desk now and, placing her hands on its central, green morocco inlay, pushed her face forward, saying, "So! What are you going to do about this woman?"

Sarah leaned back in her chair, and turning her pen between her fingers, said, "You seem awfully eager for me to meet her for some reason."

"It could be important, Sal. And it couldn't do any harm just to have a chat with the woman. Well?"

Sarah stared at the telephone numbers on the beer-mat now, saying, "I don't know, Kath. After all, she might blame me personally for not doing enough to find out if Steven had any family after he died, instead of leaving it to others."

"No, she wouldn't. She's not the type. She realises you had a lot on your plate at the time and did what you could. And the social services did find her....So, will you get in touch?"

Sarah put down the pen, saying, "Maybe...I'll have to see."

5

Jessie entered the library. "What? Jesus! Every time I'm in the middle o' summat you want me. There's a lot to do for tonight, yer know." It was now she caught sight of a man seated on the ox-blood, leather chesterfield with his back towards her. "How the bloody hell did he get in here? And at this hour!"

"Never mind that, Jess. Is Kath up yet?" said Sarah.

"Aye, she's up. She's just making a coffee." Jessie glowered at the back of the visitor's head.

"Would you ask her to come in as soon as she can? Father Rutledge is here to see her."

"Father...? Oh! Aye I'll...er, go and tell her."

Moments later, Katherine entered. The look on her face was one of profound shock when she saw the priest sitting there.

"I'll leave you to it, Father." Sarah rose from behind her desk, and in departing, questioned her sister with her eyes. But Katherine was similarly confused as to the reason for the man's presence.

Father Rutledge stood now; and walking toward the door, said, "Please, Mrs Mitchell; come and take a seat. I'm glad you were able to see me."

After shaking his hand, Katherine walked to a chair and sat like a disobedient child. He's behaving as if he owns the place, was her thought. What the hell did a Catholic priest want by coming here?

He was a bald, bespectacled old man, and as he seated himself, he appeared to engineer an awkward knee into a new position. And then he spoke: "It was your sister, Mary, who referred me to you."

Katherine leaned forward now, her former childish performance now upgraded to unalloyed petulance. But she would allow him to continue before discharging her anger at both him and his faith. And eventually at Mary!

"Mrs Wilson," said the cleric, "has informed me that your new husband is of the Catholic faith, and I commend you on your choice. Also, she would hope that – while you are in Yorkshire – you would attend Mass, as I am sure your husband would wish you so to do. So, it is my suggestion that...."

Katherine was on her feet. No longer was she the shy child in front of her teacher: she was the school principal now, and her attitude was that of a woman trembling with passion. "You will not suggest anything to me, sir!" Her voice had layers of venom in it. And as she approached the Catholic priest and towered above him, she proceeded with an unrestrained denunciation of the man and his beliefs: "I find that both you and your piousness leave an acrid taste in the mouth – a taste that has remained with me since my childhood." She turned away now, and walked to the window where she pointed, saying, "Over there stood Victoria Row. And in one of the houses that collapsed around our ears due to the neglect of our landlord, my sister Mary and I were born." She spun around to face the man. "Our father was Catholic, you know – the most evil of men you could ever come across. But Mary loved him. Yes, Mary loved the father who beat my mother black and blue in his drunken stupors. My sister is a wretched woman – a woman who denounced the marriage to my first husband because of the colour of his skin, and now she wishes to impose her doctrine on me? That will never happen. Never!"

Now, seating herself at the library desk, Katherine stared at Father Rutledge with obvious revulsion in her eyes as she said, "Even in the sixteenth century, Martin Luther had the right idea about your lot: decadent and corrupt! And you still are. Under no circumstances will you ever convince me that your faith is anything other than ungodly. The Church that you represent is one of hatred not love. I saw it when I was young, and I see it yet: manifested in the treatment of certain members of my family. And as to my present husband…well, we were betrothed on a whim. It was an amalgamation of our businesses and nothing else – certainly not as a Catholic union. So, sir" – she stood – "I suggest you go and tell my sister that your visit was in vain, because I will never again set foot in any church – least of all yours." Katherine pointed directly at the door. "You can now see yourself out, Father, and take your slimy popery with you."

Jessie and Annie were setting the table for fifteen people: they themselves; Amy Broadbent, a long-time pal of both Sarah and Jessie; Jane and Harry; Sarah's nephew Kevin and his father Wilf; Paul and Mark; Katherine and Josh; Sarah and her fiancé David; Max, and finally, Alex Stockwell.

"I never expected her to invite Mr Stockwell, Jessie."

"Well, I'll tell yer this, Annie; it were Katherine who asked he should come. Don't ask me why, but Kath always has something shifty up her sleeve."

Annie placed the cutlery beside the next plate. "Joshua's very nice, Jessie. He's a lovely colour and so handsome....Did you get the curtains sorted out for Paul?"

Jessie stood with a hand on her hip. "Don't change the subject, Annie Sykes. You've set your cap at the lad, haven't you?"

Annie went bright red.

"I knew it!" said Jess. "Eeh, you're a fast cat. Anyroad, he's far too young for you."

"Only by six years or so. Just look at the missis: David's fourteen years younger than she is. Anyway, for once, Jess, you're wrong."

"Am I? Well, whatever. Mind you," – she leaned close to Annie – "I must admit that young Joshua's got the kind of arse yer'd love to smack."

"Jessie!"

Jess was laughing her head off. "Eeh, what am I like…? Now, have we finished, lass? Aye it looks like it, so we'd best get back and you can help Amy prepare the vegetables while I get on with breakfast."

Once in the kitchen, Jessie got a box of eggs from the fridge and lit the gas under a frying-pan. And when she noticed Josh appear at the kitchen door, she said, "Hello, love. Come on in and I'll make you a coffee." He hovered over her at the stove. "Oh, you're making eggs," he said. Jessie smiled at him, saying, "No, love; the hen makes the eggs, I just cook 'em. D'yer want some?"

"Oh, no, no. Coffee would be just fine."

"So, how's yer mother after entertainin' her visitor?"

"I haven't seen her. What visitor was that?"

"Oh, she'll likely tell you herself, love."

Josh assumed that Jessie wanted to keep his mother's business private from the two other females, so put his curiosity on hold. "So," he said now. "Who'll be coming tonight, Jess?" And after he was told, he knew he'd never remember everybody's names, even though he'd briefly met them all before.

"But," said Jessie; "I don't know what your mother's reason is in asking Alex Stockwell. Last time we had a bit of a do, her sister Mary came and your mam went nuts. But this time Sarah's not invited her since it may have led to some friction between Jane and Harry." She handed Joshua his coffee. "You see Harry – the idiot –

ran off with Mary's daughter once, but Jane and him got back together eventually. Now, lad, we'll have to crack on. You can stay if you want...or go and sit in the garden if you like."

"Yes, I'll do that. I don't want to be under foot when you're busy...."

It was a beautiful morning. The sky was high and free of cloud; the garden sported an array of spring flowers, and the air about him was pure and uplifting. Joshua concluded he was going to enjoy his stay here – it was a peaceful haven compared to the manic bustle of Chicago. He sipped at his coffee....Then, as he gazed out across the fields, he caught sight of two figures approaching. They looked familiar: one with strawberry-blond hair, the other with a mane of black. He stood and watched them negotiate the brook that ran at the back of the house, and now they were coming up the path at the side of the greenhouse.

Paul was slightly in front of Mark, and as he entered the garden he stopped abruptly, staring at Joshua. Then he smiled broadly and came towards him. "Josh! It's wonderful to see you again. And from what I gather you're staying longer this time."

Joshua returned Paul's smile and shook his hand warmly. "A whole month! Maybe longer."

My! he's more gorgeous than ever, thought Paul as he looked longingly at his mixed-race cousin. It was now he noticed Mark standing beside him. "Oh...er, Mark. Remember Josh?"

"How could I forget? Nice to see you, Josh."

"And you, Mark." The two shook hands; but Joshua sensed a coolness in the greeting.

"Look you two, stay and catch up on things," said Mark, "while I go in and see Jessie." And he went.

Paul could see that Josh was feeling uncomfortable; so, he drew up a garden chair, and the lads sat side by side. "Don't take any notice of Mark," he said. "He can be a bit abrupt at times, but he doesn't mean anything by it....Now, what have you been doing with yourself these last few months?"

Josh tasted his coffee. "Well, I've been working for Mom and stepfather's company; and now, since I'm twenty-one, I'll be taking over as Managing Director – that's if I don't spread my wings instead. And what about you?"

Paul's bright blue eyes smiled. "Doing the mill's accounts as per usual. Still, I love figure work and wouldn't have it any other way. But things will probably change when Resurrection is made into a limited company later this year....Anyhow; I fancy a coffee myself," said Paul as he sprang to his feet. "Don't move and I'll join you." And as he went indoors, Josh thought, Is it so wrong to be attracted to one who's already spoken for?

Sarah glanced around the table, thinking, What is it with all the glum faces? It's supposed to be a party after all. Jane and Harry looked as miserable as sin, and her strategy of sending them away to try and sort out their problems didn't appear to have worked one bit. Well, she certainly wasn't going to suggest some sort of marriage guidance in case she had her head bitten off by both of them. And then there was Mark: he appeared not to wish to enter into the briefest of conversation with Paul even though it was his birthday. But there *were* two bright faces in those gathered, and they belonged to Kevin and Annie. She had chatted animatedly to Sarah's nephew between courses, and it looked as if a possible romance could be on the cards.

Now she leaned forward and looked passed Josh and Katherine who were seated to her right, where Alex Stockwell appeared to be struggling with his meal: every mouthful seemed an effort. Quietly she said, "Alex. Are you all right?"

Alex nodded; but Sarah knew something was troubling him. So, when the meal was over, and everyone was settled in the drawing-room chatting away as Paul opened his presents, she approached Alex, saying, "You look upset, Alex. Is there any way in which I can help?"

Alex swirled the brandy in his glass and shrugged.

"Oh, love," said Sarah as she touched his shoulder. "Come on, bring your drink and we'll go into the library for a moment."

Alex nodded and the two excused themselves from the rest of the company....

Seated on the library sofa now, Sarah patted the cushion to her side; and Alex sat down next to her. "Want to talk about it?" she said. "You know what they say about a trouble shared."

"Oh, Sarah," Alex sighed. "I thought we'd put all of it behind us...but now it seems to be starting all over again."

"What, love? What's starting again?"

Alex took a swig of his drink. "About Joseph and Uncle Phil. The police came to see me last night."

"Yes, they came to see me a few weeks ago, but that's a different story," said Sarah keeping her cards close to her chest. "So, what did they want?"

"They wanted to know if I'd seen Joseph on the morning after the fire," said Alex wearily.

"But you were still in hospital."

"Oh, no." He jerked his head from side to side. "They allowed me out about nine o'clock. Well, I discharged myself to be honest."

"Really?"

Alex nodded. "Anyway, when I got home, Joe passed me as I went in. He never said a word, so I went to find Mother. She was still asleep, so I woke her and told her about the fire, but she said that she already knew since the police had been to tell her the night before. Then, just after ten, I drove to the mill to see the extent of the damage."

Sarah remained silent. Could Alex have seen Harry in the vicinity of the house? And more to the point, could he have gone after Joseph? But could she confront him for an answer? No she couldn't. Something told her it would be reckless to become embroiled in something that was tantamount to a cross-examination of this troubled soul. So she said, "It all seems most odd to me. After all it appeared to be just a tragic accident on the face of it."

"Was it though?" said Alex. "Do you know, I've repeatedly asked myself what they were doing at the back of the garden in the first place...? I had too much on my mind at the time – what with Paul being in hospital and the problems at the mill."

"And do you know what my mother's gone and done now?" He didn't wait for a word of enquiry as he said, "She's only gone and sold Uncle Phil's shed – together with all his expensive tools just so she can buy herself some new frock or other to impress her social contacts who, I can tell you for a fact, don't give a damn about her."

"Alex," said Sarah. "Is a garden shed so important in the state of things?"

"Sarah, it was the last thing I had that belonged to Uncle Phil – and I loved him even more than I do my own mother."

"And what about loving your son? I've noticed you haven't said much to David tonight. Are you two getting on all right?"

Alex turned his head away.

"Alex, I'm talking to you. Please have the decency to give me an answer. He is your son after all."

"Is he?" He faced her now.

"Oh, for God's sake" – Sarah was on the edge of the settee now – "you know very well that he is. It was obvious on New Year's Eve that you'd convinced yourself of the fact but couldn't come to terms with it – and no doubt your mother had something to do with that."

Alexander Stockwell writhed in his seat and his head lolled. "Oh, I just can't cope with anything any more."

"Oh, come here." She wrapped an arm around his shoulders. "Look, love, don't deny what's staring you so blatantly in the face. And don't deny yourself the memory of his mother...Alice was a dear soul, and I saw your son brought into this world."

He stared at her. "How...how did...?"

Sarah took his hand. "I helped deliver him – granted I was only fourteen at the time, but I was there when Alice gave birth. But do you know, I can see in him now what I didn't see then."

Alex's eyes pleaded with her now as he said, "Which is?"

"You...! And if you get the chance, try and observe the scar on his right hand. He got that when he was speared by a rusty nail when our homes collapsed. You must recognise that it's no coincidence how he received such an injury. He's your son all right, so please treat him accordingly."

After a moment of silence, Alex turned his glass in his hands, before saying, "I shouldn't have done what I did. I know that now. But Alice was a beautiful girl and I was...."

"You were young, love. And although it was wrong, we are all enticed by something or other."

He looked at her now. She was such a profoundly astute and attractive woman. She somehow knew the sensitivity of one before it became apparent. But shaking himself out of the desultory mood he was in, he said, "I did hear recently that Alice christened her son – our son – Alan, so where did the name David come from?"

"That was odd," said Sarah, and after removing her arm from him, she rose, took Alex's glass and went to a cabinet where she replenished both their drinks.

On her return, she sat, and after handing Alex his brandy, she smoothed down her plum-coloured velvet dress. And as Alex watched her perform this brief and simple routine, he wished that it were his hand doing it instead of her own. Sarah spoke now: "Well, his name was in a way down to our Kath and the man who took him to the hospital." She sipped at her drink. "He asked Katherine for a name for the hospital records, and when she said

Alan he took it as being the family name of Allen, as in A-l-l-e-n. And then it was a woman who worked at the hospital who named the little lad David."

"So what about Alice and her father?"

Sarah sighed. "Well, since there was no other family and no money for funeral expenses, they were buried in the municipal cemetery where people in the same position were put to rest. Kath told me she'd visited the place once, and there she found the grave with a simple stone bearing the inscription: 'Allen. Father and daughter'."

Alex took a large gulp of his drink. "So they were buried in paupers' graves....Oh, Sarah; I should really go and pay my respects to them myself."

"Well, love, that will prove impossible. The remains of the many people buried there, were concreted over a few years ago for new houses to be built on the site."

Alex's voice took on a bitter tone now. "But that is sacrilege!"

"Oh, I agree, Alex. But that's just what happened I'm afraid." She rested a hand on his knee. "Look; just try and remember Alice as she was: a beautiful and caring young girl who loved life instead of someone just to be disposed of and forgotten. David would want that, you know. Now, come on, love, I think it's about time we went back and joined the others before they think we have something to hide."

But before they could move, a knock came to the door and Katherine entered. "Oh, I'm sorry, love, I...."

"That's all right. We're just coming."

"Well, I wanted a word with Alex," said Katherine.

Both parties look enquiringly at the woman in the doorway, but Sarah said nothing further until she was on her feet. "Right...I'll leave you to it." And as she excused herself, Katherine requested that her sister ask Paul to come and join them....

When the three were assembled, Katherine addressed Alex: "Now, you may be wondering why Sarah sent you an invitation to this little get-together? Well, it was me who asked her to.

"I have brought you two men together to give not just one present to *you*, Paul, but one to you as well, Alex." Katherine went to the library desk, opened a drawer, and withdrew two rolled up sheets of paper tied with white ribbons and sealed with red wax.

She seated herself now and gazed at the men who looked on in bewilderment at this elderly woman's actions. But then Katherine spoke: "I have loved – and love you both now in different ways: Alex, when you were a young man; and now you, my dear nephew, who has finally reached manhood. So" – she stood – "these pieces of paper are an appreciation of your, hopefully, reciprocated affection."

Katherine walked over to them now. And as they took the documents from her and broke the seals, she said to Alex: "You have always wanted our two families to be less disunited. Well, I sincerely hope that these small tokens may help to facilitate some kind of accord between Resurrection and Providence."

Both Paul and Alex read the papers before them. And when they were finished, Katherine said, "Now, I suggest that the only people you should tell are your mothers – for now at least. Right! Let's go back and enjoy the party."

But the smiles on the faces of the three of them faded perceptibly as they entered the hallway and caught sight of Sarah standing there with two police officers.

Sarah rushed forward and grasped her sister's arms. "Oh, I'm so sorry, love," she said, "but" – she looked down at the floor and then back up into Katherine's eyes – "it's your husband. He was found at home an hour ago. Frank's...Frank's died, Kath."

6

Edith Stockwell was sitting on the settee where, leaning over to the low table in front of her, opened her second bottle of red wine. She was waiting for Alexander coming home. And although she was still struggling to come to terms with the fact that he had fathered a child with a common strumpet, he was still her son.

It had become generally known that his bastard child – who for years she believed dead – was about to marry the woman who had been an irritation to her for all these years. And she – Sarah Crowther – who already had two previous husbands die on her, was now embarking on a life of bliss with a man fourteen years her junior. She glanced at her hands whose skin now resembled parchment. Where had it all gone wrong? Not only did she have this daunting prospect to cope with, but also her heart was heavy with memories of the destruction of her family. The loss of her husband, brother, daughter, and youngest son was hard enough to take, but when her granddaughter married a common labourer and her rightful grandson was seduced by that Crowther woman's queer boy, the bitter pill was surely laced with poison. And now Alexander had accepted an invitation to his coming of age. Oh, it defied belief.

Edith refilled her glass and cradled it between her age-spotted hands, and although she knew it was doubtful that she could prevent this sham of a marriage, she would employ everything in her power to stop Sarah Crowther getting her greedy hands on Providence mill – which had been rumoured she intended to do. Surely there must be something in the woman's background that she could use to discredit her – and maybe at the same time destroy her business ambitions – but what was it? Perhaps she could damage her reputation by hitting her indirectly? Yes, maybe she could do it that way? And by Christ! she would employ any scheme she could come up with to destroy that woman. Edith Stockwell smiled now and swallowed the wine.

Then, she heard the sound of a car's door slamming. Placing down the glass, she staggered to the window, and picking up her spectacles from off the desk in the bay, she hooked them over her ears and stared down the cobbled lane that led up to the garden gate. He was here. At last her son was back home.

Alexander Stockwell locked the car door; and without turning, looked across the land in the direction of the mill, which was now in his total control. There was a satisfactory sense of joy in his very gut. Before tonight, he had only held a forty-nine per cent stake in Providence. His mother – who had sold her forty-one per cent to Anderson's of Bradford, lacking in the knowledge that Katherine Mitchell owned this concern – had been able to purchase back twenty-one per cent for one American dollar. Now, after Katherine had transferred her remaining shares by granting certificates to Alex and Paul, Alex was in a more favourable position of owning a fifty-seven percentage of his mill. He was overjoyed by the offer – even though Paul now held a stake in the business. He turned now and walked briskly up the garden path in order to impart the news....

"How can you be pleased? said Edith. "Fancy! That woman – who had a golliwog for a husband – giving you just eight per cent, and her deviant nephew twelve."

"My God! you are a vile being," Alex growled. "You're certainly not human. The words you use degrade this household. Oh, I am so ashamed to be your son. Katherine's husband was a soldier who fought for this country just to keep you – and the rest of us – safe from Hitler's tyranny. And now her second husband is dead."

"Oh, I don't care about *her*." Edith waved her arms in the air. "It's we who matter, Alex. You must comprehend what it all means. If that thing who corrupted my grandson, and your niece are as devoted to each other as is widely believed, then together they hold one per cent more than *I* do! Or will do, when Jane comes of age."

"There you go again, Mother; demeaning Paul on the one hand and thinking of your own position in the business on the other. If it hadn't had been for Katherine's generosity in the first place, you wouldn't have a stake at all since you sold your shares to pay off some of Joe's debts. God damn it! be grateful, woman. Don't you realise, I now, by these deeds" – he waved the papers in the air – "control the business just as my father wanted. We have been given this opportunity of a fresh start, and I intend to make it a *completely new* start by employing Paul as our auditor. I intend to ask him if – perhaps once a year – he will look over our books and see that they are in order in a way that your precious Joseph would never have done. And you can't believe that your own granddaughter would in any way take sides. She is a Stockwell after all."

Edith was on her feet. And with both of her aged fists clenched, she strode to the back of the settee and beat the stuffed fabric until the dust flew. She arched her back now, and in glaring at the only member of her immediate family who now still lived, said in a tone of voice that resembled stepping on gravel: "I bowed to your judgement in employing that rogue Harry Carr to build the new warehouse, but I will never, as long as I live, allow that article who took my grandson away from me, come anywhere near the mill." She now distorted her face into what appeared as some over-painted gargoyle and began to approach her son. "And as far as your niece is concerned, she will never be a Stockwell because...." Her tirade came to an abrupt halt as she touched her breast and slumped on the sofa.

Alex went to her and pulled her upright. "Because what, Mother? Because what?"

Edith smiled enigmatically. "Oh, you wouldn't want to know, Alexander. Believe me, you just would not want to know."

7

Sarah sat on Katherine's bed watching her sister pack for the journey back to the United States. "So, Josh isn't going with you, then?" she asked.

"It's pointless really, sweetheart." She secured the second of her Louis Vuitton bags. "After all, Frank was not his father and it seems he's determined to stay here come what may. And I have already told the manager at Anderson's that Josh will be joining the company in some capacity or other." She sat on the bed now and took Sarah's hands. "You will look after him, won't you?"

"Oh, love; of course I will. But he's all grown up now: I'm sure he can manage perfectly well without me guiding him."

Katherine smiled but shook her head. "Oh, I think my Joshua needs steering in the right direction, love. He needs reins."

"And no doubt a bit in the mouth as well....Look" – Sarah shook her sister's hands gently – "Josh will be fine. You should be more concerned about getting your flight. Now, finish your packing and Max will run you to the station to get your train to London...."

Shortly after Katherine's departure, Jessie brought a tray into the library. On it was a pot of tea, together with milk, sugar, toast and a jar of marmalade. "There y'are, love." She placed the tray on the desk and was about to leave when she hesitated, saying, "Oh, and this." She dipped into her pinafore pocket and withdrew a pale-blue envelope that she handed to Sarah, before saying, "Oh! I knew I had summat to tell yer. D'yer remember Winnie Moody who used to live near your Em's? She had thin hair and her husband worked for the council."

"Yes...." The word was long drawn out as Sarah picked up a paper-knife and sliced opened the letter.

"Well, when Paul and Mark were having a coffee in Leeds the other day, he – the husband – kept popping in and out of a public lavatory. Paul told me it's called cottaging. And when he told me what it meant I was shocked to the core."

"Good God!"

"That's what *I* said. Apparently, it means...well"– she bent over slightly, and her voice turned to a whisper – "soliciting for other men."

"Not that! This!" Sarah threw the letter in the air.

Jessie straightened her back. "What is it?"

"It's only an invitation to the Wainwrights for dinner – Richard is the manager at Anderson's."

"So?"

"I haven't got a thing to wear, Jess."

"You don't mean you're going? Well, if you ask me" – she crossed her arms over her pendulous breasts – "he shouldn't be asking an engaged woman to go gallivanting off to some dinner party or whatever. It's improper. I don't know what David will think about it."

"What's he got to do with anything? I'm not married yet, Jess, and this could mean more orders coming my way if all his contacts are there. And besides, Josh is also invited – and Richard's married."

Jessie raised her arms now, saying, "Ha! That bloody doesn't stop 'em. Men! They're all philanderers."

Sarah reached for the telephone. "I'll phone Jane and see if she'll go to Leeds with me: she'll be able to help me pick out an outfit." And as she dialled the number, Jessie shook her head.

They had been in three shops already and were now in the fourth. "How about this one?" Jane passed the dress to Sarah who raised it in front of her.

"It's a bit matronly don't you think?"

"Er…yes, maybe."

Sarah sighed. "Oh, this is no good. I'll never find anything at this rate." She placed the dress back on the rack. "Let's go for a drink and then try somewhere else."

They left the shop and walked across Briggate where, down a narrow alleyway named Turk's yard, sat Whitelock's – the oldest public house in the city. It was established in 1715, and was originally known as The Turk's Head. It was a favourite of both city gents and those out shopping for the day – and also of Sarah after her first visit some years ago.

Inside, the place was a delight. There were copper-topped tables and padded, button-backed seating; dark, polished woodwork highlighted by the stained glass of the windows and the mirrors behind the bar, and what appeared to be coloured, Middle-Eastern – possibly Turkish – tiles, set into the bar's frontage. But choosing the place was a ploy on Sarah's part, since she knew it was here that Jane and Harry had first considered marriage, and now she wished to know why it had all gone wrong.

After ordering drinks and seating themselves at a spare table, Sarah said, "The last time I came here was when you tricked me into it. Remember?"

Jane smiled. "And Harry was here."

"Quite. But you knew all along that he would be. Then not long afterwards you were married." Sarah sampled her drink before saying, "How was Scarborough? Did you have a good time?"

Jane knew her stepmother was pushing for answers to her and her husband's marital situation – not out of malice but of concern. But how much she told her would depend on the amount of alcohol she consumed. She had to rid herself of the hurt she had endured for years, but would today be the day she was brave enough to confide in someone who loved her? And how would she feel afterwards? Would it be a blessed relief or cause her further pain? She drank. "We went for a sail," she said dully. "And for some reason, looking out on the vast, calm sea, I thought about my mother. It seems more than eight years since she died." Jane had cleverly turned the conversation into something that Sarah would not pursue in depth. "She would have been just your age now, with so much more life to live." But the twenty-year-old, who would shortly reach maturity and inherit ten per cent of Providence mill, showed little distress.

Sarah gazed in admiration at this young girl who had taken her mother's death with a stoicism that she herself could never match. And a tear came to Sarah's eye when she remembered Emma. "Aay, I still think of my own mam, love. She could be strict at times, but nevertheless loving. And, before she had her brain tumour, she had a beautiful head of red hair....I remember how I used to brush it on occasions. She always used to wear it in a bun, and use so many pins that the odd one used to drop off in her mutton broth."

Jane smiled broadly. "Funny that. I used to do the same with Mother's – but she never had a bun: she always wore it long. She was worried people would notice the birthmark on the back of her neck – but it was so small, I doubt if anybody would have known. Still, she always covered it up." She gulped at her drink now.

"You're drinking fast, love," said Sarah.

"Am I...? Yes...I'm nervous," said Jane.

"What on earth about?"

Jane drank again. "Oh, Mam...I've...I've wanted to tell someone this for a long time, but it's been too much for me to contemplate without feeling sick at the thought." She moved closer to her stepmother, and after putting her drink on the table, took Sarah's hands in her own. "I had as much reason to want to kill Uncle Joe as anyone else."

Sarah's heart began to race.

"Now," Jane continued, "I am going to find what I have to say most difficult – I have often denied it even to myself, but the nightmare will remain with me for as long as I live." Her eyes lowered as she removed her hands from Sarah's and clasped them together on her lap. "I was ten at the time...and was on a visit to my grandmother's.

"It was summer, and I...I wanted to play in the garden. But my grandmother was worried that I may go onto the ledge at the back where there was a steep drop down to the railway line." Jane drew in a long breath. "She insisted my Uncle Joe escort me – and I was happy to go along with her wishes.

"I never thought at the time why he wanted to take me out of sight of the house, and I was terrified at the drop over the edge of the embankment. But Joe held me close to him and I felt safe...." It was now that Jane's voice faltered.

"Are you all right, love?" asked Sarah, and placed a hand on Jane's knee. But instead of this being a show of genuine compassion on Sarah's part, the girl appeared to shrink from its contact. "Tell me what's wrong. Surely it can't be all that bad?"

After a brief silence, Jane raised her head and took a prolonged breath before saying tentatively: "I didn't know what it was at the time, but I do now....He – Uncle Joe – he...he tried to...rape me." And tears came upon her.

Sarah was lost for words. She was convinced that she must be feeling more sickened than the girl had hinted at moments before. Now in a panic, she delved into her handbag and withdrew a sachet of tissues, and tearing it open, passed Jane a bundle. This was too much for her to take in. It was as if she was in some sinister prison from which she could not escape, instead of relaxing in this popular hostelry. Then when Jane had wiped her face, she gave Sarah a pathetic look, and Sarah knew that what this young woman had just told her was obviously true.

They both sat quietly now, sporadically sipping at their drinks, before Sarah said, "You said 'tried to'?"

Jane nodded. "Philip appeared and interrupted him."

"Have you told Harry?"

"Oh God, no," said Jane, and blew her nose. "I tried to when we were in Scarborough, but I...I couldn't bring myself to." She gazed at Sarah. "I was hoping that you...might...."

"Oh, no. No, no, no." Sarah's head moved forcefully from side to side. "It's not my place, Jane. What would he think of me? What would he think of *you* for not confiding in him sooner?" She swung her head in Jane's direction, and seeing the look of desolation on the young girl's face, her stance turned to one of compassion: "This has affected your marriage, hasn't it?"

Jane nodded. "It seems that Uncle Joe's death brought it all back to me for some reason. At the time it happened, I was too young to know what it really meant and, after Harry and I married and started...making love, all was fine. But then when...Joe was killed, and I thought of he and Philip being in the same place as where he took me, every time Harry came near me I couldn't bear it." She drank now. "So, I was hoping that you could help save our marriage before...well, he doesn't want me any more."

And when Sarah saw the tears forming in her stepdaughter's eyes again, she grasped her hands so firmly that she was unable to pull away. "I'll try, love," she said quietly. "But I can't promise what the outcome might be."

8

'You are found guilty of witchery and will be put to the test.'

'No!' The woman cried out. 'I have done no wrong. Mercy! Mercy!'

Benjamin Tyler smiled. 'Very well. I will grant mercy. I give you the choice of the water, the burning, or the lingering hanging – the choice is yours. Take her away. Take her to the barn.'

'No! No!' The pleading woman was dragged screaming from the court, but not before crying, 'I curse you, sir. I curse you and your kin. Thou wilt suffer a far worse punishment than you bestow on me. I curse you with the loss of every child you sire. The devil will see to that. Curses! Curses…!'

This was an extract from An Early History of Collingley by Elias Horner – a book which Sarah had loaned to her nephew to accustom him with the area in which he now resided. No one living knew the true origin of Tyler's Barn, they were only acquainted with the dark stories told to them on stormy nights when the wind howled and the rain lashed persistently against their bedroom windows.

In 1645, legend had it that a one Benjamin Tyler was employed as a witch-finder under the auspices of the feared Matthew Hopkins. Apparently, Benjamin had a secure barn built to house those who had been tried and found guilty of witchcraft as they awaited their fate. Many were hanged or burned at the stake, and the sickening stench of their charred bodies drifted over the fields between Long Lane and High Ridge. Others were placed face down in the beck, a door placed over them and boulders piled on top, whence – eventually – they drowned in the bubbling waters of Barn Brook.…

"We were terrified, Josh," said Sarah; but she laughed. "Your Aunt Em and I would snuggle up in bed, with the covers pulled up under our chins while Dad told us the tale – not knowing whether it were true or not. Naturally, being curious, we would go to the barn just to see for ourselves – but never dare go inside, believing old Tyler's ghost, and those of his poor victims, haunted the place. And, as far as I can gather, no one has ever set foot in there since.

I'm truly surprised it's still standing. But maybe people are too scared to get rid of it. Anyway, apart from that nonsense" – Sarah finished her coffee – "your mother gave me strict instructions" – a smile accompanied the wag of a finger – "that I keep you occupied. So today, if you don't mind, how about coming with me to Woodkirk and I'll take some flowers. I thought the walk would do us good. What do you think?"

"Of course I'll come, Aunt Sarah! I couldn't let you go on your own when you're...."

"Visiting my husbands' graves?"

Josh nodded, whereby Sarah said, "I'll appreciate you being there. Come on, then; let's be off. I'll just let Jessie know in case anyone calls, and pick up a few things we'll need."

It was hard to believe they were in a heartland of throbbing industry when, after just a short walk, they came to a dusty lane between two rows of houses. And upon reaching its end, the harsh world was abruptly left behind them as vast fields of flourishing agriculture stretched far into the distance, separated occasionally by unkempt hedges and bramble bushes.

"I used to come here with your Aunt Em when we were young," Sarah reflected, as the morning sun lit up her delicately made-up face. "We'd bring a makeshift picnic and walk over to Woodkirk until we reached a crossing on the railway line and wait for the first train to come along. Then, we'd turn around and walk back home. It was such a simple thing – but it gave us so much joy." What was it about this woman? thought Josh. She was quite extraordinary: soft and caring – yet a visionary and a warrior: bold and redoubtable. And he adored everything she was.

Whilst Josh had opted for a pair of sand-coloured, slim-line corduroy jeans and a blue denim jacket, Sarah was wearing a white cotton dress with a poppy print, and a bottle-green woollen jacket made by Anderson's of Bradford. And her hair had been styled by Jane who – as Sarah had pointed out – used to do her mother's when Dorothy became too ill to attend the hairdressers. He took her arm now – and she appeared to think the act quite mundane: accepting it with a pat of her hand. And as they strolled on at the edges of fields where the hedgerows formed natural boundaries, he knew he was undeniably in the presence of greatness....

On their arrival at the churchyard, where the Norman church occupied its place slightly apart from a silvan area, Sarah led Josh to John Halliday's grave where he and his mother rested. "She was an unpleasant woman, Josh; but John loved her. And so did Paul." Sarah knelt and removed the dead flowers, before replacing them with fresh ones. "He was only four when his father died, so I don't think he remembers much of him. And oh, how I hated myself." She gazed into the heavens now. "I have always blamed myself for his death." She looked back at Josh, and seeing the perplexed look on his face, she explained herself: "You see, on the morning of his death, we had a blazing row and, as he was going out of the door on his way to work, I told him not to come back." She sighed heavily. "And he didn't: he was killed when the train bringing him home crashed into the bridge which carries the line over The Hollow. I was utterly devastated. It felt as if I'd dug this grave myself."

Josh, his heart trembling with empathy, halted in his trimming of the overgrown grasses at the edges of the black marble surrounding the grave, saying, "And you brought Paul up on your own?"

Sarah nodded. "With the help of Jess. She was always there." She pushed herself upright. "Right! That will do. Let's go and sort William out now."

After visiting William Crowther's family plot and repeating the procedure of tidying and laying new flowers, Sarah suddenly said, "It's thirsty work. Come on; I know just the place to go."

Sarah had spent the whole of the last week amusing her nephew – at the cost of ignoring her own son. But Paul had Mark to be amused by; and while she had taken a long overdue break from the mill, David and the two lads had relished looking after the place in her absence.

Settled comfortably now in the relaxed surroundings of The Railway Inn, she watched Josh order drinks. She had to admire this tall, bronzed young man whose seductively captivating eyes would make the pulses race and the mouth go dry in women of any age.

When Josh returned to the table with two pints of bitter shandy, she said, "I hope your mam is okay. It must be awful for her to be on her own to sort out a funeral. I know how grateful I was to have Jess to hold my hand when I had to go through it."

"Mom will be okay. Don't worry; *I'm* not."

Sarah looked at her nephew who was admiring the horse brasses hanging on the walls and the copper pans that were suspended from the ceiling. It was true: he seemed totally unperturbed by his mother's absence and the reason for her being away. And when he returned her gaze, he said candidly, "Have you ever been to The Hart in Leeds?"

Sarah was speechless. But after taking a sip of her drink, she managed to say, "No. I haven't. But I know *you* have: your mother told me so."

"Yes. After you told me about it, I was curious. And then on his birthday, Paul mentioned the place as well."

"Did he?" Her heart suddenly missed a beat. Was Paul's memory of Steven coming back?

"Yes," said Josh, "but he didn't mention anything about what had happened with the Stockwells. Do you hate them for what they did?"

Sarah pulled a handkerchief from her jacket pocket and patted her face, saying, "Oh, hate is such an emotive word, Josh; but I certainly detested Joe for trying to extort money from me by using Paul as bait." She replaced the handkerchief and breathed deeply. "But I like Alexander," she said. "He is not of the same mould. Edith though, is a different kettle of fish. She's the despicable woman who believed Paul seduced Mark and caused his father to exile him from the household."

The change in the conversation towards the Stockwells instead of The Hart, surprisingly came as a blessed relief to Sarah and it prompted her to say, "Oh! that reminds me – I almost forgot with all the recent kerfuffle." Josh leaned forward and peered enquiringly at his aunt. "Well," Sarah resumed. "When Max got back from seeing your mother off, he told me of a strange occurrence as they waited for the incoming London train at Leeds station to change drivers for the return journey." She paused to take a further sip of her drink. "Who was greeting a man getting off? but Edith Stockwell. And according to Max, she kissed him on both cheeks. Now, what do you think of that?"

Josh knew not *what* to think. It was as if Jessie were relating some gossip or other. But he responded, saying, "Maybe she's got a new man in her life."

"Who? Edith Stockwell? Nobody would have her! No, love; that woman's mind is set. The old witch is up to something, Josh. But the question is what?"

9

Jessie entered the drawing-room where Sarah was reading the Collingley Advertiser. Closing the door behind her, she said, "There's a Mrs Platt to see you, love. I haven't a clue who she is. Shall I show her in?"

"Ah." Sarah folded the newspaper and stood. "Yes please, Jess. And could you make a pot of tea?"

Jessie nodded, and directly ushered the woman into the room.

"Mrs Platt." Sarah approached her guest and taking her by the arm, said, "Come and sit down. I've ordered tea for us."

Bella Platt seated herself on the settee. "I'm glad you decided to see me," she said. "Ever since I met your sister, Mrs Crowther, I've been hoping and praying that you would. But when you phoned, you apologised for not trying to find me when my nephew died instead of getting help from outside; well it was not necessary. In fact, I am sorry for not letting you know about Steven's funeral, but I thought you had enough on your plate at the time."

Sarah looked at this small, grey-haired individual with the most pleasing of countenances and took hold of her hand. "We were both grieving, weren't we?" she said. Mrs Platt patted Sarah's hand and nodded, whence Sarah said, "My sister told me she had seen a photograph of him."

"Yes, she did," said Bella and then glanced around the room. "Do you not have pictures of your son? I would love to see who Steven so often talked about. He confided in me how much he loved your boy, you know."

Sarah couldn't think of anything to say in response, and was relieved when Jessie brought in a tea tray, which she placed on the long, low table in front of the two women. "Shall I pour?" Jessie asked. And Sarah replied, "No, Jess. I'll see to things. Thanks."

After pouring the tea and offering her guest milk and sugar, Sarah walked over to a bureau next to one of the many tall windows of the room. And after closing the writing area that she had been using earlier, she pulled open a drawer and withdrew an album of photographs. "I'll show you some pictures of Paul," she said as she returned to the visitor and sat beside her on the settee.

Mrs Platt placed her cup back on its saucer and slightly turned her body towards Sarah as she opened the book of photos. "This one here" – Sarah pointed – "was taken on a day trip to Blackpool when Paul was about nine – or thereabouts. And this is him in his school uniform the day he started grammar school." She flipped through a few pages now and smoothed down the next one to allow Mrs Platt to see more clearly. "Now, this was taken on his nineteenth birthday – the day he met your nephew."

The woman's look was intense as she scanned the picture. "Oh, my dear," she said. "I can see why my Steven fell for your son. He is a fine, good-looking young man. And how old is he now?" She placed her cup and saucer on the table.

"He was twenty-one last week."

"Good. I thought I was right." Sarah glanced at the woman who had a smile on her face. "Thank you for allowing me to see him – well, only pictures of him – but that brings me to why I have come to see you."

Sarah closed the album and reached for her tea. And after drinking, waited for Mrs Platt to explain the reason for her visit.

"Steven made a will," said Bella as she delved into her handbag and withdrew the said document, "and apart from a small legacy left for me, most of it was bequeathed to your son."

"Oh, I see," said Sarah. "But when he rented one of my houses, I thought he may not...."

"Be well off...? He wasn't, Mrs Crowther. He was only starting out on his architectural career and his father – my brother – was helping him get by until he found stability. And then, only a month before Steven was killed in the fire, his father died and left him the cash he had in the bank. Then Steven decided to make a will of his own and leave the bulk of that money to your Paul with me holding the money on trust."

"Oh, I see," Sarah repeated herself.

"So, when we can sort things out," said Bella, "your son with be twelve and a half thousand pounds better off."

Sarah's mouth hung open before she managed to say, "Twelve and...a half thou...?"

And smiling again, Sarah's visitor nodded.

Francis Roland Parker had been Sarah's solicitor – and good friend – since William Crowther died; but it was rumoured he was going, well, a little senile and would no doubt soon retire. But he was the only person Sarah could turn to now.

The secretary showed her into his office where she took a seat in front of the mahogany desk and removed her gloves. She felt as nervous as a child on her first day at school. She was sick to her stomach and wanted to run from the place into the arms of someone who would comfort her. In fact, she would. She sprang to her feet just as Francis entered the room through a door immediately behind her.

"Sarah! Has no one been to make you comfortable? Oh, this is not good enough." He went straight to the door through which Sarah had previously entered the office, and leaving the door open, yelled, "Miss Gledhill! Would you kindly bring Mrs Crowther a cup of coffee" – he turned to address Sarah now – "or would you prefer tea?"

Exposing her palms, Sarah said, "Anything would be welcome."

"Don't bother, Maggie! I'll see to her." And he closed the door with a bang. Seated at his desk now, he opened a drawer, withdrew two glass tumblers and a bottle of whisky, saying, "You can't get the staff these days. Sit yerself down and drink this." He poured two large measures, and before handing one to his visitor, asked, "Water?"

Sarah nodded. "I shouldn't really, though. Drinking is all I seem to do these days."

"Ah! You have a problem. I can see that."

So Sarah went on to explain the situation regarding Paul's new inheritance, and whether or not he could somehow pass it on to her son without him knowing that it came from Steven Clark. She asked Francis if it could be a further bequest from his stepfather that had been overlooked.

"Oh, my dear, you know how much I admire and respect you, but you're asking me to put my head on the block. And I must admit I want to keep it firmly on my elderly shoulders. William entrusted the two of us to take care of those he wished to benefit in the best way he saw fit. You have to admit that I cannot now hand over an extra twelve thousand pounds plus to Paul when the amount held in trust was only ten. He would be highly suspicious. And remember the number of people who witnessed William's wishes – including the Stockwells – when the will was read."

Sarah was crestfallen. Her face seemed to suddenly age before Francis's eyes. He leaned back in his chair. "Do you know, Sarah" – the solicitor looked up at the stuccoed, nicotine-stained ceiling before dropping his head once more – "many shady individuals set up paper companies to hide their income in overseas tax havens." He adjusted his spectacles now. "I may add, that I am not one of them. Yet, thinking about it now, there could be a solution.

"Sarah, the accounts that you and I are trustees of, are based in this country – this *county* to be precise. So we are not in the business of hiding these trusts for the benefit of diddling the government. Of course, you may be wondering why I am telling you this? Well, the amount we are talking about is trivial compared to the millions that these criminals deal in. So, I have no qualms in setting up an account in the name of one who would have wished Paul to benefit from their will without him thinking it odd." His eyes began to sparkle now, and Sarah appreciated now that this man had something up his sleeve when he leaned over the desk. "Now," he said, clasping his hands together. "If the money that has been bequeathed to Paul appears to have come from a different source other than from Steven Clark or your late husband, then we might be able to pull it off."

"What source, though?" Sarah asked. "I'd say the money was a gift from *me* if Paul wasn't both the mill's accountant and my own. He knows everything that goes on financially, and profits are being held in reserve for the new company."

"Think, love. There must be somebody who cared enough for Paul to want to see him set up when he became of age?"

Sarah placed the thumbs of each hand on either side of her jaw, whilst resting her fingers on her temples. And after the longest of moments, she dropped her hands, saying, "His grandmother, Martha. But she didn't have a red cent to her name."

"And who knew that?"

"Well, Paul's father was already dead when she passed away, and nobody knew anything about her situation apart from myself."

"And me now. She was quite a wealthy woman, Sarah." He winked at her. "Just convince yourself of that.... Yes?"

Sarah nodded in bewilderment.

"Good. Now, if you can persuade this Platt woman to entrust the money to you – in cash – and let me have it, then I can secrete it into my accounts with little difficulty and pass on a cheque to Paul in due course. But – and it's a big but – I will need to create the will."

"You mean forge it, don't you? No, Francis. I can't allow you to jeopardise yourself and your practice. You've already said you want to keep your head on your shoulders, so surely you're in danger of having it lopped off by doing that. There must be another way."

Francis sipped his whisky and shook his head. "You worry too much, my dear. Forgery of a will is notoriously hard to prove in court. And who could possibly dispute the signatures of both testator and non-existent witnesses of twenty years ago? The odds are stacked in our favour, Sarah."

And when he received no further discouragement from his client, he said, "Now, let me tell you more fully how I intend to go about things."

"Well, the old cow! You looked after her, fed and watered her, dressed and undressed her, and all without a word of thanks. And now it comes to light that she had all that money stashed away. Eeh, if she weren't dead already, I'd dispatch her meself. And another thing...."

"Jess! If you'd just let me finish, you'd get all the facts – she didn't have a bean." And after Sarah had told her how Francis was going to deal with the transfer of Steven's assets, and that he was going to draw up a fake will and age the document with a little weak tea, Jessie said, "Well, that's a new one on me. Do you know, I'll never be able to face another cuppa without thinking of that. Eeh! Can you credit it? The poor man *must* be going senile."

"I bloody hope not, Jess. Anyway, it sounded as if he knows what he's doing."

"Those folk do. One minute their feet are on the ground, the next they're swinging from trees."

Sarah sighed. "But there's another thing." She looked up at Jessie. "Have you heard of Maggie Gledhill? She used to work with Kath years ago and now she's Francis's secretary."

"Oh, I've heard of her, all right. Her mother were a Baker before she wed."

"A baker of what? Bread?"

Jessie threw the tea-towel on the table and glared at Sarah. "Bread? No, for God's sake! Her *maiden* name were Baker." She gazed at the ceiling now. "And if I'm not mistook, she had dropsy – used to slosh around when she walked. It killed her in the end."

"How the hell do you know all this?"

"Common knowledge," said Jessie. Looking back at Sarah now, she added, "But, Maggie...well"– she pursed her lips and shook her head – "she's a wrong 'un. She lives up Monkey Town – and a slut from what I can gather. Had more dick than a lodging house cat. Her legs have been apart so much, she couldn't stop a pig in an entry. She used to work at the Two Anchors."

"Unfortunate name for a pub if you say it quick....Oh, I wish Katherine was here: she'd know what to do."

Jessie slapped her hands on the kitchen table and pushed her face forwards, saying, "Oi! She's *not* here. So get on with it." She drew back now. "Emma would be ashamed of you if she thought you couldn't handle this piddling little thing after all you've been through. I'm sorry to say so, but it's true."

However much she wanted to rebuke her old friend for bringing her mother into the conversation, Sarah had to admit she had to deal with this fiasco single-handedly. "Right. I'll phone Mrs Platt first to arrange for the cash to be handed over; then when that's settled, get Max to drive me over to pass it on to Francis and tell him to proceed. Satisfied?"

"Satisfied," said Jessie.

10

Mary Wilson wasn't much of a cook. In fact, if her husband and daughter arrived home and didn't smell burning, they knew they were having salad.

And she considered cleaning as a demeaning chore that the wife of a businessman should certainly not undertake. So, once more, she had a woman who came in on weekdays to 'do' for her. At weekends, it was down to Laura to see to the housekeeping.

Tonight they would be entertaining Father Rutledge who was coming to dinner. But Mary's husband had seemingly ignored the fact: his mind was on other things as he strode up and down the room holding a cigar. "She has gone too far this time," he growled, as cigar ash fell onto the carpet.

"Jack!" said his wife, "Just look what you've done now. This carpet was expensive, and...."

"I know, woman. I know! But if your half-sister gets her way, there'll be no more fancy purchases for us. She'll ruin us."

"Oh, Father," said his daughter. "Don't be so bloody melodramatic." Both parents were outraged by Laura's language, but before either could reprimand her, she went on, "So what does it matter if she closes down the rag warehouse? There are plenty other mills that will keep you in business."

Jack came forward now and hovered above his only child. "Are you thick? Don't you read the newspapers?" He turned and retired to an armchair. "Mills are closing daily. It looks as if I'll be going out of business afore long, and this" – he looked at the used cigar and flung it into the fire – "will be one of the many luxuries to face the chop. And she" – he nodded toward the kitchen door – "can have her cards an' all."

As Mary's mouth hung open, Laura went to her father now, and with tender concern, said, "I'm sorry, Dad." Her father looked up, and as he touched her hand that was resting on his shoulder, he shed a tear.

"Oh, please, Jack," said his wife. "I hope you don't start moaning and blubbering while Father Rutledge is here."

And he *was* here. The doorbell rang, and because nobody else moved, Laura went and answered the door. "Please come in, Father," she was heard to say. "And let me take your coat."

Presently, the priest entered the room, with Laura following close behind. He was dressed in his usual black garb – apart from the dog-collar – and initially went to Mary who was seated at the table that was set for dinner. "My dear," he said. "May I express my appreciation of your kind-hearted invitation. It is not often I am so honoured."

Mary stood and kissed his hand. "A pleasure, Father. You are always welcome into my household. Isn't he, darling?"

Jack stood now; and approaching the priest, shook his hand, saying, "Of course. Please take a seat, Father." He indicated an easy chair at the side of the fire.

"Thank you, Jack." The priest pushed his hands towards the flames and rubbed them. "It's been a fine day, but rather cold now."

"Oh, I know your game, Father," said Jack with a chuckle. "So what will it be? Scotch?"

"I can't hide anything from you, Jack Wilson. Scotch will be fine."

"Do you want anything, Mary?" Jack asked of his wife.

"A small sherry would suit, dear."

"Laura?"

"Oh, thank you, Dad. I'll have a sherry as well."

As Jack Wilson was preparing the drinks, a woman appeared at the kitchen door. "I can bring dinner through if you're ready, Mrs Wilson."

"Oh, right, Flora. Just give us a few minutes to be seated and then you can serve."

The woman disappeared.

Now, Mary showed Father Rutledge to his place, while Jack brought over the drinks and joined those already assembled at the table.

Father Rutledge put down his knife and fork. "A truly wonderful meal, Mary. Wonderful."

"There's pudding to follow," said Mary Wilson, patting the priest's hand. "Oh, I meant to ask you, Father. Did you manage to see my sister?"

"Indeed I did," he grunted. "And I'm sorry to say it, but she was downright offensive. I was shocked, Mary. Shocked! I could certainly not understand her saying that our Church represents hatred. And then she said it mistreats certain members of her own family."

"She'll be referring to my nephew and the Crowther boy. I mean, what can two men…well, do to each other?"

"Probably what Joe Stockwell did to me – and my father to you," said Laura nonchalantly.

"Laura!" said her mother. "Don't be so crude. And anyway, I really think Sarah should have sought treatment for Paul before now. Something like that electroconvulsive therapy they give to child molesters."

"Mother!"

"Oh, Laura; it's common knowledge that it sorts those kinds of people out." Mary's horse face lengthened further. "I often wonder which one is the woman in that weird relationship." Laura promptly fisted the table, whence both cutlery and crockery rattled. "How dare you!" She almost spat at her mother. "I just don't know you any more. You appear to have been poisoned by that old bitch Stockwell. And if it comes to who needs electrocuting, I am looking at her." She leapt to her feet now and discarded her napkin. "You can finish this dinner without me."

"Come back here this instant!" Mary protested at her daughter's discourteous departure. "Come back and apologise – particularly to Father Rutledge."

Jack promptly lit a cigar, saying, "Oh, just let her go, Mary…."

In the garden now, Laura went down to the high wall which divided their house from a neighbour's, and seated herself on a wooden bench beside a large laburnum whose pendulous clusters of golden bellflowers would shortly disappear. And even though it was a chilly evening, she was heated by the incident in the house. He's right, she thought. Dad is quite right: I should go – just like the golden flowers would do when May came along. But go where? She was only thirty-one and could still bear children. And although she had lost her first born, she considered it was due to the stress she suffered at the hands of Joseph Stockwell. He wasn't physically violent toward her, but the mental anguish she endured at his hands, had worn her down. She was glad he was dead, and hoped he had experienced the fear of knowing he was going to die. So, where was she to go? Although Sarah had given her a job, it would be impossible for her aunt to also provide a place for her to live after her dalliance with Harry Carr had nearly wrecked his marriage. But where else? Then of a sudden it hit her: uncle Wilf! He and Kevin had been on their own since aunt Emily died. They had room and would likely welcome a female in the household – after all, she was their family too. Yes! Yes, that would be the best solution all round.

Then, unbeknown to those still at dinner, Laura slipped back to the house and softly ascended the stairs to her bedroom. Here she packed what she'd need for the night, put on a black, woollen coat and scarf, patted her dark-brown hair, and quietly disappeared into the growing darkness – finally escaping the prison of her restrictive and miserable life.

11

"Didn't he think it funny that his gran left all that money when she lived with us in near poverty?" asked Jessie.

"Not at all. You see, in Francis's letter that he sent Paul, he stated that some investments she had in Wales had matured and were now available for him as a bequest in her will."

"*Another* bloody lie."

"Oh, change the subject, Jess," said Sarah with not a little irritation. "Paul was only seven when Martha died so how would he know?"

"So what's all this about Laura and Wilf? He's taken her in you say?"

"He has. And apparently all three of them are suited with the set-up."

Jessie flopped onto a kitchen chair and began to clear bread dough from between her fingers. And as she tossed the pieces onto the butcher's block, she looked directly at Sarah. "And there was me thinking Wilf had all his chairs at home." She shook her head. "Well, all I can say is he'd best keep an eye out for any goings on. You know what a loose piece she is – and so much older than Kevin." When she saw Sarah's wounded expression, she stretched a doughy hand across the table. "Eeh, I'm sorry, lass. I didn't mean to say that it would be like you and David."

"I know. But I've been thinking about that myself."

"Surely you're not changing your mind about getting married?"

Sarah shook her head. "No, not that. But I am concerned about the age difference. What if he finds somebody younger and decides he prefers her to me?"

Jessie sprang to her feet now. And as she turned her fingers into doughy claws, said, "Jesus Christ! you're a handful. I could gladly strangle you if I didn't love you so much. Now! Get your act together and start planning a wedding." She went to the sink and plunged her hands in soapy water while Sarah's thoughts remained on the young man who had asked her to marry him. And her mind travelled back in time, when everyone seemed to know exactly what went on in this once small town – her mind still on David.

Gossip had it that a maid who once worked for the Stockwells, overheard a conversation taking place between Alex and his mother: 'Something has got to be done about that bastard,' Edith had said. 'Fancy getting involved with a guttersnipe like her. Thank God she's dead; and I pray that son of hers follows her to hell as soon as possible.' And Alex had gone practically berserk before marching from the room, barging into the maid who was standing in the hallway.

But Sarah mentally slapped herself now. After all, there was the future to look forward to – beginning tonight with the party at the Wainwrights. So she roused herself, left the kitchen, and proceeded upstairs where she ran a bath.

She had chosen a white, pleated, knee-length skirt with a sunshine-yellow, broderie anglaise top, and beige leather shoes with a medium-size heel. As for Josh, he had bought a modern black suit with a mandarin collar and a white, cashmere, polo neck sweater.

Driving to Alwoodley now, Sarah said, "How do I look, Josh?"

"Beautiful! What do you think, Max?"

"Madam always looks beautiful," said the chauffeur.

Sarah playfully slapped Josh's arm. "You two are so naughty. Mind you, I must say I'm a little nervous about coming here. The last time I felt like this was when Paul and I were first invited to High Ridge. Do you remember, Max?"

"I do, madam. But the weather was very different to this evening."

How true, Sarah thought. On that occasion, snow was thick on the ground and the daunting prospect of meeting Dorothy Crowther's family had instilled in her an overbearing dread since the Stockwells would be there. Her fear was compounded when she and Paul had to stay the night when the car broke down and the conditions worsened. Nevertheless, she had survived the ordeal and concluded that tonight could not be any worse than that one even though she had been treated royally.

The car turned down a tree-canopied lane now, and when the lane widened after a short distance, the Wainwright's house came into view. It was a contemporary, detached house with bay windows, and was situated amongst a grove of hornbeams and several Japanese cherries, which were just about to burst into blossom.

"Here we are, madam," said Max as he turned into an expansive driveway inlaid with bricks in a herring-bone pattern, and came to a halt at the large front door, whose steps were illuminated by two circular lights set into the adjacent walls. Max emerged from the car and went to open the rear doors. As he helped her out, Sarah said, "Will you be okay in the car?"

"I will, madam. Jessie made me up some food and a flask of tea – and I can listen to the radio."

Sarah held his arm. "We'll try not to be two long. And, from now on" – she gently touched his face – "I want you to call me Sarah."

"Very well, madam...er...Sarah."

She smiled. And turning now, she saw Richard Wainwright standing at the open door with his arms outstretched. She had not seen him for nigh on five years. He had filled out somewhat; but had certainly not lost his attractiveness – and Sarah doubted that he ever would. And she was in his presence now, along with her nephew who was soon to take a role in Katherine's business; and she felt like a little girl admiring his masculine good looks. But she halted in her admiration of the man as he approached her and took her hand. "Welcome, Sarah," he said.

"Delighted to be here, Richard. Let me introduce you to my nephew, Josh – Katherine's son. I understand you have been informed of my sister's sad loss, and of her desire that the two of you become acquainted."

Richard nodded and held out a hand. "Pleased to meet you, Josh. I hope you'll be happy with us. Mrs Mitchell has told me a lot about you."

Josh shook the man's hand, saying, "Only the best bits, I hope."

And as Richard smiled at the remark, Sarah thought the manager of Anderson's of Bradford more good-looking than ever. When they had met for the first time, she had no idea that Katherine owned the place. Her sister had instructed him to order a number of bolts of newly designed, woollen cloth from Resurrection, have them made into garments and all profits to be paid directly to Sarah. The range had been a great success, and no doubt now, with the use of pure new wool being planned for the mill, further favourable results would be forthcoming. At least, that was her hope.

"Right," said Richard. "Let's be inside where I can introduce you to the other guests."

Sarah found the long narrow hallway intimidating. The entrance to her own home was spacious and gave one a sense of freedom, whereby this one gave the feeling of being incarcerated. Several closed rooms led off to right and left, apart for one from which noisy chatter and occasional laughter emanated. Sarah's steps faltered now, but her apprehension was suddenly eased as Josh took her arm. And when she looked at him, he smiled and winked.

As they followed Richard into the room, a hush came over those assembled. Immediately, a young, smartly dressed man approached them carrying a silver tray. "Champagne?" said Richard. "Only the very best." And he picked up two glasses, which he handed in turn to Sarah and Josh. He then escorted them into the group of guests. "Councillor and Mrs Walker: Norman and Miriam," said Richard. Miriam took Sarah's free hand, saying, "Delighted, love. I understand – from many prominent individuals, I might add – that you are quite a famous businesswoman around these parts?"

"Well, I wouldn't say *famous* as such."

"Nay, don't be modest, lass," said Norman Walker. "Yer've got a great reputation all over the West Riding."

Sarah nodded graciously. "You're too kind. And this" – she turned to her left – is my nephew Joshua."

"How do you do?" said Josh. "I am pleased to meet you both."

"Well I must say, Sarah," said Miriam; "you certainly have a nephew to be proud of."

Sarah smiled. "Yes. I am very, very proud of him."

Then the whole process was repeated with George Wood and his wife Elizabeth, and Patrick and Diane Hughes.

"And last, but by no means least," said Richard, "my dear wife Amelia."

Initially ignoring Sarah, Amelia Wainwright held out her hand to Joshua. "My! Such a handsome young man. Delighted to meet you." She turned to Sarah now. "And Mrs Crowther...lovely." She then looked at her husband. "Now, darling, why don't you go and discuss business with Mrs Crowther while I keep Joshua entertained?"

To the relief of both Sarah and Josh, Richard said, "Not at the moment, sweetheart. There's plenty of time for that." He turned now and went to open some double doors that led to the rear of the house, whereby he beckoned his two guests forward. "This" – he outstretched an arm – "is our garden-room. We use it mostly for dancing."

"And do you dance a lot?" Sarah enquired.

"When we have guests we do. My wife has thought of

everything, including a sprung floor and the most up-to-date, stereophonic record player money can buy. Come and look." And he walked across the floor.

As an aside, Josh said to his aunt, "I think Mom's paying him *too much* money by the look of this place."

"I was reflecting on that myself, love. But, I have a sense that it's his wife's cash that's behind most of it."

As they were introduced to the machine, Sarah remarked: "It certainly is impressive, Richard....Sadly, at my husband's memorial service, I had to settle for the Hallé Orchestra."

Josh had to stifle a snigger. God, how he adored this woman! She was fearless – and so direct that it made the hairs on the back if his neck bristle. Yet, he was well aware that such was the character of all Yorkshire folk.

Seemingly oblivious to Sarah's acerbic remark, Richard gently closed the lid on the new acquisition, and in turning, said, "Right! I should imagine dinner is about be served, so shall we go through?"

Place settings at the table were indicated by small, silver, shell-like clips that held the names of those attending. Sarah was seated between Richard to her right and councillor Walker at her other hand. Two young servers – the man who had previously served champagne, and a female one – had presented each of the three courses with deftness, but the dishes themselves were bland. The watercress soup appeared to have more water in it than cress; the steak for the main course was as tough as a builder's boot; and the pudding – whatever it was – defied description. Jessie would have been appalled. Still, the wine had certainly aided the digestion.

Throughout the clatter of knives and forks and idle chatter, Sarah had noticed how Amelia was behaving coquettishly towards her nephew, who kept looking over at his aunt with doleful, pleading eyes as if he were being inspected. So, it came as a relief now that Richard Wainwright determined that the meal was over, and everyone should move to a less formal location. "Let us all progress to the garden-room," he announced, "where you will be served drinks of your choice."

Each of the group stood, whereby Miriam Walker went straight to Sarah and took her arm, saying, "What did you think of dinner, my dear?"

"Well," said Sarah. "It was...."

"Quite! Ghastly, wasn't it? No wonder we haven't been

introduced to the cook. Now, come and let's find a seat while the men go into the garden and smoke and talk business."

The two women found a pair of Lloyd Loom chairs next to each other and were asked as to their drink preferences by the same servers who had waited at table. "It's a bit of a mishmash all this, Sarah," said Miriam. "I'm far from being snobbish, but nothing is as it should be in this house."

Sarah was feeling at ease in the company of this elderly woman with her blue-rinsed hair; and after tasting her gin and tonic, said, "Have you been here before?"

"Never – and I won't be coming again. I suspect they only invited us because Norman's a councillor. And what about you?"

"My first time too." And Sarah went on to explain that her sister owned Anderson's but was away in America after the death of her husband. "And Josh wants to stay in Yorkshire and work there."

"Well, from what I've heard" – Miriam placed a hand on Sarah's knee – "it could do with some new blood in the place."

Sarah was concerned now. Was Katherine unaware of any difficulties that may be occurring at the clothing factory? So she was prompted to say, "How do you mean?"

"Well" – Miriam leaned close – "it's common knowledge that Richard's playing away – and with more than one woman. It goes to reason such behaviour affects staff morale."

"Yes…I…I suppose it must. Does his wife know?"

"She goes along with it, love. She's just the same, so I'd keep an eye on your nephew if I were you in case she pounces on him an' all. What do you think of her?"

Sarah looked across at Amelia who was chatting animatedly to the two other women present. "Er…."

"I know," said Miriam. "Mutton dressed as lamb. Now, I wouldn't say she's plain, but that stubby clay-like nose of hers seems to have been plonked in the middle of her face as nature's afterthought."

The two now watched Amelia drift across the room in her green, shot-silk gown and place a record on the music system. Sarah's eyes focused on the men in the garden, which was lit by six braziers now that the sun had gone down. Josh seemed happy enough talking to Richard – probably because he had been rescued from the flirtations of Amelia Wainwright. But all was about to change when the group of men – apart from Richard – re-entered the room.

Norman Walker immediately came to Sarah and his wife, saying, "Excuse my interruption, ladies, but our host would like a private word with Sarah in the garden. He wants to talk business. So, you and me, love, can test out this sprung floor."

Miriam glowered at her husband and was about to say something when Sarah stood. "Well, if it's business, I suppose I'd better go. One can't turn down any opportunity – not in this day and age." And as she started towards the french doors, Miriam said to her husband, "You bloody idiot!" But Sarah overheard the remark and, turning back briefly, said to the Walkers, "Don't worry. I am no novice when it comes to dealing with men. Please excuse me."

When she was out of earshot, Norman Walker remarked: "What a simply wonderful woman."

It was now that Josh noticed his aunt going into the garden and was about to follow her when Amelia cornered him. "Would it be improper of me to ask a gentleman for a dance?" And for the sake of good manners, he reluctantly agreed to the woman's request – not without saying, "But I'm not much of a dancer."

"I'll show you just what to do. Here! Take my hand whilst I put your arm around my waist. Like this. You know, this song, Spanish Eyes, is probably my favourite," she said, pushing herself close. Then she looked up at him. "In fact, you have Spanish eyes, not the eyes of a...."

"A what?" asked Josh, drawing slightly away from the hostess.

But she didn't answer. "Even your lovely mane is less kinky-curly than I was expecting," said Amelia touching Josh's hair, obviously ignoring his question. "And your looks are far from being – now how can I put this...? Simian." Josh thrust the woman from him and directed himself towards one of the waiters where he grabbed a drink.

Meanwhile, alone in the garden with Richard, Sarah was feeling anxious. Could she truly believe Miriam's criticism of this handsome man, who on other occasions had shown nothing but kindness toward her, or was there some fabricated reason behind her account of his apparent flirtatious nature?

"Are you all right, Sarah?"

She looked directly into his blue eyes where the flames from the brazier were reflected. "Yes. Yes, I'm fine. Maybe a little warm. That's all."

"Come. Let's find a place away from the fire." He placed a hand on her waist and escorted to the lower end of the garden where, beneath the branches of a great elm, he halted and caressed the tree's bark. "I understand this is the oldest elm around here," he said. "A fine specimen, don't you think?"

Ignoring his remark, Sarah said, "You wanted to talk about business, I understand."

"Oh, Sarah. Don't behave so naïve – I wanted to talk about *you*!" He placed a hand on her shoulder, saying, "From the first day I met you at the mill, I knew I wanted you. You must have known it?"

"Richard. You are a married man, for God's sake!"

"Oh, that means nothing. What does matter is just me – and you. Those braziers may burn out, but the passion I feel for you can never be quenched."

"Most poetic of you," said Sarah, mocking him.

But he leaned into her, pressing her against the tree, one hand cupping a single breast. She tried to push him away, but he held her there. And then his free hand moved down to the hem of her skirt and it travelled up her thigh. "Oh, Sarah," he moaned. "I'd love to suck on your...." But his words – and hands – went no further when he was wrenched away from his quarry and spun about. And there stood Josh. "Try sucking on this, you bastard!" he yelled, and felled Richard Wainwright with one punch. Then blowing on his hand, he said to Sarah, "Are you all right?"

Sarah adjusted her skirt. "Yes thanks. I am, love. But I hate the smell of men who smoke cigars. And believe me, if you hadn't arrived, my knee would have probably hurt him more than your fist."

As they turned toward the house, Amelia was standing there. "You hooligan, you thug, you...you bloody half-breed!" she screeched.

Sarah calmly stepped forward, saying, "Mrs Wainwright. I've never believed in violence, but tonight you and your husband's words and behaviour has tested my principles." And she slapped Amelia hard about the face. As the woman staggered backwards, Sarah grasped her nephew's arm. "Come on, Josh; we're leaving." And the two went back inside, crossed the room in which the other guests were standing there like hollow-eyed effigies, and departed the house into the comfort of the waiting car. "Get us home, Max," said Sarah. "I need to telephone someone."

"Are you phoning the police?" Josh asked.

"No, love. Your mother."

12

On the second day of May, High Ridge House was thrown into turmoil. Jessie was confined to bed with a heavy cold and was as fractious as a ferret: "How is it? Yer go to bed fine and yer wake up feelin' like shite!" Then Max had been called away to Scotland where his mother was dangerously ill.

Sarah was standing at the front door as her chauffeur put his bags into Mark's car. And as he came to express his regret at having to leave, she embraced him. "Take care, love. I hope everything goes all right." And after he'd thanked her, she called out to Mark who was driving him to Leeds station: "Look after him, won't you?" Mark smiled and nodded. And Sarah watched the Jaguar speed down the long drive and out of the gates....

Once back indoors, she asked Annie to bring some tea to the library while she got on with her correspondence.

After a half-hour of writing and signing cheques, the door opened. Not looking up, Sarah said, "Thanks, Annie. That was a lovely cuppa."

"So I'm in your employ now, eh?"

Sarah raised her head to see Katherine standing in front of her. "Kath!" She sprang to her feet and went and hugged her sister. "You should have let me know you were on your way back."

"Oh, I just did it on the spur of the moment. So how are you? Annie says Jessie's confined to bed."

"I'm fine; but Jess is like a bear with a sore arse. I'll ring through and get Annie to bring us some fresh tea."

"I'd prefer something stronger," said Katherine as she slumped on the chesterfield and took off her shoes.

Sarah smiled. "Well, even though it's early, I think I'll join you." She went to a low cupboard and pulled out a bottle of cream sherry and two glasses.

"Where's Josh, Sal?"

Handing Katherine her drink and an ashtray, Sarah said, "He's taken Ben for a walk – or rather Ben's taken him. They've become rather close now that Paul and Mark don't live here." She went and sat next to her sister. "In fact, I've become very close to Josh myself. Oh...."

Katherine interrupted her. "I've sold the business, Sal."

"Anderson's?"

Katherine shook her head.

"The one in America?" said Sarah. "But why?"

"Why? Because I've had enough." She lit a cigarette. "For one thing – as you know – Josh won't be going back; and for another, I'm too old to be having all the responsibility of running a large company now that Frank's gone. The lawyers are dealing with things, so I should know the outcome in a month or two. When it's all settled, I'll look for a house to buy around here, so, if it's okay with you, can me and Josh prevail on you to stay here a bit longer?" Katherine took a mouthful of her sherry and drew on her cigarette.

"Of course you can," said Sarah. "Stay as long as you want to."

"Thanks, love....Now, I must say I'm sorry, but when you phoned about going to the Wainwrights', I was in such a muddle after Frank's death and trying to sort out the business that I didn't take it all in. Did you say something unpleasant had happened?" And Sarah went on to tell her sister what had transpired. "The pig!" said Katherine. "Right! I'll take my luggage upstairs, get changed and go and sort the swine out. Same bedroom I guess? Oh, and can I borrow Max for an hour?"

"You could if he was here. He's had to go to Edinburgh to see his mother who's very poorly."

"I'll get a taxi, then. Wainwright can't get away with something like that – not on my watch." She slammed her feet back in the discarded shoes, stubbed out her cigarette, finished her drink and hurried from the room.

"You sacked him?"

"On the spot. I gave him three month's salary in lieu of notice, which after his behaviour was more than generous."

"And have you replaced him?"

"I will do – with Josh." Katherine removed her black Persian lamb coat and placed it over the back of a kitchen chair. "Anyway, apart from that, I stopped off in town and did a bit of shopping; and, you'll never guess who I saw while I was out: Maggie Gledhill!"

"Really?" said Sarah as if she knew little of Maggie's situation. "Surely it must be over twenty years since you last saw her: about the time you moved in with her before Dad died. Mind you, apart from what you've told me about her, I'd never know her if I fell over her. Want some tea?" She wished she could steer her sister away from the subject before she let slip about the false will.

Katherine seated herself at the table. "And, you'll never guess what she's doing."

Sarah passed her sister a cup. "What?" she said as though she were truly interested.

"Well, after her spell at the hospital, she took a typing course; and after working in a number of offices, last year she got a job with – now wait for this – Francis Parker: your solicitor. How she's come on after starting out as a housemaid. Do you know, she used to tell me everything that went on with the Stockwells."

The cup that Sarah had just put to her lips now fell on the table and smashed.

"Oh, Sarah!" Katherine jumped to her feet. "Let me fetch a cloth, butter fingers."

So Maggie Gledhill was the maid who overheard the conversation between Alex and his mother all those years ago, thought Sarah. Dear God! What if she'd listened in on her discussion with Francis about Steven? Oh, this was a total nightmare. "Kath," she said sheepishly. "There is something I must tell you."

13

Max returned to High Ridge on the nineteenth of May, after the death of his mother. Sarah had expressed her commiserations and told him that if he wished to take some time off, he certainly could. Max had declined the offer saying he just wanted to get on with his job. But also, today just happened to be the same day when the company West Riding Industries Limited was founded – the registered office of the company being 12, Bridge Street, Collingley.

In the new venture, Sarah took 60,000, £1 fully paid shares; Mark Crowther and Paul Halliday each held 5,000; Katherine Williams – who had merged Anderson's into the new company – took 7,000 shares. Jane Carr, having received the inheritance from her late father's estate now that she had reached the age of twenty-one, held 2,750, and the mill overlooker Albert Sanderson purchased 250. Jim Crowther – her late husband's uncle – had sold his shares in his and Sarah's partnership to the new company and fully retired to his home in New Zealand. But David had chosen not to be an investor due to his financial commitments in Bristol. Instead, he would take the post of mill manager on a salary.

David was holding Sarah's hand as they sat together on a settee in the drawing-room. "Well it's official now. You're starting afresh, so let's drink on it." He got up and went to the cabinet.

"Yes, love; let's."

He brought himself a whisky together with a sherry for Sarah, and retaking his place beside her, said, "You don't mind me not taking shares in the business, do you?"

"Not at all, love. You have your own commitments in Bristol to see to, but options are always open."

"Tell me," he said. "I know you have plans, so how about letting me in on them? Even though I'm not a shareholder, I'm still interested."

Sarah shuffled to the edge of the settee. "Well, apart from manufacturing high grade woollen cloth – maybe mixed with rayon – I have my eye on a place that makes carpets. It's not far away in Gildersome and I've heard it's up for sale. Also, I want to add more looms in the rag warehouse when it closes, and then...."

"Hey! slow down. Will you be able to afford all these new ideas of yours?"

"Yes. Paul's been looking into the costs and is convinced we can – he is the financial director after all. And, although the changes won't be cheap, a lot of the machinery can be picked up for fair prices from the mills that have had to close. Much is just lying idle and I want to grab the stuff quick before it deteriorates."

David raised his eyebrows. "So, what are the other things you have in mind, eh?"

"Wallpaper!"

"What?"

"You heard me. I want to manufacture wallpaper and have Mark design the patterns."

"I have to ask: where on earth will you find suitable premises?"

Sarah grinned like a Cheshire cat. "Providence! But first I want to get my hands on Stockwell's Field."

"But why? It's just a piece of waste land."

"You've said it, love. The operative word is 'land'. I've consulted the land registry and it can be purchased for a song. The Stockwells would be foolish not to sell, considering the state of their finances. And this is where *you* come in."

"Oh, Good Lord, Sarah. How? What can *I* do?"

"Speak to your father."

He pulled his car to a stop on the cobbled slope that led up to his grandmother's house.

It was a forbidding place. Built of locally quarried stone that at one time would have shone with a golden grandeur, it was now blackened with age and the smoke-laden air that hung over this town at times like a filthy blanket. And beyond the rusted iron gate, the broken path that led up to the front door was interspersed with dandelions and tufts of couch-grass. It was such a shame after Philip had at one time transformed it into an area of beauty when he was still alive.

Seven years had passed since Mark was last here. That was when his father had thrown him out of High Ridge due to the ill-judged remarks he made about Sarah and Paul. Oh! how he regretted the foul words that had issued from his mouth all because of jealousy. And walking through the snow-choked streets, he found himself on the doorstep of his grandmother's house and she had taken him in.

Mounting the steps now, Mark glanced at the tall stone pillars of the portico and was convinced that they bore the weight of someone's untold sadness in this cold and sullen place.

He reached the large, oak door and rang the bell; and almost immediately, the door was opened by a small, elderly woman who stared blankly at him, prompting him to say, "I'm Mark. Mrs Stockwell's grandson. Is she in?"

"Aye. She's in," said the little female. "Come in and I'll tell 'er yer're 'ere." But she didn't have to bother, when Edith Stockwell suddenly appeared in the gloomy hallway, saying, "I *thought* I heard the bell." And rushing forward now, she placed her hands on Mark's shoulders and kissed him on both cheeks. "Oh, sweetheart. How good it is to see you...Betty" – she addressed the servant – "please bring some coffee to the drawing-room." Edith looked at her grandson now. "Or would you care for something a little stronger?"

"No. No, coffee will be fine."

"Very well. Come through." And Edith took Mark's arm and ushered him into the room where she indicated that he sit on the settee next to her. "I'm glad you came, sweetheart. It seems ages since I saw you last."

"It was New Year's Eve," Mark reminded her.

"Yes. Yes, it must have been." Edith smoothed down the bodice of her floral print dress before saying, "I heard that you are a director of a company now."

Mark nodded. "Yes, I invested in Sarah's business. Design Director is my official title, and I'm here to thank you for helping me gain a place at university. I wouldn't be where I am if it wasn't for you.

"Also I wanted to let you know that I'll be away for a week from the 5th of July at a design conference in Birmingham. But, apart from all that, I wanted to see how you went on at the inquest."

"Oh, it has been a nightmare these last six months since they adjourned it, but they finally came to a conclusion yesterday."

"And what was that?" Mark asked. Edith began to wring her hands, and when Mark noticed his grandmother's agitation, he said, "I'm upsetting you. I shouldn't have asked."

"No, no; it's all right, sweetheart. I can tell you....Well, after three days of submissions and medical evidence, the jury concluded that person or persons unknown, unlawfully killed your uncle Joe with what may have been a half-inch chisel – or something of the sort – and an open verdict was recorded for dear Philip. All in all, it was a very trying experience."

It was now that the serving woman entered the room and placed a tray on a table in front of the settee. "There y'are, missis. Will I pour?"

"No, Betty; I'll see to things." And when the woman had left, Edith moved to the edge of the settee and leaned forward to pour two cups of coffee. "There's sugar and milk if you like." She took her own cup and sat back. And after taking a sip, said, "But going back to what you were saying before about my help in getting you into university, you've already thanked me, darling boy – on so many occasions."

"Yes," said Mark, "but only through phone calls and not in person." He added sugar and milk to his coffee. "And I admit, that is why I *really* came today."

Edith placed a hand on her grandson's knee. "That means a lot. ...Now, how is life in your new home?"

"Paul and I are very happy, Grandmother."

She put down her cup and coughed. "You know that I don't approve of your way of life," she said.

"We don't need anyone's approval: we love each other." And his cup was also placed back on the small table.

"I see. Well, as long as you are happy, that's all that matters. Does the dog live with you?"

"Ben? No, he's still at High Ridge. Jessie brings him to visit occasionally, but he's really Sarah's dog since Paul gave it to her as a present when she married my father."

"Oh, yes; I remember now....So, what of your neighbours? Are they duly respectable?"

"Well," said Mark leaning back on the settee, "The house to the right of ours is empty at the moment. Sarah keeps saying she's going to re-let it but hasn't done so yet, and on the other side is Amy. Amy is the kindest of souls: she'll do anything for anyone." He laughed now. "I caught her taking food to a gypsy the other day who seems to have set up residence in the old wool warehouse next door to her, but I told her not to let Sarah get wind of him....I believe, for some reason, that Sarah appears to have a distaste for gypsies."

"I'm not surprised," said Edith pulling in her chin.

"Why is that, Grandmother?"

Edith rose now and began to move around the room, and when

she stopped in front of the fireplace she shook her head. "It was dreadful," she said, raising her eyes to the ceiling. And when she looked back at her grandson, he thought he perceived a tear in her eye.

She returned to his side now, and taking his hand, said, "There was a time – before you were born – when your grandfather let the fair use the land attached to the mill for the annual holiday. And a gypsy youth...pushed Sarah's brother under one of the rides and... and he sadly died." She looked into Mark's eyes. "So, sweetheart, you can quite well understand her aversion to any of their kind."

Shortly, after further discussion about his upcoming trip, Mark finished his coffee and kissed his grandmother goodbye.

Returning to the car, his heart went out to Sarah at the loss of her brother. But he had also learned something else from his visit here today: his grandmother had been transformed from a harridan into a caring and thoughtful human being.

14

Katherine was furious with her sister for going along with Francis Parker's idiotic scheme concerning Paul's inheritance, telling her that if she had contacted her, then she would have transferred the money herself. But the deed had been done, and now she had to find out what – if anything – Maggie Gledhill had overheard of the conversation. Fortunately, Maggie knew nothing of her emigrating to America, and if she happened to ask where she was living now, she'd make something up.

She had telephoned the solicitor's office and ascertained when Maggie would be free to go on a shopping trip to Leeds. And today was that crucial day. "It's grand to see you again, Kath, so we can have a proper chat this time instead of just a few brief words."

Katherine's face was adorned with smiles, and as she hugged her old workmate, said, "Indeed, Maggie. Yes, so much water has flowed under so many bridges since we used to sit in Betty's Corner House stuffing ourselves with éclairs and cream horns. But everything changes, does it not? Now let's do some shopping. I understand that a new development has recently opened."

"It has – and it's magnificent. Come on, I'll show you how grand it really is." And the two old friends linked arms....

The huge new complex was indeed impressive. Shop upon shop of fashion and perfumes, jewellery, electrical goods and music, handbags and suitcases, china and glass and places to eat and drink – all on five floors connected by huge, shining escalators and lit by spotlights and a multitude of sparkling chandeliers.

After shopping, they were now resting in a café on the top floor with coffees in front of them, admiring the view across the city.

"Well, it's not like good old Betty's," said Katherine, "but good enough. So, the last time we met – apart from a fortnight ago – must have been when I moved in with you after my father took up with another woman after my mam had died. By! I hated that woman. Then, the time before that was probably when you had to leave the Children's Hospital after the doctor disappeared and the place closed?"

"Must have been," said Maggie. "By! what a farce that was."

"Quite," said Katherine. "And it looked as if that wicked doctor got away with murdering Alex Stockwell's son. Did you ever hear anything more about it?"

Maggie shook her head. "Not a word. Still, the old swine must be dead by now."

"Well that's all in the past....So, what did you do afterwards, love?"

"Oh loads of stuff," said Maggie, depositing her cup and wiping the froth from her lips. "But seven years ago, when I reached the ripe old age of thirty-nine, I knew it was time to get myself a proper career. So I took a secretarial course at night-school. Then eighteen months later got my first chance at a job and I stayed there for four years, before last year getting a position with a solicitor, as you know."

"Well done, love." Now Katherine had Maggie in her grasp. But she had to tread carefully in case she twigged. Katherine knew that Maggie believed David was dead by the wheeling and dealing of Edith Stockwell who blackmailed Sam Griffiths into killing him. She also knew that Maggie had no knowledge of Sarah having married William Crowther, and that Sarah Crowther was her sister. Now she had to somehow find out how much Maggie had gathered from the visit of Sarah to the offices of Francis Roland Parker. She rested her cup in the saucer and said, "I bet you hear some interesting tales working for a solicitor."

Maggie's eyes glistened now. "Interesting! Interesting?" She leaned over the table, saying, "Downright illegal!"

"Never! Surely not?"

Maggie nodded fervently. "The most outrageous thing I heard was when this woman came in a month or so ago – well-to-do woman by the cut of her jib – and she got old Parker to forge a will for her."

"No!" said Katherine faking disbelief, the while thinking, Wow! She was straight in there. What a piece of luck!

Maggie nodded again. "And it just happened to be that Crowther woman who runs Resurrection mill. Now, can yer credit that?"

"That's shocking. Some people, eh?" Katherine shook her head. "The more people have, the more they want."

Maggie finished her coffee. "Want another one, Kath?"

"Oh, no, love. But thanks anyway." Katherine looked at her watch. "It's time I was going, but it's been grand to see you again after such a long time."

"Wait for me, Kath. You can help me down those escalators. I've told you how much I hate those things."

Oh, I'll help you down all right, thought Katherine. All the bloody way down.

"I could have died, Kath," said Maggie as she sat in Leeds Infirmary nursing a broken wrist and inspecting the bruises on her legs.

"Yes, you could have. In fact, that's what I was hoping."

"What?"

"You heard me. If it hadn't been that, I would likely have thrown you under a bus – so think yourself lucky."

"But why, Kath? I don't understand?"

Katherine's eyes were afire. "After revealing details of my sister's – yes sister's – affairs with your employer, I thought that because of your fear of moving staircases, you would want to get to the bottom as soon as possible, so I gave you a push."

Instead of appearing shocked by Katherine's admission, Maggie was apologetic. "But I wouldn't have told anybody, Kath," she said.

"You told me! That was bad enough. How many more people could you spill the beans to if I didn't stop you? No, I had to do something to protect my family from your loose tongue.

"Now, I'll do a deal with you. Keep your mouth shut, and I'll pay you for the time you're off work – as long as you quit the job at the solicitor's. Also, when you're up to it, you can come and work for me at my factory in Bradford at a better rate than what you're getting in an office. But, if you ever mention a thing about what you heard, the next time you won't just be injured: you'll be pushing up daisies. Get it?

"Don't forget, Maggie, I'm from Chicago, and believe me, the people I am acquainted with would see you off in the most ghastly of ways if you cross me. I've known some folk who have blabbed like you, have had their tongues torn out by the roots. So you'd better think on."

15

Sarah owned three houses in Long Lane. One was leased to Amy Broadbent – at a peppercorn rent – and at one side of her, separated by a thick stone wall, was an old wool warehouse, which Sarah had decided to have demolished after years of it lying derelict. The middle of the three was owned by Paul and Mark, and the third which stood next to a patch of spare land, was empty. That was until Sarah chose to place an advert in the Yorkshire Post.

But the decision was needless, when Laura came in from her gardening and reported the fact that she had encountered a gentleman in The Queen public house. Sarah was wary at first, wondering what Laura was doing talking to strange men in licensed premises; but she concluded that it was not of her concern since, after all, her niece was a grown woman and it was up to her what she did in her spare time.

Apparently, he was a Londoner who required accommodation for six months until certain business matters of his were settled. He was willing to provide glowing references and two months' rent in advance. So, with Laura's recommendation, Sarah was glad to take him on.

Jessie and Amy had been dispatched to clean and tidy the premises and had been there when the new tenant arrived to look over the place.

"So what do you think of him?" Sarah had enquired when Jessie returned to High Ridge carting brushes and buckets and polish.

"Think? Think! I hadn't a bloody clue what he was talking about. I asked him if he'd like to see the bedrooms, and he says to me: 'You mean up the apples and pears.' I just gawped at him, and Amy dropped her brush. Then – get this – he says: 'C'mon then, let's 'ave a butcher's.' The man's puddled."

Sarah howled with laughter. "He's a Cockney, Jess. They talk like that."

"Nay, he sounds more like that Dick Van what's-his-face in that Mary Poppins picture…I don't know why your Laura recommended him! What's wrong wi' the girl?"

"Dyke!"

"Is she? Well I'm not surprised after being wed to Joe Stockwell."

"Not Laura! The chap in Mary Poppins."

"Is he one an' all? Eeh, what's the world comin' to? Still, I don't trust the man, Sal. He's got a lazy eye. Anyroad – and I hope I did right – I gave him my keys, so he wouldn't have to bother you."

"That's ideal, love." Sarah's face radiated tacit amusement as she got up from the library desk where several sheets of correspondence still lay, and said, "Now, these can wait for a while. I'm showing Josh around the mill this afternoon and then he can accompany me to see this new man and see what we think of him for ourselves."

Sarah was in a joyous mood.

Some days earlier, she had collared Harry, sat him down, and related the conversation she had had with Jane about Joe Stockwell – and much to her surprise, he had not hit the roof. Granted, he had used a few choice words and said how glad he was that the man was dead, but his main concern was for his wife – which was evident when he had cried in Sarah's arms. And today she was in another fulfilling situation of showing her nephew around her treasured mill.

As the two of them walked up the mill yard, Sarah remarked, "You'll be taking over the reins at Anderson's soon, won't you, Josh?"

"Third of July," he said.

"And are you looking forward to it?"

"Not really," Josh replied. "But I told my mother I wanted to work there I could stay in the country, so I guess I should."

Sarah stopped before entering the mill itself, and taking his arm said, "Don't do what you don't want to, love. When I was fourteen, my own mother took me for a job with Edith Stockwell and I told her in no uncertain terms that I wouldn't work there, and look at me now. My advice is to ask her if you could change your mind – or maybe work part-time for the moment, and who knows, when I've showed you around Resurrection you may wish to spend the rest of your time here in some capacity?" Josh smiled now and followed his aunt into the mill....

They were in the rag warehouse. "All the stuff to produce yarn, comes from the rag merchant," said Sarah. "And in here, it has to be sorted into different batches: colour, quality, new or old, and so on. Now, this is a sticky situation as far as your Aunt Mary is concerned because her husband, Jack, is one of those merchants. And, since I intend to discontinue the use of rags and use only pure new wool, I imagine there'll be hell to pay in that household when they find out – if they haven't found out already."

Josh could do nothing but love and admire this very special woman. He listened to her and revered her. Her strength of mind was boundless; she was handsome and honourable and full of charm; and more than that, she was passionate. Paul was certainly of her stock.

"So what prompted you to take a job here and not with the Stockwells?" Josh asked.

Sarah sniggered now. "Oh, love; I was young and so gauche. Edith told me that the job involved many things to be done in the household – including, as she put it, helping her with her toilet. I believed that to mean she wanted me to wipe her backside after going to the lavatory." Laughter prevailed again, before she said, "I didn't accept the position. Then, I was fortunate to get a job here" – she touched the whitewashed stone wall beside her with a noticeable affection – "and the rest, as they say, is history. Talking about history, did you know that this mill made cloth for both sides in the American Civil War?"

"No!"

"Yes.…Now, let me take you to see some spinning and weaving being done." And they walked to a further shed where the mules and looms were.

Here, Josh was in awe of the machinery. His aunt first explained the spinning process before picking up one of the weft bobbins from a basket, saying, "This is what you end up with, Josh. It's a weft bobbin that pops into the shuttle on the loom. Come on, let's go and see how they work."

There, at the other side of the shed, she introduced him to the looms. And above the noise of shuttles flying and heddles clacking, Sarah showed Josh exactly what was going on. "Some of the older weavers call the warp area" – she pointed at the lengthwise threads – "their 'lane'. I could often hear them bawling out over the noise if anything had gone wrong: 'Oi! Bert! Get thisen ovver 'ere. Me lane's up the bloody creek!'" And even though Josh had not a clue as to what Sarah had just said, he smiled nevertheless.

"You will see that warps are separate into two sheets by the heddles," Sarah continued. "This process is called shedding, and the weft bobbin flies between the sheets whence the heddles move to create a new shed. And effectively, when the weft bobbin is flung the other way, the weft is clasped between two layers of warp and is then beaten up to the cloth already woven. So there it is, Josh. Simple, eh?"

Josh shook his head. And Sarah, laughing again, said, "Come on, sunshine; let's get off and see lazy-eye just to set Jessie's mind at rest." She took her nephew's arm now, and they left the mill.

Sarah was knocked for six when she met her new tenant who was not as she had expected. He looked to be in his sixties with an overgrown beard and a mass of grey hair. Nevertheless, he had paid in advance, so he couldn't be destitute. "So, how are you settling in, Mr Jackson?" Sarah said after introducing herself and her nephew.

"Fine! It's just what I was looking for," he said as he handed cups of tea to his visitors. He seated himself at the table now, adding, "Yes, very suitable for my purposes."

Josh looked at his aunt who responded to her new tenant by saying, "And what *are* your purposes if you don't mind me asking?"

The man stroked his long beard. "Just sorting out some business affairs which my sister asked me to get settled for her. She's elderly and can't travel. And she's deaf – mutton, as we say in the East End."

Sarah sipped at her tea before saying, "Yes. The two ladies I sent to tidy the place were a little puzzled by some of the vernacular. So, is your sister originally from these parts?"

"Er...no. But some of her holdings are. Would you care for a biscuit?"

Sarah waved a hand. "Oh, no. No thank you. We'd best be off and leave you to it." She stood now. "But if you need to get in touch about any problems that may crop up, just let my son next door know and he'll pass on the message. We'll see ourselves out – and thanks for the tea...."

"So, what did you think of him?" said Sarah as she and Josh walked down the lane.

"I don't really know," Josh replied. "What about you?"

"He puzzles me, love. He puzzles me a lot."

And the joy she had felt earlier in the day had waned.

16

Alexander Stockwell was forty-seven years old, but – without exception – every woman in the district believed he was no more than thirty. He was a striking man: hair the colour of jet with not a grey hair in sight; a slim, but muscular, physique wrought through his duties in the family business; and he was possessed of blue, almost lavender eyes that were totally hypnotic. And despite his mother's attempts at matchmaking with any one of several women in her circle of acquaintances, he had rejected them outright knowing that they were all of her choice. Then on one decidedly cool day at the beginning of June, he announced his intention of courting. And it did not go down at all well with Edith.

"Good God! Are you completely mad? I could quite believe it of Joseph – God rest his soul – but not you. Laura Wilson of all people!"

"Yet apparently she was good enough for my brother. And don't forget that he gave her a child by taking her behind the hedge at the bottom of our garden and shagging the life out of her."

"You foul-mouthed piece." Edith rammed the fingers of her black, leather gloves down to her knuckles. "And I suppose you picked up that filthy language from that Harry Carr who you employed to take on the building work at the mill. Well, I'll tell you this, I'll...."

"You won't tell me anything, Mother. When you get there, you won't say or do a thing lest I throw you off the roof. Now! Are you ready?"

"Yes!" said Edith, who was wearing a cream-coloured woollen coat with an ocelot fur collar, a brown, wide-brimmed hat and brown shoes.

"You look as if you're ready to open a fête rather than just going to the mill," said Alex with derision. Picking up a large, leather handbag now, Edith said blithely, "Well, I certainly wouldn't go looking like one of the riff-raff we employ. And besides, Harry would expect it of his wife's grandmother. I wanted to dress properly to admire his splendid work and report back to her, so let's be off."

While Kevin was varnishing the desks that he had diligently constructed, Harry was installing glass into the last of the windows of the new offices. "Won't be long now, Kev. When this is done, so are we."

"I hope there's more work comin' in 'cos I'm goin' ter be a dad."

Harry chuckled. "Have no worries about that – we'll be snowed under next month. How's Annie taken the news of the baby?"

"She's chuffed. But like me, she's worried about me dad finding out."

"Well, he won't find out from *me*...oh, bloody 'ell! Alex is here – and he's brought his soddin' mother with him. Pretend we haven't seen 'em. Oh, bugger it! They've clocked us."

Alex and his mother approached them now, whence Alex said, "Well done, lads. It's just about finished, I see."

"I've just fixed the last piece of glass, Alex, and then it'll be all yours."

Edith stepped forward, and was about to smooth a gloved hand over the new desks when Harry said briskly, "No! They're still wet."

"Oh," she said. "I didn't think. How silly of me."

"So what do you think of it all, Grandmother?" Harry asked. Edith's eyes could have blistered him. "Listen, Mr Carr," she announced imperiously. "You may be my granddaughter's husband, but I am certainly not your grandmother."

"Oh, stop being so picky, Mother," said Alex. "You should take it as a compliment. Now, let's go and see the other offices." Edith grunted, but followed the three men on an inspection of the completed work.

Several of Harry's other employees were busily cleaning their stations and were about to pack away their belongings as the visitors passed through. They paused momentarily when Alex and his mother stopped to look at the results. And while the others talked at a distance, Edith, her face beaming now, walked up to one of the workmen, saying, "Do you really need all these tools?"

The chippy smiled back at her. "Oh, aye, Mrs Stockwell," he said. "Every good carpenter needs all his good tools. Those over there" – he pointed to the next desk – "are Mr Carr's personal ones. He won't let any of us touch 'em. He's very partic'lar about that."

"You keep them in immaculate condition. Are they sharp?"

"Oh, aye. The sharper the better."

"My brother was keen at making things before he died. He would have loved to have seen this lot. And so many different sizes."

"And every one needed for the jobs we have to do," said the workman.

It was now that Alex beckoned the man over, leaving Edith on her own. Then shortly he called to her: "Come on, Mother. Time to leave these good people to finish off and get away home."

"Oh, yes of course. I'm coming, dear. I'm coming."

17

Are you all right, love? You look all in."

Paul looked at his mother and sighed. "Oh, I had a restless night that's all."

"Are you and Mark…well, okay?"

"Oh yes! Nothing wrong there. It's just that…I had this weird dream that's been preying on my mind for some reason. I can't seem to shake it off. It seemed so real, and as if it actually happened some time ago. But I…I can't think that it could have."

Sarah pushed herself out of her chair and went over to the settee and sat beside her son. Placing a hand on his shoulder, she said, "Tell me, love."

Paul joined his hands together and looked at the floor. "I thought I was trapped in a fire at home. But" – he raised his head now – "it wasn't. It was somewhere else." He got up and began to pace the room, moving stealthily like a focused lion. Then suddenly he returned to the side of his mother. "It was a place I didn't recognise. A place with…sort of glass partitions and old oak desks. And I was sitting there, on my own, doing some work or other. Then I smelled smoke and heard an alarm going off and.…That's all I remember."

"Just a bad dream, love." Sarah took his hand. "Try and forget it. Now, come on, let's get to the mill where we can really do some work."

"Aye, you're right, Mam. I'll go and get ready." And as Sarah watched her son leave the room, she thought, It's coming back to him. Bit by bit it's coming back. How long would it be before he remembered Steven and everything that happened between them. And God forbid that it should cause widespread problems! Oh, what else could happen? Well, Sarah was about to find out when the phone rang.

"Sarah Cro.…" But she was interrupted. "Jane, love; slow down. Take a breath.…Yes…oh, no! When…? Shall I come over…? Right! Okay, I'll send Max to come and pick you up.…Yes; I'll be here, and try not to worry. All right, love…bye.…Bye-bye." Sarah put down the phone and raced to the garage where she told Max to go and collect her stepdaughter. Then she went to the kitchen.

"Jessie!"

"What? Me and Annie are in the middle of...."

"Jess! Listen! Harry's been arrested."

"Jesus!" Jessie dragged up a chair and slumped on it. And looking at Sarah, said, "What for?"

"For the murder of Joe Stockwell."

Annie let out a yelp of astonishment. "That can't be right," she said. "Harry? Surely not?"

Sarah nodded, and taking a seat herself now, said, "Jane's coming over. She says she can't stay on her own."

Jessie struggled to her feet. "Right! I'll finish off in here while you" – she addressed Annie – "go and make up her old room. Can yer manage that in your condition?"

"Of course I can," said Annie sourly. "I'm only a few weeks, yer know."

"Oh, by the way, Annie," said Sarah, "could you tell Paul that I can't make it to the mill and to get off on his own. But don't tell him why, love."

"Right," said Annie, and she fled.

Retaking her seat now, Jessie looked at Sarah whose normally bright green eyes appeared to have changed to a dull grey. "D'yer want a brandy, love?"

Sarah shook her head. "I need to keep my mind clear to decide what to do next."

"And what's that?"

"First of all, try and calm Jane down – which might be an impossibility – and then go and see Francis to enlist his help."

"Well, God help you with both," said Jessie. "In fact, God help us all."

"That's not my field of expertise, love," said Francis Parker; "but I know just the man whose it is."

"Then get him!" said Sarah. "I don't care how much it costs."

"Right. I'll phone him straight away and get him to visit Harry as soon as possible. Where is he being kept?"

"The jail in Collingley Town Hall until the magistrate's hearing."

Francis opened his diary. "Today's Tuesday, so that will likely be Friday. Yes. So that gives us three days. Right, Sarah; you get off and I'll be in touch – and don't worry."

"That's easier said than done," said Sarah as she stood.

413

Francis stood also. "I know, love, but the solicitor I know is very good." He shook his client's hand. And after Sarah had left, he sat at his desk and removed his spectacles, thinking, I don't care how good he is, but whatever Harry Carr may have – or have not – told the police, they must have a strong case against him. And he didn't have a chance in hell of wriggling out of this one.

The hearing at Collingley magistrates' court *did* take place on the Friday, and Jane and Sarah were in attendance as Harry pleaded not guilty to stabbing Joseph Stockwell. But unbeknown to them, this was a total change of heart. He had been thinking of admitting it after considering the options.

His mind had revisited the morning subsequent to the fire at Providence when he had returned to High Ridge where his wife was waiting for him. When Sarah had sent him on an assignment to trap Joseph into a situation that could provide ammunition against his blackmail attempts against Paul and Steven Clark, she had told him that Jane had already said she would carry out the mission – and no doubt that comment came because of her uncle forcing himself on her when she was only ten. After all, Jane could easily have followed him to the Stockwells without people noticing if they thought she had gone to bed, and killed Joe when he himself had fallen asleep out of sight of the house.

And what about Laura? She had every reason to want to be rid of him. She had told him how much she detested Joe and was stuck in a marriage she could never get out of while he was alive….Then there was Kevin. Was he the culprit since he had access to so many sharp weapons that could have caused Joe's death? He was terribly fond of Paul, and he could have blamed Stockwell for indirectly putting him in a coma. Joe after all had tried to blackmail Sarah over Paul's homosexuality.

He had also thought about Alex. He had discharged himself from hospital early that morning, and was back home just after Joe arrived. And if he found out from his wayward brother what really happened the previous night at the mill, this could have prompted a violent reaction on his part.

And then there was the evidence the police had found to confidently make an arrest – it pointed straight at him. But whatever the outcome of this whole charade, he wouldn't play the martyr and admit to something that he didn't do.

"Bridewell? Bloody 'ell! Charlie Peace were in there before they hung 'im at Armley. They say his ghost haunts the place and...."

"Jessie! Shut up!" Sarah was distraught after she and Jane had spent the morning in court where Harry had been remanded in custody to appear at the assizes at a future date for the murder of Joseph Stockwell. "I'm sorry, love," Sarah sighed, "but all this is becoming too much to take in. I just can't believe Harry could kill anyone...Jane's crying her eyes out upstairs."

Jessie came and sat with her. "Does Paul know?"

"Not yet. I'll go to the mill later and tell him. Then I'll go and speak to the solicitor and ask him if he can recommend a good barrister. He was a kind man and tried his best for bail to be granted – but to no avail."

Jessie patted Sarah's hand. "Barristers are a different kettle of fish, lass. And whoever it is, will prove Harry's not guilty."

"But how can any barrister – good or otherwise – help in a situation like this?" Sarah looked deep into her friend's eyes. "What if he did do it?" She tapped the table now. "We know Harry went out that morning after the fire at Providence and he said he'd kill Joe. He told me he didn't, but perhaps he did. The police must have some damning evidence against Harry – but what?"

"Well, we'll find out eventually, love."

Sarah nodded. "Anyway, I've retained the solicitor for now."

"Why?" asked Jessie. Surely his job's done now?"

Sarah threw back her head. "Oh, far from it." She looked directly at Jessie now. "Depending on what Harry's told the police, all of us are going to need his guidance before long. And I do mean all of us."

18

Sarah walked down St Mary's Road where, on one side where no houses existed, there was an area known locally as The Docks. She and Emily used to come here when they were younger and bring a few sandwiches and some pop. It was an odd name because it had nothing to do with sea and ships: it was just an area of sloping land covered with sycamores where, at the latter part of year, the winged seeds came sailing down from above like miniature spinning tops. And they'd sit and have their picnic and watch the trains in the distance come trundling along the line from Wakefield on their way to Leeds. They were happy days. But today, her trip was to try and alleviate any likelihood that words of Annie's pregnancy would reach the ears of Kevin's father.

She had reached Wilf's place now, and knocked on the door.

Presently the door opened. "Eeh, Sarah! It's grand to see yer. Come in. I'm just making a fresh pot o' tea as a matter o' fact."

Sarah entered the house which Wilf and her sister had acquired shortly after their marriage, and sat on a chair close to the table. It was a rented residence in a row of back-to-back terraced houses at the south side of Collingley, and Wilf had kept it in good repair. "I'm sorry to be bothering you on your day off, love," she said, "but I hardly get the chance to have a chat when we're in the mill."

"Nay, it's no bother, lass," he shouted from the scullery. "Anyroad, how's poor Harry doin'?"

"Oh, as well as can be expected in the circumstances," Sarah called to him. "Jane's in a state though: she can't settle anywhere. Now she's gone to stay with her grandmother of all people."

"Well, the Lord help her there, that's what I say." Wilf came into the front room now and passed Sarah a cup of tea. "Hey!" he said, "I got a letter from the council today, Sal. They're buying the whole row and doin' 'em up. Bathroom and inside lav – that'll be a blessin'."

"That is good news...I did read something of the sort in the Advertiser," said Sarah, noticing the enormous beam of delight on her brother-in-law's face, rarely seen since the day he married Emily.

Wilf sat at the table. "Would yer like a piece o' bilberry pie? I got it fresh this mornin'."

"Oh no, love. Just tea is fine....So, tell me more."

Wilf picked up the letter and put on his glasses. "Aye, that's right – they start next week. It says 'ere that they'll 'ave to take off a section of me and Kevin's bedroom to make the new room, so I suppose we'll have to sleep down 'ere till it's done. They're puttin' in new electrics an' all."

Sarah took a mouthful of tea before saying, "So what about Laura?"

"Oh, that's no problem: her room is staying intact."

Sarah could now possibly see a way out of her problem regarding Kevin's situation. She had already secured a promise from Laura not to speak of Annie's pregnancy, and now she had to deal with the problem of Kevin keeping the secret from his father, because Wilf was so astute when it came to his son and his changing moods. "So how long do they think the work with take?" Sarah asked.

"Months, I'd imagine. At least two."

Sarah placed her cup on its saucer, saying, "Maybe I could help out with things." She leaned slightly forward now. "What would you think if Kevin came to live with us for the duration of the work? It would give you a bit more space. And he's working all the hours that God sends with Harry being away."

Wilf remained stock-still for a while. Then he leaned back in his chair and said, "Well, I suppose that would help if yer don't mind, lass. But I don't know what the neighbours'd think of a thirty-year-old lass living on 'er own wi' a man o' forty-six."

Sarah nearly fell about. "Nay, Wilf; she's living with *two* men at the moment. Have they made any comment at that?"

"Well...no."

"There you are then....So, what do you think?"

Wilf stroked his chin before saying, "Aye. We'll do that. Should I tell Kevin, or will you? I've already packed a case for 'im, yer know."

Sarah smiled at this most special man she had known from childhood, saying, "Leave it all to me....Yes, Paul is really looking forward to Kevin staying with him while Mark is away in Birmingham."

Wilf gave a hearty laugh.

"What, love?"

417

"Eeh, Sal! Who would have thought our two lads would be livin' together after 'ow they were when they were young?"

Sarah smiled. "They hated each other, didn't they? But then, when I went with David to visit Paul in hospital last October and Kevin turned up, I was surprised at his reaction: he cried, Wilf. And prior to that, the last time he saw Paul was the day our Em died – and they didn't talk even then."

Wilf's face altered as if the mention of the loss of his wife still hurt, but it was Sarah's other remark that he was troubled by. "Nay, lass," he said, "Our Kev went straight to Leeds Infirmary the morning after the fire."

"But I sat there all night," said Sarah, "and the doctors wouldn't even let *me* see him. They told me he wouldn't be allowed any visitors for a few days at least."

"Well," said Wilf boldly, "Kev did tell me he went, lass. He even said – and I remember his exact words – 'he's been sorted out.'"

"Oh, I believe you, love. But what a weird thing to say considering Paul was in a coma."

"Ask 'im yerself, lass; but that's what he said."

"Oh, I aim to, Wilf. I aim to."

But Sarah's intention would be completely forgotten when, on the following day, a shocking event took place.

19

The evening of the 5th of July 1967.

Earlier in the day, David had told Sarah that he had to travel to Bristol to sort out some business, so it just left three of them to enjoy one another's company. And now, Sarah, Katherine and Josh were in the drawing-room enjoying a drink after dinner.

"It's a pity Paul couldn't be here." This was Josh. "But I guess he and his cousin are enjoying themselves."

Katherine was aware of the sullen look on her son's face. But Sarah wasn't, as she said, "It's about time, love. They were at odds with each other at one time."

Quickly changing the subject now, Katherine said, "Where's Jessie got to?"

Sarah twirled the brandy in her glass. "She's spending some time with Amy. She's worried about her – and I must admit, Amy's not been looking too well lately. I keep telling her to go to the doctor's, but will she listen? No! She's as stubborn as a...."

The door burst open and Max stood there. "Sarah!" he said with trepidation in his voice. "I've just seen it from upstairs. I think there's a fire on Long Lane. It could be your houses."

"Dear God. I hope it's not."

Josh leapt from his seat. "Come on let's go. We can't hang about here."

Sarah was also on her feet now. "Max," she said, "get the car started and tell Annie to look after the place – oh, and to take care of Ben."

Max hurried out as Katherine remarked, "What is it with fires around here? If it's not mills, it's houses."

Sarah grabbed the drink out of her sister's hand. "Kath! Move!"

When they arrived on Long Lane, all three houses were ablaze. Windows were cracking with the heat and clouds of dense smoke were billowing in the direction of the Hollow, from where now the strident sounds of fire-engines could be heard.

Max, having parked the car at Town End, ran up to Sarah and her family who were standing in the field at the side of the lane. "Oh, my God! I was hoping I wasn't right and it was something else," he said. Sarah grasped at his arm – and she kept it there. But she didn't shake with any bit of emotion: it was if she had been struck with what could only described as nothingness. Max looked at the burning houses in front of him and he was suddenly taken back to when he first met this exceptional woman on this very spot. It was the winter of 1958 when he was a young chauffeur to William Crowther. Mr Crowther had invited she and Paul to spend Christmas Eve at High Ridge House. He had driven through the snow to pick the two of them up, and he sensed how nervous Sarah was at meeting the family, who had also invited the Stockwells. Who would have thought she would now – nearly twenty years later – own the house in which he was employed and be the head of a new company? And now she was back to where she once lived: staring blindly and helplessly at the progressive destruction of the buildings in which people she loved could have perished. He rested a hand on her arm now, and turning away from the inferno before her, Sarah looked at him. "Oh, Max," she said. "Not my boy again." And his heart bled....

20

A thin blue mist surrounded him. But it was a warm and comforting haze that held no fear. He could almost feel it. It was reminiscent of the caress of silk velvet. Then the mist seemed to lift, and a staircase slowly appeared. And he was tempted to climb. Now the image of a man emerged, beckoning him onwards. But still he felt no apprehension as the black-haired figure was suddenly transformed into a naked, strapping blond who gestured at him to return down the stairs with the palm of one hand. He ignored the guidance since the shadowy form reappeared and urged him forward. And he went. At the top of the staircase a dull, green wall came into view; and written on it in huge red letters, was the Latin phrase Principiis Mathematica: The Principles of Mathematics. So, that's why he was here! Someone was seeking his guidance – his knowledge of the laws of numbers. Finding a compensating error when numbers are written the wrong way around and the difference is divisible by nine – and other things. Yes! Many, many other things. He was in his element. It was his raison d'être. But what was Richard Wagner doing here as well? His baton was raised, conducting the final opera in his Ring Cycle, Götterdämmerung. What a wonderful piece – particularly Brünhilde's Immolation scene. That's where she rides her horse into the flames. Oh, but the fire is so fierce, and glass is shattering, and he hasn't finished his work. Now the mist, the beautiful mist has turned to choking black smoke. Why was the blond youth trying to help him? And where is he now? Is he above a canopy of stars…? But the sickening smoke is engulfing him now, and he has to cry out: 'Help me, Mark!' But Mark isn't there – Mark is sitting in a hospital ward talking to…him! Why? Why? Why am I losing you…?

"Paul. Paul! PAUL! Wake up!"

Paul jerked into consciousness. "What? What is it…? Oh! I…I must have been…er, dreaming."

"We ought to get up. It's nearly nine," said Mark.

Paul snuggled into Mark's shoulder now and stroked the dark hairs on his chest. "Just another half-hour."

Mark raised himself, and throwing back the bed sheet, said, "No! I can't. I'm due to leave shortly. It's important for me."

"Oh, all right. Sorry. I'll make you some breakfast before you set off while you have a bath. What do you fancy?"

"A bacon sandwich would be nice." And as Paul watched his naked lover walk across the bedroom to open the curtains, his heart beat faster. He was so beautiful: tall with a neatly-trimmed beard, and how Paul loved that wisp of dark hair on his lower back. And those peach-like buttocks – God knew exactly what he was doing when he fashioned them…! Why was it that heterosexual men were obsessed with big tits when you could explore a soft, smooth, unblemished arse like that…? "It's a lovely day, Paul – and a very special one."

"Why?" asked Paul. "Because you're disappearing to Birmingham?"

Mark turned to face him. "No…! It looks like we'll be able to love each other without the fear of being prosecuted now that the bill has been passed in the Commons – it was just on the clock radio."

So, today they would be legal at last – but Mark was leaving for a whole week. Oh, just look at him, thought Paul. The sculptured muscles of his chest were covered in fine, black hair that he loved to run his fingers through. But it wasn't all over his torso: it was in a sort of Y shape that ended in a delicate line below his belly button. He couldn't control his desire for the man in front of him: he was as hard as a rock, lusting for his lover's warmth, his scent, and his powerful eagerness for sex. "Come back to bed, Mark – just for five minutes."

"No! I've got to get ready. Now, get up! You need to put the bedding on in the spare room for Kevin coming. And be quick."

Jessie got to her feet. "Right! I'll get ready and go and help Paul sort out the spare bedroom for Kevin staying. The lad'll be glad of a bit o' company while Mark's away."

"Nay, he can manage bedclothes on his own, Jess," Sarah declared. "Besides, it's your day off. I thought you were spending it with Amy?"

"I am. But men always get things wrong."

"I'll get Max to drive you over."

Jessie flapped her hand. "No, love; I'll walk – the fresh air will do me good. And I'll take them that sausage casserole from the fridge so they won't have to start cooking."

"You're spoiling them, Jess."

Jessie smiled. "I am, aren't I...? See you later, love."

Once in the kitchen, Jessie wrapped the casserole dish in a tea-towel as Ben sat sniffing at her every move. "Yours is for later, lad," she said, and placed the dish in a wicker basket. She put on her overcoat and a headscarf, grabbed her keys and went out of the back door.

It was a bright, but unusually chilly morning for the time of year, and Barn Brook twinkled in the sunlight. She crossed carefully, and upon reaching the other side, walked up the slight incline before reaching the fields that spread out between High Ridge and Long Lane. She smiled inwardly when she remembered the first time she ever set foot in High Ridge House – well, just about being carried in by Paul and Mark after she fell. Who would have guessed the changes that would occur in all their lives? Yet at first, she had found it difficult to come to terms with Paul and Mark's involvement with each other, but Sarah had told her to always remember one word that could explain everything – and that word was love....

Jessie was approaching the lane now, and could see Mark putting his suitcase in his car. She called out to him, and when he turned, he waved. He closed the car door and ran across the lane and into the field. And when he reached her, he embraced her. "I'm glad I've seen you before I set off. You can hopefully persuade Paul to get out of bed."

"Here, take this"– she passed the basket over – "I'll shift him." But when they went inside the house, Paul was up and dressed. "By! It's a good job you're up or I'd have come and thrown you out of yer pit."

Paul simulated embarrassment. "Sorry, ma'am," he said. "I won't do it again. I did make bacon sandwiches, though."

"Bacon sandwiches indeed. Now, take this basket off Mark and put it in the fridge....No! Not the basket! The dish inside. It's for you and Kevin's tea. Dear God, give me strength." Jessie shook her head with despair. "Now!" She turned and placed her hands on Mark's shoulders. "You'd best be off, love. And drive carefully.... Oh, and take these sandwiches with you to eat on the journey."

"I will, Jess. And thanks."

"Right you" – she pointed at Paul – "go and see him off and then come upstairs and help me with Kevin's bed...."

Paul and Jessie had soon made the bedroom presentable and were now enjoying a cup of tea. "Well, I'll say this: yer make a good cuppa, lad."

"Not bad....So what are you and Amy getting up to today?"

"Well" – Jessie place her palms together – "I'm taking her out for a bit o' dinner and then treating her to bingo tonight. Mind you, I didn't tell yer mam 'cos she'd say I'd be wastin' me brass....By the way, how's he next door?" She nodded at the wall.

"We don't see much of him. Keeps himself to himself."

Jessie tapped the table. "I don't trust him, Paul. If I were you, I'd watch meself. Mark my words: the man's trouble....Right" – she stood now – "I'll pop next door to Amy's and, when he arrives, give my love to Kevin. And don't forget" – she nodded at the wall again – "watch out for old lazy-eye." She put on her coat and went to see Amy....

"Are yer in, lass?"

"Oh, aye," said Amy as Jessie entered her friend's house. "I were just...er...."

"Er what?" Jessie asked as she noticed Amy wrapping something up in sheets of newspaper. "What've yer got in there?"

Amy bit on her bottom lip and sniffed. "Er...well, it's some food for...for Tom."

"Tom who? Don't tell me yer've taken in a stray cat?"

"No...! He's a fella livin' next door" – she inclined her head towards the wall – "He's just staying in the old warehouse waitin' for the fair comin'."

"Waiting for the fair coming? So how long's he been there?"

"A couple o' months."

"A couple of...?"

"Aye, Jess," said Amy in anguish. "He goes from one fair to t'other."

Jessie approached the table and leant heavily on it. "You mean a bloody gypsy, don't you?"

Amy nodded. "When he's 'ere, I give 'im a few bits and pieces to see 'im through, like."

"No!" – Jessie planted her fists on her hips – "I bloody well don't like! Do you know how much we were pestered by his lot when me and Sarah lived down Victoria Row? One on 'em killed Sarah's brother." She thrust out her arm. "Is he in there now?"

"I...I believe so," said Amy contritely.

"Right!" said Jessie picking up the small, wrapped parcel. "Take him this and tell him it's the last he's gettin'. I'm not an unkind woman, Amy, but before Sarah gets wind of this, tell him to get lost."

"But…but, Jess, he can be…a bit tetchy: he doesn't like not 'aving owt. He gets mad."

"Oh, I'll mad 'im all right! Now, while I go and sort the bugger out, get yerself ready 'cos we're goin' out. Tetchy indeed."

"I can't tell me dad, Paul, 'cos he'd thrash me – as big as I am."

Paul looked at the tall twenty-three-year-old who seemed to be in the throes of having his world torn apart. "And are you sure she's pregnant?" he asked.

Kevin nodded. "I'm sure all right. You should see the size of 'er. Eeh, I wish I were like you, Paul: you wouldn't get a lass up the duff, would yer?"

Paul gave a hearty laugh. "No. I can categorically say I would not. Look, it appears to me you need a drink or two." He got up from the table where they had just enjoyed the meal provided by Jessie, and went and lay a hand on his cousin's shoulder. "Come on. I'll order a taxi and we'll go into Leeds. I've heard The Hart is quite grand – and, apparently, they're having a party to celebrate the change in the law. It should be fun."

Kevin looked at Paul with trepidation on his face. "But it's…yer know" – his head moved from side to side – "one of them there places, isn't it?"

"Aye," said Paul, mimicking Kevin's way of speaking. "It is one of them there places! But don't worry. If anybody tries to pick you up, I'll tell 'em you're my boyfriend, but" – he wagged a finger – "make sure you keep your back firmly against a wall."

The pub was packed.

"Have yer been here before?" Kevin asked.

Paul laughed. "I haven't a bloody clue.…Come on, let's fight our way to the bar and get a drink."

Once there, an elderly woman caught sight of them waiting to be served. "Yes, lads; what can I get yer? We've got lager on draught now."

"Oh, right; then two pints of lager, please," said Paul. And as the woman proceeded to dispense the drinks, he glanced around the place. The customers – both men and women – were happily engaged in conversation. No doubt it was about the

425

decriminalisation of homosexual offences, which had been passed in the Commons after an all-night sitting; but also, it was likely to be about the restrictions enshrined in a law that still treated gay people as second-class citizens. Yet, it was a step forward – albeit a small one. Still, it wasn't the law until it gained Royal Assent, but that was a foregone conclusion.

"There you are, lads," said the barmaid placing the drinks in front of them. Paul handed her a pound note, and when she returned with the change and placed it in Paul's hand, her eyebrows turned down as though she was scrutinising his appearance. He looked down at his shirt to see if it showed signs of Jessie's sausage casserole, but no, it was clean. And when he looked up, she was still staring at him. "Oh, I'm sorry," she said quickly. "It's just that I thought I knew you from somewhere. Have you been here before?"

"To be honest with you," Paul answered. "I don't know. I realise that sounds odd, but I lost a bit of my memory after being hurt in a fire."

Bella Platt now knew that this was indeed the young man whom her nephew had loved. Yet, it would be wrong of her to broach the fact after speaking with his mother. After all, he looked happy enough in his condition and she'd hate to hurt the boy who Steven was so very fond of. But she wanted to know something, so she said, "I hope you don't mind me asking, but are you two an... item?"

Paul almost choked with unrestrained laughter. "Good Lord, no. This" – he indicated Kevin – "is my cousin. And I'm sure he'd like you to know that he's not gay."

"I'm sorry," said Bella. "I just thought that a good-looking lad like you would have been snapped up."

"Well," said Paul, "I have been. But he's in Birmingham at the moment, so I decided to bring Kevin along to see how the other half live."

"Good for *you*. Well, must get on; but hope you both enjoy the evening. There's a drag act on later – that's if the cops don't turn up and close us down." Then she laughed and left them.

"Bloody cheek!" said Kevin. "Fancy thinkin' that you and me were together."

Paul was still beaming with delight when he said, "Oh, come here, love, and give us a kiss...."

Then they cheerfully drank – and drank – and laughed raucously

426

at the female impersonator, joining in the celebrations on this very special night. But after spending over three hours in the pub, both were feeling the effects of drinking pint after pint and decided to call it a night. "Right," said Paul. "There's a phone over there. I'll go and call us a taxi."

He walked to the side of the bar and searched for some change in his jacket pocket, and as he was about to dial the number displayed on a card above the telephone, he glanced to the side. Here was a picture of a blond-haired man staring directly at him. I know him, he thought. I do know him. But from where? In an attempt to recover a memory, he shook his head, causing him to stagger backwards with the consequence of drinking too much alcohol. And yet, he still managed to dial the number, happy in the knowledge that he would soon be back to the comfort and safety of home.

21

...He rested a hand on her arm now and, turning away from the inferno before her, Sarah looked at him. "Oh, Max," she said. "Not my boy again." And his heart bled.

Now, to the four isolated people standing in the field, mayhem broke out as two large fire-engines thundered to a halt to the left of where they stood. Then, heavily-clad men jumped to the ground, hoses were rolled out, and within seconds snaked into life as water surged towards the fire-ravaged buildings.

It was now that Katherine looked towards Town End. "Sarah!" She nudged her sister who slowly turned her expressionless face towards her. "There!" said Katherine. "Look who's coming." And when Sarah looked down the lane, she saw two figures approaching. Then she ran and threw her arms about the two women. "Where have you been?" she asked.

"Bingo," said Jessie.

Sarah released her embrace, and when she looked at the two inert faces in front of her, she said breathlessly, "Thank God for that. Do you know if Paul and Kevin went out?"

"I've no idea," said Jessie as she looked in horror at the sight of burning homes.

"Mrs Crowther." The voiced startled Sarah. And as she turned, the man removed his helmet. "Fire Officer Taylor. I know you from my visit to your mill to review fire precautions."

"Oh, yes...yes of course. Sorry, I didn't recognise you in your uniform."

"And these are your houses?"

Sarah nodded and said, "*Were* my houses."

"Have you any idea if the residents were at home?"

"Well...Amy here is all right, but I...I don't know about my son?" She looked around her as if searching for her boy.

Katherine touched her sister's sleeve. "What about the new one?"

"What...? Oh, yes," Sarah said to the fire officer. "He lived in the end one" – she pointed – "...a Mr Harrison. Bernard. Yes, that's right. He's from London, but I don't know if he was in or out."

The fire officer pulled a small notebook from his pocket and wrote down the name. "Right. I suggest you all return home and I'll get back to you when we know more."

"I can't leave," said Sarah. "My son may be...." Her eyes were raw with untold emotion and her body now trembled like a leaf in a high wind.

Katherine took her arm now, saying, "We must go, love. We can't do anything here." And Sarah reluctantly complied. "Josh," said Katherine. "Help your aunt back to the car with Max while I see to Amy and Jess." And they all meandered along the lane in silence....

Then, as in a dream, through the drifting smoke, Sarah saw a taxi draw up and watched as her son and nephew get out. Paul raced to his mother, and when he stood before her, she promptly slapped him repeatedly about his arms. "You...you...." She burst into tears now and pulled him to her. "I thought you were in the house." And briefly she looked back. Then she became conscious of her nephew standing there. "Oh, Kevin. Come here." And she beckoned him into her circle. "Don't either of you go out again without telling me first. Now, get back in that taxi and follow the rest of us home."

They were all back at High Ridge trying to sort out the sleeping arrangements.

"Right!" Sarah wielded her pencil like a conductor's baton. And, occasionally consulting her notepad, indicated each member of the household in turn. "Kath can stay in her own room – as will I. Then, Josh and Jess can be next door to each other in three and four and – if you two boys" – she pointed at her son and nephew – "don't mind sharing, could have number one. And Amy can be in the spare, close to Annie and the second bathroom. So, how about that?"

"What about next week when Mark gets back?" asked Paul.

"He can go in with you and Kevin."

"Three of us in one room?"

"Er," Sarah bit on her pencil and pondered.

Jessie stuck her hand up, as would an eager child in school who knew the answer to a question. "I know! How's about Amy sharing wi' me. We could do it tonight and Kevin could have the spare and it could save me from changing a load o' bedding."

Sarah nodded. "Yes, okay. Right! Will that do?"

Everyone voiced their approval apart from Katherine who said, "Haven't you forgotten something? What about David?"

Sarah now acknowledged her sister: "Well…when he gets back, Kath, he can sleep with *me*." And as Jessie half-closed her eyes and sucked in her cheeks, Sarah concluded, "Good! Now, let's have a drink. I'm sure we all bloody well need one.… "

Paul and Josh had done the honours, and all were now seated in the drawing-room.

Jessie sat next to Amy on one of the settees and took her hand. "I'm sorry, lass. It must have come as a shock to see your home go up like that."

"Aye, it were, Jessie." Amy took a mouthful of her port and lemon and stared at the ceiling as if it was going to collapse on her head. "I bet it were 'im that did it."

"Who?"

"Yon gypsy. Yer should 'ave left 'im be, Jessie."

Jessie rounded on Amy now. "Oi, madam! I hope you're not blaming me for what's happened." Then, with her voice at the same level of annoyance, said, "And if you want to know the truth, I told 'im if he kept his 'ead down then he could stay there for the time being." But she thought, May God forgive you for lying, Jessie Dicks.

It was now that Sarah came over and sat beside the two women. "I couldn't help but overhear you talking, and I want to put your minds at rest." She addressed Amy now. "Love, I knew all about the gypsy in the warehouse. In fact, he had my blessing to stay there until the place was demolished. And whether or not he started the fire, is all down to me."

"How could you, Sal?" said Jessie. "One of his lot killed your brother."

Sarah shook her head. "No, Jess. John wasn't killed by a gypsy – he was killed by Joe Stockwell." Jessie and Amy's faces froze as if blasted by a cold reality. "It's true," Sarah continued. "Alex told me over a year ago. And so, none of us should condemn people because of our irrational misconceptions." Sarah rose now and returned to her sister.

"You appear to be taking all this in your stride," said Katherine.

Sarah shrugged. "What's done is done, Kath. We can't turn back the clock."

"But aren't you concerned? One house going up in flames maybe, but all three?"

"I'm just grateful than none of my family and friends were injured – or even killed. But yes, I am concerned: I'm concerned about Mr Jackson, and if he was trapped in that inferno – and I'm troubled by other things too. Have you ever played chess, Kath?"

"Chess? I wouldn't know how. What's chess got to do with anything?"

Sarah pointed at the table in front of them. "Imagine this is the chessboard and I'm the white queen. Well, all the black pieces opposite move in different directions just trying to hem me in so that I'm trapped." She stared at her sister, her eyes appearing like globes of green glass, and said, "But they haven't caught me out yet, Kath. Not by any means." And she downed her drink.

Paul opened another three bottles of lager. "There we go, lads. There's plenty more where these came from. The sight of those houses on fire has sobered me up."

As Kevin took his drink, he looked dejectedly at his cousin. "I haven't got any clothes left but these" – he swept his hand up and down himself – "and I can't go back to me dad's to get some more 'cos he'll start asking questions and I might not be able to stop meself from tellin' 'im about me and Annie."

Paul gently punched his cousin's arm. "Don't fret, Kev," he said. "Mam'll sort things out."

It was now that Josh said solemnly, "I wonder if old lazy-eye was trapped in the fire?" And he shuddered.

"Well, he was in before we went out," said Paul with concern. "I heard him dragging what sounded like a piece of furniture upstairs. He might have bought a cabinet or something – which now seems a bit premature considering what's happened. Aay, poor old chap."

22

In the week following the unprecedented event, Sarah had made cash available to Paul and Mark, and Kevin and Amy to purchase new clothes and any other items that they may require. And then some semblance of normality returned to the inhabitants of High Ridge House. Yet, she had to cope with more police enquiries when it was discovered that the fires had been started deliberately.

The true horror of it all was reported in today's Collingley Advertiser, describing how Bernard Jackson's body was found in his bed with the bedding fused into his flesh like pork crackling. How could the press have gone into such sickening detail? And what of the poor man's sister? She did hope that the authorities could somehow trace the poor woman.

But today being Friday, it was pay-day!

"Sweetheart," said Sarah as she sealed the fourth wage packet, "do me a favour and pass these out before we go to the mill."

David threw his newspaper aside, stood, and went to the desk where Sarah handed him four manila envelopes with the names of those in her employ. "Max is likely to be in the garage, and Amy and Annie will be in the kitchen with Jess. And I know for a fact Laura is in the greenhouse. Would you mind?"

"Of course I don't mind." He took the packets, and like a young child, repeated the names: "Max, Amy, Annie and…Laura. Right! Won't be long."

Sarah smiled as the thirty-year-old exited the library. How lucky she was to have this fine young man as her suitor. He was so like his father: tall and handsome with a shock of black hair and those extraordinary eyes; but unlike Alexander, he had a slight retroussé nose which so much resembled his mother's. And though Alexander had now conceded that David was his true son, he still could not bring himself to love him as a father should.

Jessie entered the library now. "Right. Me and Amy are off to the market. D'yer want owt special?"

"Er…oh, yes," said Sarah. "Could you pick up some different dog food for Ben? He seems to have gone off his usual stuff."

"Aye, I will. He's been looking a bit peaky lately. See yer later."

When Jessie had left, Sarah locked the cash box and replaced it in the safe. Returning to her seat, she scrutinised the papers on her desk, but knew she couldn't concentrate on a thing. Did she love David enough to marry him? Love! What was it all about?

Her first marriage to Paul's father was stressful – mainly due to his mother living with them. They argued – fought at times – but did she love him? Yes! she did, and his death was a debilitating trauma that – to this day – still affected her whenever she looked upon her son's face. And even though Paul was physically nothing like his father, there was something in him that, every now and then, came to the fore and she could imagine John standing there.

As for William…well, he was like one of the rings on her finger: a diamond. She loved him with a passion that exceeded anything she could ever have believed existed in the world. Granted, she had thought the dismissal of his son from the household unwarranted, but his actions were prompted by Mark's disrespectful words towards her. William was such a handsome man, yet his looks were surpassed by the beauty of his soul.

Then there was David. He was both a boy in appearance and character – and she was engaged to be his wife. And once more, the doubts crept in.

Now the library door squeaked open and Ben padded in. He came up to Sarah and sat at her side, his large brown eyes almost pleading to be talked to. So Sarah spoke: "Hello, love. Jessie's gone to get you some new food." She stroked the dog's head, and laughing gently, said, "Well, that's if she doesn't forget." She stood now, and after saying, "Come on. Let's go and see what David's up to, eh?" they both ambled out.

After finishing their shopping, Jessie and Amy were seated in the Co-op café. And, as usual, Jessie ordered cups of tea and fatty cakes.

"There y'are, lass."

"Ta," said Amy. "I'm ready for this. D'yer know, I couldn't eat a thing yesterday for belly-ache. I were tellin' Annie this mornin'." She tittered now. "She weren't a bit interested, though. All she could talk about was the bairn she's carryin'."

Jessie stirred two spoons of sugar into her cup. "Aye, she's smitten wi' Kevin. But he's a good lad – not always has been, though. When him and Paul were kids, by God! did they fight. Eeh! I've seen 'em tear lumps out of each other: skin and hair flying. But now…well, they've grown very close. Funny that!"

"I'll tell yer summat else that's funny, and that's Edith Stockwell." Amy leaned across the table. "She's got herself a fella."

"Never!" Jessie tore off a piece of cake and dipped it in her tea.

"As God is my judge, Jessie. Polly Sickling told me in the post office and she wouldn't lie: she's high chapel. Mind you, she said she'd been out shoppin' for bread, but 'ave yer ever heard bread clink?"

"Eeh, I say." Waving the fatty cake now, Jessie said, "That reminds me. When Max took Kath to the station when she had to go back to America, he saw Stockwell with a man an' all. I wonder if it's the same one?"

"Unless she's got two on the go….So, d'yer think Annie'll move in wi' Kevin and his dad?"

"Nay, lass, how can she wi' Laura livin' there? And if his dad finds out Annie's in the family way, there'll be hell to pay. That's why Sarah moved Kev in with us."

Amy sipped at her tea and tapped the table. "She's a fast cat – that Laura. She were all over David when he took her wages to the greenhouse – I saw 'em through t'kitchen window."

Jessie looked aghast, before whispering, "Hey. Be careful what you're saying, Amy Broadbent. Don't let Sarah hear you say that or you'll be out on yer ear." She leaned forward now. "What do you mean by 'all over' him?"

"Talkin', like."

Jessie sat back in her seat. "Talking! Is that it? Well that's hardly an 'anging offence."

"No…but…ooh…!"

"What? Are you all right, love?" Jessie asked.

Amy wiped her face with a serviette. "Aay, lass, it's this damned pain again." She held her side. Jessie now looked kindly on the woman facing her. She had often maligned Amy, but now her heart went out to her. Yet, she thought that there was more than just a gippy tummy troubling her: there was something in her head that had brought her to a low ebb. Jessie arrested her thoughts: she still dwelt upon making silly predictions. Nevertheless, she saw in her friend's eyes a soul that was suffering. "Try a drink o' tea, love. It might settle yer."

Amy nodded and raised the cup to her mouth. But the two never connected as the cup fell to the table and she let out a cry of pain.

"Oh…Jess…can you…?"

Jessie was on her feet and raced to her friend's side. And as she bent over Amy's prostrate body, she called to the woman behind the counter: "Can you phone for an ambulance, love? And please hurry!"

23

Sarah first met Amy when she came as a trainee piecener in the mill. It was during the war when women were being recruited into many professions while the men were away at the front. Then when Sarah left to work on munitions, she lost touch – that was until Amy turned up out of the blue to look after Sarah's first husband's mother, and lived next door in one of the mill cottages on Long Lane. They had been friends ever since.

Now, as she and Jessie waited in the hospital to see the surgeon who had carried out an appendectomy on the fifty-eight-year-old, she remembered that first meeting: "When I shook her hand, Jess, she had the grip of a vice. I could well believe her when she said she helped build planes in the war."

"Well," said Jessie, "I only hope she's strong enough to have got through this."

Sarah patted Jessie's hand. "She'll be fine, love…oh, the doctor's here." The two women stood as the physician approached. "Mrs Crowther?" he asked.

Sarah nodded. "And this is Miss Dicks."

"I understand you are both friends of Mrs Broadbent."

"We are, doctor," said Sarah. "Although, she never married so she's strictly *Miss* Broadbent. We've both" – she indicated Jessie with a gloved hand – "known her for nearly thirty years – on and off – and she's more like family. So how is she getting on?"

The white-coated medic did not answer at first. Then he looked directly at Sarah, saying, "You say she never married…? Well, that may be the case but" – he paused briefly – "she has certainly given birth – and by Caesarean section."

Sarah and Jessie's jaws dropped in unison.

"I see that has come as a bit of a surprise to you. In that case, I may have confided in you too much; and, if her child is still living, it would be prudent of me to say nothing further. Yet, it may be that my patient would wish to inform you of her history – it is entirely up to herself. Now, if you'd care to come along with me, I'll allow you to see her for a while."

When Amy was discharged from hospital, Sarah determined that she have her own bedroom in the house, which meant Jessie had to move in with Katherine, and neither had objected – in fact, they appeared to relish the idea.

One Sunday morning when Annie had gone to Amy's room to open the curtains, Amy had asked her for a piece of toast and a cup of tea – and had also requested if Sarah wouldn't mind coming up to see her....

Now, seated on the bed's white cotton counterpane, Sarah said, "It's good to see you eating something, love. So, what did you want to see me about?" She took the empty teacup from Amy's hand and placed it on the bedside table.

"Well, since you now know of my circumstances, I may as well tell you the whole story."

"You don't have to, you know," Sarah said. "After all, it's your business."

"Oh, I do, love. It's been preying on me mind for years – I don't know how I've kept it close this long. No, I need to." And as Sarah rested a hand on the bed, Amy began her tale:

"I'll begin in 1923 when I got my first job. I were fourteen at the time and, hearing of a position as a live-in kitchen maid in a mill-owning family, I applied and was taken on.

"The master of the house was in his thirties and the kindest of men. When he was at home – which wasn't very often – he always used to ask me how I was getting on and hoped that his wife wasn't proving difficult. I told him she was pleasant enough, but he laughed at this, shaking his head.

"They had two small boys: one aged five and one who was three. They had a nanny for them, and she kept them under control – although the younger of the two was a bit of a handful. But it was the woman's brother who seemed to have the most time for me. He told me he had just turned seventeen, but the master wouldn't go along with his wife's wishes that he should be allowed to enter the mill. And the young man was just left to his own devices: doing the garden, painting the house woodwork when it was needed, and general pottering about. But he was never allowed to eat as a member of the family and took meals in his room – even at Christmas!

"It was now that I began sneaking to his room in my time off – mainly to keep him company. I felt sorry for him. Anyhow, we developed a liking for each other; and over the months, this liking turned to love. Yes! Love, Sarah....Well, after being sick nearly every morning, I knew then that I was going to have his child. At first – when my employer found out – it caused ructions. Naturally, she soon grasped the fact that when people got wind of it – which they were bound to do – it would cause outrage. She believed folk would think it was her husband's doing and that it would ruin them. So, it was decided that I would never get any time off to visit me mam and would have to live with them until the child was born. You'll understand, Sarah, that I didn't have a choice in the matter; and there'd be no way I could keep my baby, being – as I was at the time – just fifteen. And then I'd be thrown out when it was born. They even decided – well, mistress did – that they would say she'd adopted one from the children's hospital. Of course, the two boys were too young to know it wasn't true.

"Well, the time came, and I was sent to a hospital where she were born through me belly – yes, a little girl, Sarah. Eeh, she were bonny: blonde hair and eyes of the brightest of blues. There was only one thing that marred her and that was a birthmark. But, fortunately, it was on the back of her neck and nobody would notice when her hair grew. And then she were taken from me.

"I returned home and cried for weeks – Mam believing it was because I'd lost me job. Then one day when I was out pawning some of me late dad's belongings, I happened upon the baby's father who told me how she were getting on. And as the child grew, we started meeting regularly in secret so he could let me know how she were fairing.

"Then, as time went on, I was fortunate to find work with another family who I was with for nearly fourteen years. Then they moved away and I had to look for another job. It was then I met you and you showed me the ropes at Crowther's mill. But it wasn't only yourself I met there: I met my daughter – all grown up and about to be married.

"So, Sarah, I suppose you've already guessed who the fine young lady was that I encountered for the very first time on that fateful day? Yes, she was Dorothy Stockwell, soon to become the wife of William Crowther. So you see, Sarah; Edith Stockwell is not Jane's grandmother – I am."

24

She had made her plans over several weeks – nay months – forever amending and rewriting until she was satisfied that things would work. Any changes were duly committed to memory, and any sketch, note, or idea in black and white, was subsequently burned in the grate. But a fiendish twist had struck her when her grandson had paid her a visit, and told her something that could possibly allay the discovery of the one whom she had convinced to carry out her wishes.

Edith Stockwell sat in the bar of the Leeds Northern Hotel, nervously adjusting the rim of her black, large-brimmed hat as she waited for her brother-in-law. Certainly, her anxiety was not brought about by regrets at what she had done, but lest she be spotted by someone she knew. Still, if somebody *did* recognise her, she would easily overcome the awkwardness of the situation in her own inimitable style – by lying.

Abel Stockwell was her late husband's younger brother, and he was – apart from being a hopeless drunkard – in a great deal of debt. And when she had contacted him requesting that he perform a few tasks for her that would carry a substantial pay packet, he jumped at the chance. She looked at her watch now. He was late. All he had to do was walk down the stairs from his room for God's sake!

She summoned a waiter for another glass of red wine and picked up a copy of the Yorkshire News. There it was: a report of the Collingley fire. All three houses destroyed – with arson suspected – and a poor man's charred body found in the ruins. How could anyone do such a thing?

"Edith!"

She was startled by the sudden mention of her name. And as she looked around, her brother-in-law stood there. "You're late!" she said. "But I hardly knew you without that God-awful beard and wig. I've just ordered a new drink, so go to the bar and get one on my tab – although I don't know why I'm saying that since I'm paying you enough without you sponging off me for more than you're worth."

When he returned, Edith flapped the newspaper in front of his face. "Seen that?" she said pointing at the headlines.

"I have."

Edith Stockwell tossed the paper on the glass-topped table. And when she returned her gaze on to her in-law, she grinned. "Well done, Abe. Well done. And, although you didn't rid me of the two people I wanted you to, I'm content. After all, in this life, one can't have everything. You weren't seen, were you?"

Abel shook his head. "No. Everything was done from the back of the houses where they're not overlooked by a soul. A few Molotov cocktails through the windows and boom!" His arms flew in the air. "But it was lucky about the old chap living in the warehouse. They wouldn't have found a body without him. And now the idiots think it must have been me." He swigged at his Scotch.

"Luck you say? Oh, no, Abe; it wasn't luck. I had my spies out – or should I say 'spy'."

"Who? Do tell."

Edith smiled. "My own precious grandson."

"Mark? But how did you get him involved?"

"Oh, he's not involved." She cradled her drink in her hands. "But Mark has always kept in touch with his Grandmama – albeit infrequently – and when he informed me that he was going away on business for a week, I decided it would be the ideal time to put my plans into action...."

It was the middle of May when Edith Stockwell found out from one of her many acquaintances that Laura Wilson was often to be seen in an upmarket public house in Collingley. Apparently, she was easy to talk to – which came as no surprise to Edith after Laura had wheedled her way into the arms of Harry Carr, causing her granddaughter, Jane, so much heartache. But, with her brother-in-law's fearless climbing skills, *he* had already been dealt with.

Being such a garrulous individual, Laura had put it about of the possibility of a house becoming available to rent, which just happened to be one of Sarah Crowther's properties. The cogs in Edith's head began to work overtime. She could envisage the killing of the proverbial two birds with one stone. And even though the people she wanted dead had escaped the fire that Abel started, at least she had wrecked part of Sarah Crowther's holdings. But Edith was not yet finished.

"Mark also told me about the man in the old wool warehouse, but I told him to take pity on the fellow and not tell a soul lest he be left homeless. You see, I *can* be a caring woman, Abe." She summoned the waiter to bring further drinks. "So, was it difficult to entice the man inside?"

"Not in the least," said Abel. "He actually came and knocked on the door asking if I could let him have something to eat. So, I asked him to share my table for a bite and a few whiskies; then, when he was in a defenceless stupor with the aid of the drugs you provided, I dragged him up to the bedroom for a long, long, sleep." And Edith Stockwell laughed.

The waiter arrived and placed the drinks on the table, and when he was out of earshot, Edith asked, "And how did you manage the Cockney accent?"

"Perfect. Nobody would have known that I wasn't a proper East End geezer. But why did you want me to pretend to be a Londoner?"

"Ah!" said Edith wagging her finger. "Without the gypsy being handy, a body wouldn't have been discovered in the fire, and then the police would have had to concentrate their enquiries in the capital. Nigh on impossible I would say."

"Brilliant!"

"Now, brother-in-law," said Edith, "there is just one further little job I want you to do before you pack your bags and return to Nottinghamshire. And this time, there will be no need for a disguise – just a few, tasty, morsels."

25

Josh's emotions were knotted. He needed air. He needed space.

Fortunately today, Sarah had to go to the mill to sign off the closure of the rag warehouse, before the mill was stocked with bales of new wool coming from the suppliers via the Leeds and Liverpool canal. So, on this fine Friday morning, she had suggested that perhaps he'd like to take Ben for a walk – and he was happy to concur. So, shortly after breakfast, Josh and his eager companion departed High Ridge House.

Taking the dusty stone-riddled path at the back of the house, he came across the stream known as Barn Brook; and as the dog gambolled up and down the bank, sniffing and exploring, Josh sat, picked up a large redundant twig and held it in the rushing water. It was an unusually peaceful place, seemingly miles away from the pulsating industry of the many woollen mills in the area. And the tinkling of the brook began to soothe his overbearing sorrow.

When the situation warranted it, he was considering telling his mother the truth. She knew nothing of his involvement with a man twenty years his senior who had gently taught him how to make love. She was only concerned when he fell into a deep depression when his lover died. Now, he found himself in a similar position to Paul; and even though his cousin had lost all memories of Steven, he could relate to the sadness that one day might result in a recollection of him. And if this were to happen, what would then be Paul's feelings toward Mark?

He whistled for the dog now, who came bounding to him and sat. "Oh, Ben, boy. What is all this about?" And as Ben looked at him with attentive brown eyes, Josh determined to clear these thoughts from his mind. So he decided to amble along the brook as far as it would take him.

Jumping to his feet now, he threw the twig into the distance, whence Ben shot off in pursuit; and when Josh eventually caught up, the dog was worrying the stick as though it were an enemy.

With Ben carrying the masticated branch and Josh pulling at blades of long grass, they proceeded alongside the brook for what must have been a full half-hour, whence there, on the other side of the tumbling waters, stood the barn he had read about. Granted the roof appeared intact; but the rest, well, was not in any state of repair. This came as no surprise, for if this was the actual place where such horrors took place, it certainly reflected its age.

He halted at a spot where he could cross the coursing stream without having to take off his shoes and socks, and carefully crossed to the far side with Ben splashing playfully at his heels. Walking up the incline now, he persuaded himself that his aunt's tale was made up by people to scare the wits out of children. Well he was no child – and he certainly didn't believe in ghosts.

He reached what was left of the door and pushed it open, swiftly recoiling in revulsion when a large rat scurried out and disappeared into the field with the dog in pursuit. "Ben! Back!" And the dog dutifully obeyed and returned to Josh's side. Ben sat and looked up, his pink tongue lolling. "You don't know what kind of horrible diseases those things might have," Josh reproached his companion before shuddering. Despite his scepticism of the supernatural, rats were a different story.

The two of them entered gingerly now. The place had a strange smell – almost like that of an abattoir: metallic somehow – and also that of the rank smell of vomit. Why on earth was he here? Why had he found this abandoned spot that had beckoned him to cross water and enter? He knew not; yet it didn't deter him from exploring the place – and that of his own confused feelings.

There was a wooden platform covered in sacking; and upon it, what appeared to be a partially burned candle stuck into the drain hole of an old plant pot. And next to it sat a rusted trowel with a split handle. It looked like someone else had also been in here for some reason – and recently. Still, what did it matter? He was here himself now trying to sort out his problems.

Whilst the dog carried out an investigative sniff, Josh began to scuff the ground beneath his feet. What was he to do? He couldn't express his feelings for Paul without causing hurt to so many people. He had been enchanted by his cousin on New Year's Eve when he was last in Yorkshire. But now he had to quell his desire – and soon! Maybe he should go back to the States and forget about living here? That would solve the problem. No, it wouldn't! It just wouldn't.

Josh sighed and picked up the trowel, whence he began scribbling in the earth he had previously disturbed. Then he dug. Furiously he dug at the ground: his emotions shot by his love for another man. Ben was back in front of him now, joining in a scratching of the earth between Josh's feet. And then he saw it. He saw the full horror that he and the dog had uncovered in this stifling and malevolent place; and with his eyes focused on the find, and his outstretched arm holding Ben at a distance, he recalled the words from the book: 'I curse you with the loss of every child you sire. The devil will see to that.'

The kitchen door burst open.

"God Almighty! What in heaven's name…?"

"Oh, Jess," said Joshua breathlessly as he staggered into the room. "I've just…."

"Eeh, lad, you're as white as a sheet…no, sorry…I didn't mean it like that. Here, come and sit down before yer fall down and I'll make some tea."

"I'd prefer a whisky if that's okay." Josh pulled out a chair and crumpled upon it.

"Aye. Aye, course it is." Jessie opened a kitchen cupboard and withdrew the bottle. After placing it on the table, she produced two glasses. "By the look of you," she said, "I'll be wanting one meself." And she poured two measures. "Now. Tell me what's got to yer, lad. Has something happened to Ben?"

Josh shook his head. "No, he's okay. He's in the glasshouse with Laura. Oh, Jessie, it's awful…." He looked at this woman whom he believed he could trust to provide him with a solution. He looked at her until one of her eyebrows turned down and she grunted. And then he said, "I've found a baby."

"A baby! Where? In a doorway or summat?"

" No. In a barn."

"A barn? Like a barn at some'dy's farm?"

Josh shook his head forcibly. No" – he directed his arm at the open door – "In the field. At the other side of the brook."

"And where is it now?"

"Still there. Jessie; but it's barely…formed.…It's.…It's dead."

Jessie's hands flew in the air. "Jesus! As if we haven't had enough of the police sniffin' around here." She leapt to her feet. "Right! While I get me coat on, you go and find Annie and tell 'er we're going out."

"Where are we going?" asked Josh tearfully.

"To the bloody cop-shop! That's where!"

26

"Mam's gone to work early, hasn't she, Jess?"

"She has, love. Her and David were off by six." Jessie placed a cup of tea in front of Paul. "There's a letter here for yer." She slid it along the kitchen table.

"It's got a Welsh postmark," he said. "I wonder where it's come from?"

"Wales, I suppose."

"No, I mean who could be writing to me in Wales?"

"Well, open it and see. D'yer know, you young 'uns do faff about at times. Give us it 'ere." Jessie wrenched the envelope from Paul's hand and tore it open. "There! Now read it."

And Paul did. "It say's do I know of anyone by the name of Martha Halliday? That was my grandmother's name." He looked directly at Jessie, who drew up a chair and sat next to him. "Go on then," she said.

"It's from a solicitor asking me if I'm the son of the late John Halliday."

"Which you are," said Jessie.

"And" – Paul went on – "I have to fill in the enclosed form and return it to them with proof of identity and a copy of my birth certificate."

"Eeh!" said Jessie. "I wonder what's that all about?"

"Surely it can't be about the money she left me?"

Jessie went stiff. My God! she thought. This can't be happening. They've found out. Somebody's told them something. Oh, she'd have to tell Sarah – and then *she'd* have to tell Paul about the money left to him by Steven. And what if it came out about the faked will? Dear Lord above! What was to be done now...?

"Oh, you're there, love. My! it's been a long day. I'll get you a drink and then you can tell me about that letter you got."

"That can wait for now, Mam," said Paul. "I'm more concerned about Ben. He's usually around to meet me when I get home. Have you seen him anywhere?"

"I thought he was in the kitchen eating his dinner."

"He's not now. And he hasn't touched a scrap."

"Well you know how picky he's been over his food, lately. He might have gone into the garden," said Sarah. "The door was open when I was talking to Jess; and you know how he loves it out there. Go and ask Laura – she's busy in the greenhouse. He might be with her."

Paul went out, and spying Laura stacking plants into a wheelbarrow, called to her: "Laura! Have you seen Ben anywhere?"

She came to him. "No, love," she said. "Perhaps he went down to the brook. Come on. We'll both go and look for him."

They skirted the hedge at the side of the track leading to Barn Brook, calling Ben's name as they went. And then they found him. He was lying on a patch of grass on the stone-strewn path with his head on one side.

"What are you doing here?" said Paul, as he and Laura walked towards him. But when they finally reached him, they could see that he had been foaming at the mouth.

Laura was the first to touch him. She knelt beside him and felt his chest, but there was no sign of life. Looking up at Paul, she shook her head in hopelessness, whence Paul fell to his knees and held his boy. Supporting Ben's head now, he leaned close, saying, "Come on, lad. We'll get you inside and you can go in your basket, and when you're up to it, you can try a bit of dinner. Eh?" He dipped into his jacket pocket and pulled out a handkerchief with which he wiped the dog's mouth. "There, that's better."

Laura rested her hand on Paul's back. "Come on, love. Come on. There's nothing we can do. Ben's gone, sweetheart. He's gone."

"No he hasn't," Paul said with self-assurance. "He's just worn out with being sick." Paul lifted the dog's upper body into his arms and rocked him gently. "I'm here for you, lad. Look" – he pulled a treat from his pocket – "you like these, don't you? Never mind, I'll keep it till you're feeling better." And he stayed there, rocking the black Labrador as if he were soothing a child: the child he had given to his mother when she married his stepfather.

He began to weep now, fully aware that Ben was no more. "Please don't leave me, lad. Please!" And as his heart broke in two, he wept and wept and wept....Then, when he could not find the strength to cry further, he looked at Laura who had been stroking his hair. But he didn't see her. He saw Steven: Steven Clark, the man he had loved so much after Mark had deserted him.

27

Two women were in the kitchen. Sarah was busily opening the day's mail whilst Jessie was finishing her coffee and reading the latest edition of the Collingley Advertiser.

The weeks had taken their toll on everyone who resided at High Ridge. Both Sarah and Jessie had been interviewed by the police over the allegation against Harry concerning Joe Stockwell's death, but on the solicitor's advice, had made no comments to the questions put to them. But it wasn't just the two of them who had been quizzed: Kevin had – and, according to Alex, so had he for a second time, and also his mother.

Then after the death of Ben, Paul was inconsolable for a period, during which, Sarah had to confess to her son about Steven's money since the letter he had received from the solicitors in Swansea, contained a cheque for a further thousand pounds which had been held in trust for him – this time legitimately bequeathed to him by his grandmother. At first, Paul had demanded to know the reason for the pretence; but when Sarah had told him that she only wanted to spare his feelings if he found out about Steven, he seemed to be placated – with one proviso: he wanted to know what happened on the night of the mill fire. And today was the day set aside for just that.

"Hey! D'yer know what it says here in the paper?" said Jessie.

"I will if you tell me," said Sarah.

"It says they've found an old warp lane over Morley way. Apparently, it was unearthed when they were digging foundations for a new housing estate. I wonder what a part of a loom were doing being buried?"

"What?" asked Sarah as she put down her letters. "Let's have a look."

Jessie passed her the newspaper and pointed. "There. Just at the bottom."

Sarah was intrigued. And after she had read, she glared at her friend, saying, "Jessie. It says: war-plane. WAR-PLANE! Bloody warp lane for God's sake. You get dafter by the day."

Jessie got up and began drying the breakfast dishes, mumbling to herself: How was I to know?

Sarah returned to her mail. It was when she opened the last envelope, she gasped, "Oh, my God!"

"What is it, lass? Jessie turned from the sink.

"I...I've been summoned to be a witness at Harry's trial."

"Well, you were expecting it, love. To speak up for him, like me."

"Jess! A witness for the prosecution!"

The china plate that Jessie was drying, fell from her hand and smashed on the kitchen floor. "But...."

"But nothing!" Sarah waved the letter in front of Jessie's face. "It's here in black and white!"

Ignoring the broken crockery, Jessie plonked herself on the chair she had previously vacated. "That's ridiculous! Oh" – she flapped her hand – "just ignore it."

"How can I? It's a legal document."

"Perhaps it's a mistake?"

"Courts don't make mistakes."

"They do!" said Jessie nodding her head vigorously. "Just look at that Timothy Evans who lived wi' that swine Christie. The police probably wore 'im down with their persistent questions at every hour of the day and night – and with brute force – till he was relieved just to own up even though it weren't true. And then they hung the poor soul."

"Good God! You really know how to cheer someone up, Jess.... Mind you, considering I didn't tell the police a thing, how can they believe I could help them in prosecuting Harry?" Sarah stood now. "Anyhow, I can't sit here brooding over things; Paul and I need a heart-to-heart. See you later, Jess."

"Aye, lass. And try not to worry."

As Sarah gazed forlornly out of the window, Paul stared at the photograph of Steven Clark. "It's the same as the one hanging in The Hart."

His mother nodded. "He was a gorgeous young man, love."

"Why did you keep it?"

She turned about now and faced her son. "Well, after the fire when we found out he had died, it would have seemed iniquitous not to keep something to remember him by. But that's not all I kept. Come and sit with me."

Mother and son sat on the settee as Sarah related that ill-starred night: "Steven came carrying a bunch of freesias. He looked a prince in his midnight-blue velvet jacket and white dress shirt. His naturally blond hair had been further lightened by the sun, and as he approached me I could quite understand your attraction to that beautiful young man.

"I took the flowers from him, saying, 'My favourites'. And he said, 'Well, I have to confess, it was Paul who gave me the hint.'" It was now that Sarah noticed a tear running down her son's face. "Oh, love, I shouldn't have told you."

"No. It's all right, Mam. But I want to know why I was at the mill?"

Sarah braced herself. "Well, Alex came to see me a week or so before you went there. And, he told me of his suspicions that his brother was embezzling money from the business.

"At first, I thought he was asking me for a loan – or something of the sort – but he asked me if you would be willing to look over his books."

"But why *me*?"

"Because he trusted you, love; and, knowing how good you are at figure work, he thought you were the best person for the job. I did say I would have to ask you if you would agree – and I did; and you said you'd do it willingly. Then on the night you were at the mill, a fire started. Anyhow, we all went down to Stockwell's field and...."

"And what?" asked Paul. "Go on. I want to know, Mam."

Sarah stood now and returned to the window, where she looked over the fields to the two mills. "It was terrible." Once more she turned, and began to walk around the room, her steps paced and almost waltz-like. "The firemen had difficulty breaking through the secured, wooden gates – even with their weighty axes."

"Didn't they have keys?" asked Paul.

Sarah paused and shook her head. "At Steven's inquest, Alex told the coroner that he believed his father had taken care of such things like spare keys for the fire crews, but this wasn't the case." She began her sauntering again. "Anyhow, since Steven had drawn up the plans for new offices at Providence, he knew of a different way into the mill and...."

"Mam!"

"Yes, love?"

"Will you stop walking about; you're making me nervous."

"I'm sorry, love." And Sarah retook her seat next to her son.

"Anyhow, Steven took off his jacket and gave it to me, saying he was going to go to the back of the mill and find his way in."

"To try and save me." Paul nodded knowingly.

"That was all his concern," said his mother. "All he wanted to do was to try and find you."

Paul stared down at the carpet and said nothing more. Then his face came up and he stared at his mother. "Did you say that you kept something else of his apart from the photograph?"

"I did. I kept the jacket he gave me to save for him."

"Can I see it?"

"Of course you can. In fact, I am sure Steven would have wanted you to have it." Sarah stood and took Paul's hand. "Come on. It's in my wardrobe. I sense it's been waiting there patiently for this day to arrive."

And arm in arm, mother and son left the room.

28

During the 1960s, Collingley had grown – not only in size due to electoral boundary changes, but also in status when the Town Hall was granted legal authorisation to become an assize court. And it was here on Thursday the 17th August 1967, before judge Alistair Courtney-Davies QC, that the trial of Harry Carr began.

The jury had been chosen, opening statements had been made, and counsel for the prosecution, James Reynolds QC, began proceedings: "Constable Jarvis. Please could you tell the court how you were the first to be notified of the incident that resulted in the discovery of the bodies of Joseph Stockwell and Philip Mallinson."

The policeman withdrew his notebook from the top pocket of his uniform. "On Tuesday the 26th of July, last year," he began, "we were contacted at" – he referred to his notes – "11.57 a.m., when the driver of the 11.30 train from Wakefield to Bradford stopped at Drighlington. He reported to the station manager that he believed he had run into something on the line prior to entering the tunnel at Collingley Low. Shortly afterwards, after having all trains on that section diverted onto other lines, two of us were dispatched to the scene where we found the body of Mr Philip Mallinson. Unfortunately, one of his legs had been severed at the knee – the lower half was subsequently found close to the tunnel itself."

"And at that time, was the body of Joseph Stockwell also found?" asked Mr Reynolds.

"No. It was only discovered three days later. Mr Alex Stockwell had reported his brother missing on the morning of the day after the discovery of Mr Mallinson's body; and forty-eight hours later, a search was carried out in the vicinity of the railway embankment at the back of the Stockwell residence. Eventually, Mr Joseph Stockwell's body was found lodged between the branches of a tree, half-way down the banking – some eighty feet above ground level."

"Would I be right in saying, Constable Jarvis, that the task confronting the police would have been an arduous and dangerous undertaking?"

"Extremely dangerous, sir."

"And would I be also right in saying that it would have been difficult at the time to find any evidence to support the fact that Mr Stockwell had been stabbed?"

Defence counsel, Laurence Pritchard QC, was on his feet. "Your Honour. My learned friend is making an assumption that any implement used to stab Mr Stockwell was discarded at the time of the assault."

The judge ordered that the remarks be struck from the records and asked Mr Reynolds to rephrase his question.

"Constable Jarvis. Was anything else found in your search for Mr Stockwell's body?"

"No, sir," said the police constable.

"Thank you. I have no further questions, your Honour."

"Mr Pritchard?" the judge said.

Defence counsel stood. "I have no questions for the witness."

"Very well. I think this may be a good time to break for lunch. May I remind members of the jury not to discuss anything of these proceedings other than among themselves. The court will now rise until two o'clock."

Sarah gathered up her papers from the desk and put them in a black attaché case before she travelled to the mill. But her preparations were interrupted when Jessie came into the library. "Mr Wilkinson's here to see you, lass."

"Who?" Sarah asked.

"The vet, love."

"Oh, yes. He said he'd call to let us know the results of Ben's postmortem. Will you ask him to come in, Jess?"

Jessie exited, and presently admitted the veterinary surgeon.

Sarah went and shook the man's hand. "Would you care for a drink, Mr Wilkinson?"

"Oh, no thank you, Mrs Crowther. I won't keep you more than a few minutes. I just wanted to let you know my findings on Ben."

"Yes, poor lad. He was only eight, you know. Please, do take a seat." And after the man had seated himself on the chesterfield, Sarah asked, "So what was wrong with Ben?"

"Nothing really." And seeing the understandable bewilderment on Sarah's face, the vet continued, "Mrs Crowther, Ben was a healthy dog and would have had many more years ahead of him – but for one thing."

"Which was?" Sarah asked.

"I'm afraid I found large amounts of metaldehyde in his system."

"Pardon?"

"Oh, I'm sorry. Metaldehyde is the main constituent of slug pellets. I regret to say it, Mrs Crowther, but Ben was poisoned."

"Poisoned?" Sarah staggered slightly and grasped the edge of the desk. "But how…who would want to poison Ben? He was a member of the family – everybody loved him.…" She swallowed heavily and tears formed in her eyes. "Are you sure?"

Mr Wilkinson nodded before asking, "Do you have slug pellets anywhere in the grounds?"

"Well, I…I suppose they may be some in the greenhouse…but I don't really know." Sarah reached for a tissue now and wiped her eyes. Then taking a deep breath, said, "I'll have to ask Laura – she's my niece – but.…Oh, this is awful."

"I am truly, truly sorry for your family's loss," said the vet.

"Thank you. And thank you for letting me know.…But what will happen to him?"

"That I must leave up to you, but there are two options: I can provide a coffin for him – or you may wish to have him cremated and for his ashes to be placed in a casket and returned to you."

Sarah shook her head. "No. None of us could bear to think of him being burned. No, I want him to be buried – here in the place that he loved."

The trial continued after lunch, and a second police officer was called to the stand.

"Sergeant Thompson. On the 1st of June this year, am I correct in saying that you and" – Reynolds consulted his file – "twelve other officers, were employed in a search of the area where Mr Joseph Stockwell's body was discovered?"

"You are…sir."

"And what was your own and your fellow officers' remit in this search?"

"Well, after the conclusion of the inquest when it was determined that Mr Stockwell had been stabbed in the back, we were instructed to carry out a further, more intensive, search of the area where his body was found."

"We have heard from a colleague of yours," Reynolds continued, "that the search for Joseph Stockwell's body was a dangerous endeavour. In your opinion, was the search that you took part in also extremely difficult?"

"Yes, it was hazardous to all concerned. We had to use a combination of ropes and safety harnesses to cover the terrain, which was covered in foliage, bushes, trees and rocky outcrops. Thank goodness the weather was clement at the time or it would have proved to be even more precarious."

"So what – if anything – was found?" Reynolds asked.

"Well eventually, after three days of meticulous scrutiny of the area, a half-inch chisel was discovered by one of my constables."

"Sergeant Thompson; please now look at exhibit A, which will be handed to you by the clerk....Is that the object you found in your search?"

"Yes. It has a red diamond impressed on the handle, showing it to be of the highest quality."

"And where was it found?"

"It was found beneath a ledge on the embankment, which was covered by weeds and such. And it was bagged for further inspection by the forensic department."

"Now, I understand that you were also involved in a search of the defendant's business premises. Were other high-quality tools found there?"

"Yes – all displaying the same red diamond."

"Thank you. I have no more questions."

The judge looked at defence counsel who rose.

"Sergeant Thompson," be began. "Would you say – not necessarily in your role of police officer but that of an ordinary citizen – that there must be hundreds, probably thousands, of these superior tools at large in the country as a whole?"

"I would be foolish not to."

"Indeed. Then I put it to you that it would also be foolish of anyone to hurl the weapon that had been used to take someone's life, down a railway embankment where it could subsequently be found." The policeman was silent. So Pritchard continued: "Now, after the discovery of this half-inch chisel – which I am sure the jury may construe as being remarkable considering the length of time it had supposedly lain there – was a further search carried out on the railway embankment?"

"Why, no."

"And why not?"

"Well, it was obvious that the object must have been the one we were looking for – it did have dried blood on it after all."

"Oh, Sergeant Thompson...please. You had no way of knowing

454

that at the time. It could have been paint, or some other sort of stain. And what if other articles of murderous capabilities were hiding in the bushes or under rocks?" The judge interrupted defence counsel. "Mr Pritchard. Do not test my patience."

"My apologies, your Honour. I have no more questions for this witness."

And Laurence Pritchard sat down with a smile on his face.

"Poisoned? Slug pellets?"

"I'm afraid so, love. Anyway, I told the vet we'd like to bury him. Have I done right?"

Paul sat on the settee. "Oh, yes...yes. I want to put him close to the brook – if there's enough depth so that he won't get...wet...." He burst into tears now. And when his mother went to him, she pulled him to her and rocked him like she used to do when he was a child.

Eventually he emerged from his comforting cocoon, and after wiping his face on the back of his hand and shaking his long hair, he said with anguish, "Who would do such a thing?"

"Perhaps it was an accident? Maybe Ben went in the greenhouse and ate some?"

Paul sprang to his feet now and confronted his mother. "That is totally ridiculous! Ben wouldn't do that. Somebody must have stuck them in his food on purpose." And the expression on her face prompted him to say, "What are you thinking, Mam?" But Sarah didn't need to say a word – he could read her mind. "Slug pellets," he said. "Greenhouse. My God! You think Laura did it, don't you?"

"Well, it seems that...."

"No! You're wrong! Laura would never harm Ben. She was there with me when he died and she...."

"Exactly, love," said his mother. "She was *there*."

29

It was the second day of Harry's trial.

Two diagrams of a human thorax were prominently displayed in the courtroom. The left diagram showed the twelve pairs of ribs looking from the back with the shoulder blades removed and numbered one to twelve from the top. The diagram to the right showed them from a side perspective, with the sternum facing to the right. In both cases, the heart and lungs were shown in lighter shadings to the ribs themselves. Mr Edward Ross had taken the stand.

"Mr Ross," said James Reynolds. "Are you the clinical forensic pathologist who examined both the bodies of Joseph Stockwell and Philip Mallinson?"

"Yes."

"Now, could you first tell the court your findings regarding Mr Mallinson?"

"Yes. Mr Mallinson showed all the indications of one having fallen from a great height: fractures of the thoracic and lumber spine with all the neurological complications associated with such, and those of both upper and lower limbs."

"Thank you. I would now like to move on to your examination of Mr Stockwell, and I think it may be appropriate for you now to approach the diagrams displayed on the easels to your right, and explain their significance."

Edward Ross stepped down onto the floor of the court and took his place at the side of the easels, where he explained each of the illustrations in turn. Then he was asked to mark the spot where the weapon entered the body, and then to the point where it stopped, prior to its withdrawal. "You will see from the first diagram showing the complete thoracic cage viewed from the back, that the weapon entered the victim between ribs five and six, just missing the shoulder blade." He moved to the second illustration. "This side view," he said, "shows – still between ribs five and six – the weapon puncturing the right lung to a depth of just short of two inches. I may add that death caused by stabbings in the back are rare; nevertheless, in my opinion, this incident resulted in Mr

Stockwell's death due to a massive haemorrhage, when the membrane covering the lungs is ruptured, and blood enters the cavity between the lungs and the chest wall – and pneumothorax, whereby air enters, and the lungs cannot expand. In this case, both of these occurred."

"Thank you for your explanation, Mr Ross," said Reynolds, before instructing the witness to return to the stand. "Now, Mr Ross, would I be correct in saying that the assailant in this case would be right handed?"

"Undoubtedly."

"Thank you. No more questions your Honour."

"Please remain where you are," said the judge and looked at Pritchard who stood now, saying, "It has been proved that the bodies of both Philip Mallinson and Joseph Stockwell were discovered either at the base of the embankment or on the embankment itself. I would like to put a scenario to you, as to why these two men were so found.

"Could it be conceivable that they were in some sort of fracas before they ended up dead?"

Reynolds was up like a shot. "Your Honour, this is pure speculation on my learned friend's part, and the witness is not in a position to answer it."

"Oh, I agree," said the judge. "Please move on, Mr Pritchard."

"Mr Ross," said Pritchard. "Apart from both the deceased in this case; if two individuals, say, were lying on the ledge above the said embankment – one on top of the other – would it be possible for the one underneath to stab the one on top in the back?"

Ross hesitated for a moment, before saying, "That would be highly unlikely if the perpetrator of the blow was right-handed."

Pritchard consulted his file. "I have it on record, Mr Ross," he said, "that Philip Mallinson was left-handed." There was a sudden buzz in the court. And in the dock, Harry's shoulders went back and he appeared to breathe easy. Mr Pritchard continued: "So would that be possible?"

Harry waited for an answer, but it was not the one he wanted. "I would say it most improbable," said Ross. "A personage in that position – even if he had a weapon in his possession – would not have the leverage to stab another with a force that could cause the death of the other."

Both Harry and his barrister were somewhat deflated. But it wasn't over yet – not by a long way.

"Mr Ross," said Pritchard. "Nothing – not that I am aware of – has been mentioned as to the *appearance* of the wound to Mr Stockwell's back. In your examination of this wound, was there any indication as to what type of weapon was used to cause the victim's death – for instance, could it have been something like the instrument which will now be shown to you?"

Having received the exhibit, Ross examined it carefully. "Well, wounds caused by an implement such as this, may have abraded edges which was not the case in my examination. However, square shaped objects may result in a radial wound due to the splitting of the skin at the wound's edges, which *was* evident in this case. But I must admit that any interpretation of these sorts of wounds must be made with caution as they are always open to an element of doubt."

"Thank you. I have no more questions your Honour." And as Pritchard seated himself, he thought, That's better....

After a short break for refreshments, the trial continued with the prosecution's questioning of a new witness.

"Mr Brooks," said Mr Reynolds. "Are you the assistant head in the department of forensic medicine at the Collingley Science Laboratories?"

"I am."

"Is the exhibit you have in front of you, which was discovered by the police on the embankment above Collingley Low line in June of this year – and was found to have traces of blood on it – the object that you examined?"

"Yes. Yes, it is."

"And were you able to find any fingerprints?"

"Yes. They were those of the defendant."

"Now, Mr Brooks, would it be possible that the object in question could have lain hidden for eleven months, and to still retain prints?"

"Well," said the witness, "contrary to popular belief, if the weapon used in a homicide happens to be a hand gun for instance, fingerprints would be difficult to discern, but fingerprints left behind on wood – like the handle of this chisel – are easier to detect and may last for many years. But, they are subject to weather conditions and other external factors, which could result in their obliteration."

"So, in your considered opinion, if the exhibit *was* reasonably protected from the elements, then fingerprints would remain intact?"

"I cannot say they *would* – but can convincingly say that they could – depending on the location in which the object was discovered."

"Thank you, Mr Brooks. Now, I would like to pass on to the blood found on the exhibit. Were you able to ascertain its type?"

"Yes. It was type A."

"The same type as Mr Stockwell's."

"So I am led to believe."

"Thank you, Mr Brooks. No more questions your Honour."

Now defence counsel stood, saying, "Mr Brooks. Did you inspect the area in which the half-inch chisel was found?"

"No, sir."

"So, am I right in saying that the object was presented to you without your knowledge of where it had come from?"

"Why, yes. My expertise does not extend to the solving of crimes, only to that of passing on the results of my findings to those who have enlisted my help."

"Of course. Now, you have said in your report" – Pritchard referred to his file now – "that the blood you found on the chisel was of type A. Is this a common type?"

"Reasonably so. The most common type is type O; but in Caucasian populations, the vast majority of people have only types A and O."

"Interesting. So, the blood that was found to be type A, could have been that of, say, half the population of this country?"

"Roughly about forty per cent," said Brooks.

"And are blood types inherited?" asked Pritchard.

Reynolds stood. "Your Honour. I cannot see what parentage has to do with the blood found on the chisel."

The judge pondered for a moment. Then said, "I must say I am curious. The witness may answer the question."

Anthony Brooks spoke once more. "That is a not a simple set-up; but the easiest way I can explain it is that if someone – as in this case – has type A, then his parents could both be type A; or one have type A blood whilst the other has type O. But there are variants which I am sure you would not wish for me to go into at this time."

"No. Of course not....So, in the case of siblings, would I be right in saying that they could have the same blood type or not?"

"Of course. They could have the same – or different types –

subject to the blood groups of their parents. But this would not apply if both parents were of type O. In that situation, each child would only have blood of that type."

Pritchard appeared to be pleased by the answer, but he wanted to know more. "Mr Brooks," he said. "Can blood remain on an object for a length of time?" Yet the answer he got was not what he expected, as Brooks said, "Indeed. Blood has been found on stone tools discovered on archaeological sites before now."

Somewhat disappointed, Pritchard said, "Thank you very much, Mr Brooks. I have no more questions."

"This would be a good time to break for lunch," said the judge. "We will resume at two o'clock."

Edith Stockwell entered the stand, removed her glasses and took the oath.

Prosecuting counsel now addressed her: "Mrs Stockwell, on the morning of the 26th of July last year – the day after the fire at the mill of which you are part-owner – did you at any point see your son, Joseph?"

"No. I didn't know if he was in or out due to the fact that I was quite tardy in rising. After being informed by the police the previous night that there had been a fire at the mill, I was so distressed that I took a sleeping pill."

"So, at what time – approximately – did you wake?"

"I can't really say. It was my son, Alex, who woke me and told me he was going to the mill to inspect the damage. It was only after he had gone that I happened to look at my bedside clock, which said five minutes to ten – or thereabouts."

"And what did you do then?"

"Well, I put on a robe, and went to my window and opened the curtains."

"And in doing so, what did you observe?"

"I saw a figure rushing down the path between the lawn and the shed at the bottom of the garden"

"And did you recognise the figure?"

"Oh yes I did. It was him!" She pointed directly at Harry.

"You are quite certain it was the defendant?"

"Oh, without a doubt. It was him all right."

"Thank you. No more questions your Honour."

"Mr Pritchard," said the judge.

Defence counsel stood. "Mrs Stockwell. You have already stated that the police informed you of the fire on the night that it happened. Did they also tell you that your son had been taken to hospital with smoke inhalation?"

"I believe so."

"And did you visit him in hospital?"

"No. It was awfully late, and I thought his condition didn't warrant the long journey."

"Really? But you couldn't have known what condition he was in – could you?"

"I just thought he would be all right – that's all," said Edith tersely.

Pritchard glanced briefly at the jury before saying, "Now, Mrs Stockwell; my learned friend asked you what you did immediately upon rising from your bed. Was there anything else you did before opening the curtains? For instance, switch on a light?"

"Not at all. It appeared to be a sunny day, and the room was quite well-lit for me to go directly to the window and open the curtains."

Now Pritchard referred the court to a photograph of the Stockwell house and garden. "Mrs Stockwell, if you look at the photograph in front of you, which was taken on the 26th of July of *this* year at precisely ten a.m., could you confirm that the window marked with a cross is that of your bedroom?"

"Why...yes. Yes, it is," said Edith.

"And do you see that the whole of the building – including your bedroom – is in full sun?"

"Yes...I suppose I do."

"In fact, that side of the house faces directly east; and it is my submission that to identify the defendant with the sun fully in your eyes would prove most difficult."

"Oh, no," Edith protested. "I saw him."

Pritchard smiled prudently, saying, "Returning to my previous question – and I remind you that you are on oath – between wakening and opening the curtains, did you do anything else? I urge you to think very carefully, Mrs Stockwell, before you answer."

The prosecutor was on his feet. "Your Honour, the witness has already answered the question. The court heard her reply all too well."

The judge addressed defence counsel. "Is this leading anywhere, Mr Pritchard? The question has already been answered."

"By your leave, your Honour," said Pritchard, "but the actions and credibility of the witness is most germane to this case."

The judge allowed counsel to proceed.

"So what else did you do, Mrs Stockwell?"

"I have told you. I got up and opened the curtains and that's when I saw him."

Mr Pritchard now referred to his file. "Mrs Stockwell, when you took the oath, I noticed that you took off your spectacles to read. Why was this?"

"Well, I…I…."

"Yes…?"

"…I'm…I'm…."

"Short-sighted?" said defence counsel. "Indeed you are, madam. So, if you didn't put on your glasses before opening the curtains, it would have been impossible for you to discern accurately the person who you state was in your garden."

"But I must have put them on because I saw him. I *did* see him."

Pritchard adjusted his gown now, before saying, "Mrs Stockwell. What was in the shed at the bottom of your garden?"

"The shed?"

"Yes. The shed. The shed in your garden." Pritchard was becoming infuriated, but knew he couldn't push the witness too far lest the judge intervened.

"It was my brother's," said Edith at length. "He kept things in there."

"Like what for instance? Tools?"

Edith was rattled now, but she wasn't going to be upstaged. "I have no idea," she said. "My brother's business was his business and not mine."

"And what became of the shed?"

"Well…I…er, got rid of it."

"Why? Was it not a particularly good shed?"

"Yes. Yes, it was a perfectly good, garden shed."

"Then why get rid of it?"

Edith's face reddened with frustration. "I couldn't bear to keep it," she said through gritted teeth. But mellowing now, she said in a subdued tone: "After Philip was killed, I…."

Mr Pritchard interrupted her. "Oh! So you believe your brother was killed just like your son?"

"Your Honour. The defence is blatantly badgering this witness."

The judge glared at Pritchard, who said, "I have no more questions, your Honour." And he sat down.

30

Sarah had rehearsed the limited amount she was prepared to admit to in court – which would be the minimum she was ready to disclose without causing too much harm to anyone in her family. But harm would surely occur if she did not protect her son.

Though the law had changed as regards the love of one man for another, it had become obvious in the weeks since having received the Royal Assent, that the law was still restrictive: it only applied to those over twenty-one. How many other mothers would find themselves in a similar situation to the one she had been in because their sons – even though they were old enough to die for their country – had to deny their God-given right to love? It also seemed that the police had been given a free hand to arrest people who were engaged in the most trivial of pursuits. In the House of Lords, the Earl of Arran was reported as saying about the change in the law: 'I ask those homosexuals to show their thanks by comporting themselves quietly and with dignity. This is no occasion for jubilation; certainly not for celebration. Any form of ostentatious behaviour now or in the future or any form of public flaunting would be utterly distasteful and make the sponsors of this bill regret that they had done what they had done. Homosexuals must continue to remember that while there may be nothing bad in being a homosexual, there is certainly nothing good. Lest the opponents of the Bill think that a new freedom, a new privileged class, has been created, let me remind them that no amount of legislation will prevent homosexuals from being the subject of dislike and derision, or at best of pity.' Sarah believed his words – no doubt said with an honourable motive – could have been better chosen; and then what sounded worse, were the comments of the Home Secretary, Roy Jenkins, who said: 'those who suffer from this disability carry a great weight of shame all their lives.' But nothing could come close to The Earl of Dudley's loathsome contribution in the Lords summing up the level of the opposition's argument when he said: 'I cannot stand homosexuals. They are the most disgusting people in the world. I loathe them. Prison is much too good a place for them.'

Yet, to prevent anything that may stigmatise Paul and Mark as deviants in the outside world, she had to rely on other means at her disposal. Yes! Now she was primed.

Having entered the witness-box to answer the questions to be put to her, she had chosen to affirm rather than take the oath – which did not go down well with Edith Stockwell. But what did it matter? Edith would soon be shocked to the roots of her badly-dyed hair.

Prosecuting counsel stood. "Mrs Crowther. On the night of the 25th of July last year, what were you doing prior to the fire at Providence mill in which your son was injured?"

"I was entertaining my friends and family. It was only a small gathering."

"And who precisely were present?"

She hesitated. But then said spiritedly, "There was Steven Clark – a tenant of mine – Jessie Dicks, my long-term friend, and my stepdaughter Jane Carr."

"So just the four of you?"

Sarah said that his supposition was correct, whereby counsel consulted his notes. "May I ask you where the defendant was at the time?"

Once more, Sarah hesitated. She looked at Jane in the public gallery; then, turning back to the prosecutor, said, "He had gone out."

"And had you any idea of his whereabouts?"

Sarah raised her eyes to the ceiling of the court. And then turned to look at Harry before directing her words to counsel: "I had. He was running an errand for me."

"And what was the nature of this errand?" Reynolds briefly looked at the jury.

You've got yourself into this so far, Sarah thought; best get on with it. "I asked Harry – Mr Carr – if he would try and persuade Joseph Stockwell to let him join a poker school at a pub in Leeds. The intention was to ply him with drink so that he would eventually become so intoxicated that he wouldn't be aware of where he was or what he was doing. You see, I had planned that Mr Carr would secure a...a prostitute for Mr Stockwell, whereby they could spend the night in a hotel room which I had reserved in advance. Joseph was well known for his philandering ways, and I planned to obtain photographs of him with the...the person – as one would say – inflagrante delicto."

"Before I ask you the reasons for this extraordinary conspiracy of yours, may I put it to you that surely it would not overly concern Mr Stockwell if – as you say – he was well known for his philandering ways. I would imagine he would possibly be proud of a further conquest. Wouldn't you?"

Sarah was quiet. But then she said, "The prostitute was to be a man – dragged up, as they call it." Ribald laughter now filled the court.

"Quiet!" said the judge. "Any more disturbances from those in the public gallery and I will clear the court." He paused momentarily before looking at Sarah, saying, "Dragged up? Do you mean as in…having a troubled childhood?"

"Oh no, sir," said Sarah diffidently. "It means dressed as a woman."

"Really?" said the judge. "Something like…Widow Twanky, you mean?" Stifled giggling now ensued in the gallery, but the judge's attention was elsewhere.

"Oh, nothing like that," said Sarah. "Like a really pretty woman."

"So, you had this man – dressed as a woman – hired by the defendant to…inveigle Mr Stockwell into some sort of liaison?"

"Yes, sir."

"Astonishing! Please, Mr Reynolds, do carry on before I know not whether I am in a court or a pantomime."

So Reynolds did: "Mrs Crowther. Did you have some sort of vendetta against Mr Stockwell?"

"You could say that," Sarah admitted, and went on to explain: "Shortly before this particular night, I was paid a visit by Mr Joseph Stockwell who…." She halted before looking directly at Edith, saying, "He tried to blackmail me." Many of those in the public gallery gasped. "And as I was determined not to pay him a penny," Sarah went on. " I planned to play him at his own game."

"I see," said Mr Reynolds. "So please would you enlighten the court as to the nature of this blackmail." It was now that Sarah held back. But when she was pressed by the judge, she drew in a deep breath, saying, "If I didn't pay him what he wanted, he…he was going to tell Harry's wife that her mother was not the daughter of Edith Stockwell."

Gasps occurred again, and raising her voice now, Sarah looked directly into the public gallery and pointed a finger at Edith Stockwell, saying, "And however much that malignant harpy protests that she is, she knows for a fact that I am speaking the truth."

Counsel for the defence had no questions for the witness and Sarah was discharged. But not without a warning from the judge, who told her that if she still had the photographs mentioned in her evidence, she would have to pass them on to the court for them to be destroyed, or swear under oath that she had personally disposed of them, lest she be liable for prosecution herself. And – one way or another – Sarah had to comply.

31

When she returned home on that Friday afternoon, Sarah never mentioned a word to anyone about what had happened in court. She had refused any food and had taken herself to bed with a bottle of sherry. Then, when David got home from the mill and found Sarah slumped on the bed with an empty glass in her hand, he had gone downstairs and slept in the drawing-room.

The following morning, Sarah lay in until noon, and when she came downstairs she went straight to the kitchen and asked Jessie to take coffee for the two of them to the library. And there she told her devoted friend what had transpired in court the previous day.

"I'm surprised they didn't lock you up for blackmail an' all," said Jessie. "And how could you say the other stuff with Jane sitting there listening? Oh, what 'ave yer done, Sal?"

"I know exactly what I've done – perjured myself; but it was only Joe Stockwell's real reason for blackmailing me that I lied about: he was trying to extort money from me to keep quiet about Paul and Steven's relationship, Jess. He showed me photographs."

"But to involve Jane...oh, Sarah...! So, if that's the case, who was this woman who Philip got pregnant?"

Sarah looked up at Jessie. "It was Amy."

"Amy? Amy who...? Our Amy? Never!"

"She told me herself, Jess."

"And you believe her? After all, Amy's always been dim-witted. She told me once she'd seen a four-legged pigeon. The woman's slack."

"Oh, no, Jess. Far from it. She hasn't made it up. It's a proven fact that Amy had a child." Sarah went to the drinks cabinet now and poured two large brandies.

"Don't you think you had enough booze last night?" said Jessie. "Just come and drink your coffee."

Returning to the settee, Sarah said, "Do you want this brandy or not?"

"Aye. Go on then."

"This is a total disaster," said Sarah, passing over the glass. "Do you know" – she sat forward and stared at her companion – "it means that Edith isn't Jane's grandmother but her…great-aunt – I think. And the same applies to Mark."

"Well, don't bloody ask *me*." Jessie quaffed her drink. "I'm wholly confused. Amy having her hair cut and dyed like one of those Beatles last year was one thing, but to come out with this is even more ridiculous. Anyway, none of this can be proved."

Sarah took a drink before saying, "It can."

"Eh?" Jessie bounced in her seat. "How?"

"Amy told me about a birthmark on the back of Dorothy's neck."

"Oh," said Jessie, "so I suppose now you want me to come with you to dig up her corpse and look for it, eh? Well, I'll tell yer this straight: I'm not going out in the middle of the night with a bloody shovel for anybody!"

"Don't be so simple-minded, Jess; of course not. Jane herself told me about it as well. Now, I'm just wondering about the practicalities of how we go about things." Sarah stared into Jessie's eyes. "Amy could easily tell Jane the truth about her mother's real parents, and I know what would happen then: she'd blame me like she did when Harry ran off with Laura. I can't take that chance." She looked at the half-empty brandy glass in her hands, saying, "It surprises me how Amy's been able to keep the fact of being Jane's grandmother so close for all these years. Oh, Jess, I just hope she doesn't spill the beans."

"God damn it, Sal, you've already spilt enough! And Jane's going to need some answers from somewhere."

"I know," said Sarah. "And I just hope it's Edith Stockwell who provides them."

Jessie tapped the table. "What I'd like to know, is why Amy told me at Steven's inquest that she believed Philip started the mill fire. After all, if she loved him, why point the finger at him?"

"Oh, I don't know, Jess. In fact, there are a hell of a lot of questions that need answering."

Later that afternoon, Jane arrived at the house and flung herself into Sarah's arms. "Can I come back and stay here, Mam, because I can't live with that bitch who has lied to Mark and me for all these years?"

"Of course you can. So, Edith told you everything, I guess?"

Jane nodded. "I'm sorry I berated you outside court yesterday, but it came as a total shock. And to believe that Unc…." She couldn't finish the word; but said, "Joe tried to blackmail you over the fact that my mother wasn't a Stockwell but a Mallinson. And all you wanted to do was to protect my mother's memory and spare my feelings. Please forgive me."

Sarah held the girl who had called her 'Mam' since the day she married her father, believing then that she had suddenly gained a sister for Paul. "Look. Why don't you go and take a nice hot bath until I sort out the sleeping arrangements with Jess?"

"I will. But I want to go and see my grandmother first. Is that okay?"

"Of course it is. I'm sure she'll be overjoyed to see you. But I warn you, she's more ill than she makes out."

Hand in hand, the two left the drawing room; and as Jane ascended the long staircase, Sarah went to tell Jessie that Jane would be staying.

"Bloody marvellous!" were the words Jessie used when she was told – which were said with desperation rather than gratification at Jane escaping the clutches of Edith Stockwell. "That means we'll have to move bedrooms around again." She leaned heavily on the kitchen table. "This place is getting like a hotel." Then, pulling herself upright, she said, "Do you know, me and Annie – her with a bairn inside her – are worn out, Sal." She counted on her fingers now. "Kath and Josh still haven't found a house; Paul and Mark have lost theirs, and God knows why Kevin's here when he's got a place with his dad. So, who's going to sleep where?"

"I'll have a word with Kevin and Josh to see if they don't mind sharing for the time being. When Harry gets out, he and Jane will be back in their own home."

"*If* he gets out!" said Jessie. "So where's Jane now?"

"With her grandmother."

"Sal! Not if I live to be a hundred will I ever get used to sayin' that."

"Hello, love," said Amy. "Come and sit next to me." She patted the eiderdown. "Sarah told me you went to live with your grandmother after Harry was arrested."

"Yes…but she's not my grandmother any more." Jane sat on the bed and held Amy's hand, saying, "You are."

Amy thrust her head back into the pillows. "Eeh, I'm sorry about all this, lass."

Jane gently shook her grandmother's hand. "Don't be sorry. In fact, I'm glad I found out before you…."

"Die?" Amy fixed a look on the girl who now sat with her as a grieving relative. "Oh, don't look so remorseful, love. I know I haven't long left of this life, but I'm not going anywhere at the moment. And knowing that you have finally found out about me, makes me more determined to carry on."

Jane drooped her head now. And Amy, stroking the young woman's long blonde hair, said, "Be strong, flower – not for me, but for your Harry. He will need you when his ordeal is over."

Jane raised her head, her face stained with tears. "But what if they find him guilty and they take him away from me?" she said.

Amy pulled a tissue from the box on her bedside table and wiped her granddaughter's face. She smiled now: a smile that was likened to the smile of someone who was welcoming the sun as it burst from behind a dark cloud. "Have faith, love," she said. "God will see to things. But if I don't get the chance, I want you to tell Harry I am sorry. Tell him I am sorry for being a stupid old woman who – at one time – could not see any other way out."

"I don't understand," said Jane grasping the hands of this additional love in her life.

"You will do, pet. Just remember what I have said. Amy pushed herself higher on the pillows now, saying, "I want you to do something for me."

"Of course. Anything!"

"Will you go and ask Sarah if she'll get in touch with the solicitor who is dealing with Harry's case, and ask him if he'll come and see me?"

"Yes. But why?"

Amy stroked Jane's hair away from her face. "All in good time, love. All in good time….Now, leave me, sweetheart: I have to sleep. After all, I'll be needing all the strength I can muster for what I have to do."

32

"Has your belly shrunk?" said Jessie.

Annie looked down and lifted her bloodstained pinny. "I don't think so, Jessie. Looks just like it has been all along to me."

"Maybe it's these glasses? I should really go back to t'optician and 'ave me eyes tested again. Now you crack on wi' cutting that braising steak up and I'll start on the pastry. D'yer know, lass, it's all right them saying they want a meat and potato pie for Sunday dinner, but it's us that gets the shitty end of the stick."

Wielding the knife now, Annie said, "It wouldn't be so bad if it were just the five of us, but cooking for a dozen is a different kettle of fish."

"I don't suppose Amy'll want much," said Jessie as she went to the cupboard and got out a bag of flour. "Did yer take the butter out the fridge, lass? It needs to be firm but not like a rock."

"Aye. It's on the side over yonder." And after Jessie had gathered the ingredients for her puff pastry and placed them on the kitchen table, Annie went on: "What's exactly wrong wi' Amy?"

Jessie screwed up her eyes to read the weight on the scales as she sifted the flour into a bowl, before saying, "I'm blessed if I know. It's knockin' on six weeks since she had her appendix out, so she ought to 'ave got over it be now. And of course, when the doctor's been, he's said nowt – not to us, anyroad." She went to the fridge now and retrieved the water she had put in earlier to chill. "I hope I've a big enough dish for this pie – it'll likely look like summat Desperate Dan would eat."

Annie chortled. "Aay, Jessie; yer do make me laugh."

"Well it's about time we had some fun in this house. It's been all doom and bloody gloom lately." Jessie looked at the clock on the wall. "I suppose they'll all be comin' down afore long wanting coffee. Well, they'll 'ave to bloody get it themselves."

It was now that Katherine entered the kitchen. "Good morning, ladies. It's a beautiful day out by the look of it."

"Is it?" said Jessie. "We 'aven't had the chance to see."

"Right....Well, I'll just make me and Josh a coffee and leave you to it."

"Good," said Jessie. "You know where it is."

Katherine went and poured out two cups of coffee and placed them on a tray; and without saying another word, left the hive of activity and carried them to the drawing-room where Josh was waiting for her. She placed the tray on the table in front of one of the settees, saying, "Jessie's in a funny mood. She was quite abrupt with me."

"I guess she's weighed down with work," said Josh. "It can't be easy for her with all of us living here."

Katherine looked at her son, thinking, It appears that it's not just Jessie who is weighed down. Then she said, "Are you all right, love? Is anything wrong at Anderson's? Don't tell me Maggie Gledhill is being difficult or I'll...."

"No. Everything's fine there," said Josh.

"Then is it rooming with Kevin that's upset you?"

"Oh, no. Kev's okay – apart from snoring – it's...well, I need to talk to you about something." He picked up his cup and drank quietly. Then, after placing it back on the table, he drew in a deep breath before blurting out, "I'm gay, Mom." And as his head shrunk into his shoulders, he waited for the onslaught of derision and distress from his mother that his words would surely unleash.

But he was staggered when she said, "Is that all? Good God, Josh, I'm your mother. I've known it for years – ever since you began to prefer Bette Davis to John Wayne. Mind you, *his* real name was Marion....Look, love; like your Aunt Sarah, it makes no difference to me who you fall in love with." Josh was in shock. He looked at his mother as if he didn't know her. "And are you?" she said.

"Am I what?"

"In love with someone?"

Josh got up and began to pace the room. And when he halted with his back to his mother, he nodded.

Katherine easily identified the movement as one of despair, so she went to her son. Turning him around to face her, she saw tears in his eyes. And as she read the expression on his face, she placed her hands on his shoulders and said shrewdly, "Paul."

Josh didn't answer.

"Oh, sweetheart." She held his hands now, and it was obvious from her son's pained expression, that her canny assumption was demonstrably true.

Dinner – and its aftermath – was a decidedly weird affair.

Whilst David was decanting some wine from the cellar, Sarah and Katherine were setting the table in the dining-room. "I'm glad Amy has decided to join us, Kath. It can't be much fun for her stuck in that room on her own. Yet, since she's been there – and it's most odd – she's started to speak, well, slightly posh." But when her sister made no comment, she said, "Are you all right?"

"Sorry...what?"

"I was saying how nice it is that Amy will be joining us."

"Oh...oh, yes...it is."

Sarah placed the bundle of knives and forks she had in her hand on the table. "Tell me what's wrong. I know *something's* wrong, Kath, so don't try to deny it."

"Well, if you really want to know, I...I'm going out tomorrow and...and look for a house to buy."

Sarah grasped Katherine's wrist now. "But what's wrong with that? It's wonderful....Oh, that sounds as if I want to get rid of you – I didn't mean it the way it sounded."

"I know, love," said Katherine resting a hand on her sister's. "But, I've concluded that all of us being here, has put a bigger strain on an already strenuous situation."

"Do you want me to go with you? To look for a house, I mean."

"No, love. It's Jessie's day in court tomorrow and she'll need a friend with her."

At this point, David came over to the table. "Right!" he said. "I've done the wine and put some bottles of white in the fridge for those who want it. Now, is there anything else you want me to do?"

"No...I don't think so," said Sarah. "We're just about ready, so if you go to the drawing-room and tell them all to come through, then that'll be it. Oh, yes! When you've done that, love, will you go to the kitchen and help the girls bring stuff through?"

"Will do." And as David left, Sarah and Katherine placed the final pieces of cutlery on the table....

Presently, everyone filed into the dining-room. Amy was led to her seat by both her grandchildren who sat on either side of her. And around the oval mahogany table, Sarah and Paul, Katherine and Josh, and Kevin and Max, went to their assigned seats, shortly to be joined by Jessie and Annie who were pushing a two-tiered trolley stacked with plates of meat and potato pie, and dishes of various vegetables, while David brought in three bottles of chilled wine.

As the meal progressed, noisy chatter ensued: "So what's wrong with Laura?" asked Katherine of her sister.

"Oh, it's peculiar," said Sarah, resting her knife. "Jess told me when I got back from court on Friday, that Laura had rushed into the kitchen looking like death itself. Apparently, she said she was feeling ill, and then rushed off without saying another word. Mind you, after the day I'd had, I wasn't in any mood to care. Still, she hasn't been her usual self since the beginning of August, and she looks to have lost some weight. I do hope it's nothing serious."

Katherine sipped at her red wine. "Has Wilf said anything about her?"

"Well, he hasn't phoned, so I presume things can't be all that bad. Unless she got wind of Jane coming back to live here – but I don't know how since she didn't arrive till yesterday afternoon."

It was now that Katherine cast a sideways glance at her son who was picking at his food with disinterest, occasionally looking across the table at Paul. Having her suspicious of her son's attraction to Paul confirmed, she knew he was suffering. Nonetheless, if his bubbling emotions should break the surface, a lot of people would get scalded. She had noticed before, how deeply Josh was regarding Paul's every move, and it was understandable. Paul had walked into the drawing-room earlier sporting a new, blue velvet jacket and a high-collared white shirt with the top two buttons undone. He was undoubtedly a fair-haired prince who could turn the head of anyone who encountered him.

At the other side of the table, Jessie turned to her right, and in between mouthfuls of food, said to Jane, "How's Amy managing, lass?"

And in a whisper, Jane answered, "She's doing fine. Better than I thought she would."

"So, your grandmother made a clean breast of it all, eh? Well, it makes a change for Edith Stoc...."

Now, whether it was done deliberately, or it happened by accident, the crash of cutlery on Jane's plate turned heads. "I'm sorry everyone," said Jane. And those gathered, continued with their dinner.

Jane picked up her knife and fork now and turned to Jessie. And with her voice muffled, she said with precise movements of her lips, "Never mention Edith Stockwell again. This ailing woman sitting next to me, *is my grandmother* – so remember that, and treat her with respect." And Jane resumed her meal.

Kevin nudged Annie now. "I hope nobody else goes off on one tonight, or I'm going back to me dad's."

But after everyone had finished their meal and the plates had been cleared away, Kevin's words would return to haunt him when everyone was gathered in the drawing-room for drinks.

"I've never seen that jacket before," said Mark.

"No, it's new," said Paul raising the bottle of lager to his mouth.

"When did you buy it?"

"Oh...on the day you went to Birmingham."

"But that was at the beginning of July and it's nearly the end of August now. Why haven't you worn it before?"

"I haven't wanted to." Paul was feeling awkward now.

"Well, I can't see what's so special about today for you to give it an airing," said Mark, baffled by his lover's vague explanation.

Paul was becoming riled: riled to the point where he turned on Mark. "Drop it! For God's sake just shut up about the bloody jacket!"

Sarah saw the change in her son's conduct, and excusing herself from the rest of the company, strode across the floor towards them. "Are you two all right?"

"It's him," said Paul. "He's getting on my fucking nerves."

"Hey! Curb your language, young man," said his mother. "You might be twenty-one now, but you're still liable for a thrashing." She turned to look squarely at Mark now who shrugged. "I was only asking about his jacket, Sarah. I don't know what his problem is."

"The problem is *you!*" Paul snarled. And with an impulsive movement of his arm, poured the remaining contents of his bottle over Mark's head.

Sarah moved backward just before Mark, lager dripping off his chin, calmly inspected his own bottle and hurled the liquid over the front of Paul's jacket. This action, rather than any other, could not have provoked a greater response from Paul when he dropped the bottle at his feet and landed a punch on Mark's jaw.

Now, before the row could develop into a full-blown brawl, both Kevin and Josh raced across the room. Kevin grabbed Mark by the arms and pushed him against the double doors of the drawing-room, while Josh forced Paul towards the window, saying, "No more, Paul. Leave it now."

"But look what he's done, Josh."

"It'll clean. And besides I couldn't bear to see you getting hurt."

And as Paul looked into his cousin's dark eyes, he knew that his words were more deeply heartfelt than they were conciliatory.

33

The trial resumed the following day.

Sarah had accompanied Jessie to court, not knowing when her friend would be called to give evidence. She had also handed in the photographs as demanded by the judge – and, as expected, had been given a receipt. Oh! how glad she was to be rid of them. But why had she kept them for so long after getting the ones of Paul and Steven back from Alex? Still, it was over now, and she had to hope that her revelations in court had not ruined the chances of Harry being acquitted.

The barrister had told them that Alex Stockwell was first on the list, and depending on how long he was questioned, Jessie could either be called this morning or after lunch. He also said that Sarah was free to go and sit in the public gallery or remain with her friend until she was summoned. Sarah chose the latter.

"So Jane apologised, then?"

"Aye," said Jessie. "And even though it really upset me at the time, I could understand her anger at me mentioning Edith soddin' Stockwell. Aay, Sal, I can't cope with all this – it's making me ill. What wi' Kath still not makin' any effort to find a house for her and Josh, there's me stuck waiting in this bloody hell 'ole."

Sarah took her hand now. "She'll get somewhere soon, love. And as far as this place is concerned, it won't be as bad as, say…having an operation."

"I've never had an operation," said Jessie.

"You're lucky," said Sarah, thinking how the argument of last night was just as painful. And what about Josh getting involved in the fracas? That was certainly out of character. Oh, how she wished everything was sorted out and they could all get back to normal.

It was now she saw Alex coming up the steps. My! he looked remarkably handsome in his black three-piece suit and white shirt with a blue-striped tie. And as he approached them, he said, "Hello, ladies." And in harmony, Sarah and Jessie responded: "Morning, Alex."

"I believe I'm first in," he said.

"Seemingly," said Sarah. "The barrister has no idea when Jess will be called."

Alex sat next to them now, and said emphatically, "Harry never did what he's been accused of, you know."

Sarah turned to him, saying, "Why do you say that, Alex?"

Alex rested his head against the green tiles on the wall. "I just know – somehow." And he closed his eyes....

It was almost an hour and a half before the door to the court opened and the usher called out: "Alexander Stockwell."

Alex stood. "See you later, ladies." And Sarah and Jessie watched him go through.

"It's bloody time they called him," said Jessie. "We'll be here all day at this rate."

"They'll probably break for lunch when they've finished with him," said Sarah. "I'm hungry all ready. And by God! I could do with a drink."

"Snap," said Jessie. "Mind you, I'll have to find a lav before I piss meself. So if they call me, tell 'em to bugger off."

Inside the courtroom, Alex entered the witness-box and was sworn in to give evidence; and Mr Laurence Pritchard for the defence began to question him.

"Mr Stockwell. On the morning of the 26th of July last year, did you return home after spending the night in hospital?"

"Yes."

"And at what time did you arrive?"

"I would say it was shortly before a quarter to ten, since when I entered the house, the clock in the hall was chiming fifteen minutes to the hour."

"And before you entered your home, did you happen to notice anyone in the vicinity of the house and garden?"

"No, sir."

"So what was the first thing you did when you got inside?"

"Well," said Alex as if struggling to remember. "I...I called out to see if anyone was at home, and shortly, Joseph came running out of the kitchen, in what I can only describe as being...flustered."

"And did he speak to you?"

"No, he never said a word. He just flew out of the door."

"Earlier in these proceedings, your mother, Mrs Edith Stockwell, told the court that you woke her when you returned home. Is that the case?"

"Yes."

"And did you tell her that you had seen your brother in what you thought to be a 'flustered' state?"

"I did. But I don't think she was fully awake at the time."

"So," said Pritchard, "what did you do then?"

Alex raised his head in thought. Then said, "I think I just said I was going to the mill. So, I went to my room, had a wash, changed my clothes, and then left the house."

"And in leaving, did you *then* see anyone in the grounds of your house – or did you hear anything unusual?"

"No, sir. And what I mean is no to both of those."

"Thank you, Mr Stockwell. I have no more questions."

"Mr Reynolds," said the judge, and prosecuting counsel stood. "Mr Stockwell," he said with misgiving in his voice. "I understand that you discharged yourself from hospital on that particular morning. Would I be right in thinking that was an unwise decision, considering the amount of smoke you had inhaled, and that it could have affected your…mental state for instance? And if that is the case, I put it to you that you *did* notice the defendant in your garden without realising it at the time. I urge you to think carefully, Mr Stockwell, before giving your answer."

"I was perfectly lucid – if that is what you are implying. And as I have said already, I did not see anyone in the vicinity of the house either when I arrived or when I left."

Mr Reynolds paused for the longest of moments before saying, "You told the court earlier that you found your brother flustered when you encountered him briefly. Did you not think that strange?"

"No. Joseph was never one to be consistent in his emotions. I thought he was as worried as I was about what the state of the mill might be."

Reynolds asked no more questions and Alex was discharged….

Outside the court, he saw that Sarah and Jessie were still sitting there.

"You were quick," said Sarah. "How did it go?"

"It was bloody awful. Anyway, they've stopped now till after lunch, and I need a drink. Will you join me, ladies?"

Jessie was on her feet. "Well *I* will, even if this one 'ere won't."

She was a little tipsy after lunch. Nevertheless, Jessie intended to be on her best behaviour as she entered the stand.

"I swear by Almighty God to tell the truth, the whole truth and

479

nothing but the tooth…er, truth."

"Miss Dicks," said defence counsel.

"Oh, do call me Jessie, love."

Laughter broke out in the public gallery where Sarah was sitting with her hands over her eyes.

The judge called for silence and then looked at the witness. "Madam," he said. "For the duration of these proceedings, you will be referred to as Miss Dicks."

Jessie almost curtseyed. "Sorry my…Honour," she said, aspirating the word.

Then the judge turned to the defence. "Mr Pritchard, please proceed."

Counsel returned to his question, not without a smile on his face. "On the evening of the 25th of July last year, could you tell the court where you were?"

"Nay, lad, I can't tell yer where I were last week, let alone last year."

Almost with distraction now, Pritchard said, "I am referring to the night of the fire at Providence mill."

"Oh, aye; I remember *that*. I were at 'ome – High Ridge House," Jessie said confidently.

"And were you alone on that occasion?"

"Oh, no. There were Sarah – sorry, Mrs Crowther; Jane, Harry's wife" – she pointed at the dock – "and Mr Clark a friend of… tenant of Mrs Crowther. Well, he were both really. A lovely lad an' all."

Pritchard had to clear his throat before proceeding. "So just the four of you?" he managed to ask.

"Yes, sir – oh, I forgot: Annie, our maid, was in the kitchen – she's expecting at t'present; and Max the chauffeur – he's not – preggers, I mean, 'cos that'd be a miracle. No, he were in his quarters over the garage – I think? Yes, that's right."

"Miss Dicks!" said the judge. "Are you on some kind of medication?"

"No, your worship," Jessie answered. "Well, maybe a backache 'n' kidney pill sometime. But that's all."

"Right," said the judge slowly. "Oh, please, do carry on Mr Pritchard."

Counsel wiped his brow now. "So, on the night in question, the defendant, Mr Carr, wasn't present?"

"No."

"And had you any idea where he was?"

"No. I didn't know, and I didn't ask. It isn't my place to stick my nose in to other folks' business."

Defence counsel now looked at his notes, before saying, "How long have you known the defendant, Miss Dicks?"

"Harry? Oh well, I've known him since he were fifteen – about ten years now."

"And what would you say as to his character. Have you ever considered him a violent man?"

"Oh, God forbid; never. He were a bit of a rogue when he were young, but he's worked 'ard to get where he is today. He wouldn't hurt a fly."

"Thank you. No further questions."

The judge turned to Jessie, saying, "Please remain where you are, Miss Dicks. I think there may be some further questions. Mr Reynolds."

"Miss Dicks," said the prosecuting barrister. "You said that the defendant was 'a bit of a rogue'. Well, he certainly was when he left his wife for another woman."

"Nay, that's not fair."

"We are not here to ascertain what is fair or not. We are here to deal in facts, and his extramarital affair is a fact – and a very important one: he had a liaison with the wife of Joseph Stockwell."

"For God's sake, they'd lived apart for four years."

The judge intervened. "May I remind the witness to just answer the questions put to her and say nothing else."

Jessie pointed at prosecuting counsel. "But he's saying stuff that's nowt to do wi' him."

"Madam!" said the judge. "If you are determined to continue in this manner, I will have no other option than to hold you in contempt. Do you understand?"

Jessie nodded.

"Good. Please carry on, Mr Reynolds."

"Miss Dicks. I would like to take you back to the morning of the…the morning after the fire. Were you present when the defendant returned to High Ridge House?"

Having previously had her knuckles forcefully rapped, Jessie determined to keep her mouth shut as much as possible, so she simply answered, "Yes."

"And what did he say?"

"Nothing."

"Nothing?"

"Nowt I can remember."

"So, apparently having made no comment whatsoever, then what did Mr Carr do? Did he go out again?"

"I can't be sure."

Counsel glanced at the jury. And when he turned back and looked at the judge, he said, "No further questions, your Honour."

"Thank you, Miss Dicks," said the judge. "You may stand down."

"I'm glad you and Mark have made up, Paul. It breaks me heart to see you two at each other's throats."

"Well, we're okay now, Jess. Things are sorted."

"Grand! Did yer tell him about…Steven?"

"I did," said Paul joylessly. Then, more with spirit, said, "He understood that I needed a friend when he left for nearly seven years. But I made it plain that I was over Steven and he was the only one I wanted now."

Jessie cuddled the boy who had been like a son to her since he was a six-year-old. "That's nice to hear, love."

"So, tell me: how did you get on in court?" asked Paul.

"I made a fool of myself, didn't I."

"Surely not!" said Paul.

Jessie nodded. "I slipped up and mentioned about Annie being pregnant – it were a blessin' Wilf weren't there. Mind you, thank the Lord I never mentioned who the father was. And I didn't tell the truth, either. I deliberately didn't tell them that I knew that Harry *did* go out again on that morning you were in hospital, and that he had also said he'd kill Joe Stockwell."

"Well, if they send you to jail, Jess; I'll commit a crime myself and ask them if I can come with you – I couldn't do without my Jess."

Jessie grinned now. "Bless yer, love.…Anyroad, I'd best get on and start something for us tea."

"Oh, no you won't," said Paul wagging a finger. "I'll go out with Mark and get us all some fish and chips."

"Eeh, fish and chips! I 'aven't 'ad fish and chips for years. Can we 'ave mushy peas an' all?"

"Anything you want, Jess. Anything at all." He took her by the hands now, saying with his head in the air: "Let we who are condemned, eat a hearty meal." And together they laughed.

34

As Harry was escorted into the dock by a police officer, he wavered slightly.

His black hair had not been cut, only trimmed to its usual length: just reaching the top of the jacket collar of his dark suit that looked to be a size too big for him. And the white shirt he was wearing, reflected the hue of his freshly-shaven face.

In the public gallery, Jane was holding her stepmother's hand so tightly that Sarah had to gently prise the fingers apart. Jessie was at the other side of Sarah, whilst to *her* immediate right, sat Paul – with Mark at his elbow. The judge now asked Laurence Pritchard QC to open. But his comment caused astonishment to the lay members attending court, and outrage to the prosecution when he said, "I will not be calling the defendant to give evidence. But, I intend to call another witness in his stead."

Reynolds was quickly on his feet. "Your Honour," he said with near derision in his voice. "This cannot – and must not – happen. Any other witness not listed and not mentioned in the discovery process – hence not being available for junior counsel to depose that witness – would make a charade of this trial and for the judicial process as a whole."

"Well, that would be for me to decide if, by taking the risk, it would bring my position into disrepute," said the judge. "But I do agree with you that the legal process would be compromised. Mr Pritchard?"

"Your Honour, I agree with my learned friend's comments regarding the exchange of information between the defence and prosecution, but it is only in the last few days that new evidence has reached myself and my colleagues; and the witness I intend calling, could not have been present for deposition due to ill health."

The judge was quiet for a moment. Then he addressed the jury: "You are temporarily discharged from your duties in this court. I would remind you that you should not discuss matters pertinent to the case other than amongst yourselves, and be back here at ten o'clock tomorrow morning. This court is now adjourned."

Annie was finishing off making sandwiches for the women who remained behind at home while the men had gone to the pub. "There!" she said. "Tuck in ladies while I go and see if Amy wants owt."

"I'll go," said Jane. "In fact, I'll take her up a plate whether she wants to eat or not – she'll need all her strength for tomorrow." And when she had left the room, Jessie sat down and quizzed Sarah: "What's she mean by that?"

"Oh, surely you know, Jess," said Sarah.

"Know what?"

"Amy is going to court tomorrow. You must have worked that out by now."

Jessie threw up her hands. "Why is it," she said, "that whenever summat 'appens in this house, I'm the last bloody one to know about it?" She rested her palms on the kitchen table now. "So? Why's she goin' – and more to the point, how will she get there the state she's in?"

"She'll get there, Jess. She's still a strong woman even though she's ailing."

"Oh, please; don't you dare say: 'she made planes in the war', 'cos I've heard it all before. She probably made that one I read about in the paper. She likely forgot to tighten its nuts and it fell out the sky – she's a liability that woman. So, if she can go, what's she goin' for, eh?"

"All I know is that she asked to see the solicitor a while ago, he spoke to the barrister apparently, and now she's going to court. Everything is confidential at the moment; but tomorrow…well, I'm sure we'll find out."

35

Amy was wearing a black woollen coat that reached almost to her ankles, and it sported large, deep pockets and wide lapels; and as she was helped to the stand, the judge asked if she would rather sit on the floor of the court in a chair. Amy declined the offer.

Defence counsel stood. "Miss Broadbent," he said. "Firstly, may I thank you for being here today considering the recent diagnosis of your illness." Amy inclined her head, whence counsel said, "Would you please tell the court the exact nature of this illness?"

"Yes, sir." Amy grasped the edge of the witness-box and then continued: "After spending some time in hospital and at Sarah's – Mrs Crowther's – house, my doctor visited me regularly. He took blood samples – and other things that doctors do – and eventually told me I am suffering from – I don't know the exact medical words for it, but it's known as some sort of" – she coughed slightly – "leukaemia."

A wave of both gasps and forlorn sighs seemed to encircle the courtroom, but the judge said nothing. He simply extended Mr Pritchard a slight nod who went on: "In fact it is a particular aggressive form of the disease known as acute myeloid leukaemia – or AML – and I would like to extend my deepest sympathy to yourself and repeat my thanks for your presence here today."

"Thank you, sir."

"Miss Broadbent," he said. "Earlier in these proceedings, Mrs Sarah Crowther swore on oath that you are the legitimate grandmother of Mrs Jane Carr – the wife of the defendant. You yourself are now under oath and I ask you this: Are you Mrs Carr's grandmother?"

"I am."

"And are you prepared to say who her grandfather was?"

Prosecuting counsel was on his feet. "Your Honour. Is this line of questioning relevant to these proceedings?"

"Mr Pritchard?" said the judge.

"My question is highly relevant, your Honour, as will become clear with my further questioning of this witness."

"Proceed. But make sure it is."

"Miss Broadbent. Who was Mrs Carr's grandfather?"

"It was Philip Mallinson – Edith Stockwell's brother."

The judge had now to bring the court to order as a commotion occurred in the public gallery where Edith Stockwell was sitting. But she remained rigid in her seat as the judge said that should any further disturbance arise he would have them all forcibly removed. Then, when calm was restored, the judge told defence counsel to continue.

"So, how did you meet Mr Mallinson, Miss Broadbent?" said Mr Pritchard.

And Amy went on to tell the court of her employment in the Stockwell household and the relationship she had had with Philip.

"So, would you say that Mrs...." He halted abruptly. Then, adjusting his gown, said, "Excuse me, Miss Broadbent...I will restate my question. Would you say that Mr Joseph Stockwell was also privy to this information?"

Once more, counsel for the prosecution was on his feet. "Your Honour! This is pure speculation. The witness could not possibly know."

"Mr Pritchard," said the judge. "You will withdraw this question and keep to the facts."

"Your Honour....Now, Miss Broadbent, could you tell the court what happened on the night of the fire at Providence mill."

Yet again, Mr Reynolds was compelled to get to his feet. "Your Honour. Surely this is immaterial?"

"Mr Pritchard?"

"Your Honour. I beg the court's indulgence, but the details are paramount to the outcome of this case."

"Very well. But you are on a very short lead, sir."

"Thank you, your Honour. So, Miss Broadbent, would you tell the court of the events on the evening of the mill fire."

"Well, it must have been about ten o'clock – I'd just got back from Stockwell's field after watching the fire – when a knock came to my door; and when I went to answer, Philip – Mr Mallinson – was there. Anyroad, I asked him to come in – he were in a right state: all swaddled up on such a lovely evening and...."

The judge turned to Amy. "Please, do get to the point, Miss Broadbent."

"Sorry, sir....Well, I made him some strong tea because he were shakin' and then he told me that his nephew, Joe, had made him set fire to the mill to collect on the insurance."

It was Edith Stockwell who was on her feet now. "No! Never! You liar. Liar!"

The judge spent no time in ordering Edith to be removed from the court. And after she had been led out, Amy was allowed to carry on with her evidence: "Philip pleaded with me to go and meet him on the morrow – his reason was that he was scared of his nephew hurting him if Joe found out that he had lost the keys to the mill after setting fire to the place."

"But how could you possibly help?" asked Pritchard.

"I was stronger at the time" – Amy's words were succinct and measured – "and I were more than a match for that lumbering oaf. So, in the morning, I went to the house and straight to the shed at the bottom of the garden where Philip spent most of his time."

"And what time did you arrive?"

"About ten minutes to ten, I should say."

"And what were you wearing?"

Reynolds was up again. "Your Honour. The defence has moved into the realms of haute couture now."

"Sit down, Mr Reynolds," said the judge. "The witness may answer the question."

"I was wearing what I am now," said Amy.

"So now, please tell the court what transpired in the garden shed." said Pritchard.

"Well, there was Philip: bent over his table. But he wasn't doing anything as he usually did – all his tools were stacked neatly in order on clips attached to the shed wall. 'Phil,' I said. And when he turned, he got up and threw his arms around me. 'Oh, Amy, lass,' he said. 'I'm glad yer came.' It was then we heard footsteps coming down the path. 'Get at the side of yon cupboard,' he said, and pushed me into the corner and opened the tall cupboard door so I couldn't be seen. And I heard Joseph charge into the shed and start to shout obscenities at poor Phil. Then I heard Joe say, 'You're coming with me.' and they must have gone outside. Anyroad, I peered from behind the door and they weren't there, so I picked up the first thing I could from the tools on the wall and followed them to the bottom of the garden so I could protect Phil from his nephew." Amy delved into a pocket and withdrew a handkerchief with which she wiped her brow, before continuing: "Behind some big, overgrown trees, there's a ledge that Phil and me used to go to when we were young so we could have some time on our own. And when I reached it, Joseph was kicking Philip mercilessly, and then he jumped on him trying to strangle him. I'd seen enough by then, so, I stood over Joe, and with every ounce of strength the Good Lord had blessed me with, I stabbed him with what I'd picked up in the shed. But then, I could do nothing more to save Philip, because they…they both rolled off the ledge"

The court was in shock: hushed into pathos.

Mr Pritchard then said quietly, "Miss Broadbent, please would you tell the court what you used to stab Mr Stockwell."

Amy was silent for a moment, before saying, "What I used, I kept. I hid it in the wool warehouse next to my house before it was burned down. Why, I don't know? But I'm glad I did; and glad I was able to retrieve it before I became ill. And Harry," – she looked at the prisoner in the dock – "I'm sorry for what I've put you through. Forgive me, lad." Then she put her hand inside her overcoat pocket and slowly withdrew a half-inch chisel. "I stabbed him with this, sir," she admitted. "It still has his blood on it." And suddenly – and unexpectedly – she tossed the murder weapon into the well of the court, saying bluntly, "I won't be needing it any more now."

Jessie was in tears. "Poor lass." She wiped her face with a tea-towel. "What will happen to her, Sal?"

Sarah sighed. "Well, I had a word with the barrister, Jess, and he said she won't be imprisoned. They will just keep her in hospital since she has such little time left to live."

Jessie blew her nose. Then said harshly, "That bloody judge shouldn't have told her off like he did: saying she had wasted the court's time and blaming her for puttin' Harry through so much. It were cruel….They ought to be lookin' for the bugger who must have pinched one of Harry's chisels and tossed it down the embankment using him as an escaped goat…don't you think?" Through reddened eyes, she stared at Sarah.

In this cheerless moment, Sarah did not remotely consider correcting Jess's words. Instead, she wholeheartedly supported her friend's deduction by saying, "No doubt about it, love. Yet whose was the blood that was found on it? Mind you, I do believe now, that, being dressed like she was, it must have been Amy who Edith saw that morning and not Harry. Even so, it's all a bit of a mystery, Jess. But, we can't sit here pondering. At least Harry is off the hook – thank God!"

36

"Do you know owt about Annie's belly going down?" Jessie asked Sarah. "I've just accused her of gettin' rid of her babby in yon bloody barn!" Her arm shot out. "The lass is in bits."

"God! you open your mouth and put your foot right in it at times, Jessie Dicks. You should have spoken to me before accusing the poor woman of a crime. She had a phantom pregnancy."

"Eh? Are you trying to tell me she were got at by a ghost? You must think I'm greener than a bloody cabbage."

"Oh, don't be so damned stupid, Jess" said Sarah. "It's a rare, but not unheard of condition – I looked it up. It's called pseudocyesis."

"Well, pardon me for not being a psychic bloody analyst, but how the hell was I to know?"

"Where is Annie, by the way?" Sarah asked.

"In her room, I think. She's likely resting after giving birth to a spook."

"Well, when you've finished off in here, go and find her and ask her to come and see me in the library. All right?"

"Aye," said Jessie. "I suppose I will."

"Here, love." Sarah passed Annie a glass of port. "Drink that."

"Thanks, madam...er...Sarah."

Sarah smiled. "That's better." She pulled up a chair facing Annie and sat. "Now, on behalf of Jessie, I apologise for her thinking what you might have done. It was very remiss of her."

Annie sipped at her drink and her face flushed. "I suppose anybody could have come to the same conclusion. It wasn't her fault."

"Well," said Sarah, "that is questionable. But believe me, I can certainly understand why you were convinced that you were expecting. It's because you really wanted it to be true. Yes?"

Annie nodded.

"Don't feel down about it, love. You will have a baby someday, and he or she will have two fine parents. Now, let me tell you why I really asked to see you. It's been nearly a year since you last had a holiday, and I think it's about time you had another. So, I was thinking that you might wish to visit your parents in Scarborough?"

Annie's leaden expression lightened. "I'd like that. I'd like it a lot."

"So," said Sarah, "what about taking Kevin with you? Your mum and dad wouldn't mind, would they?"

"Oh, no…no. I've told them lots about him and they've been wanting to meet him."

"Good. Then give them a ring and fix a date."

Annie's smile turned to a look of deep sorrow. "I've been wondering, though; who could possibly bury a child in that horrible place?"

"Oh, believe me, love; I've wondered that myself – but I doubt if we'll ever find out.…"

When Annie had gone, Sarah smiled contentedly to herself. That would be ideal. After all, the two could do with a break, and now that the council had finished Wilf's place, she could keep Wilf in the dark a little longer. Still, after what had happened, he would be none the wiser as to Annie's suspected condition – that's if everybody kept their gobs shut.

The telephone rang.

"Hello. Sarah Crowther. Oh, yes, and how are you? Yes…yes… oh dear, I see.…No, no, of course. Thank you for letting me know. Bye. Bye-bye."

Sarah placed down the receiver and sat there in an immobile silence. Presently she stood. And after a moment, she walked slowly out of the library, crossed the sunlit vestibule and entered the kitchen.

Jessie turned to face her on hearing the door. "Oh, Sarah. Look, I'm sorry about saying stuff to Annie, but.…"

Sarah held up her hand. "That's okay, love. Sit down a minute."

Jessie did. And when Sarah sat next to her and took her hands in hers, Jessie knew something was terribly wrong. "I'm so sorry, love," said Sarah. "The doctor at the hospital has just phoned. I'm afraid Amy has died."

In the congregation at Woodkirk, there were thirteen mourners: Sarah, Jessie, David, Mark and Paul, Harry and Jane, Katherine and Josh, Annie and Kevin, Max and Alex Stockwell. And even though Katherine had vowed never to set foot in a place of worship ever again, she had gladly retracted this pledge just for Amy.

After the singing of The Old Rugged Cross and a short address by the cleric, Jane Carr and Mark Stockwell walked to the pulpit and spoke about the dearly departed.

MARK: "We are all here today, to pay our respects to a wonderful lady who both Jane and I have only known for a relatively short time compared to others present here today. Many people outside of our family have said that Amy deserved to be punished for her crime. Well, in my point of view, she *has* been. But she did what many of us would have done in the same circumstances, and that was to try and protect the one she loved."

JANE: "It was only recently we discovered that Amy was our maternal grandmother. Initially both Mark and I took the revelation with some scepticism, but in discussions with certain members of our family, we knew it to be true." She looked at Harry now, and said, "Harry, sweetheart. Before Amy died, she told me to ask you to forgive her for putting you through the ordeal of prison and appearing in court. But she got the chance after all, didn't she?" She smiled when Harry instantly smiled back and nodded his head, and then Jane turned to her brother.

MARK: "Our uncertainty on hearing the news of our true lineage, soon turned into acceptance – and then into anger. Throughout our childhood – and adult life – we have been denied that truth. Why? Why were two young people led to believe that some other woman – who was held in high regard by them – was not of their closest kin?" He paused momentarily, and his eyes closed ever so briefly before he said, "But it also hurts that our mother was also denied the knowledge of her own true parentage. Nonetheless, after her death, we were – in a way – adopted by a beautiful woman who we are now proud to call Mam. Thank you for being there, Sarah Crowther. Thank you for being a mother to the two of us." He looked at his sister now.

JANE: "Our belief in God teaches us all to forgive those who have wronged us. Well, in time we may be able to – but not today. Today our thoughts – and those of everyone here – are reserved for Amy who is still held in our hearts with a boundless affection." She faltered momentarily now and grasped her brother's hand before finally she was able to speak: "Farewell…our dearest Nana."

When they returned to their seats and Jane sat beside Sarah, she grasped her stepmother's hand and sobbed. And apart from passing Jane a handkerchief, Sarah decided that any words of support would not be appropriate. Instead, she stroked the back of her hand in the knowledge that Paul had now truly gained a sister.

Then the vicar asked everyone to stand for the hymn, How Great Thou Art, which they sang with gusto; and shortly afterwards, Amy Broadbent's funeral ended. Then everyone exited the small church and waited for the coffin to be brought out and taken to the Crowther family plot, where Amy was buried alongside her beloved daughter.

They were all back at High Ridge House now.

Amy had written a small will, stating that the money left over from her life insurance policy after funeral costs, should be divided equally between her granddaughter Jane Carr and grandson Mark Crowther – with one proviso: one hundred pounds should go to Sarah Crowther and a similar amount to Jessie Dicks.

Jane had her arm around Jessie's shoulder. "Don't cry, Jess," she said. "Nana wouldn't want you to."

The word 'Nana' caused Jessie to sob even more. Then Harry came over carrying a glass of port, and speaking like he used to when he first encountered Jessie, he announced, "'Ere, lass. Get that darn thee neck afore I tek yer int' t'scullery an' wesh thee face."

Jessie smiled away her tears and grabbed the glass. "I could tan yer bloody 'ide, yer young bugger."

"Oh, please, Jessie Dicks. Please!"

Jessie cuffed Harry gently, saying, "I'll just go and have a word wi' Annie and Kev. Thanks, lad."

When she had gone, Jane took her husband's arm and said, "I do love you, Harry Carr."

And the one simple word that Harry said was – "Snap."

Meanwhile, Paul was saying to Mark: "What a beautiful eulogy you and Jane gave. I love you both for that."

"And I love you, Paul Halliday."

Paul looked deeply into his drink as if he were unsure of the future. Then, looking directly at this man he adored, said, "You won't ever leave me, Mark – will you?"

Mark took his arm. "Have no doubt," he said. "I'm yours for life. And you never know, in that lifetime, we may be married just like Mam will be very soon."

Paul smiled now. "I only hope she will be as happy as *we* are."

37

It was Sarah's wedding day and she had to remain composed. Today would come as a surprise to all those concerned; but, nevertheless, she must be sure that they understood her motives in doing what she had to do.

She had risen early, and Jessie had brought her a light breakfast onto the patio table around which now they were both seated. "Well, it's a grand day for it, lass, but these bloody chairs are still a bugger on the arse."

Sarah smiled. "Yes, it is beautiful, Jess; and nothing is going to spoil this day for me. They'll all be in their finery: dressed to the nines, new hats and expensive frocks, and all – or most – looking forward to an unforgettable day. And I'll make sure they get it."

Jessie reached over and touched Sarah's hand. "Who would have thought it, eh? After all we have been through and now you're...."

"Jess," said Sarah, cutting her friend short. "Would you mind leaving me for a while? I just want to enjoy a few moments alone with my thoughts."

"All right, love; but don't take too long: you'll need to be gettin' ready soon."

Sarah offered up a winsome smile, saying, "No, I won't be." And when Jessie had gone, she gazed across the long open garden in which the waters of the fountain in the centre of the lawn appeared to dance with a ponderous lethargy, whilst the summer flowers in the borders were fading. Yet Laura had told her that the floribunda roses that had bloomed in July and August would soon return for the autumn – but Laura wasn't here any more.

She began to reflect on the previous months that had almost felled her. A debilitating despondency had enveloped her when the houses on Long Lane had been destroyed and poor Ben was poisoned. And it had been proved that both these acts had been carried out deliberately. Who could have done such things? She knew for a fact that Laura had nothing to do with Ben's death after pouring her heart out to her a few days ago. Maybe it was the inhuman Edith Stockwell – or even Richard Wainwright whose advances she had spurned and had been sacked by Katherine? And what about the gypsy in the warehouse? Then there was Harry's trial when someone had set him up for Joe Stockwell's murder.... Oh, she could go on forever! She just had to admit that it was unlikely she would ever know.

A warm, September breeze began to play with her auburn hair; and a burst of festive sun now warmed her face. And she believed that both foretold the potential for a most memorable day. With this in mind, Sarah rose from her seat and entered the house. Here she met Katherine waiting at the bottom of the stairs. "So *there* you are! I was wondering if you had changed your mind?"

Sarah chuckled. "No chance, love," she said. "Come on, let's go to my bedroom and you can do your worst...."

Half an hour later, Sarah was staring at herself in the dressing-table mirror. "You don't think I look too girlish do you?"

"Compared to me, love, you *are* a girl! Now, keep still till I fix this in your hair."

Sarah was wearing a knee-length white cotton dress with a plunging neckline, and a blood-red bolero jacket. The colour of her suede high-heeled shoes complimented that of the jacket, and now her hair had been dressed in a chignon, tied with a long, silver clip.

Sarah believed – without saying a word to anyone – that she had kept to tradition: the something old was the pair of seamed stockings she had managed to find in a local shop that stocked just about everything; the something new was her outfit; the something borrowed was Katherine's set of pearl earrings, and the something blue...well, that was how she was feeling at this very moment.

"There!" said Katherine. "All done." And Sarah stood.

"Pin this on for me, Kath. My hands are shaking." Sarah handed her sister the diamond brooch William had bought her for their first anniversary. "Oh, and would you fasten David's necklace as well?"

"We all get nervous on these occasions, love – except the men: they're usually drunk!"

Sarah looked at Katherine with trepidation in her eyes. "Well, I hope that's not the case. I want my fiancé to know precisely what's going on – especially on today of all days."

Katherine smiled. Then having fixed the brooch and secured the necklace said, "Ready?"

Sarah faced her sister now. And after fingering the garnet and seed-pearl necklace and picking up her white-feathered hat, she returned Katherine's smile. "I'm ready, Kath...I'm ready."

They were all waiting at the register office: all those who had been invited to be part of this joyous occasion to witness Sarah Crowther's marriage to a third husband.

Now as everyone was assembled in the office of the registrar, Sarah stood by her husband-to-be with a broad smile on her face. Katherine and Jessie were already mopping up tears, while Paul and Mark surreptitiously held hands. And Alex Stockwell – whose son was about to wed the woman he himself had hoped to marry – was staring down at the floor in the realisation that his expectations were now at an end.

The registrar began. "Sarah, would you repeat the following words: I do solemnly declare that I know not of any lawful impediment why I, Sarah Crowther, may not be joined in matrimony to David Allen." A moment passed – and another – until the registrar said, "Sarah? Shall I repeat the declaration?"

Sarah turned to her fiancé and smiled lovingly. Then, she waited for the longest of moments before saying, "No; that won't be necessary." And she began: "I do solemnly declare that...that I... that I damned well *do* know of an impediment." An upsurge of gasps now engulfed the room; then Sarah, her words staunch like the woman she was, said, "After all, it would be unlawful to marry a man who already has a wife – and particularly one who has also cheated on that wife." She now ripped the necklace from her throat and threw it at the man at her side. "Here, take your trinket – it's about as cheap as you are." And as David bent down to pick the piece of jewellery off the floor, Sarah swung around and addressed the bewildered assembly. "This wedding, ladies and gentleman, is over before it began – but the entertainment is not. So, I would like you all to come back to my house for the reception." Sarah looked back at David now who was standing there in shock, twisting the necklace around his fingers. "You can come too, *darling*," she said, "but only for a short while."

"I don't know how you can take it so...so casually. And then still have the reception."

"Because I *am* casual, Kath. And why should we waste good food." Sarah placed the posy that she had carried with her throughout the journey back to High Ridge, on the dressing-table and threw her hat on the bed. "I'll leave these here until he's packed his bags – just to let him know that I haven't ripped them asunder in anger." She removed her jacket and hung it in her wardrobe. "No, I'm well rid of him, Kath….Come on. Let's go down and enjoy the party."

As she opened the bedroom door, David was standing there. "Sarah," he said. "Look, I want to…."

Sarah raised her hand. "No more talking. It's done. Get in there" – she pointed now – "pick up your engagement ring from my dressing-table, pack your bags, and leave this house for good. I am just grateful you never invested in the company: it saves a lot of paperwork." And she and her sister proceeded along the landing, down the long red-carpeted staircase and into the drawing-room.

Paul was the first to come to her. "Are you all right, Mam? What's all this about?" She patted his hand, saying, "He wanted my money, love – not me. Now, you and Mark sort out drinks for everyone and tell them to help themselves to the buffet…oh, but before you do that, would you ask Max to come and have a word."

"I'll go and lend a hand, Sal," said Katherine now.

Sarah smiled and nodded.

Presently, Max approached her with a glass of champagne. "Thanks, Max. I'm ready for that."

"You wanted to see me?"

"Yes, love. I want you to do a favour for me."

"Of course."

"Will you go up to my bedroom and wait till David has finished his packing? Then phone for a taxi and make sure he gets into it when it arrives – and wait until it disappears out of the grounds. Will you do that?"

"I will, Sarah. Count on me."

As he went out, Jessie came and confronted her friend. "What the bloody hell have you done? Everything was going fine till you 'ad a silly stupid strop. Married already indeed."

"Oh, calm down, Jess, or you'll give yourself a stroke."

"Stroke! I could bloody well stroke you with the flat o' me hand. That's what!"

Sarah threw back her head and laughed loudly as those assembled turned towards the two women. But then Sarah choked on her laughter, and fell into Jessie's arms and sobbed.

Of the thirty guests who had been invited, Alex Stockwell was the last to leave. But not before telling Sarah that he was always there if she needed to talk. She had kissed him on the cheek and thanked him: "I'll remember that, Alex."

Paul, and several other members of her family, had excused themselves earlier and gone to a local pub, while three women stayed behind in the kitchen, drinking.

"You both deserve answers to some questions," said Sarah.

"You're bloody right there," said Jessie.

Katherine told her to hold her tongue and let Sarah speak unhindered. "Go on, love. In your own time."

"Well," said Sarah cradling her brandy bowl. "I became suspicious of all the visits David was making to Bristol on some pretext or other, so I hired a private detective to follow him – that's when I found out the truth."

"But what did you mean when you said he was also cheating on this wife of his?" asked Katherine.

"Ah, well; the night before last, Laura came to see me. She was in a bit of a state: shaking, wringing her hands – crying almost. Anyhow, I poured her a brandy and told her to drink. And when she appeared to be more composed, I asked her – much like you asked me, Kath – to tell me in her own time. And she did."

Jessie leaned across the table. "What? What did she say?"

Katherine looked daggers at the elderly retainer and was about to admonish her when Sarah continued: "Apparently, it was she who had a fling with David."

"The bitch!" This was Katherine.

"She didn't lead him on, Kath. He did all the controlling from what she told me."

"Oh, I don't know about that. I bet she trapped him in her web as would a ravenous spider. She's her mother's daughter all right."

"Now don't bring Mary into this. I really believed you two had found some sort of…understanding."

"Never!" said Katherine, and drew on her cigarette with vigour. "That woman has been a curse on our family since the day she was born."

Jessie spoke now: "Oi, you! Do let the lass finish."

"Well, that's fine coming from you. You've never stopped butting in since we've been here. And besides…."

"Oh, will you two stop it!" Sarah reached for the bottle and refreshed their glasses as Katherine and Jessie glared at each other. But they remained quiet now as Sarah said bluntly, "Laura – and my intended – had sex in the greenhouse."

"God Almighty!" Jessie shrieked. "Well, that's it for me. I'll never touch another cucumber in my life."

"Oh! that's not all," said Sarah. "He got her pregnant."

"No!" This was said in unison by the other two.

Sarah nodded. "And what's more, she lost it just like the one she had with Joe Stockwell."

An awkward silence ensued, before Katherine asked, "But how? When? Where? Surely not at Wilf's place?"

Sarah shook her head. "No. She had a miscarriage in Tyler's Barn. And she buried it there."

"Never!" said Jessie. And Katherine said, "But surely that's a crime?"

Sarah nodded. "She turned herself in and was granted bail – and now she's back with her parents until the hearing takes place."

"Well, bugger me," said Jessie.

And Katherine remarked: "You never said a truer cotton-pickin' word."

38

It was ten days before Christmas and Mark had been invited to a reunion of students at Manchester University, which he had attended in the years after his father had dismissed him from High Ridge.

"Max will drive you, love," said Sarah.

"Oh, I won't trouble him," said Mark. "I'll take my own car. It'll be quicker."

Sarah went to her stepson and gently placed her hands on his shoulders. "*Too quick* for my liking." She lowered her arms and took hold of his hands. "Just be careful. A storm is forecast and it looks as if it will be a bad one, and those Pennine roads are terrifying at the best of times."

Mark smiled. "Don't worry. And yes, I will be very, very careful. Besides they never get the weather right. But, do one thing for me. Look after Paul."

Sarah smiled back at him. "Of course I will. Now, when do expect to be back?"

"Sometime tomorrow night, I should say."

"Okay, love. Have a safe journey...."

The storm broke at midday. The thunder was so savage it shook the house, but it was a bolt of lightning that shocked the household when it struck one of the chimneys at High Ridge and it crashed through the roof, causing damage to both Jessie and Paul's bedrooms.

Fortunately, the rain abated in the late afternoon and Harry and Kevin were able to start work. Max had cleared up the rubble that had crashed through the ceiling, and Jessie and Annie were in the process of removing bedding so they could store it in the spare room for it to be washed the following day. And the only solution left to sleeping arrangements would have to be that Jessie move back in with Kath again and Paul to share with Josh.

"Do you know, Josh," said Paul as he began to undress for bed, "he didn't have to go just to see old friends. I'm more than a friend to him. He left me once to go to Manchester and now he's gone again."

"Paul, it's only overnight."

"Ah, but when he went before he stayed away for years. That's when I found Steven. He was so different to Mark, but I loved him, and then *he* was taken from me. It's all loss: Steven, Ben and now Mark – again."

Josh put his arm around Paul's naked shoulder. "Mark hasn't left you. He's coming back."

"But is he…?" Paul felt alone. He was scared of losing out on love. Now, as he looked at his cousin, he said, "Can I ask you something, Josh?"

"Yes. Of course you can."

And Paul said candidly, "Do *you* love me?"

Joshua drew away and words wouldn't come to him. But as he eyed this epitome of beauty standing before him, he knew the time had arrived for him to speak of his desire for his cousin; but still no words sprang from his mouth. Instead, his lips settled on Paul's and he was overcome with a craving that coursed through his veins like blistering quicksilver. A burning so intense that he believed his blood would burst through his flesh and splatter the walls. What did Paul want? Was it love? Was it sex? Or was it both? Josh didn't know! But, in this moment of overwhelming passion, did he really care?

A knock came to the bedroom door. "Come on you two. Breakfast is nearly ready."

Paul yawned. "Okay, Jess. Won't be long." He nudged Josh now and said, "I'm sure we've time for a quickie."

Josh sat up in bed. "You are incorrigible – and insatiable, Paul Halliday."

Paul grinned; then, as he turned his head away from Josh's face, he said cautiously, "Can cousins commit incest?"

Josh leaned back against the bed head. "I'm not sure," he considered. "But if it is the case, then we're criminals now – and I'm worried."

Paul himself sat up now. "Surely not about that?"

"No! About Mark. He must never find out about this."

"Well we're not going to tell him, are we?"

"But what if it slips out?"

"Push it back in like you did last night." And as Paul laughed, Josh slapped him impishly, saying, "Come on. Let's be up before

Jessie comes and beats down the door." He got out of bed and gathered up his clothes that had been abandoned on the bedroom carpet the night before, knowing, without even looking, that Paul was watching his every move.

After breakfast, heavy rain began falling again. Harry and Kevin had already secured a tarpaulin over the hole in the roof before the rain began, and had told Sarah that the outside conditions were too bad to carry on with the work. Instead they decided to go and check on the progress of the demolition of the houses on Long Lane, in the belief that the task would not have been halted because of the weather.

Because it looked as if they would all be confined indoors on this Sunday afternoon, Sarah had suggested that perhaps they could start on the Christmas decorations in the drawing-room as a surprise for Mark when he got back. Paul and Josh had been recruited to dress the ceiling with large paper bells and garlands, while Sarah and Katherine would trim the tree. Jane had offered to help Jessie and Annie with dinner.

"Paul seems happy today considering Mark's off enjoying himself," said Katherine as she tied a glass bauble on a branch of the tree.

"Probably because he knows Mark will be on his way home now."

"Yes...probably...."

"There!" said Sarah. "Let's switch the fairy lights on and see what it looks like."

But before she got the chance, Jessie came racing into the room. "Sarah," she said breathlessly, "the police are here – in the hallway."

"Good God! Not again? What the hell do they want this time? Right, whatever it is, they're getting a piece of my mind."

Once in the hall, one of the two policemen approached her. "Mrs Crowther?" he asked.

"Yes," said Sarah, her voice abrasive. "How can I help you?"

"Mrs Crowther," said the officer. "I believe you may know the owner of an E-type Jaguar with this registration number?" He handed Sarah a piece of paper. "Why...yes," she said. "It's the number of my stepson's car – Mark Crowther."

"Then I am afraid I have to pass on some bad news. Would you care to sit down?"

"No...no, I'm all right standing thank you."

"Mrs Crowther, an hour ago, we were contacted by the police in Huddersfield after a serious crash occurred on the A62, and Mr Crowther's car was involved."

"Oh...is he all right? Is he in hospital?"

The officer touched Sarah's arm. "He *was* taken to hospital, ma'am...but nothing could be done for him. I'm afraid Mr Crowther has died."

There would be no Christmas lights in High Ridge House this year.

While Jessie, Jane and Annie comforted one another in the kitchen; in the drawing-room, Paul wept in his mother's arms. "What am I going to do without him, Mam?" Sarah stroked his soft red-blond hair, saying, "Endure, love; that's all you *can* do."

Josh looked at his own mother now; and Katherine, sensitive to her son's thoughts, placed a hand beneath his chin. "You must help him to do precisely that, sweetheart."

And there, in the warmth of the dimly lit room, as the rain lashed mercilessly against the windows of High Ridge House, two twice-widowed women and their sons were united in sorrow, knowing that their once divergent lives were now irrevocably entwined....